The

APPALACHIAN

Books by Kirk Ward Robinson

NONFICTION

Founding Character:
Documents that Define the United States of America and its People

Founding Courage:
Courage and Character in the United States of America

Hiking Through History:
Hannibal, Highlanders, and Joan of Arc

Notes from the Field:
A Diary of Journeys Near and Far

More Notes from the Field:
Southbound on the Appalachian Trail and Other Journeys

FICTION

August Roads
Novellas

Life in Continuum
Stories

The Appalachian
A Novel

The Latter Half of Inglorious Years
A Novel

Timewall Speaks
A Novel

The APPALACHIAN

A Novel

Kirk Ward Robinson

HIGHLAND
HOME

Nashville, Tennessee

The Appalachian
A Novel

A HIGHLAND EDITION

Copyright ©2015 by Kirk Ward Robinson

Originally published July 2015

First Highland Edition November 2017

Second Highland Edition 2021

Designed by Victoria Valentine
PageandCoverDesign.com

Printed in the United States of America

Library of Congress Control Number: 2015909872

HighlandHome Publishing
Nashville, Tennessee
37215

ISBN 10: 0-9996042-6-0

ISBN 13: 978-0-9996042-6-7

Visit www.kirkwardrobinson.com

Jeremy might see something in this

Appalachian—pronounced *ap'-ə-lă'-chən* by many from the southeast; *ap'-ə-lā-shən* by just about everybody else— derives from the 17th-century Spanish transliteration of the Muskogean word *abalahci,* meaning *other side of the river* or perhaps *dwelling on* one *side,* referring to a group of aboriginal people then living at the southern end of a long range of mountains in the northern reaches of Span- ish Florida. Driven before the superior technology and in- troduced diseases of the Spaniards, these aboriginal people would, within only a few generations, no longer recognize their world. Their mountains, of course, remain.

PART

I

ONE

It's cold, so cold. The rest of the country is hot, as dry and cracked as old leather, but not here in the state of Maine. Hard little grains of snow are skittering across this rusty tin roof like blowing sand. There are icicles dangling from the eaves. It doesn't matter that today is the summer solstice. Some of them predicted it would be like this, but too many refused to accept what was creeping up on us until it was too late. I'll just rest here a while, not too long. I need to keep moving.

I've crawled under this sagging roof to get out of the wind and the wet and the half-frozen mud. I remember this place clearly, but it's old now, maybe older than me. The floor boards are springy from damp rot. My elbow pushed through in a place, as if into a sponge, so I shifted my weight across the grain. The floor is holding for now. It smells earthy in here, like loam and termites, but also the sour reek of mouse urine. I don't care. At least I'm dry for the moment. I wish I was warm, too.

Sam has snuggled up next to me. You know a dog is smart when it doesn't have to be trained to snuggle close to keep you warm, to return to camp with a bird or a rabbit in its teeth. Sam is a smart dog. He's still wet from us getting across the stream. The old footbridge is gone now. As I recall it was little more than a slippery log with treads chopped into it, but it was enough then to keep us from having to ford the stream, which was deeper than I thought it would be, and running fast and cold. So cold. Even Sam is shivering, his skin rippling along his ribs as if his chills were no more than skin deep. But I can feel an even deeper tremor from within his core. Bluetick coonhounds have a short coat and those long, droopy ears, perfect for radiating body heat while chasing coons though the woods back home, but not so perfect here. He may need my warmth more than I need his. I think I'll keep Sam on his leash, keep him close and dry and out of mischief for a while.

My fingers are stiff as I write this. My scrawl is barely legible but I keep at it just the same, if only to pass the time, or perhaps to test my memory. Writing my recollections on these wrinkled pages allows me to make real what sometimes seems like a long dream, things that happened so long ago that they float in my mind like random passages from books I might have read as a child. It can be maddening. But my memories must be clear, otherwise I would not be here, would not have known to come. Writing them down helps me put them in order, helps temper the chaos.

This place, Rainbow Stream, was one of my favorite shelters along the Appalachian Trail. Most of the other hikers had their favorite places farther south, like McAfee Knob and Dragons Tooth in Virginia or the Presidential Range in New Hampshire, but my favorite places were all right here in Maine: Rainbow Stream, of course, and then Cooper Brook Falls, thirty miles on. If I can get over White Cap Mountain in a few days, then it'll be just twenty-three miles from there down to Cloud Pond, another of my favorites. I think I loved these places so much because of their remoteness—all in the Hundred-Mile Wilderness—and because they were either situated next to clear running streams or else aside deep, still ponds. I remember watching the moose at sunset in Cloud Pond, silhouetted against the dusky shadows, dipping their heads into the pond, rising for air and dripping water like a shaggy beard.

I liked this shelter because it fronted right up to the stream, was open to that continuous, melodic sound of rushing water, and was cool enough in its craggy hollow to keep the black flies at bay. It's not like that now, though. When did the last hiker come through here? I can't imagine. Years I think. So maybe instead I should write this as a record for anyone who might come later, like the trail registers we used to jot our thoughts into in the old days. I looked for a register when I crawled in here. It used to be kept in a wooden box on that fallen wall down near my feet. I couldn't find any sign of a register, or the box. It's all rot now. But before I depart I will slip these pages into a plastic bag and leave them here, with an extra pencil for those who may come someday and add their thoughts to mine.

So I will begin again and write with a purpose.

This shelter at Rainbow Stream was fairly typical of the shelters along the Appalachian Trail in Maine, indeed throughout much of the trail all the way down to Georgia. Built of logs, it was a three-sided box, open at the front, with a steeply canted tin roof. There were wooden pegs in the walls for hanging backpacks and other equipment, and open rafters that were perfect for drying wet clothes. It was deep enough for a hiker to lie in a sleeping bag and not have his feet dangle over the edge, and wide enough for maybe eight or ten hikers to crowd together shoulder to shoulder, sometimes head to foot. Many hikers preferred to sleep with their heads toward the open end where fresh air could waft across their faces, but I always slept the other way, head in, smelly feet on either side of my face, this in case a porcupine came along while I slept. I never knew it to happen, but the thought of having to pull quills out of my face gave me the chills back then. Still does. The wood is too rotten now but you could once see the gnawed places where the porcupines had gone after the open edge of the floor boards, much the way horses will gnaw the wood of their stalls. The shelters were elevated a couple of feet to keep the porcupines out, but this made the floor a perfect height for porcupines to teethe on, holding themselves upright with clawed paws.

I remember the view, lying in my sleeping bag, looking out past my feet. There was a fire circle of river rocks, blackened by decades of use, and some logs cut short and upended for seating. The stream was blue like once-arctic ice, frothing white where it splashed through crags and over rocks, and so clean you could smell the freshness of it. Rainbow trout would sometimes leap and splash. Maybe that's where the stream got its name. The rocky banks were sharp, glacier carved, rising quickly into a dense forest of spruce and mountain ash. Colors were vivid, earthy and alive. I once spent an entire day in this shelter, alone, watching the stream run, the ever-present rush of the water, the trees clicking and scraping. It was peaceful, it calmed the soul; just what I needed back then.

I first hiked the Appalachian Trail in 1976. Those were heady days for a teenager just out of high school. I was seventeen then, didn't turn eighteen until later that fall. The music was ridiculous, disco it was called, but it had the effect of reinforcing through our radios that nothing mattered anymore. The war was over, the president was a soft-spoken guy who didn't like to make trouble, and we had all missed the draft by a few years. The drinking age had been lowered to eighteen, and my girlfriend's favorite song was *Afternoon Delight*, which she emulated as often as she could, to my randy good fortune.

You must be thinking—how could I have hiked the Appalachian Trail in 1976 yet be writing these words now? That's because I've had plenty of time to do both. After all, I'm 128 years old. Actually, I prefer to write it this way: *one hundred twenty-eight*. It makes me feel as if I have at least accomplished something in my life. You're probably dubious. No one could be so old, it isn't possible. But it's true, really. And despite some sore joints, swollen knuckles, and having to pee once an hour I'm in pretty good shape. My pecker even still works, although I haven't used it that way in a long, long time. The last was Sofia…poor, sweet Sofia. More than sixty years ago. She is gone now. They all are.

My name is Carlton Jeffries. It's best not to call me Carl. I was born on September 27, 1958 in Nashville, Tennessee. Today is June 21, 2087, a Saturday I think. It's only about 3:30 in the afternoon but it feels later. Everything is so gray: the spindly husks of the trees, the turbid stream—the very air is streaked with gray, like a slushy winter day. Not much to elevate the spirit.

As children we all counted forward, so excited, so full of optimism about the future: How old would we be in the year 2000, when the twenty-first century would begin? For me it was forty-one. It never occurred to me to question how old I would be in the twenty-second century, but if I can hang on for twelve and a half more years (even if without the excitement and optimism this time) then I will know how it feels to cross into yet another century. *Twelve and a half years*—as nothing.

I had a granddaughter, April, who came to me on my ninetieth birthday and begged me to write out the story of my life. "A narrative," she called it, a narrative of my times; an important record of history. I wouldn't do it. There were too many things in that history a granddaughter shouldn't know. Some things aren't meant to be shared, not even within families—especially within families—where later generations would certainly view the faults and struggles of their ancestors as little more than amusing curiosities, examples of the obvious naiveté if not outright unsophisticated minds of earlier times. April's disappointment was plain, wrenching to me although I hid it well. Until then I had always been her infallible grandfather. Now I had failed her. I didn't know at the time why this was so important to her, only later, after it was too late.

I favored April over all of them. I can still see her face, those cute freckles, that petite nose. She called me *Gwampa* as a child, *Grampa* later on. She had a sweet voice and an independent streak that made her father weary. I loved that in her, though, so like her mother, my precious daughter Rachel. I don't know where the red hair came from. Mine, when I had it, was dark, the same with most of my children. April must have gotten her red hair from her father's people. But she carried my name, not his, and that sprinkle of freckles remained adorable even into her forties, the last time I ever saw her.

By the way, it's not lost on me that I am now writing for strangers what I wouldn't write for my granddaughter. If I could only return I would give her something, anything so that I wouldn't have to carry in my memory that wounded look on her face, my last picture of her. My views about writing this haven't changed, but age has given me a different perspective.

April is long gone. Forty-four years old. Breast cancer. But she made twin sons, and one of them made a son, who in turn made a son of his own, my great-great-great-grandson, whom I have never met; who I'm sure knows nothing of me, least of all that I'm still alive. After all, five generations separate us, quite a distance. And then I wouldn't write that narrative for April, something of the family she could have passed on. It's my fault, just one of many. Does he know of his great-grandmother April, though? Does he have red hair? I hope so.

Still don't believe how old I am? Listen, this is well documented: Jeanne Calment, a French woman, was 122 when she died in 1997. If someone could live to that age back in the twentieth century, with all the wars and trans-fats and everything else, then surely it's not a stretch to at least reach that age in the twenty-first century. And then there was that Bolivian guy, Carmelo Flores Laura, 123 years old and still herding llamas when he made the news in the early part of this century. I remember reading about him in the paper. That's *newspaper.* I still miss them. I never heard about him again. Who knows how long he lived? Maybe longer than me.

In actuality I'm not so rare, maybe just the first to make it this far. Poor and average folks still knock off in their sixties and seventies, but the wealthiest of the generation behind me will reach my age and then some—and be in better shape. Money will buy you a long life, a dynasty of one. Just wait and see. At least I can say I lived this long naturally, without composite bone overlays, 3-D organ replacements, or nanite treatments.

Someone came by my house about twelve years ago, a youngish man of indeterminate age, athletic looking and with a full head of the most gorgeous black hair done up with a flip, retro style like the 1950s, although to him it was probably retro 2030s. His face was as clean and smooth as a porcelain doll, tanned to the shade of autumn leaves in the old days. He worked his way up the steep hill to my house, through the scrub that covers the old driveway, not a drop of sweat coming off of him anywhere. The sun was baking. I think it was August. There was no breeze, the temperature was maybe 104 or thereabouts (that would be *40C* to you, but it still feels the same), and the desiccated leaves under his feet crackled and churned into a dust that gathered around him like a swarm of persistent gnats.

What possessed him to wear a black suit out into that heat is a mystery to me, but probably said a lot about his common sense, or lack of it. His suit and hair became powdered with that dust, as if he had just walked through the working end of a bakery, but not a particle of it clung to his skin, that's how dry he was. It was obvious that he'd had nanite treatments to control perspiration, maybe the whole package. You know how that turned out. I doubt *he* will live to one hundred twenty-eight. I doubt he's alive now. It still makes my skin crawl when I think of the people who allowed millions of little machines to circulate through their bodies, doing their business, or rather, having whoever programmed them do their business.

I knew someone was coming up the hill, I could see the dust rising above the bushes. It wasn't Belle, Sam's mother, she was in the house with me; and no varmints would be stirring around in the heat of day. There was a boy who hiked in to help me from time to time, but I wasn't expecting him. I took up my rifle and slipped outside. Belle followed along, her hackles up, but she wouldn't bark or charge unless I told her to. Belle was a smart, smart dog. She made smart pups. I still miss her.

We settled in quietly behind a cluster of prickly-pear cactus and waited. When the man came within about twenty feet I ratcheted a cartridge into the chamber. Everyone knows that sound, even if only from vids. He froze in place, one foot just stepping over a low agave. He lowered his foot slowly and raised his hands to shoulder height. He had a translucent oval flimsy in one hand. The sun caught it just right and glanced off in rainbow colors.

"I'm looking for Carl," he announced. His voice was surprisingly steady.

I groaned at that. Belle was a tight coil ready to spring.

"Are you Mister Carl?" he asked, a bit of a quiver in his voice this time. I clenched my jaw. God, it just got worse and worse. "I'm Dexter Prescott," he went on. "Maybe you've seen my net casts?"

No, I hadn't, but now I knew why he was so pretty. He was a net reporter, a cyber prima donna. He seemed to have made up his mind about something. He carefully lowered his hands.

"Look, Mister Carl—"

I couldn't stand it another minute.

"If you call me Carl again," I growled, "I will shoot you where you stand."

Now he was nervous. He licked his lips, which remained as dry as the rest of him, little nanites doing their jobs. He scanned the way ahead, trying to spot me, but I was lost in that chaotic growth of cactus.

He flicked a glance at his flimsy. Another glance. "Uh," he said, "Mister *Carlton?*"

"What do you want?" I bellowed.

"Uh," hastily, "salvagers found an old computer in the basement of the courthouse down by the river. That basement's been flooded, you know. They sent divers in. They got some data off of it—really, really old data—data that says you may be the oldest man alive. I checked Guinness. There was another guy in Canada older than you—"

"Well, they've got the climate for it."

"—but he died. Get this—*his dog ate him.*"

Dexter was grinning like the ass that he was. I threw a suspicious look at Belle.

"Damn!" Dexter exclaimed as if he had clinched it. "I can't believe I actually found you. This is *news*, Mister Carlton!"

"That so."

"Yes," he said, eagerly now, as if we were old friends. He pecked at his flimsy. I wondered what he was seeing on it. "I'd like to interview you, take some video—" He held out his flimsy and panned it around. There was nothing to see, just cactus and scrub. The house wasn't even visible from there. "—I think this story would rank high. You'll be famous. People would want to know about you, how you've lived so long; what it's like to be so old."

What it's like to be so old?

I had a grandmother—my mother's mother—who lived to 102. Her name was Villetta. She was forever old to me, although she was only in her seventies in my earliest memories, still young, in truth. I liked being around her. She was kind, always quick to offer something sweet, and she wouldn't let my older brother and sisters pick on me. She was born on the day Sitting Bull was killed, December 15, 1890. Sitting Bull was an Indian chief—a *Native American* Indian chief—the last of the great ones. His death marked a new era. There were no more Indian wars, no more Wild West. Men would learn to fly soon, and you could cross the country by rail in a week or so. It was an era of progress. This was the era my grandmother knew.

My grandfather died years before I was born, but my grandmother never remarried. She lived all alone in a white clapboard farmhouse on the western edge of the Cumberland Plateau in middle Tennessee for better than fifty years, surrounded by fields of aromatic tobacco and forests of modoc, hickory and cedar. We would drive up from Nashville to visit her every so often when I was young, and later I would visit her on my own. She wore corsets into her eighties, and heavy velour dresses with frilly Victorian collars. She had imprinted an earlier era, carrying it forward to us. Talking to her was like watching an old black-and-white western, a living history lesson. I couldn't fathom how she managed to get along in the summer heat.

Grandmother Villetta had perfectly white hair that held its bouffant shape like cotton candy. Her wrinkles fell in deep folds. I had never known her otherwise. She seemed timeless, steady, even as I grew older and the world around her rushed toward what it has become now. She spoke in the old accent, southern but without the twang. We would sit in rockers on the back porch and she would tell me about old times, old memories, people long gone. She talked about my grandfather, whom she called *Farmer.*

"Farmer took out that rock," she told me one day toward the end of her life. Rachel was still a baby then, sleeping contentedly in her great-grandmother's lap. Grandmother pointed toward a big chunk of limestone in the creek. Brush and other debris, washed down from farther up the hollow, had bent around it in a tight bow. "He and Willy got it out from over there," she cocked her head toward what was once a potato patch but was a hay field now, "and rolled it with big iron bars across the yard into the creek." *Crick.* "Took half the day."

Her face seemed to go vacant then, as if she were lost in sorrow and loneliness. This happened often when we talked. It crushed my heart. All around her in that small farming community she had seen her people go off one by one to meet Jesus, and a few the other way: mother, father, brothers and sisters; husband, cousins, friends; and then finally a few nieces and nephews. She was the last one alive, so lonely for so long. But then her wrinkles seemed to tighten, her tired gray eyes went hard, and she added tersely, "They rolled it right over my irises. Tore 'em all up."

That weighed heavily in the air for some time, and then she chuckled. A gleam came into suddenly ageless eyes and her cheeks blushed pink. "I gave Farmer heck for that, and he deserved it, too. I had 'em apologizin' to me for a month. You shoulda seen 'em tripping over himself to make it right. I couldn't of cared less about those irises. Irises grow without even askin' 'em to." She looked at me and winked. "He didn't know that, though."

She slapped her leg and laughed, caught herself as Rachel began to fuss. The mischievous glint in Grandmother's eyes made her look like a little girl off the hook for a prank. She cooed Rachel back to sleep, sobered a bit and said, "Sometimes I felt bad about what I put poor Farmer through during those years. It was easy to have my way with him." She nodded blankly at some memory. "I even spoke to the pastor about it. He didn't approve, said I shouldn't be so wild. I needed to give Farmer my all, the way the bible says. Doesn't matter now, though. Farmer's gone a long time." She chuckled wryly. "So's that pastor."

I looked away, uncomfortable hearing these things. Much, much later I realized that what I had thought all my life about Grandmother Villetta was wrong. She wasn't lonely, she wasn't remorseful and she wasn't sad—she was perfectly content. She was free.

I discovered this when my time came, when I could look back through the prison of my memories and admit that I had never been the man I should have been. I lived with remorse and regret, which grew year by year and then decade by decade, reaching all the way back to my earliest days. I remember all of it, every excruciating detail. But then it came to me, all at once after a progression of sorrows, when I felt sorrier for myself than those I had lost, that everyone I had ever known, ever encountered—every witness to every dumb, stupid, thoughtless and hurtful thing I had ever done was gone. No one sat in judgment of me. This was instantly liberating. The tightness in my chest seemed to ease. My breaths were no longer pained. My back felt straighter, stronger, and the sag went out of my shoulders. Like Grandmother Villetta I had outlived my judges. It simply didn't matter anymore. I was free.

Grandmother Villetta tripped on a tear in the carpet, fell and broke her hip. She stroked out a few days later. She would have laughed like a frivolous little girl, though, if she could have foreseen how she would eventually go, after all she had lived, like some cosmic joke, a prank on life. We all coddled her so, as if she were frail, needed us to keep her upright and breathing. She needed none of that, nor do I. If you drop something when you're young you scramble after it. When you're old you watch where it goes. Now I watch for tears in the carpet. That's what it's like to be old.

But what concerned me most at that moment was not old age, but that this guy Dexter had somehow found his way through the woods and up to my house—and that he had my name. Until then I had been opaque to the world, and I preferred it that way. I snapped my fingers, a painful mistake with throbbing knuckles, just once though, and Belle let out a single, groin-tingling growl.

Dexter backed up so quickly he got himself tangled in the bushes. A string of nettles stitched an angry red line across his face. I watched in disgust as one by one each spot of red disappeared from his perfectly porcelain face.

"How have I lived so long?" I sputtered indignantly. "It wasn't those…those damned *machines*. I take an aspirin every morning and two shots of good Tennessee whiskey after dinner. That's it."

So there you have it, the secret of my long life—well, that and not giving a damn about what has happened to the world.

"Now go," I ordered. "Don't come back." I ratcheted the rifle again, ejecting an unspent cartridge over my shoulder. Belle seconded my order with some menacing and well-timed growls.

Dexter about shat himself to get out of there. He scrambled through the brush, throwing his arms out as if he were swimming, getting poked and scratched and making those nanites work overtime. Soon he was gone, just the crunch of his footfalls far below and off a way. Later I saw his net cast. All he had to show for his journey up my hill was video of a cactus and a bit of audio, my secret of long life. Somebody zipped him a question that scrolled across the bottom of the screen. "Where can you get Tennessee whiskey?" it asked, but spelled like this: "*wr cn u gt tn wsky.*"

Otherwise no one cared about the rumor of an old man in the woods. Nothing more came of that net cast, at least for a long time. Dexter had called me Carl in his net cast. The bastard. ·

T W O

I should tell you about my house, considering the role it's had in all of this. I was four years old when Daddy had it built. We were living off 21ˢᵗ Avenue then, not too far from Vanderbilt, in a yellow three-bedroom stucco house that fit my family perfectly until I unexpectedly came along. My brother Leavitt, nine years old when I was born, had his own room, and my sisters Sadie and Elizabeth, only a year apart at seven and six, shared a room and a bond that set them apart from their brothers. My sisters never showed much interest in me, and Leavitt was just a brooding presence that sometimes stirred the dust of their otherwise insular world.

So Leavitt was *my* problem. He resented having to share his room with me. I can remember him glowering at me behind Mama's back as she made up our beds. They were bunk beds. Leavitt made me sleep in the top bunk, which for a little kid seemed as high and insecure as the swaying upper branches of a tree. The thing rocked whenever Leavitt tossed and turned below. I was terrified that I would fall out in my sleep. If I whined about it Leavitt would poke me and slap me on the back of the head and in general torment me to tears; and if I dared threaten to tell Mama then bar the doors, there was hell coming. Worse, I had to tell Mama that I *preferred* the top bunk or else face the consequences.

But his growing family wasn't the only reason Daddy wanted a new house. Richard Jeffries had come from a farming family, solid and hardworking, but simple folk. While Mama had come from a farming family, too, she had been a Smith, prominent people in middle Tennessee in those days. Daddy had married up, that was the gossip as well as the truth, so maybe he had something to prove. Daddy wasn't going to take up the life of a farmer; he wasn't going to endure the veiled disapproval of the Smiths. After the war he went to real estate school instead. Millions of G.I.s just like him were mustering out after the war, and few of them wanted to go back to the farm, either. They were going to have to live somewhere. Somehow Daddy saw this coming. Business was good and Daddy was successful. By 1963 the time had come to show everyone just how successful.

For me, the announcement that we would soon be moving into a new house came as a relief. Leavitt had become a teenager and even more cruel. But there was also the excitement of change, the first big event of my life. Maybe this is why I remember it so well. There was a whole new energy in the house, strange and important activities were underway. I remember watching my parents pile through leaves of floor plans, laying them out side by side on the dinner table, curling edges held down by empty glasses. The mimeograph smell of the blue ink sweetened the pungent smell of cigarette smoke, which trailed up from heavy crystal ashtrays to gather below the ceiling like a sea fog. Daddy and Mama didn't argue or bicker, such as it was, but I could tell that they were at odds. There were the questions of masonry or clapboard on the exterior, antebellum or modern in design. It made me feel smart to have heard these words. I would repeat them, especially when I was around Leavitt or the girls, even though I didn't know what they meant.

Then the debate moved on to tile or linoleum in the kitchen, whether they should use wood paneling or wallboard in the living room, whether or not the kids' rooms should be carpeted. Paint color became a point of contention. These proceedings went on for days, maybe weeks. Time is elongated to a child. I sat invisibly on the floor and observed all of this while my brother and sisters were in school. In a way this new house was mine from its inception.

They finally settled on a two-story red-brick ranch design with white shutters and trim. Daddy told Mama that ranch houses were the latest, most modern thing. I think Mama would have preferred something more traditional. "Can't we at least have white columns and a marble stairway, Dick?" she asked, pleaded really.

"I will not ape those holier-than-thou people in Belle Meade," Daddy answered self-righteously. He was still sensitive to class distinctions, although this is not something I would understand until I was older. "Listen, Mabel," he argued, "no one's gonna say that Richard Jeffries is trying to cozy up to those people. They wouldn't let me list a servant's shack in Belle Meade, let alone a whole property. I'm sure as hell not going to pretend I'm one of 'em. Our house will be just as good as theirs, better even. You'll see."

Mama sighed and let it go.

Daddy had bought a piece of property in Green Hills. Yes, *that* Green Hills. He would drive me up there with him from time to time to check on the progress of construction. Mama seldom came along on these trips, and of course Leavitt and the girls were in school. Sitting in the car, watching the workers, Daddy would sometimes point out a feature, squeeze my leg and ask me what I thought. I felt as if I were Daddy's partner in all of this, someone he relied on for feedback and sound advice. He made me feel big, first grade, second grade even. Sometimes there's a benefit to being the last child.

All through the spring and into the summer we watched that house going up, first a bare cement foundation studded with pipes, then skeletal boards in a naked, open frame, finally red brick walls rising in time-lapse increments from visit to visit.

Our drives to the house followed along narrow, hilly roads, steep in places. I would bounce on the seat trying to see over the hood as we climbed. Couldn't. It was as if we were launching into the sky. Giant trees branched out over the roads, casting a dappled shade that flickered across my eyes. It was an enchanted place. I thought so then. In a way it still is even now.

Daddy had bought a steep tract on the southeast side of Shy's Hill. The house was situated about three quarters of the way up, and cut into the hill such that the front door opened up on the first floor, while the back doors let out from the second floor. The house was (and is) rock solid. Situated on the southeast side of the hill as it is, it faces away from oncoming bad weather like thunderstorms and tornadoes. I don't think Daddy planned it that way—I don't think he thought about it at all—but this became lucky for me later on.

Landscapers had put in an immaculate lawn, as smooth and green as a golf course tipped up on its side. Mama would eventually try to put out some shrubs and roses, but the yard was too steep for her so she gave it up. They left one hickory tree in the yard, almost half way up the hill. The rest had been cut and cleared. This hickory was young at about twenty years, with branches still low enough that the tree was easy to climb. I liked climbing that tree. From the middle branches I could look straight across through the windows into the second floor living room. They had gone with the wood paneling. I could also see on through to the rear sliding glass doors that let out onto the patio and the back yard, which was just a small area cleared out of the dense woods that still crowned the hill. We had neighbors on either side of us, but their houses were screened by trees so there was nothing to see there. I especially enjoyed sneaking out and climbing that hickory tree at night, concealed in the branches, spying on the bright doings within, making silent curses at Leavitt as he crossed through to his bedroom.

A redwood deck came off the living room through sliding glass doors to hover over that sloping lawn. Sometimes Daddy would come out at night to smoke and take in the view, city lights twinkling below us as if we were kings on our hill and Daddy was surveying our realm. I would stay very still as Daddy took these moments. He seemed to be deep in thought. Then he would shake his head, smash out his cigarette and go back inside, flipping off the lights, setting everything into the silver glow from a television down the hall. I could see him in my mind, padding across Mama's hard-won carpet into their bedroom. The night would grow quiet, just the rustle of leaves, and then Leavitt would slip out into the darkness, gently slide the door closed, and cup his hands against the flare of a match as he lit a cigarette. His face would flash for just that moment, a devilish cast. I could smell the smoke wafting across to the tree, and fought not to sneeze. It would have been all over for me if Leavitt had ever caught me.

We finally moved in on the first of August. In our old house the boxes were taped and stacked and the walls were bare for our final night. Despite my earlier excitement I now felt a nagging sense of unease. All I had ever known was changing. There was an echoing hollowness between the walls now, and peculiar smells I had never noticed before. Bare bulbs gave off a harsh light that hurt my eyes, cast unfamiliar shadows onto once familiar walls. It was still early in the evening but I climbed into my bunk anyway and turned to the wall, away from the light. My eyes were wet and my lips trembled. Leavitt came into the room then. On the long list of bad things about those bunk beds was that Leavitt could rest his elbows on the side board and be eye-level with me as I slept. I could feel him breathing against the back of my head. I tried to ignore him, to pretend I was asleep, but it was no use.

"What's the matter, *Carl?*" he asked, but it wasn't a question really, it was a taunt. "You're not cryin' are you, Carl? *Baby Carl.*" He poked me in the back of the head, just kept on poking. And then I could feel him reaching over and he flicked my ear.

"Ow! Stop it!" I screamed, jerking upright, facing him, rubbing my ear.

Well, that was a mistake.

"What are you going to do about it, *Carl?*" He batted lightly at my face, left, right, left, right, snuck a hand in every few turns to pop my chin.

"Leave me alone!"

"Or what, twerp?" He kept on batting at my face, tugging my hair. "You were an accident, you know that? Mom and Dad didn't even know what to call you. That's why they named you after their cigarettes."

"Did not!"

But it was true that Daddy and Mama smoked Carltons, with the activated charcoal Flavor-Filter. It was all I could do not to cry. If that happened Leavitt would pile it on even worse.

"They did too. And do you know what that makes you?" He grinned and drew it out. He had some black hairs sprouting on his chin that I had never noticed before, and some pimples around his nose. "It makes you a stinky butt."

Oh, Leavitt couldn't contain himself. That last was just too clever. He was laughing as if he had delivered that line on the Ed Sullivan Show. But then...

I caught a whiff of Daddy's Old Spice cologne. So did Leavitt. He choked down that laugh, and the grin slipped off of his face like a bare bottom across a soapy tub. I scooched up to see over his shoulder, and there was Daddy standing in the doorway. Daddy was big across the shoulders, he filled that doorway up. He must not have been there long, but long enough. He didn't look angry, the expression on his face was more akin to pained disappointment. Leavitt whipped around, caught red-handed. I resisted the urge to sneer back at him for fear of retaliation later.

"Leavitt, go help your mother pack the kitchen," Daddy said. His voice was level, not stern at all, but Daddy wouldn't step aside so Leavitt had to squeeze past to get out, ducking low as if he expected to take a punch in passing.

Daddy came to me, patted my leg and gave it a squeeze. "Everything will be fine after tomorrow, Carlton," he said. "Do you want to go to sleep now?"

I chewed on my thumb and nodded.

"Okay, then. You don't have to brush your teeth tonight if you don't want to. I'll turn off the light on the way out. Sweet dreams, son."

I still love the smell of Old Spice. I have a bottle at home, the old ceramic bottle with the gray stopper. I don't wear it, never have, but every so often I'll pull the stopper on that bottle and breathe that scent just to remember Daddy.

* * *

We were up early for breakfast the next morning, just toast and cereal around our dinette table. Everything else was in boxes. Mama seemed flustered, worrying butter onto toast, rearranging our napkins. She had her apron on even though she hadn't been able to cook anything, the white one with the pink flowers.

"Sit down, Mabel," Daddy said. "Everything's going to be fine."

He folded his newspaper and set it aside. Leavitt sat next to him sullenly with his eyes down. The left side of Leavitt's face seemed redder than normal. Sadie and Elizabeth were chattering about something they had looked at on the television.

"Mabel?" Daddy said after a sip of coffee. "Carlton and I need to go for a drive this morning." I perked up at that. Mama nodded as if she already knew what he was going to say. She finally lowered herself into a chair. Did her nose seem red? "We should be back before the movers are ready to go. Sadie? Lizzie?"

My sisters went abruptly silent. "Yes, Daddy?" they said in unison.

"You two help your mother. This is a big job. And Leavitt's going to be a big help, too."

Daddy tousled Leavitt's hair but Leavitt didn't budge or look up.

Daddy drove a white 1962 Pontiac Catalina four-door with a teal interior and lots of chrome. He kept that car spotlessly clean. He was proud of it but he still intended to trade up to a Buick soon.

"Where we goin', Daddy?"

I climbed up into the car, which took both hands and both knees.

"It's a surprise, Carlton. You'll see."

We drove through downtown to Hermitage Avenue and then out Lebanon Pike, heading east. I was up on my knees so that I could see out. It was a cool morning for July, and the sky was bright and blue. I rested my arm on the door the way Daddy did, couldn't quite get it high enough but that was okay. The wind blew through my hair.

We were out of town pretty soon and then the land began to roll, long hills with white fences that rose and fell with the swells, cows grazing, some horse farms along the way. Soon we passed through Lebanon and I thought we must be heading for Grandmother Villetta's house.

"Are we goin' to see Grandmother?" I asked then. April called me *Gwampa* at that age, but if you'd ever met my Grandmother Villetta then you would know that she was *Grandmother* and nothing else.

"No, Carlton," Daddy answered, exhaling smoke. He flicked his Carlton out the window. "Somewhere else. We'll be there soon."

The hills rolled even higher past Lebanon, then the road bent around the Cumberland River toward Carthage. There was a soda fountain in Carthage. That's where I hoped we were going, but after the bridge at Carthage we went straight instead of turning left. Soon we were climbing again. The woods were thick. Daddy turned left on a dirt road that ran down a hill toward the river. We passed some farm houses, some tobacco patches. Chickens flapped in the road. Trailing a cloud of dust, we rounded a bend in the river and then pulled up at a clearing. There were tombstones in the clearing, some old ones, some new ones, some leaning over, some sticking out through stands of Johnson grass. The clearing was surrounded by a white wrought-iron fence, the white paint flaking off, black underneath. There was a gate below an arch of the same flaking wrought iron, a *C* in a circle at the top.

"Here we are," Daddy said.

He got out and I scrambled across the seat after him. He stamped out his Carlton, took his other Carlton by the hand, and led me through the gate into the cemetery. He paused before a large stone. His head was down and his eyes were closed as if he were praying. At last he said, "My daddy's name was Tom. He died in the first world war."

I was fidgeting, toeing the grass. I was *four years old.* This wasn't fun.

"I never knew him," Daddy continued. "I was younger than you, two I think. Then Mama married Pappy Joe. Pappy was a good father to me, and what with my little brother and sister, your Uncle Timmy and Aunt Jewel, I took his name, Jeffries. But I was born a Carlton."

He knelt down and looked me right in the eyes. He had an expression on his face I had never seen before, one that told me this was important business he was talking about.

"That's where your name comes from, son. From our Carlton family. I'm proud of it. I want you to be proud of it, too."

I must have grown a foot right then.

"This stone here is Mama and Pappy," he said, pivoting on his heels to face it.

I only ever in my life saw my father cry but once. He didn't cry now but it was close. He shook that off, stood, and led me to another stone.

"And this one over here is Uncle Lou Carlton. I liked him a lot. Uncle Lou sure could fish. If he took you fishing you knew you were going to catch something."

He smiled fondly and rubbed the stone with his left hand, holding me fast with his right.

"My daddy's not here," he said after a moment, his hand resting on Uncle Lou Carlton's stone. "He's buried over in France in the Argonne cemetery. Remember that." He fixed me with that look again. I will never forget it. I nodded soberly. "I've never been there," he went on. "I'd hoped to see him during the war but they sent me to the Pacific instead."

I was starting to fidget again. Daddy let me go, tapped out a Carlton and lit it.

"So," he said after a few puffs. "That's it, then. We'd better get back home or your mother will be cross with me."

* * *

I slept most of the way back. It was afternoon now and getting hot. There was a big truck taking up most of the street in front of our house. Mama had parked her Rambler farther up the block, so Daddy edged on past the truck and parked behind Mama's car. Everyone was in the front yard as we walked up. Mama still had her apron on. Her hair had fallen and was in her eyes. She kept puffing it back into place. Leavitt looked both bored and annoyed. He didn't so much as look my way as we came up. My sisters were sitting cross-legged in the grass playing with their Barbie dolls. They wore identical white dresses, as if they were twins. There were strangers in the house today. Mama wouldn't have her girls looking like urchins.

Daddy paused at the curb to take in the scene. Big, gruff men were moving up and down the driveway between the house and the truck, carrying boxes and pieces of furniture. One of the men was *black*. I gawked, but Daddy shook me and told me to stop it.

"Well that took all day," Mama said in an agitated voice. "Did you feed this boy some lunch?"

"No, Mabel," said Daddy guiltily. He lowered his eyes. "Carlton slept most of the way."

"I'm not hungry, Mama," I added in defense of my daddy.

"Get over here, Carlton," she ordered. "I'll get you a sandwich out of the basket."

Moments later I was chewing on peanut butter and jelly while Daddy and Mama went off to talk privately. It was decided that we would head up to the new house before the movers got there so that we could get everything ready and tell them where to put things. And I think Mama was ready to make a break of it with our old house, the only house she had known as an adult. I happen to know that she never returned to it, never once drove past for old time's sake. "Didn't belong to us anymore," she told me years later. "It's somebody else's house now." I, however, did visit it off and on over the years. It became a recording studio for a time, and then a lawyer's office. Now, of course, it's gone.

Daddy went into the house to speak with the movers. He came out carrying a box of papers.

"Okay then," he said. "Let's get going. I'd like to take Carlton with me, Mabel, if you don't mind taking the rest of the kids in your car."

Mama nodded and herded everyone toward the Rambler. Daddy put the box in the back seat of the Pontiac, I climbed back in, and we were off to our new life.

We got to our new house before Mama and the others. Daddy turned up that steep drive and all I saw was sky. I bounced up and down on the seat trying to see the house, but it wasn't until we were at the top that I could make it out. The garage was on the west end of the house, and was really a half basement the way the house was cut into the hill. The driveway continued on around the back of the house, though, and this is where Daddy parked the car. We got out and quick-stepped down and around to the garage. Daddy pulled the doors up, went through the garage and unlocked the inner door. It was cool in the garage. The walls were cement, very strong. There was a low door in a far corner. Daddy said it was a root cellar for Mama. In truth it was a storm shelter or, in the original plans, a fallout shelter. There had almost been a nuclear war the year before, the Cuban Missile Crisis. I was too young at the time to know that, though.

We went through the inner door into the utility room, a brand new washer and dryer for Mama already installed. Beyond the utility room was a hallway with three bedrooms, one each for me, Sadie, and Elizabeth.

"Which one is mine?" I asked Daddy.

"Which one do you want?" he asked me.

This seemed like a terribly important decision, so I walked into each of them, whirled around on the carpet, looked out the windows.

"I want the first one," I said at last. This was the one closest to the utility room. Why I wanted that one I can't say, but it felt right.

"Okay, then," Daddy said. "It's yours."

I beamed at that, bounced on my heels, and then we continued on. The hallway led to a vestibule at the front door. Carpeted stairs went up to the second floor. To the left was a bathroom, and beyond the vestibule was a den, also done in wood paneling. There was a gas fireplace at the far end of the den. Bookshelves were built into the walls, lots of bookshelves. Wide windows looked out on the front yard.

We went up the stairs into the living room. This was a big, open space that took up the whole floor from front to back. Sliding glass doors in the front opened onto the redwood deck, which was off-set so as not to hang over the front door, while sliding glass doors in the back opened onto the porch, with its views of the woods above. The room was so large and bright that a corner of it would also serve as the dining room. The kitchen was off the back of the living room to the left, with its own door to the outside. Through the living room on the east end, like a mountain aerie, would be Leavitt's room. He was the eldest, Daddy explained, and had earned his privacy. Another hallway went off to the west end of the house. Through it were another bathroom, a guest bedroom, and then finally Daddy and Mama's room.

The house was *huge*. I thought it must be a mansion, and that would mean that we must have been…rich? I pondered that, such that I could, and found that I liked the idea. Daddy did, too. I could see the pleased look on his face. What I couldn't see was the satisfaction he felt, that he had *arrived* and he knew it. Daddy was only forty-seven then. What he had achieved he had done on his own. Who in Belle Meade had a big house on a hill? Green Hills was the place to be, and he was right.

We went out the front door to wait for Mama. By the end of the day it would be unconsciously understood by everyone that our main entrance to the house was going to be either through the back doors or through the garage. If parked in front of the garage, using the front door meant walking down the hill a little and then back up the steps. Too much trouble. Mama would never put up with that, especially carrying groceries.

Daddy glanced at his watch, wondering what was keeping Mama, and then we spotted her little brown Rambler creaking up the street below. She had it in a high gear and was just barely making way. She stopped in the street ahead of the driveway. We heard grinding as she shifted into low, and then she popped the clutch and lurched up the driveway. She was about even with the hickory tree when the engine stalled.

"*Oh. Oh, oh*," we heard. There was a reflection on the windshield so we couldn't see in, but I could make out Leavitt through the door window. He was facing Mama, gesturing wildly with his hands. Finally he threw up his hands and leaned back in his seat, covering his eyes with a forearm.

Mama got the car started again, but before she could pop the clutch they started rolling back down the hill.

"*Oh. Oh, oh*," we heard, and then, "*Mom!*" this from Leavitt.

Mama slammed on the brakes and sent the car rocking, and still it rolled back a little. There was a house across the street from us, and from there the hill continued down for quite a way. A car backing out too quickly could shoot across the street to launch backward into our new neighbor's front door. Daddy was suddenly concerned.

"Mabel, honey?" he said in a panic. He sprinted down the driveway. I followed.

The Rambler lurched again, gained maybe a foot before it began to roll back—again.

"*Oh. Oh, oh*." This was Mama's flustered voice, and now the girls were starting to screech a little.

"Mom, just stop!" Leavitt was begging her. He had the door open with one leg out.

"Leavitt, you get back in this car!" I heard Mama order. The girls sounded like a troupe of monkeys in the back seat.

Gears ground and the Rambler popped forward again, stalled again. By that time Daddy had reached Mama's door.

"Dick, I have never been so humiliated in my life," Mama complained.

Daddy kept trying to say something but the words wouldn't come. He seemed completely perplexed. I caught up to them then.

"Hi, Mama," I said, waving and smiling. Mama's hair was all down in her face, and she was sweating, really sweating.

"You stand back, Carlton," she said.

"Look, Mom," Leavitt said. "Just pull the brake and let us out."

"He's right, Mabel," said Daddy.

"I have never been so humiliated," said Mama. But she took their advice and set the brake. Leavitt climbed out, looked up and down the street self-consciously.

The people across the street had come out to see what all the commotion was about. Leavitt groaned and cast his eyes down. He folded the seat and pulled Sadie and Elizabeth out of the back. Their pretty white dresses were wrinkled now, and Sadie had lost a shoe.

"You folks need any help?" the neighbors called.

"No, we're fine," answered Daddy, and then to Mama, "Mabel, just hop out and I'll drive it up."

"I've never been so humiliated," said Mama. She thrust a leg out but couldn't get herself up against the steepness of the hill. Her legs flailed around immodestly and her dress bunched up around her waist. Daddy finally took hold of her and tugged her gracelessly to her feet. Once she was out she saw the neighbors. "Oh. Oh, oh," she exclaimed in embarrassment. She spun around with her back to them and quickly went to work on her hair, which was pasted to her face in loose strands and curls. After she had made it into what she thought was presentable, and after she had patted her dress back down over her hips, she turned to the neighbors and with a forced smile said, "Hello. We're just having a little trouble with the car. Sorry to disturb you. Come children," she said then, and began to puff up the hill, still adjusting her hair.

I looked back and forth between Mama and Daddy. "Go with your mother, Carlton," Daddy said. "I'll take care of this."

So I skipped after Mama. The girls were hugging each other a few steps behind us, Sadie limping along without her shoe, and then came Leavitt, eyes down and with his hands thrust deeply into his pockets. Daddy rolled the Rambler back into the street, got it started again, waved to the neighbors, and then shot it up the hill.

Mama did not speak of that episode again, at least not in front of us. I'm pretty sure that was a Thursday. By Saturday Mama was driving a brand new Buick. Daddy's Pontiac would be around for a while after all.

* * *

We settled in, and soon our new house felt like a home instead of an adventure. Before long Leavitt and Sadie and Elizabeth started a new school year. Since my birthdays came after the school year started, Mama took me to a private school that was supposed to get me into first grade next year even though I would still only be five. Leavitt continued to pick on me but it wasn't as easy now. After all, he was upstairs on one end of the house while I was downstairs on the other end. And he was more careful about it, craftier, like the time he loosened the caps on my finger paints. Those were the first stains in our new carpet. I promised I would get him back some day.

What was really peculiar was that Sadie and Elizabeth would take turns sleeping over in each other's rooms. Elizabeth's room was next to mine, so on those nights that she stayed in Sadie's room I was happily all alone at my end of the hall, and I could slip out unnoticed through the garage at night to climb my tree.

Our neighbors across the street were the Gormans. They looked as old as Grandmother Villetta. With no kids of their own they doted on me and I shamelessly took advantage. Mrs. Gorman had this uncanny ability to always have a plate of cookies on hand, still warm from the oven. I started coming around a lot, but she didn't seem to mind.

It was Mr. Gorman who told me that we lived on a famous hill.

"It was during the War Between the States," he explained one day, "the Battle of Nashville."

My teeth locked on a cookie. There had been a *battle*—in *Nashville?* I knew all about wars and battles from television, but never knew we had one going on here.

"Now don't you worry yourself, boy," he said, patting my head. "This was a long, long time ago. The Yankees broke through General Smith's line just the other side of the hilltop," he pointed toward the woods above our house, "and drove our boys down this side and all the way to Franklin. The fighting was fierce. Colonel Shy was killed. That's where our hill gets its name."

He paused and his eyes lost focus, the way Grandmother Villetta's sometimes did.

"My papa was in that," he said quietly after a moment.

"Your daddy was in a war, too?" I asked. It seemed that everyone's daddy had been in a war.

"Yes he was." Mr. Gorman smiled. "Good thing for me he wasn't killed."

Mrs. Gorman peeked around the doorway from the kitchen. "Now you quit tellin' that boy those Civil War stories, Frank," she chided her husband. "You'll give him nightmares."

"Oh, he's big enough to hear it, Bea."

"I am big enough," I added, and I started in on another cookie. Mrs. Gorman just scowled and went back into her kitchen.

"Up there in the woods," Mr. Gorman said, pointing again, "there are still relics to this day."

"What's a relix?" I asked.

"Leftover things, metal parts, like the triggers and actions of rifles, and belt buckles and pins and lead balls and percussion caps. People still come up, and historians. They go through the woods looking for these things."

"Really?"

"Yep. I'll show you."

Mr. Gorman led me into another room, which was crowded with tables and glass display cases. There were antique rifles on the walls, a Rebel flag, a complete gray uniform with a sword and scabbard. There were models of battles on the tables, miniature soldiers in blue and gray. Inside the display cases were fragments of metal, buttons, shaving razors, a fork—all arranged in neat rows with white paper labels held down with sewing pins. I was mesmerized.

So I took to going up into the woods after school. My school let out at noon, so I had a couple of hours to myself before Leavitt and the girls got home. The woods were thick, full of brush. Our land didn't go all the way to the top of the hill, the city owned that. There was a chain-link fence in the woods, so overgrown that I couldn't even tell it was a fence until I had to climb over it. The top of the hill wasn't as thick with brush. A big, rusty water tank sat up there, like an artifact from an earlier civilization. Otherwise the woods were so dense all around that I really couldn't see anything. In later years an historical society would buy the hilltop and make a little park up there, with a split-rail fence and flags and a sign. They even hauled up a cannon and set it near the flagpoles. That cannon is still up there, half sticking out of the ground. Now it's a relic, too.

The next morning after my first trek up the hill I awoke with itchy chigger bites all over me. Mama just clucked her tongue, dabbed clear fingernail polish onto them, and sent me off to school. Later I came home with ticks on me, which Mama removed with alcohol. "Watch out for hornets and snakes," she warned me. Despite the hazards, I got to where I loved the woods. Can't say why, but I spent as much time up there as I could.

My fifth birthday came and went, then it started to get cool at night, finally down-right cold. It was the week before Thanksgiving and I was up in the woods. Everything was so different with the leaves off the trees. For the first time I could see houses down below, and hear the sounds of the traffic on Harding Place. There was a great tree up there, an ash, so old and gnarled that it seemed it would fall over soon. This tree was usually concealed from view by brush and the canopies of other trees, but with the leaves off I could see every bit of it, every naked, twisted limb. One branch hung low like an elephant's trunk, so I climbed, kept going higher and higher.

Now I could really see. I saw the roof of our house; I watched the traffic on Harding Place. I nestled down into the crook between a branch and the trunk, and hugged the trunk as I peered around for a view the other way. That trunk was too big for me to get my arms around, but there were deep fissure in the bark, perfect handholds. What I saw in that direction looked pretty much the same, more houses, a car coming up Shy's Hill Road. But then my eyes came to rest on the trunk right in front of me. There was a knot in the trunk, a perfectly round and calloused hole. I stuck a finger in it and felt something cold and metallic.

I had a pen knife that Mr. Gorman had given me, small but with a pretty mother-of-pearl handle. I opened it and began to dig into the knot. I scratched at something and saw that it was shiny. Now I was really excited. I gouged and dug into that knot and finally got whatever it was out. It was a piece of metal about the size of my thumb, round on one side but flattened on the other like a little mushroom. It was all black except where I had scratched it, which was as shiny as silver. I was sure that I had found a relic! I was so excited to show my prize to Mr. Gorman that I climbed down right then and ran down the hill to his house.

I knocked on the Gorman's door urgently, waited a second and knocked some more. I held out my hand proudly to show off my prize as Mrs. Gorman answered the door, but the grin fell off of my face the moment I saw her. She was crying big wet tears. Her nose was running and her eyes were red-rimmed and puffy. She had a shawl around her shoulders, which she clutched tight at her throat. Her fingers were strained white. I was so shocked and scared I couldn't say anything.

"You need to go home, Carlton," she said. "Go home right now." With that she pushed the door closed.

I stood rigid for a moment staring at the door, and then I spun around and raced home. I slammed into the kitchen and found Mama sitting at the breakfast table, her face in her hands. She looked up at me, her face as distraught as Mrs. Gorman's had been.

"Mama? I said, practically terrified.

"Oh, Carlton, honey."

She held out her arms and I ran to her. She hugged me so tight I could barely breathe.

"Oh, Carlton, honey," she whispered. "The president's been killed."

There was a screech of tires outside and then Daddy burst into the kitchen. He stared at Mama and me, his face ashen, and then he rushed over and held us.

I remember John F. Kennedy. I remember hearing him speak. There was something about his voice that made you want to get up and do great things, even little kids like me. What was really strange is that Daddy and Mama had always been what they called *Eisenhower Republicans*. They were none too fond of Jack Kennedy, but he was their president. It's not that way now, hasn't been for a long time. If something like that happened today I think the other side would cheer.

That was just the beginning, the beginning of times like no other. And I'm the only one left who remembers them.

THREE

This cold cuts to the quick. My fingers are so stiff and bloodless I can barely hold my pencil. I could light my stove but it's so close in here that I'm afraid I'll catch the place on fire. I can't even sit up, the roof is sagging so low. I've lost track of time writing out this story. It's gotten late now, an even dimmer gray. The treetops look black against this formless sky. It's quiet, so still. The rain has let up. I can hear the stream rustling, and the *tick, tick, tick* of dripping trees, but otherwise nothing—no birds, no animals scuttling in the bushes. Sam is dry now, sleeping beside me. He's so warm he radiates heat like an open oven. I hate to disturb him, to lose his warmth. The next shelter, if it still stands, is Wadleigh Stream eight miles farther on, with Nesuntabunt Mountain in the way. All those rocks. I almost broke my ankle on that mountain during my second thru-hike. I won't make it if I leave now. I'd better stay put for the night, hope for better weather in the morning.

The mountains will be the hardest on me. Despite my age I can still plod along, put one foot in front of the other, but mountains take all I have. I didn't go up Mount Katahdin this time, to start the hike properly, but I did find the trail. Even though there hasn't been any trail maintenance in decades or more, so many thousands had hiked that trail over the years, had packed the soil hard beneath their shoes or else polished the bare rock where it was exposed, that I could still make out a faint trace through the woods and over the rocks up the flank of the mountain. I even found remnants of the old white blazes on some of the rocks, just specks of paint clinging to the stone. It's hard to tell these old specks of paint from lichen, but stepping back from them they join like pixels into vague vertical rectangles, residual outlines of the trail markers that once showed us the way.

Nevertheless the trail up Katahdin was too steep. I had to let it go. I did get over the Rainbow Ledges without too much difficulty. That was nine miles ago, this morning. Seems like last week. The trail over the Rainbow Ledges follows an easy grade, though. Nesuntabunt is different, steeper. It's going to be tough.

I was given my first trail name coming down Nesuntabunt Mountain. I had met up with a man at this very shelter. Hank was his name. Hank had a full head of wiry gray hair streaked with black, a bushy beard to match, and a big belly held up by a wide leather belt. I think he was in his forties, but he could have been sixty or more considering the grizzled look of him. He was already flopped out in the shelter when I came up, blowing languid smoke rings toward the ceiling. I found him lying on his back, on an antique bedroll that may have once been tied behind a saddle. His head rested on a canvas rucksack, one leg propped on a knee, baggy woolen socks on his feet. Fishing rods rested against an outside wall, shiny lures twining in the breeze. A battered red-metal tackle box sat next to him, along with a pair of worn boots.

It was early evening, the sun going low. I hadn't seen anyone in three days so Hank surprised me, scared me a little, actually. I had seen the movie *Deliverance* a couple of years before, about some city guys who had been stalked and worse by some scary Georgia mountain men. Those brutal images had never left my mind. Hank resembled those mountain men in a way.

He started as I came close, sat up cross-legged and looked me over.

"Hiker, are you?" he asked. *Hiker, air ye?* He spoke in a hard-edged Mainer accent. He had a big gold tooth right up front. Not surprisingly, I learned later that his friends called him Goldie.

"Yeah." I heaved my backpack up onto the floor, wiped stinging salt out of my eyes. Although the mornings had been cool, I sweated through the afternoons, which typically became sticky and hot. "And you?"

"Naw," he said, which sounded like a growl. "Come to fish."

"Catch anything?"

"Naw, too cold yet."

I backed against the edge of the floor and pushed up into the shelter. The air smelled like sweet tobacco. I noticed that the blackflies had stopped biting.

"Don't see many hikers this early," he said. "Goin' the wrong way then, aren't you?" *airn't ye?*

Most thru-hikers went from south to north, from Springer Mountain in Georgia to Mount Katahdin in Maine. In between is about 2180 miles—3508 kilometers— that usually took four to six months to complete. Most northbound hikers started in late March or early April so that they could reach Mount Katahdin before the trails were closed in the fall. I couldn't start my hike until school was out at the end of May, so I went north to south instead. I explained all of this to Hank.

"Hmpf," he grunted, and leaned back against his rucksack. He blew a few more smoke rings from a fat cigar. "You got any food?" he asked after a time.

I tugged a can of pork 'n beans out of my backpack, wagged it in the air. Hank scowled.

"Naw," he said. "Too heavy on the stomach."

I wondered what he meant by that, just looking at the size of his stomach. I shrugged, brought out my stove and set it up on the step out front. I pumped the kerosene can, got a flame going, fetched a pot of water out of the stream and set it to boil.

"You don't need to boil this water," said Hank, somehow aware of my every movement even though his eyes were fixed on his smoke rings as they widened toward the ceiling. "This water's clean."

"The manual says to boil all your water," I said defensively. Hank gave me a sharp look.

"I don't give a damn what the *manual* says," he retorted.

I wasn't in the mood to be scolded by a stranger. "Look, man," I said then, "I'll go camp somewhere else."

I yanked my backpack across the floor and went to shut down my stove.

"Aw, settle down, son," said Hank. "I didn't mean nothin'. You can boil your water if you want. It's not my business. What's your name?"

I appraised him a moment before answering. He seemed contrite enough.

"It's Carlton."

"Carlton, huh? Don't have a trail name yet. We'll need to get you one. I'm Hank."

I had read about trail names. It was a tradition that went way back. Hikers were given nicknames, usually by other hikers, and these were the names one used on the trail. I didn't expect to get my own trail name until I crossed paths with the northbound hikers in a month or two, or unless I caught up with someone else going south.

We settled into the evening, which was pleasantly cool. Frogs croaked and skirled along the stream, and small animals rustled through the brush. The stars were crisp and bright. We didn't make a fire. Fires were too much trouble, and the fire ring was too far from the shelter to provide warmth anyway. I ate three cans of pork 'n beans, heated them up right in the can and then, with a wet bandana around my hand, poured them into my mouth like water from a canteen. I was *starving*, what we on the trail called *hiker hunger*, a gnawing pang that can never be satisfied, only assuaged. Hank, watching in amusement and perhaps sympathy as I wolfed down those beans, handed over some tough jerky, which I accepted with gratitude.

Soon night deepened. The last glow of that day slipped off the horizon until the only light we could see by in the shelter was the periodic flare of Hank's cigar ember. Hank was a talker. He was a truck driver, he said, had been all his life. He told Paul-Bunyanesque tales of hauling logs through the Maine woods, from the Hundred-Mile Wilderness to the paper mill in Millinocket. He swore that once, coming too fast down a steep muddy grade, with his wheels locked and his clutch smoking, he had jack-knifed his rig on purpose to angle it around a sharp turn ahead of an oncoming cliff. He swore that he accomplished without incident. Another time, he said, a bull moose in rut had taken up station in the middle of the road. The moose refused to move. Hank blew his horn at it, edged his front bumper right up to it, but still the moose wouldn't budge. The moose was challenging him, Hank said, so he got out of his truck, rolled up his sleeves, took that moose by the antlers and wrangled it to the ground like a cowboy in a rodeo. Apparently ashamed at itself for being bested, that moose just hunkered off into the woods while Hank climbed back aboard and continued on.

This went on late, until the bugs went silent and the cold began to press in. Hank's cigar ember moved through the dark like a conductor's baton, emphasizing points with sharp checks or else easing along levelly in time with the longer passages. Then he went suddenly silent. I was in my sleeping bag by then, snug, my eyes flickering toward sleep. That silence seemed perfectly timed to give way to the night. I closed my eyes. Sleep was just taking me when Hank took a long, contemplative puff and said, "And I was in the Nam."

My eyes popped open at that. He was talking about Vietnam. His voice had gone melancholy, almost a whisper, that hard Mainer accent tempered by haunting memories of things no one could ever understand unless they had been there. But I didn't want to hear about Vietnam, not then—not even now. I pulled my sleeping bag up around my head and turned my back to him. He mumbled for a while and then I was asleep. Thank God.

The next morning was crisp and clear, so cold and dry that the air stung my sinuses. Hank was already up and dressed when I rolled out of my sleeping bag. His cheeks were a robust red above the scraggly line of his beard, and his eyes were bright with the new day. Any lingering melancholy from the night before had been washed away by the sun. He had a pot of coffee boiling.

"Want a cup?" he asked.

"Sure, thanks."

I accepted a blue enameled cup and set it down to steam while I went off to pee, which also steamed. Then I got everything packed away, pulled on a sweater against the chill, tugged my backpack to the front of the shelter, and sat on the edge of the floor to sip my coffee.

"Here," said Hank. "Pemmican."

He handed me an oily bar the size of a chocolate brownie. I sniffed it cautiously. The smell was—unrecognizable.

"My wife makes 'em," Hank added, taking a bite of one himself. "Nothin' better to carry in the woods."

"What is it?" I asked skeptically.

"Just little bits of things, some tallow, some berries and meal. You get used to 'em."

I took a tentative bite. The taste was waxy, heavy, but not bad. I finished the bar, slurped the last of my coffee and handed back the cup.

"Thanks," I said. I shouldered my backpack and prepared to move out.

"Want some company?" Hank asked, gesturing down the trail with a tip of his head.

"Sure, why not?"

Hank shouldered his rucksack, took his rods in one hand, his tackle box in the other, and we set out.

I would not say that I have ever been a really fast hiker, but I was seventeen then. I moved along pretty well, and Hank stayed right with me. We began our climb of Nesuntabunt Mountain within an hour and a half of leaving Rainbow Stream, still early and crisp out. Hank bounded up the rocks like a much younger man, reaching the top first. We skirted along the ridge, catching views through the trees from time to time, then followed the blazes left through the woods toward our descent. Hank found a rock with a view and sat to rest. He lit a cigar, waving the smoke around his head the way an Indian would in a ritual. It was warming up now so I dropped my backpack and took advantage of the break to pull off my sweater. Blackflies were savaging my neck and ears, and my stomach had begun to ache a mile or so back. I felt miserable. My stomach ached worse when I sat, so I leaned against a tree instead. I loosened my belt and sipped some water. My stomach was rumbling like a boiling kettle, and now I could taste that pemmican in the back of my throat, grease and bile. I sipped more water and swallowed hard.

"Well, I'm ready to get goin' again," Hank said some minutes later. He knocked the ember off of his cigar and dropped the stub into a shirt pocket. I could hear his knees popping as he got heavily to his feet. "You ready?" he asked.

"Sure," I said with a grimace. I had that sour taste in my throat, and my stomach was aching bad. I would have crawled into my sleeping bag right then if I had been alone, but I couldn't—wouldn't—let Hank see me struggling so.

I got out ahead of him and started down the mountain, hugging my aching stomach. This was a rocky trail, old granite covered in moss, slippery in places. I jumped from rock to rock woozily, each impact like a knife into my belly. Hank was whistling along behind me, not a care, navigating the rocks as easily as a mountain goat. I took a long step onto a low rock and came down hard. I groaned and doubled over at the ache in my belly. My stomach rumbled loud enough to scare the birds, and then…I passed gas like a whale blowing on a breach. Oh, speaking of *Deliverance*!

"Damn, Carlton!" Hank exclaimed.

I was too relieved to be embarrassed. I felt as if I had just thrown up some bad fish, miserable one moment and then elated the next. Afterward, with every jarring step from rock to rock, the pressure in my stomach came out in rat-a-tat sputters and long bellows.

"Jesus, Carlton!" Hank complained. "You sound like you got your jake brake on going down this hill."

A jake brake is the engine brake old diesel trucks once used when they went downhill, raising a staccato racket loud enough to shake walls. I paused and looked back guiltily. Hank was waving the air in front of his face with the hand carrying the tackle box.

"That'll teach you to lay off the beans, then," he added in disgust.

But, oh, my stomach felt so good now, so light. And I got my trail name, Jake Brake. It stuck with me all the way to Georgia, although I shortened it to Jake later on.

Hank and I parted at Nahmakanta Lake. It wasn't even noon yet but the day had warmed pleasantly. The sky was perfect, not a cloud in it. Hank had a baited line in the water before he even dropped his rucksack.

"I can't tell the ponds from the lakes," I told him, looking out across the tranquil water. The ponds looked as big as the lakes to me. "What's the difference?"

"Well," said Hank, thinking. He rested his fishing rod in the crook of an arm and scratched at his beard. "If you can swim across without drownin' it's a pond."

I laughed at that.

We shook hands then, said our goodbyes, and I returned to the trail, sad in a way. I liked Hank, and he taught me a few things. He taught me that cigar smoke would drive away the bugs; that cold spring water coming straight out of the ground was always safe to drink since there was nothing on the surface to pollute it; and that the first thing I should do if I were to be charged by a moose was to find a place to hide. Apparently moose would quickly forget about you if they couldn't see you.

I made it to the Potaywadjo Spring shelter that evening, drank that icy cold water straight from the spring and never had a problem. I have sometimes thought of Hank over the years. I never learned his age or his last name, and I never saw him again.

* * *

Hated to do it, but I had to wake up Sam so that I could get into my sleeping bag. He was a bit groggy at first, but then he began to jump around and tug at his leash, expecting us to take off walking again. Sorry Sam, can't do it. Do you know that you can see disappointment in a dog's eyes? I would rather disappoint a person…well, I've done that, too, but a dog doesn't hold it against you. Soon enough they forget all about it. Sam is back to sleep now. It's going to take me a while to warm up this sleeping bag. I swear this cold just clings to me! It feels like something I should be able to brush off. I kept my hands under Sam's belly until the stiffness was gone, so now I can begin again.

I could tell you all about the 1960s, the war and the assassinations and the riots, but I'm not going to go into it. I'm sure you've read all about it in your histories. Sure it was a transformative time. What could I add? The perspectives of a child? I will only say this: The very same generation of young people that John F. Kennedy inspired to do great things, so much so that they set off a social revolution, went on to become as conservative as their parents but with an added streak of self-righteous hedonism that was responsible for transforming us from citizens into consumers. That's not what Jack Kennedy asked of us, but that's the transformation we've inherited from the 1960s. I despised it when I still cared. You would, too, you just don't know any better.

Regardless, life on Shy's Hill wasn't affected much by all the turmoil. We saw these things on television, disturbing things, but they seemed far removed from us. My main problem in life was Leavitt, not some march in Alabama or riot in Los Angeles. Leavitt never let up on me. As he became a gangly teenager he would invite his friends over and they would join in as well. I took to spending as much time as I could up in the woods, away from Leavitt. I concocted fantasies of revenge, of Leavitt and his friends committing the error of following me into the woods, the traps I would set for them, how I would lure them along a false trail into that patch of stinging nettles. It was satisfaction, if only in my mind. I never once knew Leavitt to go into the woods.

Leavitt bullied me and he got away with it. His mistake came when he went after Elizabeth. It was June 12, 1965, Elizabeth's thirteenth birthday. This was a special day, even more special for Lizzie since, for the first time, she would be having her own birthday party. Sadie's birthday was June 4, you see, so close to Lizzie's birthday that when my sisters were babies Daddy and Mama would just put on one birthday for both of them. They thought this was so cute that as the girls grew up my parents continued the joint birthday parties as if Sadie and Lizzie were twins, even dressing the girls alike until Sadie rebelled on her tenth birthday and demanded her own outfit. Both girls got presents, and both girls had little circles of candles on their cake; but between them they always knew that it was June 4, Sadie's birthday, not Lizzie's. This practice would be frowned upon in later decades, a loss of individuality for the second child it was claimed, but no one thought that way back then. Today I guess most kids would just be happy to have any kind of birthday party at all.

Sadie was the one who put an end to this. It was right after the girls celebrated their first birthday in our new house, which had been, incidentally, Sadie's thirteenth birthday. She had seemed like her usual self all during the party, chattering and grinning with her perfect little teeth, taking extra care that she didn't accidentally blow out Lizzie's candles, insisting that Lizzie open a present first. Lizzie was quiet as she always was, wearing a shy smile, eyes down most of the time, but happy. She seemed happy. Afterward, Sadie confronted Mama in the kitchen. Red in the face, she told Mama that from then on she wanted separate birthday parties or else no parties at all. Mama was shocked. Sadie was thirteen now and starting to bud. From one year to the next Mama had seen her eldest daughter go from sweet if rambunctious child to stubborn teenager. It was unsettling.

This became a family scandal in time. Leavitt and I stayed out of it. These were girl doings, something we couldn't fathom. I had my woods. Leavitt had his prick friends. This was all that mattered to us. Daddy began to have talks with Sadie in the den. Sometimes I could hear his voice rising through the air conditioner vents. Sometimes I could hear Sadie talking back. This was *brazen*. Sadie must have grown a foot or more that year. She became this svelte girl, like the British models we saw on television. She cut her hair into a thick bob that barely covered her ears. She had dark hair, brown like chocolate. She started wearing tight capri pants, and tennis shoes without socks. She actually wore these things to school! Sometimes I would see Mama in the kitchen after breakfast, after Sadie had shown off a new outfit, and I could tell that Mama was upset.

On her fourteenth birthday, June 4, 1965, Sadie went to a friend's house for a slumber party instead of having her birthday party at home. That night after dinner we all went into the den to watch TV. Mama was uneasy. She would fidget, stand as if she needed to go check on something baking in the kitchen, but then fold her hands nervously and sit back down. Daddy was calmer. He sat in his Barcalounger and read the paper. Lizzie hovered over his shoulder, whispering in his ear, smiling and actually showing her teeth. Leavitt was off with his friends somewhere, probably tormenting little kids at the Y. I was propped on my elbows on the floor watching *Rawhide*. It was one of those Norman Rockwell moments. I can still see it like a photograph in my mind. That we had skipped the girls' birthday didn't seem like such a big deal after all.

Later that week Sadie took over the planning for Lizzie's birthday party. Mama had to just step back or else get into a fight she wouldn't win. It was to be a girls-only party, no boys allowed. What did Leavitt care? He took off after breakfast that morning, said he had to go to work. That wasn't true. He had a job sacking groceries a couple of days a week at H.G. Hill's, but I knew he was off that day. For me, though, I felt as if I were being left out of something. It was noon on a Saturday. The sky was heavy. It had been raining on and off all morning. I climbed my hickory tree along with my new best friend, Kenny Batista. Both of us had binoculars, just plastic toys but they worked pretty well. We chose adjacent limbs that branched out toward the living room, and pulled ourselves along the wet bark until we could just make out the windows through the leaves. No one would ever see us. I hooked a leg around the limb and raised my binoculars.

Sadie had set up a round table right in the middle of the living room. There were six or eight girls, all wearing dresses, while Sadie was wearing her new signature look, black capri pants, a white long-sleeved pullover that left one of her shoulders bare, and strapped shoes with raised heels. Sadie was the tallest girl in the room. I got the feeling these girls did what she said. Kenny looked over at me and grinned expectantly. Although Kenny was almost a year older than me, we were both still too young to ogle at girls. He was grinning more about the subterfuge, what mysteries we might soon uncover.

The girls were arranging presents around the table, hanging ribbons and balloons. Sadie paced back and forth like a foreman, pointing, giving orders. I could see her mouth moving, could imagine the authoritative tone of her voice. After a while of this Sadie seemed satisfied. She stood back and examined the table, a hand on her hip, a leg cocked, fingers on her chin. The girls froze in anticipation, waiting with abated breath, and then Sadie nodded. Excited grins burst out. Sadie left the room, went down the hall, and returned a few moments later behind Lizzie.

Lizzie was as pretty as I had ever seen her. She came into the room shyly, wearing a pink chiffon dress, a pink ribbon in her hair. Lizzie had long, soft sandy hair, so different from Sadie. The girls were jumping up and down, mouthing *happy birthday* and whatever else. Sadie smiled demurely and held back while the girls led Lizzie to a chair at the table. Lizzie sat facing us. I could see her smiling, sincerely excited, only a hint of her usual reticence showing as a subdued, flitting quality in her eyes. Sadie was beaming. She clasped her hands and held them to her heart. And then Mama came out of the kitchen carrying the cake, a big cake with white icing and thirteen pink candles, flames dancing. Mama sat the cake in the middle of the table, kissed Lizzie on the cheek, and then, after a sharp look from Sadie that I could make out clear as day, turned around reluctantly and returned to the kitchen.

Kenny was getting antsy. Nothing mysterious at all had happened so far. He jiggled his limb to readjust himself and I shushed him lest one of the girls notice the leaves shaking and give us away. A light rain began to patter into the upper branches but we stayed dry on our lower limbs. Our view was still good through the haze of misty rain. The girls were singing *Happy Birthday to You* with Sadie joining in, while Lizzie smiled wider than I had ever seen her smile in my life. She took a deep breath to blow out her candles, leaned forward, and then…

It happened so fast I couldn't follow it.

"Whoa!" exclaimed Kenny. He pushed his eyes harder against his binoculars. I guess I did, too.

The cake erupted. Smoke clouded our view for a few moments. I could hear the girls screaming, caught a glimpse of Sadie rushing toward Lizzie. The smoke cleared into a light fog. Lizzie was standing with her arms out, a confused, stunned look on her face. Bits of icing and cake were splattered onto her like paint. She had it in her hair, on her dress, on her cheeks. Sadie wrapped her arms around Lizzie's shoulders. Mama came barreling into the room, raised a hand to her face and gasped. The girls were all screeching. They had cake splattered all over them, too. Sadie pushed Lizzie into the hallway toward Daddy and Mama's room, while Mama corralled the girls into the kitchen.

Just like that the living room was empty. Tails of smoke lingered. Lizzie's cake looked as if someone had gone after it with a baseball bat. Kenny was grinning, pressed so hard into his binoculars that they looked like a part of his face. "Cool!" he said excitedly. "So cool!"

I resented that, although I didn't know why. I felt bad for some reason. The rain was coming harder now, finally trickling through the leaves to reach us. We stayed on our limbs, though, and watched as one by one cars spun up that steep driveway to pick up girls who looked like nothing if not traumatized, even though Mama had gotten them cleaned up pretty well. I'm sure some of them were faking it, drawing out all the drama and sympathy they could. Finally we scrambled from our places and jumped onto the wet grass. The rain had let up for the moment.

"You'd better go home, Kenny," I said. "I don't wanna get in trouble."

"Aw," he whined. I could tell he wanted to go inside, sneak up the stairs with me and see what happened. Instead he kicked the grass, turned around sullenly and loped down the hill.

Lizzie wasn't at dinner that night. It was tense around the table. No one spoke. There was just the uncomfortable sound of forks clinking on plates, gulps and swallows. But I watched Sadie. She was eying Leavitt menacingly. He pretended not to notice. He had a stupid smirk on his face that made me even more resentful than usual. What had happened was that the candles on Lizzie's cake were the exploding kind you could buy at novelty stores, but they were more powerful, as if they had been packed like firecrackers. Leavitt swore he had nothing to do with it, actually got defensive and indignant about the accusation. It must have been just a bad coincidence, he argued. Somehow the store must have gotten the candles mixed up. I think Daddy and Mama believed him. I didn't, not that I would ever believe anything Leavitt said.

But Sadie…oh, Sadie. The hate in her eyes chilled me to the bone, even worse than the cold in this shelter. I think I would have run away from home if she had ever looked at me that way. Poor Leavitt.

* * *

Mr. Gorman died about a month later. I don't remember the exact day. The funeral was held at Woodlawn over on Thompson Lane. Even though I was really the only one who knew Mr. Gorman, Mama insisted that we all go to the funeral and pay our respects. Leavitt said he couldn't go because he had to work. This time he was telling the truth.

Mama dressed me in a black suit that was hotter than a sandbox on a sunny August afternoon. She would smack my hand whenever I tugged at my tie to get it off of my itching neck. The girls were dressed alike again, this time in black, but neither complained. Elizabeth had more or less recovered from her birthday fiasco except for a lingering hurt that showed in her eyes. She was still quiet, still shy, and yet she found the resolve to stand up at the dinner table a few days after the party to declare that she would no longer answer to Lizzie. She was Elizabeth, and that was that. But sometimes I would see Daddy and Elizabeth when they thought they were alone. Daddy would affectionately call her Lizzie, and she would let him, although whenever someone else was around he was careful to call her Elizabeth, pronouncing every syllable.

They had Mr. Gorman laid out in a dim room with heavy gold curtains around the walls. Sconce lights and a chandelier flickered like candles. It was cool in there, like a refrigerator. The air smelled funny. Mrs. Gorman greeted us as we came in. Mama held Mrs. Gorman's hands and spoke some consoling words that I couldn't hear, and then we all sat in the front pew as if we were in church. No one else was there. No one. I kept looking around, expecting relatives to start filing in at any moment, but it was just us.

The coffin was open on a draped table. A light shone particularly bright on Mr. Gorman's face. I craned my neck for a better view. I had never seen a dead person before. I was expecting something ghoulish and creepy, but Mr. Gorman could have just been sleeping there. Mrs. Gorman went up with wet eyes and kissed him on the forehead, and then a man whose skin looked as white and pasty as Mr. Gorman's came out to deliver the eulogy.

They didn't bury Mr. Gorman in the ground. Instead they slid his coffin like a chess piece into a square cubby in a long wall, as if he were being stored for some nefarious purpose which, as we know, is pretty much the way it went. And then we left. Daddy and Mama talked in the car about how sad it must be to die alone without family.

I visited Mrs. Gorman a few times after the funeral. She was still ready with the cookies, and would cheer up whenever I came over, but without Mr. Gorman around to tell his Civil War stories there was a heaviness in their home that made me feel uneasy. So I just stopped going. I felt bad about that. I don't know what Mrs. Gorman thought. She must have been terribly lonely. It wasn't long afterward that she moved to a retirement home. I watched Mr. Gorman's Civil War collection being loaded into a moving van, boxed and put away like Mr. Gorman had been. And then their house sat quiet and empty, their walkway gathering leaves, the Gormans forgotten by everyone in time, as if they had never been.

But I didn't forget Mr. Gorman. I still had the gifts he had given me during the two years I had known him: that pen knife, a little round magnifying glass that swiveled into a brass case, some books and a burlap field bag, and the bullet I wore around my neck. Yes, the piece of metal I dug out of the tree that day was a bullet, or as Mr. Gorman explained, a Minié ball. Mr. Gorman, as was his way, had made up a great story for me about that misshapen piece of lead.

"Now exactly which side of the tree did you find this on?" he had asked me. I held up a finger like the trunk of the tree and pointed to the place, high and on the side facing away from our house. "Ah," he said knowingly. "The north side. Let me tell you how it got there. When that tree was very young one of our southern boys took cover behind it. When the Yankees came over the hill he shot one of 'em. Pow!" Mr. Gorman pretended he was firing a rifle, kneeling as low as his old knees would let him and sighting along an imaginary barrel. "Caught that Yankee square in the chest. And then as our brave southern boy was ramming in a new cartridge the Yankees took a shot at him, missed and hit the tree."

"Wow," I said in wonder.

"And so your tree has been growing all these years, getting bigger and bigger, higher and higher, and taking that ball right along with it." He seemed to ponder something for a minute, and then: "Come with me out to the garage, son." He took me by the hand and led me out there.

At his workbench he took a drill and made a hole through my bullet. Then he found a length of leather and threaded it through the hole.

"Now you can wear this around your neck for luck," he told me earnestly, "and everybody will know that you are an experienced Civil War historian."

Mr. Gorman sure knew how to make a kid feel special. I have never understood how such a kind old man could have had so few people come to his funeral. I still have that bullet. The leather fell apart a long time ago so I replaced it with a chain. I'm wearing it now. I think Mr. Gorman would be pleased.

***

A change came over Leavitt during his senior year in high school. He seemed harried and anxious, too distracted to bully me; for that matter he was too distracted to even notice me. I could walk past him when we were alone in the house, wary and prepared to run if he tried anything, but he wouldn't even glance my way. He didn't bring his friends over much anymore. He cut his hair into a bristly crew, kept the nascent hairs on his face cleanly shaved. He began to study hard, which was so unlike him. One night at dinner, this would have been early March, just before his eighteenth birthday, he stood up and informed us that he intended to go to college and become an architect.

Sadie scowled and rolled her eyes. She was a sophomore in high school that year so saw more of Leavitt than she cared to. Her mood was perennially dark. Elizabeth ignored him, or else was just too shy to comment. Daddy and Mama were delighted, though. Daddy clapped Leavitt on the back proudly, more relieved I think. Daddy hadn't gone to college. This was something that nagged at him. He wanted better for his children, but until then Leavitt hadn't shown much promise. And Mama was as excited as a school girl. She began to rattle off colleges they would check on, people she could call.

"What's a architek?" I asked.

Leavitt wouldn't deign to answer himself, so after an awkward pause Daddy answered for him. "An architect is a man who designs buildings, Carlton."

"Or a woman," Sadie mumbled.

Daddy's brows dipped for a moment and Mama looked away, then he continued:

"Before your mother and I built this house we hired an architect to design it for us, so that the construction people would have plans to go by. Architects have an important job."

"Oh," I mouthed.

Sadie observed all of this with suspicion shadowing her face. Architect? *Leavitt?* There was more to it than Leavitt let on. I didn't know the term *student deferment* yet, but Leavitt did, and he was racing against time to get one. Somehow Sadie knew this, too.

It was the spring of 1967 and I was in the third grade. Every afternoon when the bus dropped me off out front I would sprint up the hill and into the woods where my dig was going on. Kenny would join me a few minutes later, just the time it took for him to run the couple of extra blocks from his house. We had staked out a grid maybe ten feet on a side with sticks and white string, and with spoons from the kitchen were removing layers of soil a little bit at a time. We had started our project the previous summer, but so far hadn't found anything but some pieces of broken glass that looked like they came from a coke bottle. Kenny was getting discouraged.

"This isn't a good place," he complained one day. "We need to look somewhere else."

"No way," I snapped back. I reminded him that *I* was the experienced historian and he had to do what I said. Our grid was on the north side of that old ash tree, and I was sure that somewhere within it we would find relics of the Yankee that Mr. Gorman told me our brave southern boy shot. "We'll find something," I said. "Mr. Gorman told me so."

And so we kept at it, day after day, and Kenny always showed up. He was my best friend.

Leavitt began sending out letters to colleges. He would wait by the mail box, or sometimes Mama would, and when the mail came he would sort through it right there until he found what he was looking for. I was often in my tree with Kenny, and we would watch him. Sometimes there was nothing and Leavitt would plod dejectedly up the hill. Sometimes a letter would come for him and he would rip it open urgently. The result was always the same, though. He would hold the letter for a long time, as if he were reading each line twice, and then he would angrily wad up the letter and shove it in a pocket.

But Mama wasn't discouraged. Leavitt was making excellent grades. His report cards were a source of pride for the first time. She bragged about them to her friends. Her boy was smart. He was doing well. And Daddy would throw an arm around Leavitt's shoulders from time to time. Leavitt was even taller than Daddy now, so Daddy had to hitch up on his toes a bit to get his arm up there. It looked comical.

Things were so steady at home that it became hard to remember how bad Leavitt had been to me. Even Elizabeth was perking up, now that the school year was coming to an end. Soon her solitary final year in junior high would be over and she would be able to join Sadie in high school. She talked about it all the time, with Sadie giving advice on boys and other things. Mama sighed whenever she heard this talk. Sadie had a boyfriend now. Sometimes Mama would look worried, too.

I had come up the stairs one day and was crossing the living room toward the kitchen. Leavitt was on the couch studying, oblivious to anything else. Mama was shopping and the girls were somewhere. I passed Leavitt, craning my head to see what he was reading. The writing was too small to make out, and there weren't any pictures. Boring.

I kept on, was just pushing into the kitchen when I heard, right in my ear like a whisper, "Hey Carl."

"Wha?"

I spun around and—whack!—Leavitt flicked my ear—*hard*. He had snuck up behind me and I didn't even know.

"Ow!"

"Get outta here, twerp," he sneered.

I turned to run for it but he smacked me on the butt before I could get through the door.

"Ow!"

Leavitt's laughter followed me all the way out the back door. The bastard.

* * *

I was up my tree on a Saturday when the mail came. Mama had taken Leavitt to the J.C. Penny to buy some clothes, so I dropped to the ground and went to fetch the mail myself. There were a bunch of letters in the box, inside of a folded *Saturday Evening Post*. I took them out and turned to run up the hill, but there was Sadie standing right behind me out of nowhere. She scared me a little.

"Give those to me," she ordered.

"Okay," I said, and I handed them over.

Sadie flipped though the letters absently but then paused at an official looking envelope.

"What is it?" I asked.

"Shut up."

She tore open the envelope and took out the letter. She studied the letter, her brows knitting.

"Mama says you're not supposed to read other people's mail," I whined.

"I said, shut up," Sadie shot back.

She held up the letter and a devious smile crossed her lips.

"Well, well, well," she mused to herself, "it looks like Leavitt's been accepted to Western Kentucky U. Too bad."

"Huh?"

She folded the letter and pushed it into her waistband. She took my shoulder and squeezed it hard, knelt and looked at me with cold eyes.

"Don't you say anything. Understand?"

My blood seemed to run cold. I nodded nervously.

"Good," she said. "Now go somewhere and play. Go on!"

She patted my butt, not hard, but I took off for the woods. I looked over my shoulder once as I ran. Sadie was marching up the hill. She looked triumphant.

* * *

Leavitt was drafted into the Army the week after he graduated from high school. Mama was beside herself.

"They can't take him, Dick," she pleaded. "They can't."

They were outside on the deck. Leavitt was at some kind of orientation and the girls were in their rooms. I was up my tree watching everything.

"It'll be okay, Mabel," he said sadly. He hugged Mama. "Leavitt will be fine."

"But they'll send him—*over there*."

"It's not that bad," Daddy consoled her. "It'll be over soon anyway, maybe even before he gets through boot."

Mama just cried.

I was in the den watching television alone when Leavitt came in later that evening. He had me trapped. I looked around fretfully for a way out. Leavitt sat silently, his face unreadable.

"You know," he said in a fragile voice after some moments. "Dad never took *me* to the Carlton cemetery. What's so special about *you*? Why are *you* his favorite?"

With that he stood weakly, shaking his head, and went quietly up the stairs to his room.

We were all there with him at the bus station. Even Grandmother Villetta had come. She gathered his face in her aged hands and pulled him down for a kiss on the forehead.

"You be good, boy," she said, lightly patting his cheek.

And then Mama hugged him, started crying and wouldn't let him go. Some man in a uniform rolled his eyes, and Daddy was looking left and right in embarrassment.

"Okay, Mabel, that's enough now," Daddy said firmly.

He ground his cigarette into the pavement, pulled Mama away gently by the elbow, then stepped up to Leavitt with his hand out. They shook hands, firm and strong the way men do. Daddy's face was steel and his lips were tight.

"Just do whatever your drill sergeant says and you'll be fine, son," Daddy said.

"Sure, Dad. It'll be fine."

Leavitt's teeth were clenched. His knees were shaking a little and his face kept trying to break. And then he just picked up his suitcase, spun around sharply and climbed aboard the bus. Mama wailed after him, her face red and creased. Sadie stood with her arms tightly crossed, foot tapping, the barest hint of a smile on her lips.

* * *

Leavitt died on January 31, 1968 in the opening hours of what we would come to know later as the Tet Offensive. Mama collapsed when the telegram came, and Daddy took to spending a lot of time just staring off into the distance, his jaw muscles twitching. I cried, and so did Elizabeth, but Sadie? No, Sadie didn't cry. She mumbled her grief and went through the motions, but she didn't cry.

It took a while but Leavitt's body was finally brought back. It wasn't like Mr. Gorman's funeral. We couldn't look inside the coffin. Daddy had Leavitt buried in the Carlton cemetery next to Uncle Lou. We were all there, standing in the hot sun in our black clothes. Mama had to buy me a new suit. Grandmother Villetta came to the funeral, along with a crowd of relatives whom I had never met. There was an honor guard and a flag, and maybe a dozen of Leavitt's friends. I never knew he was so popular, and wondered what these people had seen in him that I never had. Sadie stood back from it all, an arm around Elizabeth. Her eyes would cross mine conspiratorially. I never spoke of it.

Leavitt's last letter to us arrived a few days after we found out that he had been killed. Mama was too distraught to read it so Daddy did. He gathered us all in the den, stood stiffly and read aloud. Leavitt wrote about the weather over there, how hot it was, even in January. Things had been pretty calm, he assured us. He didn't care much for the people. And then he wrote:

Tell Elizabeth how sorry I am, and that I promise to make it up to her when I rotate home.

Daddy looked at Elizabeth quizzically. Elizabeth just squeezed her sweater tight around her throat and lowered her head. Sadie looked away. Daddy continued:

And tell Carlton that I miss him, and I want to hear about all the Civil War things he's found up on the hill. Love you all, Leavitt.

Mama let out an anguished cry then. Elizabeth covered her face with her hands and Sadie dabbed at a tear. And me? I ran upstairs, out the back door and into the woods.

$\mathcal{F}OUR$

I was just thinking that if getting over little Nesuntabunt Mountain is worrying me then how will I ever get over the other mountains in Maine, not to mention the White Mountains in New Hampshire? We delude ourselves so easily. A day never seems so hot or cold in our memory until we are out in it again, and mountains never seem so high until we are climbing their flanks once more. I have climbed all of these mountains twice. I know how hard it was, how much I struggled. And yet as I think back it doesn't seem that it was so hard after all. But it was; of course it was. This must be some kind of limbic mechanism in our minds, a means of insulating us from memories of pain. I can remember being *in* pain, on these mountains and the other things, but I can't remember the pain itself, not the way I can recall exactly the sweet richness of pecan pie or the feverishly alluring smell of sex.

This probably explains why people are inclined to repeat some mistakes; it certainly explains how I could embark on this hike at my age and not have been concerned about the mountains. Oh, well—I can probably skirt the mountains here in Maine by following the water courses and drainages, the easy path, my own blue-blazed route. The purist hikers would scoff, but then…there aren't any of them left anyway so who cares? Getting through New Hampshire, though, across that long arcing wall of granite, up and over Mt. Washington—I'll just have to find a way.

I met Willow on Mt. Washington. This was during my first thru-hike. It had been a tough day for me, which began with that long climb out of Pinkham Notch, followed by the rock scramble over Mt. Madison. The weather had been cold and wet for days. I carried a chill along those mountain heights that I just couldn't shake, wanted nothing more than to take a blue-blazed side trail down into the warm valleys below. But that would just add an extra climb to get back on the trail. I dreaded the thought. After more than a month on the Appalachian Trail I had lost twelve pounds to those climbs. The cold cut closer to the bone now. And hungry? I couldn't get enough to eat. My stomach would growl as I hiked.

But I remember that the sun broke out after I topped Mt. Madison. The wind still howled and it was cold, but just the sight of blue sky was enough to raise my spirits. It was only about two in the afternoon so I bypassed the warmth and shelter of Madison Springs hut, one of a series of alpine huts along the Presidential Range in New Hampshire, and pushed on toward Mt. Washington. It was a good thing, too. I wouldn't have met Willow otherwise. I would have been coming as she was going, and two hikers separated on the trail by a day could as well be hiking in two different worlds.

That long ridge through the Presidential Range seemed interminable, nothing for miles except windswept rock, scattered patches of tundra, and crags of ice that hadn't yet succumbed to the June sun. There was no cover anywhere from the wind. I was wearing my letterman jacket over a wool sweater and still I was freezing. I was six hours on that trail to Mt. Washington, pushing along miserably as the sun dropped lower and lower. New clouds blew in, and streamers of fog began to curl through the saddles in wind-driven vortices. The wind died down as the sun set but the fog grew thicker, overflowing the cols and hollows to spill across the trail like a rising tide. I topped Mt. Washington in this, the fog so thick that I was on my hands and knees looking for white blazes in the gloom. I was at the limits of myself, about to give it up for the night and pitch my tent right there on the cold hard rock, when suddenly I made out faint lights flickering ahead.

These were the lights of Lakes of the Clouds hut. Hallelujah and deliverance once more!

I had seen photos of Lakes of the Clouds hut taken in polaroid-sharp mountain light, of a European style refuge on a swath of green tundra down off the ridge and out of the brunt of the wind. There was a glistening gem of lake nearby, and hazy views of Pinkham Notch far below. This wasn't the view I got to see, though, only a deep, still fog and a few twinkling lights.

There was no glow of day remaining in the west by the time I finally reached the hut. The darkness was absolute, crushing as if it had weight. Bright light through the windows was so diffused by the fog that none of it reached the ground. I searched in the cold darkness for The Dungeon. I had been told about this by some hikers in Pinkham Notch. The Dungeon was a small emergency shelter, more like a root cellar, that had been built into the far end of the hut years earlier after some winter climbers had died of exposure. It got its name from its cold stone floor and walls. Thru-hikers were allowed to sleep in the shelter during the summer. To sleep in the hut itself cost money, money that I didn't have to spare, and the huts were usually fully booked during the summer anyway.

I found a steel door with a sign that said *Emergency Use Only*. I gave the door a yank, and a gust of funky smelling cold air wafted out. The shelter looked like a hole in the ground swallowed in blackness. It looked like...well, a *dungeon*.

"Hey!" someone shouted indignantly.

I fumbled a flashlight out of my backpack and shone it in there. I saw narrow wooden bunks along two dank walls, and these were occupied by ragged men in dirty sleeping bags. They raised hands to shield their eyes and looked out at me weakly, like refugees. Their breaths were puffs of white in the dense cold air. The floor was slick with ice.

"It's full, man," someone said. "Close the damned door."

I tried to form words but my lips were so cold that all I could manage to do was mumble.

"Close the stupid door, dude!"

I backed away numbly and gave the door a push with my hip. The wind kicked up again, shrieking and whistling and trying to lift me off my feet. I began to tremble. My fingers were stiff, my mind as weary and numb as the rest of me. I stumbled through the howling murk to the hut's main entrance, pulled the door with what was surely the last of my strength, tripped going in and fell face-first onto a wood-plank floor. The bulk of my backpack gave an extra push that flattened me where I lay. The wind caught the door and slammed it hard against the soles of my boots, giving me a little shove along the floor. It was a cold floor but at least it was out of the wind. I thought to go to sleep right there, just close my eyes and let it come.

I heard voices ahead, clinking dinnerware and scraping chairs. A gorgeous light warmed my face. I smelled food! This roused me enough to get me to my knees, my backpack skewing to the right and tipping me that way. I fumbled with the belt catch and got it open, and then my backpack slid off like ice across a tin roof. A shadow stepped into the light then. I looked up to see the silhouette of a woman, haloed in that warm light like an angel. Her hands were on her hips. Light shone through the crooks of her elbows to reveal the outline of a slender waist.

"Are you okay?" she asked. It was a young voice but firm with maturity, and not a trace of an accent in it.

I babbled a reply, tried to get my legs under me to stand. I think I drooled some.

"Oh, my, aren't you pitiful," she said with what I was certain was a hint of amusement.

I babbled again, but resentfully this time.

Surprisingly strong hands took me under the arms and drew me up. I wobbled there, tried to focus, tried to keep my knees straight.

"Okay, here we go then," she said, exasperated or annoyed, one. "Just move your feet, fella. Come this way."

She tugged me forward and into the light. My eyes were still having a hard time finding focus, but I thought I could make out rows of wooden tables, like a rustic dining hall, and benches of people who had gone silent and were staring. She turned me toward an open kitchen. A wonderful heat came off of an oven. She lowered me onto a stool next to the oven. Wonderful.

"Now don't fall off," she said, clearly amused this time, but I just melted where I sat and thought that I had found heaven.

The voices started up again, a hollow cacophony distant to my ears.

"What's the matter with him?" I heard another woman ask.

"Don't know. Cold I guess. Some hot chocolate should help."

A warm cup touched my lips. "Careful, it's hot," she said.

I slurped and burned my tongue, but no burn ever felt so sweet.

"Can you hold it?"

I nodded, held the cup close to my face with both hands and let the steam bathe my cheeks. Wonderful.

She moved off then. Pots and pans clattered. People whisked past me, back and forth, arms loaded with dirty plates. The voices gradually died down and people began to filter out. I could feel the life coming back into my limbs, pin pricks in places, a creeping warmth in others. I was beginning to sweat under my jacket and sweater so I pulled them off. Within minutes I was thinking that it hadn't really been *that* cold out.

"Okay, buster, you're looking better. Time to earn your keep."

I could see her now. She was grinning at me. She was pretty.

"What's your name?" I asked hoarsely.

"Willow. And you?"

"I'm Jake Brake."

Her eyebrows bounced at that.

Willow was my age, or maybe a year or two older. She wore khaki pants and hiking boots, and a trim, green turtleneck sweater that concealed nothing of the figure underneath. She had wry lips, high cheeks, and wide brown eyes. Her hair was light brown, pulled tightly into a long ponytail. She was tall for a girl.

"So here's how it goes…Jake Brake." She grinned again. "The hut master says you can do a work-for-stay. See those dishes?" She tipped her head toward some stainless steel sinks that were jumbled full of dishes and pans. "You get 'em all washed and they'll let you have some leftovers, and you can sleep on one of those tables. Sound cool?"

"Hell yeah."

"Then let's get to it."

I rolled up my sleeves and started washing dishes, passed them to Willow who dried them and put them away. All the others were gone now, and the lights had been dimmed in the dining hall.

"Do you work here all summer?" I asked.

"No," she shook her head, "I'm not one of the *croo*."

"Then—"

"I'm doing a section hike, Grafton Notch to Kinsman."

"Then—"

Willow must have had a habit of cutting people off, or else she had answered these same questions so many times they had become tiresome.

"This place is so beautiful I decided to hang out for a few days. They're letting me do work-for-stay, but I need to get going again pretty soon. I think I've worn out my welcome."

"You mean—you're hiking *alone*?"

She looked me up and down indignantly.

"Yeah," she said with an edge. "Aren't you?"

"Sure, but—"

"Please don't say what I think you're going to say and ruin my opinion of you."

"You mean—"

"What? That I'm a girl so I shouldn't be out here by myself?"

Now I grinned. I held a finger to my lips.

"Shh," I whispered. "You really have a habit of cuttin' people off. Did you know that? Let me finish. Okay?"

Her wide eyes went almost round in surprise, but she nodded warily.

"Okay," she said.

"Good. Then you mean…" I drew it out and smiled, "you already have an opinion of me?"

"Oh!" she exclaimed, and let me have it with a wet dish towel.

"Is it a good opinion?"

"Listen you." Her voice was stern but she wore a playful look on her face. "A little while ago you were drooling on the floor. I felt sorry for you. And now you're *flirting* with me?"

"Did I say thank you, by the way?"

"No, you didn't."

"Well thank you."

Now we were both grinning. I liked this girl.

"You're welcome. Now get back to work."

We finished the dishes and then Willow handed me a plate from the oven. It was piled high with roast beef, mashed potatoes, a corn casserole of some kind, and biscuits, lots of biscuits. I couldn't mind my manners, I had lost them in Maine. I just shoveled the food into my mouth, chewing it only enough to get it down. Willow looked on in amusement.

"I know what *that's* like," she said with a smile.

Pleasingly sated from the warmth of a full stomach, I gathered my things and carried them to a table, spread out my sleeping bag and unzipped it.

"Where do you sleep?" I asked Willow.

"On the table right next to you," she grinned. "And if you snore you're going down to The Dungeon."

"It's full," I said. "And it smells. And it's cold. And no, I don't snore, thank God."

"Okay then." She hit some switches and the room went dark. "See you in the morning."

I lay there for a long time before I nodded off, long enough to hear Willow's breathing change to the deep of sleep. I felt very content, more than I had in a long time.

* * *

It's amazing how much can change from one day to the next. Willow and I both awoke at sunrise, and what a wonderful sunrise it was. She started the coffee percolating while I hit the privy, then she took her turn. I filled two mugs with steaming hot coffee and carried them outside into the bracing air.

This day was perfectly clear. The sun blazed over Wildcat Mountain to the east, burnishing the tundra into crimson and gold. The air was still, not a breath of wind. Vague sounds carried up from the notch below, of cars and other things I was too high to see. Willow slipped up beside me quietly.

"Beautiful," she whispered.

She took her coffee, blew on it and sipped carefully as we cherished the view. A couple of thru-hikers roused from The Dungeon and draggled stiffly our way.

"We'll need to get our gear packed away before the paying guests get up," Willow said wistfully. "Those are the rules."

"Okay, then."

We finished our coffees and went back inside.

Breakfast was a repeat of dinner the previous evening. The croo attended to the guests while Willow and I, and one starving, gray-bearded thru-hiker from The Dungeon, stood out of the way and waited. Afterward we helped ourselves to the leftovers, scrambled eggs and sausage and more biscuits, got the dishes washed and then it was time to go.

"I've got to get going," I told Willow, the remorse as apparent on my face as the sun through the windows. It was already past 10:00 a.m. Burning daylight. But then Willow lifted my spirits with nine sweet words.

"I think I'll get going, too," she said contemplatively, but then with a cagy smile added, "Want a hiking partner for a couple of days?"

"Hell yeah!"

"Well let's go, then."

We moved out quickly through the first warm day I had felt in…how long? Maybe only days, but on the trail days felt like weeks. We were at Crawford Notch by midafternoon, but spent another hour or so getting down that treacherous grade. Willow was ahead of me, lowering herself from tree roots and rocks. She couldn't find a place to put her foot, poked around experimentally but then reached out a hand to me. I hadn't actually touched Willow up to then. She had long, well, *willowy* fingers, and they were strong. Touching her sent a tingle through my stomach. I took a firm grip, lowered her to better footing, and then scrambled after. By the time we reached the highway it was really too late to go on so we hoofed it up the road to a campground and pitched our tents.

I didn't usually make campfires but we made one there, sat around its crackling glow and talked into the night.

"Where are you from?" I asked her.

"California," she replied. I brightened at that.

"A surfer girl, huh?"

"No," she shook her head and laughed. "I'm from the other side. The *mountain* side."

"Oh, wow," I said in ignorance. All I knew of California was what I had heard on the Beach Boys' *Endless Summer* album, and there were no mountains in that.

"You're a long way from home, then," I went on after some moments.

"Yeah," she agreed with a sigh. "I'm doing the fall semester at Dartmouth. They let girls in now."

"Dartmouth? Hey, we'll be hiking right through there!"

"*You* will be hiking right through there," she corrected me at once. "*I* am getting off at Kinsman."

"Yeah, sure," I said quickly, "but I could see you when I come through, I don't know, a week maybe."

She was shaking her head before I had even finished.

"No, I'll be back in California with my family until August."

I was completely deflated.

"Well, it would have been cool."

"Yeah, it would have."

"Do you have a big family?" I asked.

She held up two fingers. "Two brothers," she said, and then a third finger. "And I'm the baby. What about you?"

"I have a sister," I said darkly. "I'm the baby, too."

"Well then." She tossed a stick onto the fire. "I'm going to turn in now, I think."

"Yeah, me too."

We shuffled off to our tents then. Willow ducked through her tent flaps but then turned on her heels to give me a long parting look. It was too dark to see the expression on her face.

* * *

We awoke to a red dawn. The sky looked like a painting done in oils, vivid streaks of red and pink and orange against the dappled greens of the forest and the chiseled gray of the mountain peaks. We lingered over coffee and thick wedges of pecan pie that we had bought from a camp store, just savoring the morning. It was pleasantly warm. I was wearing jeans and a white T-shirt. Willow still wore her green sweater but she had changed into a pair of khaki shorts, with her wool socks rolled down to the tops of her boots. I couldn't help but stare at her legs. Her tan was even and perfect.

"Eyes up, fella," she smiled. She put a finger under my chin and lifted. "I think I'll hike behind you today. I wouldn't want you to get distracted, trip or fall or something."

"You sure do have a high opinion of yourself," I said mockingly.

"And apparently so do you," she said with a grin. I had to laugh at that. She was right. "Are you ready to get going?" she asked then.

"Yeah," I answered reluctantly. "I guess it's time."

The climb out of Crawford Notch wasn't as tough as some of the climbs had been. Within a few hours we were above the tree line and picking our way along the ridges and over the peaks of the Franconia Range. The view was enormous, great swaths of green down below on either side, and a panoramic clear blue sky that seemed to reach all around us. Ski trails etched some of the flanks as if a giant hand had reached down and raked its fingers up the mountain sides.

"Uh, oh," Willow said into the wind. I had surreptitiously fallen back to take in the view. "Look," she pointed.

Black clouds were gathering around the peaks ahead, probably miles away and yet they looked so close. Icy white flashes sparkled in them.

"We don't want to get caught in that," she said with apprehension.

I came up beside her, dropped my backpack and took out a sweater. It was cooler at elevation. The wind was picking up. Willow's legs had goose bumps.

"There's really nowhere for us to go," I said. "There are a couple of huts ahead. I say we push on and if it starts looking bad we can stop in at one of them. Okay?"

"Yeah, okay," she said, and we pressed on.

Somehow the clouds always stayed well ahead of us. It was a peculiar sight, that menacing storm blackening the sky ahead while every other direction was basking in the full light of a warm summer's day. From Mt. Guyot the storm looked no closer, so we bypassed that shelter and kept on. At South Twin Mountain we reached our highest elevation of the day. The view was extraordinary, the crackling storm as yet ahead while long shadows fell off the mountains in the lowering light.

From South Twin Mountain the descent was precipitous into the tree line. Once into the shelter of the canopy we shook off our concerns about the storm. It could rage all it wanted to above us, and in that thick foliage we wouldn't even be able to see it.

"How much farther for the day do you think?" Willow asked.

I felt fine, Willow looked fine, and there were still a few hours of daylight left, but I thought it best to pull in at the Garfield Ridge shelter a few miles ahead and save that long ridge walk over Mt. Lafayette and Mt. Lincoln for tomorrow. Willow agreed, so we continued on at a leisurely pace. We hadn't gone far, though, before a shadow seemed to fall over the forest. Rich greens went to dull gray and the birds quit chirping. We paused and looked at one another ominously.

"Uh, oh."

And then without warning, without any preamble whatsoever, thunder shook the forest and rain came crashing in with a roar. Lightening lit the tree tops, casting them in stark outline. We were drenched in seconds. My hair was pasted to my forehead, while Willow's long ponytail splayed around her backpack in loops and tangles. Water began to sluice down the trail.

"We'd better move fast," I hollered over the roar of the rain.

We sprinted ahead, falling onto our butts in places and sliding along through the mud. The rain was warm, though, and after a time I slowed down to just let it rinse me clean. It felt good, actually. Willow did the same thing. She raised her face to the rain, held out her arms, and stood there with her eyes closed and a placid look on her face while the rain washed away the sweat and grime of a rugged hike.

It was getting dark when we reached the shelter. The rain still fell, although gentler now, and lightening cracked across the sky. The Garfield Ridge shelter wasn't a lean-to like those in Maine, it was more like a small cabin without a door. It had four walls, and stone steps up to the entrance. Willow was laughing as we went inside, as if she had rediscovered the joys of a child twirling in the rain. I was laughing, too, couldn't help it. Willow was having fun, and I was having fun watching her.

The shelter was empty. There was supposed to be a campground host on the site somewhere, but not out in this weather. Willow dropped her backpack, pulled her ponytail over her shoulder and began to wring it out. I dropped my backpack and fumbled for words. Willow was looking at me slyly.

"We'll take turns," she said. It was darkening quickly and she had become a shadow against even darker walls. "You turn around while I change into dry clothes and then I'll do the same for you. Okay?"

"Okay," I said nervously. I turned my back and stared at the dark wall.

"No peeking!"

"Okay, okay."

I heard her boots thump onto the floor, the slurping sound of wet socks coming off, a soft padding as she hopped from one bare foot to another. I heard zippers and snaps. Wet clothes slapped the floor. A rustling in her backpack. The rain picked up again, drumming on the roof. Lightening lit the shelter like a camera flash and then thunder shook the walls.

"Okay, you can turn around now," Willow said at last.

I turned—and there stood Willow, completely naked. My jaw fell. Lightening crashed and lit her in a silvery aura. I didn't say anything—I didn't need to say anything. I went to her, and took her, and we made love while rain lashed the trees and thunder made the earth shake.

* * *

I awoke to the luxurious silky warmth of Willow's lithe body pressed against mine in the tight confines of my sleeping bag. The morning was bright through the open doorway, pure yellow rays enhancing the rich greens of the forest. Water drops glistened at the ends of spruce needles like a million sparkling diamonds. Willow was propped on her elbow, watching me. She smiled. Her eyes were mellow and soft. Long fingers played in the hair on my chest, scratched at my scraggly beard, traced ticklishly along my protruding ribs. Weight loss had made my chest look like a skeleton. Her brows dipped and she pursed her lips in thought.

"How old are you?" she asked quizzically.

I slipped a hand around her bare back and pulled her face close.

"I'm seventeen," I whispered against her lips.

Her eyes went wide and she pushed away.

"What! You're…you're just a *baby*!"

"I am not!"

"Oh my God!" she exclaimed, sitting up. Her breasts stood out, firm and as tanned as the rest of her. She raised a hand to her forehead. "I think I've broken the law!"

I looked around, bewildered. "I don't see any police. And how the hell old are *you*?"

"I'm nineteen."

"Well damn, Willow. I'll be eighteen in a couple of months. Big deal."

"And I'll be twenty in a couple of months."

"It doesn't matter."

"But you're still a baby."

I was getting annoyed. "I am *not* a damn baby."

"Baby, baby," she said mockingly.

And then she wriggled out of the sleeping bag and she stood, and I could see her in the full light. My reaction was obvious and immediate.

"*Ba-by, ba-by*," she sang now. She began to dance, throwing her hips, her arms out and bent, fingers resting on air. I had never witnessed anything so singularly sensual in my life. "*Baby don't leave me.*" And now she was grinning down at me and her teeth were as bright as the sky. "*Ooh, please don't leave me, all by myself.*"

She fell on me laughing and we kissed.

"The Supremes?" I asked as she snuggled against me.

"Yeah," she breathed huskily into my ear. "One of my favorites."

"One of mine, too…now," I said, and we made love again.

* * *

The day was perfect, magical. I hiked with a fullness in my chest and a smile on my face. All those towering views looked so much…richer, grander—divine. The miles slipped by and I didn't notice them. Willow and I walked hand in hand much of the way. On the peak of Mt. Lafayette we stopped to raise our arms to the sky and bathe in the sun. We spent one more night together, camped in Franconia Notch. This time we only raised one tent.

The weather was perfect again for our final day together, but our spirits were dim. The views from South Kinsman Mountain, as magnificent as they were, did not provide the same breathless immediacy that we had experienced the day before. The descent into Kinsman Notch was steep and tricky. We took it in silence.

I walked with Willow about a mile up Lost River Road to a pay phone, where she called for a taxi. We sat cross-legged in the sun to wait. My mood was somber.

"Tell me your name," I said gently, but there was demand in it as well.

"You know my name," she said in a subdued tone.

"No," I was shaking my head, "I mean your *real* name."

She took my face and turned me into her eyes. They were earnest and wet.

"My trail name's as real to me as any other, Jake Brake," she said closely, her breath puffing against my lips.

"But how will I be able to find you?"

"Listen, Jake." She let me go and sat back. She was staring across the way at nothing. "You've still got a long way to go. Months. You'll meet people and do things…who knows how you'll feel at the end; how you'll change?"

"I know how I feel right now, and—"

"And if you still feel that way when you get to Georgia then you know where to find me."

"But—"

She stood up then and hefted her backpack. She looked down at me. Her lips were a tight line and her eyes were firm.

"And if not…" she continued, softening. She looked up to the mountains and breathed. "We'll always have this to remember."

And then she wheeled around without another word and took off up the highway, adjusting her backpack as she went. I waited, my breath caught in my throat, ready to run after her the moment she looked back, but she didn't.

${\mathcal{F}}IVE$

My sleeping bag has finally warmed up enough to drive off the damned chill. It reminds me of that morning at Garfield Ridge, although Sam is a poor substitute for Willow. She would laugh if she were here, seeing me pressed up against Sam and scrunched down in this sleeping bag like an old prune. The memory of that morning has stayed with me vividly through the years, like a moment out of time, ever present in the front of my mind and so real that I feel as if I can almost hold it in my hands.

But I have gone long in this telling. It's late and there is still much to write before the morning comes and I have to get back on the trail.

It felt claustrophobic in our house for a long time after Leavitt died, as if the very air were too thick to breathe. And then Martin Luther King was killed, and Bobby Kennedy was killed, and even kids like me wondered if things would ever be right again.

"Why won't they leave the Kennedys alone?" I asked Mama when we heard about Bobby. She just shook her head sadly and shuffled off to do something or other, leaving me standing there.

Mama went slower now, as if she had suddenly aged twenty years. She let her patio garden go. All her pretty flowers wilted and drooped and dried into hard, naked husks, and then weeds took over and her garden turned to brush. Daddy spent more time at work, and he had taken up golfing, so he was away most days. I noticed that his bottles of bourbon, in that glass cabinet in the den, weren't dusty anymore. Elizabeth stayed mostly to her room when she was home from school, and Sadie stayed mostly out with her friends. Breakfasts and dinners became mechanical. We didn't talk much over the table, just perfunctory things. I would clean my plate as quickly as I could so that I could get away to the woods, where nothing and everything changed from day to day, and in ways that I could always count on.

Our dig on the hill never turned up anything but a few rusted, jagged scraps of metal that could have been anything. Kenny and I finally became discouraged with that activity. Instead we built a fort against the big ash tree, using weathered boards and some sheets of corrugated tin that we found stacked against the old water tank. We left an opening in the roof of our fort, and nailed boards to the tree trunk like a ladder so that we could climb straight up. We played Civil War games, taking turns defending the fort. I was always the Rebel and Kenny was always the Yankee. We didn't decide on this, it just fell out that way. These games often got rough, with us hurling sticks and rocks at one another. I cracked Kenny in the head a few times, and he did the same to me. Somehow, and sometimes bloodied, we survived and didn't whine about it.

It was on a day, that same summer after Leavitt died, that I went up to the woods to get away. Kenny wasn't around. I can't remember why. It was a gray day, no rain just gray. I kicked around through the leaves and the duff, stirred up some ants so dropped down to look at them through my magnifying glass for a while. This was fascinating. A little war was going on between the ants and some little white, winged bugs that might have been termites. I was rooting for the ants because I had heard Daddy talking about termites once, how destructive they could be to houses. He kept two olive-green cans the size of old milk pails in the garage. The cans were stenciled in black with *U.S. Army*, and in big white letters, *DDT*. Daddy told me he used the DDT to kill termites.

Anyway, the ants seemed to be winning. They would single out individual termites then swarm over them until each termite was encased in a roiling ball of ants. It looked hopeless for the termites. I was glad I was too big for the ants. I moved on from this after a time, kicked up to the fort and climbed the tree. I didn't climb too high, just to the first big fat branch where I could lay flat on my stomach and look around. It was quiet on the hill that day. No birds even. I looked down, over the conical roof of our fort, which resembled half of a teepee resting against the tree, and then on to the square plot of our dig. Lying nearby, weighted with a rock, was the aluminum window screen we had used to sift the soil. We had ultimately removed about eight inches of soil from that plot. Now it was just a big square hole filling with leaves. Only about half of the bare soil was still visible, swept smooth by wind and blowing leaves. Looking down from the height of my limb, I spotted...I couldn't tell for sure.

I craned my head and looked harder. There was something like an outline in the soil, something indistinct but vaguely familiar. I moved so quickly that I skinned my arms coming down the tree. I grabbed one of Mama's soup spoons from the fort and then dropped to my knees in the hole. Whatever it was that I'd seen, I couldn't make it out up close. I scraped at the soil haphazardly with the spoon, found nothing, and then...clink. A rock maybe? I started digging. Something that looked like a tree root began to take form. I dug around it, kept digging, excited now. Something was definitely there, a shape coming out—it was a pistol!

I had to pry that pistol out of the hard clay soil with a stick. It was embedded in the stuff, as if in plaster, every niche filled, even the barrel. It was a big, heavy pistol. It took both of my hands to hold it up. I used my pen knife to chisel the clay out of the trigger guard. I scraped around the hammer and the cylinder, but couldn't do much because the clay had hardened on it like cement.

I raced home with my find, so excited that I was hollering for Daddy as I ran. I found him in the den, sitting in his Barcalounger. He had a frosted tumbler of bourbon and ice on his side table, a cigarette in his fingers. He was just sitting there, staring out the window at the dull sky. He didn't look up as I bounded down the stairs.

"Daddy, look what I found!"

He turned to me then and put on a faint smile.

"Hello, Carlton. What've you got there?"

I displayed the pistol proudly.

"I found it, Daddy. In my dig."

"Well, well, well," he said. "Look at that." He reached to the table for his glasses, took the pistol and examined it closely. "Hmm...cap and ball. It's definitely a Civil War-era handgun and, it's hard to tell through all of this dirt, but son I think you've found a Navy Colt!"

"Wow!" I said in awe. That sounded impressive. I wished Mr. Gorman were still alive. He would have been so excited.

"What do you plan to do with it?" Daddy asked.

That one caught me. I thought for a moment then shrugged my shoulders.

"Don't know," I said.

"Can I make a suggestion, then?"

"Uh, huh."

"You should probably give it to a museum or the historical society. I think they would really appreciate it."

"You mean...*I have to give it away?*"

"No, son." Daddy threw me an easy smile and ruffled my hair. "I just think you should share this with people who know how to preserve it. But you found it so it's your decision."

Daddy was back to his old self for those few minutes, making me feel big. I didn't want to let him down.

"Okay, Daddy," I agreed cheerfully, but then I frowned. "But I don't know how."

"I think I can help you with that," he said, ruffling my hair again. "Let's go make a phone call."

* * *

I wound up donating that pistol to the Tennessee State Museum. It turned out to be a Colt 1851 Navy, popular with Confederate soldiers during the war. The pistol itself wasn't rare at all, but finding it as I had *was*. Kenny and I were celebrities briefly. I gave Kenny credit too since he had helped so much at the site. Both the *Nashville Banner* and *The Tennessean* printed stories about us, the two boys who had done such a professional excavation on Shy's Hill and had discovered an artifact from the Battle of Nashville. They even put our pictures in the paper, the two of us in T-shirts and shorts, grinning wide, our arms around each other's shoulders, displaying soup spoons to the camera with our free hands.

This seemed to lighten the mood at home. We started talking around the dinner table again. The color returned to Mama's face, and Daddy smiled more. Even Elizabeth gave me a hug. Sadie patted me on the head and told me, "Good job."

Things may have been going better at home, but unwittingly I had unleashed a juggernaut on my hilltop. Men from the museum were up there every day with metal detectors. Some students from the university started a dig of their own, and then Civil War buffs from all over started showing up. Some would knock on our door and ask for permission to go through our yard, but many would just go on up there without a thought, trampling through Mama's desiccated garden.

"Dick, you've got to do something," Mama complained at breakfast one morning. "When I took the trash out there was a strange man standing right there on the patio. He scared me to death. I think he was…I think he was *peeping through the window.*"

Daddy's eyes shot to the window in alarm.

"Pervert," Sadie spat.

"That's creepy, Daddy," said Elizabeth.

So Daddy had the woods cleared of brush all the way up to our property line, and put up a tall fence to replace the old one that had become overgrown. Now I could actually see the ash tree from the house, filling a corner of the sky beyond our fence.

And so my woods lost their magic and solitude. Kenny and I couldn't play in our fort without people bothering us, getting in the way, going in our fort like it was theirs. We quit going up there. Kenny and I would play in the yard instead, or else hang out in the hickory tree. We never played at Kenny's house. I'm not sure why. Sometimes Mama would drop us off at the new 100 Oaks Mall for the day. 100 Oaks was the first indoor shopping mall in Nashville. The size of the place was astounding, and the crush and thrum of so many people under one roof was overwhelming. We had never seen anything like it. Still, I would have preferred to be in the woods.

The summer was almost over. Soon I would start the fifth grade. Kenny ran up to the house one morning, maybe a week before school started, and rapped excitedly on my window. I yanked the curtains aside and saw him there panting and sweating.

"What goin' on?" I asked. I opened the window and leaned out. My window screen was still up in the woods, where we had used it to sift the soil of our dig.

"People are moving into Mr. Gorman's house!" he answered in a rush.

I peered over his shoulder and saw a big moving van in the street. It blocked the view of the house.

"Did you see 'em?" I asked.

"Yeah."

"Any kids?"

"A girl."

"A *girl?*" I twisted my face in disgust.

"Yeah. Let's go check it out."

"Okay," I said, and I dove out the window.

We ran bare-footed down the hill through the grass, slammed our backs against the moving van and peeked around the corner. Movers were carrying things inside, while a mom and a dad and a girl stood in the yard and watched. The girl looked to be our age. She wore a pink poodle skirt with a white top, and black and white saddle shoes. She had curly blond hair, shallow round eyes, and white, white skin, as if she had never played outdoors before.

"Aw, she looks like a sissy," I whined too loudly.

The mom looked our way, shielded her eyes against the morning sun and smiled. She was wearing a black and white polka dot shift. Her hair was blond like the girl's but worn in a flip that was held in place by a high, white band.

"Those must be the neighborhood boys," she said to the dad. "Come over here boys," she shouted.

"Aw, shucks," I said, ducking behind the moving van.

"We have to do what she says," said Kenny glumly. "She caught us."

"Aw, shucks."

We came out from behind the moving van nervously and went into the yard, our eyes everywhere but on the girl.

"Hello, boys," the mom said with a friendly smile. "I'm Mrs. Hanshaw and this is Mr. Hanshaw—" Mr. Hanshaw wore a dark suit and a stern expression. He nodded quickly but his attention was on the movers. "—and this is our daughter, Evelyn."

* * *

Toward the end of October we went on a school field trip to Percy Warner Park, which was a big forested reserve on the south side of Belle Meade. Our teacher, Mr. Fennick, was a staid man whose stiff disposition belied a passion for nature and ecology. He was always going on about it.

"Rachel Carson showed us that the chemicals we use are destroying nature," he lectured one day in science class. There was fire in his eyes as he spoke, while the rest of him looked as if he had just been pressed on an ironing board. Most of the kids were twirling their hair or else trying to look elsewhere, including me.

"It will be up to you *young* people to do something about it," he went on adamantly, making withering eye contact with some unlucky kid while the rest of us looked for patterns in the scratches on our desktops.

Mr. Fennick certainly put a lot of faith in fifth graders.

Percy Warner Park was a revelation for me, though. We walked along a wooded path, the whole class, and as we each tried to straggle behind, Mr. Fennick would herd us together again with his arms out wide. "Come children," he would say impatiently. "Stay together now."

He would pause at some plant or some rock or some scuttling bug and draw us all together, leaning on our knees and peering at whatnot while he extolled with words like *harmony* and *balance*. My eyes were on the trees.

The forest here was mostly of hardwoods resplendent in the rust and honey hues of autumn, with cool, dark evergreens in sharp contrast here and there, red cedar and American holly. This forest was so unlike the woods on our hill. There was less undergrowth here, fewer of the prickly vines. In many places you could leave the trail and walk among the trees without being scratched and ripped by brush. The ground was spongy from years of falling leaves, and the smell was fecund, although I didn't know that word then. I just thought the place smelled earthy and alive, not the hard, dusty smell of the woods back home.

Kenny and Evelyn were both in my class, but Kenny wasn't really interested in the forest, and Evelyn even less so. He was standing behind Mr. Fennick, toeing the trail, while she stood off with her arms crossed looking bored. The rest of the kids were pretending to be interested in whatever Mr. Fennick was showing them.

Something just off the trail caught my eye. I knelt at a patch of wet, deep green moss, and on it was a bright orange salamander, a small one. I had never seen an orange salamander before. Most salamanders looked like slimy mud, but this one struck a vivid contrast against the green of the moss. I pulled my magnifying glass for a closer look. Now I could see that the salamander was speckled with tiny black spots, like pores, and its skin was so translucent in places that I could see blood coursing.

"Good job, Carlton!"

Mr. Fennick startled me and I jumped. He was wearing a rare smile.

"You've found one of our eastern newts, *Notophthalmus viridescens* I believe."

Notoph what? What was Mr. Fennick doing teaching fifth graders? He belonged at a college somewhere.

"Let me see! Let me see!" Kenny crowded in. They all did, except Evelyn, who remained off by herself, brooding.

"Aw, it's just a lizard," somebody whined.

"Actually, newts are amphibians…" Mr. Fennick explained academically, but I wasn't listening anymore. Somehow I had to come back here.

* * *

On the first warm Saturday of spring I embarked on my plan to ride my bicycle to Percy Warner Park. It wasn't that far, only about eight or nine miles, but it was far enough that Mama would have had a fit if she had found out. Kenny went with me, intrigued by a new adventure, but his enthusiasm waned long before we reached our goal. I was undeterred. I had my burlap field bag looped over my shoulder. It was the one Mr. Gorman had given me, and inside it were sandwiches (peanut butter and jelly, which I wish I had right now), a Golden field guide to trees, a compass, my magnifying glass, and a notepad and pencil. I was fitted out like a real naturalist.

At the northern entrance we carried our bikes up some wide cement steps to the trail, stashed the bikes in the woods, and took off hiking. All the trees were sprouting new green leaves, their branches as yet airy and light. Birds fluttered wildly, and deer popped up their heads from the thicker growth to cautiously watch us pass.

"I want to go camping," I told Kenny as we walked along the trail. I had just finished a book at school, *My Side of the Mountain* by Jean Craighead George, and if her Sam could survive in the woods then so could I.

"That could be cool," Kenny remarked.

But his heart wasn't in it. I paused to look up trees in my book and sketch their leaves, while Kenny fidgeted with disinterest.

"I wanna go do something," he would whine now and then.

I finally said okay just to shut him up, so we rode home and climbed my hickory tree and watched the Hanshaws raking and pulling weeds in their front yard. Sometimes we would spot Evelyn peering out through their picture window.

Saturdays became my day to ride to the park. There was not enough time after school, and we had church on Sundays, so Saturday was the only day I could go. I would feel cheated when I lost a Saturday to rain, but most weekends were nice enough that I could spend hours alone in the forest. Everything was so new and fascinating. The scrappy woods above our house now seemed like a dry stand of weeds. Kenny didn't go with me on these trips. He played Little League baseball instead, which had never interested me.

I came to dinner one night with my field bag over my shoulder. It was stuffed full with all my equipment, including two new books: Thoreau's *The Maine Woods* and Muir's *A Thousand-Mile Walk to the Gulf*. Everyone was already seated. Sadie and Elizabeth were gossiping about boys. Mama was pouring tea into glasses. Daddy had a newspaper open and was browsing headlines.

"Sit down to dinner, Carlton," Mama said.

I remained standing, my hands on the back of my chair.

"Daddy. Mama," I announced. "I have decided to become a naturalist like Thoreau."

Sadie snorted, and Mama looked up with incredulous eyes. Daddy folded his paper and set it aside.

"That's nice," Mama said. "Sit down now."

"I think that's cool," said Elizabeth.

"Take off that hat at the table," said Daddy.

I was wearing a floppy khaki hat that I had bought at the Woolworth's with money I had saved from my allowance. I tugged it off resentfully, stuffed it into my field bag, and sat.

"I want to go camping," I said, looking at Daddy.

"Maybe you should join the Boy Scouts," said Mama.

"*Cub* Scouts more like it," said Sadie.

"Eat your dinner, son," said Daddy. "We'll talk about it later."

We never talked about it so I hatched a plan. I would say I wanted to spend the night at Kenny's house, Kenny would say he wanted to spend the night at my house, and then we would ride to the park and camp instead. Kenny was actually excited at the prospect, but first we had to save enough money to buy a tent and sleeping bags and the other things. This would probably take a while.

School let out in May and still we hadn't saved enough. Kenny and I took to mowing yards for extra money. We would count our earnings after every yard and compare them to the lists of camping equipment we had made, lists which seemed to get longer and longer as we discovered new things that we knew we would need: mess kits, canteens, flint and steel; good hunting knives, hatchets and rope. Maybe, we thought, we would have enough money by August.

Sadie graduated from high school that May. It was both a happy and somber time, recalling that we had all gathered in the same auditorium at Hillsboro High just two years earlier to see Leavitt graduate. Sadie's mood was ebullient, though, all grins and cherubic cheeks and bouncing enthusiasm. After all, she didn't have to worry about getting drafted.

Daddy and Mama were pleased and proud. Sadie had settled down during her senior year. She didn't even smoke cigarettes, although I knew that a lot of her friends did. I don't think she ever tried drugs, either. Looking back through my memory I realize that Sadie really had been a beautiful young woman. She still had that spark of rebellion in her eyes, but she carried herself with a natural precision and poise that leant her an air of maturity beyond her age. She had never changed her hair. She kept it short and bobbed, counter to the trends of the late 1960s, and this emphasized the graceful lines of her neck. She was elegant yet studious, vulnerable yet strong. She was bound for a bright future, that's what people said.

Sadie had sent out her letters and had been accepted to several colleges. She and Mama would sit at the table to peruse catalogs and brochures, with Mama chattering like one of the girls. It took the anguish out of Mama's face and replaced it with a superior pride. This was something Mama could brag about to her friends, and she did. Elizabeth would join them at the table because it was clear that Elizabeth would also attend whichever college was chosen. Elizabeth's senior year would surely pass quickly. She and Sadie wouldn't be separated for too long.

* * *

Apollo 11 took off for the moon on a Wednesday morning in July. We all raced through breakfast so we could watch the launch on television. It was so exciting. Pride shone in all our faces. Even Sadie was giddy with expectation. Things seemed to be getting better all around, at home as well as in the rest of the country. The war was still going on, but Richard Nixon was our new president and he had a secret plan to get us out. And now we were going to the moon, too.

I stayed close to the house that week so that I could watch the updates on television. We wondered what the astronauts would find when they landed. I wondered if they would find something alive, like in the movies. On the one hand this excited me; on the other hand it terrified me a little. Some of those movies were scary. As the weekend arrived our excitement was bursting. Apollo 11 was set to land on Sunday afternoon. I didn't want to leave the house, I was so afraid I would miss something.

Sadie and Elizabeth went out together on a double date the Saturday night before the lunar landing. This had caused Daddy some consternation, but Sadie had argued as forcefully as ever. Elizabeth was going to be a senior in high school, she said. It was time she got to go out on a real date. And with Sadie there as chaperone, what could be better? The boys were from nice families. All they were going to do was have dinner out and see a movie.

They were in the den. This was earlier in the week, right after Daddy got home from work. Daddy would have wanted nothing more than to sit quietly with his newspaper and a stiff bourbon, but he had this to contend with instead. I was listening from down the hall. Elizabeth was in her room. I got the feeling that her ear was pressed to her door. I couldn't see into the den but I could picture Sadie. She would be standing with her hands on her hips, while Daddy would be sitting in his Barcalounger rubbing his temples. Sadie's fingers would be white with strain. Her chin would be out and her hair would be bobbing every time she made a point. Daddy was unmoved so far but Sadie was relentless.

"Lizzie's old enough, Dad. Boys have been asking her out all year." She said this in a harangue that the rest of us would never have gotten away with. "And after all," she went on, "you let *me* start dating when I was sixteen. It's only fair."

I laughed and quickly covered my mouth, backing into my room in case they'd heard me. Daddy didn't *let* Sadie date, Sadie just did it. Elizabeth wasn't like that, and Daddy meant to keep it that way. And then Mama spoke up.

"She's right, Dick. I'd rather Sadie be there to look out for her."

I knew from experience that Daddy had lost another battle.

"Alright," he sighed, "but I want to meet the boys."

The boys showed up right at sunset on Saturday. I was watching from my hickory tree. They pulled up the drive in a white Ford Fairlane and parked it at a slant next to our front walkway. I didn't recognize either one of them as Sadie's regular friends. Neither of them was smoking, and they were dressed nice. One wore a tan suit, the other a pale blue suit. I wondered which one was for Sadie and which one was for Elizabeth. They took the walkway to the front door and rapped the knocker. I snickered when I saw Sadie's and Elizabeth's curtains flutter at almost exactly the same moment.

Sadie answered the door and smiled brightly. She was wearing a light blue knee-high dress, white shoes, and a thin white sweater. It was so unlike her. When she turned her face a certain way she looked a lot like Elizabeth. They chatted at the door for a minute and then Sadie led the boys upstairs to meet Daddy.

I watched them cross the living room. Daddy stood to meet them. He shook their hands stiffly and said something. One boy nodded nervously, the other mopped his forehead. Elizabeth was there. She came up shyly with her hands clasped behind her back. She was wearing a white dress with a pink sweater.

They all sat and talked while the sun set, the girls on one couch, erect and with their knees pressed together, while the boys sat on the facing couch in pretty much the same posture. Daddy was going on and on. Mama wasn't in the room or else she would have shut him up. And then they all stood. Daddy shook the boys' hands again and the two couples went down the stairs.

The boy in the tan suit was driving. He held the passenger seat forward while Sadie and the other boy squeezed into the back seat, then he held the door for Elizabeth as she settled into the front seat. He shut the door after her, jogged around to his side, started the car and tried to back it down the drive. I dropped down a few branches so I could see into the car. The boy doing the driving had his arm on the seat back and was craning his neck to see over his shoulder, but on that driveway all he would be able to see were the tops of the trees across the street. He didn't like that so he pulled forward instead.

Our driveway was really too narrow to turn a car around without practice. The boy pulled forward and went around the corner toward the kitchen, but Daddy's car was parked there so the boy put it in reverse and came inching back around. He cut it at an angle until his rear bumper was almost touching the garage doors, and then he pulled forward into an even steeper angle toward some trees along the edge of the driveway. He backed up again, went forward gaining a few inches, backward and forward, backward and forward, trying to get that car turned around; and I could hear Sadie inside telling him what to do and losing her patience. I was laughing out loud now. Their windows were down but I didn't think they could hear me. I bet that boy's hands were sweaty.

"Stop. Please stop," I heard. That was Sadie's flustered voice. The car jerked to a halt. The boy in the tan suit got out and Sadie climbed out behind him, patting her dress straight as she went. She jumped behind the wheel, quickly aligned the car, and backed it smoothly down the driveway to the street while the boy who had been driving slipped and skidded on foot after her. They exchanged positions in the street, and after a few comments I couldn't make out, were off on their date. I laughed after them as their taillights disappeared down the hill. Daddy was watching, too. I saw him standing in the window, a drink in his hand, and he looked on long after they had gone.

It was a quiet night afterward, as if the world were holding its breath in anticipation of tomorrow's lunar landing. A soft breeze rustled gently through the trees. The air was warm and smelled like flowers. The moon was a bright crescent filtering through the leaves, and the stars were cast like glittering confetti across the still waters of a midnight pond. I climbed higher and higher until I could push my face through the leaves to get a good view of the sky. I squinted against the light of the moon and imagined that I could see Apollo 11 firing its rockets on approach. I reached out, stretching my fingers to close the distance that little bit more.

Just one more day, I thought. Just one more day.

* * *

The telephone woke me up. Its ring was stark in the quiet of the night, telegraphing through the air conditioner vents into my room. I sat up in the dark, rubbed my eyes and listened.

"Hello?"

That was Daddy in a drowsy voice. A long pause. I heard a light click on.

"What!"

I jumped at that, and knew in the pit of my stomach that something bad had happened.

"Oh my God! When? Where are they?"

"What is it, Dick?"

Mama's voice sounded frightened.

"Alright, alright. Be there soon."

The phone slammed.

"Dick?"

"Mabel, get dressed. The girls had an accident."

* * *

We raced through dark streets in Daddy's Pontiac. Daddy and Mama had thrown on some clothes, but I was still barefoot in my white pajamas. I recognized some of the streets shooting past and realized that we were not too far from our old house. Daddy made a hard left on 20th Avenue that sent me sliding across the back seat. He whipped into the driveway in front of Baptist Hospital's emergency room, threw the shifter into park and leapt out of the car in one motion. Mama was juggling with her door as if she were trying to escape from an oncoming train. She got out shakily, jerked my door open, and yanked me out so hard it hurt my wrist. We took off after Daddy, Mama clutching her coat closed with one hand and pulling me along with the other.

The lights were bright in the emergency room. I had to cover my eyes. Mama pushed me onto a white bench against a wall near the nurses' station.

"Stay here, Carlton. Do you hear me? Stay here and don't move."

Her voice was adamant and yet far away. I nodded okay but she was already running off. She went around a corner and then I was alone.

The hospital was busy. Telephones rang constantly. The front doors slid open and closed with a swoosh, over and over until the sound became a vague punctuation in the back of my mind. Nurses in starched white uniforms quick-stepped up and down the halls. Gurneys rolled every which way, like traffic at a busy intersection. A big round clock on the wall said it was 1:30.

It wasn't long before I was bored with it all. I kicked my legs against the bench. My feet were cold. A nurse came up to me and leaned down. She had a grandmotherly smile and curly gray hair under her winged nurse's cap.

"Are you cold, honey?" she asked me. I nodded. "Here you go then," and she tucked a blue blanket around me.

I mumbled a thank you, curled my legs and snuggled against the arm rest. A well-dressed man and woman came in, worry etched in their faces. A policeman was with them. He pointed to the corner Mama had taken. They nodded their thanks in a rush and took off around the corner. The policeman's eyes fell on mine. His expression warred between empathy and professionalism. He gave me a quick half smile and then went on through the swooshing doors.

I fell asleep clutching the blanket around my shoulders. When I awoke the sun was shooting through the front doors and the emergency room had quieted down. There seemed to be a numbness in the place, a weariness after battle. Nurses sipped coffee and studied clip boards. One of them was leaning against the nurses' station and massaging her foot.

I rubbed my eyes and stretched. Mama was sitting beside me with her hands in her lap. Her head lolled forward and her eyes were closed.

"Mama?" I asked.

She was asleep. Her hair had come down and curly wisps dangled in her lap.

"Mama!"

I poked her in the arm and her head jerked up. She looked dazed for a moment. There were dark bags under her eyes.

"Mama, I'm hungry," I said.

She licked her lips, swept the hair out of her face, and looked at me with rheumy, bloodshot eyes.

"Okay, Carlton," she exhaled wearily. She stood stiffly and took me by the hand.

We found a cafeteria. Mama bought me a honey bun and a pint of milk. She didn't get anything for herself. We sat at a big round table. Mama rested her face in her hands while I ate.

"What happened, Mama?" I asked.

"The girls are hurt, honey," she said hollowly through her fingers. She began to shake then. She sniffed and lifted her face to wipe away tears. "Are you about done?" She tried to smile but it was painful to watch.

"Yeah Mama, I'm done."

We returned to our bench and sat. Daddy came around the corner after a while. His shirt was wrinkled and the tail was out. His hair was mussed and his face was dark with stubble. He spoke quietly to Mama, which caused her to shake again. I strained to meet his eyes but they were distant.

"I'll find out what I can," he said to her, and then he left.

The well-dressed man and woman from last night came around the corner with the boy in the pale blue suit. Sadie's date. They each had their arms around the boy. He had a bandage on his forehead. The man looked down at Mama as they walked past, his expression one of sorrow or perhaps pity.

We sat there for a long time. The big clock said 10:50. A young nurse with a powdered face and red lipstick brought me a stack of *Boys' Life* magazines. Mama patted my leg, pushed some hair behind her ear with a finger, and patted my leg again. I flipped through the magazines listlessly. A radio was on in the nurses' station. Nurses would pause as they passed and lean in to hear news of Apollo.

The boy in the tan suit, Elizabeth's date, the one who couldn't get the car turned around in our driveway, came around the corner with his parents. He was walking on his own, his face set and hard. His jacket was gone and his white shirt was splattered with blood, dried like spilled coffee. He had a bandage on his head, too, but up in his hair. His face contorted when he saw us. What reserve he had been fighting to keep disintegrated right then. He covered his face and cried. His mother reached out to him and held him and they passed through the doors. Swoosh.

Daddy came back and sat with us. He and Mama leaned in and held one another, with me squeezed in between. They didn't talk.

"Daddy, what happened?" I asked.

"It'll be okay, son," he said, patting my leg. "It'll be okay." Mama sniffed and covered her face.

We waited. I fell asleep. Daddy and Mama were up talking to a doctor when I opened my eyes. Their backs were to me. The clock said 2:30, more like 2:27. The doctor said something that made Mama wilt where she stood. She was falling to her knees when Daddy grabbed her and held her up. Seeing Mama like that wrenched something inside my chest. I hadn't cried a tear the entire time but I started up then.

Daddy and Mama went with the doctor, Mama hunched and leaning into Daddy as if her legs couldn't hold her. I sniffed alone on the bench, and then that young nurse came and sat with me. She didn't say anything, she just smiled sadly and took my hand between both of hers. A while later Daddy and Mama came around the corner with Sadie pressed between them. Sadie's face was purple and swollen from crying. Her sweater was gone. She had a deep bruise on her neck. Her hair had been shaved in a place and a bandage was there. Her fingers had lots of little cuts and were stained with iodine. There were cuts on her knees, too, splotched with iodine as if she had knelt in the mud. She didn't look at me. She was walking with a slight limp. Daddy's face was white and drawn, and his eyes were red. Mama had her face pressed into Sadie's shoulder.

"Come, Carlton. Let's go home," Daddy said weakly.

"Where's Elizabeth?" I asked, lips trembling.

Mama wailed.

* * *

The Eagle landed sometime while we were driving home; and when we got home my heart ached in the way that you can only escape from by going to sleep. I went straight to bed, slept fast and hard all the way through to the next morning, so I missed Armstrong's first steps on the moon, too.

We buried Elizabeth next to Leavitt. It was Thursday, about the time that Apollo 11 was splashing down in the Pacific Ocean. I had to have a new black suit for the funeral, but it was Grandmother Villetta who took me to buy it this time. Mama didn't get out of bed until the morning of the funeral. Daddy cared for her stoically, as if no one ever questioned how he might be holding up, just assumed. And he had to look after Sadie, too. She would drift around the house in her nightgown like a wraith, to the kitchen, the bathroom, and then back to her own room with the lights out and the curtains pulled. She didn't talk. Sometimes she would go into Elizabeth's room and stay for a long time. I could often hear her crying through the walls.

Daddy didn't pay much attention to me. I didn't resent it—there are only so many hours in the day to look after people, and Daddy's days were pretty full. I wanted Kenny to come over but his parents said no, it wasn't a good time. So I started going up the hill again. The woods were a lot thinner now, but there were still thickets in which I could hide from the artifact hunters when they stamped through. I took to stalking them, moving silently from tree to tree while they waved their metal detectors and poked at the ground. I got so close to one of them that I was able to reach into his bag without him knowing. I came out with a pair of sunglasses with wire frames, the kind the astronauts wore. I crept away with my prize and then down the hill and out of sight. I held the glasses up to the sun, polished the lenses, and then tested them loosely on my face. I grinned. I had stolen that man's glasses and I didn't feel bad about it one bit.

Elizabeth looked as sweet as an angel in her coffin. They had dressed her in pink chiffon with a pretty bow in her hair, as if making up for the joy that had been taken from her at that birthday party. It seemed so long ago. I heard some relatives whisper that "they" had done a good job on her, considering…Mama sat by the coffin and stroked Elizabeth's cheek, and spoke so mournfully that I couldn't bear it. Daddy sat in the front pew, his face creased and long, trying to break but it didn't. And Sadie sat next to him, clutching his arm, her face ground into his shoulder. Grandmother Villetta was there, too. She sat as rigid as stone, a discreet space between her and Sadie. Her hands were in her lap. Not a muscle twitched. I went to a far corner, away from everyone, sat cross-legged on the floor and cried into my lap, trying not to make too much noise.

Mama started getting around again after the funeral, but what passed for routine was dark and numb. She made me breakfast alone because Sadie was sleeping into the afternoons and Daddy was taking his coffee in the den now. Mama would sit with me but she wouldn't eat. We did eat dinner together as a family, but it was so uncomfortable I would rather we had all just eaten in our rooms.

Sadie opened her wrists in the bathtub on Saturday night. This was one week to the day after the accident. Mama found her. I was in the den alone, lying on the carpet, propped on my elbows and watching a rerun of *Hogan's Heroes*. Mama screamed. *"Sadie! Oh my God!"*

I jumped and whipped my head around toward the hallway and the bathroom. A tremor coursed through me like a current.

"*Dick! Dick!*"

Daddy came rushing down the stairs two at a time, with such heavy steps the floor shook. He spun around the bannister and into the bathroom, and then:

"*Oh, no! Sadie baby! No! No! No!*"

I hurried over. Mama was in the doorway, holding her face and crying in anguished sobs.

"*Oh, no, please no, Sadie baby,*" Daddy cried. Tears washed his cheeks.

Pink water splashed onto the floor. Daddy got Sadie up across his arms and pulled her to his chest.

"Oh Sadie baby, oh God please no..." Daddy's voice broke. He rocked Sadie in his arms and dripped tears, but then he breathed sharply, a rush of air. "She's alive, Mabel! I can feel her breathing. She's alive! Move. *Move!*"

Mama backed into me and almost tripped.

"Carlton, get out of the way!" she screamed in a panic.

I slammed backwards across the hall, banged my head hard enough against the wall to see stars. Daddy came out with Sadie. She was naked. Her skin was slick like a seal and her hair hung like a wet mop about to go after the pink mess on the floor. I could see all of her, things that made me ashamed to be looking at, but I couldn't tear my eyes away.

"Get the doors, Mabel!" Daddy ordered in a growl I had never heard come from him.

Mama raced down the hall past our rooms, banged through the utility room doors, across the garage, and then she bent to lift the heavy garage door. Daddy was right behind her. He ducked under the door when it was half way up and then sprinted around the corner to his car. I was right there but trying to stay out from underfoot. Daddy flung open the car door and lowered himself in with Sadie draped across his lap. He cradled her head with his left arm while he started the car and threw it into reverse with his right. I jumped back as the Pontiac screeched in reverse down the driveway. It threw sparks when it slammed onto the street. I could hear the shifter click as Daddy flung it into drive, and then the big Pontiac lurched forward, V-8 power spinning the tires. The Pontiac shot down the hill out of sight. I could hear the tires squealing and the roar of the engine as Daddy made the right turn onto Harding Place.

Mama hurried back into the house. I stood stunned in the night. Mr. and Mrs. Hanshaw had come out onto their porch and were looking up and down the street, their questioning voices small in the distance. I turned to go inside, and just then the other garage door screeched open. Mama had thrown on a coat and was jingling her keys. She hadn't turned on the garage lights. The Buick was dark in the shadows, but stars glittered on the chrome. She jumped in, started the engine, and then she saw me in the headlights, standing small in the driveway as the night pressed down.

"Oh, Carlton; Carlton, honey," she said hurriedly. "Go inside and lock the doors. I'll call Mama to come stay with you when I get to the hospital. It won't be long. You can stay up tonight, watch television."

She tried to smile but it was an empty gesture. I stepped aside and the Buick shot out of the garage. I watched it go, down the hill and out of sight.

I did what Mama said, jumped up and pulled the garage doors down. I went through the utility room, closed and locked those doors, too. But down the hall past our rooms I began to shudder. Tears came. I looked into the bathroom with a mixture of revulsion, shame, and curiosity. There were bloody handprints on the sides of the tub, and ghoulish finger streaks. There was a razor blade in the soap dish, pink splatters all around it. I sat alone on the floor in the den, rocking and hugging my knees. *Petticoat Junction* had come on the television. I looked to Daddy's Barcalounger, thought I could see him sitting there reading the paper, with Elizabeth smiling and whispering over his shoulder; and Mama on the couch, trying to pretend she wasn't nervous or worried.

Nothing would ever be the same. It wasn't fair. These thoughts tore at my mind until they became like a vise around my head and I couldn't stand it; I couldn't stand it. I ran upstairs, out through the kitchen and then up the hill, over the fence and into the woods. Branches scraped and shadows were wicked. The gibbous moon looked like an evil omen. I went to our fort and crawled inside, curled into a ball and shivered until I was asleep

* * *

I was stiff when I awoke the next morning. My mouth was dry and my skin felt sticky. I patted at my hair but it wouldn't stay down no matter what I did. It was a bright morning, sunlight waking the trees, birds restless and chirping. Church bells tolled somewhere. I yawned and plodded down the hill. At the kitchen I could see Mama through the window. She sat at the table, her head propped in one hand, a cigarette in the other. She was wearing the same clothes from last night.

I hesitated before I went in. I didn't know if I would be in trouble or not. Mama hadn't moved. The ash on her cigarette was long. I thought that maybe I could slip in and no one would see me, but as I pondered this Mama looked up and saw me through the window.

"*Carlton!*" she screamed.

She was through the door fast, and then she had me by the shirt and she was shaking me.

"*Carlton, where have you been?*"

She was shaking me hard. Her nose was red and running and her voice was shrill. My lips trembled, and although I fought it I began to cry.

"Where have you been?" she screamed again, shaking me. My knees went out and I couldn't stay on my feet.

"*Maybelline!*" Grandmother Villetta shouted. She was standing in the doorway, her arms folded, dressed in Victorian black and as taut as a drum. The look on her face was stern, like an old black and white portrait. "That's enough of that now!"

Mama's hands fell from my shirt. She hid her face in shame. Grandmother Villetta came up and rested a hand on Mama's shoulder. "Go inside, Maybelline," she said gently. "Go rest now. I'll take care of Carlton."

Mama nodded, her face in her hands. She went into the house unsteadily, like a broken old woman.

"Well, Carlton," Grandmother Villetta said to me with a reassuring smile. She picked some leaves out of my hair. "By the look of you I think you finally got to have your camping trip, eh?"

I sniffed and smiled. I hadn't thought about it that way but I guess it was true.

"Let's go inside and get you something to eat." She took me by the hand. "You must be starving."

We stopped at the door and she reached down to smooth my hair. Somehow it stayed in place for her.

"It's going to be okay, boy," she said to me. She pressed me against her hip and took a deep breath. "We've seen such before in our family. We're strong enough for this, too. Now inside with you." She patted me on the behind. "I've a mind for hot biscuits this morning, and some gravy. And maybe a piece of pie later."

Grandmother Villetta always knew how to make me feel better.

* * *

When I asked, Mama said Sadie was in a rest home to recover her strength. I pictured a quiet country house with bright, airy windows, a gentle breeze, and frosted pitchers of sweet tea on the porch. Of course, that's not what it was. I started the sixth grade all alone down the hall, the two bedrooms next to mine empty and quiet. The kids at school whispered when I walked by, and sometimes I would catch my teacher, Mrs. Cotton, looking at me suspiciously through the tops of her horn-rimmed bifocals, as if she expected me to break down at any moment or else throw some other kind of fit. Kenny had no tact. He wanted to know everything. I told him to shut up.

Daddy and Mama did their best to make my eleventh birthday as special as they could. Daddy decorated the living room, and Mama baked a big cake. I saw her in the kitchen ahead of time, checking the candles. All the kids in my class were invited, and a lot of them came. Kenny and Evelyn were there. And Grandmother Villetta came. She sat primly on the couch with a tight smile and watched everything carefully. Daddy brought out my special present—he called it a special present—a large box that I approached with a peculiar trepidation. I ripped into it, and then I was ecstatic. Daddy had gotten me a backpack and a sleeping bag! Mama came in with another box. There was a pup tent in it! I whooped, and so did Kenny. Everyone looked at him curiously, but we shared grins and started laying our plans right then.

Afterward, when all the kids had gone home, Daddy took me aside.

"I have another present for you, son, an extra special present just between you and me." He frisked my hair, then reached a hand into a pocket and came out with his World War Two compass. "I want you to have this," he said, "so you never get lost."

"Wow!" I said in awe. I took the compass reverently. It was a solid and somewhat heavy lensatic compass in an olive-green metal case, with a built-in sight wire and folding magnifying glass. I opened the case and watched as the needle spun around toward our hilltop.

"I'll show you how to use it later," Daddy said, "because right now your mother has an extra special present for you, too."

"She does?" I said in a daze.

Mama and Grandmother Villetta came up smiling warmly. Mama took me by the hand and led me into Leavitt's room. All of my things were there, my bed and dresser, my books and my posters of Apollo 11, my clothes and my toys and my field bag. I thought I would cry but I was happy.

"It's time you were upstairs with us," Mama said. She knelt and looked me in the eyes, her cheeks quivering. "I know it's been hard, Carlton, but we love you very much."

Mama hugged me to her breast while Grandmother Villetta looked on approvingly.

SIX

Damn it all, I nodded off over this last night and now I've slept past noon! I've wasted most of another day, not that it matters. It's colder now, if that were even possible, and the rain is coming down in a solid curtain. I wouldn't hike out into this weather if I was still seventeen. Rain is seeping in. To stay dry I have had to wiggle into the tightest nook, where the roof has fallen against the floor, but the toe of my sleeping bag has caught some of the wet and now I can feel a cold dampness around my feet.

It's miserable in here. Even Sam can tell. He's curled up practically nose to nose with me right now, looking at me with those sad brown eyes, his nose tucked between his paws. If I smile at him or pet him, though, he'll thump his tail and jerk his head up in expectation. I can't bear to disappoint him again so I look away. What else can I do? I can't go out in this storm—and that's what it is, a storm, not just a spell of rainy weather. This is like a March nor'easter that got lost off Nova Scotia and didn't find its way ashore until June.

What I would give for some hot coffee, anything to still this trembling in my gut. It feels as if there is one huge convulsing shiver trying to work its way out. But there's nowhere to set up the stove; nothing I can do. I ate some hard biscuits, and washed those down with cold water. I gave Sam some dried venison, hoping he could gnaw on that for a while, but he swallowed it all in just a few jowly gulps. I could hear his teeth smacking together. His ribs are showing. I need to let him hunt, but being out in this weather would be as bad on him as it would be on me. We'll wait. I'll give up hoping to make some miles today. If the rain breaks, even if only for a little while, I'll take Sam out and I'll fire up my stove and we'll both feel better.

So to pass the time for now I'll get back to the story. I'm afraid I'm going to run out of paper before it's finished. There's so much that I want to say, about the trail and the other things, and I'm sure I won't find any paper farther on. It's possible I could still come across an old trail register preserved in a plastic bag, but not likely. It would be nice to find one, though. Or rather, it would be *comforting* to find one. To be able to read the entries of other hikers, even across so many years, would bring it all back as if they were with me right now.

We thru-hikers were a motley fellowship, at once seeking solitude yet craving one another's company. Coming up on a shelter full of hikers after days alone on the trail was an event, a chance to meet new people and share stories. All hikers weren't pleasant, though. The last full shelter I stayed in was in New York, about twenty miles out of Connecticut. That's where I encountered my final wave of northbound hikers. From then on I would meet the odd straggler now and again, but for the most part I spent the rest of my hike pretty much alone, especially from Pennsylvania and on south.

It was the middle of July, about as hot and humid as Atlanta in August. The mosquitoes were fierce. The terrain through there was pretty level, with a lot of road walking, but I was so drained by the humidity that I just drug along listlessly throughout that day, not paying enough attention to my surroundings. I missed the blazes on one of the roads, which would have steered me back into the woods, and somehow wound up skirting Nuclear Lake instead. A plutonium spill had happened there a few years earlier. The area was supposedly safe now, but the warning signs posted along the lake were ominous. I held my breath as much as I could through that part, and hoped those nuclear mosquitoes weren't injecting me with something worse than encephalitis.

This detour added hours to my hike that day. It was almost sundown when I finally reached shelter. The heat was oppressive even then. My skin was grimy and I felt sick at my stomach. There was an iron water pump out front of the shelter. I ran to it, cranked the pump urgently and let that rust-tinted water rush over my head. It felt wonderful, not quite a dive into a cool lake but close enough in that heat. I was still dripping when I went into the shelter. This shelter was a cinder-block cabin, roomy inside. It held six or eight wooden bunks, all occupied by northbounders, with even more of them sacked out on the floor. A Coleman lantern hissed from the rafters.

"There's room, dude," one of them said. "C'mon in."

Most of them looked college-aged, maybe right out of school. Some of them looked absolutely beaten. There were two girls among them, and one older guy with a righteous gray beard, like Charlton Heston in *The Ten Commandments*. He was on a bunk against the far wall and seemed to be holding forth to the group. He stopped abruptly when I came in.

"I'm Taz," he said, eyeing me up and down.

"Jake Brake," I offered in return.

"We haven't seen you before, Jake Brake," another guy said. He had long dirty hair and wore John Lennon glasses.

"I'm goin' south," I said wearily.

"*South?* Why?"

All conversation stopped and they stared. After I had begun to encounter larger groups of northbounders in Massachusetts, I discovered that there was a peculiar tribalism between northbounders and southbounders, a rivalry in a way. I had yet to meet another southbounder, so had no basis for comparison. I had explained my reasons so many times that it had become tedious. Now I just mumbled, "Got started late," and let it go.

I dropped my backpack into a corner and sat on it heavily. Taz started up again, telling tall, animated tales of the trail. His accent was a long drawl. I tried to pay attention but my mind was numb. I smacked a mosquito on my neck. My stomach rumbled.

"Here, dude, take some," John Lennon said. He handed me a paper sack that had corn flakes, pretzels, and peanuts all mixed together in it. Great idea.

"Thanks," I said, taking the sack.

"I'm Free Bird," he said.

One of the girls was sitting cross-legged on the floor next to him. She was of above average height, which exaggerated her weight loss on the trail to make her look impossibly thin. She had a petite face, deeply tanned, with high cheeks and a slightly upturned nose, and long brown hair tied back with thin braids. She was wearing tattered bell-bottom jeans and a long-sleeved denim shirt about three sizes too big. "And I'm Seagull," she added in an accent that lazed along the South Carolina-Georgia line.

"Good to meet you," I said through a salty handful of corn flakes and pretzels and peanuts.

"What's it like up there?" a hiker with haggard eyes asked from across the way.

I'd heard that question before. What he meant was: What's it like in *Maine*? My first impulse was to tell him how hard it would be, but that would have been cruel. He still had seven hundred and some miles to go, about three hundred of which are the hardest on the trail. I kept my reply generic instead.

"It's beautiful," and this was the truth. "There's cold spring water everywhere, and blueberries all along the trail." I didn't mention anything about the mountains and the bogs and the black flies.

"Yeah, man! *That's* what it's all about," Free Bird exclaimed enthusiastically.

Taz rustled around in his bunk and tugged at his beard. He seemed put out that everyone was paying attention to me. "Where you from?" he asked over the rest of them.

"Tennessee," I answered offhandedly. "What about you?" I guiltily handed the sack back to Free Bird. I had finished most of it. Free Bird waved off my embarrassment.

"Republic of Texas," Taz answered proudly, thumping his chest.

"Here he goes," someone moaned.

Taz laughed and slapped his thigh. "Y'all'll like this," he said. "You know what the difference is between a Texan and a Tennessean?" They all shook their heads, but some of them were wincing. Taz laughed again before he could get it out. "A Texan'll slap you on the back, buy you a drink, and then run off with your woman." He grinned, yellow teeth in a wild beard. The others groaned. I was feeling a little antsy.

"A Tennessean, though—a Tennessean'll show you his bible with his right hand, stab you in the back with his left, and *then* run off with your woman."

"Not cool, dude," the other girl said to Taz.

Taz exploded with laughter.

It took a minute for it to sink in, and then I realized that I had been insulted.

"Hey!" I shot to my feet. Free Bird fell over backward and Seagull edged away.

"Aw, cool it, Jake Brake," Taz said. "It was just a joke."

"It wasn't funny," I said threateningly, my fists bunching.

"Aw, c'mon, man. Here." Taz pulled out a joint, lit it and passed it around. "Peace, man."

The pungent smoke filled the shelter. Taz started talking to another hiker, his mouth running sixty miles an hour or more. Suddenly no one was paying attention to me so I let it go and fell back onto my pack.

When Free Bird got the joint he sucked it until the cherry was about half an inch long. He screwed up his face to hold in the smoke, offered the joint to me and squeakily said, "Here," with a little smoke leaking out.

"No thanks, I don't smoke," I said.

"Bummer, man," Free Bird squeaked again, more smoke leaking out. He offered the joint to Seagull but she shook her head.

The joint worked its way around the shelter. I was getting a contact high just sitting there, my head beginning to spin. The air became too thick to breathe so I rolled myself around the corner and out into the night air. It wasn't much better outside. Interstate 84 was only a few miles north, New York City about thirty miles south. The air held the hoary smell of exhaust and, vaguely, sewage. The sky was hazy. I sat at a picnic table and shook my head to clear it. The sun had set completely. The moon hadn't risen yet but there was a gray city glow off the hazy sky. Cars sped up and down the Taconic Parkway, not even a half a mile away. It was going to be like this for the next few days, until I got through that densely populated choke point between New York and New Jersey.

Seagull came out quietly and sat across from me.

"Do you mind?" she asked.

"No…no," I answered, boyishly for some reason.

We sat in silence. I saw bats scatter across the sky. Headlights would occasionally slash through the woods like spectral knives.

"Who *is* that guy?" I finally blurted. Seagull smiled ironically.

"I don't know." She kept her voice low. "He's been hanging out with us since Delaware Water Gap. I think he lives on the trail."

I'd heard the stories, of men who wandered from one end of the trail to the other and then back again as if they had no homes to go to.

"He does that to everybody he meets," she went on. "I think he's a psycho. Something bad must have happened to him. Maybe a preacher banged his wife or something. It's sad, really. The only reason the others stick around is he gives them free pot.

I'd like to get away from the guy myself. We zeroed in Unionville for two days hoping to lose him, but then we get here and," she opened her arms wide, "here he is again."

There were scars on her wrists that shone like pearl traces in the dull light. Seagull saw me looking and shrugged her sleeves down over her hands.

"I'm sorry," I said.

"No reason to be. It's not your problem."

That hung out there and smoldered while I tried to find somewhere else to put my eyes. I could hear Taz going on in the shelter. The others were laughing. Smoke wafted out of the open door to join the haze above.

"My sister's scars run long ways," I finally said, just to say something.

"Lucky for her, then," Seagull whispered gravely at the table. Then she turned to me with a forthright look. "She didn't know how to do it right."

"Look, I'm sorry," I apologized again.

"It's okay," she demurred.

"Can I ask—?"

"No!" she barked.

I leaned back. "Okay. Sorry."

I wanted Seagull to open up to me, not that her problems were any of my business, but because after Sadie I had questions that had never found answers. It wasn't going to happen. I changed the subject.

"How long have you two been together?" I asked, tipping my head toward the shelter.

"Who, Free Bird?" she said, but then it dawned on her. "Oh, man, you think he's my *boyfriend?* Hell no he's not my boyfriend."

"But—"

"I met him in Damascus," that would be Damascus, Virginia, "and we've been hiking together ever since. He smokes a lot of grass but I trust him. He's never tried to touch me."

"Oh," I said.

Seagull's face shifted into something vulnerable, almost fragile.

"Do you think I can make it?" she asked earnestly. Her eyes glistened. "I really need to make it."

"Is that why you're hiking?" I nodded at her wrists.

"Yeah, in a way."

"Is it helping?"

"Yeah, I think so. You don't have time to worry about stuff, you know? Except being dirty and tired and hungry all the time. But I can handle that. It would be better if we could get rid of *him*, though."

"He won't be with you too much longer," I said with the conviction of experience. I tried to picture Taz chugging up Mt. Moosilauke in New Hampshire, gasping for air while toking on a reefer. "Naw, I think he's just a bum looking for attention. And yeah, I think you'll make it—if it's important to you."

"It is." She circled a finger absently on the table. "What's your reason? Why are you doing it?"

"Don't know," I said. "My dad gave me a book for Christmas when I was fourteen, *The High Adventure of Eric Ryback*. He was a teenager who hiked from Canada to Mexico on the Pacific Crest Trail, something like 2600 miles."

"Yeah, I've heard of him," said Seagull.

"No one thought he could do it. He was all alone in the wilderness for months. I guess I just wanted to see if I could do it, too."

Seagull looked at me skeptically. "How old are you?" she asked.

"Seventeen," I answered truthfully, although I don't know why. By then, with my scrappy beard and unkempt long hair, I could have said nineteen and she would have believed me.

"*Seventeen!*" she exclaimed. "You're just a kid!"

"I get that a lot," I said with an edge. This had become tedious, too.

"And your parents let you do this?"

"They weren't happy about it."

"Man."

I drummed at the table. "Look, Seagull, I'm gonna clear out. This place is too weird for me."

"Aw."

"Nice meeting you, though. Good luck."

"You, too."

I went inside and grabbed my backpack. Everyone was talking and smoking, with Taz in the middle of it all. He eyed me closely as I shouldered my backpack and hiked into the night.

* * *

You hike at night when you want to put on big miles or—that night at least—get some distance on strange people. Night hiking changes all your perspectives. During the day there is the scenery, the people you meet on the trail, and long views of the terrain that allow you to anticipate your footfalls and move quickly. Time passes in discreet increments hour by hour: bugs pestering in the cool of the morning, sweat popping out as the heat rises before noon, and then the weariness that comes on through the afternoon until shadows grow long and it's time to sleep again.

Hiking at night provides none of that. Except for the rare meadow in silvery moonlight or sparkling mountain pond, the scenery is cloaked. The nearer features are silhouettes and quaking shadows that seem mysterious, sometimes menacing. The trail exists only a few feet ahead, only what can be seen from a slowly dimming flashlight or else the light of the moon. What comes next could be a steep climb or a rapid drop, there's no way to know. The darkness enfolds you like a cocoon, and time stretches out, hours merging and unmeasured. Weariness seems remote, something that belonged to the light. Outward expression is turned inward.

Seagull had asked why I was hiking. During my time on the trail she was the only one who ever did. Most people hiked for nebulous reasons, sometimes in search of an elusive idea of freedom or else self-acclamation. Not Seagull. She hiked to forget. Maybe I did, too.

My thoughts returned to that Christmas in 1972, when Dad gave me the book that all of this has come from. Sadie came down from Raleigh that year, from Meredith College where she was studying psychology and political science. It was our first Christmas together in four years, the first since—the accident. Sadie was pleasant but she wasn't the same. Her hair was longer, just touching her shoulders, and she counted her words now. Irony lingered in her voice. She said she preferred to stay upstairs in the guestroom. That was for the best. I don't think Mom and Dad would ever have let her stay downstairs alone, and any arguments about it could have opened wounds still raw even after all that time. The only hint of Sadie's old personality was that she wore short-sleeved shirts, which showed her scars. Mom wanted her to cover up but Sadie refused.

But we got through that holiday without any of the awkward moments I think we all worried about inwardly. Sadie talked about school, if not with her old exuberance at least with an engaged determination. Mom and Dad listened thoughtfully, and if they were judgmental or disapproving they masked it well. Sadie asked about my current outdoor activities. She seemed truly interested as I described my camping trips to the woods near Grandmother Villetta's house and along the Cumberland River. She smiled when I told her about stealth-camping in Percy Warner Park, where camping wasn't allowed, and how I had skillfully evaded the park rangers for two days and two nights. She was still pretty when she smiled. Mom and Dad were so relieved about Sadie that they forgot to be shocked and upset about what I had been doing without their knowledge.

Sadie stayed the week. We climbed the hill together on New Year's Eve morning, went on through the gate and up toward the old ash tree. The sky was a mournful blanket of low clouds. A biting wind coursed through naked limbs. It was cold and wet, but Sadie had said she wanted to get out of the house. Her nose was red and she panted visible breaths as we climbed.

"I've never been up here before," she said, stopping to catch her breath. She was bundled in so many layers that she should have been sweating despite the cold, but she cinched her coat tight around her throat just the same. Her fingers were stiff and white. They looked old. She gazed off to the south as if she were looking out to sea, her mind wandering.

"I found the pistol over here," I blurted at last, my voice a sudden intrusion on her quiet thoughts.

Sadie stood there, her eyes distant, but then she exhaled and turned to me with a melancholy smile. "Show me," she said.

We walked a short way to the edge of my dig. It had filled in with leaves but the rectangular outline remained visible even after all those seasons, like a sunken grave.

The fort still leaned against the tree. It looked forlorn, like an old farm shed being reclaimed by the woods.

"My, that was a lot of work," Sadie said in Mom's voice. "We were all very proud of you."

She came to me and gave me a hug that felt like something I never knew I needed until it happened. I sensed a rare moment of candor, a chance to ask the questions that had gone deep into the back of my mind but still nagged.

"Sadie?"

Somehow she knew what I was going to ask.

"No, Carlton. I can't talk about it."

She let me go and turned to look down the hill toward our house, lost in something. It occurred to me that she must have thought I meant Elizabeth—or the other. She shivered and pushed her hands into her pockets.

"I'm going in now," she said then. She shuffled through the wet leaves without looking back, and I was left wanting, knowing that to speak further might break something tenuous.

A noise from the fort snapped me out of it. I knelt cautiously at the entrance and looked inside.

"Kenny!" I exclaimed. "What're you doing?"

"Just hanging out, man," he said in a wafting voice.

The difference in our ages was beginning to show. Kenny was much taller than me now. He was thin and lanky, with thick eyebrows, the beginnings of a mustache, and the dark features of his Cuban heritage. His Adam's apple looked like a wine cork stuck in this throat. I crawled inside and sat across from him. Kenny rapped a box of Marlboros on his palm, tapped out a cigarette and lit it with a flick of his Zippo.

"Want one, man?" he offered.

"No, I don't wanna smoke. You shouldn't either."

"What does it matter?" he said, exhaling a long, blue puff. "I can't believe your sister came up here."

"Were you spying?"

"Hey, man, I was already here."

"Yeah, I guess."

Kenny and I were still best friends, but it was getting hard to find things to talk about. He didn't like to go camping anymore, and he had quit baseball, too.

"Are your parents coming to the party tonight?" I asked finally. Mom and Dad were throwing the party this year.

"I don't think so," he answered lazily. "I haven't heard them talking about it."

"Oh."

We sat in silence for a few more minutes while Kenny finished his cigarette. He stubbed it in the dirt and tapped out another.

"Well, I guess I'll get going," I said then.

"Sure, man. See ya later."
I left Kenny there and went down the hill.

* * *

The party started way past dark. Sadie had left for school right after our walk up the hill, and she had already called to say she'd made it okay, a ten hour drive. The guests parked their cars along the street and trudged up the hill on foot. No one wanted to negotiate our driveway when they were tipsy or worse—or even sober for that matter. The Hanshaws came. Dad and Mr. Hanshaw had become friends, or at least golf buddies, but Mom and Mrs. Hanshaw had never hit it off. Something about Mrs. Hanshaw irritated Mom. I could see it in the way Mom's face would tighten whenever Mrs. Hanshaw was around, but I didn't know why. My job was to greet the guests at the door, take their coats and show them the way upstairs. Mom wanted me to wear a suit and tie but I wouldn't do it. I was wearing new jeans and my Sunday sweater, and that was the best she was going to get.

The guests trickled in a few at a time, then a whole group of them came up at once, breathless and supporting one another. The Hanshaws were the last to arrive. Evelyn was with them. I took Mrs. Hanshaw's white mink coat but she held onto the stole. She was wearing a sleeveless peach dress with sequins along the hem. She wound the stole around her bare shoulders while I hung her coat in the closet. Mr. Hanshaw wore a business suit, as had most of the men. Evelyn wore a double-breasted white trench coat that fell to her ankles and was belted snugly above her trim waist. Her hair was done in a braid that was so tight it pulled at the corners of her eyes. Mr. and Mrs. Hanshaw went up the stairs. I held out my hand for Evelyn's coat but she shook her head and pushed past me to join her parents. I stood dumbfounded for a moment, shook it off and followed after.

The living room was bright and noisy, everyone engaged in conversation or idle chatter. Cocktail glasses and champagne flutes clinked here and there. I didn't see Mom. She was probably getting something from the kitchen. Dad was standing next to the hors d'oeuvre table talking to a couple of men, all sipping from tumblers of neat bourbon. Mr. Hanshaw went to join them. Mrs. Hanshaw waved and grinned at a cluster of four or five women, and moved quickly to insert herself into their circle. The television was on to the Times Square party, but the sound was muted. A Perry Como record was playing on the stereo. I cringed at that. A few couples were slow-dancing, which was even worse. I went to the hors d'oeuvre table and snagged a deviled egg.

"Hi, Dad," I said. He reached out and rested a hand on my shoulder but didn't look down. He and the men were engaged in some serious business talk. I shrugged, grabbed another deviled egg and headed for my room.

Evelyn was standing near the stairs, frowning and tapping her foot, her arms tightly crossed. I was the only other teenager there, and even though Evelyn and I really weren't friends, I felt bad about leaving her alone. So I went to the stairs instead and headed down to the den.

"C'mon," I said to Evelyn as I walked by.

She followed me quietly with her hands thrust into her pockets. There were only a couple of table lamps on in the den. A fire hissed in the fireplace. I flipped the television on and clunked through the channels, found a *Mannix* rerun and left it there.

"Have you noticed how he gets knocked out in every show?" I asked idly as I adjusted the contrast. "There. Got it."

I heard a deep sigh. Evelyn had her arms crossed again, and...a look. Something needed to be said but I didn't know what it was. I stood awkwardly still and tried to think of something.

"Well?" she said indignantly. "Aren't you going to take my coat?"

"But—uh—yeah, sure."

She unbelted her coat and let it fall off her shoulders onto the couch. I gulped. Evelyn was wearing tight white bell-bottoms that caressed every curve and crevice, and a white satin blouse that was so sheer I could clearly make out the floral pattern on her bra. I brushed past her nervously, took her coat and hung it with the others.

"What do you want to do now?" she asked. She had pulled her braid over her shoulder and was stroking it coyly.

"Uh—I don't know. Watch TV, I guess."

She pouted, leaned on Dad's liquor cabinet and stroked it as if she were petting her mother's mink.

"We can make our own party," she said with a sly smile.

"Uh—uh—naw," I fidgeted. "We'll get in trouble."

She pouted again. I sat on the couch and tried to watch *Mannix*. Smacking her braid in her palm like a golden whip, Evelyn toed on over and sat next to me—right next to me.

"Uh," I said, and scooted over a little. She scooted right with me. She smelled like Ivory soap and flowers. My face went warm. I was feeling things happen that I don't need to describe. I kept my eyes on the television, but her eyes were on me. Her hand came down gently on my thigh.

"Uh," I said, standing abruptly.

"What's the matter with you?" she asked in a biting tone. Her cheeks were turning red.

"Yeah—uh—I'm goin' outside."

"*Outside?* Why?"

"Uh, for a walk in the woods, I guess."

"*A walk in the woods?* It's cold and it's dark."

"Uh, yeah," and I shot past her and out the door.

I sprinted for my hickory tree, spun around its trunk and hid there. The air was cold but enervating after the stuffy house. It might snow tonight, or so they said. I breathed deeply and listened through the quiet night. I could hear some base notes thumping through the living room windows. Evelyn didn't follow me. I exhaled in relief, gazed up through the branches of my hickory and wished that there were stars tonight. I climbed. I was really getting too old to be climbing trees—as a matter of fact that was the last time I ever did, except...well, that's for later. I was too big now to lie out on the limbs, so I settled into a crook facing the house and leaned back against the trunk. The leaves had fallen so I could see everything.

The brightness of the living room cheered the night. It was like watching a silent movie but in exceptional color. Someone had cracked the sliding door a bit, and cigarette smoke came out in swirls as if lit by a projector. Bursts of laughter would sound and then go mellow while the revelers waited for the next joke. Some had formed a semicircle and were clapping appreciatively as a couple danced the jitterbug.

I lowered my eyes to the den. The light there was subdued, but hearthy and warm. Evelyn sat on the couch with her legs crossed, thumping her braid in her hand. The television glowed silver but she wasn't watching it.

The deck door slid open to a rush of sound and Dad came out. He slid the door closed behind him and went to the rail, lighting a cigarette on the way. He leaned against the rail and looked out contemplatively over our hill. If he had looked straight ahead he probably could have seen me. I slowly shrunk in place, but there was no hiding if he knew where to look. The door slid open again and Mrs. Hanshaw came out. She had a cocktail in one hand and an unlit Virginia Slim in the other. She walked unsteadily to the rail and proffered her cigarette regally to Dad. He lit it for her without a word and she took a deep puff.

"It's cold," she shivered. She snuggled her chin into her mink stole.

"It's not too bad," said Dad. "The fresh air is good."

He turned back to the rail and leaned on his elbows. He was looking right at me but his thoughts must have been somewhere else. Mrs. Hanshaw sidled up to him, set her glass aside and leaned on the rail.

"You can really see our house from here, can't you?" she said. Dad nodded. "It's nice up here," she added, although if she meant living on the hill or being out on the deck I couldn't tell. She reached for her glass and tipped backward into Dad. He caught her by the arms and held her up. "Oh!" she giggled.

"Jane—"

"You're so warm, Dick." She backed into his arms. I couldn't tell for sure but it looked like she was pressing her behind into his pants. It was so embarrassing to watch I had to close my eyes.

"Jane!" Dad snapped. My eyes popped open. Dad had a tight hold on the backs of Mrs. Hanshaw's arms and was pushing her away. She jerked out of his grip and turned to face him. Her look was scalding.

"What's the matter—*Dick*?" she spat.

"We'd better go in," Dad said sternly.

"Why?"

"Because you'll catch cold."

A roar of applause came from the living room, drowning out whatever Mrs. Hanshaw said next. The guests were huddled in a tight group watching the television. The ball must have dropped in Times Square. It was 1973 there now. We had an hour to go. Dad glanced over his shoulder at the activity inside and then back to Mrs. Hanshaw.

"Come, Jane," he said, and he turned his back and went in the house.

Mrs. Hanshaw blew a last puff into the wind, flicked her cigarette disdainfully into the yard, and swayed after him. And then I watched Evelyn in the den. I wondered how much longer she would stay. Hopefully not all the way to midnight. I was getting cold up that tree.

* * *

President Nixon ended the draft at the end of January. I hadn't realized until it was gone how much the threat of the draft had weighed on me, the fatal inevitability of it. Leavitt had gotten caught up in it, but that wasn't going to happen to me now. The war was still going on when I started high school in August, but you could tell that it was winding down. The Watergate scandal was really taking off by then, and this was what everyone was talking about. The war just didn't seem important anymore.

My first day in high school began on a sticky August morning. Kenny and I were loitering in a stand of trees across from the entrance to Hillsboro High as students arrived for class. It was getting hot already. Clouds were gathering for an afternoon shower. My stomach felt queasy at the unsettling thought of walking through those doors, where Leavitt and Sadie and Elizabeth had each passed. Look how things had turned out for them. Now it was my turn.

"Damn, man, this is screwed up," Kenny complained. He was scrutinizing his class schedule. He had a cigarette cupped in his other hand, shielded from view. "We don't have any classes together. Not even home room."

"Yeah, I hate that," I said.

Kenny took a hit off his cigarette and stealthily blew the smoke under his arm.

"Maybe we can get 'em to change something," he said.

"Yeah, maybe," but my voice didn't hold out much hope.

Mrs. Hanshaw's long white Lincoln pulled into the circle drive and rocked to a stop. Evelyn got out, clutching a white three-ring binder and some spiral notebooks to her chest. She was wearing a white blouse over a plaid skirt, with white knee-high socks. Her hair hung in long curls to the middle of her back. We watched her. She slammed the door with her hip, grinned at a cluster of girls and skipped over to them.

"Man," Kenny commented appreciatively. "Evelyn's a fox."

"Yeah," I said without conviction.

A bell rang. Kenny dropped his cigarette and ground it into the dirt.

"I guess we'd better go in," he said.

"Yeah, I guess so."

* * *

As sophomores, Kenny and I were on the bottom again. At least Kenny was tall. I still hadn't got my growth spurt, so the seniors towered over me, even the girls. The senior guys moved through the halls in arrogant packs, elbowing aside the sophomores and juniors who were in the way. They wore polyester bell-bottoms, and frilly shirts with the top buttons undone to show their hairy chests. They all reeked of Brut deodorant. The girls moved in packs, too, chattering and giggling and eyeing the guys—the senior guys, that is. The rest of us were below their notice.

So I kept my eyes down and hugged the walls between classes, trying not to be noticed by any of the seniors. I took elbows in the ribs from time to time, a few shoulder shoves, but I never complained because that would have only made it worse. I knew this from Leavitt's bullying. Most of these seniors would be graduated and gone soon enough. I didn't know any of them. To me they were just big faceless goons. There was this one guy, though. I don't know what it is about people. You can look out across a crowd of strangers and somehow immediately lock eyes with that one person who has it in for you.

I saw him the moment I walked into that crowded hallway for the first time. Students were scrambling past one another, lockers were being slammed shut—it was the ritual chaos before class, and yet despite all of that confusion my eyes settled on this guy and his eyes were on me and I knew right then that he would be my nemesis. He was a big, ruddy, sweaty senior, most likely on the football team. He was so freckled he looked like a walking measles outbreak. He even had freckles on his ears and lips. He had a surly sneer that only revealed his upper teeth, and he was aiming that sneer at me. I steered away from him, but before I could make it into my class he caught up to me and body slammed me into the wall and said in a surprisingly high voice, "Look out, twerp."

I later learned that he was Max Hicks, the ironically-named middle brother in a set of three. The elder brother Hicks had long since graduated, and had dated Sadie a total of once. The story went that when his hand had gone where it didn't need to be Sadie had slammed a paper cup of coke and ice in his face, and this at Shakey's Pizza Parlor on a busy Friday night. Everyone saw it. Sadie hadn't just splashed him, she had smacked him in the face—with—the—full—cup. Yeah, that sounded like Sadie. I actually felt a stirring of pride when I heard about this. Apparently hicks—er, *Hicks*—hold long grudges. The younger Hicks was my age and just starting high school that day as well. I had never known any of the Hicks brothers. They hadn't gone to my junior high, and Sadie had never mentioned them. But they knew me.

* * *

Dad took me up to the farm to teach me how to drive on the Saturday after my fifteenth birthday. Mom didn't like the idea, and she had said so over breakfast.

"He's too young to be driving, Dick," she complained with a worried look.

"Boys on the farm can drive at thirteen, Mabel, you know that," Dad countered. He had his paper open and was perusing it, and he said these things casually as he concentrated on the news. Mom wasn't having any of it, though.

"You know better than that, Dick." Her color was coming up. Dad caught the tone in her voice and wisely set his paper down. He pulled off his glasses and gave her his full attention. "Boys can drive in the fields," she went on, "they can haul hay, but they can't drive in town or—or especially on interstate."

I observed this exchange carefully. I really wanted to learn how to drive, but if we upset Mom too much we would be miserable for the trying. Dad's face took on a somber look. He got up and went to Mom, and together they walked off out of earshot to talk. I couldn't hear them but I could see them. Dad held Mom by the shoulders. He had a frank expression on his face. Mom was shaking her head in disagreement, but then she stopped. Her face seemed to fall a bit. She gave a short nod of assent. "Okay, okay," I could see her saying.

I could tell from their body language what this was all about. Mom was afraid I would have an accident and get killed, like Elizabeth, while Dad wanted to teach me the right way to drive early on so I wouldn't have an accident in the first place. Their final agreement was that I could learn to drive, but only on the farm, and that I would never drive on a city street without their permission. Sounded good to me, at least for the moment.

Dad and I went on up to Old Man Hackett's place. This was a farm one hollow over from Grandmother Villetta's house. Rumor had it that Old Man Hackett had favored Grandmother Villetta once, but nothing had come of it. Grandmother was eighty-three now. Old Man Hackett was ninety-six or thereabouts. That age difference wasn't too much for country folk, but it was too much for Grandmother Villetta. She was simply not going to go with such an old man. Old Man Hackett still pined for her, it was said. Decades and decades of unrequited love.

Dad was still driving his old Pontiac Catalina. It didn't smoke, and it didn't use a drop of oil. Dad had taken such good care of it over the years that it gleamed like new. With its narrow fins and big curved windshield, though, it looked like a rolling anachronism among the sleek and rounded cars on the road then. Dad didn't seem to notice or mind.

We pulled into the grass next to Old Man Hackett's house. He lived in a single-story white farm house with a covered porch out front. A short dirt drive led off to an enormous red barn. There were fields behind and around the side of the house, with the stubble of the summer's tobacco crop waiting to be plowed under. Old Man Hackett stepped out his front door as we got out of the car.

"Ed," Dad said, going to shake the man's hand.

"Dick," said Old Man Hackett.

"You remember my son don't you?"

"Sure," he said, working his gums. There wasn't a tooth in his mouth. "Carlton. I knew your grand pappy."

Old Man Hackett's hand was unexpectedly soft, but as boney as a catfish. He wore faded overalls that hung as loosely on him as clothes on a line. His hair was white, so thin and fine that his scalp was pink in the sun.

"Y'all sit a spell," he said.

He and Dad took rockers on the porch. I sat on an upturned paint can next to Dad. Old Man Hackett rocked slowly and looked out across the fields. So did Dad. No one said anything. This went on for a while, and then Old Man Hackett turned to Dad as if about to say something. He worked his gums a few times, shook his head, and returned his attention to the fields.

"Tabacca come in awl right?" Dad asked at last, unconsciously taking up the country accent.

"Barn'sa full of it," Old Man Hackett answered, nodding that way.

The silence resumed. The rockers creaked.

"Them Sircy boys goin' ta help with the strippin'?" Dad asked after some minutes of contemplation.

"Reckon they said they would," answered Old Man Hackett.

Dad nodded and scratched his chin. The sun had come round and now it was on me, getting hot. I thumped the paint can and tried to think of something to say or do. Country ways sure moved at their own pace.

"Well I reckon you better git that truck out," Old Man Hackett said finally, rising stiffly from his rocker. "Over to the barn. Keys're in it." With that, Old Man Hackett pulled his screen door and went inside.

Dad and I went to the barn and swung open the big middle doors. There was an old GMC flatbed inside. It was a dusty dark blue, almost black. Chicken poop was splattered on the bulbous hood. Sticks of curing tobacco hung overhead like an inverted forest. The air smelled complex and sweet.

"Alright, son," Dad said. "Get in and I'll show you how this works."

Dad cranked the old GMC to life. A cloud of blue smoke wafted up into the tobacco. The cab was dusty but mostly clean. It smelled like sweat and aged leather. Dad pushed in the clutch, pulled the column shifter down gently into first, and we were off with a jerk. We drove along a dirt road between two tobacco fields, churning up dust. Dad demonstrated how column shifters worked.

"I wanted you to learn on this truck, Carlton," he said, "because if you're too rough or get in too much of a hurry you'll jam the shift linkage and get it stuck between gears. And if that happens you have to stop and crawl underneath to free the linkage. Not much fun." He looked at me earnestly. "So the lesson is to respect what you're driving and not go too fast. Understand?"

"Yes, sir," I nodded.

I was having fun. I think Dad was, too. There was no way he would ever live on a farm again, but I could tell from the glee in his eyes that he missed it a little. He was grinning as we bounced along that road, as if reliving old times. I didn't see him outside like this often. He had his sleeves rolled up to his elbows. His skin was brown and leathery. The sun was on him, glinting off his thick glasses, and in that light I noticed for the first time that the darker streaks in his hair were just a darker shade of gray. There was no brown left in it. His knuckles looked swollen handling that big black steering wheel, and the veins on the backs of his hands stood out like ropes. Dad was old, really old. When did that happen? I guessed I would look like him someday. Would I be as tall, though? Would I have his strong jaw and soft smile? Leavitt had been going that way, but it was up to me now.

We returned the truck to the barn after a while and went up to the house to thank Old Man Hackett. Dad had his arm over my shoulders. We would come back every few weekends, he promised, until I could pop the clutch without stalling out and could handle that truck like an expert. That's not the way it worked out, though. The Arab Oil Embargo started up a week or two later, and with gas lines that sometimes stretched for a mile we couldn't spare the fuel it took to drive out to the country.

Old Man Hackett came out onto the porch. He let the screen door slam, and stood with his thumbs hooked in his overalls.

"Y'all scare up some buzzards?" he asked with a toothless grin.

"A few," Dad laughed.

"Hate them things," he said. He spat off the porch. "They'll eat the hind end out of a birthin' cow."

"I've seen it," Dad said gravely.

"After you learn this boy ta drive bring him on up and learn him ta shoot, too."

My ears perked up at that.

"One thing at a time, Ed."

A battered white pick-up truck rattled up the road and pulled into the yard next to Dad's car. A heavy guy got out to the creaking and moaning of springs. No telling how old he was, but he had the makings of a scrubby black beard and none of it was gray. He wore overalls that looked brand new, while the yellowing T-shirt underneath was torn and greasy. He was missing a front tooth.

"Howdy, y'all," he said.

"Bob," said Dad with a tip of his head.

"Bobby," said Old Man Hackett. "Whatchur got there?"

Bob hefted a burlap bag out of the bed and dropped it on the ground. Something inside whined and whimpered.

"Bitch went 'n had 'nother litter," Bob said. "Thisn's the runt." He reached into the bag and pulled out a puppy by the scruff of the neck. The puppy didn't struggle or whine, just had its legs straight out as if its mother were carrying it from danger. Long ears dangled loosely. It was a boy.

"Bluetick?" Dad asked.

"Yep."

"Whatchur gonna do with 'em?" Old Man Hackett asked.

"Put a rock in there an' toss 'em in the river," said Bob. "Got too many pups as it is. Ain't nobody buyin' of late."

"Damn, Bob," said Dad uneasily. Old Man Hackett looked down at his feet and sighed.

"Well, what of it?" Bob said defensively. "I cain't feed 'em. You feel so weak in the knees you kin take 'em home with you."

Dad was shaking his head. "Can't do it, Bob. My wife wouldn't have it." Dad's accent had shifted back to city serious.

Except for a goldfish that only lasted a few days, we'd never had pets. Mom wouldn't allow pets in the house. "I won't have filthy animals running up and down the stairs and getting hair on the furniture," she would argue self-righteously. This must have been something that went back to her childhood days. Maybe a neighbor's boy set a goat loose in her room once, or scared her with a frog. Come to think of it, Grandmother Villetta never kept pets, either, just those rangy cats that lived in the barn.

Bob gave a gap-toothed grin that begged to be slapped. "I wouldn't let no woman tell me what ta do," he said derisively.

I thought Dad was going to lay into him, but Dad just laughed instead. "Then you don't know Maybelline Smith," is all he said.

Bob's face straightened up and he toed at the ground like a nervous boy. "Well, uh, yeah I do. And Miss Villetta, too. She took a switch to me oncet."

"She still would," Dad smiled. Bob rubbed his behind. Old Man Hackett's toothless grin looked as pink as a slice of watermelon.

"Dad?" I asked urgently, tugging at his arm.

"Your mama wouldn't have it, Carlton."

"But those men…"

There wasn't a thing left to discover on our hilltop, but Civil War buffs still came, like a pilgrimage, and they trampled Mom's flowers and climbed the fence, and sometimes peeped through the kitchen window. Another man had startled Mom on the patio one morning. She went after him with a frying pan and he fled into the woods. Dad scolded Mom for that. He suspected the man had been a burglar, not a Civil War buff, so now they were talking about an alarm system for the house.

Dad was scratching his chin. "Maybe," he said. "She might go for that." And then: "Give me that pup, Bob. I'll take him off your hands. But keep that bitch put up so this doesn't happen again, hear?"

I was bouncing with excitement.

"Can I take him, Dad?"

"Yeah, Carlton. We won't tell your mama how this came to pass, though." He looked me square in the eyes. "We need a guard dog. We'll build him a dog house and keep him outside. I think she'll go for that."

"Yea!" I cried, and I snatched that puppy away from Bob before he could change his mind.

We named our new puppy Langley, after a man Dad knew in the war.

"Langley was from Louisiana," Dad told me on the way home. "He was a Cajun. His real name was something like *l'Angley*. He raised bluetick coonhounds somewhere down in the delta. He was famous for his dogs back in those days. He thought he could teach them to sniff out land mines, but the Army wouldn't go along." Dad went quiet for a time. Fencerows flickered past. After a while he added quietly, "He saved my life."

"Where is he now?" I asked.

Dad's eyes were on the road. He reached out a hand and petted Langley. "Didn't make it," he said.

It seemed that life was a minefield of sorrow. I scratched Langley behind his ears, and he looked at me with the soulful beagle eyes that I would come to know like part of myself. Somehow I just knew he was going to be a great dog.

And yes, Langley was the great-great-great-something grandsire of Belle and Sam.

S E V E N

I got in my first fight on the Friday before Christmas break. It was after third period and I was in the restroom. It was crowded in there between classes. A few guys were in the corner hot-boxing a cigarette, while others were running combs through their hair or else primping themselves in the mirrors. The place smelled like deodorant and urine and cigarettes. I finished up and worked my way through the crowd toward the door, but Max Hicks showed up before I could get there. He stood in the doorway, half in and half out, holding the door against his body. He was sneering, and of course that sneer was meant for me.

I groaned. Every guy in that restroom knew what was coming. Fighting at school was a spectator sport that drew these guys in like bread and circuses. They formed a tight ring behind me.

"Do it, man! Do it!" one of them shouted, certainly not to me.

I swallowed hard and avoided Max's eyes, went to the door and halted there in front of him. Damn, he was big. My knees were knocking a little. I stood there, looking at the door and Max's chest, and then he pushed the door open with his foot, daring me to cross. The hall was packed with spectators, too, all waiting in breathless anticipation for the action to commence.

The bell for fourth period rang, and in that moment while Max was distracted I stepped over his leg and into the hall, thinking I might just make it out after all, but then he shoved me into the door frame. I heard *ooh* and *ahh* emanate from the crowd, and felt the stares of pitiless eyes. Max lowered his smirking, freckled lips to my ear and said something nasty about Sadie. That tore it. Some teenage hormone let loose in me. I felt angrier than I ever had in my life, a red anger that comes down in front of your eyes. Some of the students began to filter off to class, moaning that nothing had happened. Max was smacking gum and grinning at his buddies, and he looked like such a slobbering jerk I couldn't stand it another minute. I spun around and cold-cocked him in the side of the face. Max dropped at my feet, his head and shoulders in the bathroom and the rest of him sticking out in the hallway.

"Whoa! Ooh!" came from the crowd. Somebody whistled.

I stood in numb amazement, knees shaking, expecting Max to get up and tear into me. But he just laid there like dead weight. It turns out I cracked his jaw, not quite broken but serious enough. I never got in trouble for it because Max couldn't admit to having been beaten by a sophomore. So I took off, shouldering through the stunned crowd to my next class, trying to shake the pain out of my hand as I went. I sat at my desk while our algebra teacher blithely chalked figures on the blackboard. Every student in that class found a moment to turn and look at me, some with awe in their eyes, some with admiration, and some with malice. My hands began to tremble as the adrenaline wore off so I kept them clasped in my lap, pursed my lips to keep them from trembling as well.

Jenny-Pea sat behind me. She leaned forward and whispered in a warm voice, "Good for you, Carlton."

My face felt hot then, and there was a tingle in my stomach. I sat a little taller and squared my shoulders, and suddenly I wasn't trembling and I wasn't thinking about Max—I was thinking about Jenny.

Jenny was a junior. Algebra was the only class we had together, but I would see her in the hallways and at lunch, and I would sneak glances at her and feel my heart flutter. She was a slim girl without much of a figure. She dressed plainly in bell-bottom jeans and solid shirts. Sometimes she would wear a brown vest or a denim jacket. She had fine brown hair that fell over her ears and straight to her shoulders, with long bangs that were cut just above her eyebrows. She didn't make heads turn, but I thought she was beautiful.

Jenny-Pea's full name was Jennifer Anabelle Peay. *Jenny-Pea* was a family pet name that had somehow followed her into high school. Although her last name was pronounced exactly the same way, you could say it with a certain emphasis and mean her pet name, or you could say it with a derisive emphasis that made it sound like *Pee*. This usually came from the popular girls or else the guys she refused to date. The thing about Jenny was that she didn't appear to care about any of it. She didn't belong to any cliques, she wouldn't pander to the jocks, and she didn't seem to be affected by the cruel things the others would say. She had friends she sat with at lunch, but otherwise she existed outside of the social order at Hillsboro High.

I had a crush on her that sometimes made it hard to breathe. I would sit there in algebra class and my mind would wander and I would have these vaguely sexual daydreams about Jenny. I felt strange new sensations stirring inside, but had absolutely no idea what to do about them, or how. I was too shy to talk to her. My breath would catch in my throat whenever I tried, and what came out sounded clumsy and inane. I'm sure she thought I was retarded. I secretly pined after her for the rest of that school year, stealing glances while my stomach tingled and my face felt hot. If she noticed at all—which I doubted—she never let on.

* * *

My second and last fight happened on the first day of school in the following year. It was another hot and sticky August. Kenny and I stepped off the bus together, but he went one way and I went the other.

"Later, man," he said over his shoulder as he made his way to his stand of trees to get a cigarette in before class.

I watched him go. He had grown his hair long and his mustache had filled in, drooping around the corners of his mouth. We hadn't seen one another but a few times over the summer, and those by accident at the fort. I would take Langley for walks up the hill, and sometimes I would find Kenny in the fort, smoking and drinking beer. A pile of empty Tall Boy cans grew in a corner of the fort throughout the summer. We would talk a little bit but I wouldn't stay long. Kenny had changed.

I went on into the school, scanning for Jenny and trying not to be obvious about it. Evelyn walked by with her boyfriend, a senior football player who walked a little bow-legged due to the size of his thighs. I waved at her but she kept her nose up and pretended not to notice me. I shrugged that off. I was feeling pretty good about my junior year. I was as tall as Kenny now, and I had started shaving over the summer— well, a few times. And Max was gone, graduated, one less thing to have to worry about; and with him his friends and their snide remarks and simmering eyes. Max had never bothered me again, too humiliated I think, but I had continued to get shoves and elbows from his friends. Every day came with the threat of another fight hanging on the barest nuance in my reaction to this abuse. I kept my eyes down and took it, knowing that I might not be as lucky a second time.

But this was a new year with a new energy. The Arab Oil Embargo had ended the previous spring, so Dad had started up my driving lessons again over the summer. I had gotten so good at handling that old GMC that Dad had let me drive us home last time. I wasn't supposed to tell Mom, though. And Nixon had resigned the presidency two weeks before school started. Mom and Dad were afraid that the country was coming apart, but I felt a renewed optimism, as if my future had just been cut loose from the dragging weight of the past. 1974-1975 was going to be a great school year, I was sure of it. And it was.

It was at the end of that first day. The halls were jammed with students. I had just put my books away and had slammed the door of my locker when a fist came in and punched me hard in the stomach. I doubled over. I was vaguely aware that a crowd had gathered around, forming a tight screen that pressed me against the wall. A guy was standing right in front of me with his fists bunched. If you've ever been punched in the stomach then you know about those desperate moments, when you want to breathe, when you fight to breathe, but you just can't. Those are the moments when you are vulnerable to anything. That's what this guy had counted on.

But my experience had been honed by years of Leavitt's bullying. Did this guy really think for a minute that he could do anything to me that hadn't been done before? Even hunched over and clutching my belly, the thought of it infuriated me. Leavitt never actually punched me in the stomach, he knew better than to go that far, but he got a kick out of taunting me with one hand then popping me in the belly with the other, never hard enough to drop me to the floor but still hard enough to knock the wind out of me. He did this quite a few times before I got wise to it, so I had plenty of chances to learn. The trick to getting your breath back after you've been punched in the stomach is not to try to breathe in, *but to breathe out*, to exhale as hard as you can, which is what I did, and I got my breath back, and then with a latent anger I didn't even know I had I drove a right uppercut into that guy's crotch.

Our roles were reversed instantly. I was up, breathing hard, and he was doubled over grabbing his crotch, a gasp trapped in his throat, his mouth open in astonishment and his face going as purple as beets in a stew pot. It was Deckard Hicks, Max's younger brother. He had Max's ruddy complexion but without all the freckles. And his lips were thinner, his face more of a slender oval in contrast to his brother's broad bullish appearance. Deckard was probably the pretty one of that family. I didn't wait. I slammed my fist into the side of his head and knocked him to the floor.

And then they were on me. Someone grabbed me from behind. I stomped down hard on the arch of a foot. I heard a yelp and was let go. Another guy took a wild swing at me, but I ducked, and that punch took out a poor kid in the crowd, a sophomore by the size of him. That kid wore braces. I saw his eyes roll as he slumped to the floor. Poor kid. But I didn't know him and I didn't feel sorry for him. It seems that there's a hapless person in every crowd, someone who doesn't have the sense to get out of the way, like the antelope that gets singled out by the lion. At least that kid's braces did some serious damage to the fist that hit him.

I kicked backward into the crowd and got away from the wall. There were three of them, including Deckard, who still wasn't much use. They were all juniors. I recognized them from around but I didn't know any of them. They were wearing jeans and boots, like farmers' kids or drugstore rednecks. The one I'd stomped limped toward me, barely in control of his rage. He had flecks of spit on his lips. I think his name was Billy—no, it was Bailey. I didn't know the other guy's name at all. That one was looking at me venomously, sucking the knuckles he'd cut on that boy's braces. I hurriedly scanned the crowd. I spotted Kenny and gave him a beseeching look. I couldn't ask for his help out loud, that would be too humiliating. He was supposed to jump in on his own, but he didn't. Instead he seemed to be enjoying the show along with everyone else.

Bailey took a swing at me. I ducked and dove at him, tackling him around the waist. He tripped on the kid with the braces, who was just then trying to get up, and we all fell in a heap, doing more damage with our elbows and knees than with our fists. That poor kid with the braces—hapless, I tell you. He was all tangled up with Bailey, getting his head knocked into the floor. I brought a knee up as hard as I could, and then Bailey got to experience for himself what Deckard was going through.

It was over as abruptly as it had started. Deckard skulked away, still clutching his crotch, and the guy with the cut knuckles melted into the crowd after him. Bailey was writhing on the floor, and the poor hapless kid with the braces had gotten unsteadily to his feet. His braces were frothy and pink from a split in his lip. I took off before the teachers could show up. Students were cheering me and slapping me on the back as I went. I saw Evelyn. Her mouth was open in amazement, and she was looking at me as if for the first time. And then I saw Jenny, and she smiled, and she followed me out of school while Evelyn watched us go.

* * *

Our principal was always telling us that the reputations we made in high school could follow us for years afterward, so be careful. I don't think he had it quite right. I'm not sure we *make* our reputations, but are made *by* them instead. From one day to the next I went from being a shy kid to a swaggering teenager. Girls wanted to talk to me now, and the senior guys steered clear. It seemed that everyone wanted to be my friend. Suddenly I found my voice and could talk to Jenny without all the clumsiness. We didn't have any classes together that semester but we would meet in the halls between classes, and we would meet for lunch, and I could feel all those eyes on us and I liked it.

We started hanging out at Shakey's Pizza most days after school. Jenny always brought an armful of books, which I carried for her of course. She would absently sip her Dr. Pepper through twin paper straws while she studied and took notes, yet somehow follow conversations with me at the same time. We were in the pizza parlor one day a couple of weeks after the fight. I thought Jenny was completely absorbed in her studies so I started preening at the girls as they walked by.

"Don't let it go to your head, Carlton," she said without looking up. She was gnawing on the end of her pen, her hair brushing the pages of her book as she read.

"What?" I said with mock indignation. She looked up at me then, an amused tilt to her lips.

"Stop," she smiled.

The girls were giggling and flirting with their eyes, daring me to make a move which, despite my new-found confidence, I still didn't know how to act upon. And Jenny knew it. And Jenny knew that I knew she knew it. I laughed.

"Yeah," I said. "Sorry."

"It doesn't threaten me," she said, turning serious. "I just don't want you to be like them."

That actually stung. Jenny reminded me of Sadie in many ways—no nonsense.

"I'm *not* like them," I said defensively.

"I know," she said, and she reached over and took my hand. I liked the feel of her hand, warm and soft. It sent a quiver up my arm.

"What are you doing for your birthday?" she asked. My birthday was on a Friday that year.

"Nothing special. Mom'll make a cake. That's about it."

"Let's go out then."

"Sure," I agreed enthusiastically, but Mom and Dad were hesitant when I asked, and I knew why, so I had Jenny come over and I introduced her. Dad thought it was strange that a senior girl wanted to date me. He said this right in front of her and I about wilted on the spot. Mom stepped in before Dad could embarrass me completely. She liked Jenny, I could tell, and that settled it.

But Dad had a point. To this day I don't know what Jenny saw in me, considering that I was a grade behind her and almost two years younger. I asked her once. It was a sunny day, cool as it tends to get toward the end of September. We had decided to eat lunch outside instead of in the cafeteria, so we went out and sat in the grass near Kenny's trees. The sun was pleasantly warm in that cool breeze. I leaned back on my elbows and let the full sun shine on my face while Jenny arranged her books around her in an arc. The seniors who drove to school were shooting out of the parking lot onto Hillsboro Road, laying rubber in a race to get to Yannie's or McDonald's for burgers and then back before lunch break was over. Jenny sat cross-legged with a book in her lap, nibbling on a sandwich as she read. I brought out my own sandwich, took a bite and watched her curiously. When the noise of the cars died down I asked her the question that had been on my mind.

"Why do you like me, Jenny?"

She looked up as if startled. Did her eyes darken, or was it just the shadows of rustling leaves?

"Why do you like *me*?" she asked, looking away.

"Uh."

She snapped her book closed.

"You're nice, Carlton," she said to the breeze.

"I'm not so nice," I objected. She looked at me then, smiling with her eyes.

"Yes you are," she said, and then she brushed that aside with a flick of her head. "You know I'm graduating early, right?"

"Uh, yeah."

Jenny had enough credits to graduate at the end of that semester. Her grades were so good that she had already been accepted to Wellesley College for the spring term.

"Good," she said, "good," and the shadows were on her eyes again. But then she brightened. "So let's talk about your sixteenth birthday party."

"Birthday party?" That shocked me. "I thought we were going to the movies."

"Hey, I asked you out and I'm driving, so I get to say where we go."

She was laughing now, clearly enjoying this, but I was a bit perturbed. Birthday parties could be…problematic.

"Don't worry, it'll be fun," she went on. "Look, there's going to be a party at Belle Meade Country Club that night. Daddy's a member so we can get in."

"*Belle Meade Country Club!*"

I already had butterflies in my stomach.

"Yeah," she grinned mischievously. "You're taking me dancing for your birthday, Carlton."

"What?" I sputtered. "But…but I don't know how—"
Her grin was so wide her face was turning red from the strain.
"You'll figure it out."

* * *

I didn't have any nice clothes to wear to Belle Meade Country Club, so I put on my black Sunday church suit. It was a little tight across the chest, and the shoes squeezed my toes, but it was all I had. Mom took one look at me and shook her head, motioned for me to stay put and hurried down the hall to their room. She came out with some of Dad's things: a maroon shirt, a pair of gold cuff links, a crimson and gold paisley tie, and a matching paisley handkerchief that she tucked into my breast pocket.

"Go put these on quick," she said. "Jenny will be here soon."

What surprised me was that Dad's shirt fit me pretty well. The sleeves were a little long, but otherwise I was able to tuck it in and button my jacket and it looked pretty good. Mom approved. She appraised me at the head of the stairs, adjusted Dad's tie until she thought the knot looked just right, and then she stepped back with a finger on her lips and considered me up and down. She nodded thoughtfully.

"You look nice, Carlton. This will do just fine."

There was a knock at the door. Dad was in the den so he answered.

"Carlton?" he called. *"You have company."*

I felt flutters in my chest and in my stomach. I exhaled. Mom smiled.

"Have fun, son," she said. "Be careful."

I went down the stairs and into the den, and I saw Jenny, and my jaw fell, and she smiled and did a mock curtsy in her full length ball gown. It was a sleeveless white gown that billowed out from her waist in airy folds. She had a blue sweater over her shoulders, and white prom gloves that came up to her elbows. Her hair was done up on top, with a long curl dangling in front of each ear.

"Jenny, uh," I said. "Uh, jeez, Jenny."

"Thank you, Carlton. You look nice, too," she smiled.

Dad suppressed a laugh. "You two have a good time," he said. "And be careful." He left us and went up the stairs.

"Well, uh, I guess we'd better go," I said. I took her arm and tried to hook it in mine, as I had seen people do at formal events, but it wasn't working out.

"Here," she said with strained patience. She cocked my elbow and rested her hand on the inside of my forearm, and we went out to her car.

It had been raining for most of the day but had thankfully let up as the sun set. Jenny was driving her dad's car, a bronze Ford LTD. It was a lumbering boat of a car, with big protruding chrome bumpers, a fancy grille, and a full vinyl top. She had parked it on the incline adjacent to our front walkway. I steered her around to the driver's door and opened it for her. It felt like a clumsy thing to do, but she was driving, and if there were rules about these things I didn't know them. I held the door while she smoothed her dress, and then I went around the other side and got in.

Jenny was dwarfed by that huge car. She had to scoot up to see over her seat before she could back up. She began to reverse down the drive but changed her mind pretty quickly, throwing it into drive and pulling forward instead. She drove around back of the house, saw there wasn't enough room to turn around so reversed at an angle toward the trees along the driveway. She pulled forward again cautiously. The headlights glared on the corner of our house, red brick about to scrape that big chrome bumper. Jenny slammed the shifter into park in frustration and dropped her hands into her lap.

"Carlton, I think we're stuck," she said, clearly embarrassed. "I don't know what to do." She had that big car wedged at a sharp angle between the corner of the house and the trees along the driveway. I felt bad that I hadn't warned her about this in advance.

"I can do it," I said.

"Can you?" She seemed relieved.

I got out and went around, had Jenny scoot over a little bit and then I slipped in behind the wheel. The seat was warm, her warmth, and her leg was pressing against mine. That set things stirring, but I swallowed hard, shifted into reverse, and nudged that car between a couple of trees; then forward almost to the garage doors, once more into reverse, and then straight down the driveway onto the street.

"Carlton, I'm impressed," Jenny said with eyebrows raised.

"Naw, it just takes practice." My face felt hot.

I put it in park and went back around to the passenger side. Once I was in and settled Jenny looked at me with a full white smile.

"Thank you, Carlton."

She bent over and kissed me on the cheek, and she left there a warm place that smelled like perfume. I covered it with my hand hoping to make it last.

We drove mostly in silence. The radio was on but the volume was low. *Bennie and the Jets* played, followed by Ringo's *You're Sixteen*. I missed the irony of that one. The streets were wet and black. The traffic lights formed smears of color on the pavement, and the streetlights looked like haloed globes through the evening mist. A few sprinkles dappled the windshield. Jenny pulled over about a block from the country club. *Time in a Bottle* was playing on the radio.

"Why don't you drive the rest of the way," she said.

"Uh, okay," I said, a little confused.

"Give them this when they come," she added. She handed me some folded dollar bills. I had no idea why.

I took the wheel and steered us through the circle drive and under the portico. A smartly uniformed black valet wearing white gloves opened the door for Jenny and helped her out. Another opened my door then took the car somewhere to park it. I joined Jenny on the steps. She was looking at me sternly and pointing with her head.

"Oh. Oh, yeah. I turned to the valet, who was hovering right there. "Thank you," I said, and handed him the bills.

"Thank you, sir, and good evening."

Jenny rested her gloved left hand on my forearm, gathered the hem of her dress with her right, and we swept up the marble steps. A doorman held the ornate door for us, and we stepped into an environment that I had only seen in movies.

I remembered Dad talking about the Belle Meade people, with their airs and their senses of entitlement and self-importance. In a way I felt that I was betraying him, because right then I was feeling pretty self-important, too. What truly amazed me was Jenny. She knew her way through this as if she had been bred for it, and yet at school she came off as bookish. She was smiling elegantly and carrying herself with poise. You would not have known she was the same girl. She stayed close to me through the receiving line. Everyone seemed to know her, these older ladies in their lemon and peach chiffon dresses and pearls, their husbands in black ties and tails. I didn't know what to say to them. Jenny introduced me as a budding historian who had discovered Civil War artifacts currently on display at the Tennessee State Museum, as well as the son of a prominent realtor. The ladies smiled approvingly and the men shook my hand stiffly.

We moved through the mingling crowd to a table set with crystal punch bowls and matching goblets. Jenny ladled some punch into a goblet and took a sip.

"Yeah, just what I thought," she said, wincing. "Go easy on this, Carlton."

I filled a goblet myself, just to have something to do with my hands. I took a sip. I don't know what the liquor was, but it was both subtle and potent. I puffed my cheeks and surveyed the ballroom. Most of the guests were elderly but there were some younger folks as well, mostly in their twenties. None were as young as me. A band started up with something light and classical.

"Moment of truth, Carlton," Jenny said with a wry smile. "Time to dance."

"But—" I sputtered. I hastily sat down my glass as Jenny pulled me to the dance floor.

I was sweating, really, and I was sure that every eye was on me.

"Put your hands here and here," Jenny showed me. "This is an easy one. A slow waltz."

I felt as stiff as a fence post set in cement, and my feet didn't know where to go. My shoes were too tight and I could hear them squeaking.

"Don't try so hard," Jenny whispered patiently. "Just one, two, three; one, two, three..."

She rested her head on my shoulder. Her hair smelled so clean and fresh, and her hand was so warm in mine; and I could feel the swell below my hand on her waist, and I felt such confidence all of a sudden that my feet found their way and we circled through the other dancers and in a moment of inspiration I gave her a twirl and she came back to me with the prettiest smile.

"Happy birthday, Carlton," she said with a grin and the sweetest breath on my face.

I wanted to dance all night, just like this, the bright lights and the noise of the crowd in some distant place, Jenny and me alone on that dance floor, turning and twirling.

We mingled for a while, with Jenny introducing me to people. She told them she had been accepted at Wellesley and they fawned their approval. But wasn't it cold in Massachusetts, though? How would she get along?

We settled in at a table and watched the guests. My head was a little light from the punch. A waiter brought me a slice of chocolate cake with a single candle.

"Make a wish, Carlton," Jenny said. I examined the candle closely before blowing it out, with Jenny eyeing me curiously.

"Well, what did you wish for?" she asked. She was resting her chin on her gloved hands and looking at me with soft eyes.

"I can't tell you," I said playfully. "It's supposed to be a secret."

She smiled. "Are you having a good time?"

"The best," I said.

"I'm glad."

I took a bite of the cake. "Would you like some?" I asked.

"Definitely."

I lifted the fork to her mouth and she took a bite, ran her tongue over her teeth to get the icing off.

"Yummy," she said, and followed that with a sip of punch.

A guy walked up to the table. He was college aged, clean cut and formal, with a sharp chin, Brylcreemed black hair, and overconfident blue eyes.

"Jenny," he said curtly. He ignored me. "It's good to see you."

"Blake," Jenny acknowledged with a frown.

"We should dance," he said. "Come on." He took her hand but she snatched it back.

"I don't want to dance with you, Blake."

He stepped back in mock offense, and then he looked at me and laughed.

"You like them young now, I see," he smirked.

"Blake—"

"Hey, man," I said, getting up.

Blake made a clownish face. He was only a bit taller than me. I wasn't afraid of him. He reached out a hand as if to adjust my tie but I slapped it away.

"Well, well, well," he said with that same smirk. I moved toward him.

"Carlton, no!" Jenny begged.

Blake puffed out his chest and we stood there, almost eye to eye. I was bunching my fists. He was looking at me as if I were trash. I was just reaching back to punch him out when an older gentleman pushed in between us, took Blake's hand and shook it.

"Blake! So good to see you again," said the man. He put a hand on Blake's shoulder, turned him around and led him away from our table.

Jenny was seething. I had never seen her so angry. As a matter of fact, I had never seen her angry at all. Blake kept glancing over his shoulder at us, his eyes condescending and with that damnable smirk. Jenny turned her back to him in disgust. I settled slowly into my chair.

"What was *that* all about?" I demanded. "Who's he?"

Jenny covered her eyes with the backs of her hands. She was trembling with rage and humiliation. After some deep breaths she dropped her hands to the table, her expression indignant and remorseful at the same time.

"I'm sorry, Carlton. Look, let's go."

She didn't wait for me to respond. She took me by the hand and pulled me through the crowd. People paused to stare as we went by. Back out under the portico she signaled for her car.

"Jenny?" I asked.

"Not yet." She shook her head. "Not here."

She didn't wait for the valet. She yanked open the door, handed him some bills and got in. I dropped into the passenger seat and we screeched out of there.

We drove in a heavy silence. There was surprisingly little traffic out for a Friday night. We swished through wet and darkened streets, around corners. I had no idea where we were going. Finally:

"Jenny?"

"I was supposed to marry him, Carlton," she spat in a single breath. Her brows were creased in anger, her eyes fixed on the road. "That was Daddy who broke it up."

"Wha—?"

Jenny flung the car around another corner. We were on Briley Parkway now. Aircraft landing lights were blazing out of the gloom in the distance. It began to rain. Another turn took us down a dark and narrow road that ended at a bluff overlooking the airport. Jenny pulled up right to the edge of the bluff, slammed the shifter into park and killed the lights. The windshield was smeared by the rain. Runway lights and the green tower strobe scattered across our view in a blizzard of sparkles. We sat in silence and watched the rain, Jenny grinding her teeth, her eyes straight ahead and unfocused. I didn't know what to say. I felt like an intruder in something deeply personal to her. At last she calmed and turned to me, her face open and suddenly tender.

"Kiss me, Carlton," she said softly.

I slid toward her uncertainly, felt a hollowness between my ears that muted the roar of the rain on the roof. I lowered my face, not quite sure which way to go, and then she took my face between her hands and pulled me to her lips and I thought my heart would leap out of my chest.

Time seemed to stop as I tasted her lips, still with a hint of chocolate on them. Our embrace became deeper, harder, and the rain pounded. And then we were in a rush, clumsily pulling at one another on that big front seat, the windows fogging, her dress bunched around her hips, my shirt open somehow, delicate hands grappling at my belt, no breath; and in a moment of fumbling awkwardness I fell into a pool of warm satin, and my mind seemed to go to some primal place, and for the first time in my life, forever embedded in memories of my sixteenth birthday, I experienced the depths of passion and the shuddering surge of release.

* * *

Blake was from one of the old families, Jenny explained, close friends of her parents. It had been decided while she was still young that she and Blake would make a perfect match someday. It was just that Jenny thought Blake was an ass, which he was. There was something else there, too, but she wouldn't talk about it. Jenny rebelled and her parents were scandalized. To keep the peace and contain the social awkwardness, they allowed her to attend a public high school, which distanced her from the gossip and drama of the Belle Meade set. She chose Wellesley College over Vanderbilt in order to extend that distance even farther.

Jenny and I were together twice more before she graduated. I keep these memories in a special place. She left for Wellesley the day after Christmas. Dad drove me to the airport so I could see her off. Jenny and I stood at the gate while the other passengers filed onto the plane. I wanted to hold her and kiss her but she kept me at a distance. Dad and Mr. Peay were off alone by the windows that look out on the runways, earnestly talking business. Dad may not have cared for the Belle Meade crowd, but he wasn't foolish enough to let an opportunity pass by.

"Jenny," I said, and then my voice broke. Her eyes glistened but her face was a controlled mask. "Jenny," I tried again. "I lo—"

"Shh," she stopped me with a finger to my lips. "Don't say that, Carlton."

"Why?" My lips were trembling. Jenny smiled sadly.

"Because it can't be like that with us. It never could. This was," her smile lifted, "really special. I'm glad we had this, but now you need to meet other people."

"I don't *want* to meet other people."

She reached out to touch my cheek, but checked herself and pulled back. Mr. Peay came up then.

"Alright Jenny-Pea," he said warmly. Whatever hardship had come between Jenny and her father was obviously long past. "They're going to take off without you if you don't get going."

I stood back as they hugged, feeling out of place and intrusive.

"Bye, Carlton," Jenny said, and she went down the jetway without looking back.

Jenny and I wrote letters to one another for a while, but time moved on and things became distant. The letters eventually trickled and stopped. I honestly can't remember who wrote the last one. I saw her father off and on over the years. He and Dad had gotten together on some real estate business, so I was able to keep up with what Jenny was doing. I never saw her again, though, at least not in person. I had a chance to once, but other things were going on with me at the time and I didn't feel up to it.

Jenny never married. She earned a master's degree in public policy and went to work for the United Nations, where she had a long career. In later years I would sometimes see her on the news, not in front of the camera herself, but in the background at press briefings and other functions. She had matured, she even had some streaks of gray in her hair, but she was still studious and slim, her smiles just as pretty. Whenever I saw her my heart would pound as if it were 1974 again. I was proud of her, proud to have known her. She was killed in the Canal Hotel bombing in Baghdad on August 19, 2003, along with more than twenty other UN workers.

That damned war.

$\mathcal{E}IGHT$

I was finally able to get out of the shelter for a little while. The rain slacked off, went from that frigid torrent into soft, warm drops that fell like a gentle afternoon shower on a Caribbean beach. It's surreal. Streamers of mist began to rise all around, joining into a smoky layer that oozed around the bases of the trees and hovered languidly above the stream. Weather systems are warring up there somewhere, like seasonal gods hurling thunderbolts at one another. I hope the gods of warmth win, and quickly.

I had a hard time crawling out of the shelter. My left elbow broke through the floor again, and it got stuck, wedged in tight. I had to squeeze my arm like a pair of pliers to get free, and now my elbow aches so much that I can't put any weight on it. Once out my knees were so tight and weak I could barely bend them. I tried to stand up straight, to stretch, but couldn't do it. So I shuffled hunched over to pee, and I set Sam loose, and I got my stove set up and made coffee. My fingers were so stiff I had to hold the cup between both hands, and I splashed a big dollop of hot coffee down my chin and neck. As much as it burned at first, it became comfortably warm where it soaked into my shirt, like a splash of hot water from a basin.

Sam wouldn't run. He nosed around the shelter, whimpering, raised his leg to do his business then came and stood trembling against my legs with his tail tucked. Something out there was scaring him. I strained to see through the mist, listened for the snap of twigs or the rustle of bushes. There had not been bears in Maine, or big cats, but that was a long time ago. Who knows what runs through these woods now? Wolves maybe, although I haven't heard them howl. Sam and I would make easy prey. I am so hobbled I can neither kneel nor stand up straight. I had to lean against a tree for support while I drank my coffee, bent over and with Sam wrapped around my legs as if he were holding me up. I couldn't have shooed off a porcupine let alone a bear. I don't think a bear would be able to take Sam, but a big cat could, so I put Sam back on his leash and kept him close.

The mist became a dense fog that closed in as if my eyes had been clouded by cataracts, and the rain began gathering weight, plopping here and there like isolated hailstones. It has been so cold and wet, so miserable, that I have looked back the way I came and thought that I could turn around and be out of here in a few days. It would take even more days, though, before I could get warm and dry. Millinocket has been abandoned. I don't know when that happened. All the houses I saw, those that still stood, were cold and lifeless, and as rotten as this shelter. I would have to walk along the old highway for a week or more before I found an inhabited place or someone who would be willing to help me. It's better to continue on. Perhaps Monson, on the other side of the Hundred-Mile Wilderness, has some residents left, or if not at least an intact building that I could shelter in. Yes, it's better to continue on. It's not as if I haven't been in these straits before.

It was the third week of September, 1976. The rain had started just as I began that long climb out of Davenport Gap into the Smoky Mountains. It had been getting colder since the Grayson Highlands in lower Virginia. I had been holding up pretty well through it, but now with the rain I was shivering as I hiked. Virginia had been a long, lonely march, more than five hundred miles along country roads, across limestone ridges and over grassy mountain balds, alone in shelter most nights, with just the occasional hunter for company. I had no sense of time anymore. I hadn't talked to another hiker since Shenandoah, and that was…weeks ago? The last people I had seen had been in Hot Springs, North Carolina two days earlier, but at that moment, climbing into the Smokies in the rain, I felt as if I hadn't seen another person in a month or more; and looking up into the desolate misty woods I believed that I might never see anyone again.

I was so close to the end, only a few hundred miles to go. And I was finally in Tennessee. I had thought for months that when I reached this point I would feel a homecoming, a sense of familiarity and belonging that would buoy my spirits and send me through these last miles with a sense of triumph. Instead I was emaciated and weak. I don't think I weighed 110 pounds. My belt had snapped right after Harpers Ferry, so I was using a length of rope to hold up my pants. My letterman jacket had ragged holes in the elbows, and was so dirty and matted that the green and gold colors of Hillsboro High were no longer recognizable. My boots were held together with airplane glue and duct tape.

The rain stayed with me as a steady drone over tall tops shrouded in mist. My tattered rain poncho wasn't keeping the weather out anymore. Cold trickles ran down my back and chest. I hiked by rote, another day, two days, then came out onto the highway at Newfound Gap. The lookout area was empty of people, no cars, not even traffic on the highway. The mist was so thick that I could only imagine what the view might have been into the valleys below. It was even colder out in the open, so I hustled across the highway and back into the woods, where at least the trees would cut the wind and deflect the brunt of the rain.

I thought back to the White Mountains and tried to remember if it had been as cold then. The White Mountains—Willow…so long ago that her face was now indistinct in my memory; and the others I had met, phantoms in my mind, just dreams. And if they had made it to Mt. Katahdin then they were home now, fed and warm, while I was hungry and cold, revising my memories of those weeks of hiking through the stifling heat of the mid-Atlantic states, thinking that it hadn't been so bad after all and longing for it to be that hot now.

The woods were deep, wet and close. Miles of dripping sameness passed beneath my muddy boots. And then suddenly I emerged from the woods onto the wide walking path that leads to the observation tower atop Clingmans Dome. It was a jarring juxtaposition from one step to the next, from the dense and rugged woods onto that open and manicured path. For some moments I couldn't reconcile it in my mind. I had to halt in the middle of the path as the rain came down, and I had to struggle to recall that I had been here before, a year ago, and that this place had filled me with wonder and excitement. I tried to focus, to find something familiar—to *feel* something familiar. There were no people here now, not in this weather. The cement observation tower was barely visible through the mist, a looming outpost on the edge of the known world.

I trudged up the ramp into the shelter of the tower, out of the rain. I was so stiff that I couldn't sit, I couldn't kneel. I set up my stove on an open cement rail and boiled coffee. I sloshed some on my chin, but in my urgency to get warm I ignored the burning and slurped that coffee until my stomach and chest were warm and the shivering subsided. Only a few hundred miles to go but they seemed like an insurmountable distance to cover, as far as where I began in Maine.

* * *

That's the way it feels when you're cold and alone. That's the way I feel now. Sam and I are back in the shelter. The rain picked up again but it was the settling cold that urged me into the warmth of my sleeping bag. Even hot coffee couldn't drive off the chill out there for long. I filled some bottles with hot water, though, and I have them in the bag with me. They help. I'm having a hard time writing this. It hurts too much to lean on my left elbow, and being right-handed I can't write if I lean that way. So what I've done is shove myself into a low corner where I can sit up a little and use my chest as a desk. I have my sleeping bag pulled up over my left shoulder, but my right shoulder is out and cold, my fingers white and stiff. I have to pause every few sentences to cover up and get warm, and then again between coughs.

I was thinking about Clingmans Dome in Tennessee, how cold and wet it had been. I should say that Clingmans Dome had been just as miserable during my second hike, but memories of my 1976 hike are what come forward so clearly in my recollection, as if suffering through it that first time has made a deeper imprint. I had been to Clingmans Dome the year before, on a warm and clear day that made anything seem possible. And I had seen the Appalachian Trail for the first time.

I had gotten my driver's license during the last week of school, this was at the end of my junior year, and then Dad surprised us a few days later when he came home in a brand new Cadillac El Dorado. It was white with a maroon interior, lots of chrome, and—big! I remember the skeptical look on Mom's face. She eyed the car, and then Dad, and then the car again. Her brows were up.

"Dick?" she asked.

Dad looked so proud, as if he had finally arrived after a long journey full of trials. He rested a hand gently on the fender, used his shirt sleeve to polish a spot. Dad had wanted a new car as far back as I could remember. I don't know why he waited so long after he gave Mom the Buick. We were well-off enough that he could have bought a new car at any time. Perhaps he had gotten distracted by all of the things that had happened; perhaps he had simply become too involved in his work. Or perhaps it was because Mom had since traded that Buick in for a newer model and he didn't want to spend any more money. Dad was frugal that way.

"Get in. Get in," Dad said eagerly. He was like a kid.

"Well," Mom said, and she fixed her hair as Dad held the door for her.

I climbed into the back seat and slid across the new upholstery. Dad reversed down the driveway with a throaty roar of power, and then he threw it in drive, screeched the tires a little, and we were off. It was strange. The El Dorado had front wheel drive, so the screeching came from the front of the car instead of the rear.

We drove through Belle Meade, past those stately antebellum mansions. Mom held her head high as we went through there. She pretended not to notice the people on their porches and in their yards, even as they noticed us. Soon we were at Percy Warner Park but Dad kept going, down Highway 100 and onto the Natchez Trace Parkway.

Dad drove along at a relaxing speed. The ride was so smooth we couldn't feel the road, and the air conditioner sent out ice cold air. Neither Mom nor Dad was smoking, as if to do so would soil that brand new car. Only Dad's Old Spice was in the air to compete with the El Dorado's new-car smell. Dad held Mom's hand. They were laughing and talking but I wasn't paying attention to them, I was gazing out the windows. The forest along the parkway was so full and green. I had camped here in the eighth grade. I remembered waking one morning to a flock of recalcitrant wild turkeys. They chased me back into my tent and held me hostage until the heat of the morning came up and drove them into the cool of the deeper woods. It seemed so long ago, like a different life.

"Well, Carlton?" Dad asked. "What do you think?"

"Huh?" I said, snapping out of it.

"What do you think?" Dad repeated.

"About what?"

"You haven't been paying attention," Dad chuckled. Mom smiled.

"Uh, sorry."

"I asked you if you would like to have the Pontiac."

It took a moment for that to sink in, but then my eyes went wide.

"Really?"

"Yeah." Dad smiled at me in the rear view mirror.

"But with some rules," Mom added sternly.

"Rules like you have to pay for your own gas," Dad said.

"Okay," I nodded eagerly.

"And you have to take care of it and keep it clean."

"Sure, okay."

Mom turned and rested her arms on the seat back. She fixed me with serious eyes. "And you have to be careful, Carlton. Do you understand?"

"Yes, Mom," I nodded soberly.

* * *

I guess most guys with their first car would have wanted to pile in with a bunch of friends and go cruising. Instead I was on Interstate 40 heading east and keeping my speed at exactly 55 miles per hour so I wouldn't get a ticket and disappoint Mom and Dad. I had asked them if I could drive to the woods near Grandmother Villetta's house and go camping for the weekend, and they had consented. I had made that drive with Dad so many times that even Mom wasn't worried. I passed the Carthage exit, though, and kept on. I was going to see for myself something that had been in my mind for a long, long time.

I left the interstate after Knoxville and worked my way south toward Great Smoky Mountains National Park. The road climbed into the foothills. A hazy range of rounded mountains stood off on the horizon. It was mid-afternoon when I reached Gatlinburg, the gateway to the Smoky Mountains, and a gaudy tourist town in those days. I stopped for lunch at Shoney's and then continued on into the park, up, up, up that winding road to Clingmans Dome, the highest mountain in Tennessee. The views were long from the mountain's flanks, of thickly forested ridges that overlapped into the distance in a vast undulating carpet of green.

I left the Pontiac in the parking area and sprinted urgently up the path toward the observation tower on top of the mountain, scanning the woods along the way for the signs that had to be there. Eric Ryback had hiked the Pacific Crest Trail way out west, a continent away from me, but he had mentioned the Appalachian Trail in his book, and the Appalachian Trail went through Tennessee. I had been fixated on this ever since, just waiting for the chance to see it for myself.

I froze in mid-step. There was a sign, a wooden sign that read *Appalachian Trail*, with a double arrow pointing north and south. Despite the warmth of the day, the wind brought a chill from the mountain tops. Mist was rolling through the woods above, like a cloud that had gotten snagged going by. The trail was a narrow, muddy parting in the woods that dropped down from the path to disappear in the thick foliage beyond. I slipped in the mud but kept my balance, and after only a few steps I was immersed in the forest. Natural sounds displaced those of the people heading up to the observation tower. I came to a T intersection in the trail. There were white rectangles painted on some of the trees, and these led off both ways, like a procession, until they were lost in the green.

I was on the Appalachian Trail! To my right, about 195 miles away, was Springer Mountain, Georgia. To my left, about 1980 miles away, was Mt. Katahdin, Maine. This was one trail, one sinuous connection between those far off places, singing with distant sounds like a telegraph line across the prairies and mountains of the old west. I felt a tingle in my stomach that rivaled my first kiss with Jenny. I breathed deeply. The air was sweet with spruce and the tickling cold of mountain mist. I would do it. Somehow I would do it.

* * *

I took a part-time job that summer sacking groceries at H.G. Hill's. The manager, Mr. Iverson, remembered Leavitt if you can believe it, said Leavitt had been such a hard worker that he knew I would be, too. This came as a surprise. It had never occurred to me that Leavitt worked hard at anything except tormenting me. Apparently there were other sides to him that I never knew. I wonder if anyone did. I was going to tell Mom and Dad about this but then thought better of it. They seemed so content lately. Why bring up that old hurt?

I met Carla Duncan at H.G. Hill's. Carla was a full-time cashier who mainly worked the day shift. I would see her on Saturdays, or toward the end of her shifts when I worked evenings. Carla had graduated from Hillsboro High the year before last and was now stuck in that period of wayward freedom between high school and the rest of her life. She had her own apartment, and drove a white Datsun B-210 with a crumpled left fender. She hadn't decided on college yet, or a career. She just wanted to have a good time and worry about the rest later.

Most of the cashiers were older women, so I would take up station at Carla's register and flirt with her between customers; and she would return this attention with a salacious eagerness that set the older ladies to gossiping. I finally worked up the nerve to ask her out, hid this in what I thought was some clever flirting in case she rebuffed me. She was quite a bit older, after all. Her brows arched when it dawned on her what I was asking. She looked me over, licked her lips and said, "Sure. Why not?"

We wound up dating all that summer in what Carla dubbed with lascivious good humor "a relationship of convenience." She wasn't interested in going with me to the usual high school hangouts, which in retrospect was probably a good thing, so we spent most of our time together at her apartment. The place reeked of cigarettes and weed. Carla taunted me with it even though I had told her right off that I wouldn't use that stuff. I kept some peppermint Binaca and an extra shirt in my car so I wouldn't bring the smell home.

Carla turned out to be a rambunctious girl with a waterbed to match. She had a wide mouth, a toothy and coquettish grin, and hair as red as a bonfire. The guys at work would tease me, ask lewdly if Carla was red down there, too. She was, but I wasn't going to tell them that. Carla taught me a lot about what I thought I already knew, bucking and rolling between the swells and with me hanging on like a rodeo rider. I didn't love her, although I did love what she could do. I never took her home to meet Mom and Dad, and fortunately she never asked. She and Kenny hit it off toward the end of the summer. I didn't mind, I was played out. And they had more in common anyway.

Kenny and I drove to school together on that first day of our senior year. I parked the Pontiac at the far end of the lot so that Kenny could finish his cigarette without being seen. He had switched from Marlboros to Kools at some point. The menthol tickled my nose.

"So you really joined the track team?" Kenny asked. He blew a puff out the window. There was no breeze that morning so the smoke lingered like an announcement to any teachers who might have been looking our way. He waved at it until it dissipated.

"Yeah, cross country" I said. He looked at me incredulously.

"Why?"

"Oh, you know, to get in shape."

"Get in shape for what?"

I shrugged my shoulders. I noticed right then that I sat taller than Kenny now. When had that happened?

"You know," I said hesitantly, "you should join, too." As much as Kenny had changed, I still missed our old times. I wished we could be that close again.

"Hell no," he said, and then he grinned. "Naw, man. I'm just lookin' for some tush."

I groaned at that. Kenny laughed.

"How's Carla?" I asked then.

Kenny flicked his cigarette out the window, looked at me and batted his eyes.

"Yeah," I said. "I get ya."

Evelyn pulled up in her mother's Lincoln and parked next to us. There were five or six other girls in the car, yammering and waving at some boys across the way.

"Look at little Evie in her mama's car," Kenny said.

"*Little Evie?*"

Kenny looked at me and batted his eyes again. My jaw fell.

"No way!" I exclaimed. Kenny just smiled, his mustache lifting at the corners like an inside joke with Pancho Villa.

Evelyn shooed the girls off and came around to my door. She rested her arms on the window sill and leaned in, her face so close to mine that I could feel her heat. Her hair looked especially soft that morning, a lustrous gold in the sun. She wore a shiny gloss on her lips that smelled like strawberries, and a loose white blouse that brought a fair amount of cleavage within inches of my eyes.

"Hi, Evie," said Kenny.

"Shut up Kenneth," said Evelyn.

Kenny grinned and drummed on the dash with his index fingers.

"Hi, Carlton," Evelyn said then, soft blond lashes fluttering over her baby-blues.

"Hi." I wasn't nervous, but this was a little weird.

"So I hear you joined the track team," she said.

"Yeah."

She reached in and fiddled with my sunglasses, adjusting them on my face until she was satisfied. I don't know why I let her do that.

"Those are cool glasses," she said. "Where'd you get 'em?"

"Oh, I just found 'em laying around."

"Well, I gotta go," she said. "See you later."

She bounced along after her friends. Kenny started laughing.

"What?" I barked at him.

"Oh, man," he said, and laughed harder.

* * *

I spotted Gracie Quinterra in the hall before class. My locker was in a corner that year, and when I turned there she was. There was no way to avoid it, she had me trapped. Gracie and I had dated for a couple of months last spring. She was exotically pretty and demure at the same time, with a surprising amount of heat to go with it, but she could be a little…clingy. And jealous, too. I had more or less broken up with her at the end of the previous school year, quietly relieved that I had managed to slip her hook without a fuss. From the look on her face, now I wasn't so sure.

"Hi, Gracie," I said uncomfortably.

Gracie was wearing a pink dress with a white collar and white frills around the sleeves. She was clutching her books tightly to her chest. The hairs on her arms were black against her brown skin. Her dark Latin eyes smoldered. I looked to see who was around in case she made a scene.

"Well, *you* had a good summer I hear," she said accusingly.

"Aw, c'mon, Gracie. You and I broke up," I whined.

"Then you should have told me," she pouted.

"I did."

"When?"

"That night at Shakey's."

"You mean that night when we—"

"No," I interrupted. "The other time."

She pondered that; then: "I still like you, Carlton."

She lowered her guard a little and pushed some hair behind an ear. Her hair was long and fine, and as black as Kentucky coal. I had brushed it for her once. That had been an unexpectedly alluring experience, but not something I would ever share with the guys.

"Uh, I still like you too, Gracie."

I winced inwardly as I said it. Gracie cheered up at that and bounced on her toes.

"I have to go now," she said, and she skipped off to class with a smile on her face.

So I guessed Gracie and I were going together again.

Evelyn cornered me about this later in the day. I really needed to ask for another locker. It was too easy to get trapped with this one.

"So I hear you and Gracie are back together," she said in a biting tone.

"Yeah, I guess so," I said. I slammed my locker. The bell rang for class.

"You're too nice, Carlton," she said in a huff, and then she spun on her heels and went to class.

* * *

The cross country team kept me busy all through September. With that and work I was able to avoid Gracie much of the time. She nailed me just before homecoming, though.

"You haven't asked me to the homecoming dance," she said, acting hurt. I had a new locker now, right across from the restroom where I'd knocked Max out, but it hadn't spared me from ambushes.

"Yeah, uh, well…I think I need to stay home and study."

She took my hand, and before I knew it we were walking down the hall like a pair of love birds. Her grip on my hand was sending none too subtle signals even as her face looked as soft as morning light.

"That's your birthday weekend, too," she said by way of argument. "We can't miss that. We have to go."

All of this *we* business made me want to run for it. We stopped in front of her class, holding up traffic but people squeezed past us without complaint. Gracie's face was beatific yet expectant.

"Yeah, okay Gracie. Sure."

"Yea!" She tipped up and pecked me on the cheek, and then ran into her class as if I might change my mind. As if I *could* change my mind.

Kenny appeared and we walked together to our government class.

"Man," he said. "Gracie's a hot chica."

"Yeah, she's hot," I said wistfully, "but she's kind of heavy, you know?"

"I can relate," he said with a roll of his eyes. "But you popped her, man."

I cringed. That kind of gutter talk made it seem cheap.

"And now she's in love," he added in an exaggerated syrupy drawl.

"She didn't tell me before—"

"Doesn't matter. You should just break up with her and get it over with."

"I don't want to hurt her, man. She's so…sensitive about things."

"Yeah," Kenny said, nodding sagely. "Her, too."

* * *

The homecoming dance was on a wet and chilly Friday, the day before my seventeenth birthday. Had someone been able to tell me where I would be exactly one year later, what I would have seen and done, I wouldn't have believed them. I picked up Gracie at eight and we made the short drive to school. She looked nice in a shapely white dress, some gold bangles on her wrists, and a white angora sweater to hold off the chill. I was wearing dark brown corduroy pants with a matching jacket, and a psychedelic satin shirt with the collar turned out.

The gym was already bustling when we got there. The bleachers had been cranked back against the walls, and the basketball hoops had been raised. The walls were laced with green and gold bunting. The letters *Go Burros*, cut from gold poster board, were taped above the doors. I spotted Evelyn at the other end of the gym doing a cheerleading routine with some other girls, with a few of the football players gathered around to enjoy the view. The guys still looked sweaty from the game. The sound system was playing K.C. & the Sunshine Band. I didn't know how to dance to that stuff. I looked for Kenny, even knowing he wouldn't be there. He didn't care about high school sports. The truth is, except for the track team I didn't either.

I walked Gracie to the refreshment table and tested the punch. No one had spiked it yet. The booster club parents were ladling the punch into plastic champagne glasses, passing them out as people came up. I took a glass for Gracie, and then we stood off out of the way while the coaches took to the mic and regaled the football team, school spirit and all of that. Girls walked by. "Hi, Carlton," they said with inviting smiles. "Hi, Carlton." Gracie stiffened and squeezed my hand hard. I sighed.

Finally all the rah-rah school spirit stuff came to an end and someone lowered the lights. A disco ball cast twirling spots all around, and a Barry Manilow tune started up on the sound system. This wasn't dancing the way Jenny had taught me, it was more like swaying in place, but at least it wasn't disco.

"So you wanna dance?" I asked Gracie.

"Yes," she answered sweetly. She had a worshiping look in her eyes that worried me.

We went onto the dance floor and swayed. The next song that came up was by B.J. Thomas, pretty much the same kind of thing, so we stayed out on the floor. Gracie rested her head against my chest. I swallowed hard and tried to play along. I had a nagging suspicion that Kenny was right, and I wasn't sure what to do about it. The next song was *The Hustle*, so I fled the floor with Gracie in tow.

"Let's take a break," I shouted over the noise. I found us a spot out of the way and we watched the dancers. Everyone was bouncing and gesticulating, and I was wishing that someone would spike the punch.

Mrs. Hanshaw was one of the chaperones for the evening. She was making merry with a group of adults on the other side of the dance floor. I could hear her exaggerated laugh all the way over here. She had a plastic champagne glass in her hand, and she sipped at it as if it held more than just punch. She was wearing a pearlescent ankle-length dress that left her shoulders bare. Her hair had a brassy look these days. Mr. Hanshaw wasn't with her. I think Dad and Mr. Hanshaw still played golf, but otherwise we didn't see much of the Hanshaws anymore.

She saw me and gave me a tipsy wave, detached herself from the group and headed our way. Her gait was less than steady. She held her glass straight ahead, and got across that crowded dance floor without spilling a drop. As soon as she cleared the crowd her elbow bent smoothly and she took a sip without breaking eye contact with me, and then we were practically toe-to-toe, with Gracie to my right and outside of Mrs. Hanshaw's field of interest.

"Hello, Carlton," she said, fixing me with a look that made my skin crawl.

"Hello, Mrs. Hanshaw," I said, looking down at my feet.

She tipped my chin up with an elegantly manicured finger. "We don't see enough of you anymore," she said petulantly, pushing her lip out to emphasize the point.

"Well I, uh, I've been busy, Mrs. Hanshaw."

"Yes, I've heard," she said, and something about the way she said it told me that she had heard a lot. "Congratulations on winning your meet. Coach Brooks says you're the best runner on the team."

"Thank you, uh, everybody trained hard."

She ran a fingernail across my chin. "All training and no fun…" she trailed off coyly.

Gracie must have felt like a scuff on the floor. I moved to introduce her. "Mrs. Hanshaw, this is—" but Mrs. Hanshaw pressed in even closer. Her breath smelled like gin, or maybe vodka. Her lipstick was flaking in places.

"Call me Jane, Carlton." She was having trouble standing still, adjusting herself with little jerks, one way and then the other.

"Uh, Mrs. Hanshaw—"

"I wonder," she said, and she took a step back. Her eyes lazed up toward the ceiling. "When are you and Evelyn going to get together?" Gracie's fingernails dug into my palm. "You two would make such a perfect couple."

"Uh."

"It's senior year, Carlton. You don't have time for these little trysts anymore."

Gracie gasped, threw my hand down like a wad of paper and fled for the doors.

"Mrs. Hanshaw!" I exclaimed. She acted as if she hadn't noticed any of it, but there was a look of smug satisfaction on her face. I glanced toward the doors then back, not sure what to do.

"Come visit," she said with a fake smile, and then she twirled around woozily and started back across the dance floor. I took off after Gracie.

Gracie had fled up the hall and into the ladies' room. The door slammed just as I came up.

"Gracie?" I called through the door. "Look—"

A girl came up behind me, Sarah Jean Connelly, one of Gracie's friends, the severe one with the strawberry hair and judgmental gray eyes.

"What did you do?" she spat at me.

"What? I didn't do anything."

"Get out of my way." She yanked the door into my face and went in.

I could hear them in there, muffled sobs from Gracie and a commiserating tone from Sarah. I started to go in.

"*What are you doing?*"

It was another girl. I had seen her around but I didn't know her.

"Uh."

"Do you mind?" she asked sarcastically. I stepped aside and she went in.

"Gracie, c'mon," I said to the door. "It wasn't my fault." The door burst open and knocked me in the head. "Ow!"

Sarah stuck her face out. "I'm taking her home, *Carlton*." She spat my name like spoiled milk. "Why don't you leave?"

"But—"

"Just leave, man!"

"Okay, okay," I waved her back. "Tell Gracie I'll call later."

"Don't bother," and then the door slammed once more.

* * *

From then on I wouldn't see Gracie except from a distance. Her friends kept a protective ring around her, and she wouldn't make eye contact with me. Sometimes though, out the corner of my eye, I would catch her gazing at me longingly, only to look away if I turned toward her. I felt bad about the whole thing, even though none of it had been my fault. My conscience was clear. Still, I could probably have gotten through to her, called her up and said the words that would have brought her back. Sometimes I felt ashamed that I didn't try.

With track season winding down I asked for more hours at work. I now saw Carla three, sometimes four days a week. She and Kenny had broken up, but she seemed as playful and lewd as always. I came into the break room one day and she was there, along with a few of the older cashiers. They were all smoking, lazy curls gathering below the florescent lights. I sat alone at a Formica table that was scarred with yellowing cigarette burns.

"Hi, Carlton," Carla said in a voice she hadn't used with me in a long time. I fidgeted a little. She stubbed her cigarette out in a tin tray and came my way with a swing in her hips. One of the older ladies rolled her eyes and exhaled an exasperated puff of smoke. "Carlton," Carla went on with a sly grin, "you are such a fox. Did I ever tell you that?"

"Oh that's enough," one of the ladies said disgustedly. She got up and left.

Carla took my face between her hands and planted a wet kiss on me and didn't let go. I scraped back from the table and broke her grip.

"Carla? Damn!"

The other ladies were shaking their heads, *tramp* written in their eyes. They smashed out their cigarettes resentfully and left as well. Now Carla and I were alone. She sat across from me. She was only twenty but she looked much older, worn and weary. She tapped out a cigarette and lit it, squinting at the smoke in her eyes. She smoked Winstons now, said they had more flavor than Marlboros.

"So Carlton," she said, "now that we're alone..." she looked around and smiled. "It works every time. Those gray old ladies can't get away fast enough."

"Huh?"

"I hear you and your little Mexican girlfriend broke up."

"She's not Mexican," I objected in Gracie's defense. "She was born in Murfreesboro."

"So what? She's a Mexican just like Kenny."

"Hey! Kenny's not Mexican either. He was born right here. And his parents are Cuban."

"If you say so."

"What's the matter with you?"

"Nothing, Carlton. Nothing." She seemed to lose focus. Her cigarette quivered between her fingers. "We're still friends, right?" she asked.

"Sure, Carla. Yeah."

"I mean real friends, not just…well, you know."

That took me a moment.

"Carla, uh, look, uh—we haven't done that in a long time, and I still, uh, I still like you—I mean as a friend."

She propped her head in her hand and twirled her ashtray, watching it go round and round.

"Do you think this is all there is?" she asked without looking up.

"What do you mean?"

"Just this," she lifted herself and gestured around the room, "working at the grocery store like these others, grass and sex and nothing else."

I thought I was beginning to understand. "You could go to college—"

"College?" she snorted. Smoke came out of her nose. "Yeah, I can go to college. But you know what?" She looked at me straight on.

"What?"

"I don't know what I want to do. No idea." She took a long puff and then exhaled. "No clue."

I hadn't really thought about it until right then, but Carla and I had the same problem. I had all these interests, but nothing specific I wanted to focus on in life. Mom and Dad had been pressing me. I had to make a decision soon, start sending out applications.

"It'll work out," I said without conviction.

"Yeah, sure Carlton. It'll work out," and she took another drag on her cigarette.

* * *

I talked about it with Sadie over the Christmas holidays. I couldn't discuss it with Dad, not that I was afraid he would be angry, but that he might be disappointed in me; and the career counselors at school were no help. Their minds were stuck in a 1950s paradigm of briefcases and gray flannel suits, or else trade schools where I could learn welding.

"I don't understand, Carlton," she said. "There are so many things you like to do." We were in my room, on that far end of the house where privacy was guaranteed.

"Nothing I can study in college, though."

"You told us once that you wanted to be a naturalist like Thoreau."

I flashed some college brochures at her. "Thoreau didn't have to deal with all of t*his*."

Sadie laughed. She had come through her morose spell and was more like the sister I remembered, only older now, and mature. Her hair was short again, a tomboyish mop of dark brown that emphasized her elegant neck and lent her an air of sophistication. The scars were still visible on her wrists, but we didn't notice them any more than we noticed the smallpox vaccination scars on our shoulders.

"Oh, Carlton," she teased, "you've always been such a serious boy, trying to make every square peg fit into every square hole before you even look at the round ones."

"Huh?" Sadie was in graduate school now. Her psychology degree had enhanced her command of metaphor.

"You don't have to be so focused. Mom and Dad will understand. Just major in English or psychology, and after a couple of semesters you'll figure something out."

"You make it sound so easy." I thought about Carla, locked in a rut she couldn't see her way out of.

"Well, it's not difficult."

"I don't want to disappoint Dad."

She touched my cheek and her eyes went somewhere. "Of all of us—" She stopped and looked up as if searching for words, then: "Carlton, that's not something I think you could do even if you tried."

* * *

1976 came on in a rush. Time was slipping away from me in what felt like blocks, a week here, a month there, and then it was spring. Kids were painting the fire hydrants in patriotic red, white and blue ahead of the upcoming bicentennial, and the girls at school were already anticipating the prom. I had acceptance letters from Middle Tennessee State, Belmont, Tennessee Tech, and even Western Kentucky U. I tore up that last one, didn't even bring it in the house. This was all good news. Mom and Dad were pleased. I should have been, too.

Kenny had gotten a job at a record store near Hillsboro Village. I drove up to see him after school on a Friday toward the end of April. The place had a small glass facade but was huge inside, narrow aisles cluttered with stacks of vinyl and a large section of eight-tracks, with the new-fangled cassettes in a rack behind the register. Kenny was propped on the counter reading *Rolling Stone* when I came in, a cigarette between his lips. There were a few customers in the aisles, flipping intently through the albums.

"Hey Kenny," I said.

"Hey Carlton." Kenny's eyes were bloodshot.

"I didn't see you in school today."

"Naw, man, my water pump went out." Kenny had bought a Dodge van from about 1967. It had faded blue paint and some rust holes along the bottom, but its most important feature, the reason Kenny bought it, was that it didn't have windows on the sides. Guaranteed privacy.

"You get it fixed?"

"Yeah. Cost me all I had."

"Sorry."

"It's not your problem."

I looked at the stacks. "What's new, man?"

"Bunch of sh—" he checked himself as a customer came near, leaned in close and whispered, "Bee Gees, man."

"Ugh."

"Aerosmith's got some cool stuff, though."

"Cool."

"You lookin'?"

"Naw, I just wanted to stop by, say hi." I toed at a cigarette butt on the floor. "Kenny, uh, can I ask you something?"

"Yeah, man."

"Have you ever heard of the Appalachian Trail?"

He seemed perplexed. "Something about cows in Texas?" he asked.

"No, it's a hiking trail from Maine to Georgia, like two thousand miles."

"No," he shook his head thoughtfully. "Never heard of it. Why?"

"I want to do it."

"Do what?"

"Hike it."

He stood back and his brows dipped. "What the hell for?"

"To see if I can. And for the experience, you know, like when we used to go camping."

He scratched his butt. "I still itch from that, man. And aren't they gonna turn you out to college pretty soon?"

Something caught me just then, something that had never come up between us because I just assumed. "Aren't you going to college, Kenny?"

"Hell no."

"But—"

"I make good money here, man."

"What about your parents?"

"What about 'em?"

Mr. Batista would be so disappointed in his only child. Could I do that to Dad?

"Well, I need to get to work," I said then, suddenly glad for an excuse to leave. "See ya."

"See ya," said Kenny, and he returned to *Rolling Stone.*

* * *

I got off of work at nine that night, felt too restless to go home so I turned the Pontiac up Hillsboro Road and just drove. It was cool out, with a soft breeze out of the south. I had the windows rolled half way up against the chill. A comforting warmth rose from below the dash. I had the radio tuned to WSM, the volume low. I liked to listen to country music when I was in a certain mood, a contemplative mood.

I drove past Shakey's and Hillsboro High. Shakey's was busy and bright, cars parked around front like wagon spokes. I recognized some of the cars but I didn't stop in. I needed to be alone. I turned right on Woodmont Boulevard just to get away from the traffic, and right again on Belmont Boulevard. It was dark in that neighborhood, quiet. Light shone serenely from the windows of the cottage-style homes. New leaves swished gently in the breeze, like the patter of soft rain.

I drove past the houses of some of the girls I knew, slowing at each one in hope of a chance meeting, a parted curtain, a glimpse of something familiar inside. I drove past Gracie's house. Her bedroom light was on, a lonely glow from that otherwise darkened house. I had only been on a few dates since Gracie, and a randy urge was stirring along with everything else on my mind. I cruised aimlessly until about ten thirty, with no resolution to my thoughts, just the encroaching weariness of a long day. I turned for home but took it slow, the throaty, melodic rumble of the old V8 stilling my mind. I paused at the base of our hill before turning up the driveway. Willie Nelson was on the radio. *Blue Eyes Crying in the Rain.* My hickory tree was full with spring growth, shielding much of the house from view. It was dark upstairs, but the lights in the den were on, the flickering silver of the television. I sighed and started up.

"*Carlton.*"

I heard my name as if it were a whisper of breeze through the trees, and then a shape came out of the darkness below and I saw who it was.

"Evelyn," I said, rolling down my window.

"Hi," she said.

"Hi."

Evelyn leaned her hip against my door and looked furtively back toward her house. She was wearing white sailor's pants that flared above her ankles, sneakers without socks, and a white pullover with red stripes. A few loose curls twined in the breeze.

She turned back to me and leaned in closer. "You just getting home from work?" she asked.

"Yeah, kind of." Her brows knitted. "What are you doing tonight?" I asked then.

"Oh, nothin'"

"Nothin'? Really?" It wasn't like Evelyn to stay home on a Friday night.

"Really," she smiled.

Silence lingered then. Evelyn twirled a finger in her hair. I couldn't think of anything to say. "Well, uh, I guess I'd better—"

"Oh, for Christ's sake, Carlton!"

Evelyn leaned in and kissed me hard, working her fingers into my hair. Her tongue tasted sweet, like vanilla icing. Her lips were…soft, full, and deliciously warm. We broke off and I took a deep breath. My groin tingled as if before a fall.

"Get in," I said, my blood quickening with feverish heat.

"Yes!" she exclaimed with the shake of a fist. She skipped around and got in, snuggled up next to me and wrapped an arm around my shoulders.

I shot up the driveway and pulled around back, got out and whispered, "Here, Langley."

Langley's nose poked out of his dog house, and then he came out, tail wagging and with his chain clinking along the ground.

"Hey, Langley." I frisked his ears and patted his back. "You know Langley, don't you Evelyn?"

"Sure I know Langley. Hi, fella." Evelyn bent down and rubbed Langley's muzzle.

"So look," I said to Evelyn. "Someone's up, probably Dad. Go around back and wait. I won't be long. Okay?"

"Oh—kay," she said dubiously.

I went in through the front door. Dad was in his Barcalounger, dozing, a newspaper spread on the floor beside him. Johnny Carson was on the television, the volume low. Ed McMahon was chuckling about something. I went quietly upstairs and to my room, locking the door behind me.

My room had a feature that I don't think Mom and Dad were ever aware of, although I'm sure that Leavitt was. It was quite a while after I moved in before I discovered it myself. My room had two wide windows, one facing front, which looked out on high over our front yard, and one on the side facing the woods between us and our neighbors. Both windows were high off the ground, but our hill sloped at such a steep angle that it was easy to reach the side window from the uphill end. I had gotten in and out of the house unobserved many times this way, usually to go camping overnight in the fort, but a few times to sneak out with Kenny when he first started driving.

I opened the window and went out, kicking my toes into the grass as I went up the hill. I found Evelyn waiting at the top corner of the house, propped against the wall and checking her nails. I startled her when I came up. She squeaked a shriek through her fingers, her hand fast over her mouth and her eyes shining with laughter. I shushed her quickly, took her hand and led her down, shoulders against the wall. She slipped in a place and grasped on to me, bent over and with her breasts dangling against my neck like fruit. I dug in my heels and brought us the rest of the way, ducked low through the window and pulled Evelyn in with both hands.

Evelyn surveyed my room. "Nice trick," she said.

"Yeah."

"Can't your parents hear us?"

"Not unless we're really loud."

I closed the window and pulled the curtains. Only my desk lamp was on so the lighting was low. Evelyn studied my Apollo posters as if they were fine art, and then my Sierra Club poster of a giant sequoia. She ran a finger absently across my desk, scanned my books, and then plopped onto my bed with a bounce and a husky smile.

"Well?" she asked suggestively.

I stood stiffly with my back to the door, my conscience at war with my hormones. Evelyn kicked off her shoes and stood. Her toe nails were painted pink. I thought to look away but somehow she wouldn't let me. As casual as an afternoon walk she pulled her top over her head and shook out her hair. Her breasts were bare. They were…perfect. She dropped her top on the floor and took a step toward me, her breaths becoming deep and rythmic.

"Well?" she asked again.

I didn't have enough spit to gulp. She thumbed a button and those loose sailor's pants fell to her ankles. She kicked out of these as unselfconsciously as a baby in a fountain on a hot day, and I saw for myself what a natural blond looks like.

* * *

I didn't say anything, and to her credit I don't think Evelyn did either, but an aura surrounds a couple who have been doing it, like pheromones. The whole school knew we'd been together. It was a cruel accident that I came out of the men's room early that next week and ran right into Gracie. She looked at me with so much hurt that my heart ached. I wanted to reach out to her, but before I could do or say anything Sarah Jean was between us, turning Gracie away and looking at me with pure hate.

So without declaring it in any way it became acknowledged that Evelyn and I were going together. I made a feeble attempt at aloofness, but Evelyn drew me back with a proprietary air and a taut body that was nothing if not hypnotic. Evelyn was insatiable, the way Carla had been, except that Evelyn was more refined, more focused—and infinitely more athletic. And she didn't smoke. Before long I was driving her to school and out to lunch. She controlled the radio. She liked soft rock and disco, thought hard rock was a lot of banging noise, and turned her nose up at country.

We were parked at Yannie's for lunch. Evelyn liked to ride with her bare feet on the dash. She was tapping along to something on the radio, mouthing lyrics and dancing in place. The food came and I passed her the onion rings she ordered. It was a nice day, not hot at all. She nibbled an onion ring. Her attention was on the radio. We needed to talk.

"Listen, Evelyn—"

"*Ohmygod* I *love* this song!" she blurted without warning. I about spilled my Dr. Pepper. She spun up the volume and the Starland Vocal Band blared from the speakers.

Gonna find my baby, gonna hold her tight…

The guys parked next to me looked over and grinned. "*Lucky bastard,*" one of them mouthed.

"Hey, Evelyn!" I shouted over the din.

Rubbin' sticks and stones together makes the sparks ignite…

Evelyn was into it now, swinging her arms, her hair flying. I had to admit that

Evelyn was a gorgeous girl, and playful when she wanted to be. I let it go and just watched her, and when the song was over she jumped half into my lap with an exuberant grin and gave me an onion-ring kiss that was sexy as hell. She looped her arms around my neck and smiled at me nose to nose.

"I can't wait until tonight," she breathed with a flush to her cheeks.

The guys next to us were watching and grinning appreciatively. "Lucky bastard," I heard the guy say this time.

* * *

And then there was the senior prom. I rented a tux. Mom helped me with the tie.

"What happened to that nice girl, Gracie?" Mom asked as she fiddled with my tie.

"We broke up, Mom," I answered nervously

"Are you sure you like Evelyn?" she asked, trying without success to mask her disapproval.

"She's okay."

"Well," she finished with the tie and stood back to size me up. "Just be careful, Carlton."

The way she said it gave me a chill.

I reversed down the driveway, and then across the street and down Evelyn's driveway. Mrs. Hanshaw met me at the door.

"My, aren't you handsome, Carlton," she gushed. "Come in."

She took me by the hand and led me inside, holding on even as we waited in the living room for Evelyn, as if I might get away. I looked around. I hadn't been in this house since the Gormans. Nothing looked the same at all. It made me sad for Mr. and Mrs. Gorman.

Evelyn entered wearing a white ball gown fit for *Gone With the Wind*, with a tight bodice that emphasized her slim and athletic waist, and delicate layers of skirt that billowed out as if she were emerging from a cloud. Her golden hair and sky-blue eyes shone with radiance, and her smile was uncharacteristically pure.

"Hi, Carlton," she said sweetly.

Mrs. Hanshaw was pressed along my right side, clutching my hand between us. I managed to snatch it loose without breaking Evelyn's spell.

"You look beautiful," I said, and I meant it. There were going to be a lot of jealous girls at the prom, as I'm sure was her plan. "I have a corsage for you."

I went to fasten the corsage above her breast, but her bodice was so tight that I was terrified that I would poke her with the pin. Sweat popped out on my brows. Mrs. Hanshaw's face was right there.

"Let me help you, Carlton," she said. Thank God.

Mrs. Hanshaw got the corsage fastened without any trouble at all, and then I took Evelyn's hand and drew her toward the door, with Mrs. Hanshaw right beside us the whole way.

"Have fun, you two," she said somewhat suggestively. I exhaled in relief when she closed the door behind us.

Our senior prom was held in the gym at school. I couldn't help but think back to the Belle Meade Country Club, a year and a half ago now, and that all of this dressing up was overkill for a dance at school. There were no valets, no doormen, no receiving line, but the punch *had* already been spiked.

We sat at a table and sipped our punch. The lights were low and the disco ball was spinning. The band was still setting up at the end of the court, so for now we were just getting music over the sound system, soft tunes by Jim Croce and the Eagles. Girls walked by. "Hi, Evelyn," they said, with only girlish glances at me. "Hi, Evelyn." *Stairway to Heaven* came on.

"Let's dance," Evelyn said abruptly. She pulled me out of my chair and onto the floor.

I held her around the waist and we swayed. Everyone else had jumped up at this song, so the dance floor was packed. Evelyn nestled her head against my chest.

"I can hear your heart," she said warmly.

"Uh, yeah."

I scanned for Gracie and didn't see her, and that was a relief, but then I saw Kenny through the crowded dancers and I was floored. This was not his kind of scene at all. When he rocked around I saw that he was dancing with Gracie and I was doubly floored.

Evelyn must have felt me tensing. "What's the matter?" she asked, looking up through soft lashes from her place on my chest.

"Nothing, uh, nothing."

Kenny was wearing a buff colored tux with black trim. He had his hair greased back from his forehead like Al Pacino, and he had trimmed his mustache up off of his chin. Gracie was wearing an off-white prom dress. Her hair was coiled on top of her head in a tall bun. Kenny saw me and made a commiserating face. I think Gracie was too short to see through the crowd. I flicked my head toward the doors and Kenny acknowledged.

When the song ended I made a break for the men's room, leaving Evelyn alone at our table. "Back in a minute," I told her hastily.

Kenny met up with me at the doors and we practically sprinted for the men's room, slamming through the door shoulder to shoulder as if we were being chased by a bear.

"Whew!" Kenny exhaled. "This is gonna suck."

"What are you doing here, man?" I asked accusingly. "You don't dance."

"My mother knows Gracie's mother," he answered, apparently taking no offense at my tone.

"So?"

"So you know my mother."

I sighed. "Yeah."

"She's traditional, you know? And besides, Gracie's hot."

That alarmed me.

"You wouldn't," I almost begged.

"Why the hell not?"

"Damn, Kenny."

"It's cool, man."

"How can we do this? I don't want to hurt Gracie's feelings."

"Maybe she's over you, man."

I looked at him skeptically. "I doubt it."

"Well anyway," he said, "we're on this end and you're over there. That ought to be enough room, don't you think?"

"Man," I said, shaking my head. "I hope so."

We went back out but then froze in our tracks.

"Uh, oh," Kenny said, his face falling.

Evelyn was sitting where I left her, one arm across the seat back and the other flat on the table. She wore a shrewd smile, and her eyes had a flippant look to them. Gracie and Sarah Jean stood across from her, their backs to us. Gracie had her arms tightly crossed but Sarah was leaning in, both hands on the table. She was wearing a blue dress with a denim vest. Her hair was done up in Indian braids.

We hustled over, not sure what to make of this. No one paid any attention to us. Gracie kept narrowed eyes on Evelyn. Sarah Jean's face was red and strained.

"You're such a slut!" Sarah hissed between clenched teeth. Gracie jumped at that. People began to stare.

Evelyn laughed. She took her punch glass by the stem, examined it thoughtfully and sipped it like a martini. She casually returned it to the table.

"How would you know?" she said offhandedly. "Since you're a queer."

Sarah Jean reacted as if she'd been slapped. She stood back from the table, struggling to form words. Gracie's mouth fell open. There were shocked inhalations from the nearby tables.

"Why don't you just take her then?" Evelyn went on as if closing for the kill. "An experienced girl like you—" Evelyn batted her lashes in mock innocence. "—and a sweet girl like Gracie…why, you could turn her in no time."

"*Holy cow, Sarah Jean's a queer!*" someone exclaimed.

"*Aw, man. And I thought she was hot,*" someone added.

Sarah Jean covered her mouth in shock. Everyone around, including me, was staring at her with a combination of salacious curiosity and disgust. Evelyn just sat there and smiled thinly while Sarah Jean bolted through the crowd, every eye following her out the doors. I didn't know what to make of Gracie's expression. It was shocked, stunned, hurt and worried all at the same time. Without even a glance at me she took off after Sarah. Kenny threw his hands out and gave me a look that said he wished he'd stayed home, and then he darted after Gracie. I sat down next to Evelyn. A few eyes still watched us. Some of the guys were grinning, their dates frowning in consternation.

"Do you wanna go?" I asked Evelyn gently, taking her hand.

"Why?" she answered flatly. "We just got here."

* * *

The night went long. Evelyn drug me out for some disco dances. I flopped around like an empty shirt and made do as best I could. Then we had our portrait made and left for dinner.

"I'm not really hungry," Evelyn said in the car. "Take me somewhere."

"What do you mean?"

"Well…" and her brows arched suggestively. "I can't go through your window dressed like this."

"Oh."

"Don't you know a place?"

"Uh, yeah."

I drove to the bluff overlooking the airport. A low blanket of cloud hid the stars, and there was a musty smell of rain in the air. Airplanes faded into the sky after take-off like apparitions.

"I love it!" Evelyn exclaimed. "I love the lights." She had her bare feet on the dash. Her dress flowed over the seat like a white tide.

"Listen, Evelyn. I need to tell you something." My voice was serious enough that it should have caught her attention, but it didn't.

"Oh, look at that one landing!" she bounced and pointed.

"Evelyn?"

She shimmied over, slipped her hand into my shirt and stroked my chest. Her lips were within a breath of mine. She had that coy smile on her face.

"So, Carlton—"

"Evelyn, look." I took her by the wrists and held her back. "I've been trying to tell you—I'm leaving soon."

"What does that mean?" She shook off my grip.

"I'm going to hike the Appalachian Trail."

"The what?"

"It's a trail from Maine to Georgia. It'll take about six months."

"*What!*" She scooted away and tore into me with her eyes. "When?"

"After finals."

"But that's—*that's not even two weeks from now.*"

"Yeah."

"But, but…what about college?"

"It can wait."

"No it can't." She seemed to be panicking. "You can't go, Carlton. This is crazy."

A plane roared over us, and for a moment we were lit in the harsh white of its lights. When things settled down I continued. Evelyn looked as if she were falling.

"I've been planning this for a long time," I told her. "And I'm going to do it."

"But what about us?" she pleaded. I thought I could see her mind racing at the implications. I found some steel in my spine.

"When I get back…maybe…who knows?"

Her eyes were flitting back and forth as she thought it through, and then her face softened and she slid over to me and she whispered in my ear, "I want you. I want you now."

And then I was back in that place where thoughts are lost in the rush of the moment, and I wasn't thinking about the Appalachian Trail or anything else except soft pale skin and silky warmth and urgent blue eyes.

* * *

I told Mom and Dad at breakfast the next morning.

"*Appalachian Trail?*" Dad spat incredulously. He didn't even pronounce it the way I did, saying *latch* instead of *lashe*, as if that most basic thing were beyond agreement between us. "No, son, I'm afraid not. I can't allow it."

I had never once, *ever*, back-talked my father; and to do so now made me feel ungrateful if not also unworthy of him. But still:

"I'm going to do it, Dad."

"Carlton?" Mom reached out a hand.

"I'm sorry, Mom, but I have to."

"Why?"

"I have to know."

"Know what?"

"I have to know if I *can*."

There was more to it than that, of course, but even then I still hadn't straightened it all out in my mind.

Mom pulled back from me. Her nose was reddening.

"What about college?" she asked in forlorn acceptance of the inevitable. Dad hadn't got there yet, but he would soon enough.

"I'll start in the spring term, take extra credits next summer."

"What are you going to do for money?" Dad asked stiffly. He folded his newspaper and pushed it aside.

"I've been saving," I answered firmly. "I have all I need. And I have all the camping equipment I need…and the experience. I know what I'm doing."

Mom buried her face in her hands. Dad sighed. "I hope so," he said.

* * *

Kenny drove me to the bus station before sunrise on May 26, a Wednesday. A sliver of moon was just coming up in an inky sky. It was in the forties, crisp and clear. Nashville slept as we made our way downtown.

"So how'd it go with Evelyn?" Kenny asked, his cigarette cherry bobbing in the dark.

"I haven't seen her in a while."

"Man, I bet she's pissed."

"What about Gracie?"

"I haven't seen her either."

"Oh, well."

"You sure about this, man?"

"Yeah, I'm sure." My backpack was on the floor in front of me. I fiddled with the straps.

"I bet your dad's pissed, too."

"He is."

"And your mom?"

"Not as much as Dad."

"Here it is."

Kenny pulled up in front of the bus station. Continental Trailways. He left the engine idling so the heater would run. I could smell some burning oil.

"You've really fixed it up in here," I said, stalling. My stomach was uneasy.

"Yeah, man. I've got a bed back there, and a sound system. It's cool."

"You could live in it, I guess."

"Yeah, if I wanted to."

"That's good." I puffed my cheeks. "Well, this is it."

"Yeah, man." Kenny reached across and gave me a hippie handshake. "Be cool," he said.

I tugged my backpack out of the van, shouldered it and went into the station.

NINE

My last days on the Appalachian Trail were idyllic compared to what I went through going over the Smoky Mountains. The sky miraculously cleared during that final steep descent out of the Smokies at Fontana Dam, as if God's own hand had reached down to wipe away the clouds. All at once the sun burst out above the ridges to the west, backlighting the forest in shadowy green, with the auburn hues of fall dappling the higher elevations. Updrafts from the valleys brought a warmth that drove the chill out of me from one breath to the next. I paused in awe at the suddenness of it, raised my arms to embrace the sun and stood greedily in its radiance as warmth filled me and the shadows of my despair vanished in the light.

The warmth stayed with me across Fontana Dam and into the Nantahala National Forest. I slept under the stars that night, on an aromatic bed of springy needles in a grove of tall pines. The air was cool, gentle, not the cold I had known for the past many days. I sat against a pine tree as the night grew deep and the mists began to rise, my sleeping bag pulled up under my arms and with a cup of hot coffee in my hands. The trees clicked and scraped in the night breeze, and small forest animals skittered through the duff. I had lain shivering in a damp shelter just the night before, my mind as dull as the sodden sky, yet tonight I sat contentedly under a wash of stars, suffused with a sense of well-being that sent warmth all the way to my toes.

My thoughts wandered back through the months and the miles. By the time I had reached Harpers Ferry, West Virginia, the symbolic half-way point between Mt. Katahdin and Springer Mountain, I knew that I would finish my hike much sooner than the six months I had assumed. This had been during the first week of August, with two months and some days behind me and about the same ahead. It had dawned on me with a start that if I pushed hard I could possibly reach Springer Mountain, Georgia on my eighteenth birthday, and that this would add such serendipitous moment to that day that I simply had to do it. This had driven me during that long march across Virginia, during those despondent days and nights in the Smokies, and now my birthday was only six days away!

I was close enough that I could see the end; close enough to imagine what might come next. Willow appeared to me then, so clearly in my thoughts, whereas days before she had been lost in the cold and the wet and the gloom of my spirits. I could *see* her now, across months that felt like years. I could *feel* her, every curve and soft place, the warmth of her lips. Journeys eventually come to an end. New journeys begin. I knew where to find Willow. I would go to her with the same determination that drove me now. This I promised.

But there were still mountains to cross, not as tall as the Smokies but tall enough to reach into the colder air. This was not a cutting cold, though, and I had the sun with me practically to the end. I made the last thirty miles from Neels Gap, Georgia to Springer Mountain under a gray sky that did not have the power to depress me. The woods were changing, more pine and oak and fewer of the hemlock and ash that formed the dense canopy farther north. Acorns fell like hail, thumping onto the trail and sometimes painfully onto my head. My heart pounded during that last mile of climb, not from exertion but from anticipation. Springer Mountain is not especially tall, but the trail was often steep. I grabbed ahold of saplings to yank myself up, scrambled on all fours in places, anything to keep moving. I broke from the trail into the small clearing at the top, shrugged out of my backpack and let it fall as I staggered shakily to the bronze plaque embedded in that floor of stone.

I collapsed onto my knees and caressed the plaque as if it were a love whom I had never met, pressed my cheek against it and fought back tears. I traced the outlines of the letters, the embossed hiker. I embraced it as if I could work my arms into the stone beneath and pull it to my heart, desperate to hold on to an indefinable something that was ebbing even as I knelt there. The tears came then, wetting the green-tinged bronze beneath my cheek. I cried hard, whole tears that washed tracks through the grime on my face and dripped from my nose, some caught by the wind and carried away. Ahead through the branches was a narrow valley of green, rising into rounded ridges that flowed like waves into the distant haze. Even in that late afternoon gray it was beautiful. It was September 27, my birthday. It was done.

The sound of voices intruded into the privacy of my triumph. I wiped my face on a dirty sleeve and looked up resentfully. A family stepped into the clearing, a mom, a dad, and a towheaded boy of about ten. The mom wore a full length white cotton dress, bulky black brogans on her feet and a white scarf that completely covered her hair. She carried a wicker picnic basket. The dad wore black trousers and a neatly tucked white shirt with the sleeves rolled to his elbows, and black patent leather shoes that shone even in that dull light. He clutched a bible to his breast. The boy was dressed identically to his father except that his white shirt was short sleeved. His hair was cut high above his ears, a cowlick sticking up in the back. They eyed me curiously but not suspiciously. I was suddenly aware of my appearance, dirty and ragged, the sharp points of my bones poking out from my shirt. My hair was long, greasy and wild, and my sparse beard must have looked like smudges on my face. I'm sure they could smell me from where they stood.

"You have fled to the wilderness," the father said toward me in a deep but smooth voice. He was maybe in his forties. "You have come to the mountain."

I stood shakily. My knees wanted to give. "Yeah," I said, feeling dizzy.

He opened his bible, paused to reflect for a moment, then read: "*The highway of the upright is to depart from evil: he that keepeth his way preserveth his soul.*"

"Huh?"

"*A man's heart deviseth his way: but the Lord directeth his steps.*"

"Amen," said the mother and boy in unison.

I tottered then, felt my knees giving. A rush of dizziness overwhelmed me and I collapsed onto the seat of my pants, a lean bag of bones that didn't even have the weight to fall over. The mother hurried to my side and knelt.

"You are weak," she said. She felt my forehead. Her fingers were red and rough, but felt just then as soft as chamois leather. She was younger than her husband yet prematurely aged, perhaps by a life of hard work. She wore no makeup at all. The austere lines of her face were sharp and stark, her eyes worried pools of golden brown. "Drink some water," she said gently, holding an aluminum canteen to my lips. I gulped the water, which tasted as if it had been sweetened with honey. The surge of sugar hit me like a jolt of caffeine, and this alone began to revive me. She took a sandwich from her picnic basket and unwrapped it. "Eat this," she said. "It will give you strength."

It was a simple bologna sandwich on white bread with mayonnaise, but it tasted so rich that I almost fainted. I meant to eat slowly, but still wolfed that sandwich down in only a couple of bites. The mother smiled. "Have another," she said.

My stomach felt as if it were bursting from just those two sandwiches. Father and son had walked to the edge of the cliff and were gazing out over the valley. The father had his bible open in one hand and the other on his son's shoulder. The mother folded the wax-paper sandwich wrappings neatly and returned them to the basket, gave me a patient smile then joined her family. In minutes I felt strong enough to stand.

The three of them were shoulder to shoulder on the cliff, the boy in the middle. They were holding hands, their heads bowed in prayer. The father mumbled scripture, too low for me to make out. After some moments he raised his head and turned to me. "Will you pray with us?" he asked.

Although I went to church most Sundays, I had never been as religious as these people. I'm not even sure I approved. Still, you don't dismiss people who are willing to help you when you're tired and hungry, and when you smell as bad as I did right then. "Sure," I said, trying to make it sound sincere.

I sidled up next to the father, not certain what the protocol was with fundamentalists. He tucked his bible under his arm, took my hand and we bowed. We stood silently for some time while I cast sidelong glances at the others. Their lips were moving in quiet reflection. My stomach began to rumble. Presently the father raised his head.

"Blessed be the God and Father of our Lord Jesus Christ," he recited from memory, *"who hath blessed us with all spiritual blessings in heavenly places in Christ."*

"Amen," they all said.

"Amen," I said, a breath late.

The father released my hand and turned to me. "We will take you from here if you want to go."

"I appreciate it, but I wouldn't want to be any trouble."

"We are all brothers in Christ," the father said. "It is no trouble."

I followed them the one mile down the mountain to the forest-service road, huffing to keep up. My knees felt like bread dough. The family had a white pick-up parked near the trailhead, an old step-side with a tall cab and a short bed. I tossed my backpack into the bed and hastily climbed in after it before they could invite me into the cab with them, not that I minded riding with them up front but because I had become self-conscious about the way I smelled. Fortunately they made no objections.

Night fell as we navigated out of the forest and onto the main highway. I had no idea where we were headed, but I guessed it really didn't matter. My hike was over. A profound sense of loss overcame me, made my lips tremble. The rushing night air chilled me, so I shimmied into my sleeping bag and leaned against the cab. Head-lights came up from behind and passed us, more and more of them as we went on. The glare blinded me. And the noise. The closer we came to ordered life the worse I felt, as if the forest had become my home and I was being ripped from it.

City lights sprang up around us. We pulled into a dark gas station. The father left the truck idling as he got out.

"This is Gainesville," he said. "Is there somewhere you would want us to take you?"

My mind was struggling. Where would I want to go without blazes and a trail to guide me?

"Can you take me to the bus station?" I asked unsteadily.

"Yes, it is not far."

They dropped me at the bus station. It was late, although I didn't know the time, or even what day it was. The air was cool, with a light fog. Moths fluttered in the street lights. I leaned against the passenger door, my backpack resting against my leg.

"Thank you," I said to the mother. The father was only a shape in the shadows across the cab, and the boy was asleep. "It was nice of you to help me. I appreciate it."

She smiled demurely and quoted from King James: *"For I was an hungred, and ye gave me meat: I was thirsty, and ye gave me drink: I was a stranger, and ye took me in."* She patted my hand. "These are His words," she added earnestly.

"Yes, ma'am." I searched my memory for an appropriate bible verse but couldn't recall anything, so I just waved and stepped back from the curb as they pulled away.

I never learned their names and they never asked for mine. I watched until their taillights were gone, took a step toward the bus station then halted in trepidation.

The activity inside was chaotic, too many people, lines forming at the ticket window and the bus stand. The lights were bright, harsh. The oily smell of diesel fouled the air. It felt so claustrophobic. My lips began to tremble again. I fought an urge to run away, to find a green place where I could unroll my sleeping bag, somewhere away from the lights and the noise and the hard pavement. A red neon sign flickered up the block, *Motel.* I sighed and trudged that way, dragging my backpack behind me.

I sat in that motel for two days and mostly stared at the walls. I slept on the floor in my sleeping bag that first night, curled around my knees and trying to conjure the trail. The worn maroon carpet smelled like cigarettes. I showered the next morning and shaved my face clean. This was the first hot bath I'd had in… well, since Hot Springs, North Carolina, however long ago that had been. I gazed at myself in the mirror, not sure who I was seeing. My eyes were hollow, pallid, ringed with yellow shadows, and my cheeks were sunken, my jaw protruding like a laboratory skull. All of the bones in my chest, clavicles, sternum and ribs, were visible in startling detail, like an anatomy lesson, or a case study in starvation. I had no body fat left, and not much muscle either. My behind felt like loose skin over concave bones.

And yet I felt fit, even energetic, with the optimism to take on another twenty miles right then. Anything was possible—*anything.* My mind was so clear. Ideas came in a bewildering flurry, unhindered by the noise and confusion and pressure of urban life. How to hold on to that; how to hold on to that? And then my spirits sank because I doubted it would last, like a brilliant dream that dissipates upon waking. The one thing, the *only* thing that could help me hold on to this feeling was to find Willow, who had shared it with me, who knew what it meant.

There was a Kentucky Fried Chicken within walking distance. I came out with a bucket of chicken and a mess of biscuits and gravy, and ate from these urgently as I walked back to my room, licking every bit of the grease from my fingers. I was clean but my clothes were foul, and now I couldn't bear that odor. I soaked my clothes in the bathtub, sat naked on the edge of the bed, gnawed on a drumstick and stared at the walls.

Willow was at Dartmouth. I could take the bus from here. I pulled my money from my backpack and counted it out, made stacks of ones and fives and tens on the bed, a few twenties. I had enough. In truth, I had finished the trail so early that I had plenty.

My clothes looked like a wicked stew in the bathtub. I drained the scummy water and refilled the tub, ate another piece of chicken and drank some cool water. My stomach began to pooch out like a taut balloon.

I needed to go home first, see Mom and Dad, let them know I was okay and what my plans were. I should call them—no, I should wait. I couldn't deal with it just then. I needed new clothes. I couldn't go to Willow at Dartmouth looking the way I did now. Would she remember me? What if she didn't? Of course she would remember. How could she forget?

I slept in the bed that night, woke up the next morning with an aching back. My clothes had dried overnight. They still looked dirty but at least they smelled better. I went to KFC for a bucket, returned to my room, sat on the bed and stared at the wall.

Willow never told me what she was studying, but Dartmouth was an Ivy League school, upper crust, and here I was not even sure what I wanted to do with my life. I began to wonder if I measured up, or if she would even accept me now. Would it be like that family on the mountain, people whom I would have avoided, even ridiculed had my preconceptions not been stripped away by the rigors of the trail? Now that she was off the trail and in her academic life, would Willow judge me differently?

I tossed a chicken bone into the bucket, not a scrap of meat left on it, took out a wing and started on it.

No, it couldn't be like that with us. What we had shared was as vivid to me now as it had been on the trail. I remembered Garfield Ridge, every moment, every word, every subtle gesture. Willow was waiting for me. She had to be.

I checked out of the motel the next morning, went to KFC for a bucket and then to the bus station. I could handle it all now. Those couple of days alone in that motel room had eased me away from the trail, and now with Willow on my mind I was driven with renewed energy.

I had to make a connection in Atlanta, and this wore away that day. My bus to Nashville journeyed through the night, stopping at every small town along the way. Dawn came through the windows at last, bathing my thoughts in golden light. It was a brilliantly clear morning, like a fine day in the Blue Ridge. The Tennessee hills meandered past. Pitch-green cedars stood out like sentinels among hardwoods turning toward autumn. Nashville was restless with activity. I didn't know what day of the week it was, but it must have been a work day considering the traffic. I called Kenny from the bus station. I didn't want a tearful reunion with Mom in that place. Kenny was startled at the sound of my voice but said he would come.

The faded blue van pulled up where it had dropped me all those months ago.

"Dude!" Kenny exclaimed. "You look like hell."

"Thanks a lot," I said wearily as I climbed in. Kenny looked exactly the same, except that his hair was longer and his mustache was back onto his chin. The air smelled like pot. I rolled down the window.

"They know you're comin'?" Kenny asked. I shook my head. "Man, you shoulda called 'em."

"What's been happening around here?" I asked.

"Same ol' thing—*nada*." He grinned my way. "Man, I can't get over you with long hair." My hair had grown past my shoulders. I had it tied into a ponytail.

"Yeah," I said. "It's something you don't think about on the trail."

"So what are you gonna do now?"

"I have some plans."

Kenny nodded and lit a cigarette. "Carla cleared out," he said after a couple of deep puffs, which he blew up toward the roof. "Took off for L.A."

"That's good. She needed something."

"Yeah, I guess."

"You still working at the record store?"

"Yeah."

"That's good," I said, and turned to look out the window.

Kenny dropped me at the foot of our hill, knowing better than to go up our steep driveway.

"Later, man," he said with a wave. "I gotta get to work."

"Later, Kenny. Thanks." His van left blue smoke as he pulled away. He hadn't asked me anything about the trail, nothing at all.

It was about nine o'clock in the morning. No one was out. I looked up the hill at the house, which seemed different although nothing had changed. My hickory tree was starting to turn, leaves curling and going dull. I looked over at the Hanshaw's house, wondered what Evelyn was up to now. Probably off to college. I shouldered my backpack and groaned. Just one more climb to make.

I hesitated at the front door. Dad was probably at work but Mom should be home, and she would cry and carry on, right out front for anyone to see. I walked around back instead, my knees aching as I made it up the grade. Langley growled low when he first spotted me, but then he recognized me and his tail began to thump. He came up to me and plopped down at my feet, sniffing me with his wet nose.

"Good to see ya, Langley," I said, ruffling his head and ears. His tail thumped even harder, and he gnawed gently on my hand. "Okay, I have to go see Mom now." He got up then, shook his floppy ears, and watched with an eager dog smile as I went around back.

The Pontiac was as clean as I had left it, which meant that Dad had been washing it regularly. I felt bad about that, as if I had failed to live up to our agreement. I peered through the windows like a stranger, like one of those Civil War buffs who used to pester us. I didn't see Mom. I tested the door and found it locked, which was a relief. It didn't feel right to just walk in. I knocked on the door, took a nervous breath and knocked again. And then I saw Mom, and she saw me. Her face went through a startled rush of emotions. She had changed her hair, from the straight collar flip she had always worn to light wavy curls that sheltered her face.

She flung open the door and paused in the door frame, taking me in with a peculiar expression that inexplicably seemed to border on sorrow, but then she stepped out and opened her arms.

"Oh, Carlton, what have you done?"

In that moment I thought she was talking about my weight loss.

She rushed to me and embraced me, squeezing the air out of my bony chest. She pushed back to look at me. Her eyes were wet.

"Why, you're just bones, Carlton, nothing but bones."

After all those buckets of fried chicken I actually felt as if I had plumped up quite a bit. Still, I had a long way to go before I got my old weight back.

"I guess I lost a lot of weight."

"And what's this?" she asked, fiddling with my ponytail.

"Aw, Mom," I whined, pulling away. "There aren't any barber shops in the mountains."

She let me go and propped her hands sternly on her hips.

"Why didn't you call? The last we heard from you was that place in Virginia with the bible name."

"Damascus?"

"Yes, that's it. That was *weeks* ago, Carlton. We were worried sick."

"I'm sorry, Mom. I was in the mountains and the weather was bad. It was…it was hard for a while."

She relaxed and rubbed my shoulders. "Let's get you inside and feed you." She picked at some loose threads on my jacket. "Your poor letterman jacket. You'll have to throw it out. Oh, well," she shook that off, "get inside. I'll call your father."

Mom made me pancakes and eggs and bacon. I finished each as quickly as she could bring them from the stove, so she kept bringing more until I couldn't swallow another bite. She looked at me in wonder. "How can you fit so much food in there?" I just grinned and patted my tight belly.

I took a shower and put on clean clothes, the fresh smell of fabric softener like an exotic aroma. I noticed all the little things: crisp sheets, bleached white towels, shampoo, toothpaste, and the marvels that can come from a bar of Ivory soap. I folded my trail clothes and put them away. I couldn't bring myself to throw them out. My sleeping bag, however, was unsalvageable. It reeked like a dead possum in a stagnant pond. I had to take it out of the house.

Dad had a busy day, so couldn't get home until late. I fell asleep before he arrived, and slept so heavily that neither fire nor Langley's barking could have awakened me. I met them for breakfast the next morning. Dad lowered his paper as I came into the kitchen. He studied me with equal parts curiosity and rebuke, but said nothing. I swallowed hard and poured myself a cup of coffee.

"When did you start drinking coffee?" Mom asked, surprised.

"When it was cold," I answered cryptically.

Dad folded his paper and put it down. His scrutiny was unnerving. He started right in.

"Now that you've finished your little walk, what do you intend to do next?"

"Dick!" Mom scolded.

Dad's eyes were on me, unyielding. I fought to control my trembling lips. Dad had never spoken to me in that tone. It stung. Mom had a fretful look. I noticed just then that she had dark bags under her eyes, as if she hadn't slept well.

"You need to go see the Hanshaws," Dad said as if he were spitting their name. This caught me completely off guard.

"The Hanshaws?" I sputtered. "Why?"

"You're the only one who could know the answer to that," he said mysteriously, and then he scooted back from the table and left the kitchen.

"Mom?" I asked, dumbfounded.

"Oh, Carlton." She shook her head slowly, dabbed at a tear with her napkin. "I'm sorry, honey," and then she backed away from the table and left as well.

I sat in shock, grasping for an explanation. I went over every telephone call I had made to them, exactly what I had said. In truth, their attitudes had seemed to improve as I progressed along the Appalachian Trail. Dad had even offered me encouragement once, during a phone call from Front Royal, Virginia. This didn't make any sense. Bewildered, and not knowing how else to get answers, I did what Dad said—I went out the back and down to the Hanshaw's house.

I was surprised when it was Evelyn who greeted me at the door.

"Carlton!" she shrieked. "You're back!"

She launched herself at me and hugged me hard enough to make joints pop. I stood stiffly, gave her a light pat on the back.

"You're so skinny," she said, stepping back to catch her breath. "And look at you with a ponytail."

She was wearing loose gym shorts and a baggy Vanderbilt sweatshirt. Everything about her looked the same, her hair, her perfect teeth and white skin, except that her face seemed a little puffy.

"I didn't think you would be home until Christmas," she went on, gushing. She took my hand and led me inside.

I caught a glimpse of Mrs. Hanshaw through a darkened hallway off the living room. The look she gave me was unsettling, or maybe it was just a trick of the light. I sat on the couch, and of course Evelyn sat down right next to me, our thighs touching. Her legs were bare and smooth, and her shorts were baggy enough to provide immodest views, yet I wasn't aroused. Much had changed during my journey. Evelyn seemed to notice.

"What's the matter, Carlton?" she asked with a concerned crease in her brows.

"Nothing, Evelyn…uh, Dad said I needed to talk to you all."

"Oh."

She scooted over a bit and twirled a strand of hair around a finger.

"Well," she hedged. "Maybe Daddy should talk to you."

It raced through my mind that five mornings earlier I had awoken in Neel's Gap, Georgia, and that I no longer had the patience for this coy foolishness.

"No," I said roughly. "Maybe *you* should talk to me."

She went from fawning to affronted in an instant.

"Okay, then." She got up and went to a chair to my left, sat with her legs together and her hands on her knees. "Carlton, I'm pregnant."

She said it without the least bit of inflection, so casually in fact that it didn't even register.

"Did you hear me?" she barked, her color rising.

"What?"

"I'm pregnant."

I blinked in incomprehension, flicked fingers across my brow absently as if chasing a mosquito.

"Pregnant?" I mumbled.

"Yes," and then she smiled girlishly and rubbed her stomach. "Nineteen weeks."

I studied her then, closely, my eyes coming to rest on her stomach. She looked… the same. I saw no bulge, nothing that would have told me anything but that she was fit and fine and able to jump on a trampoline for all I cared. She saw where I was looking, as well as the doubt in my eyes, so lifted her sweatshirt above her pale stomach and…yes, she had a rounded bulge in her belly that was stretching her navel into an oval.

"Who?" I stammered.

She leapt to her feet in indignation, her face scarlet and her eyes as angry as a spring storm.

"Who do you think?" she spat. "You!"

"*Me?*"

My mind roiled at the repercussions, settling on nothing sure and concrete. I had been on the trail, days stretching from dawn to dusk through mountains and sweat and bitter cold, every moment in the present, time elongating like one of Einstein's equations. It felt to me as if a year or more had gone by. It couldn't have been me. It couldn't.

"But…but how can you know?" I pleaded, ashamed of the panic in my voice. I thought she was about to jump me and claw my eyes out.

"*How dare you*," she hissed. "It was you and only you."

My eyes wouldn't focus on anything. I was trying to divide weeks into months, trying to remember when it could have been. She had always told me not to worry, that she was on the—it was prom night. That's when it happened. The air went out of me. I felt so hollow I thought I might collapse into myself.

"Evelyn?" I looked up weakly. "Couldn't you…shouldn't you…"

"What?" she demanded.

There are things you just can't say out loud; things you can't ask a girl to do. She's supposed to make the decision; make the offer. She knew what I was thinking. She began to shake her head slowly.

"Oh, no," she said, backing away from me. "I won't do *that*."

Those words hit with the force of a sudden gust on Mt. Washington. Mr. Hanshaw came into the room.

"Okay you two, that's enough," he said firmly. "Sit down, Evelyn."

Mr. Hanshaw sat in a rocker and laced his fingers. I'd never really had much to do with Mr. Hanshaw. He was quite a bit younger than Dad, late forties I thought. Evelyn got none of her looks from him. He had deeply parted sandy hair, with wings of gray at his temples. His eyes were hazel, leaning more toward brown than green. They looked small between his high forehead and rounded cheeks. He couldn't be called handsome, but he had a confident air to compensate. He was an attorney, and had managed to avoid all of the wars.

"There's no point getting angry about it now," he said calmly after Evelyn took her seat. "That's all done. But you two have some decisions to make…especially you, Carlton." The look he gave me wasn't especially harsh, but it withered me just the same. "Now Carlton," he continued, "I know your father well, and I know what he would expect from you. So why don't you go talk to him, and make a decision, then tell us what your intentions are. Okay?"

"Yes, sir," I said numbly.

"And I can help out, so don't worry about expenses for now."

"Okay."

"Good." He slapped his knees and stood, held out his hand to me. He had big hands. "But don't wait too long," he added.

* * *

I couldn't face Dad, so I went to Mom instead. It turned out that this was a Saturday and he had gone to the golf course anyway.

"I'm sorry, Mom," I said with a long face. We were sitting in the kitchen.

"I was afraid this would happen if you went with that *girl*." The way she said it didn't presume to disguise what she thought of Evelyn. She wrung her hands. "Oh, it's all my fault. I should have forbidden it."

"No, Mom." I went to her and wrapped an arm around her shoulders. She kissed my hand lightly. "I'm the one who did it. It's my fault."

She wiped her eyes and I returned to my chair.

"Well," she said with a sniff. "We'll just have to make due. You'll need to get your job back, honey. You need to save a lot of money."

"Mr. Hanshaw said he could help."

Mom's face tightened in anger.

"Don't you take money from those people," she hissed with righteous indignation.

* * *

I drove to the record store to see Kenny. It was a beautiful afternoon, one that should have buoyed me. The place was packed. I had to wait until Kenny's break before we could talk. We went into the stockroom and he closed the door.

"What's goin' on, man?" he asked, gathering correctly from my expression that I was in trouble.

"Evelyn's pregnant, man," I said.

"Oh, man," he said. His brows arched. "You?"

"Yeah."

"Oh, man." He sat heavily on a box and lit a cigarette. "Will she get an—?"

"No," I answered quickly. "She won't do it."

"Oh, man." Kenny blew thoughtful smoke, launched a couple of rings and watched them dissipate. "So what're you gonna do?"

"I don't know, man."

"I'm sorry, bro. Wish I knew what to tell ya."

"It's cool, man. I'll figure it out."

I drove around most of that afternoon trying to think it through, finally went home and climbed the hill to the old fort. Langley thumped his tall and yapped after me but I guiltily left him behind.

The leaves were beginning to turn but hadn't fallen, so the woods were still thick. If I closed my eyes I could imagine that I was back on the trail, away from all of this. Willow was receding farther into the past even as I fought to hold her in the present. The stark reality of the trail had brought us together, an unlikely pairing that would never have occurred in everyday life. The trail had stripped us bare of our preconceptions, but now that we were off the trail we were required to again clothe ourselves in the defenses and responsibilities that were demanded of us.

I sniffed those thoughts away, went into the fort and sat against the tree. Someone had made a small fire in there at some point, and the place stunk of damp coals. I stretched out my legs and closed my eyes, listened to the creaking and groaning of the high limbs in the wind. I had overcome everything that nature had thrown at me, the heat and the cold and the wet, the hunger and the pain. What was this compared to that?

I opened my eyes and they looked far away, to mile-high granite pinnacles and forests like an ocean; to skies of radiance that caught in the throat with their beauty, and still night pools that reflected the heavens in perfect clarity. I dabbed at a tear. What had that man said on the mountain? *The highway of the upright is to depart from evil: he that keepeth his way preserveth his soul.* I thought I understood it now.

Something glittered in the duff near the fire ring. It was a syringe, long and thin and menacingly sharp. I wondered how it had gotten there. I bent the needle and tossed it onto the coals.

* * *

Mr. Iverson gave me my job back on the spot, with a promotion to full-time stocker and a raise to an incredible five dollars an hour. I know that seems as nothing today, but at the time it was enough to live on if you can believe it, and live reasonably well. He seemed relieved to have me back. This was the Monday morning after I got home. Mr. Iverson handed me an apron and a price stamper, and I went to work right then.

I won't deny, though, that the job wasn't as fun with Carla gone. Also, most of the sackers had been friends from school, and of course they were gone now, too, off to college and whatnot. The old-lady cashiers welcomed me back, said they had never expected to see me again. They were friendlier to me now that there was no one scandalous around to rock their sensibilities. Many of the full-time stockers had been sent to work at a new store that had just opened, which explained why Mr. Iverson had been so eager to have me back.

I worked every day that week. The stockroom was so backed up that Mr. Iverson allowed us overtime to get on top of it. At time-and-a-half, I was making unheard of money for someone my age, seven fifty an hour, and I was putting in some fourteen and fifteen-hour days. When I got home I would be so tired that I would go straight to my room. Mom would see me come in and would bring me a sandwich or a plate of leftovers, but Dad stayed mostly to himself in the den.

Saturday was hectic. With boxes stacked in the aisles, the regular weekend crush made getting the merchandise onto the shelves even more difficult. The day was damp and blustery, as dismal as the way I felt at the end of that long and weary week. I had twelve cases of assorted Joan of Arc beans to price and stock on the shelves, and after that I could take a break, get a cup of coffee and maybe close my eyes for a few minutes.

I was on a knee, stamping prices with practiced speed when Mrs. Hanshaw came up and hovered over me with her arms crossed tightly and an indignant twist to her lips. She was wearing a buff trench coat over a light gray shift, natural stockings, and two strings of pearls with matching earrings.

"Carlton!" she barked loud enough to attract every ear in the aisle. "Don't you dare embarrass my baby. Marry her before she's showing like some hillbilly trash."

Shoppers froze where they stood and turned to stare. The wrinkled jaws of gray old ladies fell in scandalous astonishment, and I had nowhere to hide. Turning red from embarrassment and then from anger, I snapped to my feet, took Mrs. Hanshaw by the arm and jerked her to the end of the aisle, where we could speak with at least a little privacy. She tried to wrench her arm away but I held on tight, and I probably left some bruises but I didn't give a damn.

"Mrs. Hanshaw," I said through clenched teeth. "I'm sorry to be disrespectful, but don't you *ever* do that to me again."

I flung her arm down and loomed up in her face. She quailed at that and backed into an end-cap display of Campbell's tomato soup, knocking a few to the floor. I was conscious that eyes were still on us from down the aisle, so I stepped around the display and out of view. Mrs. Hanshaw looked afraid, as if I might beat her where she stood. I took a long breath and exhaled it slowly.

"Evelyn and I will make a decision," I said after that calming breath. "I'll see her tonight. But—" and I fixed her with a look of pure defiance, "—it will be our decision and that's it. Got it?"

She had her hand over her mouth as if she were shocked out of her senses, but from the glint in her eyes I swear she was hiding a smile.

* * *

Evelyn was still wearing her Vandy sweatshirt, this time over her sailor's pants, and she still looked fit enough to go tumbling with the cheerleading squad if she wanted to. She had met me at her front door with a cautious smile. The overcast sky was deepening toward sunset.

"Can you go out?" I asked.

"Yes!" she bounced with a cheery grin. She had her hair up in a high ponytail, and it whipped across my cheek as she spun around to close the door.

"Shouldn't you tell your parents you're leaving?"

"Oh, they don't mind," she said, and she hugged my arm on the way to the car.

I drove to Percy Priest Dam and parked in a quiet spot looking out on the lake. The sky was dark now, the cloud layer hurrying to the southeast. The full moon broke through and shimmered across the inky water. Evelyn's face was pale in the moonlight, her eyes shining like silver.

"Why are we here?" she asked, and there wasn't a hint of the usual flirtation in her voice, but maybe expectation instead.

I wrestled with words. I had rehearsed all day trying to find the best way to tell her, but nothing seemed right. Her mother's intrusion hadn't helped. Evelyn's face fell at my silence.

"Evelyn, I—" The words wouldn't come. I sat there slack-mouthed while Evelyn's eyes lost their silvery shine and went hard; and realizing that I was making a mess of it I just blurted, "Evelyn, I think we should get married."

It took her a moment. She was expecting something else. I fumbled in my pocket for the little box. I had been to Draper Jewelers over by Lipscomb University during my lunch break, and I had bought a pair of diamond rings for Evelyn that nested together to look more substantial than they really were, but they were all that I could afford, and even then I would be making payments for a while. One served as an engagement ring, the other a wedding ring, and I hoped like hell that they fit because I had no idea what her ring size was.

Her face rose in breathless surprise, and she flung herself onto me and hugged me tight. "Yes! Yes! Yes!" she cried.

I slipped the rings onto her finger, and sighed in relief that they fit. She examined the little diamonds in the moonlight, grinned wide and sprinkled my face with kisses. And then our mouths met, long and deep, and I could feel the taut ball in her stomach, her swelling breasts, and she demonstrated that she was still nimble enough to do what she did so well.

* * *

We told her parents as soon as we returned that evening. It was late but this needed to be gotten over with. Mrs. Hanshaw shrieked with giddy delight, held her daughter's hand to the light and admired the rings, then the two went off to another room, arm in arm, chittering like excited schoolgirls and without a backward glance. Mr. Hanshaw shook my hand proudly.

"You've made the right decision, son," he said. "Welcome to the family."

I got away as quickly as I could and went to tell Mom and Dad. Dad shook his head at the news and stalked out of the room, while Mom seemed to wilt.

"You don't need to do this, Carlton," she pleaded in a wounded voice.

"Yes, Mom, I think I do."

They sent for Sadie, who arrived from Raleigh at the end of the most uncomfortable dinner I had ever sat through. It was Sunday evening. We went to my room and closed the door, and I exhaled as if I had been holding my breath the whole time. Sadie sat at my desk and scrutinized me from head to foot.

"Why, Carlton?" she asked outright, not bothering with small talk.

"Evelyn's pregnant," I admitted, looking at my feet.

"So what?"

"So…because it's my fault."

"Oh, damn it, Carlton." She looked up and searched the ceiling for a moment. "Do you love this girl?" She said it as if Evelyn were some odd girl off the street.

"I think so," I answered, fidgeting.

"You *think* so?"

"Well, uh—I don't *not* love her." Sadie rolled her eyes.

"Carlton?" She was all business now. "What are you going to do about school, about money—a place to live?"

"I've got a job," I said defensively.

"And school?"

"I'll figure it out."

She sighed. "You're making a mistake."

"I think I'm doing the right thing."

"Oh, Carlton, you can't fix everything."

"I can fix this."

"This is a mistake that could ruin your life."

"Well, you would know," I said. I didn't mean to but it just slipped out, and I winced when I heard my own words.

She went hard, and fixed me with a flinty look that she had given to Leavitt once.

"Okay, Carlton." She threw up her hands. "You know what's best." And then she left me, slamming the door on her way out.

* * *

Evelyn and her mother moved quickly. They set the wedding up for the following weekend, 5:00 p.m. Sunday afternoon at Woodmont Baptist Church. They needed to hurry, they said, before Evelyn started to show. It would be a simple wedding, just family and a few friends. No need to send out invitations. Later, after the baby was born, we could renew our vows in a grander ceremony. June would be best.

I had to hurry, too. I rented a second-floor apartment at the Royal Arms on Richard Jones Road, right behind Shakey's, and filled it with second-hand furniture that I tracked down through the want ads. Kenny helped me haul the furniture in his van, and together we carted it up the stairs and into the apartment. I had to arrange all of this after work, so we weren't finished with it until Saturday. Evelyn and I went for our marriage license during one of my lunch breaks. I asked Kenny to be my best man but he declined because he and Evelyn had…well, that was a long time ago but still he wouldn't feel right about it.

Sunday, October 17 was a clear and cool day, actually cold in the morning but it warmed up in the afternoon. My hickory had turned completely and a few leaves had begun to fall. The hilltop was visibly thinner. I could see the water tank now. I skipped breakfast with Mom and Dad, just stayed in my room and stared at the walls.

Later I put on my black suit with a maroon tie. Mom came into my room, dressed elegantly and smelling like perfume.

"Let me help you with that, Carlton."

She adjusted my tie and patted down my lapels, stood back and smiled.

"It's your big day," she said. "I want you to look nice."

"Dad?" I asked. My voice broke.

"Your father will be fine. Some things take time, honey." She looked around my bare room. "I guess you won't be coming back, then." Her lips trembled a little. I shook my head, eyes downcast. She nodded thoughtfully. "Well, this is your home. It always will be."

"Thanks, Mom."

"I love you, honey. I want you to be happy." She pecked my cheek. "Now get along. You don't want to be late. We'll see you there."

I arrived at the church before everyone, went into the sanctuary and sat numbly in a front pew. A photographer was mounting cameras on tripods. Woodmont Baptist was a pretty church with a large sanctuary and a lofty ceiling. It would make a pretty wedding. Pastor Sherman came onto the stage and stood in front of the pulpit, giving everything a last lookover. He saw me and waved.

"Carlton, hello," he smiled. His rusty hair and autumn complexion seemed to warm the very air.

"Hello, Dr. Sherman," I said. He gestured me over.

"Now you will stand here, Carlton," he adjusted me just so, "and Jerry will walk Evelyn down the aisle and place her here to your left." Jerry? Oh, Mr. Hanshaw. "Don't be nervous," he went on with that same reassuring smile. "This is a small service. It'll be over soon."

He winked and grinned at me confidently while I fought to still the flutters in my stomach. The florists came in, consulted with the photographer, and began to set up their sprays of flowers.

"So wait in there," he pointed to an anteroom stage left, "and I'll let you know when it's time. Okay?"

"Yes, sir. Thank you."

"Oh, and did you remember to bring the rings?"

I patted my pocket in sudden alarm, but then sighed in relief when I felt the rings. Pastor Sherman smiled knowingly.

"Good," he said.

I peeked through the door as people arrived; not many people. Mr. and Mrs. Hanshaw came in and sat on the left side of the center pew. Mom and Dad came in and sat on the right, looking as if they were putting as much distance between themselves and the Hanshaws as possible. Grandmother Villetta was with them. She wore Victorian black with lots of lace and a high collar. She was eighty-six years old now, but still carried herself with rigid dignity. She sat in the middle of the pew, between Mom and Mrs. Hanshaw, her hands clasped in her lap and a look on her face that would brook no foolishness. Sadie arrived and sat a row back, and two of Evelyn's friends from school, and then Mr. Iverson. It was nice of him to come. A few other people trickled in, church friends I think. That was it.

There were a couple of sprays of flowers on the steps to the stage. These perturbed Mrs. Hanshaw for some reason. She got up and fussed with them, moving them this way and that.

"Let it be, Jane," Grandmother Villetta said in a firm tone subtly laced with sarcasm. "You've done your work."

Mrs. Hanshaw stood aback and gave Grandmother Villetta an icy look that didn't draw so much as a blink or twitching cheek in return. She abruptly took her seat, looking flustered.

The organ started with the bridal walk. Mr. Hanshaw went up the aisle to escort Evelyn, and Pastor Sherman gestured me to the stage. I took my place as he'd instructed, trying to look anywhere but into the eyes that were on me, swallowing hard and too mortified to wipe at the nervous sweat that was popping out on my forehead. And then Kenny slipped in stealthily and took a seat in the very back. He was wearing the same buff colored tux he had worn to the prom, his hair greased back and the ends of his drooping mustache shaved into points. He looked ridiculous. I snorted and suppressed a laugh, and suddenly I felt much better.

Then I saw Evelyn. Her dress was worthy of Belle Meade, if not also a few column-inches in the society section of *The Tennessean*. It was whiter than mountain snow, laced with pearls, with a delicate train that seemed to float along the floor behind her. Her face was alight, her eyes so startlingly blue that they seemed to light the sanctuary. Her hair was as lustrous as pure gold in the sun, done up high and with a pair of long curls that brushed softly at her cheeks. As hard as I looked I couldn't tell she was pregnant, and as much as I might have admitted to myself a certain ambivalence about our wedding, I also had to admit that she was stunningly beautiful.

Mr. Hanshaw walked Evelyn up the steps as Pastor Sherman and I looked on appreciatively, gave her a light kiss on the cheek and took his seat. Evelyn's excitement was barely contained. Her eyes danced with happiness, and her hands were warm in mine. I tried to show the same excitement, the same happiness, and I must have succeeded because Evelyn's demeanor never revealed the least shadow of concern. And yet I felt as if I were watching from outside of myself, a bystander, listening through a can at the end of a long string. Pastor Sherman was saying something.

"As we begin I will read by request from Proverbs 16 verse 17." Pastor Sherman opened his bible and adjusted his glasses, then in his sonorous voice: "*The highway of the upright is to depart from evil: he that keepeth his way preserveth his soul.*"

He closed his bible and meditated on those words for some quiet moments, then commenced with the service. I listened from afar, performing my role by rote, as if reenacting the weddings I had seen on television. *Do you, Carlton Jeffries...* I heard Pastor Sherman ask. *Do you, Evelyn Leigh Hanshaw...* I caught a glimpse of my father out the corner of my eye and I wilted inwardly. His expression was as one I remembered from long ago, a look he had once given Leavitt in our room in the old house.

Rings were slipped on fingers. Evelyn's face was a shifting light against a dizzy background. Pastor Sherman said some more words, and then I kissed Evelyn chastely, and we joined hands and went together from the church.

* * *

I worked as many hours as Mr. Iverson would allow me, socking that money in the bank while Evelyn grew fat and her pregnancy lost its novelty. She began to complain about stretch marks and other things, and that I wasn't at home enough to help her. She hated our bed, she hated our dinner table—she hated our apartment. My time at work became my only escape. Mom advised me to be patient. Pregnant women could be moody, she said. Evelyn would snap out of it after the baby was born. I sure hoped so.

I voted for Gerald Ford in my first presidential election. Jimmy Carter won. Dad called me to say that Jenny Peay was coming home for Thanksgiving. I wanted to see her but I couldn't face her, not then. Thanksgiving provided the first test of wills between me and my new in-laws. I felt as if we were being tugged back and forth across the street, finally declared that I would eat Thanksgiving dinner in the middle of the street if everyone didn't settle down—and I meant it. It was decided that we would alternate between homes, Thanksgiving with the Hanshaws, Christmas with Mom and Dad, and then the reverse next year. There was a clever ploy in that. I should have guessed because it was Mrs. Hanshaw's suggestion. As it turned out, the baby's first Christmas would be with the Hanshaws.

I wanted to name the baby *Tom* if it was a boy. Evelyn didn't like it, thought it was too plain. She wanted *Jason* or *Gerald*. So did Mrs. Hanshaw, who was as present during these arguments as a piece of worn furniture in our apartment. I stood my ground, though. They agreed to the name *Tom* as long as his middle name could be *Leigh*, after Mrs. Hanshaw's maiden family. For a girl I liked *Villetta*, but there was no use arguing over that one. *Helen* or *Jaqueline* were their top choices.

Those last weeks went by in such a fog of work and worry that even now, in hindsight, I can't recall them day by day. And then it was the middle of the night, with Evelyn tugging at me urgently, and I awoke with grainy eyes and drove her to the hospital.

* * *

Tom Lee Jeffries was born at 8:52 a.m. on February 18, 1977. It was a Friday, near freezing outside and with a gusty wind-chill, but the sun broke through the cold layers of cloud in promise of a warmer and brighter day. I elbowed past Mrs. Hanshaw to see my wife and my child. Little Tommy rested quietly on his mother's chest, swaddled in a soft blue blanket with nothing showing but one red cheek, a perfect pink ear, and the honey colored down on his head. Evelyn looked up at me with weary but proud eyes, and I bent to kiss her on the forehead.

"He's beautiful," she said dreamily, an aura of love around her like a state of grace.

I found it hard to catch my breath. I wanted to fold my arms around them both, and hold them as close to me as my own heart.

Mom had to look on from across the way since Mrs. Hanshaw was hovering over the bed with the immovable, proprietary air of the one in charge. I laughed inwardly because I had gotten the upper hand on Mrs. Hanshaw. She didn't know it yet, but on the birth certificate I'd had Tommy's middle name spelled as *Lee*.

I stayed with them until Evelyn closed her eyes to rest and little Tommy was taken to the nursery. I found Dad there, gazing at Tommy through the glass. Dad patted me on the back proudly, as if I were again his perfect son, and for some moments I longed to be back in that earlier time, up in the branches of my hickory tree, sheltered from the consequences of hard choices. I hoped that with the birth of his first grandchild perhaps I had been redeemed in his eyes. Later I went outside into the sun. Clouds mottled the sky but the day had warmed, and the gusts of wind felt like cleansing breaths from the mountains. I raised my arms to embrace the sun, and stood in its radiance as joy filled me and my lingering doubts vanished in the light—

PART

II

*T*EN

I was afraid I wouldn't have enough paper to finish my story, and sure enough I ran out last night. With your flimsies and implants you probably don't use paper very often, so you might not know that good writing paper has been hard to find for a while, and expensive if you do. I went so far as to make some home-made paper out of wood pulp, but it didn't turn out very well. I have it with me, a crinkly stack of brownish sheets I keep in a plastic bag inside my backpack. Unfortunately the stuff tears too easily to use for writing, so I use it for other things instead.

I had been writing this on loose-leaf paper from a three-ring binder that I discovered in a box in the attic a few years ago. It was one of my high school binders, I could tell by the faded doodles on the cover. My mother must have stored it up there after I left home, along with other things she couldn't bring herself to throw out, like old clothes and toys, an antique short-wave radio that had belonged to Dad, pairs of dusty shoes that maybe she thought she would wear again one day despite the missing heels and worn soles. The paper was brown around the edges and wrinkled from so many humid summers in the attic, but it was still good enough to use for writing. I have been rationing it carefully ever since I found it, and now, finally, it's all gone.

You may have noticed that, having run out of room, I wrote the last sentence on that last sheet of paper very small, squeezed along the edge and really too tiny to make out. Here's what it says: *I had a child; I was a father.* And there I had to leave it, as I had left once before, and fall asleep with those remorseful thoughts, thinking that this exercise was a ridiculous waste of time and precious paper and wishing that I could get moving again so the trail could do what I came here for it to do.

I didn't sleep well. I awoke at some point in the cold darkness with Sam whimpering and worrying after me. I must have been mumbling in my sleep, disturbing words from disturbing dreams. I soothed him until he quieted and closed his eyes, but could never get back to sleep myself. With no stars and no moon the darkness was absolute, not even the barest outline of the rushing stream. The rain had let up overnight but the air was piercingly cold, stiffening my beard with frosted breath.

The rain started up again as the gray of morning crept in, the stream now rumbling in a torrent powerful enough to roll large rocks. There could be no hiking out this morning either, no reprieve from the weather or for me.

I lay for the longest time with thoughts as bleak as the cold dawn, thinking that hours must have passed although it was much less than that. I stirred eventually, ate a hard biscuit and fed Sam some venison. And then, as I pushed my backpack away, I noticed a zippered pouch on the side with a bulge of something I didn't remember putting there. Inside was a small bound journal with a black cover and a rusty clasp. The journal was mostly blank, only some writing on the first few pages. I was dumb-founded. Here this treasure had been, tucked away all these years, but then I read those few pages and I remembered, and I squeezed my eyes tight against a grief that I thought I had left far behind. I have since ripped those pages out. They are folded in my breast pocket where they will be warm and safe.

Now and I am writing again, of another hike, another time. Think of those loose-leaf pages as *Part One*, and this journal as *Part Two*.

Here's why I had forgotten about the journal. Most of my gear, including the sturdy trail clothes I'm wearing and this little LED headlight, comes from my second thru-hike in 2008, all of it boxed and put away during these interceding seventy-nine, almost eighty years. People have been born and raised, had kids and died of old age since I completed that hike. Even I have to pause to take that in. *Eighty years*. I think I can excuse myself for losing track of a small journal over such a span of time. And besides, I had other things on my mind back then.

My gear has aged better than those things I found in the attic. My backpack, once jet black, looks washed-out now, although the rip-stop fabric has held up pretty well. My sleeping bag hung in a closet all those years, wrapped in a clothing bag to keep the moths out. It smelled musty, like one of Grandmother Villetta's old quilts, but otherwise it was fine. My tent was in good shape, too, but I didn't bring it this time. It's too heavy for me now. The rest of my gear, my stove, cooking things, trekking poles and so on, are made of titanium or aluminum, so could probably last indefinitely. Of course, even more modern gear exists now, made of carbon composites and nanoweave. They're stronger and they weigh nothing, but without eDollars how could I have purchased them? Netsellers don't accept currency or gold.

It doesn't matter anyway. My gear is light enough, obviously durable, and such a departure from the gear I used in 1976. In truth I don't know how I managed that hike, even with a seventeen-year-old body. My backpack had been an external frame model that must have weighed eight or nine pounds. My cooking set was aluminum, my stove was a steel Coleman with a fuel bottle, and my tent was canvas. I wore blue jeans and cotton shirts, wool sweaters and my letterman jacket, and a vinyl poncho for rainy days. I carried water in a saddle canteen and lit the dark with a Ray-O-Vac flashlight. The whole thing probably weighed sixty pounds! I couldn't *lift* sixty pounds now, and even back in 2008 I wouldn't have made it far if I'd had to use that 1970s gear.

I did bring my compass, despite the weight. I carried this compass on both of my hikes, even though it really wasn't necessary in the old days. The Appalachian Trail was blazed all the way, you couldn't get lost unless you tried. This time though, with the blazes mostly faded away—well, I wouldn't have found my way here without it.

Tommy loved to play with my compass. He was about three when he discovered the intriguing mystery of the needle that always pointed in the same direction. He would try to trick the compass by spinning it, and when the needle again returned to points north Tommy would laugh with the pure unbound innocence that only little children know. He never grew tired of this game, as if sooner or later he might fool the compass and win. His laughter would sound through our apartment so loudly that even our neighbors could hear it. No one ever complained. An old lady lived alone next door, Miss Martha. She would babysit for us sometimes, but she wouldn't take money. "He's such a happy little boy," she told me often. Miss Martha loved Tommy. Everyone did.

Tommy was a great kid. He slept through the night almost from the beginning, and he didn't cry much. He had honey-colored hair and his mother's piercing blue eyes. When I held him he would gaze at me with those eyes, so bright and trusting that my heart would ache. I loved Tommy; I loved being his father. I never wanted to let him down.

Tommy had his first Christmas at the Hanshaw's house as devised. We arrived just before nine on a crisp morning, the rooftops and lawns frosted in white. The sun was rising into a clear sky, already lighting my parent's house up the hill. I turned away self-consciously, afraid that Mom and Dad might be looking down on me from the living room windows.

"What's the matter?" Evelyn asked. She had Tommy on her hip, bundled against the morning chill and wearing the little Santa Claus hat that Grandmother Villetta had knitted for him.

"Oh, it's nothing," I said, putting on a fake smile. I gathered together our gifts to her parents and my field bag, which now served as Tommy's diaper bag, then went to her and pecked her on the lips. She glanced up the hill as if she knew what I was thinking.

"Well," she said, "at least nobody's in the tree."

"Huh?" That startled me. She just smiled knowingly while I blushed like a voyeur caught in the act.

Jane met us at the door with exaggerated surprise, clasping her hands to her chest and beaming. She was dressed festively in white slacks and an alpaca sweater, white with red Incan designs. She smelled like cigarettes, but then she always smelled like cigarettes.

"Come in, come in," she crowed. "How's my baby boy?" She tickled Tommy's lip and teased a smile out of him, then led us into the living room.

"Where's Daddy?" Evelyn asked.

"He'll be along," Jane answered. "Now let me hold that baby."

Evelyn and her mother sat on the sofa and cuddled Tommy while I arranged our presents around the tree. Their Christmas tree was set up in the front picture window, adorned with glittering silver tinsel and Hallmark ornaments, colorful lights twinkling.

I gazed out the window. Up the hill and through the winter-denuded branches of my hickory I could make out the Christmas tree in our living room. Mom only used clear lights on our tree, with red and gold garlands, and porcelain heirloom ornaments glazed with winter scenes and gold filigree. I thought that Sadie was probably up there, with Ryan, her new boyfriend. We would see them later in the day. I sighed and took a seat near the fireplace, the gas jets hissing with blue flames. Jerry came in with mugs of egg nog on a silver tray.

"Well, now, isn't this nice," he said. "Hello darling." He sat the tray on the coffee table and embraced his daughter warmly. He patted Tommy on the head and then held out his hand to me. "And Carlton. It's so good to have you with us."

"Thank you, sir," I said with a forced a smile. This was not only Tommy's first Christmas, but also my first Christmas away from home. I chided myself for the childish melancholy I felt.

"Here then, everybody, some egg nog before we open presents. Carlton," he winked at me, "I think you'll like my recipe."

The aroma of rum came off the egg nog like steam. I took a sip and puffed my cheeks.

"Good, isn't it?" He winked again.

"Yes, sir." My head was buzzing from just that one sip.

"Well then. Who wants to go first?"

"Me, Daddy," Evelyn blurted with excitement. She kicked off the sofa and dropped to her knees at the tree, rummaging through the presents and arranging them. I watched to see which one she would open first. She started with the biggest one, wrapped in glossy white with a gold bow. It was from her parents. My heart panged, but then my gift to her was so small it was practically lost among the others. She tore through the wrapping paper like a kid, peeled open the box and took out a fluffy angora sweater that looked as soft as Tommy's hair and as white as cotton in a summer field. It would probably become the most expensive thing we had in our apartment, and the idea of that set me on edge for some reason.

"Oh, it's so beautiful!" she gushed, holding it up to her shoulders. "Thank you Momma! Thank you Daddy!" She rushed to them and embraced them, and for a moment there was just the four of them together in a big family hug.

She got to my present last, but caught her breath satisfyingly when she opened it.

"Oh, honey, it's gorgeous," she said with a hand to her breast.

I had made another trip to Draper Jewelers, spending more than I should have but I owed it to Evelyn. We'd never had a honeymoon, and I had put off the grand wedding she wanted until so much time had gone by that the idea had become silly. My excuse was that I needed to work, which was true, but there was also having to go through that again, and risk seeing that look on Dad's face. I hoped this diamond necklace would make up for some of that.

Jane went to her daughter. "Let me help you," she said with a tight smile. I know what she was thinking, that this gesture of mine wasn't enough, but Evelyn seemed pleased and that's all I cared about.

Evelyn lifted the hair off of her neck while Jane fastened the necklace. It wasn't a large diamond, but the setting matched her rings, and together I thought they made enough of a statement to be worthy of Jane Hanshaw's expectations.

"Thank you, Carlton," Evelyn said prettily. She danced over to me and looped her arms around my neck. Her necklace glittered in the firelight.

"It looks nice on you," I whispered, brushing her lips with mine. She was wearing a white turtleneck sweater that made her look taller and more slender than she was. She had never gotten her figure back. Her hips were heavy, and even through her sweater I could see that her chest was full. But her face was as bright as ever, and she looked sincerely happy.

"I love it," she said. "Now open yours." She reached over for a slender box wrapped in red with a white bow. "I hope you like it."

Evelyn knelt and rested her arms on my lap, a look of girlish expectation on her face. I unwrapped the little box slowly, teasingly.

"C'mon, c'mon," she begged with an impatient grin.

"Okay," I laughed.

The last wrapping came off and I opened a box that held a gold Cross pen set.

"Oh, how nice," I said, but despite my best efforts it came out sounding flat. Evelyn's face fell.

"You don't like it, do you?" she pouted.

"Of course I do," I said with as much enthusiasm as I could muster. It really was a nice gift. I'm sure it was expensive, but... I bent over to give her a kiss. "They're beautiful. I love them." She cheered up at that, bouncing on her knees.

"I just knew you would," she said, happy again.

Tommy began to fuss a little. He had been teething contentedly on Jane's crooked index finger, a trick that Mom had taught me and I had taught Jane. It worked most of the time, or for a while at least, but now he was protesting and trying to twist out of her arms. She dabbed a finger in her egg nog and rubbed it on his gums, a trick her mother had taught her but one I didn't particularly care for. But the rum did settle Tommy down. Jane gave him his pacifier, which he sucked on with uncanny force.

"He's getting hungry," Evelyn said. "I'd better give him his bottle."

"Okay."

She saddled Tommy on her wide hip and carried him into the kitchen. Jane took advantage of the break to go outside for a cigarette. That was a demand of mine that she had reluctantly acceded to. Mom and Dad did the same. I didn't like anyone smoking around Tommy. I was gratified that Evelyn supported me in this.

And then the room was quiet, just the hiss of the fire. Jerry was sitting across the way, looking at me intently. I squirmed a little, tried to find some place to put my eyes. He cleared his throat and leaned forward.

"Evelyn has gained weight," he said, keeping his voice low.

"Not that much," I said in her defense. If she had heard that from him she would have been crushed.

"It's no wonder since she's stuck at home all day while you're at work."

"Huh? She has the car. She can go out." Hill's was close enough that I could walk to work, so Evelyn had the Pontiac and could go wherever she wanted.

"Having to take care of Tom all by herself is hard on her."

"She doesn't take care of Tommy all by herself," I protested with a trace of guilt. I did what I could when I was home; I had changed a few diapers. I could have done more if I didn't need to work such long hours.

"You work more than you need to, Carlton."

"But I have to work." My face was getting hot. He didn't understand. I had bills to pay, rent and gas, Evelyn's jewelry. I was still paying the hospital for Tommy.

"It would be better if she had some friends around."

"All of her friends are in college now."

"That's right," he nodded reflectively. "That's right."

The sliding-glass door opened and Jane came in, hugging herself and shivering from the cold. The harsh smell of cigarette smoke wafted across on the chill air. Jerry looked away for a moment, scratching his chin as if pondering something.

"Let's go somewhere and talk privately, Carlton," he said, standing abruptly. His voice was perfectly level, but that was an order not a request.

I followed him apprehensively into his study, the room that had once housed Mr. Gorman's collection. Jerry's broad walnut desk dominated the room now, with classy barrister bookcases along the walls. He gestured me into a dark leather wingback across from his desk then went to his liquor cabinet.

"Care for a drink?" he asked over his shoulder.

"No, thank you, sir."

He poured a couple of fingers of neat bourbon for himself then took a seat behind his desk. He sipped the bourbon and contemplated his green leather desk blotter for some long, quiet moments. I fidgeted nervously, adjusting myself in the stiff leather chair. The air was heavy and hot.

"So," he said suddenly, making me jump a bit. He fixed me with a professional gaze across that wide desk. I felt as if I were shrinking in his presence. I brushed some hair out of my eyes. "What are your plans for the future?"

"Sir?"

"What do you plan to do with yourself, Carlton?"

"Well, sir, I uh—"

"Let's get straight to it, okay?" He knocked back his bourbon and studied the empty tumbler for a moment. "You and Evelyn have been married for a year now. It's time you applied yourself to something, don't you think?" He had a patient, paternal look on his face, but his words were judgmentally sharp.

"Sir?"

"You don't want to be a grocery clerk all your life, do you?"

"It's only for a while," I snapped.

"Okay, okay," he waved me down. "Don't get defensive. We're just talking, son." He paused before going on. "I have some…ideas that I think would help you."

"What do you mean?"

"You had acceptance letters before you took off for the…*woods*," the way he emphasized it made it sound trivial, "so we know you have the grades. I've spoken to some people, and I believe we can start you at Vanderbilt in the spring—"

"What?" I was squeezing the armrests so hard that I left finger indentations in the leather. Jerry went on without pause.

"—and I'm sure your father would give you a position at his agency if you asked him. With his connections you could move Evelyn into a house. She could have her own car, and a nannie to help her with Tom, and in a few years, with a degree… you're a smart young man, Carlton. I know you can make something of yourself."

Make something of myself? I was trembling now, struggling not to lose it right there.

"Listen, Mr. Hanshaw…Jerry—" I looked away and took some deep breaths before going on, "—thanks, but I can't do that, sir."

"Why not?"

"Because…" How could I say it? That I couldn't disappoint my father again? "Because my dad would want me to make it on my own if I could."

His brows creased in disapproval and his voice became stern. "Carlton, you have my daughter to think about—and Tom. Evelyn deserves better from you."

I jumped up at that, but Jerry didn't even flinch. I had never been one to lose my temper, but it was all I could do not to slam my fist on his desk. "I'm taking care of Evelyn, sir," I managed to get out through clenched teeth. "And Tommy. We're doing okay."

"There's no shame in asking for help, son." Now he was getting testy.

"I don't *need* help, sir."

We held one another with unyielding glares for some moments before he looked away.

"Alright then, Carlton," I could tell that he was fighting for control himself, "but at least let me give you something to help you through the holidays."

"No thank you, sir," I said resolutely, and I turned on my heels and stalked out of there.

I found Evelyn dozing on the couch, tired from the rum or just tired. Tommy was asleep on her chest. Jane was somewhere. I gazed out the picture window and up the hill, not at the house but at the woods above. It was safe in the woods, steady. I wished I could have them back.

* * *

Mr. Iverson promoted me to night manager that spring, and at a salary of three hundred fifty dollars a week! This would have been in April, with warmer days and new green growth popping out everywhere. I was so excited that I ran home during my lunch break to tell Evelyn. Her reaction was not what I had hoped.

"So now you'll be working even more," she complained. She had lain Tommy down for a nap in the bedroom. I pulled the door quietly.

"Evelyn—"

"Oh, Carlton." She fell onto a chair at our dinette table. She was wearing gray sweat pants and one of my white T-shirts. Her hair fell lankly over her shoulders. She looked weary, a cumulative fatigue. "You work all the time. And now you'll be working almost every night and weekend."

"It's *three fifty* a week, Evelyn."

"We don't have to *live* like this, Carlton." She threw up her hands. "Daddy would give you money."

"Evelyn…I can't." I hated the whine in my voice.

She covered her face and sniffed back some tears. I went to hold her but she shrugged me off.

"No," she said weakly. She wouldn't look at me. "I have things to do."

She pushed herself up and went into the kitchen. Pans rattled in the sink. I came up behind her and slipped my arms around her waist. She paused for a moment but then resumed her work as if I weren't there.

"Honey, I just need some time." I kissed her neck. "I can do it. I can give you what you want, you'll see."

She locked her arms on the counter and sighed.

"When?"

"Just a few years, that's all."

"Then what?"

"Then…we'll have enough money saved to do something…I don't know what right now, but something."

She turned out of my arms then and went to the window. We could see Shakey's from that window. The seniors were screeching in and out of the parking lot in their rush for lunch. That we had once been a part of that seemed so distant now. She stood there for the longest time, just gazing out the window.

"Evelyn, talk to me," I said at last, pleaded really.

She spun around and crossed her arms tightly, which showed how much weight she had put on above her hips. Her look was not so much angry as resigned.

"What's there to talk about? You've already made up your mind."

"No I haven't, I mean—"

"Yes you have." She dabbed at a tear and her lips trembled. "It wasn't supposed to be like this."

"What does *that* mean?"

"Nothing, Carlton. Nothing." She turned to the window. "You'd better get back to work or you'll be late."

* * *

I took the car after work and went to visit Kenny at his apartment on Nolensville Pike. I had Tommy with me so that Evelyn could have some time off. Tommy loved Kenny for some reason. Kenny was fond of Tommy, too. It was hilarious to watch him dote on my son, to play and tumble and let Tommy pull his long droopy mustache like reins. I brought Tommy over fairly often, but I had rules.

Neal answered the door with a crooked grin. "Hey, dude," he said.

Neal was Kenny's new roommate. He always wore colorful Bermuda shorts, even in the winter. He had a long bristly face and knobby legs, and the curly sun-bleached hair of a California surfer. What he was doing in Nashville was anyone's guess.

"Yeah, wait a minute while we clean up, man," he added. He disappeared inside, leaving the door open.

I stood back with Tommy on my hip while rustling and scraping sounds came from the apartment. The sun was going low and it was starting to get chilly.

"Hey Carlton," Kenny yelled from somewhere inside.

"Hey Kenny."

A minute or two later Kenny came out with a couple of cookie tins. He grinned at me. "Almost ready, man. Hi, Tommy," he babbled in baby talk. Kenny's breath smelled of beer.

"*Baba,*" Tommy giggled. That's what he called Kenny. We couldn't imagine why.

"Be right back," Kenny said. He carried the cookie tins across the way and put them in his van. "Alright, then," he said on the way back, brushing his hands. "All set now."

"You feeling okay?" I asked. Kenny looked a little gaunt.

"Yeah, man. Just workin' a lot."

"I hear ya," I said. "Me, too."

I stepped inside and sniffed the air. It smelled like Lysol but not the other. Kenny closed the door and we sat on his low-slung couch. He looked at me with hang-dog eyes.

"Yeah, okay. Here," I sighed, and handed Tommy over.

"Hey Tommy," Kenny cooed nose to nose. He sat Tommy on his knee and bounced him. "So what's goin' on with you, Carlton?"

"You know, working. I got a promotion."

"Yeah?"

"Yeah. Night manager."

"Whoa, man. Night manager? Sounds like good bucks."

"Pretty good."

"What does she think about it?"

"The usual."

"Figures."

He returned his attention to Tommy, making the boy giggle with delight. Neal came in, sniffing water after having washed his face. His hair was wet, tied back with a rubber band.

"So you got a promotion, huh?" he said. "Cool." He fell back onto a worn recliner, reached for a cigarette but then caught himself and let it go. "Sorry, man. I almost forgot."

I waved him off. "No problem."

Kenny knew the rules, that I wouldn't tolerate smoking or other things in the apartment when I brought Tommy over, and Neal went along with it good-naturedly. I heard a bump in the other room.

"Is somebody else here?" I asked. Neal gave me a high-gummed grin, and Kenny turned to me with a mischievous smile.

"Got a surprise visitor," said Kenny.

The bedroom door opened and out walked Carla.

"Carla!" I exclaimed, struggling to get to my feet from the low couch.

Carla's lascivious smile was as wide as ever, and even more pronounced now because she had lost weight. Her face was more angular, her figure lither than it had been. She had a healthy tan that dampened the fieriness of her hair.

"Hello, Carlton," she said demurely. "Now let me hold that beautiful baby."

She took Tommy in her arms and cuddled him, and he stared into her green eyes as if transfixed. I gawked, Kenny laughed, and Neal looked pleased with himself.

"I thought you were in L.A.," I sputtered.

"I was," she said, rocking Tommy in her arms, "but I missed a good southern accent." Neal snorted.

"Are you back to stay?" I asked. She looked at Neal wryly.

"Maybe. I could use a job, though—Mr. Manager." Her teeth gleamed through that smile. "I heard you through the door."

"Oh, uh—"

"Don't worry, Carlton," she handed Tommy off to Kenny then went to Neal and flopped into his lap, "I've got a guy now."

"You and Neal—?"

"Yeah." She wrapped her arms around his neck and kissed him full on the mouth. He spanked her thigh playfully and came up for air.

"This little southern belle sure can surf," he said appreciatively. "No waves in Nashville, though."

"Just for a little while, baby," she purred in his ear.

"Man, I'd like to go to L.A.," said Kenny wistfully.

"You never know," said Carla. "Maybe you could get Carlton to go with you."

"Not likely," I grumbled. "I'm married now." I displayed my ring finger. All of my money had gone into Evelyn's rings. Mine was a simple gold band.

"I remember that girl," said Carla. "How is she?"

"She's okay."

She and Kenny exchanged glances.

"Well that's good. You'd better tell her to keep you happy, though," and the look she gave me reminded me of old times.

* * *

It didn't take long for Evelyn to learn that Carla was back and working at the store. She confronted me at dinner on Sunday, my only night off.

"Why would you hire that woman?"

"Carla's a friend, Evelyn." I hacked at a dry pork chop. God bless her but Evelyn couldn't cook—but then neither could I, except for beans over a Coleman stove.

"I don't trust her," she went on.

"You don't even know her."

"I know you used to date her."

"So what? You used to date Kenny."

"No I didn't," she said indignantly. There was no point in pushing that little fact so I dropped it.

"Well anyway, she has a regular boyfriend now. They're serious."

Evelyn eyed me thinly, her lips a tight line. "I don't want her around Tom."

"Oh, Evelyn." I threw down my napkin and pushed away from the table. Something passed quickly across her eyes.

"I'm sorry, Carlton." She came up behind me and draped her arms over my shoulders. "It's just that you work all the time. What am I supposed to think?"

"I have to work, Evelyn."

She didn't comment on that. She rubbed my shoulders and leaned in close. Her warm breath pattered against my ear. She smelled like the kitchen, but also the lavender shampoo she used. I found the combination to be strangely alluring. My heart kicked up a few beats. She kissed my neck and I reached back to hold her. We rocked together for some quiet moments, rare moments between us, moments that I hungered for.

"I wish you didn't work so much," she whispered softly then. "I wish you would let Daddy help you."

When she felt me stiffen she dropped her arms in resignation and returned to her chair. My shoulders felt cool as her warmth faded. She picked at her food in silence. I could hear Miss Martha's television through the walls.

* * *

The older ladies about walked off the job when they saw that Carla was back, so I put her on the night shift with me. She didn't mind, she said. As it turned out, the old ladies wouldn't have had anything to complain about anyway. Carla had changed. She didn't carry on like she used to, as if Los Angeles had matured her. She still had her playful side, only now it wasn't laced with sexual innuendo. I liked her better this way. We could talk.

Often after work we would take her car to Denny's for coffee, and we would talk past midnight. I looked forward to those late hours after work. When she was off with Neal I had nothing to do but go home to a dark apartment, lie in bed next to my sleeping wife and feel the loneliness press down like a weight on my chest.

"Why'd you come back?" I asked her one night. We were alone in a circular booth. There was a heavy-set trucker sitting at the counter, but otherwise the place was empty. Our waitress looked tired as she poured our coffee. Carla smiled almost shyly.

"I love Neal," she said. "I mean I *really* love him." She lit a cigarette and inhaled deeply. "It scared me, you know? Like am I gonna marry this guy? Me? *Married?*" She grinned then. "I lost my nerve, I guess, so I split and came home. My mom was glad to see me anyway. My dad—" she exhaled a long puff, "—not so much. Then Neal shows up at the door dressed nice and with his hair combed, and even Dad liked him." She smiled at some memory.

"I'm happy for you, Carla. I really am."

"And that means something coming from you," she said. "Thanks. We're just saving money, though—to go back. You understand that, right?"

"Yeah," I said darkly.

"Oh, Carlton," she took my hand, "you're not happy, are you?"

"I'm fine," I said, liking the warmth of her touch, "It's just that..."

"What?" She looked into my eyes.

"It's just that...you know. Things."

"Is it hard being married?"

"Sometimes."

"She's taking good care of you though, right?" Her eyes told me what she meant.

"Uh, not so much anymore."

"Poor Carlton." She patted my hand. "That girl had better be careful."

I laughed at that. "I don't think she has much to worry about there."

"Well, she should." We sipped our coffees quietly while that sank in, then: "Tell me about your great adventure. Kenny never talks about it."

"Kenny never asked about it."

"Why not?"

"Don't know. I was on the Appalachian Trail for almost four months. I think I lost a hundred pounds!" I laughed. "I saw incredible things, Carla. Incredible things. But no one wants to hear about it, like they don't care at all—like it bores 'em. I don't even bring it up anymore."

"I'd like to hear about it."

"Really?"

"Sure. Did you...you know?" She batted her eyes.

"Yeah," I smiled. "I met a girl."

"Oooh, tell me," she said excitedly, sliding closer. "What's her name?"

"Willow."

"Like the tree?"

"Yeah, just like the tree." And I went there, and I must have gone blank because

Carla was shaking my arm.

"Where'd you just go?" she asked playfully.

"To a mountain in New Hampshire," I answered distantly.

"I bet it was beautiful."

"It was."

"So then what?"

I shrugged. "So then I came home."

"You wish you were back there, don't you?"

"Yeah. I wish…I don't know. It's hard to put into words. When I was on the trail everything seemed right, even when I was cold and hungry. My head was so clear. I had ideas, so many ideas. I thought I could do anything."

"It must have been a great feeling."

"It was. It felt great. But it's gone. I could feel it going even before I got home, and now all I have is…" I plucked the name badge off my pocket and flicked it onto the table, "…a job at the grocery store."

"I thought you were gonna go to college," she said.

"Yeah. I can't afford it now."

"What about your wife…Evelyn?"

"She takes care of Tommy."

"Doesn't she want to go to college?"

I chuckled sadly. "She never talks about it. I don't know what she wants to do."

"Well," she touched my face, "at least you have Tommy. It'll all work out, it just takes time."

"Yeah, I just need a little time."

Carla stayed until the end of that summer. Neal had already gone back to California with her things. I walked her to her car at the end of her last shift. She kissed me on the cheek.

"Take care of yourself, Carlton," she said, trailing a hand on my face. "Come see us sometime. You'd love it."

"I'll try," I said.

"And look in on Kenny, okay?"

"What's wrong with Kenny?"

"Nothing. He just…sometimes he needs someone around to look out for him."

"Okay."

"Oh, I'm gonna miss you," she said. She actually had tears in her eyes.

"Me, too."

Carla got in her car then and pulled away, and I stood there alone as the night closed in.

ε*LEVEN*

It's getting late again, with nothing out there signaling a coming change in the weather. The rain is a mist now, almost a fog, and it's colder I think. It sleeted again earlier, the ground is still slushy from it. Good that I have been writing this down because I had lost track of the days. It's June 23—June 23 and ice is falling out of the sky! It's probably warmer in Alaska right now, but then Alaska hasn't had to contend with these changes in the Gulf Stream. Or perhaps it has in other ways, what with those blighted forests as far as the eye can see, like Old Testament-scale devastation. I've seen the photos. They say a bug did all of that, advancing northward as winters became milder, infecting the trees along an almost ruler-straight latitudinal line that can be seen from space. I believe it. That's something I've had a little experience with myself.

Not so in the state of Maine. It's not that this weather is necessarily unusual, but that it's so persistent and late. It started out like this on both of my earlier hikes as well. In 2008 I had wanted to begin at the end of May, on the same day I had set out on my 1976 hike, but I discovered that the Baxter State Park rangers had become adamant about keeping hikers off of Mt. Katahdin during inclement weather. I hung out in Millinocket for two days waiting for the weather to clear, as depressed as I could be. It was still wet and cold on the third day, but I couldn't wait any longer. I had to go, I had to *move*, so I snuck past the ranger shack and stealthed my way up the mountain. Evading park rangers is something else I've had experience with.

I stood on Mt. Katahdin for the second time and thought the view hadn't changed much in thirty-two years. The peak was shrouded in mist, as it had been last time, and even though I was now wearing Gore-Tex instead of wool, the cold still crept in. The weathered wood-plank sign on the summit came out of the murk like flotsam on a foggy shore. It didn't provide much of a photo opportunity, but then I hadn't come to take photos, only to touch the sign for the official start of the hike and get moving again.

It was somewhere past Abol Bridge and into the Hundred-Mile Wilderness that the sun broke through. Soon rays filtered through the trees, and glimpses of blue appeared between the limbs. The wind shifted around, and with it came warmth. This also happened last time, and in about the same place. I began to sweat. I had to stop and change out of my rain suit, and even before I reached Hurd Brook I had to pause again to unzip the legs of my convertible pants.

I pushed on. The hours spent climbing and descending Mt. Katahdin had worn into the day. I could have camped at Hurd Brook shelter and have called it a good effort at eighteen miles, but still I pushed on. Rainbow Stream wasn't necessarily my destination, I just needed to keep moving, restless from those idle days in Millinocket. And this hike was different from the first; I had come for different reasons. It didn't matter to me how many miles I made each day, whether or not I finished on my birthday or if I even finished at all. I just needed to keep moving. I hadn't come so much to hike the trail as to take a healing sojourn in the woods, some time away from the well-meaning but unsolicited sympathies of others—some contemplative solitude that would be guarded by the remoteness of the Maine woods. I gave myself my own trail name this time, *Sojourner*. Nobody would know that it hadn't come from another hiker, not that I cared if they did.

I reached Rainbow Stream after the sun had set, and truly I would have continued on had I been able. I was thirty miles from Mt. Katahdin, a long way for someone my age and much farther than I had gone in 1976, but at forty-nine years old I felt those miles as aches in my knees and lower back, and while my mind was prepared to continue on through the night, my body couldn't do it.

The shelter was empty. In a ridiculous and completely illogical way I had hoped to find Hank there, even though he had certainly died of old age by then. It was just as well, because I wanted to be alone anyway. No sooner had I rolled out my sleeping bag than I was fast asleep from sheer exhaustion, and I slept better than I had in months, deeply, without the nightmares. I knew that the trail would have this effect. That's why I came.

The next morning was crisp and clear and alive with light. The stream rushed and gurgled and held me in a contented trance. I lay bundled in my sleeping bag as the sun rose higher and the birds sang, so calming that I couldn't bring myself to break the spell. I didn't even want to get up to pee. How long had it been since I could lie idly and not torment myself? I lay there and watched as the shadows shifted with the day and the waters of the stream went from indigo to aqua and then back; and the hours passed as nothing, and in my mind I thought of nothing, just the moment, the sweet air and the thrum of the stream.

Evening came on in soft shadows and golden highlights. The frogs started up along the stream, in a chorus of slender croaks that contained a soothing harmony. My mind went along in time with them, highs and lows and double beats, and then long skirls before their song repeated. It was possible to hear them and nothing else, to be lulled into a rich world of primal life that negated all other concerns, those of thought and grief and self-pity. I lay back and closed my eyes, and slept in the comforting embrace of the song.

In the morning, though, it was time to go. If I stayed any longer I would need to hike out to re-supply, and I didn't want to do that, to interrupt this solitude. Not yet. It was another magical morning. I felt invigorated. I had coffee and oatmeal for breakfast, and in a memory that made me laugh, I could recall perfectly the waxy taste of Hank's pemmican. No pemmican this time, no beans either. I was Sojourner now, not Jake Brake. I took the trail register out of its wooden box and scanned the entries. There were no entries yet for 2008. The last entry was dated November 3, 2007, from a northbounder named Beer Poet. This is what he wrote:

> *In low mourning light,*
> *Through forest and frost,*
> *Another day comes,*
> *Beyond the dark night.*
> *Alive with the sun,*
> *So near the trail's end,*
> *The mountain I see,*
> *A journey soon done.*
> *Beer Poet, GA–ME '07*

Trail registers were full of this kind of thing. You could have gathered them together and made a book. Perhaps someone did, but if so I never saw it. I thought for some minutes before I made my own entry. I'm no poet, but I felt compelled to write some matching words, something that would join our two anonymous journeys across the long winter that lay between us, and at the same time inaugurate the 2008 hiking season with sufficient aplomb. This is what I wrote:

> *In low morning light*
> *Green forest, blue stream,*
> *Another day comes,*
> *Away with the night.*
> *Alive with the sun,*
> *A trail now to walk,*
> *The mountain behind,*
> *The journey begun.*
> *Sojourner, ME => GA '76, ME => GA '08*

I shouldered my backpack then and started out. *The journey begun,* I had written. Was this really a new journey, or just a continuation of the first? These are the kinds of esoteric questions that swirl in your mind during a long hike, and this nagged at me for some miles before I was distracted by a swarm of blackflies. I couldn't tell it then, but when you get to my age you finally gain the perspective to see all the connections between things, how this led to that, and you come to understand that causes and effects do not follow in straight lines as one might think, but in circles that demand to be completed. It may not have appeared so, but in a way this journey was a continuation of my 1976 hike, or rather it was a circle that linked with others like Olympic rings to form a chain of experience. Some circles are larger, some smaller. Some form strong overlapping links while others simply graze one another in happenstance. I can see it so clearly now, where a small circle just grazed a much larger one. Were it not for a chance conversation in 1981, none of this would have happened.

* * *

1981 was the year Dad retired. He officially retired on his birthday, August 10. Now that Ronald Reagan was president, he said, he felt more confident about the future; that he could safely retire without having to worry about the collapse of civilization as we knew it. Still, though, he dallied around his office until the end of the year. He said he needed time to sell his listings, close his office and the other things. We all knew that he was dragging it out as long as he could, but the end of the year had to finish it or else he would face tax penalties. Ironically, Green Hills was surging again after the doldrums of the late 70s. The money he made off of his listings was a nice pad to his retirement fund, but a tax liability if he kept going into 1982.

So that settled it. His grand retirement party would be held on New Year's Eve. Mom set it all up, and would brook no further procrastination from him. This would be an intimate party, just family and a few close friends, nothing raucous. I arrived at 5:00 p.m., on an evening made darker by a leaden sky and a chill wind. I chugged up the driveway in the Pontiac. The old car was starting to show its age now. Lately it had begun to blow smoke, the blue of burning oil, and it sputtered on the inclines. I worried that it would stall in the driveway, but I made it to the top and parked alongside Sadie's silver Plymouth Reliant.

I threw a glance down the hill at the Hanshaw's house. Evelyn's Cadillac Seville was in the driveway, the metallic champagne paint sparkling under the porch lights. I sighed with a hiss. Her parents gave it to her on her twenty-first birthday, which had been August 1, 1979, two years ago and still I seethed when I thought about it. Evelyn had been so ecstatic that my gift to her had been swallowed up in the commotion, a pair of diamond earrings to match her rings and necklace. She seldom wore them. They mostly stayed in her jewelry box along with the necklace, and sometimes her rings were there, too. Evelyn never understood why I was so upset about the car. After all, it hadn't cost me anything. No, but I had to pay the insurance, another bill on the list. It seemed that the more I made the more I had to spend, and that nothing I could do was good enough for the Hanshaw's daughter.

I shook my head and went on into the house. Evelyn would be along later with Tommy. Her parents had gone away over Christmas, so this was the first time she had seen them in a while. The Hanshaws had not been invited to the party. I chuckled then, not because the Hanshaws had been excluded but because I could just bet that Evelyn wouldn't deign to walk up the hill. Instead she would drive her car the few feet across the street and then up the hill. Well, she was going to have a hard time finding a place to park.

They were all in the den, Mom, Dad, Sadie and Ryan. A few of Dad's closest friends were set to show up after dinner. I hadn't seen Sadie since last Christmas. Ryan's family lived in Vermont, and that's where they had gone for Thanksgiving and Christmas this year. Sadie was thirty now, confident and poised, still as slender as a teenager but with age creeping in around her eyes. She wore white pants and a black sweater. Her hair was a soft fall of dark brown that brushed the back of her neck.

"Carlton!" she announced with open arms and a wide smile. We hugged warmly.

"Hey Sis," I said. "It's been a long time."

She stood back to take me in. I was wearing dark gray slacks and a matching sport coat over a maroon turtleneck. I didn't think I had changed much since we had last seen one another.

"You look great," she said effusively. "Where's my nephew?"

"Evelyn's with Tommy down below. They'll be up soon." Ryan was hovering nearby. "Hello, Ryan," I said, offering my hand.

"Hello, Carlton."

Ryan had long fingers, which always made for a clumsy handshake. He was tall, and as taut as a new hemp rope. At thirty-five years old, gray shoots were beginning to infiltrate his sandy hair and his distinguished, academic beard. He looked the part in a tweed jacket with elbow patches.

"How long can you stay?" I asked.

"Just till Saturday," said Sadie.

As soon as Mom got Sadie alone, she would pester my poor sister about why the two hadn't married yet. I couldn't imagine Sadie being married, but then Ryan was a nice enough guy, although difficult to talk to. He was an English professor with tenure. Mom and Dad were very pleased.

"Well, then," Mom said, rising unevenly from the couch. At sixty-one she was holding up well, but she had been having trouble with her knees. "I'd better get upstairs and check the oven."

"I'll help," said Sadie, and the two went on up.

Dad folded his paper and laid it aside. "And I'd better get dressed for the big night," he said grimly.

I took a chair near the fire while Ryan lowered himself onto the couch. He sat stiffly with his knees together and his hands in his lap. The silence was awkward.

"So—" he said at last.

"When are you and—?" I said at the same time.

We both chuckled but the silence was back. "You first," I conceded after some moments.

"So you're assistant manager now, I hear."

"Yes," I nodded.

"It must be quite a responsibility to manage such a large grocery store."

"It is," I nodded again.

I forgot what I was going to ask him. I thought to ask him about his job, but didn't have a clue what to say. The blankness in his face showed that he didn't know what to say next either. We were saved by a knock at the door.

"That must be Evelyn," I said, hurrying to the door.

Evelyn stood regally in the doorway, holding Tommy by the hand. She had on her angora sweater over a tapering, ankle-length gray skirt and white strapped heels. Her earrings were gold hoops, and her hair was soft and shiny on her shoulders. She was wearing her rings tonight. She had dressed Tommy in khaki pants and a navy oxford sweater with double white trim around the V-neck. He looked like a cute junior preppie.

"Hi, Daddy," said Tommy.

"Hi, Tommy." I lifted my boy and gave him a hug. "You look nice," I said to Evelyn. I gave her a kiss on the cheek. Over her shoulder I could see her Cadillac parked at a steep angle on the driveway. "Get in, it's cold out there."

"Hello, Ryan," Evelyn smiled.

"Evelyn," he said, standing. He kissed her on both cheeks, continental style. "And Mr. Tom. How are you, young man?"

"I'm fine," Tommy answered in his high, little-boy voice.

I sat Tommy on his feet and patted his behind. "Go find something to do, son."

"Okay, Daddy," and he scampered up the stairs.

"So tell me all about Dartmouth," Evelyn said to Ryan. "It must be exciting." She settled into my chair next to the fire, legs crossed and with her arms draped over the armrests, relaxed and open. I had to admit that she was looking good. She had been spending her days at the YMCA over on Hillsboro Circle, and the results were evident. I took Dad's Barcalounger, and Ryan returned to his place on the couch.

"Yes, very exciting," Ryan said, "and daunting at the same time."

"I understand you have tenure now."

"Yes, what a relief."

"It must be gratifying, too—to be given recognition for your work."

"Very much so."

"Will Sadie be teaching there as well?"

"She's been offered an adjunct position in the fall. She plans to move up from Raleigh this summer. Afterwards…only time will tell."

"Well I hope it works out."

"So do we all."

Ryan didn't have an accent per se, but he spoke in a clipped fashion like an upper-crust British person. Evelyn spoke with a twang right out of the South, but somehow she made it sound cultured. As for me, my accent didn't matter because I wasn't part of this conversation. I had nothing to contribute anyway. Higher education was a mystery to me. I didn't even know what tenure meant, and to ask would have made me feel ignorant. Just then Tommy's high-pitched, cackling laugh sounded from upstairs. I smiled at Evelyn.

"He's found the compass."

"Nothing else makes him laugh like that," she said with her own smile.

"I'd better go see how he's doing."

"Okay."

I left them and headed up. I followed the laughter into my old room, which Mom had done up as a playroom for Tommy. He was sitting cross-legged on the floor, spinning the compass and seemingly unaware of anything else. Other toys were scattered on the floor, some Star Wars figures and a few matchbox cars, and an old teddy bear with the nose chewed off. Tommy wasn't interested in these, only the compass. I watched him quietly, not wanting to disturb his magical fun. Beyond him was the window I had once pulled his mother through. I hoped he would never hear that story.

"You know," Dad said, startling me. I spun on my heels. Dad was standing in the doorway, an arm resting on the door frame. He had put on a white shirt and a tan blazer, no tie. He was completely gray now, with just a few dark streaks at his temples. "You were about his age when we moved here."

"Wow, you're right. I never thought about that."

"Yeah, you were already marching up the hill by now. When are you going to take him?"

If Tommy noticed us he didn't let on. The compass was more interesting.

"I don't think Tommy's interested in things like that, Dad. Evelyn takes him to the pool. They have play dates with other kids."

"How will you know if you never take him?"

"It's hard to get time off, Dad."

"I know, son." He patted my shoulder and turned to leave. "I know."

Tommy spun the compass so hard that it slid across the floor. He went to it on hands and knees, examined it closely and then began to laugh. I don't remember laughing like that at his age. I had been such a serious, perceptive boy; and with this eidetic memory. Was Tommy like that? Would he remember every word and gesture? What would his early memories be of me? I listened to my son laugh, but for some reason it made me sad.

"Okay, Tommy. Time to put that away."

"Aw."

"Go wash your hands. We're eating soon."

"Okay, Daddy."

We ate at the big oval table in the dining room, as if this were a Thanksgiving meal. Mom made her special meatloaf, which was a favorite of mine and Dad's— and Tommy's too—because Mom used brown sugar in the glaze. There were bowls of mashed potatoes and sawmill gravy, green beans and corn, squash and okra, a plate of biscuits, and sweet tea in a frosted glass pitcher.

"I must have this recipe, Mabel," Evelyn said, fawning over the meatloaf. I stifled a laugh. If Evelyn wanted this meatloaf at home then she would have to hire it done.

"It's easy, really," Mom said evenly. She still didn't approve of Evelyn, but she had come to terms.

"I wish Grandmother was here," Sadie said. She and Ryan sat across from us. Evelyn and I had Tommy between us, propped on two South Central Bell telephone books, and Mom and Dad were on the ends.

"Me, too," said Mom. "But she's getting too old to get out much. She's ninety-one, you know."

"Well, I'm going to stop in to see her on the way home."

"She would like that."

"This is wonderful, Mrs. Jeffries," said Ryan. "Southern cooking right out of Faulkner."

Mom blushed at that. I glanced at Ryan. He held his fork in his left hand, his knife in his right, also like a British person. I liked Ryan, but sometimes he was pretentious as hell.

"I've read Faulkner," Evelyn interjected authoritatively. "I struggled with *As I Lay Dying*, though."

"*Everyone* struggles with that one," Ryan chuckled.

"They tell me you have your master's degree now, Sadie," Evelyn commented then. *They* meant *me*.

"Yes," said Sadie. "I finished it in the fall."

Evelyn leaned forward, an animated look on her face. I noticed that she was holding her fork in her left hand, just like Ryan. I cut off a corner of meatloaf with my fork and chewed in aggravation.

"That's quite an accomplishment," Evelyn said. "Dick, you must be very proud."

It disturbed me that she called my father by his nickname, but then he had asked her to.

"Yes, we are," Dad said. "But—"

"Oh, Daddy," Sadie complained.

"It's so far away, honey."

"Hanover's not that far."

"It's a two-day drive up to New Hampshire."

"And two hours on a plane," Sadie chided him.

"You know I don't like to fly," Dad grumbled.

"Then I'll fly here."

"I'd love to see New England in the fall," said Evelyn. "I wish we could go."

"Why can't you?" Sadie asked.

My eyes were on my food while Evelyn's eyes were on me. I could feel them. I kept my eyes down to avoid her incriminating gaze. "I only get my vacation in the summer," I explained to my meatloaf.

"Oh," said Sadie. "Well...sometime then."

An uncomfortable silence settled in, salvaged by Tommy.

"This is good, Grammaw," he said enthusiastically. We all laughed at that.

"Well, thank you, Tommy." That started everyone going again.

"Have you told them about your book, Sadie?" Ryan asked. Sadie blushed a bit.

"Book?" Dad asked.

"It's not much," Sadie demurred. "Just an extension of a graduate paper I wrote. I still have a long way to go."

"She's much too shy," said Ryan. "It's brilliant."

"Oh, Ryan."

"What's it called?" Evelyn asked.

Sadie surrendered to the scrutiny. Still blushing, she put down her fork and knife and folded her hands primly in her lap. "*A Robin Waits*," she said.

"A robin waits for what?" Evelyn queried, puzzled.

Sadie took a hesitant breath before she explained, as if she had preferred to avoid this very thing.

"Haven't you ever watched the robins in spring?" Sadie asked. "All the other birds are flitting around like crazy, but the robins stand and wait."

"But what are they waiting for?"

"Worms, I guess."

"Worms? Ewww!" exclaimed Tommy.

"Is it fiction, honey?" Mom asked.

"Yes, Mom. It's a novel."

"What's it about?" asked Evelyn. Sadie took another breath, clearly reluctant to expound further.

"It's a multi-generational family drama."

"Oh." Evelyn's brows were creased. She didn't get it at all, and when she perked up to press Sadie further I cut in instead.

"You know," I said to no one in particular, "I've been to Hanover. The Appalachian Trail goes right through town."

"It does?" said Sadie.

"Yes, indeed," said Ryan. "The Dartmouth Outing Club even maintains a section of it. I've seen the hikers straggling across campus."

"Well I was one of those straggling hikers," I said a bit caustically.

"Of course," Ryan snapped his fingers. "Sadie mentioned that to me once. You went the entire way, didn't you?"

"I did," I said. For some reason Evelyn was scowling now.

"He was gone almost four months," Mom said. "We were worried sick."

"I should think so," said Ryan. "There's also a section of the trail near my family's home in Vermont. We live near Killington."

"Near Sherburne Pass?" I asked excitedly. As strange as it may seem, this was the first time in five years that I had talked to anyone who knew about the trail.

"I know it well," said Ryan. "There's a nice pub there now. McGrath's, it's called."

"Then you must have hiked the trail yourself…I mean at least parts of it."

"I never have," Ryan said flatly. He must have sensed my disappointment because then he added, "But I should have, since it's right there."

"Oh, well," I shrugged, and returned to my meatloaf.

"It's a coincidence, though," he went on, "now that you bring it up. I recently met someone who has hiked portions of the Appalachian Trail."

"Really?" I said in mid bite.

"Yes. It was at a symposium in Sacramento in the fall. She went on and on about it, and just like you she livened up when I mentioned where I was raised."

"*She?*" Evelyn said as if shocked. "Why would a woman want to do that? It sounds so…dirty."

"Lots of women hike the trail," I grumbled.

"You never told me about this," Sadie said to Ryan.

"What's to tell? She just happened to sit at our table for lunch. She kept us all entertained throughout. She had these colorful stories, of skirting storms on high ridges, working for food at the mountain shelters, and some of the rascally people she met along the way. Real larger than life stuff. She said she hadn't completed the entire trail, but had taken some summers off to hike different parts of it."

"She sounds like a hairy hippie to me," said Evelyn in disgust.

"No, actually she was pretty, and very bright. As a matter of fact," he turned to Sadie, "she attended Dartmouth for a term. This was only a few years after they began to admit women."

Something cold lanced through my chest just then. I dropped my fork with a clink onto my plate. There was roaring in my ears.

"Are you all right, Carlton?" Evelyn asked, more as an aside than out of concern. I ignored her.

"When?" I asked Ryan unsteadily. "When was she at Dartmouth?"

"I don't know, she didn't say, but I'd have to guess—she said it was a few years after they admitted women, and that wasn't until 1972—so 1975, 76, 77 maybe. Why do you ask?"

My hands were trembling. I squeezed my fists to still them. I had my eyes fixed on Ryan but I could see Evelyn out the corner. She was studying me with a combination of puzzlement and worry.

"What was her name?" I demanded, in a tone that brought stares from all around. Ryan seemed flummoxed.

"I'm sorry, I can't recall," he said. "It was just for that one lunch."

"Did she tell you her trail name?"

"Her what?"

"*Her trail name!*" I barked. I rose to my feet, hands on the table and cheeks quivering.

"Carlton, what's the matter?" Dad asked.

"What's a trail name?" Sadie asked. Evelyn's mouth was open in astonishment.

"Oh, right. It's the name they give themselves when they hike," Ryan answered as if he were an expert.

"*Well?*" I slapped a palm on the table. Ryan jumped in his seat and took on a wary expression.

"Daddy, what's wrong?" Tommy asked with trembling lips. Evelyn pulled him into her lap.

"Carlton, what's the matter with you?" Mom asked in a parental voice she hadn't used with me since I was a child.

"I...I..." Ryan stammered. He seemed to be backing away from the table, although he hadn't budged an inch. "I don't know that she told me."

"Sit down, Carlton," Sadie ordered. "You're making a scene." She hugged Ryan's arm. I could see Ryan's mind working, thoughts racing behind his eyes, wondering what he had said, what he had done, and if I were about to become violent.

"I think...I don't know, Carlton," he quailed. "I don't think she told us. But she talked quite a lot about a friend...uh...Jack, no, Jake! That was his name, *Jake.*"

I went icy cold down to my toes. Suddenly I felt a constriction in my chest. I couldn't breathe, not a single breath. I wobbled on my feet. Dad was up and had me by the shoulders. I could make out Evelyn scooting away with Tommy, a look of horror on her face. Dad pushed me onto my chair and kept his hands on my shoulders. I swallowed and thought while they all stared. What to ask? What could he remember?

"What was she doing there?" I asked weakly, focused now on nothing. "What was the symposium about?"

"Career paths in the arts," he answered nervously. "She was a graduate student... in the UC Davis master's program."

I dropped my head and covered my face. What had seemed so urgent just moments ago now embarrassed me to my core.

"I'm sorry," I mumbled. "I'm really sorry." And then I shrugged out of Dad's grip and fled to my old room.

* * *

Evelyn came home after midnight leading a sleepy Tommy by the hand. I was sitting in front of the television watching the post ball-drop party, barely awake myself. She didn't even look at me, just dropped her purse on a chair and padded Tommy off to bed. She reappeared a while later, moved between me and the television and stood with her hands on her hips, wearing that stern, judgmental look of hers. I groaned. I should have pretended to be asleep.

"So what was that little episode about?" she asked mockingly. "I was so embarrassed, Carlton. I swear."

"It was nothing," I answered unconvincingly.

"Oh, it was *something.* Your behavior was abhorrent."

"*Abhorrent?* You must have hung out with Ryan all night."

"What do you mean by that?"

"That he talks bigger than he needs to."

"Oh, Carlton." She threw up her hands and stalked to our bedroom. When she returned she was more conciliatory. She had taken off her sweater. The top two buttons of her white blouse were undone, the third straining between her breasts. Her throat was as smooth as porcelain.

"Who was that woman you two were talking about?" She sat on my armrest but had her arms loosely crossed. Her gray skirt formed sensually around hips that had been reshaped at the YMCA. I felt a carnal stirring that I hadn't experienced in a while.

"Just somebody I met on the trail."

"Why were you so upset?"

"I wasn't upset, I was just…surprised, that's all. You don't understand about the trail. It affects you."

"No, I don't understand," she said self-righteously. "I don't understand what made you want to do that, what makes *anyone* want to do that."

"I couldn't explain it to you, Evelyn, not then, not now. You would have to be there to understand."

"So is that what she is, someone who was there?"

"Yeah, that's part of it."

"What's the other part?"

I looked up into her eyes, which weren't harsh just then, not even dismissive, but they hardened at my silence.

"I see," she said, abruptly standing. "I'm going to bed now. It's been a long day."

The stirring I felt wilted from unrequited ardor, and I slept on the sofa that night.

* * *

Despite everything, I had never lied to Evelyn until that Valentine's Day, which was on a Sunday that year. I had to go to work for a few hours after church, I told her, which was true. Evelyn scowled as I knew she would, but what could I do? Those few hours at work unexpectedly used up the better part of the day because I wound up having to cover for a sick employee. I didn't get home until close to the dinner hour. As a peace offering as well as a Valentine's gift, I presented Evelyn with a contrite expression and dozen red roses.

"How nice," she said, almost sweetly. I kissed her cheek, and then she padded barefoot to the kitchen to find a vase.

I fell wearily into my armchair, kicked off my shoes and loosened my tie.

"Let's go out tonight," I hollered after her.

"Better not," she shouted from the kitchen. "Tom has the sniffles."

"Uh, oh."

She returned with the roses in a crystal vase and sat them in our front window. She was wearing a pale blue dress and an open thin white sweater that curved around her breasts. No more sweat pants and T-shirts for her. She looked nice. Her toenails were painted pink.

"I want to keep him in bed," she continued. "I hope he's not sick for his birthday party."

"Me, too," I said. "Oh, I'll be able to come after all. Maybe for an hour."

"Well that was kind of Mr. Iverson," she said sarcastically. She sat on the sofa and put her feet up.

"Mr. Iverson loves Tommy, Evelyn. It's just that it's hard to change schedules sometimes."

"What good is it being a manager if you can't take time off when you want to?"

"Evelyn, don't start."

"No, I'm not complaining." Yes she was.

Now started the lie.

"They're talking about giving me another promotion."

"Really? To what?"

"To general manager."

She shifted up on her elbow and looked right at me. "What about Mr. Iverson?"

"They may send him to a new store."

"That seems strange." She lay back down and rested an arm on her forehead. "He's been there forever."

He had been. I thought about Leavitt.

"I mean," Evelyn went on, "he should be retiring soon anyway, right?"

"I don't know what his plans are," I answered nervously, realizing only then, although I should have thought about it beforehand, that she knew Mr. Iverson well enough to ask him herself. I shook my head. "Well, anyway—" This was the moment. I would have to talk with Mr. Iverson. Maybe I could get him to go along just in case. "—they want to send me to New Orleans for training. I'll be gone for a week."

"Oooh," she purred, stretching her arms and twining her fingers, "I feel warmer already. When do we go?"

"Not we, just me."

She sat up with a troubled look.

"Why can't I go?"

"You can—or I mean you could, I guess, but I don't think you'll be able to. I have to leave next Sunday."

Her eyes went wide.

"*Next Sunday?*"

"Yeah." I tried to make it sound as if I were put out by the idea.

"So they decide it just like that? I have things to do. I can't just cancel everything."

"I know." I couldn't look her in the eyes. "We wouldn't have time to do anything anyway. It's all meetings and stuff the whole time. I don't know why they can't do it here."

"Well you tell Mr. Iverson I'm furious," she pouted.

"I'll tell him."

Thankfully she let it go. I'm not sure I could have kept up the act if she had pitched a fit. Now I just had to make it through the week, Tommy's birthday party on Thursday, and then if I could hold it together for just another couple of days I would have pulled it off.

* * *

Tommy's fifth birthday party was held in the rec room at the YMCA. Jane set it all up, complete with balloons and a visiting clown. I got out a little late for my lunch break, and didn't make it to the Y until the clown was just finishing up. There were more than a dozen kids sitting in an arc on the floor, as if this were a kindergarten class. Tommy was sitting in the middle, grinning and wearing a balloon animal on his head like a crown. The clown did a goodbye trip-and-stumble that set the kids to laughing, and then he slipped out a side door. I went toward Tommy to give him his present, but Jane intercepted me first.

"All the adults have agreed to put the presents over there," she said, pointing to a table loaded with presents and a blue and white cake that looked to be as tall as Tommy. I squinted to better make out the candles, then held that squint as I turned back to Jane.

"Well *this* adult is his dad," I said indignantly, and tried to push past her.

"Oh, Carlton, don't make another scene. Let Tom have his day."

"*Another scene?*"

"Let me have that."

She took Tommy's present from me and I let her, feeling more embarrassed than angry. My present wasn't as large as some that I saw on the table, but I thought it had to be the best present he would receive. I was giving Tommy my old field bag, and inside it were Dad's compass, which I had cleaned and polished, and a pair of small binoculars.

"They'll be having cake soon," Jane went on. "Let them have their fun, and let Tom choose which presents to open first."

With that she whisked away with the present and I was left to simmer where I stood. I moved around to the side to get a better look at Tommy. He was laughing the way he did with the compass. The kids were tumbling over themselves vying for his attention, while he was actually trying to give each of them equal time. He was such a good kid, so polite, but there were too many kids, and only one of him. A little girl's balloon popped like a shot, stunning them all for a moment. She was a dark little girl, three-and-a-half, maybe four years old, in a pretty pink dress and with pixie bows in her hair. When she began to cry Tommy went to her and put his animal balloon on her head. She gave him the whitest smile, and Tommy seemed to blush.

"Your son is a very nice young man."

The voice came from behind me and it sounded familiar. I turned and gawked.

"Gracie!"

I barely recognized her in a gray business suit and white hose. Her hair was shorter, professionally cut. She was wider around the waist, but still petite. She seemed solid, mature—quite a change. Gracie smiled at me knowingly while I fumbled for words.

"You remember me," she said fondly.

"Of course I remember you."

She looked me up and down. "Have you grown even taller?" she asked.

"I don't think so."

"Well," she bounced on her toes a few times trying to see over my shoulder, "maybe I've shrunk a little."

"What are you doing here?" I asked, not thinking until it was out of my mouth that it could have sounded like a rebuke. Fortunately she didn't take it that way. She pointed to the little girl in pink.

"That's my daughter, Angelina," she said proudly. "She got invited to this at day care."

"Your daughter? My God, Gracie. I didn't even know you were married."

"I'm not married," she said nonchalantly.

"Oh."

That lingered in wait of an explanation, which she finally provided with a sigh.

"It happened but I didn't want to get married."

"You don't have to tell me. I thought you were in school."

"I am. Vanderbilt Law School."

"Vanderbilt? Law School? Gracie, I'm…How did you do it?"

She puffed some hair out of her eyes. "With a lot of help and hard work. And what about you? I knew that you and Evelyn married, and now," she glanced over at Tommy, "I know you have a very nice son. But what else have you been doing?"

"I'm the assistant manager at Hill's."

"The grocery store?"

"Yeah."

She nodded in thought. "Well, I'm glad you're doing well."

"You, too."

Suddenly Evelyn was between us, as if she had materialized from a Star Trek transporter. She looped an arm around my waist.

"Gracie," she said stonily.

"Evelyn," Gracie responded similarly.

The two faced off for some moments, neither betraying whatever emotions they felt. Finally:

"Where's your friend?" Evelyn asked in a patronizing tone that made me wince.

"Which one? I have lots of friends, Evelyn." Gracie glanced at me, and I felt Evelyn's fingernails dig into my side.

"Do you have a child here?" Evelyn asked.

"My daughter, Angelina." Gracie pointed. Angelina and Tommy were playing together with balloons.

"How sweet," Evelyn said then. "Well, I'm glad you could come. Honey," Evelyn pulled me closer, "it's time for Tom to blow out his candles now. We'd better get ready."

"Okay. Bye, Gracie."

"Goodbye, Carlton," Gracie said as Evelyn pulled me away.

* * *

I had everything squared away at work. I told Mr. Iverson that a family emergency had come up on the farm in Smith County and that I needed a week off. He gave me the time off without argument, scheduling a department manager to cover for me. On the matter of the management training, though, I couldn't bring myself to draw him into my lie. I was going to have to take my chances. I stocked up on groceries so that Evelyn wouldn't need to go to the store, not that she ever went grocery shopping anyway. That was my job, she believed, since I was already there. From all the shift swapping I'd had to do, I didn't get off work until eleven o'clock that Saturday night. Evelyn was still up when I got home.

"I think I'm having second thoughts," she told me as soon I came in. She was on the sofa in her white pajamas, her legs curled. The Johnny Carson Show was on the television. "I don't like the idea of you having to go off by yourself for a whole week."

I was too weary from a long day at work to mull over the meaning of that. I tugged off my tie and fell into a chair.

"I can't do anything about it, Evelyn," I sighed, "everything's set up. I have to go in the morning. Don't worry about getting up, though. Kenny says he'll drive me to the airport."

God bless Kenny. If I'd had to go with Evelyn I think I would have lost my nerve.

"Still," Evelyn pouted the way she did. "I wish I could go with you."

"It'll go by fast, honey. I promise."

"What will you do at night?"

"What do you mean?"

"Well, you won't be working all night too, will you?"

"Oh. I'll probably be so tired I'll go straight to my room."

"Hmm."

Some comedian was smashing watermelons on the Johnny Carson Show. I got up heavily and flipped the television off.

"Come here," Evelyn said, patting the sofa beside her. I took off my jacket and slung it over a chair, then joined her on the sofa. She cuddled up next to me, hugging my arm. I smelled like a day at work, but she smelled so fresh. "It was strange to see Gracie at Tom's party, wasn't it?" she asked. With the long hours I had been working, this was the first chance we'd had to talk about Tommy's party except in passing.

"Yeah," I said. "I hadn't seen her since…well, you know. It's been a long time. I didn't even know she was around anymore."

Evelyn's fingers worked at the buttons on my shirt.

"I didn't remember how short she was."

"Yeah, she was always small."

Evelyn slipped her hand inside my shirt. Her fingers were warm. She kneaded my chest and rested her head against my shoulder.

"She has a baby and she's not even married." Her voice was suddenly husky, and her breaths tickled at my ear.

"That surprised me. Her family was so—traditional, I guess."

Her hand worked lower and found what it was after. I wasn't in a state of mind to question what had gotten Evelyn so aroused, I just accepted my good fortune and went with it; and as my blood began to rush I forgot all about Gracie and everything else. I turned my head and found Evelyn's lips, and we kissed with rare passion. She didn't talk about Gracie anymore, she didn't talk at all. I lifted her in my arms and carried her to the bedroom.

* * *

Kenny was already waiting for me when I came out at 6:00 a.m. Nashville was quiet in the pre-church dawn. It was a cool morning in the 30s, but set to warm into a beautiful day. I was groggy from last night, and my eyes were grainy. I hefted my suitcase and climbed into the van.

"Thanks for the ride, Kenny." I had told him only that I was going on a business trip, not where or why. He hadn't seemed curious to know, which was like him.

"No problema, amigo. I was up anyway."

Kenny had dark circles under his eyes. His face was pale.

"What've you been doing all night?" I asked.

"You know," he said, "just doin' what I do."

His hands were shaky on the wheel. He lit a cigarette, pulled the shifter into drive, and we rumbled off.

"You got an exhaust leak?" I asked. The smell of that overpowered even the smoke from his cigarette.

"Yeah," he sighed. "I gotta do somethin' about it."

We continued on. Kenny adjusted the radio. There was a big crack in his dashboard now. The old van was getting…well, old.

"You're gonna need a new van," I commented. *Centerfold* by the J. Geils Band started up on the radio just then. Kenny spun up the volume and that took care of conversation most of the way to the airport.

We pulled up out front of the departure lobby. Kenny brought the van to a creaking halt and threw it into park. I looked at him closely.

"Kenny, are you feeling all right?"

"I'm fine, bro," he smiled. His teeth weren't looking good.

"Everything okay at work?"

"Yeah, man. Everything's fine."

I shook Kenny's hand. His skin was cool and clammy.

"Well, thanks for the ride then."

"No problema, bro. Have a good trip."

I couldn't shake it off as I carted my suitcase into the lobby, that something was the matter with Kenny. I hoped he wasn't sick. I waited in line and got my tickets. It wasn't a long line. Sacramento, California must not have been a popular destination for Nashville flyers on a Sunday morning.

TWELVE

I spent the long flight idealizing a meeting with Willow, spinning fantasies that played in my mind with the certainty of conviction. The weather would be that perfect California climate one hears so much about. The sky would be blue, not a cloud, with the sun bursting through air that would be cool but not cold, and as crisp and clean as a spring morning on Mt. Washington. I would see her across the way, perhaps reading in the soft shade of a tree; and then she would glance up from her book and see me, as if it were preordained. Our eyes would meet, deep and soulful. A wave of joy would rush across her face, and as I ran to her she would run to me; and we would gather each other up under the full sun, and the years since Garfield Ridge would seem as nothing.

In reality Sacramento was cold and dusky. The sky was pale, washed out above a layer of brownish haze. The air smelled like a dusty attic. I sneezed all the way from the jetway to baggage claim, and then my sinuses stopped up completely. The sneezing subsided as I grabbed for my suitcase, but now my eyes were watering and I had a head full of gauze.

I should have been less impulsive in my planning. It had all seemed so reasonable a week ago, so driven with righteous resolve, but standing alone in front of the airport, in the hoary exhaust of busses and taxis, I felt so foolish and out of place that I almost turned around right then to go home. I couldn't come up with any kind of explanation for an early return, though. It was already going to be difficult to conceal the credit card charges and such. This is what kept me going, not the thought of Evelyn's caustic barbs or Jane's penetrating condescension, but a twinge of guilt and the humiliation of being caught in a lie.

I rented a car and drove down to Davis. I should have made it in twenty minutes or so, but I took the wrong exit and wound up crossing Sacramento to Interstate 80, which brought me in from the south instead of the north, and left me frazzled from the traffic and just the strange flatness of the place. I pulled into the easiest hotel I could reach from the interstate, then sat in the car quietly until the feverish tremors of that nerve-wracking drive subsided. It was earlier in the afternoon than it felt.

The sun looked like a tangerine through the haze, as if it were about to set. I took a room and fell onto the bed, and didn't wake until the next morning.

I began my search after eating a Denny's breakfast that didn't sit well in my stomach. Acid rose in my throat. I sighed a hot breath and gazed out the window. People were walking on the sidewalks, riding bikes. Cars stacked up at the lights. Everyone had a place to be, somewhere familiar to go. I didn't have a clue where to begin. It had seemed so clear in my fantasy, but now everything beyond the window looked too foreign to comprehend.

I went to the pay-phone nook to call Evelyn. This was something I figured I had better do a couple of times a day at least. I dropped a few quarters and punched our number. I got the answering machine. Evelyn was probably at the YMCA by then, wearing tights and with her hair in a ponytail, jumping and stretching to the routines in Jane Fonda's new workout book. I left a message, promised to call again later.

With no better idea in mind I walked the campus in the brown air. The campus was spread out like a suburb, divided by wide roads lined with palm and eucalyptus trees, interrupted here and there by arid open areas. Students sprinted purposefully across streets and up pathways. I followed a few, hoping they might lead me to a central place where I might be lucky enough to spy a glimpse of Willow, but invariably their paths ended at some mysterious angular building, classrooms I supposed. I couldn't summon the courage to follow them inside, for whatever good it would have done.

This went on until my stomach began to rumble for lunch. It must have taken another hour to find my way back to the car, and then even more time to work my way through the confusing traffic to the hotel. When I got there I was so tired I collapsed again, and didn't wake until late in the evening.

I ate dinner at Denny's. My stomach was settling down. I should have called Evelyn, but I wasn't up to it right then. I still couldn't breathe well. I felt tired and feverish—no, not tired but fatigued, as if I were recovering from the flu. I walked back to the hotel listlessly. The air was thick in the night, like a suffocating blanket of dust. The town really quieted down after dark.

I paused at the front desk before going up. There was a girl behind the desk, probably a student herself, propped on an elbow and reading a thick hardcover book. She wore a navy blue skirt and a white shirt with a frilly collar, the company uniform. She didn't wear the uniform well, as if she had been forced into it solely out of the necessity of holding a job. She was tall above the waist, so the tails of her shirt didn't quite tuck all the way, exposing some pale skin and a dotting of tiny moles. Her hair was jet black, draping her face like curtains drawn just enough to let in the light on a pert nose and high, white cheeks. Her lipstick was deep red, almost purple. She gave me a passing glance then returned to her reading, but as I stood there she looked up again with apathetic gray eyes.

"Yes? Can I help you?" she asked dispassionately.

"Uh, I'm trying to find someone. A girl."

She smiled at my accent, as a city person would at country manners.

"What's her name?" Her index finger stabbed at her place in the book. Her fingernails were painted the same color as her lips.

"I don't know," I said. She rolled her eyes. "I mean, I didn't get her name. She goes to the college."

"She goes to the *university*," she corrected me.

What's the difference? I thought sourly.

"Okay, then—*university*."

She closed her book with a thump, hitched her hips and folded her arms on the desk. "What's she studying?"

"I'm not sure." She rolled her eyes again. "She's a graduate student. A master's in the arts."

"That could be a lot of things. Did you check with administration?"

"Uh, no."

"Okay, look," she exhaled. She pulled a brochure from a cubby on her desk. "Here's a campus map. You can go to administration, but without a name they probably can't help you. If it was me…I'd probably hang out on the Quad. Everybody goes through sooner or later."

"Quad?"

"Here." She unfolded the map and pointed to a pair of large green rectangles toward the east side of the campus.

"East *and* west?" I asked.

"Either or," she said.

My face fell in disappointment. "It's big," I mumbled, studying the map and seeing my hopes dissolve among the serpentine paths and irregular buildings of that sprawling campus. She scrunched down so that she could see up into my eyes, so amused that she was getting color in her cheeks.

"Oh, man. You've got it bad, don't you? Maybe she doesn't *want* you to know who she is. Did you think of that? What did you do, pick her up at The Grad over on Russell Boulevard?"

The withering look I gave her wiped the smirk off of her face.

"No," I replied indignantly. "I picked her up on a mountain over in New Hampshire."

Her brows arched in surprise. "Really?"

"Really."

"That sounds so cool. So what, you two were, like, skiing and decided to do it in the snow?"

What she said may seem coarse, but the way she said it made it come out more as fascination than prurient gossip.

"No, it wasn't *like* that. We were hiking the Appalachian Trail."

"The what?"

I sighed. "It's a trail that goes from Maine to Georgia. We were hiking it."

"Seems like you had enough time to get her name then, right?"

"I did get her name."

Her brows hooded this time. "Then what's the deal?"

"It was her trail name." I could have been speaking Greek from the look on her face. "It's the names we hike with."

"How cool!" she exclaimed. "Like anonymous. I wish we had that here." She double-tapped her name badge. Her name was Paige. "So what was her name—her, uh, *trail* name?"

"Willow."

"Willow," she pondered. "That's awesome. What was yours?"

"Jake Brake."

"I don't get it," she said with a frown.

"You're not supposed to."

"Oh—well anyway, you've got your map, so good luck. And..." she leaned in closer, "...have you *been* to The Grad?"

Suddenly I could smell her, like herbs. Her face softened. I almost reached across to push the hair out of her eyes, but checked myself in time.

"I'm sorry, uh, Paige. I'm married." I flashed my ring and smiled forlornly.

"Oh man, you got problems," she said, stepping back.

"Yeah, I do," I agreed under my breath.

I went on up to my room and fell wearily on the bed. Heavy drapes shut out the brown night. A single bedside lamp cast a weak light that left the corners dark. It was only 10:00 p.m. I debated the telephone for a few minutes then picked it up to call Evelyn.

"Hello," I heard in a sleepy whisper.

"Evelyn," I said. "It's Carlton."

"Carlton," a pause, "it's so late. Is something wrong?"

"No, uh, no." I hadn't thought about the time difference at all. I felt like an idiot. "Uh, sorry. I just wanted to let you know I made it okay."

"I got your message. Why didn't you call me when you got there?"

"Uh, I was so tired...and, uh, they made me go to a meeting."

"Is everything all right?"

"Yeah."

"Good. Call me tomorrow then, okay?"

"Okay."

"Bye."

"Bye."

Subterfuge was something that I was going to learn perilously if I learned it at all. I had to be more careful.

* * *

I called Evelyn from the room before I went out the next morning. It was eight o'clock in California, ten o'clock back home, which should have been about right,

I thought, for the start of Evelyn's day. The telephone rang four times and then the machine picked up. Evelyn had recorded our message in an every-day voice, so I was thrown off for a moment when she came on the line.

"Evelyn, is that you?"

"Carlton, yes, sorry. I was just going out. How's New Orleans?"

"Oh, uh, it's fine." It could have been storming in New Orleans for all I knew, yet another potential trap. I needed to see if I could find a Sunday paper somewhere so I could check the weather report. "They gave us a break," I continued, "so I thought I'd call. How's everything at home?"

"Everything's fine, but I'm in a rush right now."

"Okay, sorry. Let me say hi to Tommy real quick before you go."

"Oh, Momma's keeping him for a couple of days."

"Jane has him? Why?"

"Just for a couple of days. It's no big deal."

"Okay. I'll call you tonight."

"That's fine. Bye."

"Bye."

It had been a hurried conversation, but I was relieved to have gotten through it without spilling anything. I went on to Denny's for breakfast, and to plan my day.

* * *

The east and west quads were actually a single broad park divided by a wide stone pathway that formed an airy, circular plaza in the middle. The grass was thick and green, and throughout were oaks and elms and varieties of evergreens that I couldn't identify, but which looked exotic compared to the pine and cedar we had back home. A few students lazed in the grass even though it really wasn't a pretty day. The haze subdued what would have been brilliant greens under a full sun. The breeze was cool. On a bright day the breeze would have been invigorating, but instead it was relentless and probing, leaching body heat like a swimming pool just a few degrees below optimum.

I walked the pathway from one end to the other, turned around to head back and realized that this activity had only consumed a few minutes of what could become a long, long day. It was as daunting as Ryan's tenure. I didn't belong here, that was obvious. Everyone, whether they were crossing the quad or studying in the grass, knew the rhythm of the place and moved in synchronization with that academic beat, while I lumbered back and forth, catching my toe in places, almost tripping. Most of them were dressed casually in hooded sweatshirts and shorts, a few in windbreakers and slacks. I wore jeans and a thick brown sweater, which set me even further apart from them.

After a while of this I sat on a bench beneath an evergreen with drooping limbs, as if it were weeping in the dull light. I wasn't catching stares. People were oblivious of me. I had carried a brown paper sack out of Denny's containing a BLT, a half dozen biscuits, and a coke in a styrofoam cup. I couldn't leave for lunch; knowing my luck that would be when she would come walking across the quad. I glanced at my watch. Only thirty minutes had passed. It was going to be a long day. I nibbled on a biscuit even though I wasn't hungry.

Every new person crossing the quad caught my attention. I followed their progress, even the guys for some reason. The people farther off were harder to make out. I should have brought my binoculars.

The morning warmed, although the light remained dull. The ice in my coke had melted. I couldn't bear sitting any longer, so got up and circumnavigated the quad, walking its gravel perimeter, straining my eyes with the constant searching. The traffic on the bordering roadways picked up during the lunch hour. Students began to mingle in the quad, clumps of them here and there, others crossing at a quicker pace. I couldn't take them all in, couldn't be done. And then I began to question myself: Would I even recognize her? Sure I could see her in my memory, her athletic form, khakis, a green sweater and a backpack; the fall of her hair and her sly grin— but here, in these surroundings, she wouldn't look the same. Suddenly I struggled to recall her face. Did I really remember her? Or did I remember what I *wanted* to remember of her?

It was as if I were hiking, my mind off on tangents, contemplating things that would never cross my mind otherwise. I turned a corner instinctively and headed west, a counter-clockwise transit of the quad. I saw blue sky and high ridges, and felt blasting gusts of clean wind. Then into the trees on the rocky trail, the sweet smell of spruce everywhere. I turned another corner and continued on. Spring water trickled between mossy rocks. A bull moose blended into the undergrowth so completely that only the snort of its breath gave it away.

I paused in mid step and looked around, disoriented. I slapped my forehead. I had been daydreaming my way around the quad, how many times I couldn't guess. Willow could have been walking right beside me for a time and I wouldn't have known it. It was well past lunch now. Traffic had thinned and fewer people were out. My stomach rumbled in complaint. I sighed and returned to the bench, ate my BLT and drank my watery coke. This was futile; futile. Defeated and demoralized, I gave up and left.

* * *

I again fell asleep when I got back to my room. Fatigue and disappointment, the shift in time zones and a stuffy nose all combined to wipe me out physically as well as mentally. When I awoke it was late evening, just like yesterday, only this time I didn't have the energy to get out of bed. I was eventually forced to rouse myself, though, because I was starving. A hot shower cleared my sinuses, but left my skin red and itchy. I never thought I would say it, but I missed southern humidity. I hesitated at the telephone. It was really too late to call Evelyn, so I vowed to catch her first thing in the morning.

I went downstairs to the lobby, heading for Denny's. Paige was behind the desk. She saw me as I came down, closed her book and smiled. Her hair was behind her ears now, and her lips were a natural pink. She looked prettier this way, younger than I had thought.

"Hey you," she said.

"Hey."

"How'd it go today?"

"Not very good." I frowned and angled toward the desk. "It's too big. She could have walked right by me and I wouldn't have known it."

"Aw, too bad. Do you think maybe you ought to just let it go?"

I rested an elbow on the desk. "I can't, Paige. I have to find her."

"Why? That is, I mean…since you're married." I could tell from the way she blushed that she wished she had that back. "I'm sorry," she demurred. "It's none of my business."

"It's okay."

That put her at ease.

"Do you mind—" she leaned forward on folded arms and lowered her voice, "—can I ask you, you know, why it's so important?"

I considered her for a moment. She seemed very earnest in her curiosity, as if we were close friends. This touched me in a way, that she cared enough to ask without seeming to pry. I puffed my cheeks. "We had a special time together," I said.

She leaned even closer. "Romantic, like?"

"Yeah, that and other things."

"What other things?"

"It was the trail, Paige. How can I explain it? When you're so free, I mean really free, and you don't care about anything but right now, and you don't think ahead any further than maybe where you're gonna sleep tonight. Nothing else is important, not a job, not school, not even if you've got enough food—you just don't care. And you can think so clearly. Everything makes sense."

"It sounds awesome," she sighed.

"It is," I sighed in return. "And then you meet someone who knows exactly how it feels; who knows exactly what *you're* feeling. And then…"

"And then?" she asked, pushing forward until our faces were very close. She must have sensed the change in my demeanor because her brows knitted.

"And then it's over," I said sullenly, "and no matter how hard you try you can't get it back."

"I've never felt anything like that," she said softly.

"You can't unless you've been there. So do you see why I need to find her?"

"Yeah. I think I get it."

"Well, anyway," I patted the desk, "I'm hungry. See ya."

"Wait a minute," she said quickly. "Listen. Try the DC tomorrow."

"The DC?"

"The dining commons. I mean, she has to eat, yeah?"

The cartoon image of the light bulb going off in your head is really true.

"Damn!" I snapped my fingers. "Sure! I never would have thought of it. Thanks!" Without thinking, I leaned over and kissed her on the forehead. She batted her eyes and smiled bashfully, like a teenager on a first date.

"Good luck," she waved as I headed for the door. "Tell me what happens."

* * *

I woke up very early the next morning, the third since I had arrived in Davis. I felt unexpectedly well, with the energy to leap out of bed and the enthusiasm to get on with the day. I went to the windows and parted the curtains. The pre-dawn dark as yet hid the haze, revealed only by the rosy haloes around the street lights. My sinuses had miraculously cleared overnight, and I was able to take my first free and full breaths of California. I cranked the window open and inhaled deeply. The air outside smelled like dirty socks, like a shelter full of sweaty thru-hikers. I wrinkled my nose and closed the window.

It was a little after 5:00 a.m. I went straight to the telephone to call Evelyn, but only got the machine, which was strange. It wasn't like her to leave the apartment so early. I shrugged and left a message, then jumped in the shower. I felt a lively optimism about the day, so much that I caught myself humming a Supremes tune as the hot shower ran over me. I laughed and dried myself, feeling prickly and clean. I threw on jeans, a white T-shirt and a navy-blue windbreaker, checked myself in the foggy mirror, ran my fingers through my hair like a comb then headed out.

The dining commons was clear across campus from the quads. I spent quite a bit of time navigating through the murky morning, but still got there too early. I found a parking place with a clear line of sight to the front doors, then sat back to wait.

The morning assembled itself as if through time-lapse photography. The odd car would scoot by. A lone male student, looking disheveled and sleepy, rounded a corner and continued on. The murk became a brighter gray. Branches shimmied in the breeze. Another male student on a bicycle coasted up and locked his bike in the rack. He leaned against the glass doors and read a book while he waited. And then another student arrived, and a few more, some of them girls. I sat up straight and studied them. No, Willow wasn't among them. The students loitered around the doors, some reading alone, some talking. I could catch snippets of conversation. Someone had a cigarette going. The harsh smell wafted across on the breeze. At exactly 7:00 a.m. a youngish guy in a white apron unlocked the door from the inside and awkwardly held it open while the students filed in, and he was still holding the door as I sprinted in behind them.

The dining commons was a cafeteria setting, with stainless steel tubs of food under heat lamps, and black plastic trays that you slid along a rail. My only work experience was in the grocery business, but I discerned an ebb and flow to food service that wasn't at all dissimilar to what I knew at the store. First were the early risers, those students who had been loitering around the doors, still groggy in the wee hours, in dire need of coffee and a donut. Later came the mid rush, coffee and some juice, pastries, preferably with sausage or egg inside. Then came the full-on breakfast crowd, scrambled eggs and bacon, with toast or an English muffin, orange juice to wash it down, and of course coffee.

I sat at a round Formica table in a far corner and watched all of this. I watched for Willow. Sometimes I would spot a girl in the serving line, a girl about the right height and with long, light brown hair, and I would stand in anticipation only to be disappointed when she turned around and revealed her face. I was on my third cup of coffee and second English muffin when the breakfast rush began. The place filled up quickly, hollow echoes replaced by a cacophony of chatter and clinking silverware. Some students sat at my table but didn't make conversation with me. They ate quickly, talked with one another about their classes and professors. One girl confessed to her friend that she'd had sex last night. Her friend giggled and fished for details, then glanced at me and lowered her voice. I looked away and pretended that I hadn't heard anything.

By 10:00 a.m. the place had cleared out. I nursed my coffee and perused a Sacramento Bee that I'd found lying on a chair. Funny name for a newspaper. The staff were wiping down tables and changing over the buffet line for lunch service. I was beginning to feel conspicuous. The guy in the white apron was looking at me suspiciously. I went to the restroom, then outside to stretch my legs. I walked with my hands in my pockets, no destination in mind. The weather was the same as yesterday and the day before that, hazy, cool, uninspiring. I grew despondent about my chances. If I didn't find her today, then what next?

I waited for a few people to go in for the lunch service before I went in myself, not wanting to attract any more attention if I could help it. I was feeling self-conscious about being there, as if I were trespassing somewhere that I didn't belong. Well, I didn't belong at UC Davis but I didn't think I was doing anything wrong. I just didn't want to have to answer any questions, to watch eyes roll as I tried to explain about Willow and the Appalachian Trail. I returned to my table in the corner. I wasn't hungry. That copy of the Sacramento Bee had been whisked away by one of the staff. I should have held onto it. I laced my fingers, waited and watched.

By noon the place was packed, just like the breakfast rush only now the food was different. I went through the line, bought a grilled cheese sandwich and a coke. The students at my table had held my place for me, which was a good thing because there was nowhere else to sit now. I chewed my sandwich and contemplated the lunch crowd. I scanned every face, ducking this way and that to see around people. Willow wasn't there. I finished my sandwich, laced my fingers, waited and watched.

The place began to empty after one o'clock, students leaving in ones and twos and occasionally in small groups. The cacophony dissipated. Voices were lowered in response. I studied the few people remaining, maybe a dozen of them in all, scattered throughout the dining area. There were only a couple of loners like myself, absently eating while they studied their books. One was a girl I could only see in a partial profile, a cheek, the point of her nose. She wore straight-legged jeans and brown suede walking shoes, and a medium blue sweatshirt with a gold UC Davis logo. She was absorbed in her book. She held a half-eaten sandwich in her left hand. She had long, delicate fingers.

I looked around at the others. There was another girl across the way, also wearing a UC Davis sweatshirt, but shorts rather than pants. I could see her full face. She wasn't Willow. I came back around to the girl with the sandwich and my mind idled, my eyes staring but vacant. They actually ached now from the strain of all the searching, the constant alertness. I was getting tired. I could have used a nap.

The girl glanced over at me then returned to her book. I barely noticed. She glanced at me again and seemed to frown, adjusted her shoulders and resumed her reading. After a moment she set her sandwich down and exhaled loudly enough for me to hear, then turned my way with a scalding look of annoyance.

"Do you have a problem?" she demanded loudly.

"Huh?" I snapped out of it and focused on her with difficulty.

"I said do you have a problem?"

I could see the others turning my way, accusation in their eyes. I didn't belong here. They knew it; they could tell. The girl screeched back her chair and stormed over, stood looking down on me with her hands on her hips. She was tall. She had long brown hair tied back with little braids. She looked like a girl who could take care of herself. She resembled Willow in many ways, but the girl I remembered from New Hampshire couldn't have an expression as severe as this one, or a tone as hostile. She had me cornered, otherwise I would have bolted.

"Uh, I'm—" I stammered.

"Why are you staring at me? I don't know you."

"Uh, look—"

"No, *you* look. Cut it out. I mean it."

"Well, uh—"

"I'm serious."

I was embarrassed; as a matter of fact, I was mortified. They were all staring at me now, even the kitchen staff from behind the serving line. But regardless of that I was also getting angry. I hadn't done anything, and this girl had no right to berate me in front of all these people. I rose to my feet and fixed her with my own contemptuous look.

"You really have a habit of cuttin' people off," I growled self-righteously. "Did you know that? Let me finish. Okay?"

She inhaled sharply. She had wide brown eyes, but they were almost round now in shock. There was something about them, something that… My eyes filled when I realized it.

"*Jake?*" she said shakily. "Is it you? Oh my God, it is! You look so…different. But your accent—"

"*Willow.*" I hastily wiped my eyes. "I was looking right at you and I couldn't tell."

Jaws were hanging open throughout the dining area. The guy with the white apron had been heading our way, but he had pulled up short at Willow's reaction, and now he was frozen in place, gawking like the rest.

Willow looked around uneasily. "What are you *doing* here?" she asked.

"I've been looking for you."

"*Looking* for me? Why?"

I slumped into my chair and hid my face in my hands. Everyone was still staring. The guy in the apron hadn't moved a step. I wasn't willing to explain any of it in front of an audience. I wiped my nose on a sleeve and looked up at Willow. I couldn't read her expression, be it anger or surprise or both.

"Can we go somewhere?" I asked. "Somewhere private."

She glanced around the dining area, at all those staring eyes, and then she flicked a glance at her watch.

"I have a class, Jake. Walk with me, okay?"

"Sure."

She gathered up her books and we got out of there.

We walked in subdued silence, following a maze of paths between buildings and across rectangular lots, some green like the quads, others worn like playing fields. I wasn't sure that I would be able to find my way back. Willow walked at a hurried pace, clutching her books to her chest. I skipped to keep up.

"Where are we going?" I asked at last.

"Voorhies Hall," she answered. "It's not far."

"Are you in a hurry?"

She pulled up then and turned to me. She smiled tightly.

"No, I guess not. Sorry."

I tried to see into her eyes, to see if Garfield Ridge was still there, but she looked away. We resumed our walk, slower now.

"Are you okay?" I asked her. "What's wrong?"

"Nothing's wrong, Jake. It's just a shock, you know?"

"It's not the way I thought it would be," I mumbled, mostly to myself. She turned smartly and stood face to face with me. She looked angry.

"What's not the way you thought it would be?"

"Uh, you. Us."

"*Us?* There is no *us*, Jake."

"But—"

"That was more than five years ago."

"I know, but—"

"What did you think? That you could just show up after all these years and everything would be like it was?"

"No, I didn't. I—"

"We only knew each other for a few days. It was nice, sure, but it was only a few days. And it was a long time ago."

"But Willow, I thought—"

"How did you find me, anyway?" she asked accusingly

"My brother-in-law is a professor at Dartmouth. He met you last fall." She glanced at the ring on my finger, seemed to notice it for the first time.

"I see," she said flatly.

"No, Willow, let me explain—" but she had already turned her back on me and was walking away. "I'm sorry, Willow," I said after her. "I'm sorry."

I had seen the best of me dissolve in the face of a stranger. I thrust my hands in my pockets and hung my head. Willow rounded a corner and was gone.

* * *

My dilemma was that it was Wednesday and my flight out wasn't until Saturday afternoon. There was nothing I could do now except torment myself, replaying that look on Willow's face over and over, futilely trying to reconcile it with the Willow I remembered from New Hampshire. The prospect of three days of this, all alone in that hotel room, filled me with dread. But if I took an earlier flight Evelyn would become curious. I wished that I had just told her the truth, that I was coming out to see an old friend—well, maybe not a friend anymore but at least an acquaintance. She would have whined, but it wouldn't have been the first time. As it was, I had trapped myself with the New Orleans story. I called her and got the machine, so I left a message. I might be able to get out early, I said. I'd call again when I knew more.

I spent the remainder of that day in my room with HBO on in the background. This would have been a novelty if my eyes hadn't been so strained, because we couldn't get HBO at home yet. I dozed for a while, woke up to a Paul Newman movie on the television, dozed some more, woke up and now it was a boxing match. I didn't care for boxing. Still don't. I rolled over listlessly and closed my eyes. Soon I was dozing again.

When I awoke after that, the room was dark except for the silver glow of the television. Paul Newman was back on the screen, and Sally Field. It was quiet beyond the windows. It felt late, early morning even. I groaned and checked the time. It was only a little after seven o'clock in the evening, but in my sleep-addled mind I thought it was seven o'clock the next morning! I got up with a start and scrambled for the telephone, trying to think of what to say to Evelyn about missing my call last night, but I came to as I fumbled with the receiver, realized that it was still Wednesday evening, and sighed in relief. I felt weary to my bones, but at least my eyes were better. I took a shower then headed downstairs for dinner.

As soon as I entered the lobby I saw Willow. She was at the desk talking to Paige. Both of them looked up as I walked in. Paige had her arms folded on the desk, leaning in close to Willow. She seemed to be relishing some female insight, some sisterly confidences. Her eyes glittered in amusement. Willow was more taciturn. She neither smiled nor frowned, but stood erect with her hands at her sides. She was wearing a blue gingham dress, with calf-high boots and an aged bomber jacket.

"Willow!" I exclaimed.

"Jake." She tipped her head at Paige. "Or should I say *Carlton*? Or maybe *Carl*."

"Definitely not Carl," I said with a grumble, "and from you I think I prefer Jake." I sauntered over. "How did you *find* me?"

"You see?" she said, and now she was grinning—well, at least a little smile. "It's disconcerting, isn't it, to show up unexpected? But tracking down a guy with a southern accent in a hotel near campus isn't hard."

"It's totally awesome, Mr. Jeffries," Paige interjected with excitement. "Judith knows my brother. Can you believe it?"

"Judith?" I looked at Willow.

"From you I think I prefer Willow," she said, and her smile lifted a bit more.

"This is so cool," gushed Paige.

"Are you going out?" Willow asked.

"Yeah. Denny's."

"*Denny's?*" she asked in disbelief or disappointment, one. "Okay then," she sighed. "Mind if I come?"

"Sure. Why not?"

Paige watched us leave. She had a fairy-tale look on her face, a dreamy girlishness that betrayed her otherwise Gothic persona.

It was a short walk across the parking lot to Denny's. We took it in silence. Before this afternoon I would have been gushing with questions, but I was an intruder now, a stalker even. Garfield Ridge was a dream; just a dream, nothing more.

We were seated in a regular booth with a view out the front toward Interstate 80, headlights glaring in the fog.

"It's really foggy here," I commented, just to break the uncomfortable silence.

"It's pretty in the spring and early summer," she said. "August is hot and September is dusty. You get used to it."

"How long have you been here?"

"Off and on since Dartmouth. This is my last semester."

"Oh."

I fiddled with my hands, tried to find something to look at on the table. I picked up a menu even though I already knew what I wanted to order.

"So your name's Judith," I said.

"Yeah. Judith Taylor."

"I thought—"

"What?"

"I don't know. I thought you would be a Rebecca or a Carolyn."

"Well, I never could have guessed that you would be a Carlton," she said sharply.

"No," I said sheepishly. "Judith's nice."

Our waitress came then, thank God. She brought coffee and poured me a cup. I ordered chicken fried steak. Willow ordered tea, and not sweet tea, either. They didn't have that out here. I sipped my coffee. Willow was gazing absently out the window.

"So," I said. "You went back and hiked more?"

"Yeah." She seemed to light up a little. "I did the Hundred-Mile Wilderness after Dartmouth, and then the next summer I did Kinsman to Sherburne Pass."

"That's what Ryan said. His family is from there."

"His family? Hey, I remember him now! He was at the symposium. Can you imagine living right there and never hiking the trail at all?"

"No, I can't. It's nuts."

"Yeah, if people only knew what they were missing."

"That's what I keep saying."

"You, too?" She looked at me for the first time with a hint of the earnest expression I remembered.

"All the time."

I smiled fondly then. The pressure eased in my chest. I hadn't realized until then how wound up I was.

"So," she went on. "This Ryan is your brother-in-law?"

"Ryan is my sister's boyfriend," I explained. "They've been together so long that I think of them as being married."

"Oh."

Her eyes drifted back to the window. So there it was, time to explain.

"I was going to go back," I said to my hands. She turned to me.

"But you got married instead."

"Yeah. And I have a son, Tommy."

"You have a little boy?" she asked in surprise, not angry, just—surprised. "How old is he?"

"He just turned five."

"*Five?* Wow. You must have gotten busy as soon as you got off the trail."

Now I could detect some hurt in her eyes, but she kept her voice level and her face under control. She seemed annoyed that she had betrayed even that much. She sat back and regarded me in a business-like way.

"No," I said, "that's not how it happened."

"It's none of my business, Jake."

"But I want to explain—"

"You don't need to. It doesn't matter anymore."

"I think it does."

The waitress came with Willow's tea. Willow took a sip then set it aside.

"I dated a girl in high school," I heard myself saying, as if I were listening in from another booth. "It was prom night—"

"Jake. Really, I don't need to hear this."

"—I didn't know," I went on from a distance. "I finished the trail on my birthday. I was in Georgia, and I was thinking, yeah, I can go straight up to Dartmouth. But I looked like hell, and I smelled bad, and I thought, no, I'll go home first. Get cleaned up, you know? And that's when I found out. It was too late to do anything."

"Jake…"

"I wanted to come. I really did."

Willow's eyes glistened. She blinked and looked away.

"Well," she said to the window. "I'm glad I know now, then."

I kept wanting to reach out, to touch her or hold her hand, but it didn't seem right.

"What about you?" I asked. I tapped my ring finger on the table. She looked at my finger with curious detachment.

"I have someone," she said.

"Oh. But not—"

"Married?" She chuckled at that. "No, I'm not married."

Our waitress brought out my dinner. I arranged my silverware, suddenly not hungry. Willow sat back and took a sip of her tea. I laughed.

"What's so funny?" she asked.

"I was just thinking—" I laughed again, "—I ordered this same exact thing at a Denny's outside of Harpers Ferry, and I ate it in—I think—two bites. Then I ordered another one. I was so hungry. But now I'm really not hungry at all."

"How was it?" she asked, leaning in on her arms.

"The chicken fried steak?"

"No, Jake," she smiled, "the hike."

"After Kinsman?"

"Yeah."

"Oh, Willow," I pushed my plate aside, "it was everything."

"Tell me."

"Oh, man. There's so much. I met some northbounders. Crazy people. And then I was alone for…forever it felt like. But it was okay. New York was hot. The air smelled like…well, it smelled like this place." I smiled at the memory. "The rocks in Pennsylvania are as bad as they say, and I thought I would never get out of Virginia. But Virginia was awesome. Lots of poison ivy, though. And the Smokies…the weather was the worst, but I got through it. I was thinking about you. It seemed like years had gone by."

She slid her hand across the table to rest on mine, I think without realizing it, but then when I took her hand and held it she didn't pull away. There was something of New Hampshire in her face now, and it lightened my heart.

"I wish I had been there with you," she said dreamily. "Do you ever think about going back?"

"Every day," I said. "Every day."

"Yeah," she nodded. "Me, too."

"We should do it."

"Oh, Jake…" Her eyes hooded but she squeezed my hand and gave me a sad smile. "I think that was our one special time. What did Bogart say to Ingrid Bergman—?" She grinned for real then, lifting the melancholy out of her eyes. It warmed me. It brought me back. "— that we'll always have Garfield Ridge."

I laughed and slapped the table, but then my eyes settled on hers and something passed between us, something as real as the thunder and the rain and the lightening crashing beyond the trees.

"Can I kiss you?" I asked. "Just once?"

"Yes," she breathed, and I leaned across and kissed her on the lips.

A charge of life shot through me, memories as present as if it were yesterday. I leaned back to catch my breath, and Willow did the same. We watched one another across the table, smiling and remembering, and in those moments I was happier than I remembered being in what felt like forever. But then her smile dissolved into a thoughtful pursing of her lips.

"I'd better go now, Jake."

"What?"

Our waitress appeared with the check. Willow gestured for a pen, then scribbled on a napkin.

"I hope I see you again," she said, sliding the napkin toward me. "Someday."

She got up without another word and hurried out the doors, while I sat frozen in place, holding back tears. I lifted the napkin and read what she'd written. It was a telephone number, and an address in a town called Oakhurst; and under that a note: *You know where to find me*. Willow sure loved to make enigmatic exits. I had to chuckle at that, although sadly. I folded the napkin and shoved it into my back pocket.

THIRTEEN

I took a flight out at ten o'clock the next morning, but with the time difference I didn't get to Nashville until five in the afternoon. I called Kenny for a ride home but got a screeching *service-disconnected* message. That was odd. Did Kenny forget to pay his bill? So I called Evelyn, but got the machine. I sighed, weary from the flight, then went out front and hailed a taxi. It was cold outside, in the 30s with a ripping wind, quite an abrupt change from central California but at least the air was clean.

I came home to a dark apartment, not even a table lamp on. I dropped my suitcase in the doorway and went around flipping on lights. I wanted nothing more than a shower and to lie down for a while, but Evelyn wasn't home and that, too, was odd. There were messages on the machine. I rewound the tape and listened to my voice from far away California. All the messages were from me, going back to Tuesday night. Had something happened? I punched Jane's number urgently, and as her telephone rang it occurred to me that if something *had* happened then they would have called Mr. Iverson looking for me. I would be caught. I braced myself.

"Hello?"

"Hello, Jane?"

"Yes. Carlton, what a surprise. How's New Orleans?"

"I'm at home now."

"*What?* We weren't expecting you till Saturday." There was a timorous note in Jane's voice.

"I got home early. Where's Evelyn. Is everything all right?"

"Yes, everything's fine. Evelyn…uh, Evelyn went out with some girlfriends."

"Went out? Where?"

"I don't know, Carlton. She didn't say."

"Then where's Tommy?"

"Tom is here with us."

It was strange all around. When had I last spoken with Evelyn? It was Tuesday morning. She had been gone for two nights. Tonight would make the third.

"Well, okay then," I said in confusion. "I'll be right over to get him."

"There's no need, Carlton. He's perfectly fine with *me*."

Something in her tone put me off, as if Tommy were only mine on loan.

"He's fine with *me*," I said hotly. "I'll be right over," and I slammed the phone.

I didn't even glance up the hill, just went straight to the Hanshaw's door and pounded on it impatiently. Jane answered with a subdued look on her face. She was positioned in the door as if blocking my way. My brows dipped in further confusion.

"Jane, is everything all right?"

"Yes," she answered, and not another word.

I blinked in incomprehension, opened my mouth to speak but nothing came out. Finally: "Where's Tommy?"

"Hi, Daddy."

Tommy rambled up to the door and I exhaled in relief. I don't know what I thought was going on, but seeing Tommy safe and sound eased the tension in my shoulders and neck just like that.

"Hi, Tommy. Time to go home."

"Okay," he said, and he squeezed past Jane to take my hand. Holding his hand, having Tommy with me, seemed to give me strength and reassurance. I had never felt so vulnerable about him before. It was a disturbing feeling.

"So…Jane?" I asked firmly. "Do you know when Evelyn will be home?"

"Mommy's on vacation, Daddy," Tommy offered innocently. Jane winced. I smiled and lifted Tommy onto my shoulder. He was really getting too heavy to carry that way. When had that happened?

"I suppose tomorrow," Jane said tartly.

"Okeydoke," I said with a sigh, and I took Tommy home.

* * *

Evelyn showed up in the morning, after Tommy and I had finished our break-fasts and I'd had my shower. I could have used a shave, too, but I left the stubble. I liked the rakish look it gave me, masquerading as confidence. I saw her pull up outside, so I sent Tommy to his room and sat stiffly in my armchair to wait. It was even colder than yesterday, with a slate sky that threatened snow. Evelyn shivered up the stairs, hugging herself against the chill. I could see her out the window. She had her fluffy angora sweater on over a short pink skirt and white platform shoes. Her hair was done up on top, held in place with pink plastic barrettes. A few wisps had come loose, as if she had put her hair up in a hurry. I wondered if she realized that she looked like a hooker.

She saw me through the window as she came to the door. She had an impassive look, and when she came in it was as nonchalantly as if she were home from the YMCA.

"Carlton," she said immediately, rubbing her arms as she closed the door with her hip. "You're home early."

"Somehow I think you are, too."

"I don't know what you mean."

She went about her business as if it were a normal morning, dropping her purse, slipping out of her sweater and heading for the kitchen, all while managing to avoid eye contact with me.

"Where's Tom?" she asked over her shoulder.

"He's in his room. Where have you been?"

She froze in her tracks, her back to me. Her shoulders rose and fell with a deep breath.

"I've been with some friends," she admitted. She made a play of adjusting some plastic flowers on the dinner table.

"You've been with some friends, *where?*"

She turned on me then with a look of righteous indignation. The wisps of hair in her face seemed to punctuate her anger. She put her hands on her hips and glared at me.

"I've been in Jacksonville, okay?"

"*Florida?*"

"Yeah. And it's nice there. It's warm. I deserve a vacation, too."

"But why didn't you tell me?" I was still in my chair, squeezing the armrests.

"Because I didn't want this."

"This what?"

"*This,*" she waved her hand as if it were self-evident, "what we're doing."

"But you could have…" I was about to say that she could have met up with me in New Orleans. The absurdity of that notion was late in coming. I lowered my eyes. "Well," I went on after that pause, "you still should have told me."

"It was a last minute thing, Carlton. And I didn't know how to reach you. You didn't leave a number."

She was right—she was right all the way, or else she had thought it through very well. I had nothing to be angry about. And yet…something didn't add up. I couldn't put my finger on it.

"Okay, then," I conceded, but she was still staring me down.

"Why are you home early?" she demanded, and if anything she was getting even redder in the face.

"Uh," I looked away, "they finished everything sooner than they expected, so they sent us home."

"And?"

"And nothing."

"So when do you get your promotion?"

"They haven't said yet, Evelyn." I got up and went to Tommy's door. "I'd better check on Tommy."

That ended that, thankfully.

* * *

On the first really nice Saturday in March, which was toward the end of the month as I recall, I drove Tommy to Smith County to see the Carlton cemetery. It was a superb day, warm and clear. We drove out Highway 70, past the horse farms and the white fences. I had the windows down, not only for the clean country air but to flush the reek of burning oil out of the car. We creaked along in the Pontiac, rolling in the dips and topping with a clunk on the rises. The car still looked okay, but it was a lumbering beast compared to the small foreign jobs that buzzed around us in the passing zones. It was well past time for me to buy a new car—and I could have afforded it—but I had become attached to that old white Catalina.

Tommy bounced impatiently in his seat, stretching up high to see over the hood on the hills. Soon the novelty wore off and he fell asleep. At the Carlton cemetery, it was warm enough in the sun to break sweat out on my forehead. I gathered Tommy in my arms and stood him groggily on his feet. He rubbed his eyes and took my hand, and together we went through the gate to visit the past.

I showed Tommy where Mama and Pappy Jeffries were buried, and then Uncle Lou Carlton.

"This was your grandpa's favorite uncle," I told Tommy soberly.

"I don't have a uncle," he commented in his small voice. I clenched my eyes at that.

"Yes you do," I said. "Right over here is your Uncle Leavitt, and this here is your Aunt Elizabeth."

"I never saw 'em," he said, looking up at me emptily.

I knelt and held Tommy by his shoulders. "They died a long time before you were born."

Tommy shrugged. "Why did they died?"

"They had accidents, Tommy. Just accidents." He looked down at his feet and kicked the grass.

"Daddy, I wanna go do something," he whined, tugging at my hand.

"Okay. Okay," I sighed. "Let's go see Grandmother."

He brightened at that, tugging me harder toward the car. "Hurry, Daddy. C'mon."

Tommy loved Grandmother Villetta. She gave him candy.

* * *

Grandmother Villetta met us at the back door to the kitchen.

"Well," she said in her pleased country voice. "Look how big that boy is."

"Hi, Grandmother." I gave her a kiss on the cheek. She knelt stiffly and smiled at Tommy.

"I bet you'd like a little candy," she said.

"Yes'm," Tommy nodded eagerly.

"Yes, *please*," I corrected.

"Yes please," he repeated shyly.

Grandmother smiled warmly and patted Tommy's head with a leathery hand that still had some strength in it.

"Sit on the porch, Carlton. It's such a fine day. I'll be back in a minute with a treat."

Grandmother Villetta shuffled into the kitchen, letting the screen door slam. Lately it seemed that she was shrinking, but it was just her back. She walked hunched over now, with a prominent curve to her spine. She hadn't been able to wear her corsets for a few years, but otherwise she still dressed like a proper Victorian lady.

We sat in the rockers at the south end of the porch, in the streaked shade of century-old maples just becoming green with the season. Grandmother returned with a glass of sweet tea for me and a Tootsie Roll for Tommy. Those were his favorite. Tommy accepted the candy enthusiastically and gnawed on it like a puppy to a bone. Soon his lips would be smeared with chocolate slobber and his hands would be a slimy mess. Evelyn would not have approved.

"It's good to see you, Tommy," Grandmother said, bending even farther to squeeze his leg.

"Me, too, Grandmother," Tommy said in return, working through every syllable of *Grand-moth-er* when his instinct was to say *Grammaw*. She had taught him early on.

"You never gave me Tootsie Rolls," I remarked fondly.

"That's because you liked cooked apples, boy. It's best not to have too many sweets."

"I do like cooked apples," I said, batting my eyes her way.

"There's no more apples in the root cellar. Used 'em all up this winter. Next time you come, bring some from your store and I'll fix 'em up for you."

"I'll do that," I said.

Grandmother dropped into her rocker with an *umph*. She broke off a piece of Tootsie Roll and popped it discreetly into her mouth, as if to hide an unladylike indulgence. Tootsie Rolls were her favorite, too. "These old bones," she mused, worrying that chocolate nugget under her tongue like a lozenge. "I never thought I'd see the day."

"What's that, Grandmother?"

"Ninety-one years old, Carlton. Ninety-two in a month or so. Never thought I'd see it. Don't know that I'll make ninety-three, though."

Grandmother Villetta wasn't speaking fatally, but reflectively. It had never been her way to whine, which is one of the reasons all her grandchildren—and now great-grandchildren—loved being around her. And she didn't preach. Still, this kind of talk disquieted me.

"Aw, Grandmother," I said. "You'll still be cookin' apples in the twenty-first century."

Grandmother smiled. "Knowin' two centuries is enough for any person, Carlton. I'd be too old to get along in a third."

"How old will I be in the twenty-first century, Daddy?" Tommy asked with boyish wonder.

"You'll be twenty-two, Tommy. Almost twenty-three like me."

Tommy's eyes widened in incredulity.

"I'll be so *old*," he said with a look of childish cleverness that made Grandmother and me laugh.

"Yep," I said. "We'll have to call you Old Man Tom."

"Nuh, uh," he objected, and we laughed some more.

After that we sat in silence for a while, watching a pair of mockingbirds dance in the yard. A lone cardinal in bright red stood out in the naked limbs of a crepe myrtle. Frogs were croaking their spring serenade along the creek. Grandmother sucked the last of her Tootsie Roll and licked her teeth. Tommy sat on the edge of the porch, kicking his legs, biting off chewy pieces of chocolate as if it were jerky.

"How is Evelyn?" Grandmother asked apropos of nothing.

"She's…" I hesitated before going on. "Well, she's—"

Grandmother must have picked up on the ambivalence in my voice. "Hold your tongue, Carlton," she said. "Little ears, even ears as sweet as these," she reached over and tousled Tommy's hair, "have big mouths." And then to Tommy, "Boy, a hen's got out yonder. See it?"

"Uh, huh," Tommy nodded. The chicken coop sat against the barn across that broad expanse of yard.

"Why don't you go round her up for me. Could you do that?"

"Yes, Grandmother."

Tommy crammed the remaining half of his Tootsie Roll into his mouth, wiped his sticky hands on his shorts and hurried off, chewing hard all the way.

"That'll keep him busy for a while," Grandmother said. "Now, what troubles you, Carlton?"

"Oh, I don't know."

"Evelyn's a handful, isn't she?" Grandmother said this mirthfully, but her face belied no trace of amusement.

I sighed. "Yeah, she is."

"What's it now?"

"It's the same. Some days are okay, some are worse. More worse lately. I didn't know it would be so hard."

Grandmother chuckled. "Farmer said that to me once. Said I was harder to handle than a heifer in a muddy pond. And you know what I told him?"

"No," I said, shaking my head but smiling at the imagery.

"I told him 'Tough. You married me, so get in here and get muddy.'"

Grandmother's eyes gleamed, and a touch of inside amusement curled her wrinkled lips. I laughed.

"And what did he say then?"

"He said he'd rather not as the water tank was empty and he wouldn't be able to wash up afterward."

She pondered that, taking on that faraway look of hers. I thought that she must be so lonely, living by herself, everyone gone now. Out in the yard, Tommy was bent over with his hands out, chasing that chicken in circles and shrieking with laughter.

"Tommy," Grandmother suddenly hollered. "Go get you some seed out of that bag there and throw it on the ground. She'll come then." Grandmother patted my leg, the way she did when I was a boy. "Thing is, Carlton, you married her, and you have this child to think of. Maybe it's time to get muddy."

I nodded in thought. I guess there were a lot of ways I could have taken that, but I think she meant that it was time for me to put my foot down. Tommy came up then with the hen in his arms, beaming as proudly as if he had wrestled a bear to the ground.

"I knew you could do it, boy," Grandmother said.

* * *

Evelyn was acting strange, outwardly no different than usual, but she gave me these furtive glances, and sometimes, if I walked in when she was on the telephone, she would suddenly lower her voice and hang up; and Jane became so placidly polite to me that it was unsettling. I began to snoop around without consciously realizing that I was doing it. I searched Evelyn's purse while she was in the bath, I went through her clothes drawers. I found nothing out of the ordinary, not that I really knew what I was looking for.

What I also didn't know at the time was that while I was snooping on Evelyn she was snooping on me. It was a call from Gracie, I think, that set it off. It was just after tax day, a wet Friday night. I had wanted to go out, but Evelyn wasn't in the mood; actually hadn't been in the mood for a while now. She was lying on the sofa, reading a People magazine. Tommy was in bed. I was in my armchair watching a Dallas re-run on the television. J.R.'s guys were trying to take John Ross from Sue Ellen at the airport. When the telephone rang I let Evelyn answer it. She always did, anyway.

"*Hello?*" I heard. A pause. "*What do you want?*" The receiver clattered on the table. "*Carlton, it's for you.*"

Evelyn walked past me as stiffly as a mannequin and flopped onto the sofa. She didn't pick up her magazine, though. I could tell that, even though she seemed to be watching television, her ears were tuned.

I picked up the receiver curiously. "Hello?"

"Hello, Carlton. It's Gracie."

"Gracie?" This was a surprise. I hadn't heard from her in more than five years, and now it was twice in just a couple of months. "Gracie, what a surprise," I said. "What's going on?"

"Have you seen Kenny?" she asked.

"Kenny? No, not since I went to Ca—to New Orleans. Why?"

"His mom called. They've been looking for him."

"Did you call him at home?"

"I tried. His phone's been disconnected."

"Still?"

"What do you mean, *still*?"

"I tried to call him at the end of February and his phone was disconnected then, too."

"Oh my God. Since *February*?"

"Gracie, what is it?"

"I don't know. His mother is worried to death."

"What about at work? Did you call him there?"

"Carlton, I thought you and Kenny were friends."

"We are!"

"Well he got fired the day after New Year's."

"What! He didn't tell me."

"I guess he didn't tell his mom either."

"Man, Gracie. I don't know what's going on."

"Help us look for him then, would you?"

"Yeah. Sure."

"Okay, Carlton. Bye."

"Bye."

I hung up the telephone and returned to my chair, deeply troubled.

"What was that all about?" Evelyn asked.

"Nobody knows where Kenny is. His mom's worried."

"So they got Gracie to call you? Why would they do that?"

Evelyn's face was pointed and hard. I knew the look.

"Oh, for Christ's sake, Evelyn. The Quinterras and Batistas are friends."

"So what? Gracie doesn't hang around with Kenny."

"I don't know, Evelyn."

I sat down in a huff. Evelyn jerked her magazine up and noisily flipped a page. I ignored her. I was worried about Kenny. Where was he? What was he doing?"

* * *

I didn't usually go out back of the store, but our dairy manager had called in sick that morning so receiving the milk and eggs was left to me. It was the Monday after Gracie's call, not a pretty day. The sky was threatening, and a steady wind brought an unwelcome chill. The dairy trailer was already backed up to the dock when I showed up in the receiving room. The driver was a big, imposing guy with a gut that hid his belt, but he was good natured and talkative. He sat on some stacked boxes of canned tomatoes in the receiving room, rattling off stories about everything in the world he had done in his life, including some bawdy things I would rather have not heard. I sighed and got to work.

I had the trailer unloaded in about half an hour. The driver slapped me on the back hard enough to knock my teeth together, but he meant this as a friendly gesture. He angled himself sideways through the personnel door and then he waddled down the steps to his tractor. In a moment the tractor rumbled to life and a waft of oily diesel exhaust filtered into the receiving room. I wrinkled my nose and waved a hand in front of my face. A sliver of gray morning widened as the trailer pulled away from the dock. I was about to pull the receiving door down when I caught sight of a van parked between a trash dumpster and a storage container across the receiving alley.

"*Kenny?*"

There was a large dent in the driver's side, and the rear door windows were covered with cardboard and duct tape, but I was sure it was Kenny's faded blue Dodge. I went down the steps quickly and crossed the alley to the van, peered in through the driver window but the curtains were pulled. "Kenny!" I yelled, banging on the door. I went around the other side to the sliding door and banged on it. "Kenny!"

The van rocked on its creaky springs. I heard a thump and a shuffling commotion inside, then the door clicked and slid open. I covered my nose. The air smelled like locker room feet.

"Kenny?"

Kenny looked as if he had been drug through a grease pit. His hair was thick and oily, and his face had a coppery sweat sheen, as if he hadn't bathed in a month. He was wearing tattered jeans and a yellowing T-shirt.

"I knew it would be you," he said hollowly. He fell back onto a gray mattress and kicked himself upright onto a stained pillow that looked as if a dog had been sleeping on it. He was barefoot. His toe nails were yellow and cracked.

"Kenny, what the hell?" I leaned into the van, which was dank and piled with dirty clothes and trash. "What're you doing here?"

"I needed a place to crash, bro. The cops hassle you anywhere else."

"What's happened?"

"Nothin', man."

He rummaged through some empty beer cans, found one that sloshed and tipped it into his mouth.

"Kenny, everybody's worried about you."

"So *now* they worry," he said ironically.

"*I'm* worried about you."

"I can take care of myself," he spat, hardening.

"Look, man, let me take you to my place, get you cleaned up."

"No way, dude. I ain't goin' near *her*."

"Then...then...come inside. You can use the employee washroom."

"Naw, man. I'm cool. But thanks."

He sat forward then, cross-legged and with his hands on his knees, as thin as a stick figure. "I could use some food, though."

"Sure, man. I'll get you something. What do you want?"

"I want..." He looked at me with the most tortured and bloodshot eyes. "I want..." He began to shiver. He hugged himself and his eyes rolled a bit, but whatever it was seemed to pass, and when he looked at me again his eyes were filling. "I want a fix, man," he cried. "I *need* it."

"*What?*"

And then he fell forward into my arms, holding onto my shoulders with vise-like strength.

"Oh, Carlton," he cried into my ear. "I'm a junkie, Carlton. A damn junkie."

"*Ohmygod!*"

I held him as if he were a child while he sobbed on my shoulder, wondering the whole time what I should do; what I *could* do. I let slip some tears myself.

"We'll fix it, Kenny," I reassured him. I patted his back. "We'll fix it." I lowered him onto his mattress. "Stay here, man. I'll get help."

"Can't go anywhere," he sniffed. "No gas."

"It'll be all right, Kenny."

I was about to pull the door, but he reached across suddenly and took my arm. "Don't tell Mama," he begged, tears running down his cheeks. "I can't...I can't..."

"Okay, Kenny. Okay. Stay put. I'll be right back."

I pushed him down and closed the door, and in those minutes of indecision I'm ashamed to admit that what I really wanted to do was get away from him, from the stink of him, the abject, disgusting condition of him. I was thinking more clearly by the time I got inside, got some distance. I called Gracie.

Gracie had connections. She was as efficient as a social worker committed to a cause. She pulled up little over an hour later, followed by a converted ambulance from one of the rehab organizations downtown. A couple of guys with lined and rugged faces got out of the ambulance and came toward me, followed by Gracie. She had on tight jeans and a plain gray sweatshirt, a worried look on her face.

"Where is he?" she asked. I pointed to the van and she nodded at the guys.

"I never knew," I told her, but even as I said it I began to recall the little things I had overlooked, the little signs I had missed.

"It's okay, Carlton," she said soothingly. "Addicts deceive; themselves and others. It's what they do."

"How do you know so much?" I asked, scrutinizing her from a new perspective.

"I volunteer with some of these groups. I've seen it all. Kenny's just lucky he has such a good friend."

"Gracie, I never knew you were so...so..."

"What?" she smiled. It was a pretty smile that brought back fond memories, but I searched her face just the same, suspicious that she might still be carrying a flame for me. I didn't see anything there except a professional countenance and sincere concern for Kenny. She had moved on. I was glad.

"I don't know, *involved*, I guess," I said after those moments.

"We all have to give something, Carlton." She shrugged. "This is what I give."

"I think he's luckier to have a friend like you than me."

"I think he's lucky to have both of us."

* * *

Gracie called every few days to let me know how Kenny was doing. He was off methadone by the first of May, and was participating in the twelve-step program with almost messianic fervor. He was doing well, she told me. He had even allowed his parents to come see him, which had taken quite a bit of courage, considering. I should visit as well, she said, but I threw up excuses to avoid it. I didn't want to see Kenny, not there, not like that. Gracie seemed disappointed but didn't push it.

Kenny got out of rehab on May 19, a Friday. It was an inspiring day, warm and bright and not too hot. If he had come out on a gray day then that could have cast a pall over the whole thing, but as it was the splendid weather seemed to be another ally in his recovery, a good omen. Gracie picked me up at work, and together we went down to the rehab center. Kenny's parents were there. We waited for Kenny in an institutionally bland room filled with rows of folding chairs, just the four of us. We didn't talk except to exchange greetings. Our smiles were forced and wary. Mrs. Batista wrung her hands.

Kenny came alone through a battered and scratched metal door that locked solidly behind him when it slammed shut, as if he were being cast into the world, ready or not. I examined him closely for some sign of a change or permanent mark, but he looked fine, clean and well groomed. He had even shaved off his mustache, which took years off of him, made him look like a teenager again. He wore crisp new jeans and a starched white T-shirt, with a pack of cigarettes rolled in the left sleeve. He was still thin, but his color was good. His eyes found me first, and he came straight to me and hugged me as if we were brothers reuniting after a war.

"You saved me, man," he said with smoky breath, clinging to me tightly. So there was something new since rehab, hugging. Guys didn't hug in those days. I untangled myself from his embrace as deftly as I could, and then held him back by the shoulders.

"You should save some of that for Gracie," I said, trying to keep it light. "She's the one who did everything."

He went to Gracie then, folded her in his arms and lifted her off her feet. Her look of surprise was comic. She dangled in his embrace like a doll.

"It was a good thing you did, *Carrrlton*," Mrs. Batista said warmly. "You are a good friend to Kenny." Mrs. Batista was a full-figured woman who favored colorful cotton dresses. Her Cuban accent had never softened. She rolled the *r* in my name like a trilling bird.

"It was nothing, Mrs. Batista," I said self-consciously, and really it wasn't. I hadn't done anything except call Gracie. But deeper still, I didn't want to accept any praise because I was afraid I might then become responsible for Kenny's sobriety. I felt some guilt about that.

"It was certainly something," Mr. Batista said, stepping forward with his hand out. Kenny's father was the picture of Latin dignity and reserve. He neither smiled nor spoke effusively, demonstrating his gratitude with a firm handshake instead.

"I'm just glad he's okay," I said.

"Okay, Kenny," said Mrs. Batista. "Time to *vamos a casa.*"

"Okay, *Mamá.*" He set Gracie back on her feet.

"Graciella?" Mrs. Batista said to Gracie warmly. "*Y tu, mi hija. Muchas gracias.*" The two women hugged.

"*De nada,*" said Gracie.

Gracie and I followed them into the parking lot and watched them pull away, and then I folded myself into her tiny bronze Civic for the ride back to work.

"It's good that they're letting him come home," she said as she cranked the engine. "He'll need structure for a while."

"I guess so," was all I could think to say in return.

Our drive back to Hill's was slow in the afternoon traffic, but I didn't mind. It was such a nice day, and I liked being with Gracie. There was no tension between us, just easy conversation without any verbal traps or double entendre to get in the way, something I didn't have with any other woman. When we got to the store, Gracie parked out front and turned off the engine. Shoppers rolled past with their carts, and crows were pecking at something across the way. The sun was getting hot through the windshield. Gracie seemed subdued all of a sudden. She absently rapped her fingers on the wheel as if she were debating something in her mind. I sat stiffly in her little car with my knees practically up to my chin. The silence lengthened.

"Gracie?" I asked finally.

She shook something off. "Oh, it's nothing."

"Okay then. I'd better get back to work. Thanks for…everything."

I opened the door, got a leg out and stretched my knee.

"Carlton, wait," said Gracie. She looked troubled.

"What is it?"

"It's…I don't know, it's really none of my business."

"I don't like the sound of that." I pulled my leg back in and closed the door.

"It's just that…well, we were at a conference in Florida, me and some of the other interns. We were only there to take messages, arrange meetings, you know?"

"Okay," I said apprehensively.

"I was doing some work for Brad Burton."

"The attorney?"

"Yeah, corporate law. I think he wants to run for mayor."

"Okay."

"Well…" she hesitated.

I glanced at my watch. "Gracie, I've got to get back to work."

"Okay, okay, but look—I was down in the lobby after dinner and I saw him going out."

"So?"

"So he was with Evelyn."

"What!"

"It doesn't necessarily mean anything," she added quickly. "Maybe they just met up by accident. I mean, Mr. Hanshaw's a lawyer. They probably know each other."

I ground my teeth and gazed out the window at the parking lot. My face felt hot, and it wasn't the sun.

"Is that it then?" I asked sharply.

"Yeah. I thought you should know."

"Thanks," I said, and I yanked myself out of the car. I slammed the door and leaned into the open window. "Thanks, really, I mean it."

"You're welcome, Carlton," Gracie said with the barest smile. "I hope everything's okay."

"Yeah, me too," I said without conviction.

* * *

For the rest of my shift I stewed on what Gracie had told me, at once trying to brush it off and yet fuming just the same. By the time I got home I had worked myself into an indignant fit. Evelyn was just coming out of the kitchen when I entered. She was wearing tapering white knee shorts and a silky lemon top, a casual but bright ensemble that did nothing to conceal the malevolent look on her face. I was too piqued just then to notice. I launched right in.

"What were you doing with Brad Burton in Jacksonville?"

I slammed the door for effect. Evelyn didn't flinch, but fixed me with an icy blue glare that held its own indignation. She pushed a hand into a tight pocket and came out with a folded white napkin, which she wagged as if it meant something to me.

"I found *this* in your jeans," she spat accusingly. It took me a moment, but then I realized what it was and I groaned. "It's a California phone number," she went on. "I checked. And a woman's handwriting…"

I stumbled for words. "Uh," I said uncertainly. "It's not what you think."

"How do you know what I think?" she practically screamed. She made a show of unfolding the napkin, as if each crease revealed a secret. "*You know where to find me.*" She chuckled darkly. "Well that's golden. You know where to find her for *what?*" She flicked the napkin at me and stood there unyielding as it wafted to the floor.

"She's just a friend, Evelyn," I answered with wavering confidence. "It's nothing."

"Strange women don't give my husband their phone number for *nothing.*"

"She's not a strange woman!"

"Oh?" Her smile was sinister. She was pacing now, as if thinking through a puzzle. "Then you must know her pretty well." She rushed up into my face. "*Who is she?*"

Couples have fights, but that's not what this was. This was a fiery eruption, long-simmering frustrations and resentments driven to the surface. I had been putting up with this kind of thing for too long, cowed by her turbulent moods and my own misguided sense of duty. Grandmother Villetta had said it. It was time to get down in the mud with Evelyn.

"Cut it out!" I ordered in a startling, commanding voice. I took her forcefully by the shoulders but she shoved back and twisted out of my grasp. Suddenly it felt hot in the apartment. I knew the neighbors would be able to hear this through the walls. In a stray glance I spotted Tommy hugging his door, wide-eyed and with his thumb in his mouth. "Calm down, damn it," I cursed after a few breaths. I turned away from her and went to Tommy. "It's okay, Tommy," I said, kneeling. I brushed some hair out of his eyes and put on a smile. "Mommy and Daddy are just having a little argument. Go in your room and play. Close the door. That's good."

Evelyn had her hands on her hips and a face going purple with fury. I stood with my back against Tommy's door and stared her down. "She's a friend from the Appalachian Trail," I admitted, but I wouldn't go further. I wouldn't tell her Willow's name; I wouldn't soil that memory by hearing Willow's name come out of Evelyn's mouth.

Evelyn threw up her hands. "That again?" She rolled her eyes but then she froze. "Is she the one—?"

"Yes," I said to wound, but she just laughed.

"And so—what? You two met up and went over old times?"

"Yeah, we did. But it's not like you think."

"Then what *was* it like?" She lurched back up in my face again.

"Evelyn, stop! Why do you have to be like this?"

She scooped up the napkin and waved it at me. "*This* is why. You keep women *everywhere*, and now you've got Gracie back, too."

"That's not true!"

"You think I don't know?" she asked mockingly. "I see the way she looks at you, and calling all the time."

"She doesn't...look at me. And she was calling about Kenny." I squeezed my temples. I had a king-size headache coming on now. It turned my vision gray.

"Oh yes she does." She looked caged. "And you encourage her."

"Evelyn, I..." My head pounded. Even the weight of the air seemed to make it worse, and Evelyn's shrill voice was like a ten-penny nail through my temples...

I saw the mountains. They were close, and quiet but for the birds and the breeze through the limbs. I had known them—I had known the peace that they could bring. And I had known Willow. I had never felt so...so free to breathe and feel.

"Hey!" she shouted.

I came to with a wince and headed for the door.

"Where are you going?" she demanded.

"Away from you! I'm not doing this anymore, Evelyn. That's it." And I meant it. Grandmother Villetta's advice had been to get down in the mud if I had to, but wrestling in the mud with Evelyn was a dirty business with no hope of coming clean again. At that moment I was prepared to walk out the door and never come back. I wasn't thinking about the repercussions, the future, or where I would go. I wasn't even thinking about Tommy. I was only thinking that I had to leave, right then, or else I might never get away.

"But you *can't* go."

"Yes I can," I growled. I had the door open. Miss Martha was peering through a part in her curtains. She snapped them closed when I noticed, but then off to the side I saw them part again ever so slightly.

"You can't leave me, Carlton. You *can't.*"

I turned back to her. There was a vulnerable quality in her voice now, transformed from one moment to the next.

"Why not?"

"Because…because I'm *pregnant.*"

That came down with a hollow numbness that sent me swaying where I stood. I closed the door on Miss Martha and dropped weakly into my armchair.

"Oh, damn it, Evelyn." I massaged my temples. The apartment was eerily quiet now. Our clock ticked on the mantle. "When?" I asked in a mumble. "When is it due?"

"November, probably." She sat on the sofa with her hands on her knees, looking at me impassively as if she were waiting for me to catch up with the inevitable.

I counted the months. It had to have been that night, before I went to California. I moaned and massaged my temples even harder. The birds went silent, and the mountains receded until they were gone.

* * *

Luke Hanshaw Jeffries was born a little after three o'clock in the afternoon on Thanksgiving Day, 1982. According to the calendar he had gone a little late. He was a big baby, almost nine pounds. Evelyn had a hard time with him.

I had Tommy with me in the waiting room, and he was getting restless. Mom and Dad didn't come this time. Jane was in with Evelyn. We had brought Evelyn to the hospital at 6:00 a.m., but as her labor had gone on and on I had taken Tommy out for a while. He was in kindergarten now, almost six years old, but despite our patient explanations, and despite watching his mother swell alarmingly before his eyes these past months, he still seemed uncertain about exactly what was going on. We had been back in the waiting room for more than an hour when Jane finally came out to fetch us. She looked fatigued and stressed, as if she had delivered the baby herself. Tendrils of damp hair hung in her eyes.

"Okay, Carlton," she said in a breathy, exhausted voice. "You and Tom can come in now."

Evelyn was propped up in her bed, holding Luke in the curve of her arm. She was pale. Her hair was damp and pasted to her forehead.

"He's big," she smiled weakly.

Tommy stood up on tip-toes to see over the bed rail. He eyed his little brother with a combination of curiosity and perhaps revulsion, the seeds of sibling rivalry taking root right then.

"He looks funny, Daddy," Tommy said.

"You did, too, when you were born, Tommy."

Luke's head had been squeezed into the shape of a gourd. Tommy's hadn't been as misshapen. The obstetrician had told me to expect this. It was normal and Luke would be just fine, but it was still disturbing to see. I think I had expected to find another version of Tommy lying there, but the two couldn't have been more different. It wasn't only Luke's size, he also had black hair. Luke was sleeping now, but later I would see that while his eyes were also blue, they were a dark, inky hue.

"Is everything all right?" Evelyn asked wearily. "You don't seem as happy this time."

"I'm happy, Evelyn." I rested a hand gently on Luke's head. "It's just different knowing what to expect and all."

"Tom, come meet your brother, Luke," Evelyn said with motherly affection. Tommy stood back and shook his head. She smiled faintly. "Okay, then. You'll have lots of time to get to know him at home. I'm so tired, Carlton," she said with half-lidded eyes. "I need to rest for a while."

"Okay, hon." I pecked her on the forehead. "We'll be back later."

She smiled and closed her eyes.

* * *

Neither Jane nor Evelyn had approved of the name Luke. Where had that come from? they asked. It was an old family name, I lied, so we settled on the usual compromise and gave him Hanshaw for a middle name. This time there was nothing I could amend that to, but Jane checked the birth certificate anyway, just in case. The truth is—and it embarrasses me to this day—I named Luke after a movie character.

You might know them as quaint classics now, if you've heard of them at all, but in that era the *Star Wars* movies were like nothing we had ever seen. The first movie came out the summer after Tommy was born. A second one came out a few years later, and we were excited to learn that a third was due next summer. The hero of those movies was a young guy named Luke Skywalker. There was a particular scene in the second movie, in which Luke Skywalker and the evil Darth Vader are fighting with their laser swords. Luke seems to be holding his own pretty well, but then Darth Vader chops off Luke's hand. As the wounded Luke struggles to evade Vader, recriminations are exchanged. Luke's father had been murdered while Luke was still a baby. "You *killed him*," Luke declares. "*No*," says Vader. "I *am your father.*" It was a powerful, shocking scene that drew gasps from the audience.

As for my Luke? I had my doubts. I know this wasn't fair to Luke, but in my defense I have never told this story until now. Luke and I fell out for different reasons.

Evelyn was in the hospital for eight days, recovering from her episiotomy and a slight infection. It was a week of unexpected contentment for me. Mom watched Tommy while I was at work, and in the evenings I cooked sloppy joes and mac & cheese, and other things that Tommy loved and were easy to make. We played games on the Atari and watched movies on our Betamax, and at bedtime I read to him from John Muir or Jean Craighead George until he fell asleep. It was like a happy lifetime compressed into a week, and then on the following Friday I took off from work early to bring Evelyn and Luke home.

Evelyn was weak, and she walked with a waddle. Getting her up the stairs wasn't easy. She wasn't supposed to lift anything heavy. Luke's weight had dropped a little—that was normal, they said—but he was still a heavy bundle. He was also a fussy baby. He cried all the time, so Jane came over to help. She practically lived with us for a couple of weeks. I slept in Tommy's room, while Evelyn, Jane and Luke slept in our room. Oddly, I didn't mind. I moved the television into Tommy's room. He liked that.

It was Mom and Dad's turn for Christmas, but we wound up at the Hanshaw's house because of Evelyn's condition. I thought she was fine now, but she said otherwise. I held Luke while Evelyn and Tommy opened presents. Jerry brought out his egg nog, and of course Tommy wanted a sip. I said no even as Jane said, "Sure, why not just a little?"

My presents to Evelyn were a couple of blouses that Sadie had helped me pick out. They were loose-fitting blouses, supposedly more comfortable for nursing women.

"How nice," said Evelyn.

"Very pretty," said Jane.

Evelyn's gift to me was a leather briefcase.

"Oh, Brad called about a case yesterday," Jerry said toward Evelyn as he settled into his chair with a mug of egg nog. I looked up sharply but Evelyn's eyes were elsewhere. "He says Merry Christmas. I told him you were feeling much better."

"That's good," she said off to the side.

I tried to get Luke to take his bottle but he kept spitting it out. Tommy came running up.

"Daddy, can I go outside and play?"

It was unusually warm for Christmas, but it had been raining.

"Well, Tommy, I don't—"

"Oh, you can't go outside, Tom. You'll get all wet," Jane interjected.

I exhaled deeply and ground my teeth, carried Luke to Evelyn then turned to Tommy.

"Sure, son. Let's go outside." Jane pursed her lips and glared at me, but I ignored that and took Tommy by the hand. "We'll be back soon," I said.

It really was strangely warm out. The sky was heavy, but the rain had let up. Tommy and I went up the hill to the house, then around back. Dad had widened the driveway up top. There was now a paved turning circle, and off of that, angled across from the house, he had cut into the woods and built a large garden shed. It was red with white trim, and shaped like a Dutch barn. The doors were open. Langley was inside, wagging his tail.

"Hi, Langley!" Tommy ran to the dog and hugged him around the neck.

"We're getting another dog," I heard from behind.

Huh? I spun in surprise and there was Dad.

"Dad!"

"Sorry to sneak up on you."

"It's okay. Another dog?"

"Yeah, another bluetick. A female."

"From Bob?"

"No," Dad laughed. "Not this time."

I looked back and forth between Dad and Langley.

"You want puppies?"

"Yeah. Langley's getting old."

"What's Mom say about it?"

Dad grinned. "Anything to get me out of the house, I think." We both laughed at that. "Are you coming in?" he asked.

"Sure, but I want to take Tommy up the hill first."

"Okay, son. We'll see you inside later, then."

"Okay, Dad. C'mon Tommy, let's go up the hill."

I took Tommy by the hand and we beat it through the brush to the clearing on top. I was going to catch hell for getting Tommy's shoes and pants so wet, but I didn't care. The hill was different. The city had taken out the water tank, and with it all the other stuff that had been laying around, including the fort. They had cleared most of the brush, and had cut the woods back. The ash tree stood alone, gnarled like an old man. I stood below its naked limbs and felt a pang of sadness.

"Kenny and I had a fort here when we were little," I told Tommy. "But it's gone now. And way up there," I pointed to the big limb, "I found a bullet in the tree."

"The one on your necklace?"

"Yeah."

"Wow."

"Do you think you can climb that tree?"

"Mommy might get mad."

"No she won't. Here, I'll help you."

Tommy scrambled up that low limb and then kept going until he reached the big limb and could nestle down in the crook, the way I had when I'd found the bullet, only he was facing outward instead.

"I can see everything, Daddy!" he exclaimed with joy.

"I know, son. Isn't it great?"

"Yeah."

He rode that limb like a horse, laughing and seeing things for the first time. I smiled on proudly. Too soon it was time to go back down.

* * *

I came home from work on the Monday after New Year's to discover that Jane had hired a housekeeper for Evelyn. It was a little after five, already dark outside, and I was so tired that all I wanted to do was lie down. Regina was her name. She was a black woman, not much older than Evelyn and me, and she was pretty. She was dressed in white pants and a thin white sweater with a pale yellow blouse underneath, and she had on the same thick-soled shoes that nurses wore. She had proud, angular features, a graceful neck, and close-cropped hair. Jane met me at the door and introduced us.

"Regina's going to help out for a while, Carlton," Jane announced. "Evelyn deserves a break, don't you think?"

Regina's smile was as white as her sweater, and it was a sincere smile. I was furious, but didn't want to make a scene in front of our guest—and that's the way I thought of her, as a guest, because we really didn't need the extra help.

"It's nice to meet you," I said, squinting through a growing headache. I shook her hand.

"You, too, Mr. Jeffries."

"Regina is going to help with the boys," Jane went on. "And do some cleaning and cooking. She will work from eleven till eight every day except Thursday and Sunday."

"That's nice," I said. I looked around for a place to be alone. Our two-bedroom apartment was too small for this many people. "Excuse me, I need to clean up." I fled for the bathroom.

"Dinner will be ready at six," Jane called after me.

I closed the bathroom door and exhaled wearily, loosened my tie and sat on the commode. I rubbed my face, tried to knuckle the weariness out of my eyes. My temples throbbed. After a few moments I turned out the lights.

A sharp knock on the door woke me up.

"Dinner, Carlton."

I groaned and pulled myself up, found the light switch and flipped it on. Pain shot through my eyes. I gazed at myself in the mirror. I had five o'clock stubble and bloodshot eyes, a haggard appearance that matched the way I felt. I splashed water on my face and went to dinner.

We all squeezed in around the table, Jane, Tommy, myself, and Evelyn holding Luke, who fussed and kicked. Regina brought out Salisbury steaks with mashed potatoes and corn, set our plates and poured our tea. It didn't feel right to be waited on like this. I wanted to get up to help but I was pressed against the wall, and doing so would mean that Evelyn would have to get up as well. I let it go.

"This is very good, Regina," Jane said.

"Thank you, ma'am."

I ate listlessly. Afterward I tried to help clear the dishes.

"Oh, Regina will do that," Jane said. I plopped back into my chair with a frown. Jane helped Evelyn up and together they headed for the bedroom. Jane paused with a hand on the door frame. She turned toward me in thought. "Carlton, don't you think it's time you moved this family into a house?"

I grabbed the edge of table and held on to keep from exploding. Regina was walking away with an armload of dishes. I wouldn't make a scene in front of her. I wouldn't. I retreated to Tommy's room. He had left the television on, and now the news was playing. I turned off the overhead light and flopped onto the bed. Tommy came in and lay down beside me.

"Regina's nice, Daddy," he said.

"Yeah, she is."

"Do you like her?"

"I think she's nice."

"Me, too."

I patted his head and looked at the news. Candidates were already scrambling to run against Mayor Fulton in August. Bradley "Brad" Burton walked up to a podium to make his announcement. I knew his name from the news, but until lately I had never paid any attention to him. I scooted up to look more closely. Burton was a slick lawyer, a big guy, wide across the shoulders, with a square jaw, dark eyes, and a shock of black hair that was combed back from his forehead and sprayed to hold its shape. He was in his mid-thirties, I thought, arrogantly handsome. He wore his success in the form of a perfectly tailored black suit and a gold Rolex that flashed from his cuff whenever he punctuated his political points. He wore a gaudy class ring on his right forefinger, but nothing on his left. He wasn't married.

Even Tommy could sense that something was off.

"What's wrong, Daddy?"

I heard him, but distantly. The anger seemed to start in the pit of my stomach, rising higher and higher until it reached my head and clouded my eyes. I felt heavy, hot. If not for Tommy I would have put my fist through the wall, or kicked the television off its stand.

I'm not trying to justify what I did, but some things can't be fixed. It's possible to hang on too long, until duty makes life poison. I couldn't do it anymore, it wasn't fair to Tommy. And Luke? Regardless, it wasn't fair to him either. I would never be able to make the life I wanted for them, it wasn't going to happen. I accepted that now. Suddenly I could breathe. The pounding in my head seemed to go deeper, where I didn't notice it as much. I bent over and pulled on my shoes.

"Where you going, Daddy?" Tommy asked. I kissed his forehead and held his sweet, innocent face. My lips trembled.

"You know I love you, son."

"I love you too, Daddy."

"Promise me you'll be good to Luke. He'll need a big brother to help him."

Tommy's little brows wrinkled in confusion. I got up. My stomach felt queasy, my ears hollow.

"Bye, Tommy," I said, and I walked out.

FOURTEEN

I tried to hike out this morning, not because the weather was any better but because I couldn't stand being cooped up in this stinking shelter any longer; that and I'm starting to get sores on my backside. I made up my mind without really thinking about it beforehand, just began to rustle around in the drizzling murk of morning, rolling up my sleeping bag, stuffing things into my backpack. Sam could tell that we were about to be on the move again. Despite the dreary cold and penetrating wet, the mud and the rot, he was jumping around like a puppy, tugging at his leash until I relented and set him loose; then he raced around the outside of the shelter, joyous and free, pausing only long enough to sniff and raise his leg.

I got into my rain suit, pulled the hood and zipped it tight around my face and neck, then shimmied out into the mud and gunk. My backpack felt heavier than before, but I got it shouldered and we were off into the gloom without looking back. I thought we could make Wadleigh Stream, even with Nesuntabunt Mountain in the way. It's only eight miles, after all. Insulated within my Gore-Tex rain suit, sealed tightly with Velcro strips and nylon zippers, surely I could shuffle eight miles, especially with the wind and the rain at my back, pushing me along. Wadleigh Stream shelter might not be any better than Rainbow Stream—it might not be there at all—but at least I would be moving again.

We didn't make it half a mile. Pollywog Stream was flashing across the trail in a roiling black torrent that had scoured the soil from the granite banks, leaving the trees to yaw on skeletal lattices of exposed roots. There was no way across. Even if a tree toppled, making a bridge, I wouldn't dare to try. One slip, one foot dangling into that relentless current, and I would be yanked away, pulped on the rocks long before I could drown.

I didn't ponder this for long, because suddenly I could feel the cold pressing in. I turned around, utterly demoralized, leaned into the wind and stinging rain and made my way back. Sam sprinted in circles around me, oblivious, daring me to play, but there was no playfulness left in me, and little hope. When we got back I found that Rainbow Stream was flashing as vigorously as Pollywog Stream, and I was—am—trapped in between.

So now I'm back in the shelter, such as it is. Sam is on his leash, shivering from the wet. My feet are numb and I've aggravated my left elbow again. I'm propped up in the corner as before, stooped under the rotten rafters and hoping to console myself with the words I am writing here. I have struggled on all of my hikes, this one is no different. That's what I keep telling myself, anyway. People didn't get it, especially Evelyn, why we thru-hikers would subject ourselves to such misery. They couldn't understand that in order to be free you have to break yourself down until nothing matters except the next step and the next breath. Beer Poet understood, but then he was a hiker. I remember that he left this at the Wadleigh Stream shelter:

> *So near me she lies,*
> *So near yet so far.*
> *I play my part well,*
> *I hold on; I go.*
> *So on just ahead,*
> *So on through the cold.*
> *I struggle and burn,*
> *I'm going; I'm gone.*
> *Beer Poet, GA-ME '07*

I don't get poetry, at least poetry that doesn't rhyme. I don't know if his poem was about Mt. Katahdin, or about some woman he had been pining for, maybe a hiker he had met along the way. I don't even know for sure if Beer Poet was a *he*. But I do know that he was tired, worn down. As a northbounder, he would have just completed some of the toughest hiking on the trail: Saddleback Mountain and The Horn, some pretty tough climbs there, and then the Crocker and Bigelow ranges, tougher yet, followed by White Cap Mountain and most of the Hundred-Mile Wilderness—pretty much what I had glossed over for Seagull, Free Bird and the others in New York that time. No longer a distant, nebulous goal, Beer Poet would have been able to snatch glimpses of Mt. Katahdin from time to time, through the trees or from the heights, right there and yet so far. Reaching Mt. Katahdin at last would have meant everything to him by that point, the culmination of it all—his Holy Grail. But after struggling through the rugged mountains of Maine, the closer he got to Mt. Katahdin the farther away it must have seemed, as if the very landscape were taunting him.

But I'm a southbounder, I have a different perspective. The truth is—and this would have aggravated the purists no end if I had ever said it aloud—Mt. Katahdin means nothing to me. It's just an inconvenience that must be dealt with in order to undertake a proper southbound hike. Springer Mountain, Georgia was my goal, my deliverance; not something I agonized toward, but something I raced toward, in

2008 and even now if I could. I race toward it because Springer Mountain is not the end for me. In a strange way it is actually the beginning. Remember, Willow was a southbounder, too.

*   *   *

Except for the turning of seasons, the view from Springer Mountain doesn't change. In the span of human time it is eternal. I stood on that wooded summit for the second time, gazing through gently swaying limbs at smooth layered ridges that looked like verdant waves piling against the horizon. It was June 21, 1983. It had been almost seven years since I had seen that view. The sun was high, the sky clear but for some light haze. The view hadn't changed a bit. I imagined that a Cherokee warrior, standing here two hundred years ago, would have had the exact same view. Or that religious family I had met last time.

I looked down at the weathered stone beneath my feet and felt certain that I was standing in the same place I had taken with them as they prayed. I had no prayer of my own to offer, just this: *He that keepeth his way preserveth his soul.* I had a giddy tingling in my chest. Breaths were easy, sweetly scented by dogwood flowers and honeysuckle. Sounds were crisp and alive: the sighing wind, trees clicking and scraping, a beetle rustling through the duff.

I had found my way; I was back on the right path. I felt it in my soul.

Dry leaves crunched on the trail behind me. I backed quickly into the tree line and pulled branches around me like sheltering arms. I wasn't hiding, just getting out of the way. This was Willow's moment, her time to see it and feel it for herself without any distractions from me.

I looked on proudly as she came up the trail. I tipped a branch just so for a better view. Willow wore an olive ball cap with an extra long bill, which hid her face from me until she was up off the steep trail and onto level ground. Her hair, bound in a thick braid, licked back and forth as she climbed. She wore khaki shorts, her bronzed legs streaked with sweat and dust, and a white T-shirt that clung to her stomach with sweat. I could clearly make out her belly button, her breasts. She drove a gnarled, improvised walking stick into the duff with her right hand, while her left hand grasped her backpack's shoulder strap. When her eyes came into view I saw that she was weary, but not beaten.

Willow paused at the top of the trail and scanned the clearing. I stood perfectly still, and if she saw me she didn't let on. Her face was not blank, just that inward expression we all take on when we've been on the trail for a while. She had flecks of dirt on her cheeks, like dark freckles. I thought they were the cutest thing, wished I could raise my camera to take her picture right then. She walked measuredly to the bronze plaque and knelt on her left knee, just knelt there and studied the plaque. After some moments she dropped her walking stick and put her hand on the plaque, worked her fingers around the figure of the hiker. Then she looked up at the view, stood and went to the cliff. She saw what I had seen, the same thing, or at least the same view. What her eyes and experience made of it only she could know. She stood there motionless for a long time.

I wanted to go to her and hold her, but not yet. It wasn't time. Presently she shrugged out of her backpack and let it fall, turned purposefully and went to the rock cache that holds the trail register. She sat on the rock and read the register, smiled when she saw the note I had left for her. The register had a pencil tied to a string. She took it and licked the tip, paused in thought then added her entry. With that she was done. She put the register away then scanned the woods for me. I was well camouflaged, she couldn't find me. Vague worry crossed her face, and with that I stepped out with a broad smile and open arms.

"Jake!"

I rushed over to her and took her in my arms, squeezing too tight, probably, but she didn't complain. She had lost a lot of weight, but not enough to make her feel boney in my arms. Her sweat dampened my shirt. Her smell was earthy and real. I took her face in my hands and thumbed some flecks from her cheek.

"Congratulations," I said close to her lips. "You did it."

"Yeah," she breathed.

I slid a hand down her back toward the swell of her behind, pressed in closer for a kiss but she pushed me away.

"Uh, uh, buster," she said with a coy grin, taking a step back. "Not with a married man."

"Aw." I hung my face, but then I brightened. "Not for much longer, though. A lot's happened since we met up at Clingmans Dome."

"That was forever ago," she said.

"Naw, only a week."

"*A week.*"

"Well, eight days, anyway."

"Feels like *months.*"

"I know, believe me."

"I believe you." She raised a hand to my face and smiled. "So tell me what I missed."

"Well…we have a woman astronaut in space now. Sally Ride."

She slapped my face lightly and faked a stern look.

"You know what I mean," she said.

"Yeah," I said, "but not here. I don't want to talk about it in this place. I don't want that memory. Are you ready to head down, or do you want more time?"

Willow spun around slowly on her heels, taking it all in once more. "You know," she said airily as her eyes grazed the valleys beyond, "Katahdin's more dramatic."

"I beg to differ." I slapped her behind playfully.

"Hey!" She skipped out of reach. "I told you, *hands off,* buster." She parked her hands on her hips as if she were angry, but her smile said otherwise. "Okay," she exhaled, "let's go." She leaned over and hefted her backpack.

"Let me carry that for you," I offered.

"No, thanks," she said. "I've got it. But when we get to your place you can wash my clothes if you want."

She said this with a grin that told me she was kidding, but I would have gladly washed her clothes—by hand—in a bucket—if she had asked me to.

* * *

I explained everything during the drive home.

"Evelyn's not asking for anything—well, just the kids, that is." I frowned in thought. "I have to pay child support—the state makes you do that anyway—but she's not arguing over how much, just whatever the court says. She doesn't want anything else from me. Gracie says it's because they want to get this over with as fast as they can. Evelyn's boyfriend is running for mayor in August. Gracie thinks they want to get this all tied up quietly so they can get married before the election. Then Mr. Perfect can have a perfect family to show the cameras. So this isn't even costing me a lot. And Gracie won't take any money from me. I feel bad about that. She should get something."

"It seems so—so…" Willow was gazing out the window, her elbow propped on the door. She had freed her hair, and it blew wild in the wind, catching in her eyes. She brushed the hair out of her face and looked over. "It's so transparent, but it's also so…fake. I'm sorry for your boys."

"Yeah, me too. But I can't do anything about it. We sign the papers tomorrow, down at the courthouse. You made great time on your hike. I thought I was going to have to postpone, which would have suited me, but everything has worked out anyway."

"Yeah," she said vacantly.

I could see that her eyes had gone back to the trail. When I had met Willow in California the previous year, she hadn't told me that she had completed every section of the trail except from Damascus, Virginia to Springer Mountain. This last section had taken her almost a month to complete. Because of my work and the divorce, I had only been able to meet up with her that one time, at Clingmans Dome. I knew she had stories to tell. I couldn't wait to hear them.

"So Judith," I said. She snapped out of the trance at the mention of her given name. "About us. I—."

"Don't say it." Her tone was serious.

"But—"

"I mean it."

"I just wanted—"

"Don't, Carlton. There is no *us* while you're still married."

I wouldn't say that she was angry, but she was definitely peeved, so I dropped it.

"Okay, tomorrow then. At about—oh," I tapped the little round clock on the dash, "—about 4:31 in the afternoon."

She snorted and smiled. "Fair enough, Carlton. We'll talk about it then. Now pull over and get me some food before I start chewing on these seats."

I slapped the steering wheel I was laughing so hard.

* * *

I was staying with Mom and Dad, but only for a little while, I told them. I couldn't bear to waste any more rent money on an apartment that I couldn't bear to walk into. Evelyn had cleared out with the boys within days after I left, as if she'd had it all worked out beforehand. They were supposed to be staying down below with the Hanshaws, but I never saw them there except when I showed up for visitation with the boys. I'm pretty sure they were living with Brad. Tommy wouldn't talk about it, and Gracie advised me not to pry. Tommy was taking all of this hard.

It was late when we chugged up the drive. The light was out in Mom and Dad's bedroom, and the den was dark as well. I pulled around our new turning circle and parked in front of the garden shed. A motion sensor light popped on from the roof of the shed, casting Judith in dull yellow. She was dozing, her head propped against the door. I nudged her gently.

"We're here," I said softly.

"We are?" She yawned lazily and rubbed her eyes. "I missed Nashville."

"Nothing to see at night anyway. I'll show you around tomorrow."

"Okay," she yawned, fighting to stay awake.

I got out and took her backpack from the trunk. Judith got out quietly and stood next to me. It was a cool night, but humid. Judith shivered and rubbed her arms. We heard a distinct *thump, thump, thump* coming from the shed.

"Oh," I said, "I know you're tired, but you need to meet Langley."

"Okay." She yawned again.

Langley was on his stomach in the circle of light, his legs splayed out, his tail thumping a happy beat. I swear he was smiling. I opened the chicken-wire gate Dad had built, stepped through then knelt to pet Langley.

"Hi, Langley."

Just then Mirabel scampered across him in a bundle of puppy energy. Langley seemed to sigh. Mirabel went after my fingers, teething. When I pulled my hand away she proceeded to gnaw on Langley's ear instead. Langley just dropped his nose to the floor, gave his tail a final thump. He looked up at me forlornly, as if begging for deliverance.

"You settle down, Mirabel," I ordered playfully. "He won't put up with this when you get bigger."

"What a cute puppy," said Judith. She knelt beside me and reached out a hand. Mirabel licked Judith's fingers then started to gnaw. "Okay, that's enough," she said, then she reached to pet Langley but Mirabel would have none of it. "Ouch!" Judith pulled her hand away. "Sharp little teeth."

I laughed. "Yeah, Dad wants puppies. I'm not so sure about Langley."

"Your father's going to mate these two?"

"When Mirabel's big enough, and if Langley doesn't eat her first."

"Poor boy," Judith said. She finally managed to get a hand in to pet him. Langley gave her two thumps of his tail in return.

"Well, let's get inside," I said. "I know how tired you are."

"Okay."

We went in quietly through the kitchen, then across the living room to my old bedroom, which Mom had turned into a guestroom now that Tommy didn't need a playroom anymore. I was staying in my old-old room downstairs so that I could be as unobtrusive as possible while I was back. I dropped Judith's backpack on the floor, showed her the closets, didn't mention anything about the windows.

"There's a bathroom downstairs you can use without waking anybody. But then, you don't really need a shower, do you?" I smiled.

Judith looked at me incredulously and held her arms out as if they were splattered with mud.

"Well maybe after all," I said, still smiling. "I'll show you where it is."

We padded downstairs.

"Here's the bathroom," I pointed. "I'm down this hall. Oh, do you need to call anybody?"

Judith waved me off. "Tomorrow's okay."

"Do you have any clean clothes left?"

"Yeah."

"Okay then…well, uh. Sure you don't need any help in there?"

Judith smiled, but she was so tired she swayed on her feet. "I'll manage."

"Okay then. Well, uh, goodnight."

"Goodnight."

* * *

I was up early the next morning. I found Mom in the kitchen. Dad must have still been in bed.

"Morning," I said.

"Good morning, Carlton." Mom poured me a cup of coffee. "Is your friend here?"

"Yeah, still asleep, I think."

"I would guess so after a month of that."

"You'll like her," I said. We settled in at the table.

"I'm sure, honey. Today's the day, isn't it?"

"Yeah."

"I wish we saw Tommy more."

"Me, too."

"Will your friend be hungry?"

"Her name's Judith, Mom."

Mom fixed me with a disapproving look.

"Then will *Judith* be hungry?"

"I guarantee it."

"Well, then. I'd better get to it."

I hovered with my coffee outside the door to Judith's room, not wanting to wake her, too squeamish to just walk in. Finally I tapped lightly on the door.

"Judith?"

"Yeah, I'm up," came her muffled voice. "Just a minute."

Judith came out wearing khaki hiking pants and a thin, white cotton T-shirt, which she had tucked in. Her waist was trim but not skinny, and her hips flared out in a way that made my groin tingle. She had on her hiking shoes, brown suede, looking worn but clean. She must have scrubbed them in the bathroom last night. She wore her hair in a loose ponytail. Her hair looked soft. I fidgeted nervously, couldn't quite figure out what to do with my free hand, finally:

"Hungry?"

"*Starving.*" She smiled with her eyes.

"Okay, let's eat."

We went to the kitchen. Mom and Dad were at the table. I introduced Judith, who held out her hand confidently. Dad appraised her and seemed to like what he saw. Whatever had been bugging Mom vanished just like that. I let out a breath, didn't realize that I had been holding it the whole time. We sat to breakfast. Mom put on the full southern course: biscuits, gravy, grits, bacon; some pancakes and eggs.

"It looks wonderful," said Judith.

"You just help yourself, now," said Mom.

I started filling my plate. Judith imitated my movements, hesitantly at first but then she dug right in.

"I'm so sorry," she said to Mom, "but I'm starving."

"Don't you worry," said Mom. "We know about that in this house." She looked at me and winked. "We have plenty."

"And I'm sorry about my clothes," Judith said between mouthfuls. "I'll need to do some shopping today."

"It's all right," said Mom. "You look better than *he* did." She pointed a spoon at me.

"I wasn't so bad," I complained.

"You were just a bag of bones, and hairy as a hillbilly. Had to throw out that… that sleeping bag. And those *shoes*." She wrinkled her nose. "Lysol couldn't cover that up."

"Well…yeah," I said guiltily, looking down at my plate.

"Judith, what do you do? For a living, I mean," asked Dad.

"Teacher." Some gravy dripped off Judith's lip. She caught it with her spoon. "I just finished my master's, and I start teaching in August."

"You must be very proud," said Mom. "What grade will you teach?"

"Fifth grade this year. Next year? I don't know yet."

"Where's your school?" asked Dad.

"Oh, it's in Fresno."

"California?"

"Yeah."

Mom and Dad exchanged looks.

"That's a long way," said Mom.

"It's near my hometown," said Judith. Her plate was empty now and she was eyeing the biscuits guiltily. Mom handed over the plate without a thought.

"What's your hometown?" asked Dad.

"Oakhurst."

"I don't know of it."

"It's in the mountains near Yosemite."

"Sounds pretty," said Mom.

"It is."

Poor Judith was getting the third-degree. I pushed back my plate and glanced at my watch.

"Well, we need to get going," I said abruptly. "Lots to do today."

I stood and gestured Judith to follow. She had her fork to her mouth and choked a little at the unexpected rush. She gulped down a last bite and took a swallow of orange juice.

"Okay," she said with cheeks full. She swallowed hard then looked to Mom and Dad. "Thank you for breakfast. Thank you for everything."

"It was nice to finally meet you," said Dad.

"You, too."

Dad had his eyebrows up as we left, giving Mom an inside look of approval. I had been holding my breath again, but now I could breathe easy.

* * *

Gracie met us on the sidewalk out front of the courthouse at a little before four in the afternoon. I didn't recognize her at first. She wore a navy blazer and matching skirt, white stockings, and black pumps that lifted her about another inch. Her hair was done up in a tight bun that tugged at the corners of her eyes. She carried a black briefcase, faux alligator, but then maybe real alligator for all I knew. I introduced her to Judith.

"So nice to finally meet you," Gracie said sincerely. They gave one another a quick handshake. Judith was still wearing what she'd had on this morning. I'd run her over to Castner Knott in Green Hills, but she hadn't found anything she liked. I was dressed in my black Sunday suit.

"You, too," said Judith. "Carlton's lucky to have you."

"Carlton's lucky I passed the Bar."

They both chuckled while my ears burned. "Uh, hmm," I said.

Gracie looked up at me with the expression she took on now whenever things went from friendly to professional.

"So it's all *pro forma*, Carlton. You'll swear before the judge that you agree with the terms, she'll do the same, you sign some papers, I file them and you're done."

"Wow, just like that."

"Yeah, just like that. You really are lucky."

I looked at Judith. "Yeah, I know."

Evelyn came walking up then, accompanied by a slickly handsome young lawyer from her father's firm. She had on a white tube dress hemmed with gold that embraced her curves down to her knees, gold bangles on her wrists, an elaborate gold necklace. Her hair fell in big curls around her shoulders. She led Tommy by the hand, and passed us as if we were below her notice.

"Evelyn?" I said with an edge. She halted and turned. I nodded toward Tommy, kept my voice low. "Did you really need to bring him to this?" I knelt then and smiled. "Hi, Tommy."

Tommy's brows were knitted and his lips were pursed. He wouldn't look at me. He edged around his mother and pressed against her hip. I sighed and stood. Evelyn eyed each of us impassively, settled on Judith and stepped forward with a smirk.

"So you were his little Appalachian-trail fling, then," she said scornfully.

"Evelyn!" I growled.

Judith didn't flinch. She didn't clench her teeth, squint her eyes or redden in the least.

"No," she said matter-of-factly. "He was *my* little Appalachian-trail fling. From what I understand of you two, *you* were his fling."

Evelyn tightened her grip on Tommy. He mouthed a whine and tried to yank his hand away.

"Evelyn, let's get inside," her lawyer warned, taking her by the shoulder.

Evelyn held on for another breath, her eyes as jagged as barbed wire, a slight twitch in her cheeks. Judith was so relaxed she could have been knocking back a beer at Lakes of the Clouds. They eyed one another, each unyielding in her own way, then Evelyn humphed and turned her back to us.

"Let's get this over with," she said to her lawyer as if scraping something off of her shoe.

They went up the steps.

"Wow," said Gracie. Judith shrugged.

The going-home traffic was picking up on James Robertson Parkway. Wafts of exhaust carried over to us whenever the lights changed, mingling with a vague odor of petroleum from the river. I looked up, absently following the lines of that eleven-story monolithic courthouse until it seemed to merge with a watercolor sky puffy with clouds. In a few years that courthouse would be designated a national historic place. We didn't know that then, or that within a handful of decades all of this down here would be flooded.

"Evelyn's right," I said, watching the clouds drift. "Let's get this over with."

* * *

Judith was tired from running around all day, and this coming back-to-back with finishing her hike. But it was a beautiful early evening, pleasant in the 70s, with long, dusky solstice rays slanting in through the trees. I went to her room where she'd been resting. The door was open. She was lying on the bead, her knees up and crossed, with her new book propped in her lap.

"Is it any good?" I asked from the doorway.

She wasn't startled. She looked up at me with a weary smile.

"Yeah, so far."

"You like westerns?"

"Some, but this isn't a western."

"*The Valley of the Horses?* Sounds western."

"No, it's a sequel to *The Clan of the Cave Bear.* Jean Auel. Did you hear of that one?"

I wrinkled my brow. "I think so."

Judith creased a corner and thumped the book closed. She set the book aside and stretched out, all long and sinuous.

"You don't read much, do you?" she asked.

"I used to. I don't have a lot of time now."

"We'll have to fix that." She sat up on crossed legs. "I liked that bookstore."

"Davis-Kidd?"

"Yeah. If I lived here I would be in there every day."

I didn't know what to say to that, so went back to my original thought.

"I was thinking about taking a walk up the hill. Would you want to come with me?"

She sighed as if she were put out by the idea, but she was only playing with me, I could tell by the lift of her brows.

"Sure." She sat up and bent to put on her shoes. "Is this like a rite of passage? Going up the hill?"

That startled me. I pondered it for a moment.

"Yeah, I guess in a way it is. I never thought about it that way before."

"Your dad told me all about it."

"He did?"

"Uh, huh."

"That's weird."

"Why?"

"I don't know. I guess I didn't think he thought about it that much."

"Well, you guessed wrong. I like your dad, by the way. Your mom, too."

"Really? Even after all that third-degree this morning?"

"It's only natural, Carlton. Wait till you meet *my* dad. Oh boy."

"Can't wait," I said nervously.

Judith jumped up and adjusted the tuck of her T-shirt.

"Okay, then," she said. "Let's go see your hill."

We went out through the kitchen. Mom was rattling pans at the sink.

"Dinner in about half an hour, you two," she said as we went out.

We went to the garden shed first so that I could let Langley out.

"He loves to run the hill," I told Judith. "He'd be broken-hearted if we left him behind."

Langley came out hesitantly when I unlatched the gate, as if unsure what we were up to.

"Go on, Langley. Go run."

Every muscle tensed as if he were about to bolt, but he stood frozen in place, and turned his head to me with a hopeful expression that seemed to beg for confirmation.

"Yeah, boy. It's okay. Go run."

He fired out of there in an instant, jumped a low bush then dove into the brush beyond, with Mirabel tumbling awkwardly after him. I laughed, and so did Judith.

"That puppy's hopeless," she said with a smile. "Her ears are bigger than the rest of her. What kind of dogs are these?"

"Bluetick coonhounds, bred in the South. I'll tell you the whole story sometime."

"Okay."

I reached for Judith's hand and she flinched reflexively.

"Hey!" I complained. I wagged my bare ring finger at her. "I'm not married anymore."

"Yeah, sorry." She reached out and took my hand. Her hand was so warm. Just holding it made my blood race. "It all happened so fast. It'll take some getting used to."

I grinned and we went up the hill, swinging our arms between us.

Despite all the work the city did last summer, the hill was going wild again, this from the explosive growth of a wet spring. The brush had shot up knee high, while hairy vines of poison ivy snaked up some of the trees. I didn't mind. In another year or two the growth would be as thick as it ever was, a sheltering curtain of green. I paused to look around. Somewhere ahead I could hear Langley scooting through the brush, and the crash and plunk of Mirabel giving chase. The sun had just dipped behind the flank of the hill, casting everything in coppery hues. Judith looked at me as if trying to read my thoughts. The lowering light was soft on her cheeks. It brought out lovely shades in her eyes, warm shades, magical shades.

"May I kiss you?" I asked in a voice that sounded too harsh in that quiet moment. She turned her nose up flippantly.

"If you must."

"Aw, c'mon," I whined.

She grinned prettily then, and pressed her lips against mine, and in that instant my blood went feverish and I could hear the thunder crashing through the trees.

"I love you," I breathed after an eternity of seconds.

Judith looked at me with those soulful brown eyes of hers, shades of gold seeming to make their own light. She rested her face on my shoulder, and when she pulled away my shoulder was wet.

"Why are you crying?" I asked, taking her face in my hands. She sniffed and knuckled away a tear.

"Because," she said.

I tipped her chin up until our noses practically touched.

"Because?" I asked gently.

"Because I love you, too. I have since I picked you up off the floor at Lakes of the Clouds. But..."

My heart skipped a beat. A breath caught in my throat. Judith pushed away and turned.

"I waited for you, Carlton. That whole semester at Dartmouth. I knew about when you were supposed to finish, and as that day came near I would look out my window and down the road, expecting to see you walking up with your backpack, just the way you looked at Kinsman. And then that day came and went, and then a week, and then a month. I quit looking for you then, but I still thought the phone might ring, or a letter might come. Before long I went home for Christmas, and when I got back I knew that I would never see you again."

My chest ached and my eyes glistened. I went to her, but she took a step away. She turned to me suddenly.

"And now here you are, and I understand what happened..."

"I'm sorry, Judith. So sorry."

"I had to forget about you. Do you understand?"

I felt numb just then.

"I never forgot about you," I said shakily.

"I know." She came up to me and touched my face, gave me a sad smile. "And I never really forgot about you, but I made it into a fantasy, like something in a book. And I don't know..." She turned again and toed at the ground. "...I don't know if this is still a fantasy or something as real as Garfield Ridge."

"It's not a fantasy." I went to her and took her by the shoulders, turned her to face me. "It's not a fantasy. It's not."

She wiped her eyes and took my hand.

"We're supposed to be taking a walk, right?"

"Yeah."

We walked on quietly, my thoughts a jumble. I wanted to marry Judith; I wanted her with more certainty than I had ever wanted anything. But did she want me? I had planned to ask her before she left for California, in some magic moment that I was sure would appear like destiny, but suddenly I felt an almost panicked need to plunge in right now, as if any delay would compound her doubts and worsen my chances. Earlier I wouldn't have been worried at all, but now, after what she'd said, after what I had put her through, I wasn't as sure. What if she said no?

Presently we reached the old ash tree. I pointed to the limbs up high.

"That's where I found the bullet on my necklace."

"Really."

She followed my finger to the place at the crook of the limb, and when she looked down again I was on one knee. She gasped a breath.

"Judith?"

"Oh my God!"

"Judith, will you marry me?"

That came out shakily, not what I had rehearsed in my mind. Suddenly I felt foolish kneeling there, worse yet when Judith's eyes lit mirthfully and she started laughing, like a child to a silly joke.

"Carlton, you can't be serious." She took my hand and tugged. "Get up. *Please.*"

She glanced around self-consciously, as if there might be spectators in the bushes. The way I felt just then, I might as well have been running naked down the street. There were no rocks nearby large enough for me to crawl under. I stood with a hang-dog look on my face and considered sprinting off through the woods.

"Poor Carlton," she tried to pout, but she couldn't make her lips form around the laughter. I was so humiliated that I couldn't look her in the eyes.

"I just thought—" I muttered, looking down and kicking at last year's leaves.

"I know what you thought. Come on, let's talk." She put an arm around my shoulders and steered me on, while I kept my eyes down and felt my best hopes slipping away. "Why do you want to marry me?" she asked after we had gone a few numbing steps.

"Because I love you," I mumbled, eyes still downcast. She tipped up my chin and studied me thoughtfully while I looked left and right to avoid her gaze.

"And I love you," she said softly, no humor in her voice now. "But really, we barely know each other."

"That's not true!" I blurted. I gave her a hard stare, but she just smiled patiently, maybe sadly in a way.

We entered the clearing on top of the hill. The waist-high grass waved in the breeze like a dusky field of wheat. A few stars were beginning to glimmer to the east, while streamers of high cloud caught the last of the sun to the west. Judith let go of my hand and looked off.

"So how well do we really know each other?" she asked into the breeze.

"Pretty well," I replied, fidgeting a little.

"Okay. So what's your middle name?"

"I don't have a middle name."

"Really?" She looked at me oddly. "Why not?"

"I don't know, they just didn't give me one."

"Hmm—okay then. What's mine?"

"It's Adeline," I answered at once. She rounded on me, hands on hips and looking perturbed.

"How did you know that?"

"I saw it on your plane ticket," I replied with a cocky grin.

"Oh." She turned in thought, mulling something, then snapped her fingers. "Okay then, so who's your favorite Beatle?"

That came out of nowhere. I stumbled for an answer.

"Uh, I like Paul, I guess. How about you?"

"George is my favorite."

"*George?*"

She grinned at me, her teeth flashing in the lowering light.

"Yeah, I like George. Didn't know *that*, did you?"

"Aw, c'mon, Judith."

"And a million other things."

"I *love* you, Judith. Isn't that enough?"

"Is it?"

Her grin descended into a thoughtful line, and then she looked away with a sigh. I turned from her and gazed back the way we had come. The old ash tree stood beyond, abiding it all. The moment had slipped away like a last shallow breath. My temples ached. I exhaled and rubbed them, pondered how I could go on. There was nothing to be done, only heartache and a fleeting glimpse of happiness.

"Okay then," I said weakly. "We'd better get back."

I turned in utter resignation to find Judith down on one knee.

"Carlton?"

"Oh my God!"

"Carlton, will you marry me?"

She asked this with a frivolous grin that should have put me off, but all I could feel was how full my lungs suddenly felt, how fast my heart raced, and how nearly perfect the lavender sky reflected in her eyes.

"Oh, yes! God yes!"

I let out a whoop, gathered her around the hips and lifted her into the air. She grinned with delight and we kissed. We kissed and spun until we fell dizzily into the grass, and then we lay together, hand in hand, gazing at the sky as the stars came out.

* * *

Mom and Dad weren't ecstatic, but they weren't opposed to the idea, either. They were more surprised than anything else. It remained for Judith to meet Grandmother Villetta before Judith had to leave for California. I noticed with a twinge of jealousy that Judith wasn't nervous or self-conscious about these things the way I was.

Grandmother Villetta was ninety-three years old that summer, and she still got out to hoe her own garden. It was amazing. She was in her garden when we pulled up, gathering tomatoes from vines that were already hanging over the tops of their baskets. I parked by the creek and we walked across the yard to her garden. The sky was overcast but the clouds were high, not rain clouds. Rain was on the way, though, according to the weather man.

"Have you ever seen such pitiful tomatoes?" Grandmother muttered as we came up. She was stooped over in her dark velour dress, a chicken-and-apple patterned apron over that, and a wicker basket hanging on her arm. "All the wet makes 'em split like old grapes. I'll have to chop these up for sauce. Not good for anything else."

"Grandmother," I said. "I'd like you to meet Judith."

Judith walked right on up with her hand out and a bright smile. "Mrs. Smith, it's so nice to meet you."

Grandmother set the basket down then stood to work the kinks out of her back, although she couldn't achieve more than a stoop by the time she was up and taking Judith's hand.

"Well, now," she said in her bygone accent, "I reckon you can call me Grandmother Villetta just like everybody else. It's what I'm used to."

"Okay."

"Let's go sit on the porch for a spell. You like sweet tea, Judith?"

"I love it."

"I didn't know you had it where you come from."

"We don't."

"Well, each has their own ways. You come on with me now."

Grandmother looped an arm around Judith's waist and off they went, like old friends walking to church.

"Boy?" Grandmother hollered over her shoulder. "You bring that basket, you hear?"

"Yes ma'am," and I retrieved that basket with all haste.

We settled in on the porch rockers. Grandmother came out of the kitchen with a tall glass of sweet tea for Judith, then fell back into her own rocker.

"So you're a teacher, I hear," Grandmother said to Judith.

"Yes ma'am."

"We used to have a school right over there." Grandmother pointed with a crooked finger to a field across the creek. "Gone now, though." She seemed to go blank for a moment, finally: "Gone a long time."

"You have a lovely house," Judith said.

"Well, it's made do all right." She patted Judith on the knee. "Carlton? Why don't you run on over to the barn and make sure those chickens are doing what they're supposed to do."

"Grandmother?"

She gave me a look that said surely Maybelline hadn't raised an idiot.

"Oh, yeah, sure," I stuttered. "The chickens. Yeah."

I loped off the porch and across the yard, went in the barn and sat on a bale of hay. I scared off some barn swallows that shot out of there like little jets. "Chickens, sure," I groused. I drummed my fingers on my chin, shifted positions a few times, got up and fiddled with the tractor, went to a knothole to spy what was happening on the porch. Grandmother and Judith were smiling and laughing and talking a mile a minute. I wondered if I would be that comfortable when I met Judith's parents. Just the thought made me queasy.

After a time I sat back down on the hay bale and rocked back and forth to the creaking of the barn. Old rusty chains clinked from the upper joists. The barn still had the aromatic smell of last year's tobacco. Grandmother didn't keep animals anymore, just the chickens, and they were all out in the barnyard somewhere. I chewed on a stem of hay, drummed my finger some more, went to the knothole for another glimpse. Grandmother was on the porch alone.

"Carlton?" she shouted. "Aren't you ever goin' to finish up with them chickens?"

"Finally!" I exclaimed under my breath.

I sprinted back to the porch, leapt up on it the way I did when I was a teenager. I was ashamed to notice that I barely made it this time.

"You'll break your neck doin' that," Grandmother chided me.

"Yeah, it's not so easy anymore."

"Nothin' is," said Grandmother.

"Where's Judith?"

"Gone to the washroom."

"Oh."

Grandmother had that sparkle in her eye. She patted my knee.

"You should of took to this one in the first place," she said wryly.

"But I did, Grandmother," and then I realized how that must have sounded, "I mean—"

"I know what you mean, boy," and she patted my knee again and chuckled.

* * *

Something felt so familiar when I took Judith to the airport, and then it came to me, the day Jenny Peay left for college. I felt just as sad, sadder, and it must have shown because Judith put an arm around my waist and pulled me close.

"Hey," she said. "I had to wait seven years for you. You only have to wait a few months. That's not fair."

I laughed. "You're right, it's just…I'm afraid something's going to happen."

She tipped up and kissed me.

"Nothing's going to happen," she said. "Not this time. I know where to find you now."

We both grinned at that.

"And I know where to find you."

A garbled voice announced her flight over the speakers.

"That's me," she said. I held out her backpack and she shrugged into it. "Thanksgiving, Carlton. Bring a coat. It'll be cold up there."

"I will."

She kissed me again, broke my hold and sprinted up the jetway. This time she paused to look back.

FIFTEEN

The Taylors lived toward the north side of Oakhurst, in a log house on a scrubby hill overlooking a cleaved valley that bristled with lodgepole pine. A creek or a stream cut through down there somewhere, or so Judith told me, but it couldn't be seen through the towering growth. She and her brothers used to fish for trout in that stream, she said, and there was a swimming hole, although the water was always cold, cold, cold. I peered into the valley. The walls were so steep that it would probably take an hour or more of hiking switchbacks just to get to the bottom, with an even more arduous climb on the way back up. Still, I was a little jealous. Back home I had my hill. Judith had this.

There were mountains on the horizon, irregular ridges studded with trees like telephone poles, and beyond these, vaguely in the distant haze, the suggestion of craggy peaks, an occasional glimpse of white. Those must be the mountains of Eric Ryback's Pacific Crest Trail, I thought, as different from the Appalachian Trail as Maine is from Georgia—or Tennessee from California. Nothing was analogous to my experience. During my few days in Davis the previous year, I had only seen the town and the university, really not much different than anywhere else. But this... The woods were green and yet the place felt arid. The soil was crumbly, in some places as fine as powder, like the tailings from the zinc mine back in Carthage. The trees were mostly evergreens that I couldn't identify, mixed together with some oaks that didn't look like ours.

Judith watched me with a curious smile.

"It's different, isn't it," she said as a statement, not a question.

"Yeah."

"You would love it here."

"Maybe," I said, and this caused her to frown.

The sun set strangely in this time zone, coming in bright and strong even though it was late in the day. Shadows fell away from the trees in long columns rather than the dappled shadows of the woods I knew. *What would it be like to hike here?* I wondered. *What would it be like to spend months in these woods?*

"No, not maybe," I said on second thought. I leaned over and kissed her on the lips. "Definitely."

That brought back her smile. She slammed the car door with her hip.

"Time to go in and meet Daddy," she said with a mischievous grin.

"Uh, huh," I mouthed. My stomach felt queasy.

"Oh, don't worry, Carlton. He's going to love you, I promise."

"Uh, huh."

I picked up my suitcase and we went inside. Mr. Taylor met us at the door.

"Call me Eugene," he gushed, shaking my hand so vigorously that my head bobbed.

Eugene was a retired civil engineer. He was my father's age, and yet his face was smooth and pink, just some crow's feet at the corners of his hazel eyes. He was a tall man, fit. His hair was iron gray and thick, combed back from a shiny high forehead and hanging to his collar, where it made a little flip. I could see some of Judith in his cheeks and nose, but it was her mother, Lois, whom she took after. There was no denying that these two were mother and daughter. Lois was a retired school teacher. Looking at her, I knew that Judith would remain beautiful all her life. The two had the same hair, although I would not dare to speculate whether or not Lois colored hers; and their eyes were the same, vaguely exotic, like Mediterranean almonds, youthfully inquisitive and warmly brown. It was unsettling to look into Lois' eyes too long because of the images that formed in my mind.

Judith's brothers, James and Michael, wouldn't arrive until tomorrow. James was the oldest, in his thirties now, and then Michael, twenty-nine, I think. Neither brother had married yet. Neither Eugene nor Lois seemed concerned about it.

We settled in on couches around a central stone fireplace that crackled and put out a lot of heat. It wasn't really that cold outside, high 40s or thereabouts. Sweat popped out on my forehead. I shrugged out of my coat and draped it across an armrest. I was wearing a black sweater underneath, over a white dress shirt and black slacks. I considered tugging off the sweater as well, but was afraid I might appear rude. I was certainly overdressed, and not because of the heat. Eugene wore faded blue jeans and leather sandals, topped with a powder-blue polo shirt. Lois wore white slacks and a pink blouse, while Judith had on her khaki hiking pants and a green sweater, I think maybe even the same sweater she wore in '76. It was worn at the elbows and around the neck—could have been. The thought made me tingle. I clasped my hands in my lap and leaned forward.

"So, Carlton," said Eugene. "Finally."

"Yes, sir."

"Judy has told us so much about you."

"Yes, sir."

"Are you hot in that sweater?" Lois interjected. "I could take it for you."

"I'm fine, ma'am."

"You southerners are so polite," said Lois.

"Mom!" exclaimed Judith.

"And that accent," said Eugene.

"Daddy!" exclaimed Judith.

"No, sweetie, it's charming. I like it," said Eugene.

"Uh," said I.

We all went silent then. Judith sat next to me and took my hand, which helped. Finally:

"This is a nice house," I said, looking around. There were no ash trays. The Taylors didn't smoke cigarettes.

"Thank you, Carlton," said Eugene. "We built it when Judy was a baby."

Every time he called Judith *Judy* I had to pause. I tried it on my tongue silently but it didn't feel right, as if I were peeping through a window on a private family moment.

"Can I get you anything to drink, Carlton?" said Lois.

"Some wine or a beer?" said Eugene.

"Uh, some tea maybe."

Judith jumped up. "I'll get it, Mom. I made something special."

"We'll go together, sweetie. I need to check on supper."

Which left me alone with Eugene and a hot, hot fire.

"So Carlton," Eugene's sudden change of tone filled me with dread, "Judy's my only daughter. She's my baby, always will be."

This was the moment I knew had to come sooner or later.

"Yes, sir," I said hesitantly.

Eugene paused.

"No need to be nervous," he said.

"I'm not nervous, sir." Lie.

"Okay, then." He didn't believe me, that was plain. After a moment of reflection he continued. "But she's always been a level-headed girl. I think you know by now that Judy is pretty good at taking care of herself."

"Uh, huh."

He fixed me with a stern expression that had me desperate to break eye contact, but I didn't dare. Then his smile went wide and his teeth were as white as piano keys.

"So relax," he grinned. "You don't have to worry about us being judgmental or anything like that. If she loves you—and I can promise you she does—then we're happy to have you in the family."

I let out a long breath that made Eugene laugh.

"I bet you're glad we got that out of the way," he went on, still grinning.

"Yes, sir. Thank you"

"But..."

Uh, oh, there was more.

"...let me ask—and please don't take this the wrong way—what do you intend to do for a living? A career? You don't have a degree, I understand."

"Not yet sir, no." I fiddled with my hands. "I meant to, but things came up."

"I understand. It happens. But what about the future?"

What about the future? I was ashamed just then that I wanted to marry Judith but hadn't given this any thought at all. To say that to Eugene would make me feel unworthy of his daughter, something I was already grappling with myself. Instead:

"I make a good salary now. They say I'll get another promotion soon."

"That's good, Carlton. I don't mean to pry."

"No, sir. It's okay."

"Good. Well then—"

Just then Judith came out carrying a porcelain pitcher on a matching tray, along with tall glasses of ice.

"Here you go, Carlton," she said proudly. She filled a glass and handed it over. I took a tentative sip.

"Sweet tea!" I exclaimed.

"Sweet tea?" asked Eugene. "You mean already with the sugar in it?"

"What do you think?" Judith asked, bouncing on her heels.

"It's great."

"Oh, good." She was beaming like a little girl. "Try some, Daddy," and she handed him a glass. Eugene sniffed the glass before he tasted, as if he were sampling an unfamiliar wine.

"Why, that *is* good," he said. "Now *there's* something new."

Judith just stood there proudly, and I thought, how could I have ever dreamed that a woman like her would love me?

* * *

James and Michael arrived separately the next morning, which was Thanksgiving morning, Luke's first birthday, by the way. I wish I could say that Luke was in my thoughts, that it saddened me to miss his first birthday. The truth is, he wasn't in my thoughts at all. It wasn't until later that I realized, and then I felt guilty.

Michael arrived first, shortly after we had finished breakfast. I'd never had a bagel before, or cream cheese, or salmon; and their pancakes were as thin as tissue paper; and they ate them rolled up with whipped cream and strawberries, like dessert. Everything tasted good, except maybe the salmon, just so different from what I was used to. Judith had been a little snippish over breakfast, and I had a pretty good idea why. She'd wanted me to sleep with her last night, said her parents couldn't have cared less, but I couldn't do it, not in her parents' house, whether they cared or not. It just wouldn't have felt right. The trouble was—and this might seem hard to believe considering everything we had gone through—Judith and I hadn't been together since Garfield Ridge. She was desperate to get on with it. Me, too, but not there.

Michael pulled up in a white four-wheel-drive Jeep that looked gray from the layer of dirt that coated its scratches and dents. There was some kind of rack on the roof for carrying things. Big round fog lights with yellow lenses crowded the grill.

The Jeep sat high off the ground, and the tires looked like some you would see on a farm truck.

"Howdy, y'all," he said with exaggerated emphasis when we met him outside. Judith's glower wiped the grin off his face in an instant. "Oh. Sorry, sis." He walked right up to me and held out his hand. "You must be Carlton. I'm Michael, Judy's little big brother." All traces of fake accent were gone, which meant—and this was something about California that I still pondered over—no accent at all.

"Good to meet you," I said, shaking his hand. His grip was a little loose.

Michael was a bit shorter than Judith, a wiry, compact guy with a lot of energy, smiling all the time, always moving. He looked more like Judith and his mother, less like his father. His hair was a lighter brown, with streaks of blond in it, and he kept it long, tucked behind his ears. But his eyes were exactly the same as theirs. He was deeply tanned, although more reddish than brown, and there were stark untanned circles around his eyes, like a Lone Ranger mask in reverse. He was dressed in jeans and tennis shoes and a thick, white turtleneck sweater.

"Sis," he said with arms open. He hugged his sister first, and then his mother, and finally his father, who embraced him in a bear hug that wasn't common where I came from. And then he grabbed a brown leather duffel out of the Jeep and we went inside.

"So James isn't here yet," Michael commented as we went in.

"No, not yet," said Lois.

"Yeah, man," said Michael. "The traffic's brutal on the 99."

"It always is on Thanksgiving," said Eugene.

"And there was a wreck north of Madera," Michael added. "A chicken truck."

Everyone groaned at something they seemed to recognize in that.

"Where does James live?" I asked.

"San Jose," said Michael.

"Oh." I had no idea where San Jose was, wondered if it was the same one in the song, but I kept all of that to myself.

"Go put your bag in your room then come have some breakfast," Lois told her son.

"Okay, Mom."

Everyone wandered off, leaving Judith and me alone. I went to her. She fiddled with my collar. This morning I had on a red plaid flannel shirt and jeans. The shirt had gotten wrinkled in my suitcase, and the collar refused to hold its shape.

"Did you sleep well?" I asked. She pouted a little.

"It could have been better."

"I know. I'm sorry."

"Don't worry about it, Carlton. If anything, I think Daddy appreciates you even more."

"He appreciates me?"

She gave me the strangest look.

"Of course he does. Don't be so self-conscious."

"I think it's a southern *thang*."

Judith laughed. "Yeah, I bet."

Lois and Eugene were starting to get worried, but then James arrived just before noon. He was with a brown-skinned woman who had perfectly straight black hair down to her waist, and was so pretty she seemed to take all the sunlight for herself. They were in a bronze Mercedes, one of the little sporty ones. James opened the door for the woman and she stepped out. She wore a brown leather jacket over a white skirt that fell to her ankles, but the skirt rode up as she got out and I could see that she had long and smooth legs. James was in a black suit with the jacket unbuttoned, and a high-collared white shirt that was starched beyond any chance of wrinkling. His collar was open, no tie, and he had a dark five o'clock shadow going on. He was tall, composed, his father as a young man, no doubt about it.

"Mom. Dad." He went to them and they hugged. "Sis." He lifted her off her feet when they hugged, which made Judith giggle. He shook Michael's hand. "Sorry we're late," he said contritely. "The traffic on the 99—"

"Chicken truck," said Michael.

"Yeah."

"Gloria," Lois said to the woman. "I'm so glad you could come."

"I'm glad I could make it."

Gloria's accent was as thick as Mrs. Batista's, but sharper, with flatter vowels.

I stood back as all this went on. After all the hugging and handshaking and cheek kissing ended, James corralled them all up and said, "Let's get inside. It's chilly out here."

"Wait, James," said Judith. "You haven't met Carlton."

James turned to me as if confused by the oversight, and I could tell right then that we weren't going to get along.

"Carlton, is it?" he asked, offering his hand.

"Yes. And you're Judith's big big brother James."

James brushed that aside and took my hand. His handshake was one of those that squeezes too tight, but I didn't let on, just smiled and nodded and watched to see if that cocksureness in his eyes would go away, but it didn't.

"Okay, then," he said, turning as if I had been dismissed. "So let's eat."

"Oh, you know better than that, James," said Lois. "It won't be for another few hours yet."

"Then something. We're starved."

"I'll make you two a snack."

"Sounds great. So let's go."

They all bundled into the house, with me coming up behind and Judith looking over her shoulder, biting her lip.

We all took spots around the fireplace, some subtle pecking order there. Judith and I wound up on an end couch, while James and Gloria took the middle couch.

Eugene sat beside them, with Michael on a couch at the other end. Lois came out with a tray of crackers and cheese and shrimp cocktail.

"So Dad," James started up. "What do you know about computers?"

I learned that James was an investment banker, that Gloria was an actress, and that Michael was a ski instructor—at least some of the time. James was investing heavily in computer companies, he said. A lot of money to be made there. I didn't understand a word of it, had never even seen a computer and wouldn't know what to do with one. Judith looked on attentively and held my hand. Eugene was leaning forward, his chin propped on steepled fingers, contemplating his son's advice. Gloria seemed fascinated if not outright thrilled, Michael seemed bored, and Lois shuttled invisibly between the kitchen and the living room, bringing out drinks and thin slices of dark bread, nodding every once in a while at something James said.

The talk rattled on about investments, with James gesticulating as if he were conducting a symphony of his own words. His hands moved up and down, in and out, fingers spread, fingers closed, punctuating points, and then, somehow unnoticed, his hand came up with a Bloody Mary in it. He took a sip, winced and sucked his teeth.

"Just right, Mom," he said. "Thanks." And then he turned to me. "So Carlton, you're a—what was it?—assistant manager in a grocery store. Right?"

"That's right," I said.

"And so…what?" he said. He looked around at everyone then took another sip of his Bloody Mary. "So someday you get to be manager, then?"

His words came out as innocent as white cotton, but I could detect the sarcasm. I refused to let him bait me, though.

"Yeah. Maybe pretty soon."

"Well that's good, because—well, you have a couple of kids, don't you?"

"Yes, two boys. Tommy and Luke, and…" Just then I realized, and my stomach knotted. "…and today is Luke's first birthday."

"Oh, well. Congratulations to Luke then." James held up his Bloody Mary in salute. "Too bad you had to miss it. So where are your kids anyway?"

"They're with their mother."

"Oh, right. She was running for mayor or something, wasn't she?"

"No, that was her husband. But he lost."

"Right."

Nobody else seemed to be catching the strain in this conversation, not even Judith. I'm sure James was a great investment banker. I think he would have made a great used car salesman, too.

"So," he went on after another sip, which he performed in such a way as to make everyone follow his every movement, "you didn't go to college, I hear."

"No, I didn't."

Were I at the Hanshaw's house this would have made me blush with embarrassment, but I didn't feel that way with Judith and I didn't give a damn what James thought.

"Excuse me a minute, Carlton," Judith said with a patient smile. "I need to use the privy."

She grinned at her use of the trail term for toilet, and I grinned back. As she came around behind James she leaned over and whispered in his ear. James nodded, excused himself, and followed Judith out of the room.

"So Carlton," Michael said. "The Appalachian Trail. Judy told us all about it. And you did the whole thing? Wow."

"Yeah. It was great."

"That's quite an achievement," said Eugene. "It must take stamina, and a lot of courage."

"Well," I nodded shyly, "I don't know about that. At least for me. But I know for Judith it took those things."

Eugene nodded appreciatively. Gloria followed politely, but clearly had no idea what we were talking about.

"I would love to do it," said Michael.

"Let's go," I grinned. "I already know your trail name."

"What's that?"

"Little Big Man."

"Ha!" Michael laughed. "Maybe Little Big Brother instead."

"I like that one," said Eugene.

"Me, too," said Lois. She came up silently and sat next to her husband.

After some minutes, Judith and James returned. It was still going to be a while before dinner was ready, so we continued our conversations, talking a lot about the Appalachian Trail, the Pacific Crest Trail, and how important it was to be able to get away from time to time.

* * *

Dinner wasn't too different from what we had back home, except these folks didn't have cornbread, or green beans and bacon, or okra. Beyond that, I guess there are only so many ways you can cook and stuff a turkey. Judith's sweet tea was popular with everyone.

After dinner I offered to help wash the dishes, but Judith and Lois shooed me away. I wandered back into the living room, where Eugene, James and Michael were huddled close, discussing something of importance. Gloria had gone to lie down for a while, tired from the long drive and probably too much turkey for an actress to indulge in. I went outside and across to a wood rail fence at the precipitous edge where the valley fell away from the Taylor's property.

The sun was setting off to my left, spangling through some tall trees on a far ridge. It was cool but not cold. The air smelled clean, with a tangy evergreen scent, and every bit of haze was gone. The mountains in the distance glowed under the sun, sharp in contrast, with streaks of burnished snow. It was so quiet, no wind, not even birds. I thought when I turned my ears just right that I could hear the trickle and gurgle of water far below.

I leaned on the rail and took a deep breath. I thought things were going well with Judith and her family, except for James, but then he was a jerk. I saw some of Leavitt's kind in him. Perhaps that's the price of having a younger sister—or sisters.

A door slammed somewhere down the hill. A car started up. I couldn't see much of the town from here, the odd red tile roof through the trees, a sliver of road, and yet Oakhurst was a fair sized town. It must have been a great place for Judith to grow up.

I sensed James' warmth a second before he leaned on the fence next to me. He had come up so quietly that I was startled.

"James!"

"Sorry, Carlton. I didn't mean to scare you."

"You didn't scare me, just surprised me, that's all."

"Well, anyway—it's pretty here, isn't it?"

"Yeah."

"I love this place. We used to play down there." He pointed into the valley.

"That's what Judith said."

"Yeah, little Judy. She's not little anymore though, is she?"

"No, she's not."

"But she'll always be my little sister. Do you understand?"

"Maybe…" I said uncertainly.

"I want her to be happy."

"So do I. So does she."

"Look," he turned to me then, "let's call it what it is. Have you really thought this through?"

"What do you mean?" I asked with an edge, standing up straight. Outside and away from the others, I wasn't going to be bullied.

"Take it easy, Carlton. I mean, you've got this history, and you people are different from us."

"*You people?*"

"Southerners, I mean."

"So what?"

"So this: Where are you going to live? Judy's job is here. Judy's family is here. Do you really think she'll be happy in…in *Tennessee?*"

"I think she'll be happy wherever we settle down."

"So what about you, then? Judy has a career. She worked hard to get it. You didn't even go to college. What do you think *you've* got to offer?"

This had gone on long enough. Something told me that if I didn't put my foot down now, or as Grandmother would say, *get in the mud* with James, then Judith and I would never be left alone; and her brother here would make every visit to the Taylor's place pure misery.

"Listen, James," I growled. I stood toe to toe with him. He was a little taller than me, but that didn't count for much. I glared into his eyes and watched them shift uncertainly. "What I've got is Judith, and we shared something you can't possibly understand. What I think is you need to mind your own damn business. Got that?"

James took a step back in surprise. Just then a chilling breeze blew up from the valley.

"It's getting cold out here," he commented flatly, as if to deflect the tension, but I wouldn't let him off that easily.

"I said, *you got that?*"

"Yeah, Carlton," he looked away, "I got it." And with that he turned for the house.

* * *

Judith had a surprise for me the next morning. She had gone off after we finished breakfast, and when she came back she was wearing her khaki hiking shorts and her green sweater. I was on the couch by the fire, talking to Eugene about bluetick coonhounds. James and Gloria had already left for the drive back to San Jose, and Michael was out visiting some friends.

"So? Are you ready?" she asked mischievously.

"Ready for—"

"We need to get going, you know?"

"Going? Where are we—"

"You don't expect me to carry all this stuff myself, do you?"

"Stuff? What—"

Her grin was as lively as a sunny spring morning. Eugene reached behind the couch and lifted up an old Kelty backpack.

"I think this should do. Don't you? It's been in the garage for a while. I haven't used it since she was, maybe, twelve or so, but it doesn't have any holes in it."

"What the—"

"We're going hiking," said Judith, bouncing on her heels. "Just you and me."

* * *

Well, it had been a while. The Kelty's shoulder straps dug into my neck a little, but otherwise it hung pretty well on my back. Judith led me around the side of the house and into a stand of low oaks at the valley edge. Between two of the oaks, through some knee-high tufts of dried grass, I could make out a faint trace, the beginnings of a trail where it started down into the valley. The tops of tall evergreens rose just above the rim, like a field of Christmas trees suspended in the air. I smiled at Judith, bunched my shoulders to adjust Eugene's backpack, then we stepped between the oaks and into the sheltering forest.

The switchbacks were shallow and long in order to cut that steep grade, maybe a half mile one way, a sharp turn, and then a half mile back, just below where we had been before. There was always the impulse to cut across the switchbacks, to grab ahold of a small tree and lower ourselves down to the next rank, but to do so would erode the valley wall and eventually wash out the entire trail system. So we stuck to the trail. Judith was ahead of me, negotiating the narrow track with her arms out for balance. The trail was little more that the width of one shoe, gouged into the valley wall by the collective footfalls of hikers over the years. A slip and tumble would fetch you up against a tree below, so there wasn't any real danger of falling, just the humiliation of having to scramble back up to the trail.

We made several turns, zigzagging our way down. I guessed we had already hiked a couple of miles, and yet Lois could probably have stood on the rim and hollered at us to come for lunch, and we would have been able to hear her clearly. The Priest, a mountain in Virginia, had thirty-six of these switchbacks, a climb for southbounders, a descent like this one for northbounders, but none of The Priest's switchbacks were this long.

We continued on, sliding in places on dry pine needles that were as slippery as oil. The woods were thick, and although the rim was not that far above us, it felt as if we were in the deepest wilderness. Judith and I didn't talk on the way down, as if to do so would disturb the quiet rustle of the forest. At last we came out of the woods onto the gravelly bed of the creek. Judith called it a stream, but it was just a thin runnel of water dribbling between the rocks. Here and there, though, it opened into still pools deep enough to swim in. Occasionally a fish would plop, drawing our attention just in time to see a silvery tailfin slip below the surface.

We dropped our packs and paused to rest, sitting on a large rock that was round enough to have rolled miles down from the mountains. It was a little past noon. The sun came through from the sliver of blue above to glint off the trickling water. The rock was warm. I put an arm around Judith and pulled her close, and she leaned against my shoulder, breathing softly.

"What a great day," I said, looking off where the creek rounded a bend, catching the sun.

"I love it here," Judith said into my shoulder.

"So this is what you call a stream?" I asked sarcastically. She looked into my eyes in astonishment.

"You should see it in the spring, when the snow melts. It roars so loud we can hear it up top. You wouldn't want to be sitting here then."

"Where does it all go?"

"Into China Creek and the Fresno River. Maybe into the San Joaquin."

"Oh."

Judith stood and grabbed her backpack.

"Let's get going," she said. "There's a place I want you to see."

"Okay. Which way?"

"That way."

She pointed to the right, more or less north.

"Alright." I shouldered my backpack. "Let's do it."

We stayed with the creek, crunching through the wet gravel, sometimes having to climb around piles of boulders that had caught like stoppers in a drain. There would usually be a pool of water beyond these, water so clear I could see fish lazing along the pebbly bottom. The chill in the air kept me from sweating, even in the full sun, but still I had the urge to dive in.

We weren't hiking with any speed, just meandering along. We hadn't seen any other hikers, no campsites. We were all alone. Judith scrambled over some boulders, reached out a hand and pulled me up. We stood at a high point and looked ahead.

"There it is," Judith said. "Do you see it?"

The water was rushing a little faster here, through braids that looked like complicated knots around boulders and jumbles of smaller rocks. Now the creek looked like what I thought of as a stream, a moving thing with some width to it. The stream turned gently to the west, and in the bow was a smooth blanket of rich green grass bordered by thick woods, with a view of a sun-lit mountain peak where the stream parted the woods beyond.

"Wow," I said in a hushed breath. Judith looked on excitedly.

"Let's pitch the tent right over there," she pointed, "with the trees behind us."

"Sure," I said. "It looks perfect."

Suddenly we were running, splashing across a shallow part of the stream and then onto that soft bed of grass. I dropped my backpack at the edge of the woods, got it open and yanked out the tent; but before I could assemble the poles, Judith grabbed me and pulled me to the ground, and we lay in that soft grass, laughing and tugging at clothes, and then we were naked in the sun, just the two of us, Willow and Jake.

* * *

Later, after the sun had set, we bundled up in our sweaters and sleeping bags and lay under the stars. Despite the light glow from Oakhurst, we could clearly see the trailing cloud of the Milky Way. The stars were like specks of glitter suspended in indigo-colored oil. There wasn't a moon, but the stars themselves were bright enough to flicker on the water and cast the woods in pale shadow.

Judith shivered and snuggled up closer to me. I kissed her and watched the stars sparkle in her eyes.

"Was it worth the wait?" I asked softly.

"Yes, since I had no choice." She pretended to pout, but then she giggled and nuzzled my neck. "So now that you've met James," she went on, "do you still want to marry me?"

"Ha!" I laughed. "If I'd met James when I first came off the trail, I think you'd hate me today."

"No way," she said incredulously, lifting onto an elbow, cupping her face in a hand.

"Uh, huh. He reminds me of a guy I ran into on the trail in New York. Kind of full of himself. I think back then I probably would have punched James out."

"Ooh, poor James. That would have been bad."

"You know it. So—maybe sometimes things just work out for the best."

"It didn't feel that way to me a few years ago."

"How about now?"

"Yeah…" She kissed me warmly. A shooting star streaked across the sky, gone before I could say anything. Judith turned onto her side and pressed against me, her head resting on my shoulder. "Carlton?" she whispered.

"Yeah."

"I want a June wedding."

"But…" I scooted onto my elbows. Judith sat up then, gathering her sleeping bag around her shoulders. "…but that's so long from now."

"It's not that long."

"It's *months*." I counted quickly. "*Seven months*."

"Don't you think it will be worth the wait?" she asked with a grin that shone in the starlight.

"Yeah," I chuckled, "since I have no choice."

"You're bad," she said mockingly. If we'd been out of the sleeping bags I think she would have slapped my behind. But then her face went serious and she lowered her voice. "I want to get married here, in California. Is that okay?"

I hadn't really thought about it, but it didn't matter to me one way or the other. "Sure it's okay. Why not?"

She relaxed at that and we lay down again, holding one another close.

"Carlton?" she whispered doubtfully in my ear. "Where are we going to live?"

I hadn't thought about that either, just assumed.

"Where do *you* want to live?"

"I want you to be happy."

"Well, I want *you* to be happy."

"I'd like to keep my job," she said hesitantly.

I had to pause a moment to think. Maybe James was right. I really hadn't thought this through. I could feel the warmth of her lips on my ear, her waiting breaths. I turned to her, nose to nose. Her brows were knitted with worry. I smiled faintly.

"*Ba-by, ba-by,*" I sang huskily "*Baby don't leave me.*"

She giggled and kissed me and nuzzled into my neck, and I worked my hands into her sleeping bag and under her sweater; and the stars wheeled above as we made love in the silver light.

* * *

Judith could have said she wanted to live in Timbuktu and I would have followed her without question, but that didn't make it any easier to tell everyone back home. Mom and Dad weren't overjoyed by the idea, but they weren't overly distressed either. Evelyn was unexpectedly pleased, and I wondered why. They all lived in Belle Meade now, in a classy antebellum not-quite-mansion at the end of a long, hickory-lined drive. I ground my teeth every time I drove up that thing to get the boys, the house getting bigger as I drew closer, the old Pontiac looking more like the Mexican gardener's car than a car that should have belonged to the father of Evelyn's children. She seemed to enjoy my unease at these meetings. I'm sure she did.

We were sitting in gold embroidered wingback chairs in the drawing room when I told her my plans. A nursemaid was looking after Luke upstairs, and Tommy was in his playroom. And Brad? I never saw him, didn't care to anyway.

Evelyn was dressed in white, a full skirt and a crochet sweater. She had changed her hair, permed it, a lot of oily looking curls that didn't so much as quiver as she spoke. It was January. I hadn't seen them since I got back from California. They had all gone off as a family over Christmas, someplace warm, Cozumel, I think.

"How wonderful," she said in that put-up air of hers. I was certain I could see little wheels turning in her head. "We're so happy for you."

We? That's the way she spoke now, not I, *we*.

"I don't know what to do about the boys," I said.

"Oh, the boys will be fine, Carlton. It might even be for the best—you know, the disruption."

"Disruption?"

"It's hard on them, having to go back and forth. You can see that, can't you?"

"Now wait a minute—"

"And Tom's been so upset since…well since you left us."

Damn her.

"It wasn't like that and you know it, Evelyn."

"Well, what can we say? One minute you're there, the next you're gone. And now this, moving across the country for that…that woman? What are we supposed to think? And Tom?"

"He can come visit."

"Not until he's much older. No, we wouldn't be comfortable having him so far away at his age."

"We? Who's we?"

"Why, Brad and I, of course."

"Brad doesn't have anything to do with this."

"Oh yes he does, which you will find out if you make trouble."

"*What?*"

"Don't make a scene, Carlton. Tom might hear."

I was barely in control of myself, squeezing the armrests, clenching my teeth. Evelyn smiled her scheming smile. She was hoping I would blow, wasn't she? I took a deep breath and thought of Judith instead, of the forest and the stream and our last night together.

"Just go get the boys, Evelyn. I'll have them back on Sunday by five."

"Of course, Carlton." She rose with the poise of a stalking cat. "But you should know that Tom will probably not want to go with you."

"Why not?"

"Well, what have we just been talking about? Give me a minute to bring them down."

She left the room and I sat there as if waiting in a doctor's office. A fancy clock on the mantle chimed. The day was lifeless through the gilded window, damp, cold. Fallen leaves had caught in the patio shrubs. After a minute Evelyn returned. The nursemaid, a matronly black woman, held Luke, who was asleep. Tommy stood next to Evelyn, clutching her skirt.

"Hi, Tommy," I smiled. "Are you ready to go?"

"I don't wanna go," he whined.

"It's okay, Tom," soothed Evelyn. "Go with your father now."

"No!" He shrugged away from her and turned his back.

"Tommy? C'mon, son." I moved toward him.

"No! No! No!" he cried. "I don't wanna go!"

Tommy was pitching a fit worse than anything I had ever seen. He sat on the floor and folded his arms, and wouldn't be moved no matter what I said. My impulse was to lay a hand across his backside. The nursemaid seemed to sense this. She clucked her tongue and shook her head just barely. Luke woke up and began to fuss and twist in her arms.

"I'd better go see what I can do to calm this baby down, Mrs. Burton," she said.

"Yes, Carmella. Please," said Evelyn, as if she were deeply concerned, which I doubt.

Carmella turned for the door. "Tom? Come with me now," she said in a voice that would brook no foolishness. She held out her hand for Tommy and they left, with Tommy kicking his heels on the carpet.

"Evelyn? What's the matter with him?"

"He's upset, Carlton. Maybe we should skip this visitation. I'll speak with Brad and see what he thinks. Maybe we can try again next time."

"But—"

"You should go, Carlton. Before you make things worse."

I have never hit a woman in my life, but it was all I could do to keep from slapping her off her feet. I had to get out of there before I did do something foolish, so I left, stalking out, slamming the door and squealing tires below those stately hickories.

* * *

Gracie didn't sound hopeful. We met at her place, a cozy two-bedroom brick house off of Antioch Pike.

"We can go in and file for a modification, Carlton, but the court will appoint a guardian *ad litem* for the boys; and they'll want psychological tests. It could get expensive—really expensive."

"She did this on purpose, I bet. She turned Tommy against me."

"Unfortunately, this happens a lot. And I wouldn't put anything past Evelyn. But..." She hesitated as if to carefully choose her words, "...well, Carlton, you *are* moving away. You're not going to get to see much of Tommy anyway. And Luke's just a baby. He won't know anything about any of this. Maybe it would be best to just let this go for now. In a couple of years—who knows? Tommy will be older. He might be more understanding."

"You're probably right, but I can't stand the thought of letting her get away with this."

"She only gets away with it if you lose your cool. Once you and Judith are married and settled in, we can take another look at a modification, set it up where you get them for alternate summers and Christmas breaks. Then you can spend enough time with the boys to build a good relationship, and there won't be anything she can do about it."

"Yeah, you're right." And she was. It was a blow to my pride, but it was the right thing to do.

"Good," she nodded in approval. "Then stay on the visitation schedule for now. When you're ready to go out to California I'll let the court know and we'll see what happens then."

"But what if Tommy still won't go with me?"

"I can't do anything about that unless we go to court, and then you'll be into all that expense I told you about. Maybe get your Mom to go with you, or your Dad. Tommy might be more open to them."

"Yeah, okay," I agreed reluctantly. "That's a good idea."

Angelina came bouncing into the room just then. She was a darling little girl. She had her mother's petite features and Latin eyes, and the long black hair with straight-cut bangs that Gracie had worn when we were in high school. Her mouth was different than Gracie's, though, wider, with pink gums that showed when she grinned. She had on Oshkosh denim overalls, which made her look like a tomboy, and considering the energy she was putting out, I suspected she could tumble with the boys, no problem.

"Angelina, say hello to Mr. Carlton," said Gracie. She had moved subconsciously from a professional voice to a Spanish-inflected accent. She rolled the r in my name, and her daughter's name came out as *Anhelina*. Gracie hadn't talked like that when we were in school. I wondered if she had been hiding it so she wouldn't sound like an outsider; so she would fit in. She had been such an insecure girl. Not anymore.

"Hi, Mr. Carlton," Angelina said shyly, toeing the floor. No Spanish accent there. Angelina spoke like a little girl born and bred in the South.

"She's really grown," I said to Gracie.

"Yeah, she'll be six soon."

"Wow."

"She's a smart girl. I'm trying to get her into an advanced school. If I can, guess what?"

"What?"

Gracie grinned. "She would be going to school with Tommy."

"Really?"

"Yeah, but one grade back."

"Huh. Looks like you might be seeing more of Tommy than me."

"Maybe so."

"And Evelyn, too."

Gracie groaned. "Yeah, that too."

* * *

I took Gracie's advice, but I took Kenny with me to get Tommy instead of Mom or Dad. This was two weekends later. Tommy had loved Kenny so much that I thought surely it would work, and Kenny didn't hesitate when I asked. I hadn't seen much of Kenny the past year. He looked thin, almost emaciated, with dull eyes, lanky hair, and that long, droopy mustache. He reeked of cigarette smoke, but fortunately not the other. At my look of concern he swore he was okay, just doin' what he had to do to get by.

Evelyn met us at the door. She was formal and tense, eying Kenny with something like loathing.

"Hello, Kenneth," she said tightly.

"Hi, Evie," Kenny said with old, toothy familiarity. Evelyn's face went hard, but she recovered quickly and told us to wait in the foyer. The boys would be along shortly.

"She's still a fox," Kenny said under his breath as Evelyn walked away. I sighed and groaned. Kenny played drums on his knee, and then Evelyn came out with Tommy and Luke.

Tommy eyed me with suspicion, but Kenny made a face and Tommy went right to him like old times. Kenny knelt, and Tommy poked a finger in Kenny's mustache.

"It's so big," said Tommy.

"Just the way you like it, huh guy? Umph." Kenny tried to lift Tommy but couldn't do it. "You're too big for that now," he said, so took Tommy by the hand instead.

"Just Tommy tonight. Okay, Evelyn?" I said. You would think the floor had just fallen out from under her.

"But Carmella's off tonight," she complained.

"So?"

"So what am I supposed to do? No, Carlton. It's your weekend."

So I took Luke in my arms, feeling as strange to him as he to me. He babbled and reached out a hand to his mother.

"Mama," he said.

"When did he start talking?" I asked in surprise.

"Since about when you took off for California. He can walk a little now, too."

"I missed his first steps?"

Evelyn just shrugged.

"Here," she said. She hung Luke's diaper bag on my arm.

Somehow while all this was going on, we had been discretely herded out the door.

"Sunday by five," she said. She wasn't asking, she was telling. And with that she closed the door in our faces.

We drove over to Kenny's house. Kenny kept Tommy occupied in the back seat, while the steady drone of the old Pontiac put Luke right to sleep. I caught glimpses of Tommy and Kenny in the rear view mirror. Tommy seemed to be doing well back there.

"Maybe we could hang out at your place a little bit," I said to Kenny. "To give Tommy time to adjust, you know?" I was afraid Tommy would throw a fit if he were left alone with me. The thought of it hurt.

"Yeah, man. No problema."

Kenny was roomating with some guys in an old two-story brick-and-frame house near downtown. It was a seedy neighborhood, but all Kenny said he could afford these days. After rehab he hadn't been able to find a regular job, so instead he traded his van for an equally aged Econoline box truck, which he used as a mobile car repair shop. The truck was parked out front on the street. Kenny had his tools in there, his sole means of support, but the truck was so old and rusted and dirty that no one would ever deign to break into it.

We went into the house, with me carrying Luke, still asleep, and Kenny leading Tommy by the hand. It was dark now. A bare bulb hanging by a wire lit the front porch. Someone had taped newspaper to the insides of the windows, old and yellowed. Big flakes of white paint were peeling off the window frames.

It was almost as cold inside as out. The carpet was brown shag. It felt sticky under my shoes. Kenny flipped on a light. I looked around warily at the filthy room. Kenny misunderstood my expression.

"Naw, man, it's cool. We don't do that anymore. Don't worry."

Oh. He thought I was looking for drugs.

"Isn't anybody here?" I asked.

"Doesn't look like it," he shrugged. "Have a seat. I'm gonna grab a beer. Want one?"

"No thanks."

"Okay."

I sat on a threadbare couch with Luke in my lap. Tommy fiddled around, then blew out a breath and fell back into a mismatched but equally worn recliner. Kenny came out with his beer tipped to the ceiling. He took a last slug, crushed the can and tossed it into a cardboard box that was overflowing with similarly crushed cans.

"Okay, big guy," he said to Tommy. "That's my chair, so hop up."

"Aw."

Kenny dropped into his chair, then grabbed Tommy around the waist and tickled him. Tommy giggled in delight then scooched up onto Kenny's lap.

"Ugh, Mister Tom. You're so heavy now."

"Am not."

"Are, too."

"Am not."

Kenny laughed, his gums showing. His teeth didn't look that great.

"So Kenny," I said, "what's been goin' on lately?"

"Just tryin' to make money, man."

"Been getting any jobs with your truck?"

"Some. Kinda slow right now, though."

I looked around. "How many roommates do you have?"

"Five."

"What do they do?"

"Music wannabes. You know how it is."

"Oh, yeah." I spotted a guitar with a broken string. "So they're, what, all out playing gigs right now?"

"Guess so. Hop up there, Mister Tom. I need to grab a beer."

Kenny slouched across to the kitchen, and then I heard some thumps coming down the stairs. A woman walked in, our age but looking rode hard and put up wet. She had stringy brown hair and a waspish waist. She wore ratty jeans and a black AC/DC T-shirt. A barbed-wire tattoo encircled her right arm just below her sleeve.

"Hey," she said tiredly.

"Hey," I said back.

"You Kenny's friend?"

"Yeah."

Kenny came out of the kitchen chugging his beer.

"Oh, hey Stacie," he said. "I didn't think anybody was home."

"I was sleepin', man."

"Stacie, this is Carlton and Mister Tom, and that little guy is Luke."

"Good to meet you," we said as one.

Stacie pulled a flattened cigarette out of her back pocket. Before I could say anything she had it lit.

"Got another beer?" she asked Kenny.

"Oh, hey Stacie. We don't smoke around the boys," said Kenny.

She blew out a long, disdainful puff.

"Sorry, man." She picked something out of her teeth. "It's my last one." She turned and trudged up the stairs, trailing smoke all the way.

"We'd better go, Kenny," I said then. Stacie's acrid smoke draped me like a filthy blanket.

"Already, man?"

"Yeah, we'll be late for dinner. C'mon, Tommy."

Surprisingly, Tommy didn't whine at all, he just fell in behind me and we went out. Kenny crushed his beer can and threw it in the box.

"See you around, man," he said.

"Yeah, see ya."

* * *

Probably worst for me was when I had to quit my job at Hill's. Mr. Iverson's eyes misted when I told him the news. He was so old now, with deep folds in his face, silver hair that was as fine as silk, and eyes that were once handsomely blue but seemed to be growing paler as time went by. He was like a grandfather to me. I felt a pang that went deep. He should have retired long ago—I wish he had retired before this came up, then I wouldn't have had to witness his pained affection for me; wouldn't have had to feel that I had let him down. I promised Mr. Iverson that I would stay through Memorial Day weekend, even though I was barely hanging on during those months and months away from Judith.

Judith and I talked on the phone from time to time, but mostly we wrote letters, Judith's in her smooth and even script, so lovely to read, and mine in my coarse scrawl, which sometimes I couldn't even read myself but Judith said was just fine. She wrote about her kids, her teaching, and how much she missed me. I wrote that Tommy was getting better, although he still wouldn't let me hug him and he wouldn't go up the hill with me. She wrote that I should be patient. I wrote that I missed her terribly.

Sometimes Judith's letters would include a Polaroid. One was of her and her kids in the classroom, all the kids making faces and showing off, Judith smiling so prettily that my heart ached. My favorite was a Polaroid of her standing at the fence rail overlooking the valley. She was wearing cowboy boots and jeans, and a denim shirt with the sleeves rolled to her elbows. She stood toward the camera with her arms crossed, but her face was in profile, looking off into the distance, contemplative. It must have been a breezy day because a wisp of hair was caught on her lips. The sun was low when the photo was taken, afternoon I think, because the glow on her skin looked amber and warm. I kept that photo with me in a pocket. Months on the Appalachian Trail seemed to go by quicker than this.

In early May the water pump went out on the Pontiac. I called Kenny, thinking that he could probably use the work, but I got Stacie on the phone instead.

"He hasn't been around," Stacie said. The tone of her voice made my call sound like a major inconvenience.

"He hasn't? Where is he?"

"It's not my job to keep up with him, man."

"Look, sorry."

"Tell ya what. I'll let the guys know you're lookin' for 'em. They probably know where he is."

"Thanks, Stacie."

"Sure, man," and she hung up.

Kenny called late that afternoon.

"Hey Kenny."

"Hey man."

"I called the house and Stacie said you were gone. Everything okay?"

"Yeah, it's cool. I've been doin' some jobs is all."

Kenny's voice didn't betray any sense of worry or concern. He sounded fine, so I told him about the water pump. No problema, he told me, so we set it up.

He came by the next day, parking his truck in the street at the foot of the hill. There was no way he would ever be able to get that lumbering box of a truck up the driveway, so I put the Pontiac in neutral and coasted it down the drive, angled it around the corner and parked it with the right wheels rolling up into the grass along the street. Kenny was rattling around in the back of his truck. He hopped out with a red toolbox in his hand. He had on greasy jeans and a yellowing T-shirt, a blue bandana around his head.

"Did you get the pump?" he asked.

"Yeah."

"And the fan clutch and the belts, too?"

"Yeah, I got 'em all, just like you said."

"Oh, and the antifreeze?"

"Yeah, that, too."

"Good."

He flipped the lids on his toolbox, took out wrenches, and started banging around under the hood. He seemed subdued, didn't talk much. I didn't probe further, as if to do so might reveal something I would rather not know about.

I watched him work for a while, old and greasy parts coming out of the car. Some he tossed into the grass, while he laid others around his feet. He skinned a knuckle and cursed, but kept at it, not saying much. After a while of this I wandered over to his truck. The box had a roll-up door, like a moving van, and it was open. Inside was his big upright toolbox, strapped to the wall with bungee cords. The floor was filthy with granular oil-dry, like kitty litter. I saw a flimsy card table and folding chair, a styrofoam ice box, and a stained mattress from a twin bed. A coffee can was over-filled with cigarette butts. Opened cardboard boxes had dirty clothes flung over the flaps. One was full of crushed beer cans. There was a rectangular mirror on the wall, some greasy handprints, and a Playboy centerfold of a girl in a baseball cap leaning naked on a bat.

And there in the corner, almost concealed in the litter, a syringe.

My stomach rolled in disgust. How long had this been going on? Kenny had held my son—he had held *Tommy*—in his lap. Had he been doing it then?

He seemed to know what I had seen when I walked back to him.

"I got it under control, man," he said. He was fitting the fan back in place. A cigarette bounced in his lips. He didn't look up at me as he spoke.

"Kenny?"

"It's cool, man," he said. He did look up at me then, flashing his gummy smile, holding his cigarette between his teeth. His smile looked more like a grimace.

He resumed his work, fitting the radiator shroud into place, spinning his ratchet.

Then:

"Go start it up, man."

I sat numbly in the seat and turned the key. The Pontiac chugged a little but then roared to life. I let it run while Kenny checked his work. The sun shone brightly that day. It was getting hot in the car. I could smell grease burning, but this passed.

"Okay, man," Kenny shouted. He slammed the hood and wiped off a handprint, then bent over to put his tools away.

I shut off the engine and got out. Kenny was already carrying his tool box to the truck. I watched him until he disappeared around back of the truck, and then I followed, dread pulling at my steps as if I had lead weights in my stomach. I found him squatting on the lip of the box's floor, gangly bare arms resting on his knees. I looked for tracks, didn't see any. He noticed where my eyes had gone but made no comment.

"You're good to go," he said instead, as if nothing in this scene was out of the ordinary. "Take that old pump to the parts house and they'll give you the core exchange for it."

"Why don't you take it, Kenny? It's a couple of bucks, isn't it?"

"Naw, man. That's your money."

"Okay."

There was a battle going on in my head, whether to push this or let it go—actually, whether to push this or get away.

Grandmother Villetta told me something once, something that shames me even now when I think about Kenny. It was a warm summer day during the time when Dad was teaching me how to drive Old Man Hackett's truck on the farm. Back then, Grandmother had her trash hauled to a dry pond in the woods out past the barn, where the trash was thrown in and left for nature to deal with. Over the years that pond had filled with successive generations of trash: rusty tin cans beneath shiny aluminum cans; old canning jars with the wax seals still in place, their contents murky and sinister after having been discarded perhaps decades ago; oxidized plastic bottles, and a 1950s Frigidaire peeking up through the refuse like a berg in the sea. I hauled the trash for her that day, and as I tossed the trash out of the bed of the truck I got splashed with something wet and nasty.

"Oh, gross!" I cried, flinging that stuff off my hand.

Grandmother overheard me from the cab of the truck. She turned around in her seat and said to me, her voice muffled through the rear window, "Well, Carlton, you can't work with trash without getting a little on ya."

I didn't push it with Kenny. Instead I took a step back and thumbed through my wallet.

"How much do I owe you, man?" I asked him, averting my eyes.

"Naw, man. I don't charge friends."

"But Kenny—"

"It's cool, man. You'd do the same for me."

Silence fell. Kenny jumped down and pulled the door closed. He walked toward the driver's door but I didn't follow, just stood there with my wallet out, my stomach turning. He climbed in with a creak and the rocking of springs, slammed the door and fired up the engine. Blue smoke belched around me, then Kenny stuck his head out the window.

"I hope you have a good wedding," he hollered. His face went thoughtful and then he frowned, his mustache drooping past his chin. He killed the engine and sat there for a minute, just looking at the ground. Then he turned back to me. "You know," he said, his voice seeming to break, "you never introduced her to me."

Without another word or backward glance he fired up the engine again, threw it into drive and sputtered off. I stood there as the blue exhaust dissipated, and the rumble of his truck no longer carried to me on the wind.

* * *

Judith had everything organized on her end. She lived in a small rental house in Fresno, but she didn't mind moving if I didn't like the place. I would be staying with her parents until the wedding. Everything would be southern-proper. I could just picture her smiling on the other end of the phone as she said this. I had to laugh.

"What?" she asked, still smiling I was sure.

"What makes you think we're all so proper?"

"Are you telling me I'm not marrying a proper guy?" She tried to make herself sound hurt, but I knew better.

"Well," I hedged, "I've done some things in the woods."

"Oh, Carlton, you're so *bad*."

We both fell out laughing.

"See you soon," I said when I caught my breath.

"Not soon enough."

"I love you."

"I love you, too."

"Bye."

All of my stuff was packed. I was shipping some things, and Mom let me store some other things in the attic. For a while I thought I would drive the Pontiac out there, but then after the water pump I was afraid the car might break down in the desert somewhere and leave me stranded. So I flew out on the Tuesday after Memorial Day, carrying nothing but a suitcase.

It was a bright morning, cool and clear and welcome after a gray and humid holiday weekend. Mom and Dad drove me to the airport in the El Dorado. Dad focused on the driving, while Mom leaned on the seat-back and scrutinized me with proud eyes.

"You look nice," she said.

I had bought a casual suit, navy slacks and a brown tweed jacket.

"Thanks."

I wasn't nervous, I was so excited I could barely sit still. In a few hours I would be with Judith. Just a few more hours.

We pulled up out front of the airport. I wanted to go in alone because I was afraid Mom would break down crying, but her eyes weren't wet at all.

"We're very happy for you, Carlton," she said. "We'll see you in a couple of weeks. Sadie's going to fly here first, and then we'll all come out together."

It saddened me that Grandmother Villetta was too frail to make the trip herself.

"Are you excited?" Mom went on.

"Crazy excited," I smiled.

I got out and hugged Mom. Dad shook my hand. If anything, his were the eyes that were wet. And then I grabbed my suitcase and hustled inside.

S IXTEEN

Judith and I were married in the open air of Yosemite Valley during the afternoon of June 25, 1984. Lois and Eugene drove me up from Oakhurst the day before, while Judith made the drive from Fresno separately with her friend Susan, who would be Judith's bridesmaid. We each had rooms in the Ahwahnee Hotel, but things had been carefully arranged to prevent Judith and me from seeing one another beforehand, accidentally or otherwise. Judith, it seemed, was very traditional about some things, less so about others. There would, for instance, be no rehearsal. Fate would shape how smoothly things went, and if things didn't go smoothly, then…well, we would have to dwell on the meaning of that later.

She was also very clear on the kind of wedding she wanted. I didn't interfere with the planning, not that I felt excluded in any way, it's just that her face lit up whenever she described her vision for the wedding, and I was afraid any ham-fisted input from me might diminish a little bit of that excitement. I was perfectly happy to go along. I knew I was in good hands this time.

Judith wanted a white wedding—all white—down to my tuxedo, my tie, my shoes and socks. In the hours before the wedding I was terrified of getting a smudge on that tux or a scuff on those shoes. There would be no way to hide the least imperfection, and no way to do anything about it on short notice. It was the same for Michael, who stood as my best man. There would be no other groomsmen, and Susan would be the only bridesmaid. Judith didn't want a crowded wedding. She thought the ceremony would be more intimate with just we few, and she was right.

The wedding took place in a grassy glade set within a thicket of dogwood trees. The ivory-white dogwood bracts had all turned to summer green by then, but in their places were white silk flowers, hundreds of them painstakingly tied onto the limbs. It looked as if the sky had opened up with pure white confetti, catching in the trees, dappling the green grass all around. The sky was clear blue, the sun coming in at a slant, lighting those flowers in myriad ways, like a freak blizzard from a cloudless sky. A couple of dozen white folding chairs had been set up for family and guests, and behind these, at the entrance to the glade, a white arched trellis strung with ivy.

I wandered out earlier to survey the preparations, leaving that immaculate white tuxedo coat hanging in my room, wearing my street shoes in place of those glossy patent leather ones. A white podium had been set up in the soft grass for the minister. The Taylors were a non-denominational family. The minister, Everett Wilkins, was from a Unitarian church in Fresno. I had met with him the previous evening. He was a heavy guy in his forties, with a thin blond comb-over and round eyeglasses that looked too small for his face, quite a contrast to Dr. Sherman at Woodmont.

"Don't worry, Carlton," he told me. "The service will be pretty much what you're accustomed to, maybe just a little more free-form. We like to have fun when we marry people." He chuckled at some internal imagery. "I won't ask you to repeat things you can't remember. Other than that, just follow along. Are you nervous?"

"No, not really," I said. What I didn't say was that I'd had previous experience with this.

"Good. We wouldn't want you breaking out in a sweat. It's supposed to be warm tomorrow, maybe in the 80s."

He smiled. I expected him to put a comforting hand on my shoulder, but apparently the paternal aspect wasn't one of their practices.

I stood at the podium, looking beyond it at what would fill my view while Everett performed the service. Ahead, through some tall pines, was the towering gray limb of Glacier Point, and off to my right, the wispy ribbon of Yosemite Falls. Judith would stand with the massive, rounded side of Half Dome in view to her left. It was an almost overwhelming vista. Nothing along the Appalachian Trail looked like this, not even the White Mountains. There couldn't have been a more spectacular place to say our vows.

Michael came up quietly, a mischievous smirk on his face. He was wearing his full tuxedo, although his collar was open, his tie dangling around his neck.

"Be careful, man," I said urgently. "If you get dirty…"

"Don't worry, I've been careful. Judy won't have anything to complain about."

"That's good. Do you have the rings?"

"Yeah, got 'em in my pocket." He patted his right leg.

I had been back to Draper Jewelers in the spring. They knew me so well by now that they had been kind enough to let me trade in my old ring. Who knew what Evelyn did with hers? These new rings had been specially made for me, from a vision that had come to me in a dream. It was going to take a long time to pay them off. If not for my relationship with Drapers, I doubt that I would ever have been able to afford them. The rings were bands of polished gold, the edges encircled with tiny diamonds. Judith's ring held a larger diamond that was mounted in such a way as to seem to swirl into being from the smaller diamonds, like the brightest star in a galaxy. The truth is, Judith probably would have been happy with plain gold bands—and I mean that—but I wanted her to have something special.

"Are you ready?" Michael asked.

"I can't wait," I said.

"You don't look nervous."

"I'm not nervous. I've never been more sure about anything."

"That's good. Do you know how to tie one of these damn ties?"

I looked at him and laughed.

"I have no idea."

"Do you think she'd notice if we left them off." My arched brows gave him his answer. "Yeah, well," he went on, "it was a thought. I'd better go find Dad, then. He'll know how to do it. See you back at your room?"

"Yeah, in a little while."

"Oh, your parents just showed up. I saw them at the reception desk."

"Finally. I was starting to get worried."

"Man, your sister's a babe."

"Dude!"

"Well," he fidgeted self-consciously, "she is. Anyway, see ya later."

I surveyed that view a final time before I went to find Mom and Dad. I could see Judith's vision now, a fairytale of pure winter white in the heat of summer. It was beautiful. I hoped I was worth it.

* * *

I caught up with Mom and Dad in the reception area. Ryan was with them. Sadie had gone off to the restroom.

"Mom. Dad." I went to them with my arms open. I hugged Mom. Dad waited for a handshake. "And Ryan. Good to see you again. Thanks for coming." Ryan and Sadie hadn't been back to Nashville since Christmas before last. He looked more or less the same, except that he now wore a goatee rather than a full beard.

"I'm glad to be here," he said. He gave me his clumsy handshake. "I look forward to meeting your fiancé…again." He smiled at that. I smiled, too.

"Yeah, and she can't wait to meet you either. If you think about it, we wouldn't be here if it weren't for you."

"Yes," he stroked his goatee, "the vicissitudes of fate can be singularly perplexing or, in your case, wonderfully serendipitous."

I looked at him slack-jawed. Nope, Ryan hadn't changed at all.

"Uh, huh," I said, "and Judith will think so, too."

"Carlton, you're so…*white*," Mom said.

"Yeah, Judith wants a white wedding."

"Well I think it's very nice. And this place…have you ever seen the like?"

"It is incredible, isn't it? Dad, you've been here before, haven't you?"

"A long time ago, son, in '41 right before we shipped out. Me and some of the fellas drove up from San Francisco, thought it might be our only chance to ever see it." He went somber for a moment before continuing. "It's a beautiful place alright."

Just then Sadie came out of the restroom, saw me and gave a wide smile.

"Carlton, look at you," she grinned. We hugged and then I stood back, holding her by the shoulders and looking her up and down.

"You look great, Sadie."

"Thank you, Carlton."

Sadie wore her signature look, black pants and a sheer white three-quarter-sleeve shirt. Her hair was much shorter now, tapered at the nape of her neck, almost boyish but as always she made it look elegant. I examined her fingers for rings, saw none so gave her an inquisitive look. Mom noticed.

"Ryan? Sadie?" she asked. "Will I get to see you two married before I die?"

"Mom!" Sadie scolded, aghast. "We're fine the way things are." Ryan laughed. Mom looked at Ryan skeptically, but he just shrugged with a smile. "Anyway," Sadie went on, "I can't wait to finally meet Judith."

"You'll like her."

"I know I will. But for now we need to freshen up. That trip was long."

"Okay, then. Try to save some time to meet Mr. and Mrs. Taylor before the wedding. The wedding's going to be out there," I pointed toward the windows, "so I'll see you all at three."

Mom sniffed a tear and gave me another hug, and then they all went off to their rooms.

* * *

Michael and I took our places off to the side of the podium and stood with our hands clasped in front of us as the families and guests arrived, each ushered through the arched trellis by white-gloved attendants. I could hear Everett wheezing behind us, as if his white tuxedo were a little tight around the neck. Eugene and Lois were brought in first, seated to my right, and then James and Gloria. James winked at me as he came up the aisle, but in a conciliatory way. Gloria was beautiful although she wore a plain white shift, nothing flashy. This was an unspoken agreement among women, which Judith explained to me about a year later when James married Gloria: one never draws attention away from the bride.

Then Mom and Dad were brought in, seated to my left, followed by Sadie and Ryan. Afterward the guests were led in, friends and relatives of the Taylors, maybe aunts and uncles and cousins. I hadn't met any of them. None of Judith's grandparents were still living. The right side was filling up, only my small family on the left. I felt a twinge of momentary remorse. I had once had a larger family. But demonstrating that Judith had thought of everything, as her friends were brought in they were seated on the left, filling in that side so that it didn't seem so forlorn. Some of her girlfriends giggled with one another, others eyed me curiously. There were some guys, whether friends or old boyfriends I didn't know. Anyway, I wasn't jealous of them, although I'm sure they were envious of me.

After everyone was settled the bridal march began to play from speakers in the dogwood trees. Eugene rose and went to fetch Judith while everyone looked on in anticipation. Eugene was wearing a gray suit, the only man in the wedding to have escaped a white tuxedo. My stomach felt ticklish. A little girl came down the aisle scattering white flowers. Who was she? I didn't know. A cousin? A friend's daughter? And then Eugene stepped back through the arch with Judith on his arm.

Yes, my jaw did drop, although no one noticed because all eyes were on Judith. She was so purely, elegantly white. Her dress was not elaborate, no frill or bustle, just a fall of satiny white that rivaled Yosemite Falls across the way for unencumbered beauty. Her shoulders and arms were bare, as if she were rising from a crystal-white fountain. The dress tapered suggestively at her waist then gathered around her feet like a cloud. There was no train, nothing to catch in the grass behind her. Her hair was up as I had never seen it, a long looping fold at the base of her neck; and in her hair some delicate white lace that hovered gently above her eyes. Her lips were deep red, her smile as white as her dress. There were appreciative gasps from the guests, low murmurs of admiration. Susan followed in step behind Judith, holding a bouquet of white flowers lightly at her stomach. Her dress was similar to Judith's except that her shoulders were covered.

Every eye followed Judith to the podium. Eugene placed his daughter at my side, squeezed her hand and kissed her cheek, then took his seat. Judith and I gazed into one another's eyes with excitement and also something deeper and full of meaning. We turned to face Everett. My hands were shaking, not from nervousness but from anticipation.

"Ladies and gentlemen," Everett said, giving Judith and me a quick smile of confidence before turning his attention to the gathering beyond. He had a pleased expression on his face, kindly eyes behind those tiny glasses. "We have come to this divine cathedral…" He paused and raised his arms as if to emphasize the obvious. "…to witness and celebrate the joining in loving marriage of this man, Carlton Jeffries, and this woman, Judith Adeline Taylor."

Judith and I stole expectant, breathless glances into one another's eyes.

"Marriage is a joyous estate," Everett continued, "but also a solemn one, as we are elevated by love yet also challenged by obligation…"

I found a place for my eyes just over Everett's shoulder, where Glacier Point loomed, seeming to come closer and closer, grow larger and larger, filling my view as the hypnotic cadence of Everett's words numbed my senses.

"And so Carlton—" I came to with a start. Everett winked at me discreetly. I caught sight of a photographer out the corner of my eye."—will you take Judith as your wife?"

I almost blurted *I do*, but caught myself in time.

"I will," I said.

"And you Judith? Will you take Carlton as your husband?"

"I will," Judith said in a joyous breath.

"Then please face each other, hold hands and repeat together after me—"

Judith's hands felt so warm, so soft in my own.

"I will love you and cherish you—"

"I will love you and cherish you."

It felt as if we were the only two there, speaking to one another intimately under a starry sky. My lips trembled, and Judith smiled with glistening eyes.

"—support you and defend you—"

"Support you and defend you."

Her breath was on my lips, warm and sweet.

"—until the end of my days."

"Until the end of my days."

I saw starbursts in my mind, lighting a journey across miles and emotions. We stood there mesmerized, gazing into one another's eyes. Time seemed to fall away, leaving us outside of it, the mountains and the forests rushing below.

"Uh, hmm," said Everett, grinning. "Are you two still with us?" That drew laughter from behind us. Everett leaned in closer. "You did remember to bring the rings, didn't you, Carlton?"

"Uh…" It took me a moment to come out of the spell. Judith fought back a laugh. "Uh, yeah."

"Then now would be a good time to put them on," said Everett to more laughter from behind.

Michael stepped forward and handed me the rings, grinning like a fool. I passed my ring to Judith, and squeezed hers so tight I was afraid I might bend it, or worse, drop it. I looked to Everett for instructions, but he just smiled mischievously.

"Well," he said as if he were impatient to get on with it, but this was just a guise, "you're married now. Don't you think you ought to put 'em on?"

We both laughed, Judith and I, couldn't help it. We slipped those rings on together. I again looked to Everett for instructions. He sighed, but this, too, was an obvious guise. He seemed to be having a lot of fun with this.

"Some couples kiss now," he said mirthfully. "Some couples share their own words. It's really up to you two, but don't keep these people waiting too long. They came a long way to see this."

Laughter erupted. I could hear Dad booming the loudest, and that relieved me. I wondered what Grandmother Villetta would have made of such an irregular service. Somehow I think she would have been laughing, too.

Judith and I kissed warmly for an eternity, and now there was riotous clapping at our backs. When we pulled apart she looked into me with an earnestness and honesty that teared me up.

"You will always be my Jake," she breathed.

"And you will always be my Willow."

We turned then to ebullient faces. Sadie was dabbing at tears, the same with Mom and Lois. Gloria didn't bother to wipe away her tears, they ran down her cheeks. The voices of Diana Ross and The Supremes began to sound from the speakers. I smiled at Judith in fond memory, took her hand, and we went together up that aisle of green grass and white flowers.

* * *

While the wedding was going on, Judith's and my things had been moved into one of the cottages away from the main building. We went there now, and careful not to muss her dress or hair, comically did what newlyweds do the moment they're alone. The reception was to be held in a banquet room in the main building. We had one hour to freshen up, make ourselves look presentable, then head on over. Somehow Judith got through those gymnastics without so much as a loose hair, but I came away with a lipstick smudge on my shirt collar that couldn't be removed or hidden no matter what we tried. We finally just shrugged and opted to ignore it.

It was obvious when we arrived at the banquet room that everyone else had come right over after the service. Half-filled champagne glasses were scattered about on tables and trays. A few couples were dancing to a slow tune. I spotted Dad with Eugene off to the side, deep in conversation. Mom and Lois had found one another and were sitting on a plush couch, chattering like schoolgirls. Sadie, Ryan, James and Gloria were standing in a little knot, sipping champagne and talking. I didn't see Michael. Susan spotted us and came swooshing over.

"I think it went perfectly," she said jubilantly as she approached, her eyes only on Judith. Susan worked in Los Angeles, and had only arrived at Judith's place in the past couple of days, so I hadn't been formally introduced to her yet. She was an attractive girl of average height, which meant that she was shorter than Judith. She had a slender build, dark brown hair braided and coiled at the back of her head, and a proprietary note in her voice when it came to Judith. "Even if," she went on, "it was the weirdest wedding ever."

"What?" Judith looked shocked but not really, just some play between friends.

"I mean," said Susan, "this is the only wedding I've ever seen where you don't get to meet anybody until the wedding's over. I mean, c'mon." Her jaw hung open for emphasis while Judith laughed. "But don't worry about it," Susan added after a breath or two, "everybody's been introduced now, except..." She turned curious eyes on me, noticed the lipstick stain on my collar. "Oh, you guys," she grumbled in annoyance. She licked her thumb and rubbed at my collar.

"Carlton?" Judith said with a laugh, "This is Susan Wagner. We've been best friends since—"

"Eighth grade," interjected Susan. She gave up on my collar.

"—eighth grade," Judith finished.

"And of course I know you," Susan said to me. "I thought you'd be taller."

"Suzie!" exclaimed Judith.

"Just kidding." Susan scrutinized me from head to toe. "I guess you'll do." I grinned at that.

"Yeah, he'll do," said Judith with a warm smile. She pressed against me and rested a hand on my chest.

"Okay, you kids," harped Susan. "I mean, go out and mingle and dance and stuff.

I'm going to go find Michael. He's around here somewhere."

Susan took off as if on a mission. Judith looked at me and grinned.

"Best friends?" I asked with my own grin, "or the Odd Couple?"

"Both, I guess, or…well…second best now."

"Good to know."

"I need to go hug Daddy, okay?"

"Yeah."

"Be listening for our song," she said with a smile as she glided across the room.

"You know it."

I wandered over to Sadie and Ryan and their group. James gave me a challenging look, but then thrust out his hand with a big smile.

"Welcome to the family, Carlton."

"Thank you."

"No hard feelings?"

"About what?" I shrugged. James laughed and slapped my shoulder.

"It was a beautiful wedding," Gloria fawned. She turned her eyes suggestively on James, who lifted his own eyes to the ceiling and whistled nonchalantly.

"Congratulations," offered Ryan. We shook hands.

"Good job, Carlton," this from Sadie. She leaned in for a hug and whispered in my ear, "*Finally.*"

"Ha!" I laughed.

"Ryan's been telling us about your sister's book," said James.

"Book?" I asked.

"Yes, Carlton," said Ryan. "*A Robin Waits*. You remember, don't you?"

"Sure, yeah," I said, snapping my fingers. "It was at Dad's party a few years ago." Sadie smiled tightly, as if the mention of her book pained her somehow.

"That's right. And now UNC Press has published it," Ryan added proudly.

"Congratulations, sis."

"Thanks, Carlton," Sadie said shyly, not like her at all. "It's not a big deal. No one will read it."

"Certainly they will," boasted Ryan. "It's a brilliant novel."

"Well anyway," I said, "I was told to mingle."

"Susan?" James laughed.

"Yep." That earned me another slap on the shoulder from James.

"Well, as I said, Carlton," he said wryly, "welcome to the family.

I worked my way over to Mom and Lois, being intercepted here and there for an introduction or congratulatory handshake. That loopy song from Wham! began to play over the sound system, and with that the younger couples crowded onto the dance floor, clearing the way for me. *Wake me up before you go go…* I cringed, then turned to Mom and Lois. They were getting on like old friends. From the animated looks on their faces, they were certainly gossiping about something. I smiled, as happy for Mom as I was for myself.

"Hi, Mom," I said. "Lois."

"Carlton." I had never seen Mom look so proud. I went to her and we hugged.

"We couldn't be more pleased," said Lois. She stood with her arms open, and we hugged as well.

You know that a marriage is right when the mothers like one another. This was a weight I hadn't even realized I was carrying until it lifted just then.

"I'm sorry you all didn't get to meet until today," I said with a note of embarrassment. "I wish we could have done something before."

"Don't worry about it, Carlton," said Lois. "It's a long trip to make. But," she looked at Mom and winked, "I hope we can get out to Nashville soon."

"We would love to have you," said Mom.

"I'd better go see Dad now," I said. We all looked over there. Judith had moved off to talk with some friends, and Dad and Eugene had resumed their close conversation.

"Those two are up to something," said Lois.

"Up to no good if I know Dick," chuckled Mom.

"Well, I'll find out," said I. I left them and headed on over.

"My money's in gold," I heard Eugene confide to Dad. Dad seemed skeptical.

"I don't know, Eugene." Dad was rubbing his chin. "The prices are so volatile, up one day and down the next. I've always felt more secure with real estate."

"But the trends," said Eugene. "If you follow the trends since the 70s then—oh, hello Carlton."

"Hello, Eugene." He stood and offered his hand.

"Your father and I were just discussing some things."

"I can tell," I said with a smile. Dad shot a glance over at Mom.

"Well, uh," Dad stood and shook my hand. "That was a beautiful wedding, son. Unusual, but I thought it was beautiful. And Eugene? Your daughter…Judith…she was beautiful."

"We're very proud of her," said Eugene, the color rising in his cheeks. "And proud of this man, too." He patted my shoulder.

The Supremes came over the sound system just then.

"I've got to get going," I said quickly, searching for Judith.

There she was, across the way, and her eyes seemed to catch mine at the same instant. We met on the dance floor, in a dream, and I took her hand, folded an arm around her waist, and we danced, swaying gently. The others had left the floor to us, crowding the periphery as if in silent understanding, although I'm sure Susan had a hand in that. Judith and I danced as if we were all alone with the mountains and the music, and nothing as witness but the birds in the trees. I kissed her trembling lips, breathed in her scent, lost in her spell.

And then…a mischievous grin from Judith, a knowing sparkle in her eyes. The music picked up pace and she twirled. She threw out her hips and raised her arms, her fingers resting on air, and she sang to me coyly, "*Ba-by, ba-by. Baby don't leave me.*"

"Never," I whispered, and I took her and spun her like a southern belle. The other couples took that as their cue to return to the floor, shoulder to shoulder, clapping and dancing and it was magic.

The reception went late, morphing into a dance party. The older folks had all long since gone off to their rooms, while the waiters were looking disheveled and tired. Judith had the weary look of a twenty-mile hike, game to go on but not for much longer.

"We should go," I almost shouted in her ear. The music had gotten louder. Most of the guys had loosened their ties, and were dancing with their collars flying.

"Yeah, I think so," she said woozily.

We said our goodbyes to Susan and the others, then walked out into the night toward our cottage. Judith shrugged out of her dress the moment we crossed the threshold. She had a slip on underneath, a delicate little thing that fell only as far as her thighs. Her toned legs were so alluring I couldn't hide an immediate reaction. She laughed and wagged her finger.

"Eyes up, buster."

"Aw."

She padded off to the bathroom to get ready for bed. After a few moments the door squeaked open and she looked out, a toothbrush in her mouth.

"Don't you need to get ready for bed?" she asked around her toothbrush.

"Uh."

"Oh for goodness sake, Carlton." She whipped out her toothbrush. "Get in here."

"Uh."

You have to understand, Evelyn *never* let me in the bathroom with her, so sharing one now almost seemed indecent to me. I went on in uncertainly, shouldering next to Judith at the sink. She slipped off to bed while I finished up, then followed with eager eyes as I crossed the floor to join her. I shinnied under the covers, feeling strangely displaced. Judith reached over and turned off the lights. We lay quietly in the dark for a while, not even touching. Her breaths were deep and steady. I could imagine her chest rising and falling, the tickle of her fingertips on my stomach, the heat of her body, and yet suddenly I felt lost as to what to do.

She shuffled onto her side, propped on an elbow, and I knew she was staring at me through the dark. She exhaled in frustration.

"What's the matter, Carlton?" she asked flatly.

"I—"

"Is something wrong?"

"It's just that—"

"Just what?"

I clicked on a light and saw that her lips were tight, her brows creased in puzzlement.

"It's just that," I explained hesitantly, "well, we've never slept together in a bed before. Or..." My eyes roved up and down her body.

Her puzzled expression gave way to a mirthful grin that had us both giggling.

"Turn off the light, Carlton," she said in a sultry voice, "and we'll pretend we're outside in the forest.

* * *

We spent our honeymoon right there in Yosemite, four days and four nights of splendor. The weather was uniformly perfect all week. We hiked to Half Dome, to Yosemite Falls. We made love under the stars on Glacier Point, lights twinkling above us as well as those twinkling from the Ahwahnee Hotel below. We lay on our elbows and gazed into the valley, the lights down there seeming to have dropped from the sky like sprinkles. We turned onto our backs and lost ourselves in the stars. It was another moonless night, so sharp and clear that the stars seemed to spangle all around us like fireflies. Judith reached up and twirled her fingers, as if to spin the stars into new constellations.

"I wish we could stay here, just like this," she said airily, pale light dancing on her lashes. It was getting cold so I pulled her close, the softness of her warmth flowing into me like breath.

"I love it here, being with you," I said.

She flipped onto her elbows and studied me closely.

"Me, too. Will it always be like this with us?"

"I want it to be."

"I don't want us to ever argue or fight."

"We won't."

"You can't say that. It's not fair. But promise me that if it does happen we'll just stop and remember tonight."

That wouldn't be hard. Every night with Judith had been like this for me, vast yet intimate at the same time. I couldn't imagine us arguing. I couldn't fit it into my mind.

"I promise," I whispered through a gentle kiss. She rested against me and we dozed off, up high in the soft velvet of night.

* * *

We had to leave on Friday ahead of the Fourth of July rush. If not for that we might have stayed another week and gotten lost among the days. Judith drove a 70s copper-colored Mercury Capri that was showing its wear but still shined in the sun. We squeezed into it for the drive to her house in Fresno, which I needed to start thinking of as *our* house, but I couldn't just yet.

Fresno was a flat and dusty town, very dry and very hot. Judith lived on San Ramon Avenue over near Fresno State, in a modest white stucco house that had a red tile roof and deep eaves to ward off the summer sun. The house had a postage-stamp of a front yard, dry grass and some spindly shrubs, but a secluded and green patio out back, with a tall redwood fence, an herb garden, and a lot of ivy.

"Well, what do you think?" she asked as we pulled into her driveway.

"I think it looks great," I said, and I meant it. I saw no reason to trade this house for any other, and Judith had an option to buy it, her rent going toward the purchase. It seemed like a good deal to me. Still, I did look around wistfully at the sparse trees.

"I know what you're thinking," she said with a smile. "Don't worry. We can go up to Sequoia or Kings Canyon any time we need to get away. You haven't seen a sequoia yet. I can't wait to see the look on your face when you see one for the first time."

"Me, either," I said. "Ready to show me around?"

"Yeah," she replied, her excitement barely restrained.

I felt a bit like a voyeur as Judith led me through her house, as if I were peeping through the window into her private spaces. She kept a neat house except for the books. There were books everywhere, askew in shelves, stacked on tables. Her furniture was aged but clean, looked as if it belonged to the 60s. She ate at a white Formica dinette in a nook off the kitchen. Her refrigerator was a plain white model from Sears, and her stove was gas. The kitchen was small but tidy, with pans hanging from hooks, and narrow shelves of spices.

"Oh, I forgot to ask," I said with a wry smile. "Can you cook?"

"Now he asks," she smiled back. "Maybe you should have thought about that a week ago."

"Uh, oh."

"Yeah, I can cook. Can you?"

"Uh, a little."

"Good. You can cook for me tonight." I groaned while she laughed. "But don't worry, I'll help you."

"Whew!" I exhaled, "since I don't have my Coleman stove here."

"Oh, you." She tugged at my ear, then led me to her bedroom.

Her bedroom had a pale blue theme, from the paint on the walls to the curtains to a blue and white floral bedspread. The furniture was white: end tables, a dresser with a mirror, a small desk, a few stand-alone bookshelves. There were stacks of books in here as well, even on the floor in one corner.

"I never knew you read so much," I said in awe.

"You know I love to read," she said, a touch defensively. "These in here are mostly for school, though, curriculum planners and things like that. I should really use the other bedroom for an office, but Mom comes to visit, and Susan, so I do all of my work in here.

"That's fine," I said.

I scanned the walls. There were photos of her family, some shots taken in her classroom, and a picture of her and Susan in graduation gowns. On the wall above her desk was a framed Sierra Club poster of a giant sequoia.

"Wow," I exclaimed, pointing at the poster. "I have that exact same one."

"Do you really? Sequoias are my favorite trees."

"Mine, too...well, sequoias and hickories."

"But you've never seen a sequoia."

"I've seen the pictures."

"Not the same." She shook her head. "Imagine a tree so big that you can camp inside it."

"There's nothing like that on the Appalachian Trail."

"Nope."

We went silent then. I gazed around some more, and then my eyes fell to her bed. It was a small bed with a white wicker headboard, just big enough for two people but roomiest for one. I felt like a guest, as if I should have been in the other bedroom and was violating her privacy. Judith must have sensed this.

"Look," she said suddenly. She hopped to her closet, which had sliding doors, opened the right side and...my clothes were all there, hanging neatly, my shoes lined up on the floor.

"What? How did you—"

"And look over here." She skipped to the dresser, pulled open some drawers, and there were my socks and underwear and T-shirts.

"When did you—"

"And in here," she said, taking my hand and hurrying me into the bathroom. Arranged around the sink were my shaving things, my hair brush, my toothbrush.

My jaw fell.

"I don't know how you managed—"

She put a finger to my lips, yanked me back into the bedroom and pushed me onto the bed. We were both laughing by then. I took her by the waist and drew her on top of me. She brushed some hair out of my eyes and gazed longingly into them, her expression softening.

"Your mom sent me your things," she said huskily. "I want you to feel at home here."

I blinked away some gathering tears then kissed her, long and sweet. It would still take some time to get used to all of this, but I was already feeling less self-conscious. Judith raised herself up and put on a stern look.

"But I get the right side," she demanded, and then her face broke playfully and I tickled her, and she collapsed onto me, giggling like a kid.

* * *

That night Judith taught me how to make spaghetti sauce from scratch. While she chopped tomatoes, she sent me out back to the herb garden for basil and rosemary, which I recognized from the produce department at Hill's but had never used before. We had always used dried spices, but the wonderful aroma of the fresh herbs left me wondering why we hadn't used these ourselves back home.

Judith put everything into a pot while I watched over her shoulder. She set the flame to low then turned to me.

"So you get tonight off," she said with a humorous glint in her eyes, "but tomorrow night I'm looking forward to seeing what you can do."

"Why wait till tomorrow night?" I asked. "I'm making you breakfast in the morning."

"Oooh," she purred, "I can't wait. Will it be breakfast in bed?"

"In bed?" I asked as if put out by the idea. "Well, it'll be crackers, then."

"Oh, you!"

"Naw." I held her and breathed deeply. The rich aroma from the bubbling sauce vied with her own intoxicating scent. "You get breakfast in bed whenever you want."

"I like that," she said coyly.

* * *

Judith was already under the covers when I came into the bedroom that night. She was propped on pillows with a book in her lap. I slid in beside her.

"What are you reading?" I asked.

"Your sister's book."

"Really?"

"Yeah. Ryan gave it to me. It's pretty good so far, but it's dark. It follows a little girl named Robin from a coal town in Kentucky during the Great Depression, a dreary place. Sadie's imagery is perfect. I think I can actually feel the coal dust on my skin. Did your family ever live in a coal town?"

"No."

"Well, she did her research then. Listen to this paragraph:

Black soot settled into cracks and crevices in weathered clapboard walls, tracing maps of peeling paint and buckling wood. Soot powdered window sills, sifted through screens onto fine lace doilies. It caught the wind off of rusty tin roofs, streaming like fine black snow. We all wore it around our eyes and noses like ghoulish Halloween paint. We left handprints on the door posts, little black fingers and palms on the lower part, bigger ones up high, like the gnarled, coal-skeined hands that found me in my nightmares, probing in the dark, as suffocating as the deepest mines."

"Damn. Sadie wrote that?"

"Yep."

"What does that last part mean?"

"I'm not sure yet, but I think this character, Robin, is being abused."

"Damn."

"Yeah, this is going to be a tough one to read."

"Hmpf."

I lay back against the pillows and pondered that. Judith resumed her reading, flipping pages like a metronome, following lines with an index finger, biting her lip at times. In that silence I began to think about the present. The past week had gone like a dream, the days joining into a single seamless event that was receding even as

I tried to recall each day individually, forcing my thoughts into the here and now, to this town, this house, this bed. The honeymoon was over. I needed to find a job.

"Judith," I said. She lowered her book patiently. "I think I need to go home and get my car."

She seemed startled.

"But why?" she asked.

"I need to start looking for a job."

"You can use my car."

"No, you need it."

She marked her page and set the book aside, turning to me thoughtfully.

"I thought you were afraid your car wouldn't make it," she said.

"I'll just have to take the chance. We can't afford to buy another car right now."

Her brows dipped in thought.

"When do you want to go?"

"In a few days maybe."

She nodded at that. "Yeah, that's good. I have a couple of weeks before I need to start prepping my classroom."

"You don't need to go." I leaned up on an elbow.

"Why not?"

"Well—"

"I've never driven across the country before."

"But—"

"I think it would be great."

"But Judith, it's a long—"

She was smiling now, that mischievous smile of hers. Willowy fingers caressed my face.

"And besides, Carlton, I only saw Tommy that one time. I need to meet your boys."

"Yeah," I sighed.

"Good. That settles it then."

So the honeymoon wasn't over yet.

* * *

Dad was out playing golf, so Mom picked us up at the airport and drove us to the house. When it came to the bedroom arrangements I felt a little strange, but Mom just rolled her eyes and said, "Carlton, you two are married now. You can stay in the same room and it won't cause a scandal." She looked at Judith and whispered as if I couldn't hear, "Not that it would have caused a scandal before, but you know how he is."

Judith grinned. "Yeah, he's got that weird prude streak. Where do you think it comes from?"

"Must be his father." Mom shook her head. "I'll start lunch while you two get settled."

I turned to Judith as Mom went off to the kitchen.

"*Prude streak?*" I asked.

"No, Carlton, not at all," she said with a straight face, struggling to hold back a laugh. "I'll put this stuff away. Go call Evelyn so we can see the boys."

"Right," I said, outflanked again.

There was no answer at Evelyn's house so I called Gracie's office.

"Carlton," Gracie answered. Her practice wasn't large enough yet to afford a secretary. "I know why you're calling. The news isn't good."

"What's happened?" I asked with an unsettling feeling in my stomach.

"They've taken the boys out of the country. On vacation, they say."

"What? She *knew* we were coming."

"It gets worse, Carlton. They've filed to terminate your parental rights."

"*What?* They can't do that."

"Well, they can try."

"What can we do?"

Gracie exhaled deeply into the phone.

"Not much at the moment. I'll petition the court for a hearing, but it's going to take some time."

"Damn her."

"I never thought she would take it this far. I'm sorry, Carlton."

"No, I should have known she'd pull a stunt like this."

"Will you be okay?"

"Not really, Gracie, but there's nothing I can do about it."

"How long will you be in town?"

"I don't know, a few days maybe. Judith needs to get back."

"I don't think we can do anything that fast, but I'll try."

"Okay," I sighed. "Well, thanks Gracie."

"*De nada.* I'll be in touch."

"Okay. Bye."

I gave the news to Mom and Judith. Mom just dropped onto a chair, her face tight, while I saw something in Judith that I hadn't seen since Davis—anger.

"I should just march down there right now," Mom spat righteously.

"I'll go with you," Judith said through clenched teeth.

"Won't do any good," I told them. "Even if they were here it would just make a scene."

"I'm so sorry, Carlton," said Judith.

"I *hate* for you to have to be involved in this," I hissed.

"So what do you want to do now?"

I shrugged my shoulders. "Gracie says this is going to take a while, so I guess we should just go home."

Judith lifted a little despite the anger in her eyes.

"You know," she said, "that's the first time you've called it your home."

That startled me. I went to her and held her.

"It's home if I'm there with you," I said.

* * *

As she feared, Gracie wasn't able to do anything on such short notice. We met with her at her office late the next day. She sat behind an imposing desk that practically dwarfed her. Judith and I took the chairs in front.

"Burton has this judge's ear," Gracie revealed contemptuously.

"It's so unfair," said Judith.

"There's never anything fair about this process, even when things go smoothly."

"I feel so…helpless," I said.

"We're not helpless, Carlton," Gracie said, "they're just one step ahead of us right now. There are still things we can do. When are you all going home?"

"We thought in the morning, but if I need to stay…"

Judith tensed subtly.

"No, no," Gracie said quickly. "It might actually help us if you leave right away, catch them off guard. I know the guardian *ad litem*, he taught one of my classes. If I can get Tommy in a room with him, and they don't see it coming, it's possible I could get a hearing."

"It all sounds so Byzantine," Judith remarked in disgust.

Gracie didn't have anything to say to that. Her eyes fell on Judith's ring.

"I wish I could have come to your wedding," she said wistfully. "I hear it was beautiful." Judith blushed.

"It was," I said.

"Well," Gracie stood, "so you're going to drive that old car the whole way?"

"Yep."

"*Aye*," she mouthed with a nostalgic shake of her head. "Hope it makes it."

"That's three of us," Judith smiled.

"It'll make it," I added without confidence.

"Okay, then," said Gracie. "Call me when you get home."

* * *

Judith and I backed down the driveway at 8:00 a.m. on a clear Saturday morning. There had been fog earlier, but it had all burned off by then. We couldn't have asked for better weather to start our journey. The Pontiac was running great. As a wedding present, Dad had put it in the shop. The old Catalina had a fresh tune-up now—new plugs and points and wires—as well as new wheel bearings and brakes. Dad must have spent a fortune.

Mom and Dad waved to us from up top as I backed into the street. Judith was looking down at the Hanshaw's house. I couldn't see her face, so didn't know what it held. I lingered on the Hanshaw's house myself for a moment. Everything down there, from Mr. and Mrs. Gorman to Evelyn and all that had happened in between, seemed to belong to a different life, a life I recalled in the third-person—someone else's life.

I shook it off, waved at Mom and Dad, clicked the shifter into drive, then Judith and I headed for home.

S EVENTEEN

According to what I've written, I've been five days in this old shelter. Has it been that long? The walk I tried yesterday morning didn't do anything to loosen my stiff joints. My hand is like a claw around this pencil. I can't straighten my fingers, they hurt when I try. One of the sores on my backside has gotten worse. It burns, as if I were sitting on an ember, so I've had to tip over onto my hip a little but now it aches, too. I should go, I should go now. The stream is down this morning. It's still raining, but softly, like a wispy veil over everything out there. From time to time it sheets to white, and snow falls, and then it dribbles back to gray and rain.

I should go. The weather's no worse now than it was when I got here. Sam and I could make it through this, just zip up in the rain suit, put one foot in front of the other, and be at Wadleigh Stream by dark.

Today is June 25, Judith's and my anniversary, our...*one hundred and third anniversary*. Is there a special color for that, silver or gold or whatnot? I doubt it. Anyone old enough to have that kind of anniversary wouldn't be writing etiquette books, they wouldn't have the energy and they probably wouldn't care. I care, though. Maybe this should be our *gray* anniversary. The way things look out there it fits, but I don't like that. There was nothing gray about Judith.

No, I'm not going to hike today. This will be a legitimate zero-day for me, as it was during my 2008 hike. Back then I had made it to Garfield Ridge the night before. I hadn't planned it that way, but sometimes improbable things just land by accident. I wasn't looking for any cosmic meaning in it, at first I wasn't even aware what day it was, but later I realized, so I zeroed in that shelter the next day, alone with my thoughts and an ugly blister on my heel. I'm not going to tell you anything else about that day—I will keep those memories for myself—just this, something Beer Poet had written on the wall:

> *There are peaks ahead,*
> *Hiding in the cloud.*

> *What may come I cannot know;*
> *What I know may never come.*
> *But this I do know,*
> *Of the journey on.*
> *Days go by and days unfold;*
> *And I will be there waiting.*
> *Beer Poet, GA–ME '07*

I would like to have met Beer Poet. I don't necessarily understand his poetry, but he seemed to have had a good handle on things, an inner eye that saw clearly. I could have used some of that in 2008. I scratched this on the wall next to his poem:

> *I wish you were here, Beer Poet.*
> *I can wait, but only a day.*
> *Sojourner, ME => GA '76, ME => GA '08*

Anyway, I'm rambling now. I fell asleep again over this last night, so I need to read back a little bit, see where I left off. Oh, our drive across the country... I don't have enough paper to describe that journey in detail, so you'll have to use your imaginations. Just know that you could still travel freely back then. It took us five days to get home to Fresno, five wonderful days in which I was able to put aside most of my worries.

The Pontiac made it in great shape. Judith and I stayed in a couple of motels, one in Arkansas and one in Texas, but after that we camped each night. Neither of us had ever seen such desert landscapes as those in New Mexico and Arizona. We saw towering formations of red rock standing in open plains, like giant chessmen on a vast board of sand. There were canyons that seemed to have been clawed from the earth by talons large enough to carry off the moon. There were mighty rivers in these deep canyons, although looking down from the rims they appeared as little more than muddy trickles. During our drive through that country we were astounded from one view to the next, as if we couldn't catch our breaths.

We camped on Navajo land in Arizona, beneath rocky spires that reminded me of old John Wayne westerns. It was surprisingly cool at night, and so quiet, just the wind rustling the pink sand. The lowering sun set the far horizon into so many shades of color, at once pink, orange, and red, violet and the deepest blue. The stars seemed as close as they had from Glacier Point, flowing across the sky from the east like an incoming tide. The songs of coyotes came to us in long, mournful notes that might have traveled miles on the wind. We sat bundled in our sleeping bags, watching all of this with a kind of awed reverence until the sky was as black as obsidian and the stars danced on the sand.

We didn't make a fire. An old Navajo man named Joseph Begay had given us permission to camp where we were. Joseph had steel-gray hair that was braided, and a face that looked like the canyons we had crossed. He spoke mostly with his eyes, deep, penetrating and gray, and those eyes told us, "You can stay, but be respectful and don't make a mess." We didn't make a fire because we didn't want to leave a scar on that pristine pink sand. Instead I set up my Coleman lantern, which washed away the night, holding us in a cocoon of light.

We ate Indian fry bread that we had bought at a trading post, washed that down with water then snuggled deeper into our sleeping bags. Judith brought out Sadie's book and began to read. I watched her out the corner of my eye.

"Stop it," she said without lifting her eyes from her book.

"Stop what?" I asked innocently.

"Stop staring at me while I read." I could see her scanning lines as she spoke. Her lips rose into a smile. "Really, Carlton, I mean it." She turned to me then, her eyes catching the lantern glow like an owl in moonlight. "Would you like me to get you something to read? A comic book maybe."

"Aw, c'mon."

"I'm just kidding." She smiled softly and stroked my face. "But really, I want to finish this."

"Okay."

I turned on my side away from her and tried to make out the details beyond our wall of light. I saw a pair of eyes dart behind a bush, small eyes, nothing to be alarmed about. I heard thumping like drums in the distance, some vague animal calls. Maybe the Indians were doing a dance or a ceremony somewhere in the night. My eyes grew heavy and I must have slept, because suddenly I was jerked awake by the sound of Judith snapping her book shut. I sat up and rubbed my eyes. Judith dialed the lantern down, letting the night back in.

"Did you finish it?" I asked groggily.

"Yeah."

"So tell me about it."

"Well," she said. I was fully awake now, watching her teeth flash in the starlight. "It's very moving in places, disturbing in others. It's an empowerment story—empowering women, that is, which goes with Sadie's Women's Studies degree so I get why she wrote it. But..."

"But?"

"Well...okay, here's the story: The little girl, Robin, refuses to be a victim. The coal town, I think, represents society as a whole, repressive, you know?"

"Uh, okay."

"There are individual people who abuse her, authority figures. Each represents some component of society, like the police, or bosses at work. Then there's her mother and an aunt, who look the other way. They're the enablers."

"Uh, huh."

"She has a scar on her arm where she was cut while struggling with one of her abusers. The scar is a theme as she gets older. She's carrying scars. Do you understand?"

"Yeah, she has a scar on her arm."

"It's not just that, Carlton. It's figurative as well. Everybody has scars, only some are more visible than others."

You might think that Judith's tone with me was condescending, but that's not the way it was at all. She was only being patient with me. Judith was a teacher, after all.

"Okay. Yeah, I get it."

"Good. Here's the really dark part. She is so determined not to be a victim that she plots her revenge and she waits for just the right moment. One of her abusers stumbles drunk into a running gutter. She could help him, but instead she squats next to him and watches dispassionately as the water runs up over his nose and mouth. He drowns.

"Another is an uncle who trips on one of her toys while he's coming down the stairs. He's lying at the foot of the stairs, moaning, and before anybody can come to see what's going on she jumps on his neck and breaks it."

"Oh, man."

"Yeah. But the worst, I think, is her older brother. She waits years for him. Now she's a teenager and the war is on. Her brother was always domineering and cruel to her, but in reality he's a coward. He's waiting for a letter that will get him a deferment from the Army, so she watches the mail box every day."

They say that the pit of your stomach can just go cold, like a block of ice. It must be true because it happened to me right then.

"One day," she went on, "her little brother gets to the mailbox first and finds the letter. She snatches it away from him, and intimidates him into keeping her secret. You see? She's corrupted an innocent kid. Now she's turned into what she hates. Anyway, she tears up the letter, her older brother is drafted, and he gets killed in action within a week or two of being sent overseas."

The fry bread I had eaten wasn't sitting well. I leaned over to be sick, but nothing came up.

"Carlton?" Judith asked. Her eyes seemed darker than the night.

Was there an implied question in those hooded eyes? I wanted to blurt it all out right then, but I was afraid that doing so might leave a taint that would cling to my family like a sickness. *That's not my family, Judith,* I wanted to say. *It's all fiction. Nobody abused Sadie, we weren't from a coal town, Mom and Aunt Jewel never got along, and Uncle Timmy seldom came to visit. It's all fiction, except...*

...Leavitt. Damn it, Sadie.

* * *

I woke up still fretting about Sadie's book, but then we reached the Grand Canyon. All of my worries suddenly seemed so small. I can't adequately describe the Grand Canyon to you, it overwhelms the senses. It was astoundingly deep, tiered with color all the way to the bottom, where the muddy Colorado River flowed. There were areas of deep green in the depths of the canyon, like looking down at a riverine forest from an airplane. Any people down there would have been too small to see. It was like discovering patches of green while looking at Mars through a telescope, patches that might be lost civilizations, visible but forever beyond reach. Today, of course, the Grand Canyon is...well, you know.

We camped in the Angeles Crest during the last night of our journey, with the anonymous, checkerboard lights of Los Angeles washing against the mountains like ocean waves. Carla and Neal were down there somewhere. I wished we had kept in touch. I would have loved for Carla and Judith to meet.

We got home late on a Wednesday afternoon. It was blistering hot, desert hot, but at least we had none of that Tennessee humidity to deal with. There was a message from Gracie waiting for us on the answering machine. She had managed to get a hearing scheduled for next week. I didn't have to come, which was a relief. She would be in touch later.

For the rest of that week, Judith showed me around Fresno. She showed me where the grocery store was—it was a Safeway—where her favorite bookstore was—it was called Fig Garden—and she took me to her school, Margaret R. Robinson Elementary. The school was only a few blocks from the house.

"See?" she said. "I can walk to work. You could have used my car."

We were in her classroom, which was still bare. The chalkboards had been washed, the desks were stacked in a corner, and the linoleum floors had been polished to a high luster. Her empty wooden desk looked naked. It had scratches and burnished corners, where generations of kids had grazed it with their hips. I sat on her desk top, took her hands and pulled her to me.

"Would you really have wanted to miss out on that trip?" I asked coyly.

"No," she smiled. "I'm glad we went. It was great."

"Am I allowed to kiss you in here?" She looked around and grinned.

"For about another week it's okay."

I kissed her, then lifted her onto my lap. She looped her arms around my neck and bounced her legs like a kid.

"Do the kids bring you apples?" I asked with a smile.

"They haven't yet."

"Would you eat one if they did?"

"Sure. Why not? I'd wash it first, though."

"That's good," I laughed, "sticky little fingerprints and all. You really love this, don't you?"

"Yeah," she said dreamily. "I love kids."

"Little monsters."

"No they're not," she exclaimed prettily.

"Well, I was, anyway."

"I don't believe you," and we kissed again.

Judith started setting her classroom up the following week, and I started looking for a job. I went to the Safeway, but they weren't hiring. I tried a couple of the independent grocery stores, but with the same result. Fresno didn't seem to be a very up-wardly-mobile town. Some of the geezers in those stores looked as if they had been there forever. I went to the Fashion Fair Mall, which was pretty close to where we lived, and applied at a department store called Gottschalks. They were so amused by my accent that I thought I had landed a job for sure, but they never called me back.

I wasn't discouraged—not yet, anyway. I had money saved from Hill's, and in truth, Judith made enough money to support both of us. I couldn't live like that, though. I couldn't be a deadbeat. Judith didn't pressure me in the least, just offered encouragement, told me to be patient. I asked her if they needed a janitor at her school. She thought I was serious, pondered that a moment, then said she would look into it.

Gracie called me with an update at the end of that week. It was midafternoon. It was hot. I had just gotten in from another futile day of job searching. Judith was at school.

"We had the hearing, Carlton," she said the moment I answered the phone. "It went our way."

"That's great," I said. "So what's happening?"

"We have another hearing next week—"

"You had a hearing to have a hearing?" I barked. Maybe it was the heat. Gracie exhaled into the phone before going on.

"It was a hearing to show cause," she explained tersely.

"I'm sorry, Gracie. It's been a hard day."

"I understand, Carlton. Evelyn has to show up with the kids next week or else be held in contempt. The guardian *ad litem* wants to see Tommy—alone."

"That's good, then."

"That's *very* good. It's what I was hoping for."

"That's great, Gracie. What do I need to do?"

"Nothing for now. Just stay tuned."

"Okay. Thanks again and, uh, sorry I snapped at you."

"No problem, Carlton. *Hasta.*"

* * *

I started applying at gas stations that next week, that's how desperate I had be-come. As always, Judith was supportive. What I saw as failure she saw merely as a challenge. It hadn't even been two weeks yet, she said. These things take time. And she had checked—they didn't need any janitors at her school.

I didn't hear from Gracie that week. It was the first of the following week that she called.

"Great news, Carlton. She has to send you the boys for a week."

"She does? A week? When?"

Judith was home this time. She heard the excitement in my voice and edged in close.

"August 27 to Labor Day. They'll fly out with your Mom. I've already talked to her, and the court approves. The guardian *ad litem* really dressed down Evelyn. I wish you could have seen it."

"Wow, a week out here? And Mom's coming, too?' I winked at Judith. She smiled in return, bouncing on her heels.

"Yeah." Gracie's tone shifted. "But Carlton, listen: There'll be another hearing after. They're going to ask Tommy who he wants to live with."

"*What?*"

"I know. It's a stupid thing to do to a kid, but it's all I could get."

"That's not fair to Tommy," I said. Judith's brows were creased with concern.

"I know, Carlton, but that's the way it is. You'd better start making plans."

"Okay, Gracie. Damn, but okay."

I explained it all to Judith. She was livid.

"I couldn't care less about Evelyn," she spat, "but to do that to a child is cruel."

"The only other thing we can do is give up."

"No, no," she said quickly. "We'll just have to make the best of it, give the boys a good week."

"How are we going to manage it? You'll be at work most of the time." Classes started on August 13.

"I'll figure something out," she said. "Don't worry."

* * *

I don't know how Judith did it, but she got the week off from school.

"It's not that big of a deal," she told me. "Friday's an in-service day anyway, and then Labor Day weekend. So I'm only missing four classes."

It seemed like a big deal to me, to be given time off when she was still so new at that school.

"Maybe I should be a teacher," I said. Still no job prospects.

"Then we'd better get you enrolled now," she came back with a grin. "It takes a while."

We waited inside Fresno Air Terminal and watched through the green tinted windows as Mom's plane touched down. Waves of late-afternoon heat rippled off the runway. We shielded our eyes against the reflected glare, which was painful even through the tinted glass.

The stairs were rolled out, the hatch was opened, and Mom emerged with the boys soon after. Mom paused at that first blast of heat, as if she were having second thoughts and was about to retreat back into the plane, but then she jostled Luke higher onto her shoulder and descended the stairs carefully, with Tommy thumping along behind. We met them at the gate.

"Thank God," was the first thing Mom said. She set Luke on his feet then fanned her face. "That was a trial. We've seen the inside of four airports today. It must be easier to get to Outer Mongolia than this place. And I've never felt such *heat*."

"But it's a dry heat, Mom," I laughed. I went to her and we hugged. "Hi, Tommy," I said with a painted smile. He was looking down at his feet, his hands in his pockets.

"I'm s'posed to be in school," he remarked sullenly.

Mom shrugged and gave me a defeated look.

"Hello, Mabel," Judith said fondly. She knelt and opened her arms. "And hello, Luke. I'm Judith."

Luke smiled wide. He had little pointy teeth now. His black hair was thicker, and long enough to be plastered in the sweat on his forehead. He hadn't so much as looked at me, but he ran into Judith's open arms as if he had known her all his life. Mom smiled. Judith scooped Luke up and rode him on her hip. "You're such a big boy," she said.

"Judy," said Luke. He aimed a finger at Judith's eye, but she swept it away with a laugh.

"Well, I guess we'd better get going," I said.

Judith was going to drive, with Mom in the front so that I could sit with the boys in the back, but Luke threw a tantrum and wouldn't settle down until Judith slid in beside him, so I wound up driving instead. We got to the house and got everyone inside. Tommy found a corner in the living room and stood there sulking, while Luke went on a tear trying to touch every one of Judith's books.

"You have a nice house," Mom said to Judith. "Isn't it nice, Tommy?"

Tommy didn't respond. I was about to snap at him, but Judith stepped in first.

"Give him time, Carlton," she said in a low voice. "This must all be very strange to him." She checked her watch. "I thought my mother would be here by now." She turned to Mom. Just then there was a knock at the door.

"*Hello!*" Lois announced. She let herself in and met us in the living room. "Hello, Mable. Are you ready to go?"

"Go?" I asked.

"Lois is taking me to Las Vegas for the week," said Mom.

"Vegas?"

"We're going to see Wayne Newton," she blushed.

"And some other things," Lois added with a wink.

"But I thought you were going to stay with us."

Suddenly I felt uncertain about handling the boys for a week.

"It was a last minute thing, Carlton," said Mom. "I'm so excited."

"But—"

"We'll be fine, Carlton," said Judith.

"And I'll have Mabel back in time to take the boys home, so don't worry," added Lois. She glanced around the room, took note of Tommy's posture and made a silent decision to forego introductions. "Well, let's be off, Mabel."

"Bye, Mom," said Judith. She sensed my unease. "It's okay, Carlton. We'll be fine."

"I hope so."

"Don't worry. Tommy's just acting out. He's confused. It takes time and patience. Okay?"

"Yeah, okay."

That night after dinner, Judith put a cartoon tape into the VCR then set Tommy up in front of the television. She walked Luke into our bedroom. I found them sitting on the bed, Luke in Judith's lap. She was reading a picture book to him, *Mice Twice*, showing him the words and sounding them out. He alternately gnawed on his stubby fingers then pointed them at the book.

"Cat," he said.

"Yes. That's very good, Luke. Cat."

I don't know that watching the sun rise over Mt. Washington would have made Judith as content as she looked right then. She seemed to have a glow about her. She flipped pages and read to Luke in the most patient and soothing voice. He took to her as if she were his mother, but he was a stranger to me, a stocky, black haired kid with dark blue eyes. Judith looked up at me with a beatific smile.

"He's yours," she said softly. "No question."

* * *

A couple of days later we all piled into the Pontiac and drove up to Sequoia National Park. Judith had gotten through to Tommy a little bit. He would speak with her, although without enthusiasm, and he would do as she asked. He still wouldn't look me in the eyes.

We parked and walked the path to the General Sherman tree, claimed to be the biggest tree in the world. Standing on the wooden viewing platform, dwarfed by the sheer mass of that tree, I believed it.

"My *God!*" I exclaimed in awe. Judith beamed.

"I told you."

"It's *huge.*"

I looked over at Tommy, hoping to see some sense of wonder in his eyes, but he was as sullen as always. He looked bored. Where was my Tommy, who had played so happily with compasses, who had walked up the hill with me and climbed the old ash tree? I wiped my eyes and swallowed hard against a knot in my throat.

We continued along the path through the grove, Luke between Judith and me, holding our hands, Tommy kicking duff off on his own. We came to a tree that was open at the roots.

"It's like a cave in there," I said in astonishment.

"Fire does that," explained Judith. "Sequoias have a fire retardant in their bark. They actually need fire to help their seeds germinate."

"Really?"

I left them and wandered between the roots into a cavern of wood. The hollow was bigger than any shelter on the Appalachian Trail.

"You're right," I hollered out. "You could camp in here easy. I wished we had these in Tennessee." My mind spun. What would I have made of these as a kid? I think I would have wanted to live in one of them.

"There's one up ahead," Judith hollered back, "that fell centuries ago. In the 1800s they used it as an army barracks and a stable for their horses."

"Wow," I whistled.

We got home well after dark. Both of the boys had fallen asleep in the back seat. Judith carried Luke in while I carried Tommy. He was getting so big, almost seven. His hair was still that honey color. It brushed softly against my hand. My face broke, and I looked away so Judith wouldn't see. I missed Tommy, I missed being his dad. Judith would have chided me, would have said that I was still his dad no matter what. But it didn't feel that way now. He had become so distant that I couldn't even touch him unless he was asleep. I missed him. My beautiful boy.

* * *

Mom and Lois showed up on Labor Day morning. It was early, yet already baking outside. Mom had a fancy new hair-do and the beginnings of a tan on her nose and cheeks. She looked as if she'd shed a few years in Vegas.

"So how was it?" I asked.

"We had a great time," Mom gushed. "I have got to get your father to bring me back there soon."

"Ha! Good luck with that," I said. I couldn't imagine Dad in Las Vegas, around all the lights and the gambling. He would grumble the whole time.

"Hi, Mom." Judith came into the room, drying her hands from washing the breakfast dishes. "Win any money?"

"Puh," Lois groused, "not a dime."

"Lose any money then?"

Lois looked away guiltily. "Don't tell your father."

"Why not? He does worse than you."

They both laughed and hugged.

"Are the boys ready?" Mom asked.

"I'll drive them to the airport, honey," Lois said to Judith. "It's on my way."

"Okay," said Judith. She seemed wistful.

"They're ready to go," I said. "Thanks, Lois."

Judith went off to round up the boys while I stood with Mom and Lois. Mom looked at me inquisitively and I shook my head.

"I don't think so, Mom. Tommy's doing better with Judith, but he still doesn't want to be around me."

"I'm so sorry, Carlton," said Mom.

"Me, too," said Lois. "It must be hard on you."

"It is."

Judith came in with the boys and their little suitcases. Mom knelt and ruffled Tommy's hair.

"Did you have a good time, Mister Tom?" she asked.

"Only Uncle Kenny calls me that," he mumbled.

"Uncle Kenny?" Judith asked with arched brows.

"Long story," I said. "Tell ya later. Okay, let's get going."

We got everyone out to the car. Luke started to fuss when Judith slid him in next to Tommy.

"It's okay little man," she said. She kissed him on the forehead. "And you, Tommy. It was good to meet you." She held out her hand and he shook it limply.

"You, too," he said with a stone face.

"Do you want to say goodbye to your dad?"

Tommy looked at his knees. "Bye."

When they were around the corner and out of view I shook my head.

"I don't think that went very well."

"It wasn't so bad," said Judith. "Tommy was starting to open up a little bit. That's an improvement. And at least we're sending Luke back potty-trained now."

"Do you think that'll be enough?"

Judith bit her lip and didn't answer.

That night when I came to bed, Judith set her book aside and cuddled against me, laying her head on my shoulder.

"Luke's adorable," she said, working her fingers on my chest. "I already miss him."

"Yeah," I said without enthusiasm. "He's a good kid."

"Still don't believe me?" she asked, looking up at me searchingly.

"I don't know what to believe about Luke."

She pondered that with pursed lips.

"Why haven't I met your friend Kenny? Tommy seems to love him."

"Kenny is an..." I hesitated. "Kenny has some problems."

"What kind of problems?"

"The kind that rubs off on other people."

"Can we help him?"

"Some people can't be helped."

She let that go and we lay quietly for a while. My eyes were just getting heavy when Judith whispered, almost shyly:

"Carlton, I want a child. Do you think..."

My eyes popped wide open. I scooched up a little on my pillow.

"Do I think what?"

"Well, we really haven't talked about it before."

You're probably thinking that this was a conversation we should have had before we got married, and you're right. But I always assumed that Judith would want children, while she assumed that I'd already made all the children I wanted. That's what happens when you assume things. But more than that, I didn't realize until just then that she had been willing to marry me even thinking she might never have kids of her own. I couldn't imagine Judith never being a mother. The thought made my heart ache.

I drew her lips to mine.

"You'll make a great mother," I said against her lips. She lit up at that.

"Are you sure?" she asked, still with a note of trepidation.

"I'm sure," I smiled softly.

She lay back on her pillow with her hair fanned out, a look of joy on her face. I could tell she was thinking, calculating. After a moment she turned onto her shoulder and rested her head on my chest.

"You know..." she said coyly, her breath warm on my skin. "If we started right now our baby would be born in the summer after school lets out."

I pulled back in surprise.

"But Judith, I don't even have a job."

"You're going to find a job, Carlton. I'm not worried about that."

"But—"

"Shhh." She put a finger to my lips. "Let's make a baby, Carlton."

Before I could agree or protest or anything else she sat up and shimmied out of her nightie, and she sat there with her proud breasts and her bronzed skin and an eager smile that left me defenseless.

There's a different attitude about lovemaking when you've decided to make a child. I experienced it for the first time that night with Judith. Passionate eyes quest deeper, kisses are softer, and fingertips have a lighter touch. I did my best to give Judith what she wanted, what we both wanted. There would be other times, other nights like this, but I always believed, because of how tender it was, how sweetly our bodies went together, that must have been the night we made Rachel.

* * *

The very next morning, after Judith had left for school, I answered an ad in the Fresno Bee and landed a job as a delivery driver with an outfit called Stefanelli Distributing. They handled wine and spirits, selling to liquor stores and bars in three counties. It must have been my perfect driving record that got me the job, because I didn't know anything about booze. It wasn't the kind of job that I'd been hoping for, but it paid okay, and by that point I had been willing to take just about anything.

I told Judith when she got home that afternoon, watching her closely for signs of disappointment or disapproval. I needn't have worried.

"Congratulations!" she exclaimed sincerely. She dropped her book bag and skipped over to give me a hug. "See? I told you you'd find a job."

"It's not much," I said guiltily.

"No, it's great," and she meant it. She was animated, her eyes gleeful. "You're going to be able to learn your way around the Valley so fast now. And you'll meet so many people. Good things are going to come from this, Carlton. Just wait, you'll see."

"I hope so."

I started Wednesday morning at 7:00 a.m. My trainer was a driver named Dave Gurney. I was supposed to ride with him for a week to learn the ins and outs of the business. We met outside of the warehouse, next to a chalky-white cargo van with sliding front doors and a roll-up door in the back. I was already cooking in the early sun. I couldn't tell how old Dave was. He had mischievous blue eyes, sandy brown hair that curled at his collar, and a wide goatee that rode up his jawbones. There was no gray in his hair, not even in his goatee or at his temples, and yet fine wrinkles etched his face like the bark of an old elm tree. He wore cowboy boots and jeans, a crisp white T-shirt, and a straw hat.

"Howdy," he said with his hand out.

"Howdy." His hand was as rough and cracked as a worn-out buckskin glove.

"You Carlton?"

"Yeah."

"Can I call ya Carl?"

"No."

His eyes did an amused little dance.

"Awlrighty then, Carlton. You from Tennessee?"

I winced at the put-on accent he came up with, but held my tongue. I didn't want to get into it with anyone on my first day.

"Yeah, I'm from Tennessee."

"Okay pardner." He laughed and slapped me on the shoulder. "Sorry about that. We just don't hear yur kind of talk around here too often. I ain't from around here neither."

"Where are you from?"

"Wyoming. Came down for the Clovis rodeo a while back. Got unhorsed, lost my saddle, my tack, and a couple o' teeth," he grinned to show me the empty places behind his cheeks, "and been workin' this booze wagon ever since."

I smiled. Dave was a good-natured guy after all. He reminded me a little of Hank back in Maine.

We spent the first couple of hours that morning just loading the van. Dave showed me where to find the pick tickets for our route, how the booze was organized, and where to turn the tickets in for invoices.

"Check it all careful," he warned me. "Yur responsible if any comes up missing."

We loaded the van ourselves, positioning the merchandise in a certain order so that we could get it back out with as little shuffling as possible. My skin was so dry in that San Joaquin Valley air that the cardboard boxes scuffed my hands and left fine cuts in my fingers.

"Bring ya some gloves tomorrow," Dave advised. "And a hat, too."

It seemed like lunchtime to me before we got on the road. There was no air conditioning in the van. Heat came up through the floor, and the baking wind through the windows just made it worse. I had salty grime on my skin, but not a drop of sweat. Dave rolled a one-handed cigarette and lit it with a Zippo that he struck by swiping it across his jeans.

"You ever been ahorseback?" he asked, blowing smoke out of his nose.

"A little, on the farm."

"You got a farm?"

"My family does."

"Whatcha doin' out here, chasin' a girl or runnin' from the law?"

I laughed.

"It's a girl. I married her."

"Well good fer you. Congratulations, Carl, er, Carlton."

"Thanks."

We drove into Clovis, a town adjacent to Fresno, passing under a green sign that read, *Clovis, Gateway to the Sierras.*

"First stop's at Don's Place," said Dave. He handed me an invoice. "You get the stuff on the dolly and I'll show ya where to put it."

Don's Place was a bar in a blue stucco building on a side street. We pulled around back and parked. While I squeezed into the back of the van to pull the order, Dave got out and rapped his rhino-skin knuckles on a gray steel door. Even from inside the van I could hear the door locks unlatching. There were four deadbolts on that door, *click, shunk, clack, snap.*

"Mornin' Cowboy."

"Mornin' Don."

I hopped out and stacked boxes on the dolly.

"This here's Carlton, Don. New driver."

I walked over to introduce myself. Don had on olive shorts and a white polo shirt that bulged out around his middle as if holding in his enormous belly like a net. He was mostly bald, a few strings of black hair combed across his pink scalp, and his eyes were bloodshot.

"Good to meet you, Carlton."

We shook. His meaty hand was damp.

"You too, sir."

"I ain't no sir, but thank ya anyway. Bring it on in, Dave."

It smelled sour inside, stale alcohol and cigarette smoke, a reek that I would soon get accustomed to. I stacked the cases where I was told. Don checked them off the invoice then signed. Dave went off to pee, leaving me alone in the backroom with Don.

"Where you from?" Don asked.

"Tennessee, sir."

"You kinda sound like Festus, you know?" I winced. He meant Festus from *Gunsmoke*, one of my favorite shows when I was a kid. But did I talk like Festus? No way. "He lives here, you know," Don went on. "See 'em from time to time."

"Really?"

"Yeah."

Dave came out, shaking his leg and zipping his jeans. "All set?" he asked.

"Looks good," said Don.

They went off together to talk privately, so I loaded the dolly, pulled and latched the cargo door, and climbed into the van to wait. It was too hot to stand in the sun. Dave came out after a few minutes, rolled a cigarette, and then we chugged off.

"Next stop's the Starlite," he said, his wrinkled cigarette bouncing in his lips. I pulled an invoice off the clipboard. "Looks like yur nickname's gonna be Festus," he added with a chuckle. I groaned into my hands. Nicknames stuck as hard as trail names. Dave laughed. "Better git used to it."

I was worn out by the end of that day. Judith met me at the door with an expectant smile.

"How did it go?" she asked.

"It went okay," I answered wearily. She tried to kiss me but I pushed her back. "Not until I've had a shower."

She sniffed and wrinkled her nose.

"Yeah, you smell bad," but she said this in fun.

After a shower I collapsed on the couch. Judith brought me a glass of sweet tea brimming with ice.

"I know you need this," she said. She handed me the glass and sat, pushing her bottom against my hip.

"You know it," I said. I held that sweating glass to my forehead.

"Is it hard work?" she asked.

"It wouldn't be so bad if it wasn't for the heat."

"Oh, look at your poor hands. I'll get you some lotion."

She hopped up and went into the bathroom. My hands were a mess. The little cuts stung. When she returned she took my hands one at a time and massaged the lotion into them. It was an arousing sensation, which made itself plain. Judith's eyes went humorously wide.

"Shouldn't we have supper first?" she asked with a smile.

I laughed and tried to lift my tea glass, but my hands were too slippery now.

"Maybe I'll just rest for a while."

"Just rest till you're ready."

She stretched out alongside me, complimenting every curve as if we had been made as one, and I fell asleep with her warm breath on my lips.

* * *

Judith's birthday was on September 15, a Saturday that year so we were both off. Lois and Eugene asked us to come up to Oakhurst for the day, but we wanted to stay home and relax instead. That night we went to The Outpost over on Olive Avenue for dinner. Dave and I had made a delivery there earlier that week, and it seemed to be the fanciest restaurant around. The place was packed, but they had held a table for me in a far corner, which offered a bit more intimacy than the tables out in the open.

I held Judith's chair for her then went around to my own. I wore a gray suit that night. Judith was dressed in a white cotton dress with short sleeves, a chaste collar, and a pleated hem at her ankles. With her hair in a ponytail and gold bracelets on her wrists, along with her wedding ring, she had a fresh and youthful, but at the same time mature look. I had noticed some wandering eyes as we crossed the dining room to our table.

Our waiter was a lanky Mexican kid named Diego. He came over and I ordered shrimp cocktail, the only appetizer on the menu.

"Would you like some wine?" I asked Judith.

"No," she shook her head, "I don't think so, Carlton."

"Well, I know they don't have sweet tea."

"No, I don't suppose they do," she said with knowing smile. "Maybe just regular tea, then."

I propped my elbows on our blood-red tablecloth and gazed appreciatively at her. She sat in perfect contrast against The Outpost's dark wood decor. Diego brought out candles and placed them on the table. I gave the candles a furtive glance as he lit them, then leaned forward after he moved off.

"Happy twenty-eighth birthday," I said softly.

"Thank you," she demurred.

"It's hard to believe I've known you since you were a teenager."

"And that I've known you since you were a minor. I still worry about the statute of limitations."

"I don't think you have anything to worry about there," I laughed. "But you know? This is the first time we've been together on your birthday."

"Oh my God, you're right! So much has happened, I hadn't thought about it. And your birthday, too, in a couple of weeks...maybe we should just split the difference and have one birthday together."

My eyes hooded for a second but she didn't notice.

"No," I reached for her hand, "I like it like this."

We sat in silence for some moments.

"I start my own route on Monday," I said.

"Already?"

"Yeah. I pick up on things pretty quick."

"Tell me about it," she said, batting her lashes.

Diego brought out a vase of white roses and set them in the middle of our table. He stood back with his finger to his lips, considered the arrangement, then slid the candles closer to the roses.

"Oh, Carlton, they're so beautiful," Judith fawned.

"I wanted to get you red roses, but everything else in here is so red already."

"No, they're perfect. I love them."

Diego stood off to the side, beaming. I looked up at him in appreciation. "Thank you," I mouthed silently.

"*De nada*, Festus," he said with a crooked grin, and then he whisked away.

"*Festus?*" Judith asked incredulously.

"It's the handle they gave me," I explained sourly. "I'm stuck with it now."

"*Festus,*" she laughed, leaning in on her elbows. "Couldn't they have just called you Jake?"

"I would have been happy with Carlton, but they all wanted to call me Carl. I don't know which is worse. Anyway," I shook that off, "look closer at the roses."

The lighting was dim in there, so she squinted to see better.

"Carlton, is that—"

"Your birthday present?" I answered for her.

"Is it a—"

"Necklace?"

"It's so—"

"Beautiful?"

She smiled prettily and I grinned.

"I got *you* this time," I said.

"Yes you did," she pretended to pout. "You're so bad."

"Let me help you with that."

The necklace was looped around the stems of the roses. Drapers had made it for me, a custom design. It had only arrived yesterday. I had worried all week that it wouldn't make it in time. It had a delicate gold chain and an equally delicate pendant, a willow tree. The detail was so fine that you could make out individual limbs and leaves. I stood and worked the necklace loose from the roses which, what with the thorns, wound up being more difficult than I had intended; but I finally got it loose, went up behind Judith, and fastened it around her neck. The pendant hung tastefully below her collar, a dash of glittering color against her white dress. Judith was fingering it gently when I returned to my chair.

"Carlton, it's so beautiful. I love it." I think my cheeks were flushing. "And I love you," she added.

The rest of that night was perfect, everything going as I'd hoped it would. When we got home we kissed our way through the dark to our bedroom.

* * *

My route had me shuttling up and down Highway 99, from Madera to the north of Fresno to Tulare down south. In between were other towns, some right on the highway, like Selma and Kingsburg, others farther out, like Dinuba and Reedley. Sometimes I went down dusty farm roads to reach my customers, past flickering rows of vineyards, rich green fields of lettuce and spinach, and shaded groves of almond trees. The little towns out there were often nothing more than a gas station, a few bleached houses, and a bar with whitewashed windows. Always in the distance, to the east and north, were mountains that curved along the horizon like an arching spine.

I developed a deep reddish tan, especially on my left arm. I wore a straw cowboy hat, a red bandana around my neck, and a pair of aviator sunglasses like the ones I had taken from that guy on the hill all those years ago. I kept a pair of buckskin work gloves in my back pocket.

We finally got a break from the heat around the first of October, as well as a little rain, the first I'd seen in California. By November it was getting cold enough at night that we had to light the pilot and get the furnace going.

It was the second week of November—the Tuesday after Veterans Day—that I learned about the San Joaquin Valley's infamous fogs. We'd had some rain over the weekend. The air that morning was so still that I could hear my own heart beating. It was already a foggy morning, but not so thick that I couldn't see. In retrospect, Judith had mentioned something over breakfast, Tule fog, which I had heard as *tooly fog*, a strange name, I thought, for a little autumn mist.

I took off from the warehouse that morning, heading up the 99 to Madera. There was a lot of traffic on the road, a lot of trucks. I was just going along, fifty-five miles an hour, being passed by the big eighteen-wheelers, the chicken trucks and the cantaloupe trucks and all the rest. The fog thickened so suddenly that I couldn't anticipate it at all. From one moment to the next I could no longer see the road right in front of the van!

Completely blind, I wobbled the steering wheel in fright then cut over onto the shoulder, which was invisible in the murk. I left the van running and got out to see how close I was to the edge. I could still move over a few more feet, so I got back in and inched the van over as far as I dared. I killed the engine, hit the emergency flashers, and sat back to wait it out. To my left I could hear the roar of speeding trucks but I couldn't see them, not even their passing swirl in the fog.

This went on for a long time. We had CB radios in the vans, but mine had a blown fuse. I thought belatedly that I should have gotten it fixed before I left the warehouse. And then I heard it, coming from behind: The scalloped, hoarse chirping of a tractor-trailer jackknifing. It went past me and kept on going, a juggernaut of violence that was invisible in the fog...and then the hollow crunch of a collision. Air horns blared. Car tires shrieked as brakes were locked. There were more crunches, more shrieks, and other impact sounds that I can't describe. A terrible wreck was underway. It went on and on, like steel dominoes falling from there to Madera. My first impulse was to jump out and go help—people might be hurt—but I couldn't see a thing; nothing.

I listened for screams or cries for help, but heard none. It occurred to me that someone might come flying through there and sideswipe me right off the shoulder, so I got out and hoofed it through the fog into a field. After a time I hiked north, thinking I might be able to see something or help someone. I strained to make anything out ahead. My eyes actually ached from the effort. I tripped on bushes, stumbled into a ditch, and then I scrambled out onto damp concrete, probably the Avenue 7 exit.

There were sounds off to my left. I could hear people speaking urgently but I couldn't make out what they were saying. I was about to go to them when I heard another vehicle screech in and slam into something. It was too dangerous to walk onto that highway, where people didn't have the sense to pull over when they couldn't even see the hoods of their cars. I heard sirens coming up, saw a hazy red glow flash through the fog as a sheriff or ambulance sped past. There was nothing I could do to help. I returned to the van, leaned out my door to follow the white stripe on the pavement, crept along the shoulder to the exit, then made my way slowly back to Fresno.

The fog thinned after lunchtime and I was able to finish my route. I got home late, though, way after dark. Judith met me at the door. I had phoned her earlier.

"I was so worried," she said, hugging me in the doorway.

"Man." I wiped the grime off my forehead with the back of my hand. "Even Mt. Washington wasn't that bad—or the Smokies."

"I should have warned you."

"You did, I just didn't understand."

It was on the news. The latest chain-reaction crash on Highway 99 had involved sixteen cars, three tractor-trailers, and the obligatory chicken truck. Miraculously no one was killed. Over in Visalia, Dave had crashed into a telephone pole and had broken both of his legs. They say he was found when the fog lifted, sitting on the ground against his van's bent rear wheel, smoking a cigarette, drinking from a broken bottle of Jack Daniels and bitching like a cowboy, unhorsed again.

* * *

We had Thanksgiving in Oakhurst that year. Judith and I had originally talked about flying to Nashville for Thanksgiving, but with Dave out I was running extra routes. There was no way I could ask for time off. Judith had the holiday week off, but she hadn't been feeling well.

I had shuffled in from work the night before, bone tired and looking forward to sleeping late in the morning. Judith had dinner waiting, so I washed up quickly and went to the table. She was making dinner most nights now. I felt bad about that, but then I was getting in so late from all the extra work. She said it was okay, she understood. And besides, since Dave's wreck I was making more money than she. And we were going to need it.

"What for?" I asked.

She looked fatigued. Her eyes were a little puffy, but when she smiled they sparkled all the same. She reached across and took my hand.

"Because I'm pregnant, Carlton."

That didn't register right away. I was looking at her hand in mine, in a kind of a gauzy haze after the long day. I fiddled absently with her wedding ring and then it hit me, and suddenly I was wide-eyed and out of my chair.

"Oh, honey," I said joyously, going to her. I held her and rested a hand lightly on her stomach. "When's our baby due?"

"June," she said. "About the first week."

I had no words, only a feeling of joyous wonder. I pressed my ear against her stomach and she giggled.

"It's too early for that."

"No, I can hear the baby's heartbeat," I swore.

"No you can't. That's just my stomach rumbling because I'm starved."

She waited until we were in Oakhurst to tell Lois and Eugene. It was a cool day, hazy in the distance, pretty much identical to last year. We parked the Pontiac by the wood fence and went right on in without knocking. James and Gloria were sitting in the living room by the fire.

"There you are," James said, standing. "I'm usually the one who's late."

He set his Bloody Mary on the table, kissed his sister on the cheek then shook my hand.

"Hello Judith. Carlton," Gloria said with a bright smile. She looked Judith over and something seemed to trigger in her eyes. "Come sit," she said to Judith, eagerly patting a place on the couch.

"Where's Michael?" I asked James.

"Canada. Great powder in Banff this year, it seems."

"Oh."

He leaned in to whisper.

"Judy told us about your sons. It's too bad."

"Yeah."

"But you get to see them...what? Every other summer?"

"Alternating. Summer after next."

"Hmm."

Eugene came in with a platter of crackers and cheese, followed by Lois with the shrimp cocktail.

"There you two are," they said together.

"Sorry we're late," said Judith. She was sitting and holding Gloria's hands. The two were giggling, like a school-girl conspiracy. "You go first," she said to Gloria.

We all stood there, puzzled, except for James, who was either smirking or beaming, hard to tell with him. Gloria displayed her long elegant fingers, and her shiny new rock.

"Oh, Gloria," Lois practically swooned. She set the shrimp cocktail down and bent over to hug Gloria. Then to James, "Why didn't you tell us?"

"We wanted it to be a surprise, Mom."

"Well, you've sure surprised us. Congratulations, son," said Eugene.

"Yeah, congratulations," I added sincerely. "Have you set a date?"

"Not yet," said Gloria. "There's so much to plan. And other news, too."

"There's more?" asked Eugene. "You're not..."

"No," Gloria blushed.

Somehow all eyes seemed to instinctively fall on Judith. She sat shyly, pressing her hands between her knees.

"I'm pregnant," she announced at last, barely restraining her excitement.

Lois actually squealed with delight. She rushed over to hug her daughter. Eugene slapped me on the back proudly, and James offered his hand once more. "When is it due?" he asked with a happy grin.

"June," I said.

"We are so blessed in this family," Lois said, her eyes red and misting.

I did feel blessed. I used their phone to call Mom and Dad with the news. Dad was pleased, and Mom said she would move heaven and earth to be there when the baby came. At dinner we held hands and said a prayer, something the Taylors didn't usually do, and then Lois started taking the lids off the dishes. There was the usual, turkey, stuffing, and mashed potatoes, but also cornbread, a green-bean and bacon casserole with fried onions, black-eyed peas and okra. My eyes went wide in surprise. Judith patted my leg and smiled warmly.

"I can't wait to try this southern food," James said eagerly. He tucked a napkin in his shirt and dug in.

* * *

The call I had been dreading came on New Year's morning. Judith and I were still in bed. We hadn't gone out last night, but we had stayed up late so were sleeping in. I was awake. I had a hand on Judith's stomach, kneading it gently. I couldn't feel the baby yet, but Judith's stomach was beginning to pooch, like a soft pillow. Her obstetrician, Dr. Petrosyan, already knew the baby's sex, but Judith and I wanted to keep it a mystery, which irritated Susan, who wanted to throw a baby shower.

Judith jerked up when the phone rang. She reached over groggily and answered it. I don't know how, but before she said a word I knew who it was.

"Hello? Dick? Yeah, he's right here." Judith turned to me with a troubled look. "Carlton? It's your dad."

I squeezed my eyes tight and took the phone.

"Dad? Good morn—"

"*Did you know about this?*" he cut right in. There must have been no question in his mind that I knew exactly what he was calling about. I hadn't heard him this angry since...since Evelyn.

"Dad, I was just a kid," I found myself pleading. Judith squeezed my arm and searched me silently for an explanation.

"*Did Sadie do that to Leavitt? Well did she?*"

"Dad, I...I don't know."

"*Weren't you there?*"

"It was so long ago."

"*He was my son, damn it! He was your brother.*"

Dad slammed the phone, and I fell back on my pillow.

"What is it?" Judith asked, her face drawn with concern. "What's happened?"

I didn't want to tell her. I wanted those memories gone, erased. To speak them just kept them alive, kept them going. There would be no end of it. But she was involved now, so I told her everything. When I got to the part that sounded like what she had read in Sadie's book, she gasped and bit her knuckle.

"Did it really happen?" she asked. "Your brother?"

I nodded, no words left.

"Oh, Carlton. Poor Carlton." She cradled my head. "You were just a little boy. It wasn't your fault.

It felt good to hear that from her, but down inside I knew better.

I talked to Mom later that day. I could tell from her voice that she had been crying. Damn you, Sadie.

"Why didn't you tell us, Carlton?" she asked.

"I don't know, Mom. It was so long ago. I was scared."

"Have you talked to your sister?"

"No."

Mom explained what had happened. They'd thrown their regular New Year's party. A few of the ladies who came happened to be in a reading group. I didn't know this, but *A Robin Waits* had been nominated for some kind of award. The ladies all knew who Sadie was, of course, so they took the book up at their last meeting. Actually being in the childhood home of an up-and-coming author must have lent an air of notoriety to their chatter and gossip. The ladies discussed the book in detail with Mom, and one of those details struck close to home. Sadie had never given Mom and Dad a copy, which seemed strange in itself but then she had always been so shy about the thing. One of the ladies produced a copy from her purse, and Mom tore through it until she found the passage. When she showed it to Dad, she said he blew up.

I thought to call Sadie, but I couldn't bring myself to do it right then. Dad had called her and screamed at her through the phone. He told her he never wanted to see her again. I lay in bed with Judith that night, worrying over things I had thought were too far in the past to matter now. Our bed was warm. Judith was asleep, her hair tickling my nose. I felt her stomach and I thought, it's all so far away, so long ago. I had my wife and my baby right here, my family, and we were happy. I wouldn't let anything interfere with that.

* * *

Judith was even more beautiful when she was pregnant. As tall as she was, she was able to carry her ever-swelling stomach without having to waddle. She had a maternal aura about her, a blush in her cheeks. Her hair seemed softer, with lighter streaks that caught the sun. Her students had done crayon drawings for her, which we taped to the walls in the spare bedroom, soon to be the baby's room. Most of her students were ten-year-olds, but she had a few Mexican and Hmong kids who had only recently been brought to America. Their drawings were mostly stick figures, a woman with a bump on her stomach, a woman holding a standing baby by the hand. Some were little better than scribbles. In every drawing, though, the stick figures wore smiles, one with exaggerated teeth. Most were set outdoors, with a yellow sun, blue sky, and a green tree in the background. They were cute.

We had our regular birthing classes on Thursday evenings, where we would sit on the carpet with other expecting parents while our instructor told us what to do, Judith leaning against my chest for support, my arms around her stomach. I always felt odd at these classes. People revealed personal things, private things that I wouldn't have discussed with my own mother let alone strangers. Some of them were planning to take cameras into the delivery room, which I found almost pornographic. Fortunately Judith shared my sensibilities about these things.

Judith got bigger and bigger. I was afraid our baby would be as big as Luke was, but Dr. Petrosyan said no, everything was fine. The baby was due around June 10. It was normal weight at this stage, whatever that meant. Judith's ankles began to swell, but then school let out for the summer and she was able to stay home and off her feet. Stefanelli's had hired another driver, so I was back to regular hours, which got me home in time to cook dinner. Afterward I would sit with Judith and rub lotion onto her stomach. Her only complaint was the stretch marks she was developing.

"They don't go away, you know," she told me one night.

"I don't care," I said, working the lotion onto her belly. Her navel was inside out now.

"Easy for you to say," she snapped. "You don't wear bikinis."

"Aw."

"Oh, I'm sorry, honey. It must be my hormones. And my breasts are killing me."

"Don't be sorry." I nuzzled her ear and reached a hand to her breasts. They were hard as rock.

"Mmmm," she moaned as I massaged the ache out of them; then: "I want this baby *out*, Carlton."

"Soon," I said soothingly. "Real soon."

* * *

My route finished up in Visalia on Tuesdays, part of Dave's old route that I had been able to keep after his accident. It was the fourth of June, a little after four o'clock on a clear and comfortable afternoon, not too hot. I was just taking the Highway 198 interchange to Visalia when my CB radio crackled.

"Breaker one nine. Got your ears on, Festus?"

"Yeah, I'm here," I said, thumbing the mic.

"Better call home. I think your missus wants to have that baby."

I hung on those words for a moment, thumbing the mic but no words would form. I shook my head in incomprehension, and then it hit me in a panic. I threw the mic to the floor and heaved that van across traffic to make the next exit. A case of something fell in the back, glass breaking. The tang of whiskey filled the air. I bumped and walloped into a Unocal station, yanked the emergency brake and sprinted for the pay phone, digging into my pockets for quarters as I ran. Our phone rang and rang until the answering machine picked up.

"*Ohmygod!*" I exclaimed in a sweat.

I beat it back to the van and hurled it onto the highway, passing cars and eighteen-wheelers as if they were just piddling along, although they were speeding as always. It took me almost an hour to get to the hospital. I got stuck at a red light on Divisadero Street, thought my heart would burst before that light finally turned green. I edged around some cars, rolled over a curb to avoid the light at the hospital entrance—losing another case of something in the back—and floored it into the first parking space I saw. I knocked my hat off coming out of the van, but I was in too much of a panic to waste time picking it up. I left it on the pavement and raced inside, searching wildly. I spotted Lois in the reception area.

"Thank God, Carlton. Hurry."

She took my hand and yanked me down a corridor to the delivery room. When I got inside I pulled up fast, out of breath, my heart pounding. A nurse was snapping gloves onto Dr. Petrosyan's hands. He winked at me, his dark Armenian eyes simultaneously reassuring and professional. Judith was on the table, her legs draped. She saw me and smiled tightly.

"You made it," she breathed, but then she winced from a contraction.

I was about to rush to Judith when a nurse stepped up and blocked my way.

"Here, Mr. Jeffries." She held a blue paper gown open for me and I urgently slipped into it, but before I could get to Judith the nurse stopped me again. "And this." She squirted a dollop of hand sanitizer into my palm. I worked that into my hands impatiently while the nurse looked on. She waited with her arms crossed until she was satisfied, then at her nod I pushed past her and finally got to Judith.

"I'm here," I said, taking Judith's hand.

"Push now, Judith," said Dr. Petrosyan.

Judith's hair was pasted to her forehead. She grunted and clenched her teeth as she pushed, sweat breaking out all over her face like rain drops on Grandmother Villetta's peaches. Judith had wanted a natural childbirth without a spinal block. Dr. Petrosyan had warned her that she might change her mind at the last minute, but she hadn't. She was feeling everything.

"Push, baby," I said gently. A nurse handed me a damp towel. I wiped Judith's face and forehead. "Now push again."

I kept looking over at Dr. Petrosyan for some sign. The drapes over Judith's legs hid everything from us. Judith was straining, puffing breaths, then she convulsed with a massive contraction. She screamed, and I almost toppled over in anguish. I felt so helpless, so inadequate. Dr. Petrosyan leaned under the drape and then...a baby cried.

"Well now, mom and dad," he said with a smile that was startlingly white against his dark skin, "you have a baby girl."

"It's Rachel," I smiled at Judith softly.

Judith had collapsed into her sweat-soaked pillow, her face wan, but she managed a smile.

"Rachel," she breathed, reaching out weakly for our baby.

We had decided it would be Rachel for a girl, Samuel for a boy. Samuel was my choice. There was no particular reason, I just liked the sound of it; but Judith wanted Rachel for a girl. It was important to her. Judith admired Rachel Carson, the environmentalist who had taken on the chemical industry in the early 60s. Judith had read all of Carson's books. She even used one of those books, *The Sense of Wonder*, in her classroom. I knew of Rachel Carson, too, from Mr. Fennick's fifth grade class and those walks we took through Percy Warner Park. It seemed like fate, and anyway, I thought the name Rachel was pretty.

A nurse put Rachel on Judith's chest. The motherly bond was already there in Judith's eyes, a deep softness tinted with pride and affection. I sniffed and wiped my eyes. Rachel was red and wrinkled, still streaked with blood and fluid, but she was beautiful, so beautiful.

"Hi, Rachel," I said in wonder. "Hi, baby girl."

I stroked the soft spot on her head lightly, her little tuft of caramel-colored hair. Her eyes were clenched tight, as if she were about to cry, but she lay quietly on her mother's chest, questing with her lips, her fingers bunched into tiny fists.

"Okay, another small one, Judith," said Dr. Petrosyan. Judith squeezed her eyes and gave an involuntary push. "That's got it."

Dr. Petrosyan stood and snapped off his gloves. Instruments rattled in a pan. A nurse came up and smiled.

"Time to get this baby to the nursery," she said. "We'll have her back soon."

The nurse swaddled Rachel in a pink blanket and took her away. I stayed with Judith, cradling her head in the curve of my arm.

"You did it," I told her.

"A girl," she smiled dreamily.

I patted her face with the towel, gazing into her weary but proud eyes. She smiled and gave my hand a weak squeeze.

A shrill beeping alarm pierced the delivery room. Judith shuddered and her eyes rolled up, just the whites showing. Her hand went limp.

"Judith?" I shook her lightly and her head lolled to the side. She felt cold. "*Judith!*" I looked around in a panic. "*What's happening?*"

"*Oh, no!*" I heard a nurse exclaim. "She's hemorrhaging. Get Dr. Petrosyan! *Get Dr. Petrosyan!*"

Someone shoved me out of the way. Nurses swarmed around Judith, blocking my view. Dr. Petrosyan elbowed his way in, sweat beading his forehead. I stepped back, tripped on some wires or tubing and fell.

"I can't stop it!" someone shouted.

"Get me a central line," this from Dr. Petrosyan. "Hang a unit of O neg. Let's get her to the OR. *Now!*"

After those few frenetic seconds I was suddenly alone in the delivery room, on my butt and tangled in some black wires. Everything was a mess. There were blue towels on the floor, turned purple with blood, a thickening pool, and crimson splatters leading out the doors. I stood numbly and followed them—

$\mathcal{E}$IGHTEEN

It's a cruel coincidence that I got to this part of the story on this day, our anniversary. Sometimes improbable things land in droves also. It's only natural, though, even unavoidable if you live as long as I have. It's not old people like me who invent religions and other things to explain these coincidences away, but rather the younger people who haven't seen enough yet.

I still shudder when I remember that day, Judith going lifeless in my arms. I needed a break before I could go on with the story, so I crawled out and stood in the mud, let that chilling rain numb me. Poor Sam. He was so anxious to go that he began to whine and chew on his leash. He almost pulled me off my feet while we were out there, his paws digging into the slushy mud, his nose down. I had to jerk him back. "Stop it Samuel!" I growled at him, and then he took on that hurt look, his eyes drooping like his ears. I felt bad doing that to him. I rustled some venison out of my backpack, and stroked his neck as he lapped it out of my hand. "It's okay, boy. It's okay." In minutes he had forgotten all about it. Dogs are lucky that way.

But to continue, now that I'm wrapped up in my sleeping bag again and I've got feeling back in my fingers:

I followed that trail of Judith's blood into the corridor, swaying as I went. My head felt hollow. An orderly was already going after Judith's blood, swirling it around with a gray mop, like finger painting on white linoleum. Lois was there. Her nose was red and some hair had come loose, dangling on her cheek.

"Carlton? What happened?"

"I—I don't know."

"Is she—" Her lips trembled.

"I don't know."

I dropped onto a bench, transfixed on Judith's blood on the floor. I felt dizzy. Lois sat beside me and held my hands. I looked into her anguished face and I thought, *This is what Judith would look like if something bad happened to me.*

Dr. Petrosyan came out after a while. How long? I don't know, but the sun was coming in duskily through the front doors by then, an orange sheen on the floor where Judith's blood had been. His face was unreadable. He was wearing green scrubs, a surgical mask hanging below his chin like a napkin. He smelled like antiseptic. Lois and I rose together, partly numb, partly in shock. She was leaning on me heavily.

"Carlton," Dr. Petrosyan said. He stood a pace farther back than he normally did whenever he spoke with me. "Judith has suffered a uterine rupture." Lois moaned and buried her face in my shoulder. "It's very rare, especially in the absence of dehiscence." I had to shake my head at that, as if my ears were plugged and I needed to clear them to make out what he was saying. Dr. Petrosyan exhaled. "I'm sorry. That means a Caesarian scar or other incision."

"But Judith's never had that," I countered at once, as if that assurance alone would make all of this go away.

"I know," he nodded thoughtfully. "She probably had a congenital weakness in the uterine wall."

"Is she—" Lois asked but couldn't finish.

"She lost a lot of blood, and the peritoneum has been breached. Dr. Evans is an outstanding surgeon. He's doing everything he can. I need to get back in there now."

He left us with a quick, parting nod. Lois drug herself to the phone to call Eugene. I thought that I should probably call Mom, but what could I say to her? She had tickets to fly out this weekend, closer to what we thought would be the due date. She had no idea that any of this was going on. It was better to wait until...until we knew more.

The sun had fully set by the time Eugene arrived. Lois got up and went to him, her face red and drawn. He hugged her then walked her back to our bench. Eugene was stoic.

"Have you heard anything?" he asked steadily. I shook my head then looked away. He and Lois sat beside me, his arms around her. No one spoke.

It was hauntingly familiar, sitting in that hospital corridor as the night deepened and the florescent lighting became glaringly white. The nurses all wore scrubs now rather than the smart white uniforms they used to wear, but otherwise everything smelled and sounded as it had before, a long time ago. The institutional clock on the wall turned just as slowly. It was cold in that antiseptic air. I hugged myself and drifted off.

I came to with a start. Sadie's birthday—Rachel and Sadie had the same birthday! Why hadn't I realized that before? My mouth was sticky. I looked around in confusion and noticed that gray dawn was diffusing through the windows like mist. I turned grainy eyes to the clock. It was a little after 5:00 a.m.

Lois and Eugene were asleep. Lois had a white shawl over her shoulders, and was huddled into Eugene's chest. Eugene's head was back, his mouth open, his arms limp at his sides. I stood and stretched, went to the water fountain for a sip. A nurse was at the desk, arranging clipboards. No one else was around. The place was eerily quiet. I went to the nurse. She knew me but I didn't know her.

"Mr. Jeffries," she said. "We have coffee if you'd like."

"Yeah," I said groggily. "Can you tell me—"

"Dr. Stepan should be out soon. He can explain."

"Stepan? Where's Dr. Petrosyan?"

"He went home, Mr. Jeffries. Dr. Stepan is the attending. He'll be with you—oh, there he is now."

I had never met Dr. Stepan. He was a tall, handsome guy with blond hair, younger than I would have expected.

"Mr. Jeffries," he said with a weary smile. He offered his hand and I shook it. My hand came away with a film of antiseptic on it. "Are these Judith's parents?"

"Yes."

Lois and Eugene roused at the commotion. They trudged over, hugging one another as if they were freezing. Dr. Stepan looked from me to them then back. He focused on me squarely. He exhaled.

"Judith came through the surgery," he said. I felt my knees buckling. Lois stifled a cry. "She's in the recovery room. The anesthesia should be wearing off soon. You can go in, but quietly. Okay?"

I thought my legs had gone out from under me. Dr. Stepan took me by the arm.

"Steady," he said. "Come, I'll take you."

Eugene shouldered forward, but Lois held him.

"Let Carlton go, Gene," she said. "It's his place."

I gave Lois an appreciative nod as Dr. Stepan led me to Judith's room. Once we were out of earshot he explained the situation.

"Her uterus ruptured, Mr. Jeffries. We had no choice but to perform a hysterectomy." He took a breath and smiled reassuringly. "But she's going to be fine now. She's had major surgery, though. She'll be weak, and she needs to be still so the incisions can heal, so keep the excitement down. Okay?" He patted me on the back.

"Thank you, Doctor."

"No problem. It's just this way."

He pushed a door open for me and I went inside. Judith was tucked into a hospital bed, the side rails up. The low light of dawn fell through cracked blinds onto her face, like an apparition. She had IV lines in both arms, held in place with white tape, and an oxygen line in her nose. Her hair lay in a bundle over her shoulder, bound in links with rubber bands. Rachel was asleep in a glass baby warmer beside the bed. I went to them, wanting to touch them both at once. When I leaned over Judith to kiss her forehead, I could smell Rachel's clean, baby freshness. My face broke. I wiped my eyes then reached out a hand to Rachel. She was so warm, so pretty.

Judith's eyes fluttered open, as if from a dream.

"Hey," I said softly, but even that seemed garishly loud.

Her lips were moving, trying to form words. Water, she wanted water. I found a bottle with a straw and held it while she sipped. That exertion alone seemed to drain her. She took some deep breaths and winced.

"What...happened?" she whispered hoarsely.

"It's okay, baby. You're okay. Rachel's here. She's perfect."

I smiled but tears came anyway. I pulled over a chair and sat.

"Everything's fine," I said. "You're going to be fine."

And then I buried my face in my hands and let it all come out.

* * *

Mom arrived on Saturday afternoon. Judith was still in the hospital, so we went right over. We were roasting in the heat because the air conditioner had gone out in the Pontiac. Mom fanned her face with her hand, and when that wasn't enough she took a checkbook out of her purse and fanned her face with that.

"I still can't get over the heat here," she said.

"It was really nice until this week."

She fiddled with the A/C vents to no effect, threw up her hands in frustration.

"So how's Judith doing?"

"She's doing great."

Judith could sit up now to nurse Rachel, and she could swing her legs gingerly over the side and get out of bed by herself. She couldn't stand up straight, though. When she went to the bathroom she shuffled hunched over, a hand pressed to her stomach.

"Have you talked to your sister?"

"Yeah, I called her the other day."

"How is she?"

That came out as a question begging for elaboration, but I had little to tell.

"She's busy, I guess. Too busy to come out here, or so she says. I don't know about that. I think she's avoiding us on purpose, because of...well..."

"That book," Mom muttered.

"Yeah. So how's Dad?"

"Keeping busy outside." Mom shook her head and sighed, then added, "Thank God."

"What does *that* mean?" I didn't know if I should laugh or frown.

"It *means* I don't have to put up with him as much. He's building a greenhouse right off the garage."

"A *greenhouse?*"

"And a kennel, too."

"What? Did Mirabel have her pups?"

Mom laughed. "Sure did. Six of 'em. All the puppies together are bigger than she is. I meant to tell you, but with all of this going on—"

"Six pups!" I slapped the steering wheel. "Well I know Dad's happy now."

"Such as it is," she said tightly, but then she smiled. "They were born on Tuesday."

"No way," I exclaimed in disbelief.

"Yep," she laughed ironically, "Sadie, Rachel, and six puppies all on the same day."

* * *

When we walked into her room, we found Judith sitting upright against her pillows, bright sunlight canting in through the blinds. Lois was brushing out Judith's hair. Rachel was asleep in the white wicker crib that I had brought from home.

"Hello, Mabel," Judith smiled. She had her color back, and her energy. Now that the IV and oxygen lines were out, she looked perfectly normal.

"Hello, Judith," Mom said with smile. "How are you?"

"I'm ready to go home," Judith answered, biting her lip.

Mom nodded in sympathy. "Hello, Lois." She and Lois hugged like old friends, then Mom bent over and kissed Judith gently on the forehead. "Now let me see that baby."

The three of us gathered around the crib, with Judith looking on proudly. Rachel fussed for a second but didn't wake up.

"She's so beautiful," Mom fawned, clasping her hands to her heart. "And so quiet."

"Tommy was that way, Mom. Remember?"

"I remember, Carlton," she said in fond memory, but then she fixed me with a hard look. "They sure didn't get that from you."

"Aw."

Everyone chuckled at that.

"When do you go home?" Mom asked Judith. Judith flashed a cheery smile.

"Tomorrow. Yea!"

"Well, I hope I'm not a bother," Mom said.

"No, Mabel," Lois assured her. "We're glad to have you with us."

We took Judith and Rachel home on Sunday afternoon. Lois drove us in her car so that we would have air conditioning. I helped Judith into the front seat, then Mom and I got in back. Mom held Rachel. She cooed and tickled Rachel's lip, and Rachel rewarded her with an adorable toothless smile. Judith grinned and tried to look over the back of her seat, but she couldn't twist that far.

Once home I helped Judith into bed then rolled the crib into our room. Lois went to the kitchen to make us some lunch, and Mom brought Rachel in, who was fussing now.

"She's hungry," Judith said in a motherly voice.

"Starving's more like it," Mom said, "if little Rachel has *his* appetite."

They both laughed, sharing something only mothers can know.

It was crowded in that house with so many people. I wanted nothing more than to be left alone with Judith and Rachel, but at the same time I appreciated the help. Things were going to be difficult until Judith fully recovered. Stefanelli's had given me the week off, but I had to get back to work the next day. Lois was heading home that evening, while Mom was going to stay for a week to help out.

That night in bed, Judith showed me her scar. It was an ugly welt, still puckered, warm to the touch. It looked like an angry red zipper, with Judith's navel as the top button.

"Does it hurt?" I asked her.

"Not really, but it throbs. I get the stitches out next Friday. It'll be better then. But oh," she pouted, "I'll never be able to wear a bikini again."

I was about to blurt that I didn't care, but I caught myself in time.

"You're beautiful no matter what," I said instead. "That night at the hospital, I thought...I thought—"

"Oh, honey." She held me as if I were the one with the scar. "Everything's okay." We both gazed at Rachel, sleeping peacefully in her crib. "She's so beautiful. I'd go through it all again if I could."

Her eyes seemed to darken a shade.

"You made a beautiful little girl," I whispered in her ear. "As beautiful as her mother."

* * *

Time eases along when you're happy. It flows like a lazy summer stream from day to day, days always remembered somehow as having been sunny and warm. I had never lived such a stretch of contentment, as if I had spent each of those days on Cordell Hull Lake back in Smith County, lazily casting lines, feeling the nibbles but not particularly concerned about reeling in a fish; and this while the sun rounded overhead, with egrets skimming the water, the forest deep and green.

The school district had allowed Judith to substitute teach, only a day or two a week. This made it easier for us to look after Rachel, one less thing for us to have to worry about. I couldn't get home quickly enough in the evenings, to hold Rachel, to play with her and, well, the other things you have to take care of with babies. But I didn't mind. I really didn't.

I went to work every day, I did my job, and I did it well enough to earn a raise, although there's not much about work during that time that I can recall now. It simply wasn't my focus. I do remember where I was the morning the space shuttle *Challenger* exploded. That was January 28, 1986. It was a cold morning, drab and dusty beneath a high layer of clouds. The farm fields looked desiccated and colorless. I was already on the 99, heading down to Tulare when I heard it on the radio. President Reagan spoke well later, but his words couldn't console the ache I felt, or the fear that we had lost more than seven astronauts. One of the crew had been a school teacher. Judith only had one class that week, so she used it to teach about space, about Apollo, and how we had once walked on the moon. Maybe we would go to Mars one day.

Yeah, I wish it had been us.

We flew to Nashville on a Saturday at the beginning of Spring Break. It took three flights and most of the day to get there. Our flights were hard on Rachel. She fussed and cried, twisting in our arms like a bundle of taut springs. At nine-and-a-half months old, she had two little teeth up top and was pushing up two more on the bottom. Judith and I passed her back and forth, giving Rachel her bottles, patting her back, letting her teethe and drool on our knuckles.

A stewardess on our second flight came up the aisle and gave us a commiserating look. She returned with some cold applesauce, which settled Rachel down until I could finally coo her to sleep. I had her on my lap, wrapped in her pink blanket. She had hair now, a cute topknot that Judith had tied with a pink bow. Rachel's hair had darkened a little since she was born, but it was still lighter than Judith's. It looked like honey and cinnamon swirled in a glass.

We didn't get into Nashville until after six in the evening. It was chilly out. The sun was already below the hills, casting the thin clouds in pink. We straggled down the jetway wearily, Judith carrying Rachel while I drug along behind them with Judith's purse and Rachel's diaper bag. Mom and Dad met us at the gate. Mom smiled wide and went straight to Judith.

"Oh, I *love* your hair," Mom said to Judith in that praising tone that women use with one another. Judith had cut her hair. It now fell in long curls only as far as her shoulders. The rest she had donated to some project that made wigs for cancer patients. Judith claimed it was easier to take care of her hair now, easier to handle Rachel. Her hair looked nice, but I was still getting used to it. It made her look more mature, not older, just more settled in life.

Mom looped an affectionate arm around Judith then leaned in to peer at Rachel, sleeping in Judith's arms. The women started off together toward baggage claim, chattering and in their own world. And Dad? Dad looked fine. He was trimmer than he had been when I last saw him, which was at the wedding. He was more angular, especially around his jaw and shoulders. He had developed a deep tan. He smiled and held out his hand.

"Hello, son," he said in his reserved way.

"Hi, Dad. You look great."

That seemed to embarrass him. He looked down and cleared his throat.

"Well, uh, hmm," he said, "let's get you loaded up."

Dad drove us home in the El Dorado. It was dark when we pulled up the driveway, but I couldn't miss the new greenhouse.

"Holy—"

"It took a lot of work," Dad said.

Mom humphed at that. She got out and went around to help Judith. Dad and I went straight to the greenhouse.

"Jeez, Dad," I said. "I was thinking it would be plastic, you know? Like the ones at Grandmother's place. You did all of this by yourself?"

Dad looked on distantly, as if he were recalling every stage of the construction.

"Yep," he said.

The greenhouse extended from the corner of the garage, across the top of the turning circle toward the garden shed, leaving just enough of a gap for a car to get through. The greenhouse had a cement floor, and a knee-high stone wall supporting an arched lattice of angle-iron that held clear glass panes. It looked like something from a botanical garden.

"Are you growing anything in there?" I asked.

"I've got tomatoes and green beans started," he said. "I've been thinking about some citrus."

"I never knew you were interested in this kind of thing."

"You've got to keep busy, son. Want to see the pups?"

"Yeah," I said eagerly.

He took me around back and my jaw fell. Dad had excavated into the hill behind the greenhouse, about where my trail to the hilltop used to be. The kennel was built of wood, with airy windows and double doors. We went inside. It was warm in there, smelled like dog food and a whiff of urine. Dad flipped a switch and a bank of florescent lights came on. There were gated stalls strewn with old blankets and straw, and in each of these a boisterous adolescent puppy thumping its tail. I spotted Langley right away. He looked up at me with a dog smile, his tail thumping the loudest.

"Hey, Langley." I unlatched his gate and knelt. Langley came out wagging, a little slow. He was getting to be an old dog now. Some of his whiskers were thick and gray. "Hey, boy." I frisked his neck and ears. "Did you do all of this, Langley? Look at all these pups."

Dad opened a gate and Mirabel slinked over. She nosed at my hands then flopped against me. I frisked her with one hand, Langley with the other. Mirabel was a big girl now. The last time I'd seen her she was younger than these pups.

"These aren't all from Mirabel," Dad said. "I've done some trading."

"Not with Bob," I said in alarm. Dad just shook his head and laughed.

"No, not with Bob."

I sobered after a moment and said, "Dad? About Sadie." Dad's cheeks twitched.

"I don't want to talk about it."

"But—"

"Let's go inside now."

The ladies were in the den, sitting on the couch and gossiping. Rachel was asleep between them. A fire was going.

"Well," Dad said, lightheartedly all of a sudden. "Can I hold my granddaughter now?"

Judith lifted Rachel and carried her to Dad. Dad rocked Rachel gently in his arms, gazing on her proudly, as he had once gazed on Sadie.

* * *

We went to see the boys on Monday. I didn't call Evelyn to set this up, why bother? I called Gracie. There was something in the legal papers that said Evelyn had to accommodate reasonable visits if I came to town, but defining *reasonable* was something best left to lawyers. Gracie made her calls and arranged the visit for 3:00 p.m. We would have one hour at the Belle Meade house. Gracie asked if she could come with us in case there were problems, but I think she really just wanted to see Rachel. I said sure.

Gracie met us at Mom and Dad's house, and came in to visit for a while before we went over to Belle Meade. She had Angelina with her. Angelina astonished me. She was eight years old now, a little shy, dark complexioned and slender, with her mother's smart eyes, round cheeks and pert nose, but a toothy smile that couldn't have come from Gracie. It was obvious even then that Angelina would one day be much taller than her mother.

We sat in the den, Judith and Gracie ogling over Rachel, Angelina off to the side toeing the floor. Mom brought in sweet tea and joined them.

"Angelina is so pretty in that outfit," Mom said to Gracie.

"Thank you, Mrs. Jeffries."

Angelina had on a maroon school blazer over a blue and green plaid skirt, her hair in a ponytail. She blushed at the attention.

"Carlton, Rachel is adorable," said Gracie.

"Yes, she is," I said. "She has her mother to thank for that."

Judith flashed me a smile as she played patty-cake with Rachel.

"Say *Mama*," Judith teased. "Say *Mama*." Rachel just smiled and drooled. "Well, she said it the other day."

"She did?" Mom asked me in astonishment.

"No, I think that was *Dada* she was saying," I laughed.

"Oh, you," Judith pouted.

Gracie flicked a glance at her watch.

"Well, I guess we'd better get going," she said.

Dad let us take the El Dorado so that we could all fit in. The El Dorado was getting old now, too, but still looked stately enough to pass along those Belle Meade boulevards. I gritted my teeth as we pulled up that long drive into the circle in front of Evelyn's house. I sighed.

"They're richer than whatnot," I said in disgust. "But they still cash my child support checks every month."

"Now Carlton," Gracie chided me. "That money's for the boys, not them."

"What's the difference?" I mumbled.

Carmella met us at the door, cracking it suspiciously as if we might burst in. She eyed our entourage curiously.

"Mr. and Mrs. Burton are away," she said. "You can see the boys in the drawing room."

Judith gave me an arched brow, and Gracie rolled her eyes. We followed Carmella to the drawing room, passing through that ornate hallway, past the grand staircase. Carmella announced us.

"Boys," she said, "Mr. Jeffries is here."

I gave Carmella a dirty look, but what she gave me back said that she didn't give a damn. I went in first. Tommy was standing at the window, looking out, his hands clasped behind him. He wore a maroon blazer just like Angelina's, with navy slacks. He was only nine, but he looked like a prep school kid. Luke was playing with some matchbox cars on the floor. At three years and some months old, he had grown tall enough to trim out and be less bulky across his shoulders. He froze in place and looked up at me warily, as if I were a stranger about to snatch him and run. Tommy turned to me with a diffident air, came toward me stiffly and offered his hand.

"Hello, Father," he said formally.

I was caught off guard, shaking his hand as if he were a man.

"Tommy, I—"

"I prefer *Tom*, please."

"*What?*"

Judith pushed in beside me, Rachel in her arms. She knelt and gave Tommy her patient, professional smile.

"Hello, Tom," she said pleasantly. "Would you like to meet your sister, Rachel?"

Tommy scrutinized Judith as if she were someone off the street, the muscles in his face working at control.

"I don't have a sister," he said flatly. "You're not my mother."

"No, Tom," Judith said, breathing patiently, "I'm not. Your father and I are married, just like your mother and Mr. Burton are married.

"Where's Daddy! Where's Daddy!" Luke abruptly whined.

He jumped up and raced for the door, pushing between Gracie and Angelina to get out. When Angelina stepped to the side, Tommy caught a glimpse of her. His face softened and he gave her a faint smile, which he quickly concealed. Angelina waved at him shyly and he wagged his fingers in return.

I was so disoriented by then that I didn't know what to say or do. Judith stood, a disturbed look on her face.

"Father," Tommy said frankly. "I can't go to summer camp this year because I have to go to *your* house."

I wasn't disoriented now, I was so angry I was trembling.

"Go to summer camp, then," I spat. I turned to Judith. "Let's get out of here."

"Carlton," she pleaded.

"Let's go, damn it."

I stormed out of there, through the hallway, past the stairs, and I would have knocked Carmella over if she hadn't shown the sense to get out of the way. We all piled into the El Dorado, and I left twin strips of rubber on the pavement on the way out.

* * *

Judith was furious with me. She glowered at me on the way back, while Gracie explained some legal maneuvers we could try. I didn't hear half of what Gracie was saying. When we got home I threw open the door and went straight for the hill, having to swing around the greenhouse first, then around the kennel.

I hesitated before going up. The hill was overgrown, really thick with brush, and my old trail was gone. Everything looked different. Colonies of bushy boxwoods arced out like umbrellas, cutting off the view above. I couldn't even see the old ash tree; I couldn't even convince myself that this was the same hill. I plunged into the growth, using the slender boxwood limbs like ropes to pull myself up. The fence was laced through with nettles, but a big limb had fallen across it, collapsing it in a place.

I went on, high-stepping through the brush, ducking beneath tangled vines. The area around the ash tree was mostly clear, its twisted, ancient limbs blocking the sun from competitors. Johnson grass as high as my shoulders had taken over the hilltop beyond.

I sat on a big root and looked around, fingering the bullet hanging from my neck. There was no trace that I had ever been here—the fort carried away when they'd cleared the hill those years ago, and even our excavation, buried so deeply beneath the loam that not even a shallow depression showed where it had been.

I heard footfalls coming up, and turned to see Judith emerging from the brush.

"You'll get chiggers," I warned her.

"I'll take my chances," she said.

"You may regret that tomorrow. When you get back, throw everything in the washer then jump in the shower."

"I'll do that."

She sat beside me and looked around wistfully.

"It's really changed up here," she said.

"Yeah."

"I don't recognize anything except this tree."

"Yeah," I sighed.

"Carlton, you can't blame the boys."

"I don't blame Luke. He's too little. He probably doesn't even remember staying with us. But Tommy...Tommy's big enough to know better."

"They're just kids."

She put an arm around me and leaned against my shoulder. I sat stiffly at first, but then leaned into her as well.

"It all seems so pointless," I said.

"It's not pointless, just hard. Gracie has ideas."

"Yeah, she'll get something done in court, and that'll work until the next time. It'll be like this until they're grown, and maybe then, too." I cupped her face in my hands, tucked a curl behind her ear. "I don't want Rachel around this. She'll get bigger and she'll start to understand, that she has brothers who don't care a thing about her."

Judith's brows dipped in sadness.

"She'll be okay," she said unconvincingly.

"Maybe, maybe not. But I know she'll be better than okay if she never has to deal with this...this crap."

"Well," Judith stood, trailing fingers on my face, "time will tell."

"Yeah."

She left me and quietly picked her way down the hill. I took a deep breath, stood and looked around a last time. A single tear splashed off my cheek. I turned my back and walked away.

* * *

We went to Grandmother Villetta's place on Wednesday. Dad dropped us out front then sped off to take care of some business he had in the county. We went up the walkway and onto the porch, where I clanged the old brass bell. It was still early in the season, but everything was greening up. The lawn could have used a mowing already. Clusters of buttercups ringed the trees, their yellow blooms waving in the warming southerly breeze. Grandmother's irises were sending up bright green shoots.

The front door creaked open.

"Well," Grandmother greeted us warmly. "Come in, come in."

We followed her into the parlor and sat on a green embroidered settee that was probably older than Mom. It was dim in there, smelled dusty. Grandmother hobbled to the window and yanked open a lavender velour curtain.

"Now then," she said. "Let's see that little girl."

Judith held up Rachel and smiled proudly as Grandmother tottered over. Grandmother was ninety-five years old. Her spirit was as fierce as ever, but her body was rickety. I was afraid she would fall, so I leapt up and supported her by the arm.

"That's all right, boy," she patted my hand, "these old bones still get along. What a sweet baby." She teased Rachel's lips with a swollen knuckle. "And a pretty smile. I'd hold her but I don't think I'd better." She chuckled and looked at me with a mirthful glint in her eyes. The pink rouge on her cheeks seemed to brighten. "I might drop her, you know." She chuckled again, and then she went vacant, looking around as if confused. She shook that off after a moment. "It's so nice out. Been shut up all winter. Let's go sit on the porch."

We went out through the kitchen, following slowly behind Grandmother. I got out ahead and held the screen door, then helped Grandmother into her rocker. When she was settled she said, "I think I can hold that baby now."

Judith lowered Rachel into Grandmother's arms, then pulled another rocker close.

"Oh, look at her," Grandmother said sweetly. "Pretty girl. She doesn't even cry," and then playfully to Rachel, "This old lady doesn't scare you, does she."

Grandmother rocked and hummed something from a long time ago. I stood watching them. Judith's eyes were moist.

"I meant to tell you something," Grandmother said to Judith, "but I lost the thought." She gazed out over the yard distantly, then: "It's a little cool out here, isn't it? Carlton, why don't you go in and find my shawl. The white one."

"Sure, Grandmother. Where is it?"

"Oh, just look around." She waved me off. "You'll find it somewhere."

"Oo-kay, then."

I left them and went in search of the shawl, the white one. I searched drawers and closets, went through and old steamer trunk. I found a red one and a pretty green one with embroidered flowers, but I knew she would harangue me if I returned with one of them. I finally found the white one draped over the rocker in her sitting room. When I got to the screen door I overheard Grandmother speaking to Judith, so I hovered by the door until she was finished.

"Well, honey," Grandmother said soothingly, "I know, I know. I only had one, though, and look what's come from that." Judith sniffed and rested her forehead on Grandmother's arm. "There, there, girl," Grandmother said, "bear up."

Judith looked up and smiled. Her nose was red.

"I found it, Grandmother," I hollered. I waited a moment, then pushed nonchalantly through the screen door. "Here it is."

"Thank you, Carlton. Just put that around my shoulders."

When Grandmother was younger, that shawl would have wrapped around her neck and hung inside her overcoat like a scarf, but now it covered her hunched shoulders like a blanket.

"That's better, boy." She patted my hand.

Judith stood. "I need to use the bathroom," she said. "I'll be back in a minute."

I took Judith's place in the rocker. We sat quietly for a time, Grandmother's eyes looking out over something I couldn't fathom. She had coaxed Rachel to sleep. After a time, Grandmother seemed to come to.

"I heard about your boys," she said. "People tend to go on about things. It's a bad business what Evelyn's done, but we country people usually make do. You'll catch on to it yourself, just see."

The rockers creaked beneath us as I mulled that over, and then Grandmother patted my hand and told me her story about Jackson Smith, the man she called Farmer.

* * *

Time eases along, and children grow. Rachel and I had a game we played when I got home at night. She would ride me like a horse, and I would prance from room to room on all fours. When we went into a dark room she would giggle and shout, "I can't see, Daddy! I can't see!" She would cover her eyes and hold on tight with her legs, and then I would crawl into a lighted room and she would throw up her hands and exclaim, "I can see, Daddy! I can see!" I would make the rounds, laughing, Rachel giggling, until Judith would step in and put an end to it with, "Time to eat," or "Time for a bath," or worse yet, "Time for bed."

"Aw."

"Aw."

And then I would carry Rachel like a monkey dangling from my neck, tickling her stomach as we went off to do whatever her mother had asked. If I tried to cheat, if I tried to make the rounds one more time, she would hop off, cock her hips, point a finger at me sternly and say, "No, Daddy. Mama said."

Rachel shed her pudgy baby cheeks during her toddler years. She became a taut bundle of energy, lean and willowy like her mother. Her hair grew long and straight, as fine and soft as satin, and she had Judith's wise brown eyes. At the same time, I could see some of Sadie in the way Rachel carried herself, with her chin up, wearing that mysterious smile that had so many variations.

She was three years and a couple of months old when Dad called to tell me that Langley had died.

"He went peacefully," Dad said with a tremor in his voice. "I found him lying there this morning. At first I thought he was asleep."

"Poor Langley," I said. My voice was a little shaky, too. "I loved that dog."

"Yeah, Langley was a good boy. Even your mother got to where she loved him. And he gave us two generations of puppies. I cleared a place on the hill and buried him there. I think I'll get him a stone."

* * *

I bought a new car when Rachel was four. They were talking about giving me a promotion at work, hinting that I would need something more dependable than the old Catalina. I pulled into our driveway on a hot Saturday afternoon in July behind the wheel of a 1989 Pontiac Firebird convertible. Judith came out outside, with Rachel hopping and rolling around her feet like a bear cub. Judith took one look, and her brows rose into incredulous arches.

"A *convertible?*" she asked dubiously.

"It's beautiful, isn't it?" I grinned, not yet the least self-conscious about deviating from the LeMans hatchback we had discussed earlier that week. I might catch grief from her about it later, but for now...

Oh, that Firebird was pretty! It was white with a black folding top, sleek and nimble, with clean, raking lines that cut through the wind like an arrowhead. It had retractable headlights, mag wheels, and a spoiler on the trunk lid. With a six-cylinder it wasn't a hot rod, but it sure looked it.

"Wanna go for a ride?" I asked with a flirtatious smile.

"I wanna go for a ride, Daddy," Rachel screeched, bounding barefoot into my arms. I hefted her onto my hip then beckoned toward her mother.

"Okay," Judith sighed in resignation.

I did ultimately feel bad about making such a large and impulsive purchase without consulting with Judith first, but she went easy on me.

"You've been driving your dad's car ever since I've known you," she said to me in bed that night. "You deserve something of your own. I'll miss that old car, though."

"Well..." I hesitated.

I couldn't bring myself to trade the old Catalina in. The Herwaldt Pontiac dealership would only offer me five hundred dollars for it, and my salesman admitted that they would just sell it for scrap. And then I wanted to hang onto it for nostalgic reasons, reasons that I didn't think Judith would appreciate. So I put the Catalina in storage instead.

"That's fine," Judith said. "I understand. And your dad will be happy to know that you kept it."

That was a relief. Judith didn't like driving with me when the top was down, though. The wind blew her hair into tangles, and we had to shout to be heard. But Rachel loved it. Sometimes on hot weekends I would drive Rachel up to Kings Canyon or Yosemite, banking into those winding mountain roads, climbing above the haze, the brisk wind carrying the chill from the mountain tops. Belted in, looking tiny in her car seat, Rachel would tip her face into the wind, squinting and grinning, her hair streaming and whipping like a fountain on a blustery day.

She loved the Wawona Tunnel in Yosemite. When we entered it she would play her game, covering her eyes and shrieking, "I can't see, Daddy! I can't see!" And when we burst out the other end into that brilliant, majestic view, she would grab hold of the seat as if she might fly away, and she would scream, "I can see, Daddy! I can see!" The joy on her face tugged at my heart, and had me circling around to do it again. I just couldn't bring myself to disappoint her. I vowed I never would.

* * *

On Rachel's fifth birthday I answered a knock at the door and found Sadie standing there.

"Sadie!"

"Hello, Carlton," she said with a hesitant smile.

"What are you doing here?"

"I came to finally meet my niece. Is that okay?"

She said that sarcastically, but there was still a wounded note in her voice.

"Sure, sure. Come in." We hugged clumsily. "They're not here, though. Judith took Rachel to buy some clothes. Rachel's birthday party is this afternoon."

"It's a perfect day for it." Sadie looked up at the sky. The first weeks of June were almost always nice in Fresno. "I can wait," she went on. "I've got plenty of time."

"Okay."

I showed her around the house, and then we went out back and sat at the patio table next to Judith's herb garden. The air was sweetly scented with oregano.

"It's so peaceful here," Sadie said.

Our tiny backyard was like a private oasis. Besides the herb garden, there were beds of elephant ears and poinsettia. Ivy had overtaken the fence. Potted flowers hung from our trellised awning, and a eucalyptus tree gave us nice shade. Wind chimes sang gently in the breeze.

"Judith has a green thumb," I said. "She did all of this."

"You're lucky."

"Thanks."

I looked Sadie over. She was wearing all black: black pants, black shoes, and a svelte black pullover. Her hair was as short as a boy's now, giving her a haunted, spare look. Her face was pale, as if she hadn't been out in the sun for a while. Her graceful neck was uncannily similar to Rachel's. How long had it been since I had seen Sadie? Not since the wedding, although I had seen her on the television.

"I saw you on Donahue," I said. Sadie blushed and looked down.

"I hate those shows."

"Why?"

"Because they all try to one-up each other. They send me there to talk about my books, but someone always pries into personal stuff, trying to dig out some gossip. They'll take one word out of context, and then they play it over and over again. The cable shows are the worst."

"Well, uh...so how's the new one doing? What is it? Kingdom—"

"*Kingdom Spring.*"

"Yeah."

"It's doing okay."

"What's it about?"

"It's...Oh, let's not talk about that, Carlton. It's been so long. How are you?"

"I'm fine."

"And your job?"

"It's great. I'm in outside sales now."

"Liquor?"

"Yeah."

Sadie took a little blue box from of her purse and picked a cigarette out of it with her nails. She lit it and took a deep puff. Her fingers trembled, making the smoke dance.

"Oh, do you mind?" she asked.

"When did you start that?"

She chuckled darkly and pushed the box around the table with an elegantly manicured finger.

"Gauloises," she said. "They're French. I only use them once in a while, when I'm nervous."

"Why are you nervous?"

She blew smoke and smiled ironically. "Just things," she said.

We sat in awkward silence. The question was still hanging out there even after all this time. It demanded an answer. Finally I just came out with it:

"Sadie, why did you have to put that in there? In *A Robin Waits*?"

That could have meant anything, but she understood exactly what I was asking. I tensed, expecting her to lash out at me in anger, but she just sat back calmly and blew smoke at the sky.

"I didn't do it on purpose," she said, looking far away. "It wasn't a plan. I was writing that scene and it just happened, like a confession, like it needed to come out."

She looked around for an ashtray. I scrambled for an empty flower pot and she stubbed her cigarette out in that. Then she looked me straight in the eyes.

"I told myself it didn't matter," she went on. "*It was a university press*, Carlton, academic, short run—I didn't think anybody would actually *read it*, let alone Mom and Dad."

She reached for another cigarette but checked herself and popped a mint into her mouth instead. Some chickadees flittered around our bird feeder. We watched them for a few minutes, and then I asked:

"Will Dad talk to—"

She shook her head sadly before I could finish.

"No," she said. "I talk to Mom on the phone sometimes, though."

Her lips trembled but her eyes were dry. It was wrenching to see. I changed the subject.

"So how's Ryan?" I tried to make it sound upbeat. Sadie forced a smile.

"Ryan's fine. He's a little jealous, but then he's the one with tenure."

"Aren't you two ever going to get married?"

"No. We like it the way things are."

"Kids?"

She snorted and smiled genuinely this time, showing her teeth.

"Definitely not. I'm getting too old anyway."

It was Sadie's birthday, too. She was thirty-nine now. Was that too old? Except for some fine crow's feet at the corners of her eyes, she looked much younger.

"*Carlton?*" I heard from the house.

"Judith's back," I said. "C'mon."

We met Judith in the kitchen. She was flabbergasted when she saw Sadie.

"Sadie! My God! What a surprise. I didn't know you were in town."

Even though they hadn't seen one another in years, barely knew one another, actually, they hugged like sisters.

"I'm signing books tonight in Sacramento," Sadie told her, "so I thought I'd drive down."

"I read *Kingdom Spring*," Judith gushed. "I loved it."

"Thank you."

"Where's Rachel?" I asked.

"She's coming."

Rachel came in proudly, wearing new jeans and a pink western-cut shirt with mother-of-pearl snaps. She had her thumbs hitched in her jeans, and she walked bow-legged as if she had just come off a horse.

"I thought you were going to buy her a pretty dress," I complained to Judith.

"She wanted that," Judith said to me over her shoulder.

Sadie knelt and grinned.

"Hello, princess," she said.

"I'm not a princess," Rachel corrected her. "I'm a cowgirl."

"Well...you're a pretty cowgirl."

"You're Aunt Sadie," Rachel stated flatly.

"That's right. How did you know?"

"I saw you in Daddy's picture book. Why are you sad?"

Sadie was taken aback. Judith shifted nervously.

"I'm not sad, honey."

"I think you're sad. Did somebody hurt you?"

"No, honey. Nobody hurt me."

"Alright, then," I said to break that up. "Rachel, honey, you'd better get ready for your party, don't you think?"

"Okay, Daddy. Bye-bye Aunt Sadie."

Rachel spun around and horseshoe-walked to her room. Sadie stood and watched her go.

"She's a precocious little girl," said Sadie.

"Reminds me of her father," said Judith.

"Reminds me of her mother," said I, but Rachel also reminded me of someone else.

* * *

Rachel was six when she discovered modesty. She banished me from bathtime about a week before she started the first grade. I followed her to the bathroom after dinner that night, to sit with her while she bathed, like I usually did. Only this time she hugged the door when I tried to go in.

"No, Daddy. It's private," she scolded me.

Judith watched this, laughing with her eyes as Rachel closed the door on me. I stood there slack-jawed.

"What happened?" I asked Judith, stunned. She just shrugged coyly. "Well, it was okay yesterday," I whined as she turned for the kitchen.

Rachel was seven when Grandmother Villetta tripped on that tear in the carpet. It happened the day after Christmas, not even two weeks after Grandmother's hundred-and-second birthday. Mom called with the news. Grandmother was in a coma, she said. We should make plans. On December 29, Grandmother died.

The funeral was held on the third of January, a Sunday, at the Sanderson Funeral Home in Carthage. Getting to Nashville from Fresno on short notice wasn't easy, what with the holiday crowds. We arrived late Saturday evening after more than twelve hours in transit. Judith and I were exhausted, barely able to shuffle off the plane, while Rachel hopped and bounced and tugged at our hands. We had flown to Nashville the previous Christmas, so I figured that Rachel would remember all of this. Nevertheless she wanted to explore everything as if it were a new adventure.

Mom met us in baggage claim. She was bundled in a heavy coat against the damp chill outside. Her eyes and nose were red, her face creased with wrinkles that I hadn't noticed last year.

"I'm glad you could make it," she said wearily. She patted Rachel's head with a hand that was beginning to resemble Grandmother's hand. "And you, Rachel. You've grown a foot."

"I'm in second grade," Rachel said proudly, holding up two fingers.

We drove out to Carthage the next morning. It was a dull day, cold with a light drizzle. Grandmother's coffin was closed.

"I don't want people starin' at me when I can't do for myself," she had told me once.

We took our places in the front row. The sanctuary was small, and filled up quickly. People had to stand along the walls. Some of the Hacketts were there, a lot of Smiths. Except for a few, they were all young or middle-aged people. Most of the old-timers had passed by then. From the Case family, Grandmother's maiden family, there was no one. Grandmother had outlived them all.

Brother Jeff, the Methodist pastor at Grandmother's church, came out to give the eulogy. He paused to pray over her coffin, then turned to us, opening his bible.

"I will read from James," he said soberly, "chapter four, verse fourteen: *Whereas ye know not what shall be on the morrow. For what is your life? It is even a vapour, that appeareth for a little time, and then vanisheth away.*"

He stood in silence for a moment before he continued:

"Villetta Case Smith was with us for a century. *A century.* Why, I knew her when I was a little boy."

Brother Jeff was in his forties, tall and fit, with oily dark hair and surprisingly white teeth. He was a pastor on the weekends, a tobacco farmer the rest of the time. Despite the hours he spent in the sun, his skin looked winter-pale against his black suit.

"Miss Villetta was always kind," he went on. "She made us treats, and would have us kids over any time we wanted. I remember her cooked apples." He smiled while his eyes went back to that time. "When my daddy was having his problems, Miss Villetta would often feed me dinner and tuck me into her spare bedroom for the night. A child felt special with her. I know she was that way with many of you, too, I can see you nodding at your own memories. James is telling us that all things pass, but Miss Villetta will remain with us as long as we remember her."

"Is Grammy in heaven?" Rachel suddenly blurted.

We all laughed despite ourselves, even Brother Jeff. No one had ever gotten away with calling Grandmother that except Rachel.

Grandmother Villetta was buried next to Farmer in the Smith cemetery on that bluff over the river. It was a gray procession. We huddled under umbrellas, shivering in the stinging rain as her coffin was lowered into the ground. Mom clung to Dad tightly, her face red and raw in the chill wind. Rachel began to bounce on her heels, her patience wearing away. She kept turning around to look at the other mourners, perhaps looking for other children. Judith put out a hand to hold Rachel still.

"Shhh, Rachel. Behave, now."

"Look!" exclaimed Rachel, twisting in her mother's hand. "There's Aunt Sadie."

I turned around to see, catching a glimpse of Dad. He just stood there, as weathered and unyielding as barn wood, his jaw muscles bunching as he gnashed his teeth. He wouldn't look. He wouldn't turn. Sadie stood alone next to a black walnut tree, its bare limbs like arthritic fingers reaching into the gray above. She was gauzy through the drizzle, tucked so deeply into her heavy black coat that her face showed only as a small oval of wet eyes and red nose. One bare hand looked starkly white and naked where it held her umbrella. When the service ended, I pushed through the crowd to find her, but she was gone.

* * *

The very next summer, when Rachel was eight, we found out that Dad had lung cancer. It was an aggressive cancer. I spoke to Dad on the phone.

"No, it's not that bad," he told me. "The doctors think I'll make out all right." He covered the phone and I heard a muffled cough. When he came back he said, "I'm glad you never smoked."

Mom wasn't as stoic. The worry in her voice came through clearly over the phone, even though she tried to conceal it by sounding upbeat.

"It may be just a small spot," she said. "We have to go back for more tests."

"Do you need help, Mom? Should I come?"

"Oh, no, honey. We're fine."

I wanted to take that as a sign that it would all be okay, but I had a disquieting tremor in my stomach that said otherwise.

"Mom?" I said. "I'm glad you quit smoking when you did."

"Me, too," she sighed. "I wish your father had."

* * *

Meanwhile, Rachel decided that she wanted to be a ballerina. That lasted long enough for us to get her into a pink tutu and see her skip adorably across a stage. But then, out of nowhere, she told us she wanted to play baseball instead. There were no teams for girls in those days, so I bought gloves and a bat, a black-and-white striped shirt and a ball cap for her, then took her to the playground at Robinson Elementary to teach her how to hit, catch, and throw. I looked forward to those outings because they were a chance for me to play with her again. She had outgrown our old game. "I'm too big, Daddy," she had told me firmly when she was seven.

After a few weekends she got to where she could throw the ball over-handed, and tip a short grounder without losing her grip on the bat. One day, while batting easy pop-ups to her, I accidentally tapped one too high and it came down and thumped her on the head.

"*Ohmygod, Rachel!*"

I dropped the bat and ran to her in a panic.

"Ouch, Daddy," she said, rubbing her head, more annoyed than hurt. She looked at me and smiled one of her variations. "What's the matter, Daddy?"

"I hurt you, baby. I'm sorry."

"No you didn't, Daddy," she said earnestly. "You won't ever."

I hugged her then, working my fingers into her hair to find out if she had a knot on her skull. She wiggled out of my embrace.

"Daddy," she scolded me. "I'm too big for that."

Once she wore out baseball, she informed us quite frankly that she wanted to learn karate. Judith did a double take—so did I—but inwardly I was relieved that I wouldn't have to worry about her getting hit by another baseball. I started looking around for karate schools that would teach a little girl, but before I got far with that, Mom called.

"Dick's in a bad way, Carlton," she said. Her voice was shaky from crying.

It was the end of October, still warm in Fresno. In Tennessee the leaves would be turning.

"Mom—"

"The radiation and the drugs—oh, honey, all his hair has fallen out."

"He's going to be okay, though. Right?"

Mom sniffed and set the phone aside for a minute. I hung on the silence, an icy chill in my chest.

"Mom?"

She came back to the phone, her voice breathy and weak.

"I don't think so, honey."

* * *

Rachel was in a school play the day before Thanksgiving. We were all so proud. Lois and Eugene even drove down to see it. Rachel played an Indian girl who brings a bowl of corn to the Pilgrims. She wore a beaded headband with a feather. Judith had braided Rachel's hair, so Rachel really looked the part. At her age I would have been mortified to be in front of an audience like that, but Rachel wasn't shy on stage at all.

Afterward we went out to Carrows for dinner with Eugene and Lois, then stopped in at the new bookstore on the corner of Blackstone and Shaw. Judith and Lois chased Rachel into the children's section, while Eugene and I mulled along through the aisles with nothing particular in mind.

"How's your father?" Eugene asked. I shook my head. "I'm sorry," he said then.

He rested a hand on my shoulder. We could hear Rachel laughing over the tops of the aisles. She must have found some children to play with back there. We weaved through the aisles to join them. Judith and Lois were standing back from the kids, looking on with a combination of mirth and pride. Rachel was sitting cross-legged on the floor, a half-circle of kids arranged around her. She was reading Dr. Seuss to the kids, laughing with them at the funny parts.

It was late when we got home. There was a message on the answering machine. It was Mom.

"You'd better come," was all it said.

* * *

I spent Thanksgiving in the air, arriving in Nashville at about four o'clock in the afternoon. With just a carry-on bag, I went straight to the taxi stand and had the driver take me to Baptist Hospital.

It was eerily dislocating to be at Baptist Hospital again. My driver dropped me at the main entrance. I suppressed the urge to rush inside, instead taking a moment to look around, to compare fragments of memory with what I saw now. The sky was so heavy that mist oozed through the tree tops. The streets were wet. Nothing looked familiar in that featureless dusk. Perhaps at night, under the harsh street lights, I might remember something of the place. I rubbed at the weariness in my eyes and went inside.

It was cold in Dad's room. One table lamp in a corner cast everything in dull shadow. Mom was asleep in a plastic chair, leaning against a wall for support, a blanket over her shoulders. Her hair had come down, giving her a frail, desperate look. I didn't recognize Dad at first, thought there must have been a mistake and some stranger had been brought in while Mom slept. Dad was in bed, his sheets tucked around him like a mummy. He looked desiccated and abominably thin, with one skeletal arm lying uncovered at his side. A few strands of gray hair held out on his bald and shockingly white scalp. An oxygen mask covered his mouth and nose. His breaths were hollow and halting.

I went to Mom and nudged her gently. She came awake with a start.

"Oh, Carlton. Thank God." She sat up straight and felt at her hair. "I must be a sight." She groaned, trying to stand, but I gestured her back.

"It's okay, Mom." I hugged her lightly. "How's Dad?"

She looked at me and her eyes misted over, her cheeks quivering, and then we both turned to Dad.

"Go sit with him, Carlton. While you still can."

I pulled a chair over and sat next to Dad, then reached out hesitantly and took his hand. It felt as fragile as a bird's wing, as if I could crush it if I weren't careful. Dad gripped me in return, weakly, but still firm enough to show that he had some strength left. I leaned in closer, put on a feeble smile.

"How are you, Dad?" I asked softly. He turned his eyes to me and they were clear, no pain in them.

He exhaled a shallow breath that fogged his oxygen mask. "O—" another shallow breath, "—kay. Glad—you—came."

That little bit of exertion seemed to take all the strength he had. I struggled to keep my face straight. Dad wouldn't want to see me cry. He worked his head toward me as if trying to close the distance. I leaned in even closer, practically touching his sunken cheek.

"Dogs," he exhaled, and then another breath that barely lifted his chest, "you."

"Yes, Dad," I sniffed. I couldn't help it, some tears spilled down my cheeks. "I'll take care of them. Don't worry."

Somehow he found the strength to pat my hand, like dry paper on my skin. He settled into his pillow and seemed content.

I sat with him in silence, not wanting to sap his strength by speaking. I held his hand, which was remarkably warm. I counted his labored breaths.

The door wafted open and Sadie was there. Ryan stood behind her. He met my eyes sympathetically and clenched his teeth. Sadie's face was puffy and purple from crying, her cheeks glistening, slick like the skin of a seal. I felt a pang of suppressed memory, reaching back to the only other time that I had seen her vulnerable and wounded.

Dad cocked his head weakly and his eyes searched across the room until they found Sadie's. Her face contorted and she spilled fresh tears.

"Daddy?" she cried, pleaded.

Dad let go of my hand as he inhaled, as if he needed every bit of his energy to breathe, and when he let that breath go into his hollow mask, with it also came, "Sadie baby."

A single tear followed the fissures in his cheek, like the rivers in those Arizona canyons. Sadie broke down then, crying in full. I stepped back as she rushed over and knelt beside Dad, taking his hand, kissing it, holding it to her face.

"Sadie baby," Dad exhaled again.

"Oh, Daddy," Sadie cried. "I'm sorry, so sorry."

Dad sunk into his pillow, exhausted from that effort, but he grazed Sadie's face lightly with his fingertips; and he smiled, faintly, but he smiled. Mom stood and I held her, and when Dad released a final, lingering breath, we were all with him.

NINETEEN

Dad's funeral was on December the first, a cold and dismal Wednesday. It had been like this all week. I had hoped for a clear day. I didn't mind the cold so much, but just to have some sun and blue sky overhead when we lay Dad next to Leavitt and Elizabeth would have raised my spirits.

We were back at Sanderson's in Carthage. An Elder from Mom and Dad's church in Nashville came up to give the eulogy. Henry Kirby was his name. He had a grandfatherly presence, and spoke in the old accent, the way Grandmother had. Lois and Eugene had come out with Judith and Rachel. Sadie and Ryan were there, and also Gracie and Angelina. Gracie was getting heavy as she aged. She already had a few gray hairs, like specks of paint that wouldn't come out. Her determined and confident eyes told of the courtroom skills she had mastered, but her face was as petite as ever. Angelina had grown into a stunning young woman. She was taller than her mother, with straight black hair to her waist, thin lips, and a mouth that might have seemed too wide for her slender features were it not for her shy Latin smile.

We took our places up front. Mom sat between Sadie and me. The sanctuary filled up as it had with Grandmother, only this time I didn't recognize most of the people. They were middle-aged and older, many of them business types dressed in sharp suits, with Brylcreemed hair and graying wings at their temples. Some might have been Dad's golfing buddies. One old man wore his World War Two army uniform. Mom could have had Dad buried with an honor guard in the veterans' cemetery, but he wouldn't have wanted that, she said. He would have wanted to come home.

They had done a good job with Dad. He looked peaceful and natural in his coffin. They had filled his cheeks somehow, and you couldn't tell that his hair was a wig.

Elder Kirby didn't quote from scripture. Instead he reminisced about Dad through the years, how hard work had built a successful business; how Dad had helped develop Green Hills into the coveted zip code that it was now. He shared golfing anecdotes that made many of the mourners chuckle. Mom held my hand throughout, squeezing so tightly that my fingers turned white. She didn't cry, but sat as if she were wearing a mask. I didn't cry, either—I was cried out—but Sadie sniffed and wiped at her eyes.

We gathered in the lobby after the service, shaking hands and accepting condolences ahead of the procession to the Carlton cemetery. I had Rachel with me. Judith was talking to Gracie across the way. I shook hand after hand, nodding solemnly as sympathies were offered. Rachel began to fidget. She slipped away, weaving between people toward something that must have caught her attention. I followed her out the corner of my eye.

"Hi," I heard her say in her high-pitched voice. "You're my brother Tommy, and you're my other brother Luke. Why are you scared?"

I whipped around in shock.

"I'm not scared," Tommy said, although I wouldn't have recognized his voice.

"I think you're scared," said Rachel. "How come you never see me?"

"I saw you once."

"I don't remember," she said. "Maybe I was too little."

I pushed through the crowd and pulled Rachel to my side, steering her around behind me while I eyed Tommy warily. Luke's hands were in his pockets, his eyes downcast.

"Hello, Father," Tommy said with an unreadable expression. "It's been a long time."

"What are you doing here?" I asked more gruffly than I had intended. Tommy backed up a step, as if afraid I might lurch at him. Luke lowered his face farther until all I could see was the top of his head.

"We wanted to say goodbye to Grandpa."

I looked around quickly, dreading to find Evelyn in the crowd, but I didn't see her.

"How did you get here?" I asked then.

"I drove."

"*You drove?* All the way from *Nashville?*"

"I have my license."

"But," I sputtered, "you're only..."

I had to stop and think about it. Tommy was born in 1977, in February, so...

"I'm sixteen, Father," he said testily. I hung there with my mouth open. I was about to say sixteen, but he had beaten me to it.

I looked Tommy over. He was a good looking kid, tall, although not as tall as me yet. His hair was well groomed, with a clean part on the left. It was more of a sandy brown color now, darker than it had been but still light enough to make his eyes stand out, like sapphires on a beach. He wore khaki slacks, brown suede loafers, and a white Oxford sweater with black piping around the V-neck and cuffs.

And Luke? He was...I'm ashamed to admit that I really had to think long about how old Luke was. He was born on Thanksgiving, in...1982, so he had to be eleven. He had graceful features now, considering how broad and stocky he had been. His hair was still jet black, but his skin was pale. He wore a sweater that matched Tommy's, but with black slacks instead. He seemed fragile.

"Daddy," Rachel whined behind me, trying to twist out of my grip. "Let me see."

Judith edged up beside us just then. She took Rachel's hand, looked at Tommy and smiled.

"Hello, Tom," she said. "It's so good to see you. And Luke," he looked up at Judith and put on a delicate smile, "you just had your eleventh birthday, didn't you. You've gotten so *big*." His smile turned into a shy grin.

"Happy birthday, Luke," Rachel chirped. "I didn't get you a present. I'm sorry."

"It's okay," Luke muttered, averting his eyes.

"Look," I said then. "Thanks for coming, boys, but we have to drive to the cemetery now."

"We'll come, too," said Tommy.

"You don't have to."

"I know we don't have to, Father, but we want to."

I hadn't been nearly that self-sure at his age. I was about to object, but Judith cut in first.

"That's nice, Tom. You can follow us. You won't get lost."

"Can I go with Tommy?" Rachel asked sweetly.

"No, baby," I said. "Tommy wouldn't want to have to drive you around."

"I don't mind," said Tommy.

"See, Daddy?"

"No, baby."

"But Tommy said."

"And I said no."

"Aw."

Gracie and Angelina came over.

"Hello, Tom," Gracie said. "You look nice."

"Thank you, Miss Quinterra."

"Hi, Tommy," Angelina said demurely, blushing.

"Hi, Angie," Tommy said in return. He was blushing, too, and all that formality in his voice was gone in an instant.

I looked back and forth between them, wondering what was going on. Judith smiled.

"I think they're ready for us in the limousine," she said.

We rode over in Sanderson's limousine, along with Mom, Sadie, and Ryan. Judith was giving me mysterious looks.

"I saw the boys," Mom said.

"Yeah," I muttered. We left it at that.

It was gray and cold, but at least the rain had let up by the time we got to the cemetery. The grass was wet, though. Mom stepped through it carefully, clutching her collar against the cold. White folding chairs had been set up near the grave.

Mom trailed a hand on Elizabeth's and Leavitt's stones as she passed by. We took our seats. Not everyone had come over from the funeral home. Those who had come stood behind us, including Lois and Eugene. It didn't look as if Gracie and Angelina were there.

Dad's coffin was pulled from the hearse by solemn-looking men whom I didn't know. Elder Kirby walked along beside them. The coffin was draped with an American flag. The Army had sent two officers. They played Taps and gave their slow, traditional salutes, then folded the flag meticulously and brought it to Mom. She had been holding herself steady, but broke down as she accepted the flag.

On behalf of a grateful nation...

Afterward, people wandered back to their cars. The weather was too poor to linger. Sadie and Ryan guided Mom to the limousine, while I gathered Judith and Rachel together. Tommy and Luke approached us.

"I remember you bringing me here," Tommy said.

"Yeah," I said wistfully. "That was a long time ago."

"I'm glad you did," Tommy said.

That caught me by surprise. He had been so indifferent for so long.

"Luke," Judith said as cheerfully as she could muster, "why don't you walk us to the car."

"Okay," he muttered. He held Judith's hand as they walked, and that surprised me, too.

Tommy and I watched them go, and when we were alone he said:

"I liked those soldiers, the way they did things. It makes you feel good, you know?"

"Yeah," I said. "They did that with Leavitt, too."

"Leavitt was your brother?"

"Yeah."

"And he was in the Army?"

"That's right. He died in Vietnam."

"And Grandpa was in World War Two?"

"Uh, huh."

"And your grandpa was in World War One. How come you didn't join the Army?"

"I didn't want to, Tommy. And Dad wouldn't have wanted me to, either."

"I think I'd like to join the Army."

I looked at him in disbelief, but saw that he was serious.

"Well," I said, "I hope you change your mind."

"That's what Mom says."

"Then we agree about something."

We seemed to have run out of small talk. Tommy looked away, as if trying to think of something to say. Judith and Rachel were in the limousine, waiting.

"Look, Tommy, it's time to go."

"Father," he said quickly. "Uh, Dad." I shot him a look of surprise. "Uh—" he toed at the wet grass, "—Uh, I'd like to come out and see you."

"What?"

"This summer. A week, maybe."

I should have been excited, but I wasn't.

"Oh, I don't know, Tommy."

His face fell.

"Uh, okay. I just thought, you know, maybe you wouldn't mind."

Judith came striding over. She eyed us curiously then said:

"The driver wants to go, Carlton. You two will have to finish your conversation at the house."

"There's nothing to finish. We can go now." I turned to leave.

"I wanted to come visit," Tommy said in a rush. Judith paused and smiled.

"That's great, Tom. We'd love to have you. Wouldn't we, honey?"

I groaned inwardly, and wondered how Tommy had learned to manipulate people that way. But then of course I already knew the answer.

"We can talk about it," I said reluctantly. Judith's brows dipped. "C'mon, we'd better go."

I took Judith's hand, probably squeezing harder than I should have, and left Tommy standing there under the Carlton arch.

* * *

Judith and I couldn't talk about it on the way back, not with Mom, Sadie, and Ryan in the car—and especially not in front of Rachel—but there was no way Judith was going to let it rest. She confronted me later as we were getting ready for bed.

"Carlton, those boys deserve their father," she erupted suddenly, as if this had been boiling in her head all day and could finally get out.

"They had their chance," I snapped back.

"What does that mean?"

"You were there, when Rachel was a baby. You saw how Tommy acted."

"He didn't know any better, Carlton."

"Well *I* know better," I barked at her, slapping my chest self-righteously. Judith's brows went up.

"You must really want to sleep alone tonight," she warned me, pursing her lips.

"Judith—"

"Why are you so defensive about this?"

"Defensive? I'm not—"

"Oh yes you are."

"*Damn it, I'm not—*"

"Oh, you are *definitely* sleeping alone tonight."

I hung my head in exasperation. Judith had gotten into bed, and had the covers pulled to her chin. Her brows were creased, and her eyes simmered. I exhaled wearily.

"Look, Judith—"

"I think this conversation is over, Carlton."

"No, wait," I pleaded. She began to open her mouth to object. "*Please.*"

I stood there half dressed, searching for words, while she pierced me with that unmoving, granite look she took on whenever I annoyed her beyond her limits. I sighed in defeat, and spoke the only words that I knew would get through to her:

"Glacier Point, remember?"

Her hardened expression reluctantly dissolved.

"Oh, you," she pouted. She pulled the covers over her face. I could hear her breathing purposefully under there. She resurfaced after a moment and tossed a pillow at me, still vexed but also with the hint of a smile. I caught the pillow and hugged it to my chest.

"Well, you're the one who said—"

"I know what I said, Carlton." She patted the bed. "Come here. Let's talk."

I flopped onto the bed, relieved, and scooted up to lie beside her.

"Why, Carlton?" she asked softly after a moment. "They're your boys."

"They *were* my boys," I said, absently rolling one of her curls around my finger. "At least Tommy was. But now they're *hers.*"

"They're still yours, too. And besides, Rachel should know her brothers."

I groaned and rolled away.

"What is it?" she asked.

I covered my face with a pillow and took a few breaths, then turned to Judith until we were nose to nose.

"It's Evelyn. It's like she can reach right through Tommy and get to Rachel, too."

"Is that what this has all been about? That somehow Evelyn will corrupt our daughter?" Judith chuckled. "My baby's tougher than that. And besides, you can't protect Rachel from the facts. She can handle it."

"I'm sure she can handle it," I sighed, "but I don't want her to *have* to handle it. I don't want her to have this mess in her head."

"But you're her dad. We're already dealing with this mess, Carlton. You brought it with you."

"Well, that makes me feel good," I muttered ironically.

"It's not supposed to make you feel one way or the other, it's just the way things are."

Judith was so patient when she put on her teacher persona. She wasn't judging me now, and she wasn't angry, she was only waiting for me to come around to her way of thinking, as if she knew full well that it was inevitable.

I lay there wrestling with my thoughts, her warm breath on my face.

"I knew this would happen if we came back here," I said at last. "In Fresno...I could keep a distance. You know?"

"But only for a little while, Carlton," she smiled sagely. "Children grow up."

* * *

For a few days, the house was full again. Lois and Eugene were in the guestroom, Sadie and Ryan were in Sadie's old room, Rachel was next door in Elizabeth's room, while Judith and I were upstairs as usual. I think all the activity helped distract Mom. She wasn't depressed, just melancholy and a little dazed. But with laundry to do and meals to cook, and with Lois there to talk to, Mom came around pretty well. Judith and Rachel needed to get back to school, so they flew out on Sunday morning with Lois and Eugene. Ryan left for Dartmouth later that afternoon. That left Mom in a suddenly quiet house with Sadie and me.

"It's fine," Mom said, patting my hand wistfully. "I'll be fine."

I needed to get back to work pretty soon myself. I felt bad about that. Sadie said she would stay with Mom through Christmas, so that relieved my guilt a little.

Even though Sadie was the eldest, Dad had put me in charge of his affairs. We read Dad's will. He had left some investments for Sadie and me, which showed that he had forgiven Sadie long before they reconciled. Everything else went to Mom, but there was one startling provision: When Mom's time came, Dad wanted me to have the house. If that bothered Sadie, she kept it to herself. And then this: Dad wanted me to go fishing. Why he would put that in his will was a mystery to all of us. Mom thought it was probably because I worked so much. Dad fished to relax, not to actually catch fish. Perhaps he thought the same would work for me. I made a mental note to give it a try come summer, but then other things needed tending and I forgot all about it.

I needed to find a gardener for Mom, and someone to look after the dogs. Mom wouldn't be able to keep up with the mowing and trimming, and I had promised Dad about the dogs. But I couldn't take the dogs with me to Fresno. We didn't have room for four frisky bluetick coonhounds, plus Mirabel, who was the matriarch now. And besides, I think Mom liked having the dogs around. She even let Mirabel in the house sometimes.

I called Gracie to find out if she knew anyone we could hire.

"Have you thought about Kenny?" she asked.

"Kenny? Uh—"

"When was the last time you saw him?"

There was something in her voice, something with an edge.

"It's been a long time, Gracie. Have you seen him? How is he?"

"I see him around. He does odd jobs." And then she whispered, "He lives in his truck, Carlton. I worry about him."

"Does he still—you know?"

"I don't know. What happened between you two?"

"Kenny's problems…Gracie, you know more about this stuff than I do, but they have a way of making their problems your problems."

"Yeah," she sighed. "Addiction is hard to live with. Still, it's Kenny we're talking about."

"I know, but I don't think it would work out."

"Oh well, then. I'll ask around for you."

"Thanks, Gracie."

We wound up hiring a service for the yard. Mom said she could look after the dogs, not to worry about that. I did worry, though. It was a lot to do, but then maybe that's what she really needed.

On Monday I went by Hill's, just to look around and reminisce. I found out that Mr. Iverson had finally retired. He lived in Florida now. I introduced myself to the manager, who shook my hand awkwardly. He was older than me, but not by much. He seemed uncomfortable to have me there, anxious to get away, as if the history of the store had only begun with him. I didn't recognize anyone, none of the cashiers or stockers. I wanted to go into the receiving room, but I felt like a stranger, too self-conscious to ask—and they would probably turn me down anyway. Instead I went out and walked around back, thinking the receiving door might be open and I could look inside.

The receiving door was closed and locked. The receiving alley looked cold and abandoned in the gray damp of that day. A few plastic bags and styrofoam cups tumbled along in the wind, and there was an oily sheen on the wet concrete. I felt foolish being there. I was just turning to leave when I spotted Kenny's box truck parked at the end of a line of trash dumpsters. I felt a chill of dread, backed away quickly, and as I rounded the corner I saw Kenny coming toward me. And he saw me, too. I couldn't get away. There was nowhere to go.

"Carlton," he said without emotion.

Kenny looked like hell. His hair was lank and oily, and he wore a week's worth of scrappy growth on his face. His eyes were dark and hollow, and his mustache drooped around the corners of his wide mouth like walrus tusks. The cuffs of his jeans were tattered. His hands were shoved into the pockets of a navy pea coat that looked as if it had come from a second-hand store.

"Kenny," I said nervously.

"Whadaya doin' here, man?"

"Just lookin' around, you know?"

"I heard about your dad. That's too bad."

"Yeah."

"So you're livin' in California."

"Yeah."

"Ever see Carla?"

"Naw, we lost touch a long time ago."

"Me, too." He shivered and shrugged deeper into his coat. "Wish I was in California. This place blows." He picked at a tooth and turned solemn. "I needed you, man. I *needed* you."

My stomach felt queasy.

"Kenny, I—"

"You left me, man. You just left."

"Look, Kenny—"

"I was *always* there for you, dude," he spat with unveiled resentment.

That went too far.

"Really?" I spat back bitterly. "Like that time in the eleventh grade when those guys jumped me? You just stood there and watched, like it was a good show."

He rolled his eyes. "Man, you're really reachin'. That the best you got?"

I trembled in anger, at all of it, the years of Kenny plodding along, wrecking himself and now blaming it on me. Or perhaps I was angry at myself for letting him get away with it—or looking the other way while it went on.

"Look, Kenny, what do you want from me, huh?" I should have added, *You did this to yourself*, but knew it would be futile to say more. My skin crawled just at the sight of him. I felt a desperate need to get away, to flee before I got splashed worse by his mess.

I shouldered past him at a fast clip, kept my eyes straight ahead and pretended not to hear what he shouted at my back.

* * *

Tommy walked up to the house after school that day. I was in the den, in Dad's Barcalounger, still trying to shake off my confrontation with Kenny when Mom came downstairs with Tommy.

"Carlton, look who's here," she announced. Tommy was a step behind her. He looked clean and sharp in khaki slacks, white shirt, and a maroon V-neck sweater.

"Hello, Father."

"Tommy," I exclaimed. I got up out of habit. "Uh, have a seat." Tommy took the couch.

"Well, I'll leave you two to talk," Mom said. She gave me a curious, inside look as she turned to leave.

"What brings you by, Tommy?"

"I was down with Grandmother and Grandfather, and I thought, you know, I would just come up for a little bit."

"Well, it's a surprise."

Tommy shrugged. "It shouldn't be."

I opened my mouth to say something but found no words. We sat silently while the fire hissed. Tommy squeezed his hands between his knees and shifted a little, looking around.

"Hey," he said with a forced smile. "I saw Grandpa's kennel when I went around back. It's nice."

"Yeah, Dad worked hard on that."

"I saw the dogs through the windows. Is one of them—"

"Langley? No, he died a long time ago. Dad made a little cemetery for him on the hill."

"Can I go see?"

"I don't know, Tommy. It's wet up there."

"I'd like to."

I sighed and pulled myself up.

"Okay, then."

We went out through the kitchen door. Mom and Sadie were sitting at the table, drinking coffee. They followed us with curious expressions. It felt colder now than it had when I'd been to Hill's earlier. Water dripped from the boxwood limbs, and fog had come down over the hill. I shivered against the chill. We rounded the kennel and went on up. Dad had cleared a path, so the going wasn't too difficult. The little cemetery was just before the fence, a small gray stone standing alone in the murk. *Langley*, it read, *September 1973 – August 1988. A Fine Dog.*

Tommy stood in thought, gazing at Langley's stone. Finally I broke the silence.

"I would have thought that you knew about this."

"Naw, we never came up here. Mom...well. I only saw Grandpa and Grandma a few times, and they never said anything."

"Well that's too bad."

"Look...Dad," he said, fidgeting. "I really want to come out to see you."

"Tommy, your mom—"

"I'm old enough to come by myself."

"Maybe, but it'll make trouble."

"I don't think so. They always take off during the summer anyway."

I exhaled and gazed up the hill into the fog. I wanted nothing more than to berate his mother right there to his face, but I couldn't bring myself to do it. What had Judith said? *He didn't know any better.* Maybe not. Still, I was a kid once, too, and I don't think anyone could have turned me against Dad.

"I remember when you took me up there," Tommy said, looking where I was looking. "That hill was so steep...man, I was miserable."

"What!" I turned to him as if he had slipped a knife into my ribs. "What I remember is how proud you were up in that tree."

"Yeah," he said, looking down at his feet now. "Maybe."

This was so futile. We couldn't even come together on something as basic as this, something that had felt important to me.

"I still have the compass," he said then. "It was Grandpa's from the Army, wasn't it?"

"Yeah. Do you remember how you loved to play with it?"

"I do." He smiled. "And I still have your bag, too."

"Do you really?" That surprised me. "I thought that thing had been thrown away a long time ago."

"Nope. I hid it."

"Why would you do that?"

"So nothing would happen to it."

I mulled that over.

"Okay, Tommy, look." I took a deep breath and rubbed my temples. "Judith wants you to come out, so I guess it's okay. But I don't want any trouble with your mother."

"You won't." He was bouncing on his heels and smiling. "I promise."

* * *

So much time had gone by that the notion of Tommy coming for a visit had receded to the back of my mind. He called us the week after Rachel's ninth birthday. I was at work, so it was Judith who took the call.

I got home late that afternoon, went straight in and flopped on the couch. The weather was still mild, but I had covered a lot of territory that day, three hundred and some miles. I was beat. Judith came out of the kitchen with a glass of cold sweet tea.

"Here," she said. "I bet you could use this." She set the glass on an end table.

"Oh, thanks," I exhaled. "Man, I'm tired."

She sat down and leaned in for a kiss. "How far did you go today?"

"Over three hundred miles."

"Poor man, you must have driven all the way around the valley."

"Yeah." I took a sip of tea then held the glass to my forehead. "And get this, there are these weird billboards on the 99 saying we should impeach President Clinton. What's that all about?"

Judith chuckled.

"Some of our valley farmers think we're still in the 1800s. They'd like to turn the San Joaquin into its own state. It's just crazy politics."

"Huh. I never really think about that stuff. Oh, well, I didn't vote for Clinton anyway."

"Guess what?" she asked with a mysterious smile.

"What?"

"Tom called today."

"He did?" I sat up straight and put the tea glass down.

"Yeah. He wants to come out over the Fourth of July, and...he wants to bring Luke, too."

"Luke, too? No way. She won't let that happen."

"I think she will. Tom says she's going to Aruba that week. And anyway," she leaned in to kiss me again, "Tom's seventeen, Carlton. I bet he can handle her."

* * *

We picked them up at the airport late in the afternoon on July 1. Tommy could have picked a better time to come. It was over one hundred degrees out, and the air was hazy with dust blown in from the dry fields. Tommy was wearing a white T-shirt and jeans, while Luke was in black slacks and a white long-sleeved shirt. Luke's skin was pale, and his hair had grown out. A wavy black forelock of it hung over his eyes.

"Hi, Tommy," Rachel said with an eager grin.

She skipped up and took his hand. Tommy stiffened for a moment, but then he relaxed and walked Rachel over to us. Luke hung back. I dipped my head trying to see into his eyes, but his hair hid them.

"Hello...Dad," said Tommy. He didn't seem too nervous, but I might have been. "Hello, Tommy."

"And Luke," Judith beamed. "I'm so glad you could come, too." She went to him, draped an arm around his shoulders and steered him our way.

"Hello, Luke," I said with an uncertain smile. Luke kept his eyes downcast.

"What's the matter, honey?" Judith asked him. "Are you feeling all right?" Luke mumbled at his feet. "What's that, Luke?"

"I don't know what to call him," Luke said to the floor.

"He's Daddy," Rachel said with an innocent grin.

"Oh." Tommy slapped his forehead. "That's what he calls Brad."

"Oh, don't worry about it, Luke," said Judith. She knelt and brushed the hair out of his eyes. "I know it's a little weird." Luke met her eyes then. I couldn't get over how dark and brooding his eyes looked. "Why don't you just call him 'Father'?" Judith whispered. "That would be okay, wouldn't it?"

"Yeah, I guess," he said nervously. He still wouldn't meet my eyes. "Hello, Father."

"Hello, Luke." This was a pathetic exchange. I tried to keep my voice level, but my anger was beginning to rise. Judith shot me a warning glance, but Rachel calmed the whole thing by stepping up and taking Luke by the hand.

"Let's go Luke. Let's go Tommy." She had them each by a hand, bouncing and swinging between them toward baggage claim. Judith came up to me.

"That was awkward," she said.

"Yeah." I was biting my lip.

"Give them time, Carlton." She grazed my face with the backs of her fingers. "Please?"

I sighed and said okay.

* * *

I was off of work through the fourth, so we were all together those first few days. Luke did finally begin to open up. Judith pampered him as if he were her own child. I never understood her devotion to him, still don't, but looking back I think that maybe she had already sensed his estranged nature and was trying to help him through it, to fit in.

Rachel was inseparable from Tommy, and to his credit, he didn't seem to mind. I won't deny that I felt a pang of jealousy when suddenly my baby wanted to spend more time with Tommy than with me.

Our house was really too small for so many kids. We set up folding cots in the living room for Tommy and Luke, and in the mornings Rachel would skip barefoot from her room and pounce on Tommy to wake him. She used to do that to me in the mornings, now she did it to Tommy. After breakfast she would grab his hand and drag him laughing outside. They would walk to Rachel's school, swinging their hands together as they went, then work their way around the playground, Rachel showing off Tommy to her friends. Rachel felt safe with Tommy. I guess that said something.

Luke liked our big new bookstore. Judith and I took him a couple of times while Tommy and Rachel were at the playground. We would sit upstairs in the cafe, sipping coffee and following Luke's progress through the maze of books below. Luke spent a lot of time looking at art and photography books. I asked him once if he liked to draw or paint, but he just shook his head.

Judith and Rachel always read together in the evenings after dinner. Rachel had a seemingly endless supply of *Boxcar Children* books, which she would read aloud in her sweet high voice while her mother looked on warmly. Luke took to joining them, sidling in close until they were all huddled over the pages. Sometimes Judith would gaze at him in that soft way of hers, brush the hair out of his eyes and smile. I wondered what was going through her mind, what it was about Luke that touched her so.

Tommy wanted to drive my Firebird. That made me anxious for many reasons, but Judith gave me her amused yet patient look and said, "Carlton, he's *seventeen*."

So I relented.

With the top down and Tommy behind the wheel, I guided us out to those long, straight country roads through the raisin vineyards beyond Clovis. Rachel wanted to come with us, but that's where I drew the line.

"But Daddy, why?" she pouted.

"Tom and your daddy want to go alone," Judith consoled her. "Come on. Let's go to the bookstore with Luke."

"Okay," Rachel chirped, recovering just like that. She took Luke by the hand, then looked up at her mother. "Well," she said impatiently. "Let's go."

Tommy had a grin on his face, motoring along in the Firebird with the mountains rising in the distance.

"I'd like to take it up there," Tommy shouted over the wind.

"I don't think so, Tommy. They're farther away that you think."

"Aw."

I did let him drive us into the foothills up near Millerton Lake, sweeping through turns that had me gripping the armrest. Tommy was wearing aviator sunglasses. In his white T-shirt and with his hair blowing in the wind, I was reminded of my first drive up to Clingmans Dome; and with every mile I felt more like his father again.

The Fourth of July fireworks show at the stadium in Fresno was always crowded and congested, so instead we went to see the show at Buchanan High School in Clovis. I preferred the small-town, carnival feel of Clovis anyway. We got hot dogs and cokes for the boys, cotton candy for Rachel, then climbed the bleachers to watch the show.

It was a warm night, but comfortable in the sighing breeze. Luke sat next to me. Judith had taken him to the mall and had bought him some blue jeans and T-shirts. With a little color in his cheeks now from the California sun, he looked more like a typical eleven-year-old rather than the shy, shadowy kid who had walked off the plane. He was even smiling.

"I love fireworks," he told me excitedly as the first tracers went up.

Explosions danced across the sky, expanding balls of color that sent streamers raining down like falling stars. Luke gazed raptly at the sky, his eyes sparkling in the flash and color. I squeezed his knee and he let me, so I put an arm over his shoulders. Luke leaned against me as if we had always been close. I studied his silhouette for some resemblance, something of me in his face, his expression, his demeanor. Judith always swore he was mine. A simple blood test would have confirmed it, but that seemed so unfair. And what if the test proved that he wasn't mine? What then?

I looked over at Judith. She had her eyes on Luke and me; wise, patient eyes. She was pleased with what she saw. I was pleased, too. Tommy hefted Rachel onto his shoulders and then he stood, lifting her into the night. She giggled and shrieked and held onto his head, but then when she felt secure she raised her hands to the sky; and with a look of wonder and enchantment she twirled her willowy fingers among the starbursts, as if to spin them into new patterns of light. Judith leaned against my shoulder, and I held her, and we watched Rachel and Tommy, and for a time I felt as if this was the way it had always been.

Friday came too quickly. We drove to the airport that morning in Judith's mini-van, and walked the boys to the gate. I was afraid that Rachel would cry, but she was as chipper as always.

"Bye Tommy, bye Luke. Thanks for coming to see me."

Rachel hugged them both, and they hugged her back, and then Tommy approached me.

"I had a good time, Dad," he said. "I'm glad we came."

"Me, too, Tommy."

I held out my hand, but to my surprise Tommy stepped up and gave me a hug. It was an awkward hug between men, but it had been so long since I had held my son that way that I had to choke back a sob and pass it off as if I were clearing my throat. I was surprised again when Luke came up and hugged me as well.

"I liked being here, Father," he said. "I hope I can come back."

"Sure you can, Luke," I said. "Anytime you want."

Judith kissed them both, and then they boarded the plane.

"I like my brothers," Rachel beamed.

"They like you, too, sweetie."

"See?" Judith said to me with a wink. "I told you. Tell me you didn't have a good time."

"Yeah," I sighed.

Judith smiled and whispered in my ear, "And Rachel's just fine."

* * *

Tommy graduated from high school the following May. He and Luke came to visit for a couple of weeks in June. They missed Rachel's tenth birthday because Luke still had some classes at school, but they made it out a few days later.

From one year to the next, Tommy now stood eye to eye with me, a confident young man. He had been accepted at Vanderbilt for the fall term to study business. He wasn't enthusiastic about it.

"Mom and Brad want me to be a lawyer," he groused. I had a disquieting flashback to a time when Tommy was a baby. "Miss Quinterra does, too," he added.

"You're in touch with Gracie?" I asked in shock.

"Yeah," he averted his eyes, "I see her around."

"Hmm. Well Tommy, what is it *you* want to do?"

"I applied at West Point and Mom had a fit."

"*West Point?*"

He shook his head and muttered, "Doesn't matter now, anyway."

Luke had grown as well. He was taller, but skinnier. He was so thin that his jeans wrinkled around his waist when he cinched them down. But his demeanor was positive, if not still a little shy. He smiled more, and he still liked to read with Rachel.

Later that summer we got our first computer. Judith insisted. She drug me over to Circuit City on Blackstone, where we spent a ridiculous amount of money for a Windows 95 machine. We set it up on her little desk in the bedroom—a hulking white box, a monitor that was as heavy as our television, and so many *wires*.

"I think this thing is an electrical hazard," I told her. The monitor and keyboard overwhelmed her desk. I was afraid the whole thing might topple over.

"We're going to have these in the classroom someday," she said proudly.

"God, why?"

She just smiled.

Judith said she needed the computer for writing papers and curricula, and for looking things up on the World Wide Web. Sometimes Rachel played games on it. I didn't have much use for the thing myself. It's funny when I think back on it. Today, even your nanites and ocular implants have more processing power and memory than that computer, but back then it was the latest and greatest gadget on the market.

The year after that, I booked a cottage at the Ahwahnee Hotel for Judith's fortieth birthday. We drove up after work on Friday. The weather was splendid, so on Saturday we made the steep hike to Glacier Point, carrying a couple of blankets from our cottage, a bottle of red wine, and a picnic lunch. I was panting and sweating when we got to the top. Judith leaned on her knees to catch her breath.

"Was it that hard last time?" she asked me between gasps for air.

"Whew," I wiped the sweat off my forehead, "I don't think so."

"We're getting old, Carlton."

"Maybe me," I said with a laugh, "but not you, babe."

Judith gave me an appreciative smile. She didn't look older, not a bit. She might have been a little bigger around the hips from having Rachel, I think, but she was still lean and well-toned. I was already getting wrinkles at the corners of my eyes, but not Judith. Her eyes and cheeks were smooth and clear, her smile just as bright.

If she were to grow her hair out again she wouldn't look much different than she had when we were married.

"We just haven't gone hiking in a long time," I added then.

"Yeah, a long time," she mused.

The road to Glacier Point was open, so there were a lot of people up there. We tramped through the woods, following the ridge around to the north until we found a secluded place on an outcrop covered in soft, springy tundra. Half Dome loomed ahead, like a falling moon. I spread our blankets, and we lay down on our elbows to take in the view.

"It's so quiet up here," Judith said. "Just the wind. Can you hear it?"

"Yeah."

"I mean really listen. It's like voices over the rocks and in the trees. Different voices. And out there," she pointed over the deep valley, "it's like a thousand people whispering. It reminds me of Mt. Washington, you know, if you hike up to the top when nobody's around?"

"You should tell that to Sadie," I said, cupping Judith's cheek in my hand. "That would sound great in one of her books."

Judith smiled and looked softly into my eyes.

"Maybe I should write a book," she said.

"Maybe you should."

"What could it be about, do you think?" She chewed her lip in thought.

"How about the Appalachian Trail?"

"Now there's an idea." She nestled close to me. "It's been twenty years, you know?" And then airily, "*Twenty years.*"

"Long time."

She hitched onto her side and faced me. The wind caught her hair and fluttered it around her eyes.

"Do you still think about it sometimes?" she asked. "The trail, I mean?"

I gently tucked her hair behind her ear.

"Yeah, all the time. I wish we could go back."

"Me, too. Maybe in a few years, when Rachel's in college."

"Then we'd better start getting in shape now," I laughed. "We barely made it up here. We'd never be able to make the climb to Lakes of the Clouds."

"Yeah," she chuckled. "You barely made it last time."

"Hey! It was the weather."

"Sure it was." She rolled her eyes playfully, then went soft and contemplative. "Let's promise to go back, at least to Garfield Ridge."

"I'd love that."

She rolled onto her back and gazed into the panoramic blue sky. There wasn't a cloud in it.

"We're happy, aren't we, Carlton."

That wasn't a question. I nuzzled her neck and she giggled.

"I'm happy when you're happy," I said. "And I'm happy, so you must be, too."

"We've been blessed, I think."

"It feels like it." I rolled atop her, and I kissed her and caressed her face. "I love you, babe," I breathed onto her lips.

"I love you," she breathed in return, and the sky turned indigo with the setting sun, and the stars came out, wheeling above us.

We were blessed.

TWENTY

The new century finally arrived. I ticked off the hours, the minutes, and then the seconds, as giddy and full of optimism as I had been as a child; and in some peculiar way I was relieved that I had counted accurately back then. I was forty-one years old, just as I thought I would be, a silly thought, I know, but here I was, in the future, and I had been right.

We celebrated in Oakhurst with Lois and Eugene. There were no fireworks because of the fire danger in those dry winter woods. We could have seen fireworks if we had stayed in Fresno, but I accepted the invitation to come up to Oakhurst without even consulting Judith. None of the crazy stuff that had been predicted came to pass. Computers did not melt down, mobs did not run riot—the only incident in the whole country was in Anchorage, Alaska of all places, a bomb threat that proved to be a hoax. Still, just in case, it seemed prudent to get out of town.

Suddenly Rachel was a teenager. She wore earrings and makeup and grew her hair long. She looked like her mother on a mountain top long ago, with the sun coming in and the air so fresh and clear. She had Judith's build, not as tall yet but you knew she was going to get there. I would catch myself gazing at Rachel sometimes over dinner, when the sun came through the windows just right, limning her face with a burnished glow.

"Stop staring at me, Daddy," she would complain. "It's weird."

Judith would laugh, put on a fake pout and pat my hand. I could have done the same to her. Rachel didn't want to hang out with either of us anymore. She came home to eat and sleep, but the rest of her time was spent at school or out with her friends. Judith said not to worry, it was natural, part of growing up. She assured me that in a few years Rachel would come around and be my darling again. I just needed to be patient.

On a Saturday in the summer of Rachel's fifteenth birthday, I got a call from the security office at Fashion Fair Mall. Rachel had been in a fight, and had been detained by the guards. Judith was out shopping, so I raced to the mall, searched in frustration and rising panic through the maze of dull corridors that led to the tiny security office. My stomach felt weak as I rattled through the glass door into the office. The lighting was dim in there, from bare fluorescent bulbs that flickered and buzzed. The walls were institutional green, scuffed where furniture had rubbed against them.

A teenaged boy sat on a plastic chair just inside the door. He looked at me sullenly then looked away, pressing a baggie of ice to his cheek. Rachel sat across the room in a varnished wooden chair, her arms crossed and her eyes simmering. She was breathing impatiently through her nose, I could hear her from where I stood. Between us was an old steel desk, where the security chief was sitting. He was heavy and sweaty. The collar of his white uniform shirt was open, revealing a pink and hairy chest.

"Daddy!" Rachel exclaimed. She jumped up but the security chief put out a hand.

"Now hold on little lady," he said as if bored, then to me, "You Mr. Jeffries?"

"Yeah," I said, bewildered. "What's goin' on?"

"Your daughter here started a fight with that boy."

"I did not!" Rachel countered, stamping her foot. "Bobby was bothering us."

"Bobby?" I asked. "Bobby *Boudreaux*?"

I glanced at the kid but he wouldn't look me in the eyes. I knew who he was, he was the son of one of the guys at work.

"That's right," Rachel spat. "He wouldn't leave us alone, and he called Chrissy a dirty name." Chrissy was one of Rachel's friends, the blond girl.

"And?" the security chief prompted.

"And, well..." Rachel looked down at her feet. "And I called him a dirty name back."

"*Rachel*," I said in shock.

"And?" the security chief prompted again.

"And nothing," Rachel retorted, indignant now. "Bobby grabbed my arm so I flipped him on his face."

"You *hit* him, honey?"

"No, I didn't hit him. The *floor* hit him."

I shook my head in confusion and looked at Bobby.

"Bobby, I know your dad, so tell me right now what happened."

Poor Bobby looked as if he wanted to crawl into a hole.

"It's what she said," he grumbled.

"*See*, Daddy?"

"Mr. Jeffries," said the chief, "this is serious. The boy could have been hurt."

I kept a concerned look on my face, but inside I was laughing so hard I could barely contain it. So Bobby had tangled with Rachel, a brown belt in karate... I had never been more proud. When this got out, which it would, no boy would ever dare to touch my baby. I bounced on my toes, but then caught myself and put on a hard expression.

"Mr. Chief?—er..."

"It's Grimley."

"Okay. Mr. Grimley, I think this is just a thing between kids. I know Bobby's dad—"

"He's on the way."

"Good. Then when he gets here I think we can settle this between us."

"Fine," sighed Grimley. "Then it won't be my headache to deal with."

* * *

Another year, Rachel was sixteen, and now she wanted to date boys. She asked us during breakfast on a Wednesday morning.

"Mom? Daddy? Can I go on a date Friday night?"

She asked as innocently as that, or more like an aside, a trivial thing. Judith and I had been talking about the last presidential election, what a disgrace it had been. And see? The country had not come to an end under President Bush after all. Those were her sentiments, not mine. She knew I didn't like Texans, and she knew why. And besides, I *had* to vote for Al Gore because he was from Smith County, not to mention that Mom was his fourth cousin or some such.

Rachel had tuned out of this conversation. She was twirling her spoon in her cereal bowl, looking bored. She spoke up the moment I paused for a breath, as if she had been waiting for just that opening. With her mother and me distracted by all this political nonsense, I bet she thought she could just slip that in. My jaw dropped, and whatever criticism of Bush I had intended to launch next was gone.

"Oh, I don't know, honey. You're not old enough—"

Before I could finish that sentence—before Rachel could even get her color up—Judith reached over and touched my hand, and I saw in her eyes exactly what I was supposed to have said.

"Or..." I said hesitantly, checking with Judith for confirmation. She nodded discretely and smiled, so I went ahead. "Or maybe it would be okay."

That cheered Rachel up in an instant. She bounced in her chair.

"Thank you, thank you, Daddy!"

"Now wait a minute," I said in my practiced, fatherly voice. Judith's brows dipped, and Rachel froze in mid grin. "Who's the boy?"

"It's Bobby, Daddy," Rachel answered guardedly.

"Bobby? *Boudreaux*? But he was the boy you—"

"Oh, Daddy," she chided me, rolling her eyes. "That was a long time ago."

Judith was laughing behind the straight face she was hanging on to, while Rachel bored into me with a pair of wide brown eyes that dared me to say no.

I sighed. Judith nodded again, so I said okay.

Bobby pulled up on Friday evening at seven. Rachel was in her room getting dressed. Judith was rattling pans in the kitchen, so I let Bobby in. I took his measure the moment I opened the door. I think he gulped. Bobby wasn't a bad looking kid. He had sandy hair, buzzed on the sides and gelled on top so that it stood up like a brush. He had nervous brown eyes—probably nervous because of the way I was scrutinizing him—and some acne on his chin. He wore jeans and a brown short-sleeved shirt with the tails out.

"Come in, Bobby."

"Thanks, Mr. Jefferies."

I didn't offer him a seat. That was probably cruel, but tough. He just stood there, looking at everything except me. Judith came in and smiled.

"Hello, Bobby."

"Hello, Mrs. Jeffries." He relaxed a little and took a deep breath. I guess he had been holding it the whole time.

"Rachel will be out in a minute," said Judith. "Have a seat."

"Uh, okay."

He took the couch on the farthest end from my recliner.

"So what are you all going to do tonight?" I asked. He wouldn't make eye contact with me. He answered to Judith instead.

"Uh, go to the movies, you know? And the mall."

"That's nice," said Judith. "What're you going to see?"

"Uh, *Tomb Raider*. Rachel wants to see it."

"And what about you?"

"Uh, yeah, I guess I do, too."

"Angelina Jolie's a pretty girl," I said. Bobby blushed.

"Yeah."

Rachel came out of her room and I stood. So did Bobby.

"Hi, Bobby," Rachel smiled.

"Hi, Rachel," Bobby said nervously. He thrust his hands into his pockets.

I gawked at Rachel, and not for the reason you might think. She was wearing tight jeans that she must have put on with a shoe horn, the kind of jeans that taper at the ankles and have silver beadwork on the back pockets. She wore a loose yellow pullover above that, and had her hair tied into a high ponytail. I glanced at Judith and got the nod, so I let it go.

"Okay. Well let's go," Rachel said to Bobby.

"Just a minute," I said. "What time are you coming home?" That was directed at Bobby.

"Uh," he fidgeted, "maybe twelve midnight."

I cleared my throat.

"Uh," he paled, "maybe eleven thirty."

I cleared my throat again.

"Uh, maybe *eleven*?"

I smiled and checked my watch, fiddled with the crown and made sure he noticed.

"That sounds good, Bobby. You two have a good time."

"Wait a minute, sweetie," said Judith.

She handed Rachel a cell phone. Rachel flipped it open, checked it, and then slid it into her back pocket.

"Thanks, Mom."

"Seat belts," I added.

"Okay, Daddy."

I stood in the open doorway as Rachel and Bobby left, but then Judith came up and made me close it.

"Don't be so mean, Carlton," she said in mock annoyance.

I closed the door with a sigh, but then went to the blinds and peeked out. Bobby was driving his dad's pick-up truck, a high four-wheel-drive. Rachel climbed up in her side, while Bobby climbed up in his. I shook my head.

"I don't get it," I said, shaking my head. "Boys don't hold doors for girls anymore? And they don't dress up for dates?"

Judith chuckled.

"Times have changed, honey. Kids like to do their own thing."

"Yeah—well," I sputtered, "so did we. But still—"

"You're getting so set in your ways, Carlton." She came up to me, smiled softly and kneaded my neck. "You're going to stay up all night waiting for them, aren't you?"

"You betcha."

Her eyes went sultry and mischievous.

"Wouldn't you rather stay up all night with me instead?"

* * *

The rest of that summer was unremarkable. Politics had cooled off, Rachel started the eleventh grade, I was trying to think what to do for Judith's forty-fifth birthday—and then the 9/11 terrorist attacks happened.

I know that to you the terrorist attacks of September 11, 2001 are just a historical curiosity, the way my generation looked back at the sinking of the Titanic, but for us at the time those attacks were deeply unsettling. We never considered such a thing as even being possible.

The attacks were mostly over before we had even gotten out of bed. That day started for us like any other. Judith woke up first and padded into the kitchen to make coffee. I drug in a little while later. We sat at the table, groggily sipping our coffees. Rachel was still in bed.

"I'll get her up," Judith said wearily.

I heard the television click on as Judith passed through the living room, then a knock on Rachel's door.

"*Time to get ready for school, sweetie,*" I heard Judith holler.

I sipped my coffee in the following silence, and then:

"Oh my God! *Carlton!*"

The strongest coffee couldn't have brought me that alert that quickly. I stubbed my toe getting out from the table, winced and limped hurriedly into the living room.

Judith was standing, staring at the television, a hand over her mouth.

"What is it?" I asked in a panic.

She didn't say anything, just stared at the television, her face creased in shock. I looked at the television in confusion. Both towers of the World Trade Center in New York City were burning.

"What the—"

As we watched, one of the towers collapsed.

"Ohmygod!"

Did I say that or did Judith? Maybe it was both of us. I couldn't understand what was happening, and then I read the scroll across the bottom of the screen: Hijacked airliners had been deliberately flown into both towers. The Pentagon had also been hit, and maybe the State Department. Contact had been lost with another plane over Pennsylvania. All U.S. flights had been ordered to land immediately, and foreign flights had been ordered to turn back. It was thought that another hijacked plane was still in the air. No one knew where the president was.

Rachel came out of her room, rubbing the sleep out of her eyes, but when she saw us she froze and her eyes went wide with alarm.

"What is it, Daddy?" she asked.

I called into work, so did Judith. We kept Rachel at home that day. So many people had died in the worst possible way. All I wanted to do—all any of us wanted to do—was go to New York and try to help. But three thousand miles separated us, and the planes weren't flying—and wouldn't fly again for days afterward.

We sat in front of the television all day. Later, the Secretary-General of the United Nations, Kofi Annan, stood behind a podium to speak. Behind him and to his right, clutching a handful of papers, stood Jenny Peay.

September 12 was eerie. We stayed home again, numb, as if we had just ridden out a tornado, and yet the sky and the air were the clearest I had ever seen them. Sounds were muted, as if Fresno had been evacuated. Eventually we found out that the sky was so clear those few days because the entire U.S. air fleet had been grounded, no jet planes to trace contrails across the sky. All those people who didn't believe that humans could change the weather should have taken notice.

The phone rang that afternoon. It was Evelyn, who for once didn't have condescension in her voice but something more akin to hysteria.

Tommy had joined the Army.

* * *

With the resources the country had at that time, I would have thought that we would have just sent a crack Special Forces team to Afghanistan to root out those terrorists like groundhogs from a cornfield, but no, the president had to go and make a war out of it. I said as much to Don one morning at his bar. This came out as stray banter while I scanned his shelves and wrote his order, so the vehemence he hurled back at me was unexpected and stunning.

"That's bull—, Festus!" he exploded. He couldn't catch his breath between the profanities he spat at me. His blubbery pink face went red, and the few strands of gray hair across his scalp became damp with sweat.

I quailed at first, backing away from him as if he were a deranged stranger on the street, not someone I had known for more than fifteen years. But as his insults turned personal, directed at me rather than politics or the war, anger rose and clouded my eyes.

"I can't believe you just said that to me," I spat in return. "I thought we were friends."

"Talkin' like that, you're no friend of mine."

"What? C'mon, Don—"

"I don't need your kind comin' in here talkin' that trash."

"My kind?"

"Go on. Get on out of here." He flicked his fingers toward the door. "And tell 'em to send me a new salesman out."

I stood there with my mouth open while he ripped me with his eyes. Finally he spun around and stamped into his office.

I wasn't worried about losing my job. These kinds of altercations happened all the time in the booze business, but still— I screeched out of Don's gravel parking lot, spinning some of that gravel into his white-washed windows. I cut over to the 99, heading south to Visalia and my next customer. I was so angry that I cursed under my breath and pounded the steering wheel, which made me part of the problem as well.

Until the 2000 election, I had never really paid attention to politics. I think most people were the same way. We went in, voted for whomever we thought would do the best job, and then we got back to more important things, like our families and our jobs. Whoever won...well, we took it in stride. It was nothing to get worked up about. Not anymore, though. Now people were always angry, ready to fight at the slightest slip of the tongue. It didn't matter if it was election time or not.

But what really churned my insides was that we had soldiers dying over there, and a military top brass that didn't seem to know what it was doing; and yet despite all of that, there weren't any billboards on the 99 calling for President Bush's impeachment.

* * *

Throughout 2002, the president put the spurs to that war-horse of his and kept it galloping full-out for a war in a country that used to be called Iraq. It was a sorry mess. Calmer heads around the world thought we were off our rocker. There were accusations, counter-accusations, and meetings of the heads of state. Some of them came out of those meetings shaking their heads. The evidence to justify a war was flimsy. Anyone not blinded by politics could see that.

The United Nations got involved. Secretary-General Kofi Annan gave speeches, cautioning against war. We would see him on the news, speaking in measured tones but with an obvious edge of disgust. I would often spot Jenny Peay in the back-ground, ready to step forward with a memo or fact sheet for the secretary-general. She always looked prim and competent, like the *Jenny-Pea* I had known, although she now had gray streaks in her hair and a looser aspect to her face.

"Look, there's Jenny Peay," I pointed out to Judith one night.

"Your high school girlfriend?"

"Yeah," I said wistfully.

"She's pretty."

"Yeah. She was then, too."

Judith gave me a knowing smile. She wasn't jealous, no need to be. And she wasn't like that, anyway; never had been. I just knew that if we three could meet, Judith and Jenny would take off, gossiping as if they were old friends, and I would be sitting there with my ears burning.

Tommy was back at Fort Benning, Georgia. We got short emails from him every now and then. He had been sent to Virginia after he completed his basic training at Fort Benning, but he either wouldn't, or couldn't, tell us why. He was a lieutenant, he wrote to us, a commissioned officer.

He stopped in to see us between Christmas and New Year's. He was heading somewhere on military business, but had a few hours to layover before his next flight. I met him at the airport that morning, and didn't recognize him until he smiled and said, "Hello, Dad."

"Tommy?"

He wasn't taller than me, but he sure looked it. He was dressed in desert camo, his posture as rigid as steel rebar. Crystal blue eyes shined from a face that was lean and taut, and his hair was cropped short in a military flat-top that looked sharp enough to shave ice. I thought I would break when he hugged me.

"Tommy, you look so...so..."

"Thanks, Dad." He waved off my astonishment and looked around. People dipped their heads at him as they walked by. "Where're Judith and Rachel?"

"They had to do something. We'll see them at home."

"Okay, then." He hefted his duffel. "Then let's get going."

Tommy wanted to drive.

"I still love this car," he said, handling the wheel with one hand. His other hand rested on the floor shift. His fingers were rough and calloused, and looked as if they were strong enough to crack hickory nuts.

I studied him, trying not to be obvious about it. He wore dark wrap-around sunglasses that completely hid his expression, but he was smiling as he jockeyed the Firebird along. I had the top closed against the cold, so Tommy seemed to have to duck his head to keep from punching through it. How had he gotten so *big*?

"I'm glad you still like it," I said after some moments. "I've been having some trouble with it, though. It's not holding up as well as the Catalina did."

"You still have that car?" he asked.

"Yeah. I'm thinking about having it restored."

"Good. That's a sweet car. Check the prices. It might be worth a lot of money now."

"Really?"

"Yeah, Dad." He looked at me but I couldn't see his eyes. "It's an antique, you know?"

"I never thought about that."

Rachel came scampering out as we pulled into the driveway. "*Tommy!*" She jumped on Tommy the moment he got out of the car, straddling his waist and looping her arms around his neck.

"Hey, little sister," Tommy said with a laugh.

Judith came out. Tommy set Rachel down and went to give Judith a hug.

"It's so good to see you, Tom," Judith said. "You're so...so..."

"Yeah, that's what Dad says," Tommy said with a wink toward me.

We went inside and sat at the kitchen table. Judith poured coffee for Tommy and me.

"So what's it like?" Rachel asked Tommy. He smiled and sipped his coffee.

"It's busy. Luke says hi, by the way."

"What's he been doing?" asked Judith.

"Oh, just going to school and arguing with Mom. Same as always."

"Tommy?" I asked, turning serious. "What's next?"

"I don't know, Dad. I haven't been given my orders yet."

"Will they be sending you...*over there?*"

"Don't know. Maybe." He didn't seem the least bit concerned. "Nothing to worry about," he added. "It'll probably be over soon anyway."

I wished I could share his confidence.

We all went together to take Tommy back to the airport. We couldn't go to the gates anymore, not since 9/11, so we said our goodbyes out front.

"When can you come back?" Rachel asked him. She was starting to tear up a little, but when Tommy lifted her off her feet for a hug she giggled her tears away.

"I don't know," he told her. "But soon, I hope."

He hugged Judith, then opened his arms to me. I stepped back instead, and held out my hand the way Dad would have. We shook hard and long.

"God, be careful, son," I said.

"I will, Dad."

We watched him wend his way through security, and I wished that I had hugged him.

* * *

March brought us three jarring announcements.

Evelyn called early in the month and shakily informed me that Tommy had been given his orders. No one knew what that entailed, but we could pretty much guess.

I hung up that call with a dark sense of foreboding, and no sooner had I put the handset down than the phone rang again, making me jump. It was Gracie this time. Tommy and Angelina had eloped the day before Tommy had shipped out.

"*What?*"

That yanked me out of my stupor.

"Yeah, it surprised me, too."

"I didn't even know they were together. Did you?"

"I thought they might be, but I wasn't sure."

"Why didn't you *tell* me?"

"Carlton—" She exhaled before going on. "It wasn't my place to spread gossip, and Evelyn would have had a fit. You know that."

"Yeah, but still—"

"C'mon, I didn't know they would do *this*. I thought if they were serious they would tell us."

"Where's Angelina now?"

"She's here."

"Does she know where Tommy is?"

There was a pause on the line, then:

"No."

* * *

The third shock came over breakfast on a Saturday toward the end of the month. The three of us were at the table. I had rolled a television over so that I wouldn't miss any of the news from Iraq. Footage was being played of the aftermath of a suicide bombing in which four American soldiers had been killed. And then Secretary of Defense Rumsfeld came on the screen, cavalierly rambling about how our guys would be met with cheers and roses in Baghdad. Yeah, sure. Rumsfeld was a real snake in the grass. I couldn't stand the guy. I drummed my fingers, impatient for the news to cut back to Iraq. Tommy was over there somewhere.

"Did you hear that, honey?" Judith asked.

"Oh, huh? What?"

"There's a career exposition Monday night. We should take Rachel."

"Oh, yeah." I looked over at Rachel. She seemed preoccupied with something. "So what about it, honey?" I asked her. "Do you want to go to that?"

Rachel twiddled her spoon, then looked up hesitantly.

"Yeah, about that..." she said, trailing off. She fiddled with her spoon some more, tucked some hair behind her ear. "I've been meaning to tell you all something."

"What's that, honey?" Something was off, but I couldn't put my finger on it. I looked a question at Judith, but she just shrugged.

Rachel gathered herself and sat upright. Suddenly I was anxious.

"Mom? Daddy?" She paused and smiled weakly. "I want to hike the Appalachian Trail after graduation."

Just like that it was out, but it didn't make it through my head because it made no sense. I just sat there, befuddled. Judith stiffened. And then Rachel's words came together and I realized what she had just said.

"What?" I stood abruptly and leaned on the table. Rachel crossed her arms tightly and scowled at me with her eyes. Judith looked dazed. I took a calming breath and sat back down. After a moment and a sip of coffee, I tried to laugh it off. "Baby," I explained lightly, "you can't do that because you have to start college in August."

"I'm not a baby!" she threw back at me, reddening.

"Sweetie?" Judith said with forced patience. She tried to smile. "You've never talked about this before."

"No," Rachel barked at her mother. "But you guys talk about it all the time. So I want to do it, too."

It was only then that I realized she was absolutely serious. I fought to frame my words. There was no way I was going to allow Rachel to take off for the Appalachian Trail.

"Honey," I said, trying to reproduce Judith's patience. "It takes a long time, and it's not safe." Judith was nodding, and that gave me confidence. I knew I must be in the right because she was taking my side for once. "And really, you're too young for something like that."

Rachel's eyes narrowed. She stood and jabbed a finger at me. "I'm older than you were when you went."

"Sweetie, it's not the same," Judith said, trying to remain calm.

Rachel jerked her eyes to her mother.

"And why not?"

Judith searched me, speechless, or rather, with words on her lips that she didn't want to speak.

"It's because, honey," I said weakly. "It's because...well..." I looked at Judith in anguish. I think she was begging me to say it so she wouldn't have to. "Honey...it's because..." I leaned back and rubbed my face. Judith's nose was red. I couldn't look Rachel in the eyes. "Well...it's because you're a girl."

That was a bomb that deadened everything around us. I sniffed and covered my eyes.

"Oh my God," Rachel trembled. "*Oh my God.* Mom? *You* went." A tear splashed off Rachel's cheek. "Why can't I?"

"Times have changed, baby," Judith answered in misery.

"I'm not a baby!"

Rachel rushed around the table and to her room. I was stunned, like those people in Iraq. Judith shook her head and wiped at her eyes.

"I never knew anything about this," she said in a pale voice.

"I don't...I don't know what to do," I said helplessly.

* * *

Rachel had made up her mind, and there was no turning her from it. I thought about trying to scare her with stories of assaults, animal attacks, and the few murders that had happened on the trail, but I couldn't bring myself to fill her mind with fear. So instead I tried a different approach. I told her about the blisters and the poison ivy and the bugs, the cold and the heat; but above all, the staggering weight loss. How would she feel, I asked her, when her athletic figure was sickly thin and her socks smelled like something that needed to be taken out and shot? She gave me a hard look.

"I don't know," she replied levelly. "How did Mom feel?"

Judith took her aside to discuss inconveniences of a more intimate nature to women; how difficult it was to stay clean and so on. Rachel just shook her head.

"If you could handle it, Mom, so can I."

There was no use in forbidding her to go, she would just go anyway. Judith and I both knew that, so we stayed away from that tactic. Instead we hatched a plan to take Rachel on a weekend backpacking trip. A few miles under her feet, some steep climbs, and a couple of nights sleeping on the cold ground might just dissuade her.

We drove up to Oakhurst right after school let out on a Friday a couple of weeks later. We took Judith's minivan so that we could haul our backpacks and gear. I wish we could have taken the Firebird, not for any sporty reasons, but because then I could have put the top down. It had been warm in the 70s in Fresno. It got colder as we climbed toward Oakhurst, not much colder than the 50s, but the wind carried a tangy dry chill that tickles the sinuses and promises a crispy night ahead. With the top down, Rachel would have felt the change in the air. Perhaps that alone might have planted some doubts.

We didn't visit long with Lois and Eugene because we only had about an hour and a half to get down into the valley before the sun set. When Lois insisted that we at least stay for the night, Judith took her aside for a talk. Rachel sat on the couch by the fire, looking bemused, as if she knew exactly what her mother was saying in that whispered conversation. I stood near the front door with Eugene, waiting, and then I caught sight of something in Rachel that put a knot in my throat. I swallowed painfully and gazed at my daughter. She didn't see this, she was watching her mother. Rachel was wearing khaki hiking pants, a green turtleneck sweater, and a pair of suede hiking boots that hadn't even been scuffed yet. Although she still had a girlish cast in her eyes, she suddenly looked as tall and sinewy as her mother. This very same scene could have played out more than twenty years ago.

I furtively wiped my eyes. As Judith and Lois broke their conversation, I overheard Lois whisper, "So now you know how *we* felt."

We went outside and shouldered our backpacks. Rachel had brought a pair of trekking poles. I had never used trekking poles myself. I thought they looked silly, as if we were going to ski down the mountain rather than hike. I took a last look at the lowering sun, shivered against the incipient chill, and then we started down.

I took the lead, with Judith following, making what I thought was good time down those endless switchbacks. We hadn't made it far, though, when Rachel hopped across a narrow switchback and took off ahead of us, her trekking poles clicking on the rocks and her hips swinging with determination. Soon she was out of sight. Judith paused to give me a look of startled amazement. I wiped my forehead, caught my breath, and we continued on.

We didn't see Rachel again until we came out of the woods at the stream and found her sitting on a rock, eating an energy bar. The sun had dropped beyond the limb of the mountains by then, and a waxing moon shone brightly in the velvet sky. The woods and the stream looked soft in that light, and Rachel looked a lot like her mother had once looked in a similar setting.

"What took you all so long?" she asked nonchalantly, not even looking our way. She finished her energy bar and stuffed the wrapper into a pocket. "I was going to go on," she said then, "but I didn't want to leave you two by yourselves." She stood and shouldered her backpack. "Okay, let's go."

I looked at Judith, and she looked at me.

"That was our rock," I said.

"Yeah." She didn't have the breath for more than that.

"You ready to go on?"

"No."

"Oh, God, me neither."

I shrugged out of my backpack and fell onto my butt. Judith did the same, leaning against my shoulder. Rachel went around some boulders ahead and was soon out of sight, the clicks from her trekking poles merging with the scattered sounds of the stream.

"I guess we should have practiced first," Judith said with an ironic laugh.

"No kidding."

I opened a water bottle and offered it to Judith. She took a slug then passed it back to me, where I finished off most of it in one gulp.

"We'd better get going," she said then. "It'll be dark soon."

"You worried about Rachel?"

"No," she laughed. "I'm worried about *us*."

The sky was black by the time we reached the bow in the stream, although the moon cast enough silvery light for us to see our way. Rachel was sitting in the grass, resting against her backpack with her legs crossed. She had her LED headlight on and was studying a map. We splashed across the stream toward her light, like a beacon in a gauzy night.

"Oh, there you are," she said. "I was starting to get worried."

"No worries, ba—honey," I said with a forced and weary smile.

"I made some soup if you're hungry," she said. Judith dropped her backpack and flopped into the grass.

"I'm not hungry, sweetie," Judith said. "I just want to wash my face and go to sleep. Carlton? Do you mind? Can you set up the tent?"

"Sure, honey."

"Already?" Rachel exclaimed. "You want to go to bed already? You just got here."

"We're old, sweetie," Judith sighed.

"Yeah," said Rachel. "I know."

I was too weary to banter with my daughter, and I had a burning place on my right heel that promised a big blister in the morning. I shucked out of my backpack, pulled out the tent and began to separate the poles.

"Okay, then." Rachel hopped up. "I'm going to put my tent over there by the trees."

She went off and I sighed. Judith looked at me with amused albeit weary eyes, made wearier still in the pale light.

"Look where she's going, Carlton," Judith whispered.

"Is that the same—"

"Yeah, I think so."

"Isn't that a little—"

"Weird? Maybe."

"Think we should—"

"Tell her? Absolutely not! But could you please set up the tent? *Please?*" She said that with a begging smile and the flash of white teeth, so I got after it.

My knees were soaked through from the damp grass, and the evening chill was coming down like a curtain. I fumbled with the tent poles in the dark, looking over my shoulder from time to time to give Judith a reassuring smile. Somehow I got my foot tangled in one of the lines, and I tumbled into the grass. Rising on wet elbows, I saw that Rachel's tent was up. She was inside, silhouetted in the light of her headlamp. She looked to be reading a book.

"Carlton?" Judith beseeched me. "*Hurry.*"

I finally got the thing up, although it drooped in the middle. I didn't care. Judith and I crawled into our sleeping bags and shivered.

"Just whose idea was this?" she asked drowsily as her eyelids fluttered toward sleep.

"Uh, I think it was your idea."

"No, honey," she said, and she turned onto her side to sleep.

There was a rime of frost on the tent when I awoke the next morning. The tent had slumped into my face overnight, pestering me in and out of broken dreams. If there was one thing I remembered about the Appalachian Trail, it was that a good night's sleep was crucial. Well, I hadn't had that.

I climbed stiffly out of the tent. Judith had burrowed toward the foot of her sleeping bag, like a fetus in a womb. I tried not to disturb her, but I tripped into a guy line and pulled the whole tent down.

"Cut it out!" Judith complained from underneath. "I'm trying to sleep."

It was a cold morning, a saturating chill that went straight through the skin. My breaths were puffs of white in that still, frigid air. I hugged myself and shivered, and went off to pee.

"Oh, you're up," Rachel said cheerily from the distance. She was sitting on her backpack, heating something on her stove. It smelled like coffee.

"You drink coffee now?" I hollered.

"No, Daddy," she smiled. "It's for you and Mom."

She had already taken down her tent and packed it away. Her trekking poles were stabbed evenly into the ground beside her. I looked around. The sun was coming in brightly, although the mountains were shrouded in cloud.

"What time is it?" I asked.

"Oh," she said, pretending to check her watch. "About nine."

I shook my head and went into the woods to do my business. When I came back, Judith was up, bathing her face in the steam from a coffee mug. She had her sleeping bag over her shoulders like a cocoon, just her head and hands showing. Rachel sat next to her.

"Did you save one for me?" I asked, shivering my way over.

"Of course, Daddy," said Rachel. Her mood was ebullient. "So what are we going to do today?"

"Uh," I said. Judith looked at me resentfully. Her hair was a mess of tangles. "I think just camp here, you know?"

"Naw," said Rachel. She stood and hopped her backpack onto her shoulders. "I want to hike on up the stream. That okay?" The look she gave me told me that I had better agree. I turned to Judith. She gave me a shivering nod, so I nodded, too. "Great, then," Rachel smiled. "See ya later."

She clumped off through the grass and around the bend. I followed her until she was gone.

"Well, she sure showed us," Judith laughed, her teeth chattering, but there was something else there, pride, I think.

"Yeah."

I searched the damp, cold grass, perplexed, then finally sat in the flattened and dry place where Rachel's tent had been.

"I'm starved," I said.

"Me, too," said Judith.

We both looked over at our collapsed tent. We both groaned.

That day did brighten and become warm. In a few hours we barely remembered our cold start, as if it had happened ages ago, and really hadn't been that bad anyway. I got the tent set up properly, and we cooked a dehydrated camp meal that tasted surprisingly good. It was so warm in the sun now that I pulled off my shirt.

"We need to get out in the sun more," Judith commented. I was as white as a Yankee in a snow bank, and Judith's once-proud tan had become more of a pale olive rather than bronze.

"Yeah," I said. "It's been a long time. But it seems like yesterday, you know?"

"Yeah. Goodness, Carlton. What have we done?"

"I think we forgot how it was," I said. Judith nodded at that, but I think she thought I meant that we had forgotten what it was like in the outdoors, when what

I really meant was that we had forgotten what it was like to be Rachel's age. "I mean us," I added quickly, "when we were on the trail."

"That's what I was thinking," said Judith.

"Oh."

"It's not fair, you know?" she said.

"What's that?"

"Our parents trusted us."

"Well, maybe yours did."

She looked at me sharply.

"Yours did, too, and you know it."

"But they weren't happy about it, going on the trail, I mean."

"Of course not. Neither were mine. But we went anyway, and look what came from that."

"Yeah, but...Rachel's not like we were then."

"I think she's more like us than you want to admit."

"I just want her to be my little girl again."

"Well, you can't have that. We're going to have to accept this, you know."

The clouds had burned off of the mountain tops. I gazed at the icy crags and the wisps of snow off the peaks.

"Yeah," I sighed.

* * *

The Hoover High School graduation ceremony was held in the early evening of May 28 at the Selland Arena in Fresno. It was unusually hot for a day in May. The sun was going low when we arrived at the arena, but that was little relief. I regretted wearing a black suit. Rachel was riding to the graduation with friends, so it was just Judith and me. Lois and Eugene wanted to come, but Eugene hadn't been feeling well. Lois thought it best to keep him at home.

We were early enough that we found seats in the bleachers down near the stage. People were filtering in, finding their places. Rows of gray metal chairs sat empty on the court. I loosened my tie, and tilted my head toward the cool air coming down from the ventilators. It wasn't long before I was dry and almost freezing under that continuous draft.

"Whew, it's hot in here," Judith complained. She fanned her face with our graduation program.

"I'm fine, now," I said, readjusting my tie.

She looked at me with something like resentment.

"You men are lucky that way."

My brows dipped in confusion, but then...oh, yeah.

"Well anyway," I said to change the subject. "We did it, honey. We got her grown up without anything bad happening."

Judith understood me. She squeezed my hand.

"Yes we did, Carlton. Yes we did."

The place filled up quickly, with people pressing into us. A few of them carried pompoms in the green and white school colors. Some guys on the other side unrolled a banner: *Patriot Pride.* That *rah-rah* school spirit stuff had never been one of Rachel's interests. She had always been focused on her studies, which made her mother proud, me too, prouder than I have words to describe.

I put an arm around Judith's shoulders and held her close. Principal Jones and others of the faculty came out and took their seats on the stage. Introductions were announced to the audience, and then the graduation march began. The graduates filed out of both corners at the far end of the court, moving briskly along the sides toward the front before turning back down the middle to fill their chairs from the rear. I searched urgently for Rachel, but couldn't make her out among so many, all wearing satiny green gowns, their faces hidden below mortarboard caps with white tassels, some paired green and white.

Principal Jones gave a speech, looking out proudly over his graduates, and then the roll-call began. It moved along well, and finally, as the alphabet approached *J*, I saw her.

"There she is, Judith!" I pointed excitedly. Rachel looked regal and dignified, sitting erect, hands on her lap, eyes forward. From then on I could spot her easily because of her paired tassel.

I followed the names in anticipation: *Howard, Hudson, Hughes; Irvine, Jackson—* and then...*Rachel Lynn Jeffries, cum laude.*

They had asked us not to cheer as this would slow down the process, but I couldn't help myself. Rachel looked our way with a beaming smile. Some boys whooped somewhere. My baby walked across the stage with poise and grace. She accepted her diploma from Principal Jones, then she held it up in triumph. I stood and clapped, my eyes welling.

"Sit down, Carlton. Sit down!" Judith chided me, looking embarrassed. No one behind us complained, though.

When it was over we met Rachel out front. It was boisterous out there, but we found a place out of the crush.

"Let me get a picture, baby," I said eagerly. Rachel struck a pose, clutching her diploma over her heart, her smile as exuberant as a bluetick puppy. I pulled out an old Kodak 110 and raised it for a snapshot.

"Daddy, you really need to get a digital camera," Rachel said through her teeth while holding her smile.

"Why?" I asked. "This one works just fine."

Her friends thronged around her after that, chattering and carrying on. There was going to be a party, but Rachel shook her head. She was leaving for the Appalachian Trail in the morning.

* * *

We had to leave at 4:30 a.m. to get Rachel to the airport and through the Homeland Security checkpoints in time for her flight. Rachel had an odyssey ahead, not just the Appalachian Trail, but actually getting to it. She couldn't take Continental Trailways as I had, they weren't around anymore. Instead she would have to fly first to Los Angeles, then to Chicago, then to Boston, and then take the Concord Coach Lines bus to Millinocket. From Millinocket she would have to—and this caused me the most anxiety—*hitchhike* to Baxter State Park.

We went in Judith's minivan, but I drove. Rachel sat beside me. Judith was in the back. My hands were sweaty on the wheel. It wasn't only Rachel who was on my mind, we hadn't received an email from Tommy since the dust had settled in Baghdad. I had no end of worries.

"Honey, listen," I said, breaking a palpable silence. "Buy some cigars. Don't smoke them, just light them. The smoke will help keep the blackflies off, especially in shelters."

"Okay, Daddy. You told me."

"Check for ticks every day; check behind your knees. The bad ones are little. They look like specks of dirt. You can get 'em off with alcohol, or hold a cigar close, but not too close to burn yourself.

"Okay, Daddy."

"The water's okay from the springs."

"I know, Daddy."

It was too dark in the minivan to see her clearly, but I bet she rolled her eyes. Judith was silent and pensive.

"And your trekking poles," I went on anyway, "they're like spears. Keep them beside you when you're asleep."

We pulled up out front of the airport just then. I got out reluctantly and went around to fetch Rachel's backpack. Her new backpack and gear were amazing. They weighed practically nothing, yet everything she would need was there: sleeping bag, alcohol stove, a titanium pot; rain suit, ultralite tarp, fleece jacket and extra socks—the only thing that would add weight was the food she would need to carry when she got to Maine. A pang of jealousy rose from the pit of my memory.

Rachel came up and hugged me. In the dark, with my eyes squeezed tight to keep from giving them away, it could have been Judith I was holding. Rachel took my face in her hands and made me see.

"I'll be fine," she smiled. "You taught me everything. Nobody knows more than you."

I couldn't help it, the tears came. I wiped my eyes and looked away. Judith hugged her daughter, then stood back and adjusted a lock of Rachel's hair. Judith's eyes were set and dry. She looked at Rachel with an expression only women possess, a motherly way of knowing.

"Don't be afraid to fall in love," Judith said, almost a whisper. "But please be smart about it."

Rachel nodded earnestly.

"Okay."

"And be careful, sweetie," Judith added. "Email us."

"I will, Mom."

Rachel slung her backpack, took up her trekking poles, and went inside. She didn't look back.

TWENTY-ONE

It must be past midnight. I can't tell for sure because the damned battery in my watch has died. A watch is a valuable navigation tool on the trail; a watch helps you set your pace and locate yourself on a map. I couldn't have gotten along without one before, but I guess I move so slowly now that it really doesn't matter. I wish I still had one of the old-fashioned watches, the kind you had to wind up every morning, but they haven't made them in decades. Too bad. You could always count on those. Having to regularly wind a watch isn't as inconvenient as having a battery die in the Hundred-Mile Wilderness.

It's so quiet out there. The air is like a heavy wall in this crushing cold, keeping everything out. Even the stream is muffled, little more than the hollow rush of blood in my ears. There is no light, not a glimmer. The sky was dense with malevolent clouds when the sun went down. The clouds must still be as thick because no light is making it through; not the stars or the moon, if there is one tonight. I could as well be floating in space or on a dark sea, at least that's what it feels like.

I can't sleep. The sore on my backside is worse, and there's no way to lie down without aggravating it. Sitting up makes it hurt less, though. I had hoped that even if sitting I might still nod off by and by, but no, not in this position. Or maybe I just have too much on my mind. At least Sam can sleep, lucky dog. He's lying across the foot of my sleeping bag, keeping my feet warm while in turn my feet keep his stomach warm. That's a fair trade, except now I'm getting a cramp in my right foot. I need to move it, but I don't want to disturb Sam. It seems I have no end of worries.

Rachel worried me. I couldn't sleep that night, either. I tossed and turned while Judith lay with her back to me. She didn't complain once. She was probably awake herself, just less fitful than I was—or less willing to show it. When morning finally came I hopped out of bed and went straight to the computer, where an email from Rachel was waiting for us. I clicked on it urgently, like tearing into an overdue letter. She had sent the email from Portland, Maine last night. She had made it okay, she wrote. She was in Portland to switch to the bus that went to Millinocket. She was tired, but excited at the same time. Everything was so different back east.

I woke Judith, who was asleep after all.

"Rachel's in Maine," I whispered as Judith's eyes fluttered.

"That's good," she said sleepily. "That's good."

I checked the clock. With the three-hour time difference, Rachel was probably already in Millinocket, maybe even making her way to Baxter State Park. There was nothing surreal about this now, it was as real as slamming your fingers in a door. Rachel was on her way to the Hundred-Mile Wilderness. No matter how I felt—how much I worried—she wouldn't be able to contact us again for a while.

* * *

We received an email from Tommy on Rachel's eighteenth birthday.

Hey Little Sister. Happy birthday. Hi Dad. Hi Judith. Hope you all are doing okay. I'm doing fine. I don't know when they will rotate me home, but I will let you know. Love, Tom.

That was it. No other news. He didn't even mention his marriage to Angelina, as if he assumed we already knew or else was trying to keep it a secret. But I wanted to know how he really felt. What was it like over there? Had he been shot at? *Had he killed anyone?* He either wouldn't or couldn't say. According to the news, though, things did seem to be settling down in Iraq. Maybe he *would* be home soon. Of course he didn't know about Rachel. Judith typed out a reply and gave him the news, while I studied a calendar and tried to figure out where Rachel might be.

Getting supplies in Millinocket and then making her way to Baxter State Park would probably have used up her first day. If she had climbed Katahdin on the second day, then camped at Baxter on the way back, she could be five days into the Hundred-Mile Wilderness by now. She might have made it to the Newhall shelter at mile 78, or maybe even as far as Cloud Pond. The black flies would be terrible. It made me miserable to think about her having to endure that. I prayed that the weather was good, that she wasn't cold.

* * *

I finally had to shuffle my feet. Poor Sam, he was so comfortable. He looked at me with the closest thing dogs have to resentment, but then he sniffed out a new place next to me and he is asleep again. I wish I was. My eyes are so heavy that the letters are blurring on this page. I feel that I should be able to just drop off, but I can't. There's too much stuff whirring in my mind; Rachel, Tommy—damn. It was so much for a father to have to cope with all at once. So much.

As I learned later from Rachel's journal, she had made it through the Hundred-Mile Wilderness in six days. It had taken me eight days to hike those same miles. She was a fast hiker—God she was fast! She was faster than I ever was. Her trail name was *Swift*.

The weeks rushed by anxiously for Judith and me, although I know that for Rachel it would have felt like months. We didn't get but a couple of emails from her in Maine, and then suddenly she was in Gorham, New Hampshire, about to take on the White Mountains. I doubted that we would hear from her again until she reached Hanover, New Hampshire and Dartmouth. Lakes of the Clouds and the other huts in the White Mountains didn't have computers (or electrical outlets), so I would have been surprised if she came across a computer before she got to Hanover. She planned to stay with Sadie and Ryan for a few days, to rest and recover before she went on into Vermont. That was good, and then we would actually be able to talk to her on the telephone.

I did stop in at Lakes of the Clouds hut during my 2008 hike. The weather had been perfect that day, clear and warm down in the valleys. There had been a brisk wind around the peaks, but just hiking in the bright sun made that gusting cold wind bearable. The view was enormous, what I had missed last time. For a while I could forget everything that had happened and just be in the moment, a part of that view. It's why I came, why I was so lucky with the weather that day.

I reached Lakes of the Clouds in the middle of the afternoon, the lake sparkling like glacier melt. The hut must have been refurbished at some point. It looked newer—still rustic, but newer. I walked past the steel door to The Dungeon and laughed. I didn't need to open that door this time. I wasn't going to stay at Lakes of the Clouds, it was too early for that; I stopped at the hut because Lakes of the Clouds keeps bound trail registers going back to Roosevelt—that would be the first Roosevelt, Theodore.

The interior did look the same—same plank floor, same dining hall, same kitchen—although in the warm light of day if felt different to me, smaller somehow. The place was deserted; all the guests would be out hiking on such a nice day. One of the croo was in the kitchen, a young bearded guy with long, wavy brown hair under a red stocking cap. His name was Alex.

"'S'up, man?" he asked with an irregular grin.

I told him my story, or at least the part I was willing to tell.

"Whoa, dude! That's awesome," he said. "Man, *nineteen seventy-six*—that was like the Wild West."

He didn't mean that as commentary about my age, but rather the conditions on the trail in those days. It *had* been something like the Wild West then; rugged and remote, sleeping in the woods most of the time, bathing in the lakes and ponds—few services. Now there were hiker hostels along the way, food and hot showers. Once you cleared Maine, you almost didn't even need to use the shelters anymore because of the hostels. Fast-food restaurants had popped up near some of the road crossings, and I heard that down in Pennsylvania they would even deliver pizza to one of the shelters!

Alex led me into the dining hall, where the more recent trail registers were lined up on a mantle. The older ones were in a closet somewhere. I asked for 1976 and he went looking. While he was gone, I pulled out 2003 and carried it over to a table that I might have slept on once. I thumbed the pages. The trail may have changed, but not the hikers and their entries. Some of the trail names were as colorful and outlandish as they had ever been—*Goosedown Felt, Ragin' Reiver, Blister Man, Sarah One-Sock, Miles Slayer*—and some hikers still drew caricatures and cartoons, of exaggerated feet with blisters the size of apples, snarky double entendres, and occasionally a truly skilled portrait.

Rachel had reached Lakes of the Clouds on June 25, another of those improbable coincidences—or perhaps she had planned it that way. She had only taken one zero day, that was in Gorham, New Hampshire, which meant that she had raced through the rugged Maine woods without a rest, and then had taken only one day off before the climb into the White Mountains. I wiped away a tear of pride, turned another page and found her entry:

My poor little toe. It has a blister all the way around it. The nail fell out—yuck! I look like a mutant. These guys let me wash the floors for food. Yummy. The way I look I should just sit out front with a sign that says: Will wash floors for food:) *Maybe if I hold out a cup the people will give me money:) Naw, I feel pretty good. I love this place. This is where Mom and Dad met.* Tollbooth Tom *wants to stay a few days. I think I wore him out getting here. Serves him right. I want to go on to Garfield Ridge, so...bye bye,* Tollbooth Tom.
Swift, ME-GA '03

A tear dripped on Rachel's page. I sniffed and caressed her words as if I were caressing her, my baby. But Rachel had been right, she wasn't a baby. Look how tough she was, how determined. I had to smile despite it all. I even wanted to rip out that page while Alex was still gone, put it in my pocket—but no, Rachel had left her mark here; she had earned it. She deserved to keep her place.

Alex must have been having trouble finding the 1976 register. It was strangely quiet in the hut. My sniffs echoed in the high rafters. I put the register back on the mantle, paused, then pulled out 2007. I found Beer Poet's entry, which was dated October 8. I bet it was cold then, but he didn't mention that. As always, he left only a poem:

> *Through forests high,*
> *A howling wind.*
> *No bow breaks,*
> *But what we rend.*
> *Where are they now?*
> *My fellows,*
> *My band of friends.*
> *At the mountain,*
> *At the end.*
> *Beer Poet, GA-ME '07*

Beer Poet was alone, I could tell. It was late in the season and he had only made it as far as Lakes of the Clouds. He should have been deep into Maine by then. His friends must have all gone on ahead. Something had held Beer Poet up. But what?

Alex came out and startled me. I thumped the register closed self-consciously, as if I had been prying into matters that weren't my business.

"I found it!" he grinned. "I didn't think I would. Someone had stuck it on the bottom, but...well, here it is."

He sidled up next to me as I opened the register, looking over my shoulder as if to be a part of what I would find. I would rather have been alone, but it didn't seem right to run him off. I found my entry:

Damn it's cold out there. It's warm in here, though. Good food. Glad I made it. I met a girl. Too bad I have to go in the morning.
Jake Brake, ME-GA '76

That's all I wrote that night. It seems anticlimactic now. It must have been, because Alex snorted and said, "Yeah, man—well, I got to get back to work."

"Sure thing," I said.

"I got some baked goods coming out of the oven in a minute," he added in parting. "Hang out and you can have some."

"Sure, man. Thanks."

He went away and I was glad, because then I found Willow's entry:

It's crowded tonight because the weather's terrible. The place is packed! A southbounder came in kind of late. He was a mess, but there's something about him...I don't know, it's a silly thing to do, and I wanted to stay a few more days, but I think I'll head out tomorrow.
Willow, Grafton Notch to Kinsman Notch '76

Judith had told me about this, what she had written, but it never seemed real until I saw it myself, as if I were back there in '76, seeing her for the first time but knowing how it would all turn out. Would I have done anything differently? Yeah, a lot of things—for one, I wouldn't have let her go at Kinsman.

I took out the 2008 register and jotted quickly:

Pushing on to Garfield Ridge, another day and a half, maybe. Willow, I'm coming.
Sojourner, ME=>GA '76, ME=>GA '08

I didn't wait for the baked goods. I thanked Alex anyway, shouldered my backpack, and headed out.

* * *

Another call from Gracie, another shock, and I wasn't sure how to take it.

It was the Fourth of July. Rachel had left Sadie's place the day before. She would be in Vermont's Green Mountains now, a rolling, densely forested ridge of hardwoods, especially sugar maple. From the trail you could see the pipes coming off the maple taps and then through the woods, miles of pipes that canted down the steep mountain sides like thrown ropes, eventually disappearing into the undergrowth. Sometimes the pipes crossed the trail itself. They had been buried in the trail once, but a million footfalls had exposed them in places, scuffed and gray in the duff.

I thought that Rachel had probably made it as far as the Thistle Hill shelter that previous day. There was a nice stream nearby, as I recalled. I found out later, though, that she had made it all the way to Winturri shelter, with its little stone spring out front. That was more than 26 miles in one day! Rachel's two-day rest in Hanover had paid off in big miles.

So on the Fourth, by the time Gracie called, Rachel would have been at Kent Pond and that miles-long boardwalk through the swampy woods, only a day or two from Sherburne Pass and Ryan's parents. Rachel had promised to call us from there, and then I would be able to tell her that she had a niece or nephew on the way.

Angelina was pregnant.

* * *

Things began to fall apart in Iraq in August. We hadn't heard from Tommy since the day in July that Saddam Hussein's depraved sons had been killed. People had celebrated that, but then there had been a bombing at the Jordanian embassy. On August 19, when the Canal Hotel was bombed, Rachel was somewhere in Shenandoah National Park, hiking along Skyline Drive, wary of bears, and having to compete with Boy Scouts for shelter at night. The UN envoy, Sergio Vieira de Mello, had been killed in the blast. People were shocked by his senseless death. Many UN workers had also been killed. I read the names in the paper the next day, and I saw Jenny Peay among them.

* * *

Rachel's pace was slowing. She called us from Damascus, Virginia on Judith's birthday. It was a Monday evening. Judith and I hadn't planned anything special for that day, so I brought home a nice Italian red wine, and I cooked dinner. We ate by candlelight on the back porch. It had been hot that day, but the evening was cool and quiet, the air fragrant with herbs. Judith had slipped into a clingy white shift that molded seductively to her hips and flat stomach, but she looked weary.

"Long day?" I asked.

"Yeah," she sighed. She sipped her wine. "Some of the kids we're getting...well, they act out. Their parents don't care. They expect us to handle it. I try—we all do—but it's hard. It takes away from the other kids. It's not fair."

"I'm sorry," I said.

"Well," she shrugged and finished off her wine, "it's just the way it is."

I took her bare feet into my lap and worked my thumbs into her soles.

"Mmmm," she moaned.

"Better now?"

"Lots. Don't stop."

She settled into her chair and closed her eyes while I worked at the soreness in her arches. And then the phone rang.

"Oh, please don't answer it," she groaned, eyes languidly closed.

"It might be Rachel," I said. "Stay put." I patted her silken calf. "I'll be right back."

I answered the phone and sure enough:

"Rachel? Honey, where are you?"

"I'm in Damascus."

I had been noticing that Rachel's voice was becoming huskier, deeper. Judith thought I was imagining things.

"But honey, you should be in the Smokies by now. Are you all right?"

"I'm fine, Dad. I've just been taking my time."

"Rachel?" Judith came on the other line.

"Hi, Mom. Happy birthday."

"Thanks sweetie. Where are you?"

"I was just telling Dad—I'm in Damascus. Me and some friends are going to hang out for a few days."

"But honey," that was me, "it's going to start getting cold. You need to get through the Smokies."

"We will, Dad. Don't worry. I just wanted to say 'happy birthday' to Mom. I'll call again, maybe from Erwin or Hot Springs. Love you. Bye."

I hung up the phone, feeling perplexed. I went to the calendar I had hung on the wall in the kitchen, each day of Rachel's hike marked with an *X*, with notes from her calls and emails. I made a notation for September 15: *Damascus.* Judith came up behind me.

"She's slowing down," Judith said, perusing my calendar closely.

"Yeah." I counted the days. "If she doesn't get moving she won't finish until October."

"Oh, no," Judith said with a sarcastic smile. "She'll miss your birthday."

"Aw c'mon, Judith."

Judith went thoughtful, then softly stroked my face.

"I know you hoped she would finish on your birthday, Carlton, but this is her hike. She gets to do what she wants."

"I know, but still—"

"Poor man." She pouted the way she did when she was teasing me, but then she leaned in and kissed my cheek. "Let Rachel finish what she's doing, and you come and finish what you were doing."

She smiled seductively and I smiled back. Not sure if I could still lift her but determined to try anyway, I swept her into my arms and carried her to our bedroom.

* * *

There were bombings every day in Iraq, fighting between rival militias that caught our soldiers in the middle. It was jarring to watch this on the news, a sorry business. Tommy sent abbreviated emails, short on words and even shorter on details. He was fine, hoping to rotate home soon. He wanted to be there for Angelina. He was excited. Had we talked to her?

Gracie called periodically, but there wasn't much to talk about. Evelyn was a nightmare, she said. Otherwise we were all waiting; waiting for Angelina, waiting for Tommy—and waiting for Rachel.

* * *

Rachel called on October 11, a Saturday. It was midafternoon.

"Rachel!" I exclaimed. "Honey, where are you?"

"I'm in Gainesville, Dad."

"Gainesville? *Georgia?*"

"Yeah."

"Then you mean—"

"Yeah, Dad. I finished a few days ago."

There was a melancholy note in her voice, while I wanted to shout my joy into the phone.

"Honey, why didn't you call?"

"I don't know, Dad. It felt weird. I needed to be alone, you know?"

"Yeah, honey, I know."

I remembered my days in that Gainesville motel room clearly, those feelings of displacement, mental fatigue and loss. I had tried, but had never been able to satisfactorily explain these feelings to others. No one but thru-hikers really got it. Everyone else thought it was strange, or at the least, eccentric. Of course Judith understood. Now Rachel had gone through it, too.

"Can I talk to Mom?" Rachel asked.

"Oh, sorry, honey. She's at the grocery store."

"Oh, well..." Her voice trailed off; then: "Dad? I'm ready to come home."

"That's great, honey. That's great." I wiped my eyes.

"I'll see you soon."

"You too, honey. Love you."

Rachel got home on Monday the thirteenth, Columbus Day. Her plane didn't arrive until four in the afternoon, but I took the whole day off anyway. Judith went into work, but she came home for lunch and stayed. We were so anxious we couldn't be still. Judith washed all of Rachel's sheets—again—then fussed around cleaning the house. I made a stew in the slow-cooker, big chunks of meat and potatoes. And I toasted some baguettes with cheese. Rachel may have been off the trail for a few days, but she would still be starving. I remembered.

Judith and I went into baggage claim to meet Rachel. We were a little early yet. There were only a few people there, either waiting for passengers or else waiting for the luggage carousel to start up. We peered through the glass security doors toward the concourse, looking for the sudden swarm of disembarking passengers that would tell us that Rachel was on the way.

It wasn't long. Suddenly the concourse was a flurry of activity, passengers trailing their carry-ons, cutting across one another to head in different directions. A mob of them came into baggage claim all at once. I tipped up on my toes to see over their heads, but I didn't spot Rachel. After some minutes a buzzer sounded and the luggage carousel began to turn, and then the luggage abruptly began to come out, like a tight procession. It reminded me of the students at Rachel's graduation, suddenly emerging from the hidden corners, filing along evenly before turning to march down the middle.

In a brief flurry, passengers grabbed their bags and then scattered, draining out of baggage claim like water from a rusty cattle trough. Judith wore a puzzled frown. She walked up to the security door and peered through. I spotted Rachel's backpack on the carousel. I recognized it right away, although it was worse for the wear since the last time I had seen it. The black rip-stop fabric was sun-bleached around the top. There were duct-taped patches in places. One of the shoulder straps seemed to be holding on only because of the tape. Rachel's trekking poles were tied together and fastened between the shoulder straps, again with duct tape. The poles were scratched and pitted. One of the carbide tips was missing.

I went to fetch Rachel's backpack. Judith wandered over with a worried look.

"Where do you think she is?" Judith asked.

"You didn't see her in there?"

"No. She would have called if there had been a problem."

I looked over at the security doors.

"Hey! There she is!"

Judith spun around with a smile of expectant joy, which was only slightly tempered by what we saw. Rachel was as thin as I knew she would be, but it was still hard to process. She wasn't wearing anything that she had left home with. She had on olive cargo pants with duct-taped knees, a faded long-sleeved denim shirt under a green fleece vest, cheap sneakers, also bound in duct tape, and a red bandana Aunt Jemima-style on her head. She had cut her hair, and not evenly. What little ponytail she had remaining looked like a worn out broom.

Rachel grinned and waved and picked up her pace a step. Her teeth stood out brightly from a dark, coppery tan. I dropped her backpack, then found myself in an undeclared race with Judith to reach Rachel first. Rachel banged through the doors triumphantly, and I scooped her into my arms.

"Oh, Rachel, honey," I practically cried. Even though I knew what to expect, it was still a shock. Rachel felt like a bundle of sticks, her sharp bones poking into me. She seemed as light and frail as balsawood, although there was a ropey hardness in her muscles. She still smelled like the trail—wood, smoke, DEET, soil and sweat— all combined into an earthy scent that wouldn't wash away for a while.

"Dad," Rachel smiled. "Sorry it took so long. I had to run to the bathroom. I think the food they gave us on the plane wasn't very good."

I kissed her cheek.

"I'm just glad you're home."

"Me, too. It feels like—"

"Years?"

"Yeah. It's weird. But you look just the same, Dad." She scratched the whiskers on my cheek and grinned.

"Well, *you* look a little different."

Rachel chuckled.

"Yeah I guess." She pushed back and looked over my shoulder at her mother. "Mom!"

Somehow Rachel loosed from my embrace then swooped into another embrace with her mother. Both women held fast, nose to nose, eye to eye. Judith's cheeks were wet, but Rachel's were as dry as a pleasant night in shelter. I noticed some freckles that hadn't been there before.

"Oh, sweetie," Judith cried. "We're so proud of you. So proud."

"I missed you, Mom."

"I missed you, too. I want you to tell me about all your adventures. But oh, sweetie, your hair—" Judith ran tentative fingers through the stubby brush of Rachel's ponytail, as if afraid there might be another surprise in there somewhere. I had to laugh. Rachel couldn't weigh more than ninety pounds, and she was tanned darker than a coconut shell, but Judith was more concerned about Rachel's hair.

"It'll grow back, Mom," Rachel said self-consciously.

I hefted Rachel's backpack.

"Okay, ladies," I said. "Time to go."

They walked behind me, arm in arm, gossiping about this and that, speaking faster than I could follow, as if in some mysterious language between women. I loaded them into the minivan. Rachel took the rear seat and held her backpack close as if it were a talisman.

"Oh, Dad," she blurted as we pulled out of the airport. "Can you stop at a KFC on the way? I am *craving* fried chicken. What's up with that?"

"I remember that feeling," I laughed. "I've got a *huge* stew waiting for you, but I bet you could eat a bucket of chicken *and* the stew."

"Yeah, I think so," she grinned. Judith looked over the seat and grinned with her.

When we got home I carried Rachel's backpack into our spotlessly-cleaned house. Rachel followed along absently, grazing from her chicken bucket.

"Uh, Carlton?" Judith said, wrinkling her nose. "Why don't you put that in the laundry room."

She meant Rachel's backpack. I laughed and pinched my nose.

"Uh, yeah."

Rachel spent an hour in the bathroom. I could hear her in there, scrubbing her skin, draining and refilling the tub. When she came out she wore baggy jeans and a white shirt with the tails tied around her waist, what waist she had left.

"I lost some weight," she said, smiling. "Nothing fits."

"I told you," I winked.

"I know," she said, still smiling.

We all went to the table outside. Rachel and Judith sat while I dished out the stew.

"Still hungry?" I asked Rachel. The look she gave me was irreplaceable.

"Please hurry," she said, fork in hand.

We all laughed, and when the stew was gone, and Rachel took on that warm sated glow, her eyes heavy, I walked her to bed, turned out the light, and gazed at her while she slept.

* * *

It was the very next weekend, Sunday. I got up that morning and found Judith and Rachel already at the breakfast table. I poured a cup of coffee and joined them.

"When did you start drinking coffee?" I asked Rachel. She was already beginning to get some weight back. She couldn't quite tie the tails of her shirt anymore, although her arms still looked like chicken bones. She hadn't been feeling well for a couple of days. There were yellowish circles under her eyes.

"Oh, Dad," she replied, trying to smile but she seemed pensive. "You know how cold it gets up there."

"Yeah, I do."

I flipped open the newspaper, glanced over it at Judith. She was unusually quiet this morning. Her eyes and nose were red.

"I hope you're not getting sick, too," I said to Judith. I turned to Rachel. "You checked for ticks, right? You didn't get Lyme Disease, did you?"

"No, Dad. I didn't get Lyme Disease."

"Maybe just a cold then."

I returned my attention to the paper, but then a thought occurred to me.

"We haven't talked about your plans, Rachel. You know, school? You can still enroll in January."

"Yeah, well, Dad—I don't know about that."

"Huh?" I lowered the paper. Judith's eyes looked as if they were about to spill. "What do you mean?" I asked with rising apprehension.

You might have thought that Rachel would hedge and stall, that she would fiddle and fidget while her mind worked around it, but the trail had matured her. She looked me right in the eyes, firmly, forthrightly. She didn't blink.

"Dad, I'm pregnant."

It took a moment. I couldn't understand those words. I twitched my head in confusion.

"What did you just say?"

"I'm pregnant, Dad."

No, that couldn't be right.

"Don't say things like that, honey. It's not funny."

I rattled my newspaper, scanned a column and tried to put her words aside.

"I'm not trying to be funny, Dad."

There was something in her tone. I lowered the paper slowly, glanced between Rachel and Judith. Rachel looked subdued. Judith had a hand over her eyes. The newspaper fell from my hands and wafted onto the floor.

"Honey," I explained, leaning forward. I fought to keep my voice level. "You can't be. You're only eighteen. You just have a cold or something."

"Carlton?" Judith reached out a hand. Her face was red and strained. I had never seen her look so distraught. Suddenly my chest felt heavy.

"Dad," said Rachel. Her lips were trembling a bit. She had a flighty look in her eyes. "I took a test this morning. It came out blue."

"What does that mean?"

"It means—"

"Carlton," Judith interrupted in a feeble voice. "We're going to have to deal with this."

I looked back and forth between the both of them, still puzzled, still in denial, and then the reality of it distilled out of my bewildered thoughts and I stiffened.

"You mean," this to Rachel, "when you were on the trail you—"

"Yes, Dad."

I pushed back from the table with a screech and leapt to my feet.

"Oh, God damn it, Rachel!"

"Carlton, *please*," begged Judith.

"It was an accident, Dad," Rachel said with a quiver in her voice, although she held onto her composure otherwise. "I didn't think I could. We were hiking so hard. I didn't have my period in forever."

"*Stop!*" I shouted, covering my ears. I didn't want to hear these things. "I *knew* this would happen! *I knew it!*"

"*Dad?*" That beseeching aspect in her voice would have cut right through me in any other circumstance, but at that moment I was too furious to notice.

"*Who did it? What's his name?*"

"It doesn't matter, Dad."

"*The hell it doesn't!*"

"Carlton," Judith said sternly. "This isn't helping. Please sit down."

"*I don't want to sit down, damn it!*"

Judith flinched at that outburst, but Rachel just sat there, a portrait in stone with a chiseled edge of—not anger, not indignation, not defensiveness, but...disappointment. I felt my stomach fall out.

"Oh, damn it—"

I spun around and gazed out the window, seeing nothing. Every hope and dream I had ever had for my daughter had fallen apart in an instant. Every fear that I had ever dared to contemplate lay before me. I buried my face in my hands and fought back a sob.

"Dad?"

Rachel was at my back, her arms around me, holding tight even as my arms fell to my sides and I stood there as unyielding as an enraged moose in the Maine woods. I tried to shrug away but she wouldn't let me.

"Dad?"

She got around me and held me from the front, burrowing into my chest and clutching me so tightly with her subtle, ropey strength that I couldn't catch my breath. She pressed her cheek to mine, holding tighter still so that I couldn't turn away.

"Dad," she whispered in my ear, her humid breath filling me with shame. "It's okay. It'll be okay."

She took my face in her willowy fingers and looked into me with her mother's familiar earnestness. I trembled. A gurgle rose in my throat.

"I can see, Dad." Her lips moved against my cheek, warm, soft and sure. "I can *see*."

My heart throbbed and ached. These weren't the innocent, playful exclamations of my little girl, my baby, but the measured words of a young woman. My knees went weak. I thought I would fall but she held me. My face broke then, and there was nowhere to hide. Judith came up and embraced us, holding us together.

"It'll be okay," Judith breathed soothingly. She brushed the hair out of my eyes. "Carlton, it'll be okay."

* * *

Rachel told us the story. I didn't want to hear it even as I *needed* to hear it. This was the hardest on me yet. I sat numbly and listened.

The father was Tollbooth Tom, a Southie from Boston whose off-trail name was Thomas Tiller. They met at the hostel in Gorham, shared some pizza and beer, then started out together toward the White Mountains. It was innocuous enough, but then he started flirting with her, carrying on all the way to Lakes of the Clouds. These attentions annoyed Rachel, so she took off alone out of Lakes of the Clouds, hiking at a brisk pace, thinking she would never see him again. She had forgotten all about him when, more than a month and a half later (which on the trail seems like a year), he managed to catch up with her at Harpers Ferry.

Rachel was a much stronger hiker. Tollbooth Tom drove himself hard to keep pace with her, sometimes hiking late into the night in order to reach her at the next shelter. It was pitiful to watch, Rachel said. He would drag in, hours late and bone-weary, with stripes of poison ivy blisters on his legs, and yet somehow he still had the wherewithal to flash his cheeky wide smile and crack wise in his peculiar Boston accent. By the time they had transited Virginia she was feeling sorry for him. At the same time, she admired his effort. It had happened at a hostel in Damascus.

"Do you love him?" I asked soberly. My eyes were still damp from before.

She shook her head. "No, not really. I mean he's nice." She turned to her mother and smiled faintly. "Wicked good looking, too. I like him a lot, but I don't want to marry him or anything."

"We can call Dr. Petrosyan," I said uncertainly. I looked to Judith. Her lips were pursed. She shook her head sharply in warning.

"Why?" asked Rachel.

"Well, uh...never mind." A quarter century later and there was still no way to broach that subject. I shook it off. "Honey, what do you want to do?"

"What *can* I do, Dad? I'm going to have a baby."

She didn't say this cavalierly. If anything, she was behaving more maturely than I had when I learned about Tommy. But still, I thought she was shrugging this off too easily.

"Rachel, it's hard. You're too young for this—and you have your whole future to think about."

"I have thought about it, Dad. I know I can handle it."

"*How* do you know?"

"Because *you* did."

Children are worse than sea lawyers. They dissect your stories over the years, memorizing every detail and drawing conclusions where they will, and then they throw them back at you as if citing doctrine. I sighed and massaged my temples.

"That was different, honey. I got married."

"You want me to *marry* him?"

"No, honey, that's not what I meant. But doing it all by yourself—"

"You'll help me. Won't you?" I sat back and sighed once more. Rachel turned to her mother. "Mom, you'll help. Right?"

"Sweetie, of course we'll help, but..."

"I don't mean all the time," Rachel added quickly, "just sometimes."

"Rachel," I asked wearily. "What will you do for money?"

"Starbucks," she chirped with a smile. I couldn't tell if that was youthful optimism or naiveté. "And I'll get an apartment. Maybe after the first, if that's okay."

"We'll talk about that later." I drug myself up. "I need to go lay down for a while."

"You just got up," Judith said.

"It doesn't feel like it."

* * *

We were still sorting all of that out a week later when we received an email from Tommy. He had managed to wrangle two weeks of leave out of the Army, and expected to be in Nashville no later than November 5. He wished he could come out to California, but there wouldn't be enough time. He was sorry about the short notice. Maybe we could fly out to Nashville for a few days. He would love to see Rachel. He wanted to hear about all of her adventures on the Appalachian Trail, but he understood if we couldn't make it.

Rachel was ecstatic to go. I'm not sure she had thought through what might happen when Tommy found out about her...well, *condition*. Maybe he would be supportive, maybe he wouldn't. I should have known him well enough to anticipate how he would react, but really, I didn't, and that brought a pang. I probably could have gotten some time off of work. Judith wasn't as sure whether she could, but it wound up not mattering anyway.

On November 2, Tommy boarded a Chinook helicopter bound for Baghdad International Airport and his flight home. The Chinook was blown out of the sky near Fallujah by a surface-to-air missile. Tommy and sixteen fellow soldiers died.

***

Gracie is the one who called with the news. She reached me on my cellphone at work the next day. She could barely speak through her sobs, crying as if Tommy were her own son. But then, yeah, he was in a way; not only as her son-in-law, but also all that had come before. I brought home a bottle of bourbon that night, took one guilty sip then poured the rest out.

Evelyn and I argued on the phone. I shouted with such pent-up rage and frustration that Rachel covered her ears and fled the room, dripping tears. Judith dropped onto the couch and looked on, her eyes puffy and red-rimmed. I wanted to bring Tommy home, have him buried in the Carlton cemetery with his family. Evelyn wanted him buried at Arlington National Cemetery. He had earned it; he deserved it. The country owed it to him, she spat bitterly. She had been to Dover Air Force Base to witness the Dignified Transfer as Tommy's flag-draped coffin was carried solemnly from the tail of the C-130 by the honor guard. She had made all the necessary inquires, she said. Why did I have to argue about this?

In the end, it wasn't up to us. Angelina was his wife. It was her decision to make, as much as that chafed Evelyn. And I wasn't going to argue with Angelina, it wouldn't be right. Angelina wanted him buried in the Nashville National Cemetery, where he would be close and she could visit him often. That was her decision. Evelyn and I had no choice but to accept it.

The funeral was held at noon on November the twelfth, the day after Veterans Day. Thousands of flags still lined the pathways and adorned every marker, a field of red, white and blue flapping and snapping in the gray breeze. There hadn't been enough space left for a coffin burial at Nashville National Cemetery for ten years or more, so Tommy had been cremated.

I sat in the open-air memorial shelter, protected from the chill spitting rain, if not the wind. Rachel and Judith were beside me on one end. Gracie and Angelina were in the middle, while Evelyn, Brad and Luke took up the other end. Mom was in the row behind us with Jane and Jerry. I felt as if I had abandoned her to them, but there was no more room up front. At least she had Sadie between her and the Hanshaws. Angelina was stoic, her firm mask given away only by her trembling lips. Her hands rested on her swollen belly. Evelyn looked old, her face red and wet. She held a handkerchief to her nose. Her hands shook.

Now I knew how Dad felt when Leavitt was brought home, and that twisted something inside me that I thought I had put away long ago. I glanced at Sadie over my shoulder, wondering if she was having similar thoughts. She sat somberly, her eyes as dark as winter. She had Mom's hand in her lap and was kneading it absently. She looked up and acknowledged my gaze with a pained nod. I nodded in return, hovering for a moment before turning back to the service.

Tommy's urn was a polished wooden box no larger than a shoe box. The honor guard drew it from the hearse as if it were a full-sized coffin, exercising the same solemn decorum. An officer stood to the side with a flag that had already been folded into a tight triangle. It didn't seem right. It couldn't be possible that all that remained of Tommy, of my son, was contained in that little box; all of his laughter as a child, his sparkling blue eyes, the way he doted on Rachel. It just couldn't be.

"Are you okay?" Judith asked me quietly. She took my hand and squeezed. I sniffed and nodded.

The familiar ceremony was performed. An officer presented Angelina with the flag. *On behalf of a grateful nation...*

Angelina broke down then. *Gracie* put a comforting arm around her. Evelyn looked over grudgingly, tears streaming down her cheeks. I expected her to wail and make a scene, but she didn't. Her clasped fingers were strained white and her teeth were pressed hard together, but she kept up appearances. I clenched my jaw to hold back my own bitterness and tears.

That damned war.

Afterward, Rachel ran to Luke and they hugged one another, rocking slowly as they cried into each other's shoulders. Luke would be twenty-one in a little over a week, but in that moment Rachel looked more like his big sister. She was his height. Luke would never be as tall as Tommy or me. He had mature features now, an angular, masculine face, a thin goatee, but he still seemed withdrawn, fragile. His face was pale under a wavy forelock of black hair. Evelyn pretended not to notice this display between siblings, something she couldn't control. She and Brad stood together grimly, not even holding one another. She dabbed at her eyes and avoided looking into anyone else's.

Once Luke and Rachel had cried themselves out, Luke approached me with such a forlorn, broken look on his face that I took him into my arms without a thought, and held him as I had never held him in his life.

"Father," he cried.

There was so much need in his tremulous voice, but what could I give him?

"I know, Luke. I know."

I hugged him to my chest as Judith looked on, signaling her approval with tight lips and a slight nod. I gave him a light pat on the back.

"Go to your mother, Luke. She'll need you now."

I didn't mean that the way it sounded. If Luke took it that way he didn't let on. He stood back from me and wiped his nose, a vulnerable longing in his eyes.

"Yes, Father," he said emptily. He went and stood by his mother, anonymous in her shadow. What more was there? Nothing.

Judith squeezed my hand.

"He needs you, Carlton," she said.

"I don't know what I can do for him."

"You can be his father."

"He's got Brad for that."

"It's not the same, Carlton."

"Isn't it?"

She shook her head sadly.

"You can be so blind sometimes."

"What does that mean?"

"It means..." She gave me a cross look. "Forget it. I need to give my sympathies to Angelina and Gracie. Are you coming?"

"Sure."

Angelina and Gracie were still seated, holding one another. We eased through the people gathered around them. Judith bent over and took Angelina's hand.

"I'm so sorry," Judith said somberly. "If there's anything I can do."

"Thank you," Angelina sniffed. She held the flag to her chest as if it were her baby, born early.

"How long can you stay, Carlton?" Gracie asked me.

"We have to leave tomorrow."

"So soon?"

"It's work," I said. "I wish you all could come out."

"I don't think that's possible." She glanced at Angelina's stomach.

"When's it due?"

"End of the month, first of December."

"Gracie, I—I hate to leave you alone with this, and with..."

Gracie and I looked over at Evelyn. Gracie shrugged and put on a pained smile.

"It's okay, Carlton. We'll be fine...or as well as we can be."

* * *

Tom Lee Jeffries, Jr. was born the next day, November 13, while Judith, Rachel and I were still in the air flying home from the funeral. It was the stress, we were told. At least three weeks premature, he only weighed five and a half pounds. But Gracie said he was fine. Mother and son were fine.

"How does it feel to be a grandfather?" Gracie asked me on the phone.

"I feel old," I said. "How about you?"

* * *

Judith and I flew back to Nashville for Christmas. Rachel was desperate to go with us, but she had landed a holiday job at the bookstore, which had moved from its old location on Shaw to a larger building on North Blackstone across from our new mall, the River Park Shopping Center.

"I want to go so bad," she told her mother and me, stamping her foot in frustration. "My manager, Dusty—he's a real nice guy, but I can't ask him for time off. Not now, anyway. I mean, that's why he gave me the job, to work at Christmas."

"That's what you get when you have responsibilities," I told her with undisguised paternal smugness. She was starting to show now. Her shirt formed around her softly rounded stomach. I averted my gaze uncomfortably.

"Yeah, thanks Dad, I know," she flipped right back at me.

Judith stayed out of this one. She was always wiser than me that way.

We arrived in Nashville on a brisk but clear evening, feeling almost as if we hadn't been home at all since the funeral.

"Is it me?" I asked Judith. "Or are those flights getting longer and longer?"

"It feels that way" she sighed.

Judith rested her head wearily on my shoulder as we walked to baggage claim. Mom met us there. We gathered our bags, and then Mom led us out to her new Buick Rendezvous, an SUV. It seemed a peculiar car for an eighty-three year old woman to be driving, but then, Mom always did like Buicks.

"The new Buicks are too small," she complained. "This one's easy to get in and out of."

I laughed. Mom seemed so small behind the wheel of that thing. I tried to visualize Grandmother Villetta driving something like this, but couldn't. And yet...with the right expression Mom looked just like Grandmother now. Even her cotton-candy white hair. That gave me a disturbing pang. I shook it off. Mom was still healthy and spry, with good color in her cheeks. If she went as long as Grandmother had, she would be with us for a long, long time to come.

The first thing I wanted to do after we put our things away at the house was to go out and see the dogs. There were only two of them now, Dolly and Daisy. Mirabel had passed away the year after Dad died. She had only been eleven years old. The vet said Mirabel had died of the dog equivalent of a heart attack, nothing we could have done.

Dolly and Daisy had been sired by Rockford, who had come from Patton, a male from Mirabel's and Langley's last litter. Their mother had been sent up from a kennel in Louisiana that Dad had established a relationship with. Dad had kept a detailed breeding book, which Mom still had. There had been so many puppies from Langley and Mirabel—and now their descendants—that it was impossible to keep them straight otherwise. Mom wasn't breeding them anymore, though. It was too much work.

Mom came out with me to see the dogs. She wrung her hands.

"Rockford was such a frisky boy," she said with a trace of guilt. I knew what was coming next, but I listened patiently as she told me again, as if she needed the confession to assuage her conscience. "He got out of the kennel. I thought I had locked the door."

"I'm sure you did, Mom." I put an arm around her.

"And then...well, you know. He got onto Harding Place and was hit."

"I know, Mom," I consoled her. "Rockford was a handful. He probably got his paw through somehow and slipped the latch." I had said the same thing before, and with the same lack of effect.

The familiar sound of thumping tails greeted us at the door. I went inside and knelt to pet Dolly and Daisy. Even though they had come from the same litter, Dolly was larger, like a big sister. At three years old, they still had puppy ways, mischievous and over-eager to play. They both jumped on me and slobbered on my jacket.

"Okay, girls, that's enough." I turned to Mom. "I'll take them out for a long walk tomorrow if the weather's nice."

"They'll like that," she said. "I can't take them far anymore."

The dogs would have to wait, though. First thing the next morning, Judith and I went to see Gracie and Angelina, and of course, Tom, Jr. Angelina was staying with Gracie for the time being. It was Angelina who met us at the door. She didn't have her figure back yet, but it wouldn't be long now. She smiled broadly, still with a tinge of sadness. I couldn't get over her smile. She had her mother's petite, exotic face, but that smile came from someone else.

"Hello Judith, Carlton. Please come in. Mama has Tommy in the bedroom. She'll be along."

For just a moment I thought she meant my Tommy. I winced inwardly when I realized how foolish that was.

"You look beautiful, Angelina," said Judith. Angelina blushed.

"Thank you, but I don't feel that way." There was a charming combination of southern and Latin in Angelina's accent these days, precisely-pronounced syllables and an emphasis on *ee* sounds, all mingled with the lazy *ah* vowels of southern-speak.

"You will," Judith said knowingly. She rested a reassuring hand on Angelina's shoulder as we went inside.

We settled in the living room. Gracie's law practice had grown over the years. She could easily have afforded an airy house in Brentwood, or one of the new Mc-Mansions that were replacing the stately homes in Green Hills, but she preferred her cozy brick house off of Antioch Pike. The place was looking aged, though. The air smelled like cilantro and garlic.

"Carlton! Judith!" Gracie came out of the bedroom, a cloth diaper over her shoulder. "I'm so glad you're here." We hugged and then Gracie gave me an eager look. "Are you ready to see your grandson?"

"Sure."

We went into the bedroom. Tom Junior was asleep in his crib, on his back in a blue onesie, his little arms splayed like a puppy spreading its legs in the shade on a hot day. He had gained a healthy amount of weight. His lips made sucking motions as he slept. I looked for some resemblance to Tommy, but there wasn't any that I could see, at least yet. He had Latin features: black hair, black brows, and olive skin. Judith clasped her hands and fawned.

"He's such a pretty baby," she said admiringly to Angelina.

"Yes he is, and so hungry all the time."

Gracie laughed.

"Well, Carlton?" she asked me. "How does it feel?"

"What's that? Oh, yeah. I don't know. Strange, I guess. How about you?"

"I feel like an old lady."

"Oh, Mama," moaned Angelina.

"Let's go visit while Tommy's sleeping," said Gracie.

We returned to our places in the living room, but then Angelina stood abruptly.

"Oh," she said. "I'm sorry. I need to go and—" She looked at me and blushed, then turned to Judith. "I have to...you know." She made a pumping gesture with her hand.

"Uh...right," said Judith, standing. "Let me help you with that."

"No, it's okay."

"I don't mind, Angelina."

They went off to the kitchen, leaving Gracie and me alone.

"Poor Angelina," I said. "I remember when Judith had to do that."

"Sometimes they get so full it hurts," Gracie said, raising a hand to her breasts.

"Uh, yeah." Now I was bushing. "So," I said to change the subject, "how's it going with Evelyn?"

Gracie exhaled an exasperated breath.

"I want her to know her grandson, but she's making us crazy. The other day I had to tell her to stop it, you know? She acts like we're the hired help, but I'm not going to put up with that and I told her so."

"Ouch! What did she do then?"

"She got all high and mighty the way she does, but I think she got the message. I mean, it's been a whole *day* since she's called."

We both laughed.

"I'm sorry, Gracie. I wish there was something I could do."

"Not unless you can go back a long time and turn right instead of left."

That was just an old saying, but it happened to be uncomfortably true in my case.

"I wish I had," I mumbled. "Who could have thought, after everything, that you would be stuck with Evelyn in your life?"

Gracie chuckled. "Yeah, I would never have predicted this."

Our conversation trailed off after that. I rubbed my palms. They were sweating for some reason. I pondered Rachel's situation. Gracie had been through it, and she had done well for herself. She didn't know about Rachel's condition. We hadn't told anyone except Mom, Lois and Eugene.

"Gracie?" I asked. "How did you do it, raising Angelina by yourself, I mean?"

She blew a breath.

"It was hard, but it wasn't terrible. Mama and Papa helped me. You have to be strong, Carlton, that's all."

"And you were still able to go to college, too."

"Yeah."

"I never did."

"I know."

"Will it be like that for Angelina? Do you think the kids today can do what you did?"

"I don't see why not. Angelina will be fine. Anyway, she already has her degree, so it won't be as hard for her."

"But without Tommy..." I mused darkly. "Did Angelina's father ever help you?"

"No." She shook her head sharply. "He doesn't even know."

"A father should know he has a child," I blurted without thinking.

"Not this father," she said with an edge.

"I'm sorry, Gracie. I didn't mean that. But..." I wasn't sure I had a right to ask, but someone out there was also a grandfather to my son's child. And I had been scratching at an itch for a long time, an itch I couldn't quite reach. "Gracie? Who is Angelina's father?"

"That's not important, Carlton." She had crossed her arms and was looking at me with smoldering eyes. I shuddered, remembering that look from long ago.

"Well—okay, never mind."

She looked up and took a deep breath, seemed to be working through something.

"Okay, Carlton." She wouldn't look at me. She rolled her tongue around her cheek, glanced at the kitchen door, then exhaled. "Okay, damn it, it was Kenny."

Of course! I should have put it together long ago, but still—

"*Kenny?*"

"Keep your voice down."

"Gracie?" lower now, "*Kenny?*"

"Yeah," she muttered morosely.

"But...but..."

"Ahh!" She tugged at her hair with both hands. "I must have lost my mind telling you. Carlton, you had better keep this to yourself. If you tell anyone..."

"I won't, I won't." My palms were really sweating now. I wiped them on my pants. "But Gracie—why Kenny?"

"Look." She fixed me with a hostile glare that resurrected an old wound. "We graduated, and just like that you were gone."

"Appalachian Trail," I mumbled.

"Uh, huh. The next thing I know, you and Evelyn are married. *Evelyn?* I never saw that coming. And all my friends were gone, off to college and such. It gets lonely, you know? Or I guess not. That never seemed to be one of your problems."

She spat that last out like long-awaited retribution.

"Gracie—"

"Carla had taken off for L.A.," she went on, "and Kenny was all by himself... It just happened. One time," she chuckled ironically, "that's all it took."

"I'm sorry, Gracie."

"I'm not. I have Angelina, and now Tommy Junior, so it all worked out. I was even going to tell Kenny once. Remember when he got out of rehab?"

"Uh, huh."

"I tried to look after him, to help him. You know I did."

"I know, Gracie."

"But he wouldn't stay clean. I won't bring that into our lives. Believe me, Angelina's better off not knowing."

"Have you seen Kenny?"

"Not for a long time."

* * *

That weighed on me as I took Dolly and Daisy for their walk. I took them up the hill, pausing at the cemetery, which had four stones now: Langley, Mirabel, Patton, and Rockford. Mom couldn't make it up the hill anymore, but she'd instructed the gardeners to maintain the cemetery. The grass was brown right now, and the trees were bare, but everything would green up in the spring to make a pretty, shaded refuge. Mom had put in a cement bench and a wrought-iron trellis. Dad would have been pleased.

I didn't take the dogs any farther up the hill. It was cold and wet, and besides, I didn't want to be reminded of Kenny, the way he had been when we were kids. I felt bad about him. Maybe I could have done something for him after all. I tried to shake that off. Why had it fallen on me to rescue him from himself? I remembered our last, painful meeting, that look of betrayal.

I needed you, man.

No he didn't. Just thinking about it made me angry, as if he were blaming me for his own damned weakness. And now we were tied together, the same way Gracie was stuck with Evelyn, carrying these hates and burdens with no way to escape them. I wouldn't live like that. I wouldn't. Why did Gracie even tell me? Had her burden become too heavy? She was right, though. No one could ever know. I wouldn't tell, not even Judith, because to do so would put that right in the middle of our lives. No, I wouldn't tell. And if I ever saw Kenny again, I wouldn't tell him either.

* * *

Rachel was offered a permanent position at the bookstore after Christmas, which kept her busy as her stomach swelled. We were talking over dinner one night in April.

"I still want my own apartment," she said firmly. This was directed at me, but Judith responded.

"After the baby's born, sweetie. Until then it doesn't make sense."

Rachel acquiesced to her mother, which is why Judith had cut in. If I had said the same thing there probably would have been an argument.

"How much longer are you going to work, honey?" I asked. Like her mother, Rachel was tall enough that she didn't waddle when she walked. Still, though, her belly was huge.

"Dr. Petrosyan says I can work all the way through May if I want to." I winced at that. Her ankles would swell and her feet would hurt, just as Judith's had. I still had trouble seeing a woman sitting there, and not my little girl. "And anyway," she went on, "I like working at the bookstore."

Well, at least it kept her distracted; me, too, for that matter. There was a topic we danced around every night, whether or not she should contact Tollbooth Tom—Thomas Tiller. A father should know he has a child, I thought, but at the same time I dreaded the idea of having to confront the man who had done this to my daughter. Rachel hated it when I said that, even though I clothed it in more gentle terms in her presence. It wasn't his fault, she argued. She had been there too, after all. Judith wanted Rachel to contact him for a variety of reasons, not the least of which would be child support. Rachel had been going back and forth with this, although of late she seemed less inclined.

"Maybe after the baby comes," she said. "I'll think about it then."

Soon it was May, and then June. Sometimes, when Rachel padded barefoot across the living room, her back arched and her belly leading the way, she looked so much like her mother during that time that I would get a knot in my throat and have to swallow hard. Rachel kept working all the way to the end. Dr. Petrosyan said it was okay, but that was little consolation to me.

"Remember what happened to Judith," I reminded him.

"I know, Carlton," he said soothingly.

Dr. Petrosyan had gone completely gray. He had bushy white eyebrows under a full head of platinum hair, which made his dark features even more pronounced. But he was handsomely lean and athletic, with the straight jaw and high cheeks of his lineage.

"Judith's case was very rare," he continued. "That's not going to happen to Rachel. She can work as long as she wants. It helps keep her from building up fluid."

Rachel was at the bookstore when her water broke. Her manager, Dusty, called me on my cellphone. I had met him, and I liked him. He was young, early thirties I think, with engaging eyes and an inviting smile. He didn't sound rattled on the phone, he was controlled and to the point: An ambulance had taken Rachel to the hospital. He had already called Judith. They were all fond of Rachel at the bookstore. He hoped we would call later and tell them how it went.

It was about noon on a Thursday, June 17. I was writing orders in Madera, not too far from Fresno, but I still found myself in a flying rush down the 99 that brought back memories of nineteen years earlier. I got stuck at the same red light, hopped the same curb and, for all that I could remember, hastily parked in the same place.

Judith met me in the lobby.

"It's a girl," she announced with a joyous smile. "They're both fine."

We went into Rachel's room. Rachel was in bed, propped up against some pillows, holding a sleeping baby to her chest.

"Hey Dad," she smiled weakly but proudly. "Come meet your granddaughter, April Swift."

TWENTY-TWO

April was a darling baby girl, bubbly and good-natured from the beginning. She won my absolute devotion the moment I set eyes on her. But that Viking red hair—

"Did Tollbooth Tom have red hair?" I asked Rachel after she and April had come home from the hospital. Referring to Thomas Tiller by his trail name helped me keep him in the abstract, easier to overlook. Both Rachel and Judith, having been imbued in Appalachian Trail culture themselves, never seemed to notice how I skirted around the identity of April's father.

"No," Rachel replied thoughtfully. "It was a kind of reddish brown, nothing like April's."

And then there were April's eyes. She was born with blue eyes, as bright as Tommy's had been, but they changed over the months, becoming as startlingly green as spring daffodils against late-season snow.

I had to hold her whenever I was home, before work in the mornings, after work in the evenings. I would rock her in the curve of my arm as she slept, all the while gazing hypnotically at her blushed cheeks and fine red lashes. The curve of her chin and her cute button of a nose were so much like her mother's as an infant. It wasn't long before April could grasp my finger in her tiny hand and draw it with surprising resolve to her mouth, where she would gum it contentedly.

"Gee, Dad," Rachel would chide me half-heartedly when she saw this. "Do you want to nurse her, too?"

Rachel was working full-time at the bookstore now, saving her money and talking about getting her own apartment. I was still ambivalent about that.

"What will you do with April?" I asked her, trying once more to deflect her from the idea. It was a weekend. Judith and I were at the breakfast table. I had April in my lap, while Rachel crossed back and forth getting ready for work.

"The same thing I do now, Dad," she answered in a harried tone laced with annoyance.

We had worked out a schedule in which Judith or I could look after April while Rachel was at work, but April still spent two days a week in daycare. I hated that.

After twenty years at Stefanelli's, I had the seniority to cut back my work load, perhaps to two or three days a week. I told Rachel as much.

"No, Dad," she objected. "I won't let you to do that. I told you, I can handle this."

"Carlton?" Judith reached over and patted my hand. "Let it go for now."

Judith wasn't enthusiastic about Rachel moving out either, but she was more accepting of the inevitable. And so when April was ten months old, coincidentally in the month of April, Rachel moved into a one-bedroom apartment at Jackson Park Place off of Herndon Avenue.

It was a nice apartment in a nice neighborhood. Judith and I helped her with the move, although it didn't take but a few trips in the minivan to get Rachel's things over there, mostly clothes and books. We let her have her bedroom furniture, which looked puny and girlish in its new environment of gold carpet, high ceilings and white walls. Lois and Eugene gave her a living room set, and her friends at work chipped in for dishes and cooking things. We got the whole move done before one o'clock on a pleasant Saturday afternoon.

I lingered, holding April, while Judith and Rachel ran around discussing curtains and such. Much too soon, they had discussed it all and it was time to go. I handed over April reluctantly. Judith squeezed my hand.

"Thanks, Dad," Rachel said. She gave me a good-bye kiss on the cheek, which contained a finality that made my chest ache.

"Maybe I should stay for a little while," I said. "You might want to move the couch over there, or—"

"It's time to go, Carlton," Judith said with damp eyes. She was doing only barely better than me. Her cheeks trembled.

We went home to our quiet house. Rachel and April had awoken there that morning, like any other day. Now they were gone. When Judith went out shopping after we finished lunch, I sat alone at the breakfast table and stared at the wall.

* * *

Gracie and Angelina finally came out to see us over the Fourth of July week. At nineteen months old, Tom Junior was a handful. Angelina wrestled with him as we headed out from baggage claim. It was late afternoon, hot of course. The air was hazy and bitter from exhaust.

"Poor Tommy," Judith commented to Angelina. "He must have been miserable cooped up on the plane."

"He was okay most of the way," said a weary Angelina. Tom whined and yanked at her hand. "But after we changed planes in Los Angeles I think he decided he'd had enough."

Gracie knelt tight-lipped and tapped Tom on the nose. That got his attention.

"He's a good boy," she said to us but looking at him. "He behaved very well most of the time."

Tom settled down under his grandmother's scrutiny, some subtle understanding between them. Gracie stood and shared a motherly, inside look with Judith, then the two walked on together, talking close. Angelina took Tom in tow, and I bundled after them with the luggage.

We had turned Rachel's room back into the guestroom it had once been. It would be a little tight with all three of them in there, but Gracie waved off my concerns with a polite smile.

"You know how small *my* house is," she said. "We'll be fine."

We went out back to the patio table and let Tom loose in the yard. Judith brought out cold sweet tea.

"It's very nice out here, Judith," Gracie commented, assuming correctly that our patio was Judith's creation and not mine. "I wish I had a nice place like this to sit outside."

"Oh," Judith demurred with a casual wave of her hand, "it's easy with our weather. It would be harder for you in Nashville, I think."

Tom had gotten his hands into some soil and was running it through his fingers. I watched him, thinking that at least he had his father's curiosity and ready smile. He didn't look like Tommy. Not at all. He was a well-balanced kid, though, taller than average for a toddler his age. He had dark eyes and a dark complexion. Maybe there was some of Tommy in his cheeks and around his eyes after all, but what I really saw when I looked at him was Kenny in a white T-shirt and shorts, with scuffed knees.

"When do we get to see that pretty baby girl?" Gracie asked.

"Rachel's on the way," I answered, turning away from Tom.

"So what do you think of your grandson?" Gracie asked expectantly.

"Oh, uh, he's a fine looking boy."

"Yes, he is," she said proudly.

"Knock, knock. Hello everybody."

Rachel came out through the kitchen with April on her hip. I hopped up and ran over with my arms out.

"Can't wait, huh Dad?" Rachel laughed.

She pecked me on the cheek then handed April over. I tickled April's lip and got a wet smile in return.

"Oh, look at that pretty girl," Gracie and Angelina gushed at the same time. "And Rachel," Gracie said with her arms open. "You look wonderful."

Rachel was wearing snug designer jeans and a satiny champagne shirt that tapered at the waist, and of late, a speck of a diamond in her right nostril.

"Thank you, Gracie." The two hugged, and then Rachel went to hug Angelina in turn. "Angelina, you look gorgeous," Rachel enthused to her sister-in-law.

Angelina had on a yellow pastel dress that hemmed at her knees, gold hoop earrings, and gold bracelets. She reminded me of a younger Gloria, James' wife. Angelina still wore her wedding ring.

"Gracias, Rachel," Angelina blushed.

I bounced April on my hip and carried her over. Judith and Rachel looked on warmly as Gracie and Angelina hovered over my granddaughter. I beamed at their praise, but then Gracie cleared her throat and gave me an inferred look.

"Aw."

I handed April over, then stood abjectly as Gracie adjusted April into the crook of an arm.

"Hi pretty girl," Gracie cooed.

"Hi," April said back with an adorable bunny-toothed grin.

"Oh, that's so precious."

April's repertoire of simple words was expanding fast, although she still didn't have an intelligible name for me, just a burble of syllables. She called Rachel *Mama*, and she called Judith *Mamam*, but I was still waiting.

"Where's Tommy?" asked Rachel. "Oh, there he is."

Rachel skipped over to Tom, kneeling in the grass at his side.

"Hi, big guy," she said, patting his head. "What have you got there?"

"Dirt," Tom answered with innocent glee. He displayed a handful and let it slip through his fingers.

I took a seat next to Judith and sipped some tea. Gracie and Angelina took their seats, April in Gracie's lap. We made small talk, Judith's school, Gracie's practice. Angelina was clerking in a law office and studying for her MBA. Gracie had gotten Evelyn under control, she claimed, although I doubted that. Rachel joined us and announced that she was going to be promoted to supervisor soon.

"What about college, Rachel?" Angelina asked. "Are you going to enroll?"

"I don't know." Rachel shrugged. "I like my job, and I'm doing okay."

"I wish you'd register for some classes," I said sourly, drawing *that* look from Judith. This was a sore topic.

"We've talked that to death, Dad," Rachel sighed. "Maybe when April's a little older."

"Mama," April whined on cue, throwing out her arms. Gracie laughed and passed her squirming bundle to Rachel.

"She's strong," Gracie commented. "I was afraid I would drop her."

"Strong-willed is more like it," Rachel said in exasperation. April continued to twist and struggle, so Rachel set her on her feet and patted her behind. "Go play with Tommy, then."

April waddled off across the grass. Angelina followed April thoughtfully then turned to Rachel.

"Have you decided about her father?" she asked. I tensed. Another sore topic.

"Not yet." Rachel shook her head. "One minute I want to, the next I don't. I can't make up my mind."

"He should be responsible for his daughter," Judith said for the hundredth time.

"I know, Mom, but—"

"I think things are fine the way they are," I threw in. Rachel glared at me.

"You told me a father should know he has a child," she snapped.

"Sure, honey, but...well—"

"I wish I knew my father," Angelina mused.

It was not something I think she meant to share, but there it was. I was more stunned than Gracie, she didn't miss a beat.

"We've talked about that, *mi hija*," she said, patting her daughter's hand gently but still firm in her resolve. She gave me a conspiratorial look. "And now is not a good time to discuss it."

Angelina looked wounded. This had obviously been a sore topic in *their* household. Judith came to the rescue.

"Well, time works these things out. Would anybody like some wine?"

Gracie jumped at that ruse. "Yes, I would. Let me help you with it."

Gracie and Judith got up and went to the kitchen, while Rachel and Angelina exchanged commiserating looks. I sat flustered, and decided that it was best if I held my tongue. Just then, April let out a cry. I looked over in alarm as April plopped onto her diapered bottom and then opened up with a full wail. Tom was throwing dirt, not directly at April, but around. I jerked myself up and raced over, swooped April off the grass then glowered at Tom.

"*What did you do to her, Tom?*" I shouted, more brusquely than I had intended. Tom froze in place, a clod of soil still in his hand. His lips trembled. Suddenly Rachel and Angelina were beside me.

"For God's sake, Dad," Rachel scolded me. "They're just playing."

"Tommy? Are you okay?" Angelina blurted in a rush, lifting her son into the sanctuary of her arms. She threw me a wary look and backed up a step. Tom buried his face in her shoulder.

"What happened?" Judith and Gracie asked in unison. They came out of the kitchen and hurried over.

"It's nothing, Mom," said Rachel with a roll of her eyes. "Just Dad being Dad." She lifted April out of my arms.

"Is Tommy all right?" Gracie asked, worried.

Angelina shot me a defiant look. "He's fine."

"I'm sorry," I sputtered. "I thought—"

Everyone moved off except Judith. She came up to me crossly, and under her breath said, "You know, you're *his* grandfather, too."

* * *

Rachel contacted Tollbooth Tom the week following Gracie and Angelina's visit, which had become uncomfortably strained after that first day. Rachel didn't tell me in advance, and she must not have confided in her mother either, because Judith would not have kept something that important from me.

Judith was pleased with Rachel's decision. I was outwardly supportive, if not enthusiastic. Inwardly I harbored the selfish hope that Tollbooth Tom would deny his part in this and brush the matter aside. If that happened, Rachel wouldn't go after him in court. She wouldn't force him into anything, she said. Judith didn't like that, and although I put on a solemn face about the matter, I felt reprieved. After all, it was going on two years since Rachel had been on the trail, and Tollbooth Tom lived clear across the country...

There was a knock at the door a little over two weeks later.

It was a blisteringly hot Saturday afternoon. I answered the door to find Rachel standing there. Puzzled, I wondered why she hadn't just come in. Then my eyes wandered to the right, to a young man in a brown suit, his beige tie cinched up tight around his perspiring neck. He was of average height and solid build, with wavy chestnut hair and a freshly-shaved ruddy complexion that was beginning to break out in the prickly heat. He had a gregarious smile and pale green eyes. April was in his arms.

"Hi, Dad," Rachel said cheerily.

"*Who is it, Carlton?*" Judith called from the other room.

"Uh, uh," I stammered. Rachel looked amused.

"Well? Can we come in, Dad?"

With a hop and a bounce, the man shifted April to the left side of his hip then held out his hand.

"Nice to meet you," he smiled eagerly. *Nice tah meechjah.* I recognized that accent from the trail. It was a Massachusetts accent, Boston more specifically. This was Tollbooth Tom.

I shook his hand in a daze, and then Rachel kind of pushed us inside and closed the door. Judith met us in the hallway.

"Who is this?" she asked, and then she smiled in realization. "You must be Thomas," she said cordially, offering her hand. Thomas shook it gently. "We've heard so much about you," she went on. "It's good to finally meet."

"Thank you, Mrs. Jeffries," he said bashfully.

"Come in and sit down," Judith offered then. "May I take your coat?"

"Ah, yeah." He passed April to Rachel then slipped out of his coat. "It's wicked hot out there."

Judith laughed. "Rachel didn't warn you?"

"Well, yeah, but—"

"Here," Judith took his coat, "you all go sit and I'll bring you some iced tea."

I was still in a clouded daze as I dropped into my recliner. Rachel and Thomas sat on the couch, a discreet space between them. Rachel held April in her lap. Thomas blew some damp hair out of his eyes and looked for something to focus on.

"Uh," I mumbled uncomfortably, saved when Judith came out with a tray of iced tea. She passed them around.

"Thank you, ma'am," said Thomas.

"So, Thomas," Judith said as she settled into her chair. "When did you get in?"

"Late last night, ma'am."

That set off a warning alarm. Had he stayed with Rachel?

"How was your flight?"

"Long, ma'am."

"Yes, I imagine. Have you ever been to California before?"

"No, ma'am."

"Well, what do you think so far?"

"It's nice, ma'am."

Judith was doing her best to break the ice, but this was like pulling teeth. I gritted my own.

"Tollb—uh, Thomas," I managed to mutter. "Should we call you Tom?"

"No, sir, just Thomas—or Tollbooth Tom if you want. Trail names kind of stick, if you know what I mean."

"I remember. How did you get yours?"

"Ah, Mr. Jeffries," that seemed to set him at ease—wish it had done the same for me, "I work a tollbooth on the Turnpike, so, you know, it was kinda obvious. I heard about *your* trail name, but I don't get it."

"Well, uh...long story. Anyway, this is a surprise."

"Surprised me too, sir, but in a good way."

I wasn't sure what to make of that. "Really?"

"Yeah. I mean, you know what it's like on the trail. Bigger than life, you know? Swift here—ah, Rachel—she was the best." I cringed. Thomas did, too. Hastily: "What I mean, sir, is she was a great hiker, great to know."

Rachel blushed. "Thomas..."

"Sorry, Rachel, but it's true."

"Well," said Judith. "You seem to be taking it well."

"I am, ma'am. Excited, too. April's beautiful, isn't she?" He smiled fondly at April. "I love her name. And you should see my mother. She wanted to come with me but I wouldn't let her."

"I'd like to meet her," said Judith.

"I hope you can," Thomas said sincerely.

There was a lull then. Thomas gestured to Rachel and she passed April over. That felt like a knife in my side. It took everything I had not to jump up and snatch April from him. He played with April and made her smile, which seemed to drive that knife even deeper.

"Well then, Thomas," I said. "Uh, I guess you should tell us what you think about all this."

"Well," he said, bouncing April on his knee, "I want to help out, you know, do what's right. I would have," he looked over at Rachel and his brows dipped, "if I had known."

"I know," Rachel said glumly. "I'm sorry. I was afraid—"

"No problem," Thomas cut in. "I get it."

It wasn't until then that I noticed a ring on Thomas' finger.

"Thomas, are you married?" I asked.

"No, sir." He flashed his ring. "Engaged."

"Does your fiancé know about April?" Judith asked with a note of concern.

"She does, ma'am," he answered directly.

"And?" That was from me.

"She was upset at first, but she knows it happened before we got together, so she's cool with it now."

"She must be an understanding person," said Judith.

"She is, ma'am."

Realizing that Rachel wouldn't be marrying Thomas must have relieved me visibly, because then Rachel chimed in with:

"What, Dad? Did you think we were going to get married or something?"

"Honey, I didn't know what to think."

Thomas seemed to slump a little. He straightened up, forced a smile and added, "That's not in the cards, sir." *cahds.*

"Let's not talk about that, then," said Judith diplomatically. "Thomas, tell us about your family."

We talked into the early evening, ultimately straying into our Appalachian Trail experiences, which then dominated the conversation. Later on, we sat for dinner outside on the patio. As much as I wanted to, I couldn't dislike Thomas. He was affable and enthusiastic, made no demands, and had actually worn a dark suit out in this heat trying to impress us. And he seemed to come from a good family.

After dinner, Rachel put April down for a nap then helped her mother clear the dishes, which left Thomas and me alone.

"It's a big responsibility," I said out of the blue. He seemed to have been anticipating that.

"Yes, sir, I know it is." He rubbed his hands in thought.

"You're going to be getting married, starting a family—it takes a lot of money. But you work in a tollbooth?"

It was the first and only time I had seen him bristle all day.

"It's a good job, sir," he said hotly. "It pays good, and good benefits. I mean, you just sell whiskey, right? Seems like you're doing okay."

Now it was my turn to bristle, but Thomas was right.

"I'm sorry, Thomas. I didn't mean that the way it sounded."

"It's okay, sir. I was only trying to say you don't have to go to college to make something of yourself." I mulled that, and then he added, "I just wish Rachel and April didn't live so far away. It's wicked hard to get here."

"Yeah, clear across the country. We've done it. I have a sister who lives at Dartmouth."

"Oh, man," Thomas slapped his forehead, "no love lost between New Hampshire and us Massachusetts men."

"Massachusetts men, huh?"

"Yeah. We got a strong thing going back home."

"I can see that." I swirled the last of the ice in my tea, gathered my thoughts. "Well, Thomas," I said finally, "I'm glad you came. You and Rachel can work out whatever you think is right. I won't give you a hard time.

"I appreciate that, sir."

"It would be nice to meet your parents, though. Maybe the next time I go visit my sister."

"That's great, Mr. Jeffries. Just don't tell my dad your sister's a New Hampshire-woman."

I chuckled. "I guess she is, now. She even talks like them these days. Your dad must have been beside himself when you were doing the Whites."

"Oh, man, if you only knew what New Hampshiremen call people from Mass." I arched a brow. "Nah, I'm not going to repeat it. I would've been beside myself, too, if it wasn't for Swift."

"I had the worst weather when I went through there, but it's where I met Rachel's mom."

"Yeah, she told me about that."

"Do you still think about the trail?"

"Every day, sir."

I had never been envious of young people until that moment. My time on the trail had been almost thirty years ago. Those experiences never left my mind, but they had receded into a distant place, like a childhood memory. I mentioned it to Judith in bed that night.

"Thomas makes me feel old," I said, groveling for sympathy. Judith would have none of it.

"Oh, Carlton, you're becoming so stodgy."

"*Stodgy?*" That wasn't the response I was expecting.

"I remember when you were a little more fast and loose. A little like Thomas, actually." Her eyes were full of mirth. She snuggled close and absently traced patterns on my chest with her fingernail.

"Yeah, well," I said sourly, "I didn't have a grandchild then." Her brows dipped.

"You mean *grandchildren*, don't you?"

"Yeah, that's what I meant."

"Well anyway," she went on, "Thomas is a fine young man. I can see what Rachel liked about him."

"Liked too much, if you ask me. But, yeah, he's a good guy. I think we got lucky."

"It wasn't luck, honey. Did you really think that Rachel would take up with someone we wouldn't like?"

I sighed. "No, you're right. I trust her, just sometimes I forget."

"That's what dads do," she laughed, and then she reached across me to turn out the light.

* * *

The weather was with me when I left Garfield Ridge. I pushed hard under the bright sun, trailing memories like litter blown from a truck bed. In and out of Franconia Notch, over Mt. Lafayette and then across Franconia Ridge, weaving between ice-carved blocks of granite—the views were spectacular but I didn't really see them. I was pushing hard with a single purpose, to reach Kinsman Notch that day.

The sun made its steady descent. The wind became chill, but then I was into the tree line, murky shadows going deeper as I went. I scrambled down into Kinsman Notch in the dark. That was hard enough to do in the light of day. Supposedly, the Dartmouth track team ran up that broken incline for practice. I couldn't see how.

I stumbled onto Lost River Road. It was cold. A biting wind shot through the notch like ice water through a funnel. Clouds were gathering above, glowing ghostly from the lights of North Woodstock nine miles away.

I looked for our place but couldn't locate it for sure. The area had changed— signs had changed—and there weren't pay phones anymore. I paced along the dark road, scrutinizing the pavement like a tracker looking for sign. About a mile, as I remembered. A lonely car sped past, long headlights making the treetops quaver in shadow. I gave it up finally and fell back in the cold grass alongside the road. After some twenty-eight rugged miles that day, fatigue and pain pounded in my feet, ankles and knees.

I gazed up the road and relied on my memory to recreate what I had been searching for: Willow walking away, not looking back...

I had also found Tollbooth Tom's entry in the register at Lakes of the Clouds. He had written it on the morning of June 26:

Swift took off before I got up! She's wicked fast. I'll never catch her. I want to go now, but first I have to wash some dishes for these guys. Dammit! I thought we had something. I'm sure we did. I know this sounds dumb, but I'd marry that girl if I could get her to stand still long enough. There's a long way to go yet. Anything could happen. I'm going to catch her. I don't know how, but I'm going to do it.
Tollbooth Tom, ME-GA '03

Tears chilled my cheeks. In the surreal displacement of that night, my mind fogged with pain and memory, I conjured an alternate life, a parallel reality in which Willow looked back and Rachel stayed that extra day at Lakes of the Clouds. Little gestures can turn things. Sometimes the big things just get in the way. I shivered in the cold grass and dreamed. I dreamed of that alternate life, and in my dream it was warm. The sun was shining and the sky was blue. In my dream I was happy.

* * *

Judith's fiftieth birthday fell on a Friday. She had been glum about it all week, dragging around the house lethargically, not much beyond wan utterances for conversation. Not even the new school year had been enough to distract her. I knew better than to tell her that she was still beautiful to me, that being fifty didn't matter. She would have just dismissed me out of hand, saying something flat and biting like, "Easy for you to say, you're not fifty."

But it wouldn't have been simple flattery coming from me, it would have been true.

Judith kept her beauty in middle age. She may have had a few gray strands in her hair, but I thought these implied experience and wisdom; she may have had fine etchings at the corners of her eyes, but I thought these leant character. She took care of herself. Her cheeks and neck were still taut, her arms were still firm. She had some bulging veins in her calves, so she took to wearing flesh-colored stockings whenever she went out; but I knew, although she would never have believed me, that her deliciously toned legs would still have drawn lustful stares from men.

And then if anything, Judith was aging better than I was. My hairline was creeping up my forehead. My temples were gray, the way my father's and his golfing buddies' had been. My chin was ominously beginning to sag, and no amount of exercise would coax my stomach back behind my belt. These were disquieting things to notice in the mirror every morning. But unlike Judith, I was more alarmed than depressed, or perhaps wistful.

Judith didn't want to go out or do anything special for her birthday, so Rachel and I conspired to create an intimate evening for her at home. I took off from work early to start the meal: clams steamed in the shell, bow-tie pasta in butter and tossed with herbs from her garden, a white cheese sauce, fresh asparagus; and for desert, tiramisu. I brought home four different wines, from pale to bold, dressed our patio table in white linen, and set out candles.

When Judith got off work, Rachel intercepted her and took her shopping, with instructions not to bring her home before 6:00 p.m. Meanwhile, I got everything ready. I used Lysol to mask the aroma from the kitchen, to preserve that surprise, then ran a hot bath with the lavender salts she liked so much.

Rachel's timing couldn't have been more perfect. She dropped her mother off promptly at six. I met Judith at the door and kissed her cheek. She sniffed the air.

"Have you been cleaning?" she asked wearily.

"No, not really," I answered in an evasive air. "Are you ready?"

"Ready for what?"

I smiled while she frowned in suspicion, and then I lifted her in my arms and carried her to the bathroom.

"Carlton!" she squealed. "What are you doing?"

"I'm taking care of you, baby," I said softly, and when she saw the bath her frown reversed itself. I set her on her feet, kissed her and nuzzled her neck.

"See you soon," I whispered in her ear.

She came out of the bath pink and fresh, wearing a knee-high white dress without stockings. I gazed longingly at her legs while she stared at me in incredulity. I was wearing a white tuxedo—white shirt, white tie, white socks—even white shoes. I offered her my arm.

"Dinner is on the patio tonight," I said with a debonair smile.

The incredulity slipped from her face, replaced with girlish glee. Her eyes sparkled. She rested a hand on my arm and I escorted her out.

The sun was below the rooftops, the sky a wash of sheer salmon clouds. A few stars twinkled in the east.

"Carlton. I—I—"

"Just sit."

I held her chair until she was settled, poured two flutes of Pinot Noir, then took my place across from her.

"Happy birthday, darling," I said sweetly.

"Oh, Carlton," she blushed.

"You look beautiful tonight."

"Oh, stop it."

"I will not."

That softened her. She leaned forward on an elbow and touched my face.

"I'm so lucky I found you."

"Uh," I said, grinning. "I think *I* found *you*."

"Oh, hush. You're so bad." She sipped her wine with flirtatious lips.

"No, just lucky."

We ate as the sun set. It was almost too cool out, so I fetched a shawl and laid it across Judith's arms.

"I wish we could go back," she said dreamily, clutching the shawl to her throat. Candlelight glittered in her eyes. Her skin glowed warmly.

"Back where?"

"To the trail."

"Why can't we?"

"Oh, how would we ever find the time?"

"Yeah," I had to agree. "But maybe tomorrow we can do something kind of like that."

"What do you mean?"

"It's a surprise," I smile coyly.

* * *

I was out of bed before dawn to get everything ready. When Judith came out sleepily, I had coffee waiting for her. She rubbed her eyes, yawned, and lifted her cup. Her hair was adorably disheveled in a way that tugged at my memory and my heart.

"Something's up," she said groggily.

"Yeah."

"Am I going to hate it?"

"I don't think so."

Pale morning light filtered through the windows. She woke up enough to notice how I was dressed. Her brows arched.

"Are we going hiking today?"

"Yeah," I said. "It'll be a little cool up there, so be sure to wear your green sweater."

Her brows arched higher.

"Where are we going?"

"Yosemite."

Judith was nineteen again when she came out of the bedroom. She was wearing khaki hiking pants, the kind with the zip-off legs, and a green sweater that was not a turtleneck but close enough for memory. Her hair was in a ponytail.

"Okay, here I am," she said, displaying herself with a sigh of surrender. "Lead on."

I walked behind her to the door, then covered her eyes with my hands.

"Carlton? What?" she objected.

"Hush," I said. "It's a surprise."

We went out the door clumsily, and then I took my hands away. She stared, and then:

"Oh, Carlton, it's gorgeous!"

"Yeah," I said airily. "It's taken more than two years."

She rounded on me. "But you never said anything."

"It wouldn't have been a surprise, then," I shrugged innocently.

The morning sun flickered through the palms and eucalyptus, shadows dancing on gleaming white paint. I opened the door of the fully restored 1962 Pontiac Catalina, and held it while Judith slid in.

* * *

If we'd had more than a weekend, I would have turned that Catalina east for Arizona and the desert country, but the drive up to Yosemite was nice just the same. The morning warmed to a perfect 72 degrees, with none of the usual haze. The air became crisp as we climbed, pure like the water from a Maine spring. The Catalina hugged the turns, nimble on its new shocks and springs. Once an anachronism, now people paused to stare. Some gave us an appreciative thumbs-up. A crowd of bikers roared around us, slowing to gawk, but whether at the Catalina or at Judith I wasn't sure. Judith blushed as they went by, turning away to tuck a stray lock of hair behind her ear.

"It sounds more powerful now," she commented over the rushing wind. "Like a big dog growling, or maybe a bear."

"Yeah," I laughed. "The guy at the shop told me he couldn't resist. He put cherry-bomb mufflers on it, and a four-barrel carburetor. It'll lay rubber now if I gas it."

She grinned. "You're like a teenager again."

"You, too, babe," I said, and I meant it.

Judith covered her eyes as we approached the Wawona Tunnel, and when she felt the air go chill and knew we were inside, she shrieked, "I can't see, Carlton! I can't see!" I turned to her in fond remembrance, seeing Rachel in Judith's playful side.

When we burst into the sunlight she whipped her hands away and added, "I can see, Carlton! I can see!"

We both collapsed into laughter. I put a hand on her thigh and squeezed, stole a few glances at the genuine joy in her face. I felt proud.

I had a room reserved at the Ahwahnee Hotel, just one night but we had that whole marvelous day to enjoy. We dumped our things hastily, grabbed our daypacks, and took off for Glacier Point.

The climb was tougher than it had ever been, but we made it, breathless in that expansive view. We followed the ridge around to our place and collapsed onto the turf.

"So you still want to hike the Appalachian Trail again?" I laughed.

"Maybe I was a little hasty with that," she smiled, wiping sweat off her brow.

The air was chill, but we were warm in the sun. We spread out a blanket and lay side by side, holding hands and gazing at the sky.

"Sometimes it's like a dream," she mused after a while. "If I close my eyes it's like we're on Franconia Ridge right now and not thirty years ago."

I rolled over and stroked her brows. Her eyes were clinched tight, as if she were transporting herself to another time.

"I like it right here," I breathed into her ear. "With you. Just like this."

My hand strayed south. I studied her face as it went. She kept her eyes tightly shut, but then her lids fluttered and she giggled, and when her eyes popped open they were eager and hungry and as young as yesterday.

* * *

Rachel's car was in the driveway when we got home the next afternoon.

"*Hello*," I hollered as we went inside.

"*Gwampa! Gwampa!*"

April came stumbling across the floor, too fast for her little feet. I scooped her into my arms just as she tripped on her last step.

"Whoa there, princess. How are you today?"

"Fine," she answered distractedly. Her enthusiasm waned just like that, and she reached out to Judith. I laughed and handed her over.

Rachel came out of the kitchen, a dish towel over her shoulder.

"Well," she smirked, "from all the dishes in the sink I guess the birthday dinner went pretty well."

"Yeah," I chuckled. I went and gave her a hug.

"So, Mom?" asked Rachel. "Feel better now?"

"You know I do, sweetie."

"Good. Glad *that's* over with." Rachel noted the light sunburn on her mother's cheeks and legs. "Uh, hmm," she made to clear her throat. "Dad, if you've got a sunburn on your back I think I'm going to cringe."

"You'll never know," I said with a laugh.

"Thank God. Well, I've got the kitchen all cleaned up for you."

"Oh, sweetie, you didn't have to do that," said Judith.

"I know I didn't have to, Mom. I wanted to." She puffed some hair out of her eyes, and then with an eager smile, "So...do I get to go for a ride now?"

Rachel couldn't see herself as I saw her, sitting up to peer over that long hood as we drove around the neighborhood, looking small enough in her seat to put a knot in my throat. For just a moment she was my precious little girl again, spell broken when she asked, "Okay, Dad, when do I get to drive it?"

I snorted my nostalgia away and pulled over. "Okay," I said, presenting the Catalina to her with both palms open. "Have at it."

She hopped across my lap, clicked her seat belt and we were off, making a circuit that took us up Blackstone and through the parking lot of her bookstore. I saw Dusty through the window. He waved and gave us his even-toothed grin, while Rachel preened like the Queen of Fresno. I thought we would stop in, but she kept on to the Sonic Drive-In, made the circuit of that place, waved at a few people.

"Okay, honey," I said then. "Time to head home."

"Aw."

Judith had dinner ready when we got there. April was still down for her nap.

"So, what did you think?" Judith asked Rachel.

"That car's a lot cooler than I remembered," Rachel replied with an adolescent grin.

"I thought you might say that. Dinner's ready, by the way."

We ate inside. Rachel asked probing questions about our weekend, especially the nights, which caused Judith to blush and finally change the subject.

"So, how's Thomas doing?" she asked. Rachel fiddled with her fork. She seemed not to want to go there. "Sweetie, has something happened?" Judith asked, this time in concern.

"No—well—yeah." Rachel answered reluctantly. "He broke off his engagement."

"Oh, no," Judith moaned, legitimately saddened.

I dropped my fork, leaned back and exhaled. In her concern, Judith couldn't see the repercussions. But I could. I could see them clearly.

"When's he coming?" I asked Rachel frankly. Judith looked at me in confusion.

"He wants to come for Thanksgiving," Rachel answered with downcast eyes.

"And you said...?"

"I told him he could."

Judith caught up to it then. She took a sharp breath and studied her daughter.

"Is it what you want, sweetie?" she asked.

"I don't know, Mom. Maybe."

"But you would have to—"

"Go live in Boston? Yeah, probably."

I pushed back and threw down my napkin, eyed Rachel with an uneasy combination of anger and remorse.

"Don't be that way, Dad," Rachel said, not in anger or hurt, but maybe in sorrow. "We don't know what's going to happen."

"You know *exactly* what's going to happen, or else you wouldn't have brought it up."

"But he hasn't *asked* me."

"He will."

"Carlton, stop," said Judith.

I stood. Rachel was withering under my gaze. It wasn't like her to yield that way, and that disturbed me even more.

"I'll be in the other room," I said, and I stalked out.

* * *

Things weren't right between Rachel and me after that night.

"Carlton, if you push her away I promise you'll regret it later," Judith warned me. "I thought you liked Thomas."

"It's not that. She'll be across the country. We'll never see her. We won't see April."

"Oh, honey, he hasn't even asked her. Maybe he's not going to."

I shot her a sharp look. "You know better than that. I could see it the first time we met him."

Judith came up behind me and wrapped her arms around my chest. I could feel her lips at the back of my ear.

"Does Thomas remind you of anyone?" she asked, her soothing breath on my skin. I leaned into her.

"It's not the same."

"Isn't it?"

"I came to you."

"Well here's a little secret." Her lips were on my ear now, I could feel them smiling warmly. "*I* would have come to *you*."

I turned in her arms until our breaths were on each other's lips.

"I'm glad it worked out the other way," I said tenderly.

"Are you?"

"Yeah." I dropped my hands to her hips and we rocked in place.

"Why?"

"Because we didn't have to live with all of that...well, you know."

"Uh, huh. And why is it any different for Rachel?"

"It's completely different."

"In what way?"

"Because she has April."

"You're not April's dad, Carlton, Thomas is. You see the way he is with her. He loves her."

"I know, but so do I."

* * *

Judith was right, of course, but that didn't make it any easier for me to accept the inevitable. The countdown to Thanksgiving was like a death watch to me as I stubbornly held on to the frailest hope that I had been wrong about Thomas, that he wouldn't propose to Rachel, that I could have her and April back, the way it had always been.

Things remained awkward between Rachel and me as we went into November. She would come over with April, peck me on the cheek and I would peck her back. We trod carefully around the subject of Thomas, like navigating those slippery bog-logs in the Hundred-Mile Wilderness. Rachel's smiles were fragile. When she went off with her mother, I would play with April, running her until she was worn out, as if to fit in as much as I could. I plied her with candy, which was wrong of me but I couldn't help myself.

Judith was up early on November 18, a Saturday. She was already dressed to go out, was sitting at the table writing something when I padded into the kitchen for coffee.

"Something happening today?" I asked groggily.

"I thought I told you. Rachel and I are driving to San Jose."

"What on earth for?"

I plopped onto a chair and rubbed the sleep out of my eyes.

"We're going shopping, she and Gloria and I."

"Can't you shop here?"

"Carlton?" Her hands were on her hips, so that meant I was being a nuisance. I wisely diverted my attention to my coffee. "Today is our ladies' day. Rachel needs some nice clothes for next week, and Gloria's going to help."

"Oh," I groaned. There wasn't enough sugar in my coffee. I reached for the bowl.

"It's perfect for you," she went on, "you get to have April all day. *But*—" That was my signal to take note of her stern expression. I set the sugar bowl down warily and did so. "—no candy this time. Okay?"

"Aw."

She ruffled my hair, kissed the top of my head.

"Well," she reconsidered, "maybe one piece."

Rachel showed up with April soon after. I met them at the door.

"Hi, Dad." She pecked my cheek.

"Hi, honey."

"Is Mom ready?"

"Yeah, she's coming."

She set April on her feet and scooted her along. I paused to look out before closing the door.

"It's a little foggy this morning."

"It's not too bad," Rachel said over her shoulder as she followed April into the living room. "Oh, hi Mom."

"Good morning, sweetie. Are you all set?"

"Ready to go. Your car or mine?"

"Let's take the minivan. More room for things."

"Okay."

"Honey?"

That was Judith calling me. I joined them in the living room, standing aside as they hung their purses and checked each other's hair and makeup. There was a flowery smell of perfume in the air.

"We'll be back late," Judith went on. "I'll call you before we leave."

"And I made lunch for April," Rachel added. "It's in her bag."

"Okay."

"Bye, honey." Judith kissed me on the cheek.

"Bye, Dad." Rachel didn't.

I followed them as they went out, two women, same height, same hair, both dressed in beige pants and white sweaters, like twins.

"Be careful. It's foggy," I said after them.

"Oh, it's not so bad."

Same voices.

I lingered in the doorway for a long time after they had turned the corner and were out of sight. I felt unsettled and didn't know why. I went woodenly to gather up April, maybe holding her a little too tightly.

"Ow, Gwampa!"

April squirmed in my arms. Suddenly it was hard to breathe, as if something were closing in around me, cutting off my air. My stomach felt weak. I sat with April in the kitchen, clutched her to my chest even as she struggled to get loose.

"Gwampa, Gwampa, *let me go*," she whined, but I held on, scarcely aware. I held her and stared at the wall as my coffee went cold.

I didn't jump when the phone rang. Somehow I had been expecting it.

"Hello?"

"Carlton?" The line was crackling, like cellophane wrapping paper.

"Judith?"

"Yes, honey, it's me."

"Where are you?"

"Almost to the 152 interchange. The fog is terrible, you can't see anything. I pulled over. We're going to wait here until it lifts."

"I can come get you."

"No, honey. You don't want to be out in this."

I heard something in the background, hollow and distant and chillingly familiar…

"Judith? What is that?"

"What, honey? I can't hear you."

…a scalloped, hoarse chirping; louder, coming closer…

"Judith?"

…rubber skewing violently against pavement; the plaintive wail of an air horn, like a desperate final plea…

"Carlton?"

"Mom!"

"Oh my God!"

There was a shrill squeal over the line. The phone went dead.

My heart pounded, rising into my throat. April was suddenly still in my lap. I dialed Judith's number feverishly—ring, ring, ring—it went to voicemail. I stabbed the redial button—

"Gwampa? Why you scared?"

—and got voicemail again...and again...and again.

* * *

If the sky had once been blue, it wasn't anymore; if there had been sunny days, I couldn't remember them.

Thomas made it in the next evening. Michael and Susan picked him up at the airport. James and Gloria were at home with me. I sat with April, holding tight and rocking her in my arms as she slept, rocking, rocking. All else was dull and distant. Time meant nothing, only April in my arms. Her hair was wet from my tears, pasted to her forehead as if she had just broken a fever. Gloria wanted to take her elsewhere, to bed or for a bath. She begged me with stricken eyes, but I held on even tighter.

It was dark outside when Thomas came in the house. I noticed him numbly, registered his silhouetted outline in the open doorway with a bare croak across cracked lips. Michael and Susan were with him, blending formlessly into the darkness that limned my vision. Thomas reached out with shadowed arms, his silhouette quavering from headlights passing anonymously on the street. Gloria leaned over and dripped a tear that joined mine in poor April's hair. Gloria begged me once more, no words, just pain. Her trembling lips formed *Please*.

I offered April up even as I warred outside of myself to hold onto her, to never let her go. I stood with uncertain knees. James rushed to my side and supported me, as if I were Grandmother Villetta going down the back steps. Thomas staggered forward, one step, two. We didn't so much meet as fall into one another, and then we embraced, pitiful and shuddering, and we cried, we cried for so long.

Lois and Eugene wanted me to bring Judith and Rachel to Oakhurst. I wanted to take them home instead, but then I realized...this *was* their home. So I did what I was asked, making decisions as if I were someone else far away. Mama suffered a grief-stricken spell—she would have been too frail to come out anyway. Sadie flew down to be with her, torn between coming here or staying there, where she might be needed most.

I haven't forgotten that drive to Oakhurst, but everything is jumbled in my memory even now, shuffled images, colorless—black suits, gray winding roads, bowed heads and tears. It rained the day we laid Judith and Rachel to rest—

—and that's all I'm going to say about it. Damn it! I don't *want* to remember.

* * *

Thomas came to me afterward, still ashen but steady, or as well as could be expected.

"Mr. Jeffries? About April..."

I heard him, but only as if his words were echoes from far below. I mumbled something.

"...I think she should be with me..."

I clung to a granite peak. Cold stone. My grip was slipping. Everything was dark. Clouds flickered and roiled.

"...I'm her father, Mr. Jeffries..."

I held on by my fingertips, legs dangling in the void.

"...Rachel would have wanted..."

Oily black clouds enveloped me, suffocating.

"...You can visit any time you want..."

I clawed the sharp granite. My fingers split and bled. I fought for breath, spared *a glance into the void, saw nothing but darkness there.*

"...It'll be better this way..."

I let go.

* * *

Enough! That's it! No more—

PART

III

T WENTY - THREE

The paper is gone. All I have left are my homemade sheets, brown and almost tissue thin. I discovered that a dull pencil will work. Too sharp of a point tears the stuff, but writing lightly and carefully with a rounded lead—as much as this cramps my fingers—leaves legible marks that might actually last a while if I can keep the paper dry. If it gets wet, that's it. Even one stray drop of water from this rotted ceiling could destroy what I've scribbled so far. I've even had to shield my work from Sam lest his slobbering tongue ruin everything.

This story should have ended where I left it. It would've ended there if I hadn't somehow managed to live another eighty years. Cruel fate. Bringing all of that back darkened me so deeply that I crawled out into the muck, doffed my coat, and offered myself to the stinging cold, praying that it would take me quickly. Sam knew something was wrong. He twined between my legs and whined, pushed his nose against my knees as if trying to steer me back under cover. But I wanted to go. I truly did.

I didn't even notice the cold after a while. It's strange, but as I began to convulse I actually felt hot, as if my skin were burning. I ripped off my shirt for relief, exposed my flaccid skin to that frigid air, yet still I burned. I must have been hallucinating by then. I saw hell in that dark before dawn, a ring of cold fire in the tunnel of my vision. *Take me*, I begged the night. *Please make it stop*. Poor Sam. My pitiful lament must have burrowed into a primal place. With tail tucked between trembling legs, he sat back and howled a mournful dirge that shuddered through the woods and made everything still. No wolf could have howled such woe into the darkness.

Muddy slush oozed between my toes. My skin was afire. Sam howled and I waited. Dark went to gray as somewhere the sun rose—not over me, but somewhere. A rising gray. The trees formed and took shape—as trees rather than sinister sentinels in the night. The stream burbled, carrying on despite me, lapping at gray granite mottled with lichen. A fleeting flicker of light glanced across my eyes, and I looked up to see a trace of blue in the gray above; just a trace, like an errant brushstroke on a painter's canvas; only for a moment, but it was there. I saw it. I'm sure I saw it.

Another day comes,
Away with the night.

Those words stirred from somewhere deep inside, returning me to another time when I had come through the darkness. My skin no longer burned. Suddenly I was so cold and numb and desperate for warmth that I scrabbled on stiff fingers and knees to the shelter. Pitiful. I couldn't feel my feet or ankles as I shoved myself into my sleeping bag. I tried to call Sam but could make no sound except a hoarse grunt, so I waved him over weakly and zipped us both into the sleeping bag. So warm. Sam has saved me again.

It is now noon or thereabouts, judging from a brighter gray almost overhead. I don't know if it's because of what I put myself through this morning, but it feels warmer now. The rain has stopped. The sky seems to have lifted, still gray although not as heavy. I could hike out now, but I seem to have come down with a fever. I don't know if this is from exposing myself to the cold, from being short of sleep, or if I've caught something. I took some aspirins. Hopefully they'll help.

Despite my fever and this throbbing sore on my backside, I feel better. I was able to get out and fire up my stove. I boiled water and added a pouch of chicken-broth powder, drank that down, and that made me feel better yet, well enough that I began to get restless just lying here; well enough to continue with my story if I could find a way. So I took out that homemade paper, whittled a pencil and wrote some experimental sentences, tore some sheets so will save those for other uses. Where to go on from here? Perhaps into that haze afterward.

* * *

Everyone left eventually. How many days? I don't know. I woke up one morning, or maybe it was night, I'm not sure—but I woke up and dragged myself out of bed. My sheets smelled rank. I smelled worse. I saw myself in the mirror and didn't recognize who I was looking at, turned away from that and stumbled into the kitchen, where I sat and stared at the wall.

And then it was light outside. It hurt my eyes. I shielded them and went back to bed. And then I awoke again.

The good thing about working in the booze business is that it's easy to get whiskey. I managed a call to one of the guys in the warehouse, and he dropped off a case of Jack Daniels on my doorstep. It was decent of him not to knock or insist on coming in. Two fingers of straight whiskey warmed me. Two more fingers set my mind on a far shelf between a couple of Judith's books, and two more after that made it tolerable to stay awake. I sat in my recliner and drank. I kept the lights off. I didn't need those. Every once in a while I would go into the kitchen, scavenge something to eat, then retreat as quickly as possible to the sanctuary of my recliner and my whiskey.

It was too bright in the house. I hung blankets over the windows.

The phone rang. I ignored it.

I discovered that I liked good Tennessee whiskey, pondered why I had deprived myself of it all these years. My head swam in and out of folds in the air. The floor rose and fell.

The whiskey ran out. I called for more, scratched at the bristles on my face. Why was my shirt wet? I should find a dry one. Later. Maybe later.

The phone rang again. Again I ignored it.

I plopped into my recliner and poured a glass. Somehow the remote had fallen off the side table into the recliner, and my butt switched the television on. The television flared, blinding me. It came on to some fatuous news show, pundits raging frothy-mouthed against a black guy who wanted to run for president. Hate. Hate. Hate. I covered my ears and begged it to stop, reached for an empty bottle of Jack and hurled it at the screen.

Elvis Presley had famously fired a gun at a television screen over something he hadn't liked. His screen—at least in the movie that came out after he died—erupted in the most brilliant and satisfying shower of sparks and glass; but my new flat-screen television only sizzled and toppled over. I shrugged and poured another glass.

The knock at the door was insistent, but I ignored it. Soon it was coming from the windows around back, keys rapping on glass, piercing. I fled to the bedroom with a bottle, curled up around it and plugged my ears—and yet the knocking and pounding continued, on and on endless, anger rising.

"*What?*" I shouted at no one. "*What?*"

My bottle was empty. I went to fetch another, and still the pounding. *Pounding. Pounding.* My skull was cleaving in two. I charged the door like a raging moose and jerked it open.

"*What?*"

It was Dave Gurney. He looked me over with a grimace and shoved his way inside. I glared at him in righteous fury, dismissed him out of hand and fled to my recliner. He followed with his bow-legged gait. Dave was too old and broken to get bucked off horses anymore. These days he gave riding lessons in Clovis and worked part-time at the warehouse.

I ignored him, or tried. He bent over and lifted a bottle, swished it around, took a sniff, then finished off the dregs with a smack of his lips.

"Good whiskey," he said. "You left a little."

"I got more."

"So I hear."

I fixed him with a frosty glare.

"Waddaya want, Dave?"

"Hey, pardner," he held out his palms, "I just came fer the whiskey."

"Have at it."

I turned away and stewed.

Dave mused around the living room, high-stepping over dirty piles, his hands clasped behind him. He kicked an empty and it spun off into the kitchen. He looked in after it and waved a hand in front of his face.

"*Shoowee*, Festus! This place stinks."

"So hold your breath."

"Yeah, I think I might at that. You reckon maybe you oughta hire somebody to clean this up?"

"It doesn't bother me."

"Yeah, I reckon."

I tried to ignore him, but my glass was empty. So was my bottle. But I didn't want to get up or encourage him in any way. I fumed and ground my teeth. He hovered near a window, and then without warning yanked down the blanket. Bright light blared in, piercing my skull like serrated knives.

"Damn it, Dave!"

I lunged at him but he fended me off. Too easily, I thought in my addled mind.

"Whoa now, pardner." Somehow he got my arms up behind my back. "*Shoo*, Festus. I've wrangled buffalo what smelled better'n you. C'mon now."

"Let me go!"

"Don't reckon I will."

"Damn you!"

"Too late, Festus. Been done."

He practically pulled my arms out of their sockets dragging me to the bathroom. He reached over, just about bending me backwards off my feet. I heard the water running in the tub.

"Now this next here is pure hateful," he said, "but it's gotta be done."

"Oh hell."

He plunged me into the cold water, held me under while I thrashed and kicked.

"*Whooee!*" He grinned like a maniac as I twisted and sputtered. "You fight like a pissed off bull with bob wire up its hind end. I swear, Festus, I'm gonna tie you off if you don't settle down."

"Like hell you will."

"Well, that'll show me fer bein' nice."

I caught a glimpse as he tugged a stretch of braided latigo from around his waist, fought harder but it was useless. In a breath and a half he had me tied off like a calf in a rodeo. He stood up then with his hands on his hips, me on my belly in the tub with my hands and ankles hog-tied behind my back, sloshing as that cold water rose.

"I only ever had to do this once before, Festus. Hated it then, don't care so much for it now." He turned off the tap while I glowered and spit. "Holler all you want. I reckon the neighbors're all at work right now. I'm gonna go off and make some coffee. When you settle down a little I'll let you have some."

"Dave! *You son of a—*" He closed the door on me as that last came spewing out.

The water was room temperature by the time he returned. He walked in nonchalantly, whistling *Git Along, Little Dogies* or some such, which made me want to get free more than ever so I could kick him in what teeth he had. But I just lay there, straining my neck to glower up at him. I was so hollered out that my throat was scratchy. He placed a stack of clothes on the toilet tank, then sat on the lid and appraised me with calloused fingers to his whiskered chin.

"I found these clothes in a drawer," he said. "Reckon they oughta fit." He paused for a moment to take in my reaction, of which there wasn't one. "So here's the deal, Festus—I reach down there and slip that leather off ya, you git dressed in these here clean clothes, and I'll see ya out yonder when yur done. Fair enough?"

I glowered.

"Suit yurself." He slapped his thighs and stood.

"Wait," I gargled in the water lapping over my chin.

"Change o' heart, then," he grinned around his missing teeth. "I thought as much. But listen up—you carry on or come at me and I'll have ya back on the ground and tied off like a heifer in heat. And I can do it, you know I can. Git me?" I burbled some water and creased my brows. "I'll need you to *act-knowledge* that Festus. Give us a nod or an *a-firmative* else you git to soak there a bit more."

I nodded. And glowered.

"Well that's more like it."

He reached down and undid the knot with one hand, wrung the water out of his latigo and tied it back around his waist. I rose shakily to my knees, rubbing my wrists while wincing at the pin pricks stinging my feet. My fingers were pruned like pickles in vinegar.

"Awlrighty, then," he said with a self-satisfied smile. "See you in a bit."

I came out of the bathroom wearing clean jeans and a fresh white T-shirt that I had somehow overlooked during these interceding...weeks? Months? Hell, I didn't know. They had probably been in a bottom drawer, too much effort to bend over and get when all my whiskey bottles sat waist high or higher.

I moved lethargically into the living room, too weary to fight or even cause a commotion. Dave had kicked all the junk to the side, clearing a space around the couch and coffee table. He sat on the couch sipping coffee, his booted feet on the coffee table. His sweat-stained cowboy hat rested on the couch beside him.

"There's you a cup right there," he said, pointing.

I lifted the cup unsteadily and sipped. My stomach protested, but I swallowed hard and kept everything down. After a few sips, the coffee began to do its work.

I looked around as if in a trance, noted that things had changed. Dave had pulled down all the blankets, channeling daylight onto the mess I had made of my house. The windows were open despite the chill outside. Goose bumps rose on my arms. I rubbed them absently.

"If yur lookin' fer a bottle, give it up," he said sidelong to me, as if he were more interested in his coffee. "I poured it all out...well, 'cept two I put in my truck. Shame to waste good whiskey. I'm keepin' those'ns fer myself."

"Damn, Dave." I fell onto my recliner, splashing some coffee onto my clean T-shirt. My head throbbed.

"I got some pizza comin'," he said then. "Nothin' else in this place worth foolin' with—hey, you don't got twenty bucks, do you?"

I shook my head in misery. "Christ, Dave."

"Well hell, Festus." He acted offended. "This ain't *my* mess."

"I don't know, Dave," I said woozily. "Look in that jar over there."

He hopped up without spilling a drop and peered into my change jar. "Well, there's plenty enough in there. Take a while to count it out, though." He returned to the couch and plopped down. "On second thought," he added, "you might need it. It's a shame about yur job, but I reckon under the circumstances they'd have ya back if ya asked."

I groaned and drained my cup. "Tell them I'm sorry, will you?"

"I think they git that awlready, but sure, I'll tell 'em."

He sat back, crossed his legs casually and sipped his coffee. I hauled myself up for another cup. When I returned to my recliner, Dave was skewering me with his intent blue eyes. His hair was as coarse as flax these days, and his wild white goatee was yellowing at the roots.

"So listen, Festus," he said seriously. He set down his cup. "You got dealt a raw hand. I ain't gonna tell you I know how it feels, 'cause I don't. I ain't got no kids, and no woman ever stuck with me long. But I know this—Some folks are built fer drinkin'. I never saw you as one of 'em. You'd best leave that stuff alone."

I wanted to wave him off, but looked away guiltily instead.

"If you want ta kill yurself," he went on, "go walk out in front of a bus or hop on a mean bull. Drinkin' like this just wastes time and good whiskey. It don't kill you but slow, and it tends ta git other folks mixed up in yur mess."

"That's some speech," I muttered. Something familiar tugged at the back of my mind.

Dave shrugged. "'Bout all the words I know. Don't make 'em any less true. We was all fond of yur wife and girl, you know that. I hate thinkin' of 'em lookin' down on you like this."

My anger rose at that, but when Dave stood, looking as menacing as an outlaw on the high plains, I cowered back. He fitted his hat onto his head.

"Advice usually ain't worth the time it takes ta git it out," he said, stepping toward the door. "Sometimes a man gits hisself caught 'tween horn and hoof. I don't hold that against 'em. But if it happens twice he's just plain dumb and I won't give 'em spit after that. If I was you I'd clear outa this and head on home to that farm of yurs."

Since Grandmother Villetta died, there isn't a farm anymore, I wanted to inform him, but I bit my tongue instead.

"Take care of yurself, Festus," he said from the door. "Look me up sometime."

And then he stepped through, a cowboy in silhouette, and I never saw him again.

* * *

I shaved, I bathed—properly—I ate a lot of pizza. I filled fifty-gallon trash bags and drug them to the curb. I paced a lonely circuit through my clean, quiet house—kitchen to living room to bedroom and back. I trailed my fingers across Judith's books.

Sometimes I could smell Judith in the bed sheets, on the pillows. One day, while cleaning up the mess in the living room, I caught her scent in the carpet. I lay flat and pressed my cheek against it, scratching and grasping to bring her closer, but I couldn't pull her any nearer than that. She was everywhere in the house, wherever I looked or breathed, shimmering in the air and yet my arms closed on nothing. Sometimes I smelled her in the kitchen, a rich tomato sauce, oregano, rosemary and chopped basil. I couldn't go out back now, not into her garden. She lived there most of all, and if I strayed into that place I was afraid I wouldn't make it back.

I put a few things in a box, some photos and letters, Rachel's trail journal. I put the box in the trunk of the Catalina along with my clothes. The rest...

A few sober phone calls, a realtor to organize an estate sale. I signed some papers. All in good hands. It was April—*April*—a cool morning, the sun coming up. The Firebird was parked in the driveway, dusty, forlorn, its tires sagging. The keys to it and the house were under the mat where the realtor knew where to find them. I backed the Catalina into the street, rumbled away and didn't look back.

Mama was surprised to see me. I was surprised in return, because at first I thought she was Grandmother Villetta come back to straighten me out. She was a little unsteady on her feet, her back was bowed a bit, but her color was good and she had her cottony hair done up nice.

"*Oh, Carlton.*"

I hugged her gingerly, noted the fragile bones I could feel beneath my embrace.

"Can I come home, Mama?"

"Of course you can, honey. Of course you can."

* * *

Gracie called it my healing summer. But I wasn't healed. Scarred over, perhaps; functional and far enough along to be able to look back without breaking down; able to speak Judith's and Rachel's names, sometimes even with a wounded smile, but by no means healed.

I kept myself busy with the yard and the shrubs and the dogs. I mowed the hill all the way down to the street every few days, belaying the mower on the steeper parts, digging in and pulling it up in jerks, my biceps and quadriceps throbbing. I wore a straw hat under the humid sun. Sweat ran out of me not in drips but in drizzles, like a cleansing fountain. I went shirtless, earning a reddish tobacco-patch tan. I never groused about the work, I relished it. It kept my mind in a manageable place.

I cleared a path along our fence line and took Dolly and Daisy for walks up there. Our excursions were limited to that boundary now that the Battle of Nashville Preservation Society had turned the hilltop into an historical park. They had put in a trail on the other side of our neighbor's house. It zigzagged through the woods to the top, opening my hill to strangers from all over. Tour busses would now creak along our narrow street, disgorging Civil War aficionados and clouds of diesel at the trailhead. Those who made the climb on a hot day would loiter in the shade of the old ash tree and know nothing of the true history of the place. My window screen was still buried up there somewhere.

Gracie came by with Tom Junior every once in a while. At three-and-a-half years old he was attentive enough to take some interest in me, even if my demeanor was often vacant. I read to him sometimes, the way I used to read to Rachel, and when I had to pause to wipe my eyes he would go on ahead, flipping pages, sounding out words on his own. He was a good-looking kid, well-mannered and empathetic for his age, with Kenny's gummy grin, Gracie's Latin eyes, and Tommy's unbridled exuberance, or at least the way I remembered it. It was good to finally see something of Tommy in the boy. Mama loved him. She doted on him and gave him sweets, too many, perhaps. This seemed to pain Gracie, although she was kind enough to let it pass beneath her notice.

Gracie and I would often talk outdoors, wandering around the yard, keeping conversation on the surface while I clipped shrubs and weeded flower beds. During one visit I asked her why I never saw Angelina.

"She's in Knoxville," Gracie informed me, "taking some summer classes." She sighed and flicked a drop of sweat from her brow. "But really it's because she met a guy."

"Oh," I said, startled, but why should I have been? "She's young," I added clumsily. "It's only natural."

"I know...but still—" I put a comforting arm around her and she leaned into me, her cheek resting tentatively against my salty skin. "I wish...Oh, I don't know."

"What?"

"It's nothing." She pulled away and straightened her hair. The gray streaks really didn't make her look old, but rather dignified—and perhaps a bit weary.

"You did a great job raising her," I said. "Both of them. You should be proud of yourself. *I'm* proud of you."

"Oh, Carlton." She turned away to compose herself. I heard what might have been a sniff.

"Hey, did you hear about the Hanshaws?" I asked, changing the subject to spare her from any further embarrassment. "They moved to Florida."

"Really?" She gazed down at their house.

"Yep, snowbirds. Can't say I miss 'em, though. How's Evelyn these days?"

"We haven't seen her much lately. Something's going on with Luke. I don't know what."

"Luke?"

She gave me a quizzical look. "Haven't you talked to him?"

"No. Not since—" I bit that off and leaned to pull a dandelion. Gracie winced.

"Well," she said with a strained smile. "I'd better go rescue Mabel from Tommy."

"Okay," I said dimly, and leaned to pull another dandelion.

* * *

Mama couldn't get up and down the stairs anymore. She'd installed a chair lift along the handrail, but its jerky motion left her unsettled, afraid of falling. She didn't drive anymore, so only came down every week or so to do the laundry; otherwise she had pretty much closed off the downstairs. I had decided to stay in my old room down the hall, not for privacy, but for propriety. A grown man living with his mother seemed odd, if not to others then at least to me. By living downstairs I felt more as if I were simply renting an apartment below.

I met Mama for breakfast every morning, though, squeezing past the chair lift to climb the stairs. Were she not eighty-seven years old, and resembling Grandmother Villetta in almost every nuance, our morning routine could have been right out of my childhood, with us sitting at the kitchen table, reading the paper and drinking our coffees. Mama glanced out the window one morning and caught her breath.

"Bless me," she said with a hand to her breast. "For a minute I thought Dick was home."

The Catalina was parked in Dad's old place, looking as new as it had when we'd first moved here. That caught me wistfully, too, when I thought about it.

"Maybe I should start putting it in the garage, Mama."

"No, it's fine. I like seeing it there."

A lifetime of hurt and memory passed behind her rheumy eyes. I understood it. I understood it too well.

* * *

The leaves dropped in the fall. My hickory tree was enormous now, dominating the hill like a sheltering giant. That grand old tree could still be standing long after we were gone, but for now it dropped leaves like New England snow. It took weeks to gather them all. I set to it diligently, raking and bagging. We weren't allowed to burn them anymore, city ordinance.

When it grew cool and wet, I fled indoors and looked for projects to keep me busy. I dusted every one of Dad's books in the den; I greased the chain on the chair lift, hoping to get it running more smoothly; I re-plumbed the downstairs toilet. There was always enough to keep my mind occupied, or distracted.

I had hoped to see Sadie for Christmas, but she couldn't make it. It was just Mama and me. No gifts, we promised one another, but I got her some flowers anyway. She smiled warmly and gave me a colorful quilt that she had made out of Dad's old dress ties. My lips trembled when I picked up just the faintest trace of Old Spice.

Hill's had been closed to make way for a new shopping mall, so for Christmas dinner we sent out to the Kroger for rotisserie chicken, potato salad and green beans. It would have felt foolish to spend all day in the kitchen for just us two. It was a nice enough dinner, though. We ate at the big table. Mama and I sat together at one end, and as we ate my eyes wandered to all the empty chairs. Judging by her distant gaze, I'm sure Mama was doing the same thing.

We were surprised when the bell rang, not out back but at the front door.

"Well, who could that be?" Mama asked in wonder, breaking our contemplative silence.

"Be right back," I said hastily.

I got up, went past our anemic Christmas tree in the front windows, down the stairs and around the chair lift. I opened the door with a curious look and found Luke there, dressed smartly as always in a navy blazer, white collared shirt, khaki slacks and brown loafers. A Christmas gift-bag dangled from his fingers.

"Hello, Father." He gave me a reserved smile.

"Luke!" I exclaimed. That wasn't, perhaps, the most welcoming greeting I could have offered my only surviving child, but I was too flabbergasted for anything else.

"May I come in?"

"Uh, sure, sure. What a surprise."

I led him upstairs. When Mama saw him, she brightened to an affectionate pink and stooped forward for a hug.

"Oh, Luke." She reached up to busy that forelock of black hair out of his eyes. "I'm so happy to see you."

"I'm happy to see you, too, Grandma." That didn't come off of his lips as naturally as it should have, but then, how long had it been since they'd seen one another? A year or more, probably; and I hadn't seen him since...well, I wasn't sure.

"Sit. Sit," Mama busied on. "Would you like something to eat, Luke? We've got plenty."

"No, thank you. I ate already with Mom and Da—uh, Brad."

We took our seats. Luke sat with an empty chair between us. I picked up my fork, but then paused to appraise him indirectly. He had grown to become a real looker, with his dark blue eyes, dimpled chin, and subtle vulnerability. Evelyn probably made herself crazy trying to fend off the girls. Maybe that's what had been going on between them last summer. Luke was still pale, though, and somewhat shorter than me. He seemed nervous. His hands trembled ever so slightly. I put my fork down and pushed my plate away.

"That's enough for me, Mama," I said.

"Oh, honey. There's pecan pie yet. I'll warm it up."

"Mama—"

"Don't you *Mama* me, now. I can't eat all that myself," then to Luke with a coercive smile, "You'll have some, won't you, Luke? And some coffee?"

Luke began to protest, but then he must have thought better of it. "Yes, Grandma, I'd like that."

"Good."

Mama bustled off, leaving me alone with Luke. I cleared my throat, searched for something to say.

"Uh—so Luke, what have you been doing with yourself?"

"Just going to school."

"Still?"

"Yeah, well—" He looked down uneasily and seemed to notice his shaking hands. He laced his fingers to steady them. "—you know how Mom is."

"Uh, huh," I sighed.

"I don't really want to be a lawyer."

"What *do* you want, then?"

"I don't know, Father. I don't know..." He trailed off with a troubled look, but then snapped his head up and blurted, "Here. I brought this for you." He placed his bag on the table then sat back expectantly.

"Well, Luke—uh—I don't know what to say." I opened the bag and timidly looked inside. "Is that—"

"Yes, Father." Luke seemed to straighten up a bit. His smile was sincere. "I've been keeping them. I wanted to give them to you last year, but—" He went gray then.

"It's okay, Luke," I reassured him weakly. "But this—I thought it was gone forever."

I lifted out my old field bag, which was musty and brittle with age, and stained in places from Tommy's baby slobber and whatever else it might have encountered over the years. Beneath it was Dad's compass! My eyes misted.

"I thought you'd like to have them," he said, wet-eyed himself. "Tommy would have wanted you to."

"Maybe they should go to Tom Junior."

"No, Father," he shook his head, "I don't think so. They belong with you."

Deep emotion welled up in me right then, jumbled emotions, a lot of things. I stood without thinking and opened my arms, and Luke stepped into them. When he hugged me he held fast, digging his forehead into my shoulder. He shuddered and sniffed, as if he had been waiting for this all his life. I patted his back and gave him his time, and when Mama came back with the pie we were still standing there.

* * *

I was restless on New Year's Eve. Mama had gone to bed earlier. She'd lived her fair share of new years; nowadays they just came and went. I stood gazing out the living room windows at the dark hill below. Mist lingered in wisps from the rain earlier. The Hanshaw's house was cold and quiet, still vacant after their move. Lights from beyond our hill twinkled through naked and dripping trees, illuminating the overcast sky in a greenish hue, like an inverted night sea. Everything was still. So much New Year's revelry had taken place exactly where I stood, year after year, brilliant and boisterous. I had watched from that limb on my hickory tree, now grown large enough to support a gaggle of curious boys. What would I see from there now?

Someone was shooting off fireworks already. Lonely tracers arced above the trees only to die in flight with a distant pop, falling somewhere, falling unnoticed. I went out onto the deck and leaned against the rail. The air was cool and damp, although not cold. Another tracer shot skyward. I followed it as it sped to its death, waited impatiently for the next. Probably just boys with bottle rockets, I thought. Not enough to make a show. The big show would be downtown by the river, invisible from our side of the hill. Shortly the tracers fell silent. The boys had probably fired off the last of their certainly-illicit stash, a few exciting moments for them, no more.

I would have liked to go out and see the fireworks downtown, but the thought of mingling alone through jubilant crowds only depressed me further. I couldn't ask Gracie to go with me, not this late in the evening, but beyond her there was no one left, no friends, no family, only...Luke! He loved fireworks, he had told me so. When was that? It had been that Fourth of July at Buchanan High School in Clovis, when Rachel was nine. I remembered he had been so entranced by the light; and then with a pang I remembered the warm, motherly look Judith had given him as he grinned at the sky.

I called Luke's cell phone. It rang and rang. I was about to hang up when his harried voice came on the line.

"Father? Father, hello."

"Luke?" There was a raucous noise in the background, clinking glasses, tinny music, men's husky voices, cheering—a real party.

"Sorry, Father. It's loud in here. Just a minute."

Sounds warbled high and low from Luke's phone as he worked his way through the party to someplace quiet. A door clicked shut and then the party sounds were muffled.

"Yeah, Father, sorry about that. What's up?"

"I was thinking—but no, you sound like you're having a good time. Never mind. I'll call you tomorrow."

"No, Father, wait. Tell me."

"Uh, I was thinking of going to see the fireworks. I remembered how much you liked them, so I called."

"That's great, Father. I'd love to."

"Really?"

"Sure. I need to get out of this place anyway. It's getting out of hand in here."

"Uh, okay. Tell me where you are and I'll come get you."

He went quiet for a moment. I could hear him breathing into the phone, along with thumping bass beats through the door.

"Uh, I've got a better idea. Meet me on the Shelby Pedestrian Bridge, say half an hour? We can make it in time that way."

"But it'll be crowded. We won't be able to find each other."

"Sure we will. Just go to the middle. I'll find you or you'll find me. But we'd better get moving or we'll miss it."

"Okay, Luke. If you think so."

I took the long way around to avoid the traffic, parked on a street near LP Field across the river from downtown, then sprinted for the bridge. People were lined along the north rail like starlings on a limb, stacking deeper as I raced ahead. Crowds clogged the bridge. I shouldered through them to reach the midpoint. Music was blaring from the far bank where the clubs were, an amplified din. Shouts and hoots carried through the crowd and over our heads. Empty beer cans rattled underfoot.

I neared the middle of the bridge, searching for Luke through the confusion as I went. He could have been standing right next to me and I would have missed him in that throng. I wavered in place, being buffeted by the swarming crowd. I wouldn't be able to find Luke in this, it was futile. The fireworks would go off, the crowd would cheer, and I would be left standing there, alone.

A hand reached through and took my arm.

"Father," Luke grinned. "I told you we would make it." He got knocked by a shoulder but he held on.

"Luke!"

"C'mon over here. I got some guys holding us a place."

He tugged me through the crowd to the rail, squeezed in beside me and squared his shoulders.

"This is crazy," I shouted. "I've never seen it like this."

"Nashville's becoming the new *It* city," he shouted back. "Better get used to it."

I wedged my elbows onto the rail and looked up the river toward the iron lattice of Woodland Street Bridge, where the fireworks would be set off.

"We'll have a great view here," I said near his ear.

"Yeah, it's perfect."

It was too hard to speak over the roar, and I couldn't think of anything to say anyway, so I held my place against the rail and waited.

The countdown rang out from below, urged on by the crowd—*ten...nine...eight.* Luke turned my way with a look of boyish anticipation that erased twenty years from his face. I grinned, caught up in it myself, and rested a hand on his shoulder.

...three...two...one—Happy New Year!

The first pops were perfunctory, but they sent the crowd into an orgasm of cheers and shouts that were even more deafening than before; then followed a rapid-fire succession, like a distant battle line. Plumes of smoke wafted over the river in a suddenly breathless lull, and then the sky exploded with color.

The crowd bellowed its excitement in a thrilling rush and ululation. Streaks one after another grazed the sky, expanding into orbs of brilliance that sparkled off the river in a parallel show. We were cast in scarlet, in green and yellow and blue, our shadows flashing between the bursts like still images. The light danced on Luke's grinning face, sharpening his cheeks and nose, bringing out familiar features that tugged disconcertingly at something in my memory.

I looked away quickly and cheered as the next rocket blossomed in the night. Out the corner of my eye I saw Luke studying me, some inner debate plain in his expression.

"What is it?" I asked him.

Another thrilling burst of color exploded above us just then. I cheered and shouted with the others, glancing at Luke to see if he had come around and was joining in as well. He was looking right at me instead. His expression had gone sober.

"Father?" he shouted over the din.

"Yeah, Luke." I leaned my ear closer.

"Father, I need to tell you something."

"Okay, go ahead." My attention was back to the fireworks, but I kept my head tilted so that I could hear.

"Father, I'm...I'm gay."

I couldn't have heard him right. It was so loud... I laughed it off, slapped him on the shoulder and grinned. Kaleidoscopic light glittered in disquietly somber eyes.

"I'm happy, too, Luke," I said to him sidelong through the roar. I parked my elbows on the rail and whooped as another rocket went up.

"No, Father, not that," he hollered testily. "I'm *gay*."

That struck with the force to knock the grin off my face. I turned to him with brows creased, considered him up and down as if he were pulling a prank on me.

"Don't say that, Luke. It's not funny." The crowd was so loud that I wasn't sure if he heard me. But he had.

"No, Father, it's *not* funny. It's who I am."

"What?" That vanquished the last of my naive reserve. "No you're not, Luke." I examined him for some flaw, some tell-tale sign. "We don't have that in our family."

"It's not a sickness, Father."

The crowd and the noise seemed to recede around us.

"The hell it's not."

His eyes began to fill. What passed across his face would have been wrenching under other circumstances.

"I thought you would understand," he said with quivering cheeks.

"No, I don't understand," I growled back at him. And I didn't. I'd only ever known one homosexual, Sarah Jean Connelly from high school, and I hadn't known her well. And anyway, she had gone off after graduation. Who knew if she really was that way, or if it was just gossip?

"Father, *please*," he begged me, as if he were dangling from a rope fraying on jagged rock. His eyes revealed his anguish. They were dark, tortured pools, about to spill.

I know my reaction was wrong. I heard enough about it later from Sadie to last me until even now. But those were different times. And coming on top of everything else, Luke's confession struck with a finality that I couldn't accept just then. If only Judith had been with me. If only...

I turned my back to him as anger and disgust rumbled up from my belly. My son? A queer? It wasn't possible. It couldn't be. I rounded on him in a fit of rage, rage that took me over, rage that embodied every misery, disappointment and loss I had ever endured. I stabbed a shaking finger at his chest and he quailed. The crowd around us went on, oblivious.

"We don't *have* that in our family," I seethed through gritted teeth, eyeing him with a suspicion that must have been evident.

Something stiffened in him. He stood erect, wiped the hair out of his eyes and pushed back at me with his chest.

"I knew it!" he spat. Tears streaked his cheeks now. "Well let me tell you, *Father*, we *do* have it in our family." He laughed acidly. "She never told you, did she?" He shook his head ironically at my dumb expression. "Just like her, I guess. Well I'll tell you now—Dad made her do the test, you know? When I was little." I gawked at him, confusion churning with anger. "Yeah, Father. Sorry to disappoint you, but I'm yours. Always was." He chuckled darkly. "But it explains a lot, you know?"

I didn't know whether to scream or cry. I stood there with my jaw hanging while the crowd cheered around me.

"Goodbye, Father," he said weakly, then he turned and pushed through the crowd.

* * *

I didn't sleep worth a damn that night. I gave it up at the first dim light of dawn, threw off the sheets and trudged upstairs for coffee. I sat quietly at the kitchen table, sipping coffee and rubbing at the worry in my eyes. The morning came up in dull layered shades. A front had come through in the early hours. It was crackling cold outside, mid 20s. A dusting of snow powdered the trees like a confection.

What little sleep I had managed hadn't done anything to temper my anger. It simmered, hotter than my coffee. I slammed a fist on the table hard enough to startle a red-winged blackbird off the window sill. I knew what Judith would have done. She would have taken Luke under her arm, steered him someplace quiet, and they would have talked about it; and then she would have come to me, planting her hands on her hips, giving me *that* look, and somehow I would have found a way to accept Luke.

But Judith wasn't here, and no amount of pained memory could make this right.

Dawn rose higher. Dolly and Daisy were barking for their food. I went out to them, hugging myself through the bracing cold. They looked up at me with eager dog smiles as I filled their bowls, then set to it as if they hadn't eaten in a week. I knelt and patted their heads affectionately. Dogs didn't betray you. They loved you no matter what. And if they were ever angry, they forgot about it soon enough anyway. Dogs know how to forget. I wished I did. With those troubled thoughts mulling around inside me, I shivered down the hill for the newspaper.

Mama was in the kitchen when I got back, sitting at the table, sipping her coffee. She seemed pale.

"Are you feeling all right, Mama?" I asked, rubbing the chill off my arms.

"Oh, I didn't sleep well." She absently worried at her hair. "I heard you go out last night."

"You did? Sorry, I didn't mean to wake you up."

"You didn't. I just tossed and turned all night. Where did you go so late?"

"I went to see the fireworks with Lu—uh, I went to see the fireworks." Too late.

"Did you say you went with Luke? That's nice. He's such a sweet boy. He and Tommy both. They're sweet boys."

Did she mean Tommy or Tom?

"Mama, are you sure you're feeling okay?" She seemed distracted this morning, out of focus.

"Oh, I'm fine," she answered with a dismissive wave.

"Hmm."

I refilled my cup and sat, paged through the newspaper with disinterest. The news was mostly about the presidential campaign. Clinton, Obama, and Edwards were duking it out even harder in advance of the primary, their barbs growing caustic; and on the other side a host of candidates with less control over their tongues than a frothy preacher in a revival tent. I folded the paper in disgust and put it down.

"This election," I commented sourly. "I don't know if I can vote for any of them."

Mama was staring out the windows as if hypnotized, her eyes glassy and vacant. I glanced over my shoulder to see if something was out there, saw nothing out of the ordinary.

"Mama?" I waved a hand before her eyes and smiled uncertainly. "What is it?"

She turned to me with a faraway look.

"I wish Leavitt would come home, Dick," she said distantly." It's been so long."

A foreboding chill tingled in my spine. "Mama?"

"And Elizabeth," she went on. "Why won't she visit? I should call Sadie. She would know."

"Oh, Mama," I moaned in dread realization. I rose numbly to my feet.

Suddenly Mama jerked herself up, looking around in a daze. Her lips drooped. Her left eyelid fluttered.

"Mama, what's the matter?" I whined like a child. Tears spilled.

She wobbled, raised a hand to her temple, probed in puzzlement as if something were there. She winced at a sudden stab of pain.

"Oh, no! Mama, *please*," I cried.

I started toward her, but before I could reach her she fell over, dead.

TWENTY-FOUR

Anger tricks you. It robs you of your senses. It distracts you from the here and now. It turns that which is not in your control into a struggle that cannot be won. It makes you believe you are self-righteous and superior, when all it really does is sequester your mind into a dark place.

I had been grumbling since New York—hotter than sin, no water, many of the shelters taken over by bums. New York is also where I encountered the brunt of the northbounder wave. Some hikers left earlier, some later, but most northbounders and southbounders departed their prospective mountain within a window of a couple of weeks—early spring in the south, late spring in the north—which inevitably brought them together in New York. And of the few thousand who attempted a thru-hike each year, ninety percent began in the south.

The northbounders came on like a tribal storm surge, insular packs of hikers who had been together since Springer Mountain, suspicious of anyone going (what was to them) the wrong way. There were so many hikers on the trail now that I only met them obliquely in passing. They overwhelmed the shelters at night; they stuffed the hostels to capacity. They scooped up the *trail magic* before I could get to it. Many local people, known as *trail angels*, would leave styrofoam coolers of cokes, beer, cookies and whatnot along the trail for the hikers. In Maine they would even float the cans in the cold streams, a welcome and invigorating surprise on a hot day. This truly was trail magic. Especially in humid and hot New York, I stumbled toward these luxuries as to a desert mirage. Glimpsing a styrofoam cooler along the trail ahead, I would run to it in salvation, only to seethe bitterly when I found it full of empties.

On and on the northbounders came, on through New Jersey and the rain; across Delaware Water Gap into Pennsylvania, and still they were there, an endless tide. Anger was robbing me of the trail. I recognized this clearly in my rare moments of solitude, so I steeled myself to maintain objectivity. The northbounders were as equally deserving as I. It wasn't right to begrudge them anything. I began to hike with a mantra, which I voiced out loud every four steps until whatever had set me off had passed: *Don't use anger; don't use anger; don't use anger.*

With so many hikers on the trail, the registers were soon filled and replaced. The last poem I had seen from Beer Poet had been at RPH shelter just off Taconic State Parkway in New York, on a re-routed section of trail that wasn't too far from where I had met those northbounders in 1976. It was dated July 23, so Beer Poet had still been making pretty good time up until then. This poem disturbed me:

> *Onward and on,*
> *Where I may rest.*
> *Somewhere beyond,*
> *Where I may sleep.*
> *I journey long,*
> *In search of peace.*
> *Perhaps to sleep,*
> *If not to dream.*
> *For my dreams cry,*
> *They cry to me.*
> *Beer Poet, GA–ME '07*

This was the last poem from Beer Poet that I would ever find. Had I known, it would have seemed a melancholy note to end on. I sensed despair in his words. Knowing how late in the season he had climbed into the White Mountains, I worried that he wouldn't make it, wouldn't find his peace at last; but then I remembered with an ironic laugh that I had been following his journey in reverse. In the end he *had* made it. I had to smile. I had become kindred with him in a way that I didn't share with the other hikers. I felt a gathering sense of loss as the trail went on, when it became apparent that I would find no more poems. Eventually, in that time-elongating way of the trail, Beer Poet slipped the present and joined my memories.

* * *

I met my last northbounder in Palmerton, Pennsylvania, in a basement under the town hall that Palmerton offered as a shelter to thru-hikers. We were the only two there. When I met him he was sitting on one of the bunks, probing his teeth with dental floss. The local Girl Scouts distributed free hygiene kits to the hikers, plastic baggies containing a toothbrush, toothpaste and dental floss. It was a nice gesture from true trail angels.

His trail name was, unoriginally, *Rye Lee*, which came out as Riley, probably his off-trail name. He could have been about my age, but it was hard to tell. He looked haggard, used up, with a wild mop of greasy brown hair, patchy skin, some angry welts on his ankles, and a scattered look in his eyes. It was already July 29. There was no use saying the obvious out loud, that he would never make it to Mt. Katahdin before it was closed for the season, although he held on that he would make it with time to spare.

"I twisted my ankle on the rocks," he said right away, as if he needed to apologize to me for his tardiness. I didn't care. I had just come off that long, denuded ridge above Palmerton, which offers no shelter from the sun. Due to generations of zinc smelting, that ridge was an EPA Superfund site, and it looked it. More than thirty years of clean-up and restoration had yet to bring the trees back. On top of that I had barely missed being bitten by a rattlesnake, was penetrated instead by thorns after throwing myself into the brambles to dodge its strike; and then came that torturous, rocky decent into Lehigh Gap. I was wobbly on my feet, scratched, sweat-streaked and bone-tired. I wanted to sleep, not talk. But Rye Lee was a talker.

"I was a good hiker," he went on, "until I twisted my ankle." I couldn't place his accent. "You can see that, can't you? Sure you can. I'm a good hiker. I'll catch up. You wait and see."

"Well, good luck," I said. I heaved myself into a bunk.

"Say, you wouldn't want to go out for a beer would you?"

"Not right now," I answered wearily.

"Oh, sure, sure. You're tired. But later we should go out. I met a girl up the street. I bet she'd buy us some beer."

I looked at him skeptically. "Riley, are you *living* here?"

"No, no," he said, apparently not offended at all. "I'm a hiker just like you. I've been hiking. I just twisted my ankle is all."

"Okay then." I closed my eyes.

"So which way you goin'?" he asked. I sighed.

"South."

"Sure, sure. I shoulda gone south. But then I'd still be here now, wouldn't I?"

"Yep."

"Wouldn't have twisted my ankle, though."

"Maybe not."

"These rocks in Pennsylvania are awful. Everybody talks about 'em."

"I know."

"Never seen anything like it. Can't get your footing, you know?"

"Yeah, Riley, I know," I said with an impatient sigh. "But if you don't mind, I need to get some sleep."

"Sure, sure. Sorry. I don't mean to go on and on, I just haven't had anybody to talk to for a while."

"No problem." I yawned and turned to the wall.

"Say, I met a *SOBO* a couple of weeks ago. *Rocklayer*. Young guy, kind of tall. You know him?"

I squeezed my eyes. Sleep was right there, begging to come.

"Yeah, I met him in Maine," I mumbled to the wall.

"He was a good kid. And fast. Man, he was fast."

"Uh, huh."

"Say, you think you'll catch him?"

I didn't answer. Sleep was taking me, heavy and sweet. I thought that maybe he would take the hint, but no—

"Be nice if we had some other hikers here—to talk to. You know what I mean? I was in a good group. We stuck together, at least until I twisted my ankle. They were all young and fast, but I caught up to them most nights. Sometimes I had to sleep outside because there was no room left in the shelters, but they would have let me in, you know, if there'd been room. That's all it was. I liked them a lot. I wish I hadn't twisted my ankle. That's what did it. I'd still be with them if I hadn't twisted my ankle. That's all it was. Could happen to anybody."

He wouldn't stop; he just wouldn't stop. The veil of sleep lifted and I exhaled in frustration.

"Riley," I said with an edge, "I really need to sleep."

"Sure, sure. But it's not even dark yet, you know? Maybe if you stayed up a while it would be better. Sleep, I mean. Sometimes when I can't sleep I stay up real late, and then, guess what? I fall asleep just like that. I remember in Tennessee all the shelters were so full, everybody snoring—I couldn't sleep at all. So I said to myself, hey, don't think about it, just keep your eyes open as long as you can. And you know what? Next thing I know it's morning and I slept like a baby."

There was something pathetic about this guy, and I couldn't take it anymore. I rolled out of my bunk and rubbed my eyes.

"What's wrong? Can't sleep?" he asked inanely. "Maybe you should try what I do." I reached for my backpack and pulled it over. His face seemed to fall. "Hey, where you going?"

"Next shelter," I answered in disgust. The George W. Outerbridge shelter was only a couple of miles away, but I would have to climb out of the gap to get there which, in my weary state, would be excruciating. *Don't use anger; don't use anger; don't use anger.*

"Hey, don't do that. *Please.*" He was groveling like a beaten dog now. I swear his eyes were filling. "Stay here. At least for a little while."

I blinked my eyes to clear them, shouldered my backpack and looked away. It was too depressing to watch a man carry on so. When he put a weakened hand on my arm, I snapped around to bat him off. The look in his eyes, though—pathetic. I shrugged angrily out of his grip, but then winced at his cowed reaction.

"Riley?" I asked in exasperation laced with pity. "What are you *doing* here?"

"Oh," he seemed to brighten a little if that were possible. He lowered himself onto a bunk and looked off somewhere. "My boy and I—we always talked about it. Even when he was a kid. We were going to do it together. The whole thing."

I looked around blankly. "So where is he?"

"Oh, sure, sure. Yeah, I'd wonder about that, too." He looked up and gave me a strained smile. "My boy's in Afghanistan. He's a soldier over there. He's brave. You know what he did? He and his squad had to hold a firebase in the mountains all by themselves. Those Taliban started shooting down on them, you know? Picking them off? First this guy then that guy—well, my boy, he grabbed a machine gun and went after 'em, and all the time they fired down, killing his guys, but he fought back, going after them all by himself. He showed 'em. He sure did. He made them pay. He made them pay..."

Riley trailed off, his eyes about to spill, and I felt something heavy and hard sink in my stomach.

"Riley, what happened to your son?" I asked in dread.

"Why—" He shuddered. His lips began to tremble. "—why he killed them. He killed them all, and...and..." He lost it then, sobbing into his hands like a spanked child. Tears leaked between his fingers. "*Oh, Shane,*" he wailed. He looked up and I saw a broken man. "*I'm so sorry. I tried. I tried so hard. But I can't do it. I hurt, Shane. I hurt so bad.*"

"Oh, hell." I dropped my backpack and battled my own emotions, found myself taking that broken man into my arms. I patted his back and searched for comforting words. "It's okay, Riley. Shane would understand."

"He always wanted this," Riley cried. "I wanted to do it for him. But I can't. *I can't.*"

"Sure you can, Riley. You can do it." I peered into my darkest hours and shuddered. This could have been me in other circumstances. It easily could have been. "You're tired, that's all." I took him by the shoulders and stood him up. "C'mon, let's go have that beer and we can talk about it."

"You mean that?" he asked, as if it might be a trick.

"Yeah. C'mon now."

We went to a bar up the street, where I bought the beers and sat drowsily while Riley poured it all out to me, becoming more coherent as his burdens fell away. There wasn't much more than what I had already deduced back in the basement. Riley wasn't the crazy man he had appeared to be, he was just a distraught father from Milwaukee who had been broken beyond his limits through a combination of grief, physical extremes, and shame. He was who I might have been if I had attempted this hike last year. What he needed most was not empathy or pity, but someone to talk to, someone who would listen.

By the time we finished our fourth beers, he seemed a different man entirely. He still looked fragile, but at least his eyes weren't as flighty now.

"I can't make it, can I?" he asked hollowly, knowing the answer but clinging to hope anyway. I would have liked nothing more than to encourage him on. It felt defeatist to say otherwise, but Riley needed the truth.

"I think it would be tough," I hedged, but then saw a glimmer of hope take hold in him, a glimmer that, in his condition, could cost him his life in the Maine woods if not beforehand in the White Mountains. I gritted my teeth and plunged in with the truth as I saw it. "Actually, Riley—yeah, I don't think it's a good idea to go on."

His eyes watered and he wiped them. I reached across and patted his shoulder. My advice to him then, worth less, perhaps, than the time it took to spit it out, was to go home, to get well, then return in the spring and start from here. There were no rules on the trail, no judges except ourselves. He could climb Mt. Katahdin next summer. His son would have been just as proud, and then maybe Riley would find some peace.

* * *

I reached Virginia a week later. We southbounders were strung so sparingly along the trail that I never saw anyone anymore. That kind of solitude hadn't helped Riley, but it's what I yearned for most of all. I had spent only a few weeks in the midst of the northbounder wave, but those weeks had seemed like months. I hadn't been aware of the stress this put on me until I passed through Harpers Ferry into Virginia and suddenly discovered that I could breathe again.

Beyond the occasional hunter or fisherman, I spent each night alone in shelter. I lazed contentedly on the sleeping platforms, spreading out my gear, shamelessly taking up all the space. The evenings were redolent of honeysuckle and pine, the nights a serenade of frog song. Most evenings I would lie against my rolled sleeping bag, cross my legs and just gaze out as the bronze hues of sunset shaded toward dusk, descending into night and the hooting of owls. No other therapy could have been as effective.

Barely a week beyond the half-way point of the hike now, my body had become fully adjusted, what Riley had not been able to achieve. I had lost about forty pounds. I may have appeared emaciated to others, but I felt wonderful, cleansed, light on my feet. I hiked fast, four to five miles per hour, covering thirty miles or more a day. Discomforts became minor annoyances, the dirt and the sweat, the bug bites, the inflamed scratches and intractable blisters. Starving though I was, my stomach didn't rumble anymore. I had reached that magical state of equilibrium.

I hiked along those Virginia ridges like a man born for the mountains, deftly side-stepping poison ivy without losing pace, hopping from outcrop to outcrop in a fluid motion, scaring up wild turkeys and hollering at the bears. I was in a state of grace until I hiked into Shenandoah National Park.

Those three days of congested trail felt interminable. I gritted my teeth as day-hikers plugged the trail, picking their ways along, shoulder to shoulder from one side of the trail to the other, taking no notice of who or what was coming up behind them. "Excuse me. Excuse me," and they would turn, startled, then idiotically bunch together right where I needed to pass. They were so unaware of their surroundings, so hapless, that a bear could have picked them off one by one and they wouldn't have noticed.

"*Don't use anger; don't use anger; don't use anger,*" I seethed as I went, sometimes hopping up into the woods to sprint around them. I picked up some poison ivy stripes that way.

The shelters were full of Boy Scouts. They weren't supposed to do that, they were supposed to tent out and reserve the shelters for thru-hikers, but what could I do?

Fight them? Rachel had gone through this, she had written about it in her journal, and that made me even more angry.

Don't use anger; don't use anger; don't use anger...

I pushed on as if I were fleeing an invading horde, hiking late into the night, thirty-seven miles one day, forty-eight miles the next. I outpaced even Rachel's time through Shenandoah, and then I was out of it, alone again, and soon I couldn't recall what had gotten me so worked up.

The woods grew deeper, the nights colder. The Grayson Highlands, Roan Mountain—that gnarled, eerie stretch of dark forest along the Tennessee/North Carolina line, where hillbillies hung fish-hook traps to snare unwary hikers, and wild-looking men dug for ginseng—and then the Smokies.

It rained again. Mist filled the hollows, and the rounded peaks were shrouded in fog. It was cold. I pushed on, oblivious. I passed local hikers like a wraith through the mist, so fast that they stopped to gawk after me. The woods, the mist, and the cold merged into a blur in passing. Bears tumbled out of my way. When I emerged onto the paved path to Clingmans Dome I felt that I had been yanked out of reality. The cement observation tower loomed in the mist like a Cold-War relic. I considered it distantly. There were no people out, not in this weather. I shrugged, plunged back into the woods and rejoined the trail.

It was going to end soon. As much as I was hiking briskly at thirty miles or more per day, I didn't want it to be over—and yet at the same time I was desperate to reach Springer Mountain. Strange dichotomy, that.

The weather cleared at Fontana Dam, as it had before. At my pace I would make Springer Mountain in less than a week. That could as well have been a year in trail perspective, but I slowed down anyway, or tried to. I thought I was just ambling along leisurely, but then night would come and I would discover that thirty miles had passed beneath my tattered, duct-taped shoes. I scrambled up Springer Mountain on, yes, September 27. I was fifty years old.

I expected to see Baptists, but there were none. I reached out for Judith's hand, but she wasn't there. Elongated trail time had allowed me to sense years in passing, and this in only a matter of months. It was why I came, what I knew would happen, even as I felt the stabbing pang of loss. Judith was in the past now, always to be. Rachel was with her, and Mama. They were all memory now.

It was midafternoon, bright and warm. I stood at the cliff, gazing out at the view that doesn't change. I felt strangely numb, displaced. My eyes were dry. The breeze roared in my ears, my breaths as loud as the puffing exhalations of a steam locomotive. All sound fell away, just my breaths and the hollow breeze. I took a last look around, walked past the trail register without signing it, and headed home.

* * *

As before, it took a few days alone in a motel room for me to come to terms with the end of the trail. I ate fried chicken and stared at the walls. I was not wracked with loss and confusion this time, but rather with a peculiar detachment, as if my mind were a half step out of phase with the moment. I felt neither grief nor joy; neither angst nor surcease. Instead I inhabited some middle place, a dispassionate refuge in which all that had been was kept just out of focus. This presented no dilemma to me, no emotional conundrum. It just was.

I left for home on the fourth morning after Springer Mountain, clothed in a numb reserve that insulated me against the bumping and bustling of people. It was October 1, a fine, clear day. I took bare notice of anything until my taxi pulled to the foot of the hill and I looked up into the yard.

"What the hell?"

I jerked myself out of the taxi and stood there gaping. My driver was a foreign guy, Middle-Eastern or some such. He leaned across to speak to me through the passenger window.

"The electricity company cut the trees of all the people. They are very angry."

"Those bastards!"

My hickory tree had been mutilated. Huge limbs had been hacked off indiscriminately on the side facing the street, leaving the tree obscenely lopsided, like a man with half a face. In my absence, a death sentence had been pronounced and executed. The old hickory might eventually send out some spindly limbs, might even appear to recover for a time; regardless, such massive wounds would never heal. Rot would set in. Bark would crack and fall. The tree was dead already, it would just take time to show.

I grabbed my backpack and cursed my way up the hill. Sadie met me at the front door. We embraced with a closeness that was new between us, an unspoken acceptance of the reality of things, that it was just us now. I pulled away only when the plight of my hickory tree intruded into the moment.

"Were you here when it happened?" I asked. She didn't need an explanation, she knew what I meant.

"No, it was that way when I got here. Hermano said they did it right after you left."

Hermano was the caretaker I had hired to look after the house and the dogs while I was on the trail. He was a thin old Mexican with the calloused hands and the rank smell of a dirt-poor farmer. I didn't think he was legal, but Gracie had vouched for him. He had proved to be trustworthy and dependable.

"Your poor tree," Sadie added ruefully.

"It wasn't even that close to the power lines," I spat. "I'm gonna get those bastards."

She pursed her lips in a disapproving way that was eerily reminiscent of Mama, but there the resemblance ended. At fifty-seven years old, Sadie was as prim and svelte as she had ever been. Her skin was smooth and clear, delicately pale from northern winters. She still wore her hair short, in a feathered continental style, and she still dressed in some version of her signature black. Only her tortoise-shell eyeglasses gave away her advancing age, although these, more often than not, made her look studious rather than old.

"Do that later," she said. "For now, get inside and tell me about everything. You're so skinny! My God, I had forgotten."

I smiled wanly. "Yeah. Is there any food in the house?"

"We'll find something."

We hauled ourselves around the chair lift and upstairs to the kitchen. I dropped my backpack next to the table, went to the cupboard and fished out two big cans of beef stew. I poured the stew into a pot, and Sadie came up with some bread that she had bought earlier in the week. That would be enough to tide me over until we could go out.

"Did you get it all done?" I asked her as the stew bubbled. This was about Mama's room. I had closed it off after she died because I couldn't bring myself to go in there to clean it out, afraid that I might see things that no mother's son should ever see. Sadie had promised to take care of it for me while I was on the trail.

"Yes," she answered darkly. "It's all done. I kept some pictures and some jewelry, if that's okay."

"Sure," I said. "She would have wanted you to."

"I gave the rest to her church."

"She would have liked that." I pondered this for a moment, then: "I just couldn't go in there, you know?"

"I understand. Oh, and I found this." She reached for something on the counter top.

"What is it?"

"A journal."

"Hmm."

She handed over a small black journal, which I accepted with some ambivalence.

"Well?" she asked in expectation. "Aren't you going to look at it?"

"I'll look at it later," I said uneasily, and I stuffed it into one of my backpack's pockets, hoping that would end it. Sadie sighed.

"Okay, then."

We settled in at the kitchen table. Sadie looked on in amusement as I shoveled stew into my mouth.

"You ate like this when you stopped at my house." She smiled at the memory. "Well, anyway—we thought we would hear from you again. You never called or anything after that. So how did it go?"

"It was different. There were a lot more hikers than before, and everything seemed so modern. You don't have to rough it as much. Parts of the trail have been relocated since last time, off of the roads and into the mountains, so there was a lot I didn't remember. If anything, I think it's harder now, more climbs. And there are these huge shelters in Pennsylvania and Virginia, like two-story cabins. They call them *Hiker Hiltons*."

"You sound as if you're disappointed."

"No, not that, but—well, being older this time, I guess I knew what to expect."

"You seem...oh, I don't know."

"What?"

"A little off. Distant, maybe."

"It's probably just the trail," I deflected.

"Did you at least find what you were looking for?"

"I think so."

"I'm glad. Oh—and did you get to see April?"

"Uh, huh. Thomas brought her when I crossed over the Turnpike. There's a campground right there."

"So how was she?"

"She's getting big. Jabbers a lot, you know, the way Rachel did."

Sadie winced at the mention of Rachel. It seemed to pain her more than it pained me.

"We invited them up," she mused, "but—well, you know."

"Yeah, I do. It's the New Hampshire thing."

"I honestly don't understand that."

"Massachusetts men got a strong thing goin' on back home. Or so they say."

"Right," she smiled, but then her brows furrowed. "So—what now, Carlton?"

"What do you mean?"

She raised her arms and swept them around. "This house. Everything. What are you going to do?"

"I don't know. Keep the place up, I guess. The way Dad wanted."

She became pensive at that, or maybe it was something else.

"What about Luke?" she asked guardedly.

"What about him?"

"*Carlton?*" she prompted in irritation.

"Well, you heard what he said to me at Mama's funeral, that he was done with me. *Done with me?* What kind of thing is that to say?"

"Well, you *were* awful to him."

"Only because he brought that *man* to the funeral," I sputtered.

"That man's name is Nick."

"I don't care. He didn't know Mama. He didn't belong there."

"Oh, Carlton, Luke just wants you to accept him for who he is."

I rubbed my temples to ward off an incipient headache, thinking that if I had just hiked slower I would still be on the trail now.

"Sadie," I said, hollow-eyed, "I was on the trail for more than four months, so I've had plenty of time to think about everything...and what I think is, he doesn't want anything from me. So please just drop it. Okay?"

Sadie moved to object, but I cut her off with a sharp look. She shook her head sadly. "Okay, Carlton."

"Good. What room are you staying in by the way?"

"Downstairs in my old room. Nothing else felt right. But still, it's strange. It's so quiet at night. I keep expecting to hear Mom coming down the stairs, or Dad clinking the ice in his glass. I couldn't live here alone, Carlton. Too many memories."

"I'll be all right. Anyway, how long can you stay?"

"Only a few more days. I need to get back."

"Teaching or writing?"

"Both."

"Well, I'm glad you were able to come, even if only for a little while."

"Me, too," she said. She rested her hand on mine and looked at me with a worried frown. "Carlton, are you sure about this?"

"I'll be fine," I answered, averting my eyes. I rattled my spoon in my empty bowl and forced a smile. "So now let's go out and get something to eat."

She laughed at that. Good.

* * *

When winter cleared, and spring returned leaves to the half of my hickory tree that still lived, the workers arrived to install my new solar electricity system. It was the best revenge I could think to take against a faceless electricity company that felt sufficiently empowered to destroy people's property without fear of reprisal. Yeah, I got them back. Not only would I no longer have to pay them money, but on certain sunny days they would actually have to pay *me* for the excess electricity I generated.

It took about a week to get it all done. In retrospect, looking back more than forty-five years, the decisions Dad made when he sited our house seem to have been almost prescient. This prescience would demonstrate itself again later, but in the meantime the house—or specifically that long, canted ranch-style roof—was perfectly positioned to capture the most sunlight throughout the year. Iridescent solar panels were installed from one end of the roof to the other, precisely angled on adjustable legs like something NASA would use out in space; and to help during the darker days of winter, the workers perched a compact windmill generator on the peak of the garden shed. My house was now completely self-contained, requiring no outside power source.

I relished the control this gave me, the freedom to exist independently of, for lack of a better cliché, *the powers that be*. I had a strange dream shortly after the work was completed. In my dream, a storm came. Lightening crackled from a roiling black sky, splintering trees, striking homes from their foundations with malicious impunity. Then Nashville was inundated by a biblical tide. Towering waves lapped at the upper floors of the high-rises downtown, flowing around my hill until I was cut off from the world, an island in a new sea. Other hilltops poked above the turbulent waters, creating a forested archipelago upon which ragged survivors clung and scraped for survival; and all this while I resided safely and comfortably with all the modern conveniences. I awoke shaken and troubled, but at the heart of it there was something else, a sense of pacific isolation that was disturbingly alluring.

Those thoughts passed as one day led into the next. Nashville did flood a year later, in May of 2010. It wasn't the biblical flood of my dream, but still epic enough to do significant damage to the lower areas along the river. The Cumberland had been mostly tamed by a series of dams up river, but after days of unusually constant rain, the Army Corps of Engineers was forced to do releases to relive the pressure on its dams. The river swelled over its banks, pouring into downtown. Some lives were lost. The recriminations let fly almost immediately afterward, and recovery took a long time, but on my hill I wasn't affected in the least.

In the meantime, I stayed busy around the house, looking after the dogs and gardens, doing minor repairs. I slept in the room upstairs, my old room, Leavitt's old room. Sadie had also refurbished Mama's bedroom while I was away. It had new paint and carpet, but I still couldn't bring myself to use it, as if to do so would somehow intrude on Dad's and Mama's privacy. It was their room and always would be. I kept that door closed and locked, and so it remains, even now.

In the world beyond my hill, politics had become disgustingly vitriolic. That was the genesis of our undoing, I think, or perhaps it started a few years earlier with those billboards I saw on Highway 99. Shameful. I avoided the news shows on television because of this, but still got splashed in the muck from the newspapers. You couldn't escape it. At the same time, the economy almost collapsed. Considering the upheavals that have happened since then, this little episode is probably not even in your history vids. Why would it be? Supposedly we barely averted another Great Depression, but you wouldn't have known it from the high-priced SUVs that raced up and down my street or the lines to get into the better restaurants. None of it affected me, my inheritance was secure. As for the rest, I no longer cared.

Instead I enjoyed quiet evenings on the deck, sipping straight whiskey over ice as the sun dipped beyond the hills. Gracie often joined me. While I was on the trail, Angelina had remarried and moved to Knoxville with Tom Junior. This seemed to have cast Gracie adrift. Despite her law practice and her volunteer work, Gracie still couldn't manage to fill her days, as if looking after Angelina and Tom Junior had been her true vocation, everything else just a necessary distraction.

We would sit on the deck like two old warriors whose scars and secrets had been laid bare for so long that there was nothing left for us to hide from one another. I sipped whiskey while she sipped wine, and sometimes we wouldn't speak at all, just watch the sun go down.

On one such evening in August, when the humidity was only a percent or so from driving us indoors, Gracie asked me, "Carlton, don't you ever get lonely?"

She asked this abstractly while gazing at the sky, her feet propped on the rail, her wine flute resting lightly between her fingers. I mulled her question for a moment. No, I wasn't lonely. It was casually comfortable to have Gracie there, but more as a familiar routine than a need for company. In truth, I would have enjoyed the evening just as much if I were alone on that deck, but to say as much would have been deliberately cruel.

"I don't really think about it," I answered vaguely to spare her feelings. "Why do you ask?"

"It's just...oh, nothing." She looked over and gave me a faint smile. There were times when her expression could be as fragile as it had been when we were kids in high school, and this was one of them. Her eyes darted away as I pondered that. "What's going on over there?" she asked then, tipping her flute toward the Hanshaw's house, which was no longer there.

"Oh, you know," I answered sourly. "It's going on all over."

The Hanshaw's house—once the Gorman's house—had been torn down to make room for two, possibly three soulless McMansions on the same lot. This had been going on all over Green Hills for the past few years, spoiling the rural character that Dad had helped to create here. As a result of the financial crisis, though, the hammers had lately fallen silent, the lot left churned and raw and all but abandoned. The contractors would be back when the money started flowing again, but for now I just enjoyed the quiet.

"Too bad," she said. "And your poor tree can't hide it anymore."

"Yeah. I'm thinking about putting in some shrubs, maybe privet. They grow fast, and can maybe hide that mess."

"I hope that never happens to your house."

"It won't," I said with a bitter edge that I reinforced with a gritting jolt of whiskey. "Ever."

"Some things never change, do they Carlton?"

She turned to me then. Her eyes seemed to darken, but maybe it was only the low light.

"No, this house is here to stay. I can promise you that."

"That's something, I guess," she said with peculiar irony. She sipped her wine thoughtfully and looked off as shadows merged toward night and the fireflies began to glow.

* * *

Thomas brought April for a visit the following summer. It was a couple of weeks after April's sixth birthday, still June and a pleasant day. I was down near the foot of the hill planting privet shrubs when they pulled up in their rental. I doffed my gloves, wiped a sleeve across my forehead, and watched eagerly as they drove up to the house. As soon as Thomas threw the car into park, April flung open her door and came running down the lawn, a freckled red sprite with an even white grin and wide green eyes that seemed to know more than their years.

"Grampa! Grampa! Grampa!"

"Hey, sweetie!" I exclaimed with an umph as she leapt into my arms. "You're so big!"

"I'm a big girl," she grinned proudly. "I'm gonna be in first grade."

She displayed a single index finger as I bounced and got an arm under her. Thomas came down with an easy smile.

"Hello, Mr. Jeffries," he said, offering his hand. I had to jostle April onto my hip to get a hand free.

"Thomas. It's good to see you." I shook his hand while April tightened her legs to keep from slipping. "I told you, though, first names are fine now."

"Sure, Mr. Jef—uh, *Carlton*. If you say so." He smiled wide.

"Let's go up to the house—but you, big girl," I tickled April's stomach and she giggled, "are too heavy to carry up the hill."

I set April on her feet and she took my hand, and we trudged up the hill to the house. I had let Dolly and Daisy inside. As soon as we were in, April ran off to play with them.

"Can I get you anything, Thomas?"

"No, sir, I'm fine."

"Okay then."

We sat in the den and appraised one another. Thomas looked good, a little older, a little more mature. He fiddled with the ring on his finger.

"So how was the wedding?" I asked him. He rubbed his hands and looked down. "It's okay, Thomas. You couldn't stay single forever."

"Yeah, sir, well, uh—I just didn't want you to think—"

"I said it's okay, Thomas. I mean it."

But did I really? Thomas deserved his happiness, but this meant that Rachel had to slip that little bit farther away. I guess he sensed this conflict in me despite my best efforts to conceal it.

"I'll always love her, sir," he said to his hands. "And April is so much like her. Sometimes it just catches me, like she's still here."

I could see then what Rachel had loved in Thomas, his gentle devotion. I smiled sincerely to put him at ease, and maybe myself, too.

"So—about your wedding?"

"Oh, yeah. It was great. April was our flower girl. I wish you could have come."

"I'm sorry I missed it. So how does she—"

"Pam?"

"Yeah. So how does Pam get along with April?"

"They love each other, sir. It couldn't be better."

"I'm glad."

"And April knows all about her mother. You don't have to worry about that."

"I'm sure it's fine, Thomas. You don't have to explain."

That seemed to have settled everything we needed to get out in the open. We sat in silence for a minute or so and then I stood.

"Well," I said, "we'd better go check and see what April's gotten into."

They could only stay the weekend. I set them up in Elizabeth's and Sadie's rooms so that neither one would have to stay downstairs alone. April was too big to share a room with her father now, or else I would have put them upstairs in the guestroom. She wasn't too big to play with me the way her mother had, though. The house was so much larger than what she was accustomed to that after dinner that night she just had to go and ferret out all of its hiding places.

April was a delightful little girl, every bit as precocious as her mother had been. We scrambled up and down the stairs while Thomas looked on, laughing with genuine joy. I let her ride Mama's chair lift, which was like a carnival ride as far as April was concerned, and she even rode on my back the way Rachel had.

And then she wanted to play hide-and-seek. We were in the den. Thomas was on the couch, looking at the television. Night had fallen and the fireflies were lighting up, a constellation beyond the windows.

"Close your eyes, Grampa. No cheating," April instructed me forthrightly.

She hitched her hips and wagged a finger at me, and in that moment a knot caught in my throat. I laughed it off, though, covered my eyes and promised not to cheat as she bounded up the stairs. I counted to sixty, and then again for good measure, and then I made my way stealthily upstairs to begin the search. I had a feeling that she was hiding in the guestroom, so I made it a point to go to every other room first, announcing myself as I went.

"Come out, come out wherever you are."

At last I went to guestroom door and cracked it open. It was dark in there, just a shaft of light from the hall. I looked surreptitiously around the bed, got down on hands and knees and peered underneath. She wasn't there, which meant that she had to be in the closet. I padded silently to the closet door, grinned and jerked it open.

"Found ya!"

"Grampa!" April shrieked giddily in the sudden light. "I can see, Grampa! I can *see!*"

That was almost more than I could bear. I wilted onto the floor beside her and wiped at my eyes.

"Grampa?" She took my face in her little hands and looked at me with such knowing eyes that I had to fight to hold it together. "Grampa, why are you sad?"

"I'm not sad, baby." I sniffed and put on a smile.

"I think you're sad."

"No, sweetie, you just reminded me of somebody."

"Who? My mommy?"

"Do you remember your mommy?"

She chewed on a finger and shook her head.

"Well," I sighed, "you were little then."

"I'm big now," she piped up cheerfully.

"Yes you are." I tousled her hair and made myself smile. "My turn now."

"Okay."

She covered her eyes and began to count, and I was carried away to another time.

* * *

Angelina and Tom Junior were in town, so Gracie brought them by the next day. It was another pretty day, perfect for being outdoors. We adults sat around the deck table in the shade of an umbrella while April and Tom Junior played on the lawn below. I brought out sweet tea, while Gracie set out a tray of chicken-salad sandwiches that she had made at home. Thomas and Angelina were already into a long conversation about weddings by the time Gracie and I settled in. I scooted my chair closer to the rail so that I could watch the children, and Gracie did the same.

"He reminds me of his father," Gracie said, crossing her arms on the rail and resting her chin.

"And she reminds me of her mother."

"I feel so old sometimes, Carlton. And then sometimes I feel that I'm too young to have a grandchild, like we're still in school and all I have to worry about is what to wear for our next date."

"I don't feel old," I said. I crossed my arms beside her. "Well, that's not true. But it's not so much that I feel old, but that I'm full of old memories. Do you know what I mean?"

"I think so. Maybe."

The kids were chasing one another in circles around the hickory, laughing with the abandon that only kids can know. My grandchildren—Gracie was right, it was hard to process. Tom Junior was six that summer, too, although three-quarters of a year older and a head taller than April. You couldn't have guessed they were cousins, not with his dark Latin features and her fair Irish ones, but when they laughed they were the same. They were Tommy spinning a compass and Rachel riding me like a pony.

I laid my face on my arms and looked lazily into Gracie's eyes. She met my gaze and smiled softly. Behind us, Thomas was getting worked up in whatever he and Angelina were talking about, slipping deeper into his Southie accent, this juxtaposed against her precise, Latin-inflected diction. Gracie caught that, too, and grinned.

"We have a strange family, don't we Carlton?"

"Yeah, I'd say."

"If we had been together I think it would have turned out the same way."

"You think so?"

"Yeah..." She trailed off with a sigh, and then after a moment: "Who would have thought, back when we were in school, that one day we would be here like this with a grandchild together?"

"Nobody would. At least not me."

"It's almost like we've been together all along, like it was supposed to be—like Evelyn came along and messed up some plan."

"Well, I don't know about that, Gracie."

"Don't you ever think about it?"

"No, not really. Things just happened, and this is the way it worked out."

"Do you really think that?"

"Sure, what else would I think?"

Her eyes glistened and she turned away.

"What's the matter, Gracie?"

"Nothing, Carlton," she mumbled. "I'm just tired."

I puzzled over that, and then April hollered up at us:

"Daddy! Grampa! Look at me."

She had somehow gotten herself up the hickory and was straddling a limb, grinning triumphantly and swinging her legs as if she were atop a galloping horse. Thomas made it from his chair to the rail in a single stride.

"Baby, get down from there before you fall," he shouted, worried like a protective dad and powerless to do anything about it.

"Tommy, you help her down," Angelina added in a stern tone.

I laughed, and was gratified to see that Gracie was laughing as well.

* * *

It only took two seasons for the privet hedge to grow so tall and thick that I couldn't see the street from the deck anymore—or the Hanshaw's former lot, although the hammering had started up again.

"It is very big, Mr. Carlton," Hermano said, clearly impressed. "*Muy grande.*"

"Yeah. I didn't expect them to grow so fast."

We were up ladders, trimming the top of the hedge, he from the street side and me from the other. The hedge had grown too tall and wide for me to handle this chore by myself, and so thick with intertwined limbs that even the puppies couldn't get through it.

"*Mira allá,*" he gestured with a crooked grin, "*los perros.*"

I turned around to see five puppies tumbling over one another like big balls of cotton in the wind. Dolly was lazing in the shade, worn out from nursing her pups, and Daisy was keeping a wary eye from the front steps. I laughed. Puppies were always cute until they got a little older. That outfit in Louisiana that Dad had worked with had provided a stud for Dolly, and in exchange would receive four of these puppies. I already knew which one I was going to keep, the biggest male of the litter. I named him Beauregard.

After we finished with the hedge, Hermano helped me clean out the greenhouse. Mama had made only a half-hearted effort to keep it up after Dad died, until eventually the greenhouse became just another storage shed. The windows were opaque from years of accumulated grime, and the interior was dusty and stale. We hauled out cracked and weathered garden hoses, and crumbling cardboard boxes of magazines and outdated Christmas decorations. We discovered an old lawn mower, which I didn't need so I gave it to Hermano, and stacks of flower pots in all sizes. Some of the pots still contained soil, turned gray and sterile by time. A few held the desiccated remains of plants that had probably been set by Dad. I tossed these out wistfully, yearning to reanimate them somehow.

It took the rest of that day, but the windows gleamed again when we were done, the irrigation and sprinkler system was working, and pots were lined up on the slatted teak shelves, ready for new soil and new plants. I thought that I could already smell the scent of oregano and basil, and knew I would plant those first. It was still early enough in the season to put some tomatoes in, and I was also thinking about trying my hand at roses.

After Hermano left that evening, I carried my whiskey out to the greenhouse and sat there instead of on the deck. The light coming in had a greenish cast, and the air smelled like fresh rain. Looking around, it was easy to re-conjure Dad's vision. The greenhouse was like a refuge, a place of green and living solitude. He must have spent hours alone in here, tinkering with grafts and hybrids, watching his labors grow and produce. I sniffed for the scent of Old Spice, which I didn't smell, of course, but I could still imagine it. I sat back with a satisfied sigh and sipped my whiskey. Everything I needed was right here.

* * *

Within three years I had planted privet all the way around the property, and keeping it trimmed had become such a big job that Hermano brought his son and grandson to help. Even Gracie chipped in, although the hedge troubled her.

"It's like fortress walls, Carlton," she said to me during a pause to wipe the sweat off her brow. It was unusually hot for a Saturday in June, mid 90s or thereabouts. She was wearing white shorts and a T-shirt, her hair tied up and off her neck with a red bandana. Her arms were scratched from the privet, and sweat pasted her shirt between her shoulder blades.

"You think so?" I said.

"Yeah, I think so. Carlton—" She set down her clippers and took a swallow from her water bottle before going on. "—are you trying to keep people out or keep them in?"

"Neither, Gracie. I just like the way it looks."

"Uh, huh," she said with a roll of her eyes.

"It does keep the people in the park up there out of my yard, though," I smiled.

"And your neighbors, too."

"I've never had any problems with them."

"Well," she picked up her clippers, "as long as I can still get in."

"Of course you can, Gracie. We've been all through that."

She considered that a moment before turning back to her work. We clipped the hedge in silence for a time, but I could tell from the tight set of her lips that she was debating with herself whether or not to take it further. She finally came out with it, although she kept her back to me and seemed to be speaking to the hedge.

"Sometimes, Carlton, I'm afraid that I'll come over one day and you'll turn me away."

There was that fragile quality again. I didn't know what more I could do to reassure her except give her what she wanted, which would have been dishonest. I reached over and took her hand before she could snip the next limb.

"Gracie?" I paused until she reluctantly met eyes, and when she did I gave her an affectionate smile. "You're my last friend, like we're the last two left. We've known each so long...you're like a sister to me, as close as Sadie, and that's not going to change. Can't that be enough?"

She sighed. "It's enough, Carlton. I told you it was."

"Good." I sighed in relief myself, and then I gave her a buoyant smile. "Now let's finish this and get lunch."

"I'd rather finish this and get air conditioning, if you don't mind." She was smiling now, too.

"How about lunch *and* air conditioning?"

"Even better."

We went off to the house, two old friends, and if Gracie still wanted more from me she did a good job of hiding it.

* * *

When April turned sixteen, she browbeat her father into letting her fly across the country by herself. Thomas called me, at about his wit's end.

"Was Rachel like this?" he asked rhetorically. Of course he knew the answer.

"Yep," I said in commiseration. "Handful, isn't she."

"Gosh, Carlton, she's always been a handful, but she's been wicked hard to deal with since she became a teenager."

"She's a good girl, Thomas."

"I know that, but *damn.*"

"At least she hasn't asked to hike the trail yet. Or has she?"

"No, thank God. I don't know what I'd do if she asked."

I had to laugh at that. Poor Thomas.

"Oh yes you do," I said, still laughing. "You'd let her. What choice would you have? And then maybe she'd meet a guy, and the next thing you know you'd be a grandfather."

"That's not funny, Carlton."

"Oh yes it is—*Tollbooth Tom.*"

He must have been able to sense how wide my grin was.

"Okay, you got me there. At least so far she's never talked about it."

"Neither had Rachel."

"Ugh."

"Cheer up, Thomas. Maybe she'll just want to join the army, or play pro football or something like that."

"You're getting a kick out this this, aren't you, Carlton?"

"You know it."

"Anyway, she's going to spend the summer with the Taylors, and she wants to fly through Nashville on the way back. That would be about the first week of August. That okay with you?"

"Of course it is. I won't be anywhere else than here."

"Sounds good. But Carlton—*please* don't encourage her too much."

"I would *never* do that to you, Thomas," I said, tongue actually in my cheek.

* * *

April made it in on August 8, a Saturday. Her layover in Denver had been short, so she arrived early in the afternoon. Baggage claim was as chaotic as always. I stood aside and searched the crowd, but April spotted me first.

"Grampa!" she shouted over the din.

I spun around with an expectant grin, which fell in puzzlement when I didn't see her.

"Grampa!" she shouted again, and a hand waved above the heads around her.

My jaw fell in astonishment, and I gawked. She was wearing khaki hiking pants, suede hiking boots, a white T-shirt, and a bright smile. I hadn't recognized her because she had her otherwise unmistakable red hair all tucked beneath an olive ball cap. She clutched a backpack over one shoulder, and came toward me with a long-legged stride that made me dizzy from flashbacks that went through my mind like shuffling cards. I opened my arms warmly, and she dropped her backpack and rushed into them. I hugged her and felt something so familiar in her embrace that I had to clinch my eyes. She smelled earthy, and her muscle tone was firm in my arms.

"Grampa, I'm so happy to see you."

"You too, sweetie." I let her go reluctantly. "C'mon, let's get out of this crowd."

We went out to the parking garage. The day was stagnant, not a bit of breeze, and hoary exhaust etched the back of my throat.

"Gosh it's wicked hot here, Grampa," April commented as we went.

"Quite a change from Oakhurst, huh?"

"You betcha. It was cool in the mountains, but everything's so dry. And Fresno? I don't know how people can live there."

"That bad?"

"Yeah, terrible. Everything's dried out, and there's so much dust you have to wear a mask."

"Well, at least it's not that bad here. It'll be better at home—still hot, but the haze won't be as bad."

We maneuvered through traffic while the Catalina's air conditioner struggled to keep us cool, but then once we got into the hills we did climb above most of the haze. April hadn't seen the gate at the driveway, and she laughed as I pushed the remote on my sunshade to open it.

"This place has really changed," she said, craning in an attempt to see over the hedge.

"Not that much since you were here last time."

"It's been two years, Grampa."

"That long?"

"Yeah. What do you need the gate for?"

"Mainly to keep the dogs out of the street."

"So it's for the dogs, huh?" she said sarcastically.

"Sure, what else?"

I pulled into the garage, so we went into the house through the utility room. I led her upstairs to the guestroom, and she shucked her backpack onto the bed.

"I used to hide in that closet," she mused nostalgically.

"I remember," I said with my own fond recollection. I shook that off. "So look, you know where everything is. Get cleaned up or whatever and I'll see you in the kitchen when you're ready. Are you hungry?"

"Starved."

"Good. See you in a bit."

I left her then, and when she joined me in the kitchen after she had freshened up, I had sweet tea, ham sandwiches, and chips laid out on the table. She had changed into a fresh T-shirt and had left off the ball cap. Her hair was shoulder length and curly, not like her mother's by any stretch, but her trim T-shirt revealed a figure that was identical to Rachel's. I couldn't help but stare, and this made her blush.

"C'mon, Grampa. Stop that," she smiled. "It makes me feel weird."

"I'm sorry, sweetie. It's just—"

"I know. Dad says it, too. And so does Uncle Jimmy."

"Uncle Jimmy? Oh, James! How is he?"

"He's fine. Gloria too. They say *hi*, by the way."

She took a bite of her sandwich, but then seemed to go somber.

"Grampa?" she asked hesitantly. "Do I really look like her? Like my mother?"

I tried to smile off her discomfort, but the truth was that with brown hair and fewer freckles April would have looked just like Rachel.

"Well," I said, searching for the right words, "your mom didn't have red hair or green eyes." That drew a tentative smile. "But you do look a lot like her."

She contemplated that, nibbling her sandwich in silence. Her eyes were looking at something I couldn't see, but then she glanced at me and said, "Uncle Jimmy took me up to the cemetery. I saw my mom and Gramma, and Mama and Papa Taylor, too. I wish I could have known them."

"I know, sweetie." My heart ached, not only with my own loss, but also for what April had never had. "Just know how proud they would be of you."

"I'm not her, Grampa. You know that, right?"

That took me by surprise.

"Of course you're not—"

"It's the way you and Dad look at me, like I'm supposed to be like her."

"Oh, sweetie—"

"I mean, all my life Dad's told me stories about my mother, how she did this, how she did that."

"I think he just wanted—"

"But I'm *me*, Grampa. I want to do what *I* want."

She was so much like her mother that I could barely hold it in, and there was some of Judith there as well. But that's not what she wanted to hear, at least not right then.

"You're taller than your mother was," I said. It was the only thing that came to mind. "I bet you're good at basketball."

"I'm *great* at basketball."

"So see? Your mother was lousy at it."

"She was?"

"Yeah, it was really embarrassing. I never told her that, of course." I smiled and tried to make light of that, which drew a snicker from April.

"Thanks, Grampa," she grinned. That ended it, thank God.

Later in the evening, when it was cooler out, we went for a walk up the hill. With a conspiratorial wink I showed April my secret passage through the hedge and up to the park on top. We wandered around the site, the split-rail fences, the flagpole and the cannon. The grass was ankle deep. Not too many people came up anymore, and the place was starting to look unkempt. I told her about the old ash tree, which still spread its limbs over the meadow. I tugged the bullet out of my shirt and explained that as well. She seemed to marvel at it, not that I had made such a discovery, but at how long ago it had happened. It was incredible to her that I had climbed that tree more than half a century ago, an unimaginable eternity to someone her age.

We paused at the dog cemetery on the way back down. Dolly and Daisy were in there now, having joined their ancestors. April clearly remembered them both, and this made her wistful.

"It's like a history lesson," she said to me reverently. "All the people, and even the dogs—they're like steps to get here. Do you know what I mean, Grampa?"

"Yes, sweetie," I answered in a hushed voice. "I do."

"And the family's so spread out—Boston, here, and California, too." She shoved her hands into her pockets, shrugged her shoulders and looked down. "And I never got to meet any of them."

"Yes you did, you just don't remember." My eyes were beginning to fill at this talk, but I didn't want April to see that. I wiped them furtively.

"Grampa, will you take me to the other cemetery? I'd really like to see it."

"Why, sweetie?"

"Because I want to know about us; because I don't want us to forget."

I had to turn away to conceal my face, and if April let on she was perceptive enough not to show it. It took me a moment, but I said okay, and then we meandered back to the house, where I poured a whiskey and went into the greenhouse.

* * *

The next morning was a Sunday, so with most people off work and out of their cars the air was clearer, although the heat seemed to come up the moment the sun topped the hills. I drove us out to Smith County on the interstate instead of tak-ing the back roads, this to make better time in the heat. April took it all in with a sense of wonder, even if very little resembled what it had even ten years ago. South-ern-pine saplings were beginning to pop up along the way now, crowding the ma-ple and hackberry trees like the irregular vanguard of an encroaching army. Most of the cedars were brown and tinder dry, having fallen prey to some invasive pest. There were still a few farms, but these were being squeezed between strip malls and clusters of apartments. Even the old highway up to Carthage was lined with new construction, miles and miles of retail baking in the sun. It wasn't until we turned off and headed down toward the river that it actually felt as if we were in the country.

The Carlton cemetery was in poor shape. It hadn't occurred to me until just then that I was probably the only one left to look after it. Uncle Timmy and Aunt Jewel were buried in other states, and we hadn't been in touch with their families since Dad died. I made a mental note to make arrangements when I got home, but for the moment I parked in the tall Johnson grass and we went through the rusty arch. It shamed me to see boxwoods sprouting at the bases of Dad's and Mama's stones, while the stones toward the back were completely overgrown now. Our decrepit surroundings didn't seem to perturb April. After all, she had never known what it looked like before.

"So this is Dad and Mama," I said, high-stepping through the grass to show her the way. "And Leavitt and Elizabeth, who would be your…" I couldn't think what the relation would be. Great uncle and aunt? "Well, they would be like Sadie to you."

"I call her *Aunt Sadie*," she said with a chipper smile.

"That's good," I said. "Uncle Leavitt and Aunt Elizabeth, then. Leavitt gave me a hard time when I was little, but he came around before he died. I wish I could have known him when I was older. Maybe he would have been better to me then. And Lizzie was…well, Lizzie was special. I still think about her sometimes. And over here is Uncle Lou Carlton. He was my dad's favorite uncle. And this stone here is Mama and Pappy Joe Jeffries."

She grazed the weathered stone lightly with her fingertips, her mind wandering off, as if the stone were a link to a time she could only imagine or read about in books.

"These are my great-great-grandparents, then?" she asked in a kind of awe.

"Yes—well, uh, Mama Jeffries is. She was married first to Tom Carlton, Dad's father, but he died. So then she married Pappy Joe Jeffries."

"Oh, so Jeffries isn't our real name then?"

That startled me. In all of my life no one had ever asked that question, and to have it come out so unexpectedly sent a defensive spike through me for some reason. My reply was harsher than I had intended.

"*No*, April. Jeffries is our real name because Dad *wanted* it that way."

"I'm sorry, Grampa." She gave me a hurt look that was shattering.

"No, sweetie, *I'm* sorry. I guess…I just never thought about it like that before."

She recovered with a tentative smile, and glanced around inquisitively.

"Where is he buried, then? I mean you dad's dad?"

"He died in World War One. He's buried in France."

"He was a soldier in *World War One?*" she asked, further awed by a connection to something so distant that schools didn't even teach much about it anymore.

"Yeah."

"Have you ever been over there?"

"No, I haven't."

And then I caught my breath sharply enough to draw April's notice. Dad and I had stood right here fifty-eight years ago, and he had told me to always remember that his father was buried in the Argonne cemetery in France. Dad had never been able to visit his father's grave, and now I felt such an urgent and pressing need to go myself that I wanted to turn around with April right then and get moving. I had never been much interested in traveling abroad, but suddenly I *needed* to go, to fulfill something like an implied promise that I had never made but weighed on me just the same. If I didn't, then my father's father would be lost and forgotten, and all of us would have come from nothing.

TWENTY-FIVE

The way I felt when we got home from the cemetery, I was ready to pack up and rush off to France right then. First I had to apply for a passport, though, and this took the better part of two months. By then it was getting on to winter, not the best time to travel, and Hermano and family had gone to Mexico for an extended visit, which left no one here to care for the dogs. I could have asked Gracie to help out, but she was still pouting about not being invited to come along. To ask her to look after the dogs instead would have been an added insult, so I pushed the trip off to the following spring and wound up cooling my heels all winter.

And a strange winter it was, too. I had never experienced a milder one in Tennessee. It only got down to freezing a few times, and the poor confused trees started budding toward the end of February. Even my enfeebled hickory leafed out early, putting on enough new growth by the end of March to hide the deep rot in its wounds for another season, although the big slabs of dead bark littering the ground beneath it still revealed its mortal struggle. A pileated woodpecker had also been at work on the dying trunk, pecking a hollow into the base that revealed dying roots. I couldn't bring myself to cut the old tree down, not while it fought on so gamely, but it was apparent that it had few seasons remaining.

We had our first heat wave in April which, after a week of temperatures in the 90s, was doused by a sudden influx of cold air that dropped temperatures near freezing. It was a stormy spring, loosing enough rain to flood downtown Nashville yet again. Tornadoes one after another danced across the plains states that year, eventually tearing along the Tennessee/Kentucky line. We were spared in the Nashville area, but Clarksville would never be the same. And farther south, tornadoes devastated parts of Alabama, Mississippi and Louisiana, followed a week later by Hurricane Carma, which rearranged the Delta and much of the coastline. New Orleans came through the hurricane in pretty good shape—the levees and flood walls held—but Biloxi and Mobile looked like third-world disaster areas. The media couldn't help but wink and call it *karma*. After all, the Alabama and Mississippi congressional delegations had been some of the primary drivers behind the defunding of many government services, including the Federal Emergency Management Agency. Now these same congressmen were whining the loudest for help. No wonder no one cared.

None of this caused me any problems on my hill—no damage, no downed trees, and especially no power outages. Nashville was wringing itself out again, but if not for the newspaper I could have gone on oblivious. Of more concern to me was France. Their winter had been the harshest on record, which affected my travel plans. I had intended to go over there by the first of May, but now I was advised to wait until the first of June in order to give the French time to clear the roads and clean up the mess. I compromised and settled for the week before Memorial Day. It seemed fitting.

Hermano had died while the family was in Mexico. His grandson, Alfonso, brought me the news during the hot spell in April. Alfonso was in his mid-twenties by then. I had practically watched him grow up. Once an awkward and somewhat bashful teenager with a pair of rusty hedge trimmers, he was now a handsome young man with his own landscaping business. I gave him my condolences. I had liked Hermano. We had never been close in the way of friends, but Hermano had still been good company, seeming to know when to plant a helpful word while at the same time knowing when to keep his thoughts to himself. He had also been a hard worker, never once complaining in all the time I knew him. And he had been great with the dogs, los *perros bonitas* as he affectionately called them. I would miss his subtle wisdom.

Alfonso assured me that he would continue in his grandfather's place. His family liked me, he said. I was their *buen gringo*. I could only take that with a smile, knowing that it was meant as a compliment. We made arrangements to get started on the hedge right away. The unseasonably warm weather had caused the privet to explode with growth. It almost looked wild enough to take over the hill like kudzu. And then there were the dogs, which Alfonso promised to look after personally while I was away. As much as I had watched Alfonso grow up, he had also grown up with the dogs. He loved them, and asked if he could have a puppy from the next litter. I happily said yes.

When the day came to leave for France, Gracie insisted on driving me to the airport. I resisted, fearing a guilt-lashing along the way, but I should have known Gracie better than that. She had too much self-respect to conduct herself in that manner, although I could tell from the subtle, unrequited longing in her eyes that she was wrestling with it just the same.

It was a blustery morning, caught somewhere between a weak northern and a humid low over the Gulf. The sky was mottled like marble, while the wind alternated between sticky gusts from the south and cooling blasts from the north. Rain splattered the windshield in fat, errant drops. Gracie pulled along the curb in the departure area, and I reached awkwardly for the door handle.

"Are you ready for this?" she asked with a weak smile. "It's a long flight."

"Yeah," I nodded. "Eleven hours from Atlanta, plus that layover. I would have been better off just driving to Atlanta and leaving from there."

"It'll go fast, don't worry."

"God, I hope so."

"I understand why you want to go alone—"

"Gracie, look," I interjected curtly. This is what I had been afraid of. "We've talked about this."

She reacted with an offended expression.

"No, Carlton, that's not it. You haven't left home in...years. Things are different now. I just wish you had somebody going with you."

"Oh." I sat back and mulled that, feeling like a heel. "Yeah, Gracie, sorry. I'll be all right, though. Don't worry."

She reached over and brushed at my thinning hair with her fingertips, let them linger for a moment before she pulled away.

"Your dad would be proud of you for doing this," she smiled. "Have a good time. And be safe."

"I will."

"And send me a postcard."

"Do they still have those?"

"I hope so."

"Then I promise."

She smiled prettily at that, and then as if out of old habit I leaned over and pecked her on the cheek. She went soft then, closing her eyes as if to relish the moment, but then her eyes popped open and she smiled enough to show some teeth.

"You'd better get going," she said, still smiling. "Security takes forever nowadays."

I considered her for an elongated moment, and then I hopped out with my suitcase and headed for the security line.

* * *

I felt scruffy and glazed when we landed at Charles de Gaulle Airport in Paris. The disembarkation concourse was the usual mayhem but with an international flavor, and I was shuffled through customs like a cow through a shoot. I stumbled wearily on, catching glimpses of an orange orb through the hazy air outside. My watch said it was past midnight, but here it was the next morning. I was so jet-lagged that it would have been a comfort to just collapse where I stood and sleep on the floor.

I rolled my suitcase outside to the crowded arrival area, dazed, searching as I went for a sign or some other clue that would mean salvation from this misery. A guide was supposed to meet me but all I saw were blurry faces, and all I heard was the incomprehensible rattle of French. My stomach rumbled sourly. I thought to buy a coffee, maybe with a lot of milk to ease my stomach, located a cart and waited in the press of people, mingling my body odor with theirs. After some minutes I seemed no closer to a cup of coffee, then finally made eye contact with a harried, diffident barista with an oily forehead and stringy black hair. He babbled something at me.

"Coffee, please. With milk," I said.

He babbled in response. I clenched my grainy eyes.

"Speak English?" I asked.

"Non!"

I was too weary to argue, too dazed to puzzle it out. I turned my back on him and stood at the curb. Busses lumbered in and out. Taxis honked. The air felt too thick to breathe. I sat on my suitcase and rubbed my face. Where was my guide?

Once, during my second hike, I came out of a shelter in New Jersey one morning and turned the wrong way in the fog. I hiked north for the better part of two hours before the disquieting feeling began to take root that I had gone in the wrong direction. The trail looks completely different going the other way. The grade is opposite. Tell-tale markers like moss at the bases of trees are shifted, making the woods feel foreign. I became confused, disoriented among unfamiliar surroundings. That's the way I felt on that curb—disoriented, everything foreign beyond my experience. Were it possible to turn around and board a plane for home right then I would have done it, no less miserable but at least I would know my way.

The crowds thinned, the traffic lessened, and the orb of the sun hovered at a new angle. I must have dozed while sitting there because I suddenly jerked my head up to realize that I was now mostly alone on that curb. There must have been a lull between arriving flights. Even the baggage handlers had pushed their carts inside. I rubbed my arms. The air carried a chill that added to the foreignness of everything.

Soldiers with assault rifles at the ready made their rounds, eyeing me suspiciously as they passed by. Across the way, a woman with a worried expression was trotting up the sidewalk at a hurried clip, her thumb busily working at a smart phone. She caught my eye for no other reason than she was something I could focus on. She was young, certainly no older than thirty, dressed in a conservative navy skirt, sensible black shoes, and a white collared sweater. Her hair was black, cut in a nondescript style that brushed at cheeks that were as pale as a daytime moon. She wouldn't cause heads to turn but she wasn't unattractive either, just plain.

I turned away and yawned. This had gone on long enough; it was time to call it quits and hail a taxi. I was just about to force myself up and do that very thing when I was suddenly enveloped in a cloud of sweet perfume.

"Monsieur Jeffries?" a soft French voice asked tentatively, pronouncing my name *Je Freece*.

I gathered the wherewithal to look up, and saw that it was the woman I had been watching earlier. She was glancing back and forth between me and her phone, her brows creased. When I returned a dull nod, she perked up with an uncertain smile.

"Désolé, um, sorry to be delayed. I am your guide, Sofia Fontanier."

***

As if to make amends for being late, Sofia would not allow me to get more than two steps away from her before she came running to the rescue—except when I was asleep, which I did for the rest of that day, that night, and well into the next morning. When I hauled myself out of bed at last, feeling a little better although still muzzy and fatigued, Sofia was waiting outside my door. How she had known when I would wake up was a mystery compounded by a question: How long had she been waiting outside my door? If I had been in a clear frame of mind I would have asked her, but my stomach was growling furiously and I was desperate for coffee.

"*Bonjour Monsieur* Jeffries," she greeted me with an inquisitive smile. "You are feeling better now?"

"Yeah," I answered weakly, rubbing my eyes. "Is there coffee around here some-where?"

"Yes of course," she chirped. "Down the stairs there is breakfast ready for you."

I shook my head in confusion, glanced at my watch, and took note of the sun coming through the window. I didn't have the mental faculties just then to calculate the local time, but the sun looked high enough for lunch.

"Isn't it lunchtime by now?" I asked.

"*Lonch?*" she asked with a laugh. "*Non*—it is only 1130, too soon for the *lonch*. Please come with me."

I was staying on the third floor of the *Hotel Américain*, a gilded nineteenth-century edifice of wrought iron, gold drapes and scarlet velour that was, I had been told by the travel agency, near the Seine and within walking distance of all the iconic Paris stuff. Just the idea of a walking tour made my knees tremble, though. Maybe later—several days later considering how I felt at that moment.

We took a small caged elevator down to the first floor. Sofia kept her eyes on her phone the whole way, seemingly steering us into the restaurant with a sixth sense. She didn't look up until we were at our table, where she smiled and rattled some-thing off to the waiter before returning her attention to her phone. Distracted as she was, I had the opportunity to discreetly study her in more detail.

She had on the same outfit as yesterday, a little rumpled since then, and her per-fume—or whatever it was she was wearing—was almost overpowering. Her skin was practically translucent, laced with delicate blue veins. I noticed that she chewed her nails. Her eyes were small and brown, made weary by the pronounced bags beneath them. Nevertheless I thought she could be modestly attractive if she tied her hair back out of her face—or better yet, if she kept it short the way Sadie did. Sofia's neck was long enough to do that look justice.

Our waiter was a rigid guy with a haughty demeanor. He brought out a basket of croissants and two coffees in dainty porcelain cups. I downed my coffee before he could even get away from the table.

"Uh, could I have another, please? Or maybe three?"

He babbled something at me and I shrugged my shoulders. Sofia looked into my empty cup and her brows lifted in surprise. She said something in a business-like tone to the waiter, who made a brusque response then flitted away.

"Americans have their coffee fast," Sofia commented, perhaps amused but it was hard to tell.

"Americans have bigger cups."

"Yes, everything is big in America. He will bring more, not to worry."

"Good."

Sofia set her phone aside, crossed her arms on the table and leaned forward.

"So," she said, "your appointment at *Meuse-Argonne Cimetière Américain* is for two days from now—so, you have some days to see Paris and have a good time."

"I don't think I have the energy to have a good time."

"This will pass soon, not to worry."

"I hope so. By the way, why do I have to have an appointment?"

"This place is very big. The man will help you to find what you need, but he is busy so you must have the appointment."

"Oh."

There was something charming in the way she spoke, with her French-inflected vowels and the bird-like way she gestured with her hands. I wondered what else I could ask to keep her talking. Our waiter reappeared then, balancing a tray with at least six coffee cups on it. He positioned the cups in the middle of the table, making a show of doing this one cup at a time. I was sure the coffee would be tepid by the time he was done. He spun off with his nose in the air, and I downed two cups in succession. Sofia watched in amazement.

"Well," I said as if caught at something, "he could have just poured them all into one big cup."

Sofia laughed. "It is very different here, yes?"

"Yes it is," I laughed in return, knowing full well that if it weren't for Sofia's intercession with our waiter I would be grumbling and indignant as hell right now.

The waiter came out again with a carafe of orange juice and two plates of delicate crepes with crème filling. He set these down and left, wiping his hands as if he were finally rid of us. My face fell and my stomach growled when I realized that this was all that passed for breakfast in Paris.

Sofia went to work on her crepes with fork and knife, cutting small bites and chewing them thoroughly. I stabbed mine with a fork, got it down in one bite, then polished off another cup of coffee. My stomach rumbled loud enough to disturb the people sitting at the next table over. Sofia winced like an embarrassed hostess.

"Well," I said with a shrug, "I can't help it. How about some biscuits and gravy, and scrambled eggs with bacon?"

"Oh, sorry." She seemed worried, almost fretful. "We do not have these things. Maybe you have some bread and *fromage*, um, cheese?"

"No thanks." I picked up a croissant in resignation. "I'll make due."

* * *

Afterward, Sofia led me on a short tour of the neighborhood. I didn't have the energy for much more than that. We walked along the Seine for a time, with its gardens and its weather-stained brick embankments. I caught a few views of the Eiffel Tower poking above the buildings down the way. It was sunny but hazy, and the breeze was uncomfortably chill. I zipped up my jacket and plunged my hands into my pockets. There were armed soldiers all over the place.

"What's that all about?" I asked Sofia, tipping my head toward one of the soldiers.

"Oh," she darkened. "I am told not to talk about this with the clients."

Something about that rankled me.

"Why the hell not?"

"Because it is—how do you say?—not appropriate to discuss."

"Tell me," I said hotly. "I want to know."

She looked down, clutching her sweater nervously around her throat.

"It is because of the austerity," she said after a moment of consideration. "Also the winter was very bad. The government does not want to give this impression."

"I don't understand."

"Oh, you see—" She cut that off and looked up at me. Her nose was beginning to run in the chill air. "Maybe you need some rest. I do not want to say the wrong things."

I had put her on the spot and felt bad about that, but I still wanted to know.

"It's okay, Sofia. You can tell me." I gave her a patient, paternal look and reached gently for her arm, touching her for the first time. She was really a tiny woman under that sweater.

"It is not proper to talk about these things. My employer could be angry."

"I won't tell anybody. I promise."

She seemed torn, but went on reluctantly. "There are no jobs here, no money because of the government austerity, so the people make the riot and burn the cars. And the immigrants have no jobs. But the winter was very cold, so the people burned the wood, and some places burned down and some people did not live."

I barely kept up with the news at home, so this was the first I'd heard about any of this.

"So why are there soldiers everywhere?"

"Because they are afraid there will be some problems. Many people have no food. This is bad for the tourism." She looked away. "Please no more. It can make trouble for me."

"Okay, I'm sorry." And I was. She wasn't just reluctant to talk, she was scared.

I had endured about all the sightseeing I could handle, so Sofia guided me back to the hotel. It was only about two o'clock in the afternoon, 1400 in the local parlance, but I fell exhausted onto my bed and was asleep almost immediately.

I awoke near midnight, feeling much better and too restless to get back to sleep. I padded through the quiet halls and then downstairs in search of coffee and a snack, pulling up in surprise when I found Sofia sleeping on a chaise lounge in the lobby, her sweater wrapped around her shoulders like a blanket. The desk clerk had gone off somewhere and there was no coffee to be found, so I tiptoed out without waking

Sofia and returned to my room.

* * *

I was up with the sun the next morning, and sure enough Sofia was waiting at my door. She hadn't knocked, but the scent of her cloyingly sweet perfume announced her presence just the same. I put on a mischievous smile and yanked the door open.

"*Bonjour* Sofia!"

"*Bonjour Monsieur* Jeffries," Sofia replied with a start, jockeying a cheery smile into place even as her tired eyes said otherwise. She was wearing the same clothes, now three days running, and it had become apparent that she was pouring on the perfume in lieu of a morning shower. It wasn't my business so I pretended not to notice, but Sofia was definitely going through something in her life, something that tugged at my latent fatherly instincts.

"So where are we off to this morning?" I asked with my own cheery smile.

She paused to thumb something into her phone, then: "Ah, first some breakfast for you and then today we will see the sights."

"Good, I'm looking forward to it."

Sofia walked me out of the hotel and around the corner to a bistro that served eggs and some reasonably-sized pancakes, and used coffee cups that were more in line with what I was accustomed to. We sat with a view of the street, in what would have been open-air seating were it not for a clear plastic tarp that hadn't been rolled up yet. It was still a little too cool out otherwise.

"So, you may have anything you want," Sofia said, browsing the menu for me. "They have the eggs and the pancakes, and I think for you maybe the sausages also."

"That's perfect," I said with an appreciative smile. "And coffee too, yes?"

"Yes of course. I am learning much about Americans."

We both laughed at that. She motioned to our waiter, who brought a single cup of coffee to the table.

"Aren't you having any?" I asked her.

"Oh, no," she said. "I have had coffee for today, so not to worry."

I eyed her as I sipped, suspicions taking shape in my mind. The food came out on three plates, which I coveted like a first meal after finishing the trail. Sofia looked on in astonishment as I dug in.

"It is so much, *Monsieur* Jeffries. Are you not afraid to become fat?"

"No," I laughed, spearing a sausage with relish. "This is exactly what I need. Aren't you going to have *anything*?"

She shook her head, although her eyes were glued to the sausage on my fork. "No, I have had the breakfast. It is enough for me."

"Okay, then. Oh, and from now on, please call me Carlton."

"But *Monsieur* Jeffries, this would not be proper."

"The heck with proper, just try it out."

The way her face darkened you would have thought that she was caught in a moral dilemma, but after a few tries she managed to pronounce my name, and even smile when it didn't bite.

"Carlton," she mused. *Karl-tone.*

"That's better. Sure you wouldn't like one of these sausages? They're good."

"I am sure."

I inhaled that breakfast in record time, and then we were out on the streets to see the sights. We took a different route than yesterday, up narrow bricked streets that were fronted with stately architecture like nothing I had ever seen. There were wrought-iron terraces, leaded windows and gas lamps, ground-floor boutiques with tri-color awnings, and bicycles chained to every pipe and post. I kept my head craned about as high as it would go trying to take it all in. Presently we emerged into a circular plaza, or *place* as Sofia explained. There was a green-tinged bronze statue in the middle of it, and benches all around. We sat to rest for a minute before going on. It was still uncomfortably cool, but at least the sun seemed brighter this morning.

"I can't believe how cold it is," I commented, shivering in my jacket.

"Yes, this is strange. The winter does not want to go away."

"But it's almost *June.*"

"Yes, this is what I say also."

There were a lot of ornate flower boxes around, but these as yet displayed only a few intrepid blooms. There weren't many people around either, which surprised me considering that this was *Paris* after all.

"Where is everybody?" I asked. "I thought there would be crowds of tourists."

"At the Louvre and the Tuileries, possibly."

"And there's not much traffic either."

She frowned at that. "It is as I told you—there are not too many jobs, so the people are in other places."

"Hmm."

Looking more closely, there was a background of dinginess to our surroundings, nothing overt or immediately evident, but more like the beer cans and other garbage lurking beneath the surface of Cordell Hull Lake back home, easy to overlook unless you chose to notice. An accumulation of little things revealed the struggle that Sofia had tried to keep from me: broken glass glittering on the paving stones, flaking paint on the wrought-iron benches, trash cans filled and overflowing, and a hint of sewage in the air. I spotted a street person sleeping in a doorway, and then on further inspection I noticed more of them, like piles of discarded clothes.

"Well," I shrugged, slapping my thighs and standing. "Ready to go on?"

"Yes," she said with a twinge of anxiety. "We will go to some places that are more interesting to you."

We continued on, winding up along the Seine once more, and then into the Tuileries gardens. There were more people here, but not so many as to be stifling. We walked the manicured paths while the sun fought to break through the haze. Sofia was a chatterbox of information, explaining this and that as we went along. Most of what she said didn't register, but I did enjoy the melodious sound of her voice.

We crossed at last into the magnificent grounds of the Louvre, and here Sofia lit up with more exuberance than she had shown yet. There were indeed crowds here, tour groups from every part of the world being marshalled and corralled by their harried guides.

"You will enjoy this *musée*," Sofia said expectantly, as if to compensate for some perceived dissatisfaction in the tour so far.

"If you don't mind," I said, "I'd rather pass for now. I don't think I can concentrate on a museum at the moment. I'd rather just keep walking around."

"But...but...it is part of your program."

That came out as a panicked plea, which caught me off guard and made me frown in puzzlement.

"Sofia, what's the matter?" She seemed almost petrified. I slipped a comforting arm around her shoulders without thinking, and felt her trembling beneath. "What is it?"

"You must have a good tour, Carlton. My employer will ask you, and they will be angry with me."

It dawned on me then—so she thought I wasn't enjoying myself; that I would complain and she would be in trouble with her boss. Poor girl. No wonder she was trying so hard.

"It's okay, Sofia." I turned her until she would meet my eyes, and then I gave her a reassuring smile. "I'm having a good time. You're doing a great job, and I'll tell them that. Promise." She seemed doubtful, but her trembling did ease a bit. "C'mon," I said with an easy shrug, "let's go see the Arc de Triomphe."

"It is far, Carlton."

"That's okay. We have all day...and I like to walk. It's been a long time."

We retraced our course through the Tuileries, then turned away from the river to follow the Champs-Élysées. Sofia walked stiffly for a while, but eventually found her voice and resumed her running commentary. She seemed to know everything about every building, statue, and landmark we passed, and to sincerely enjoy explaining them to me. I continued to enjoy the sound of her voice, and although she probably would not have believed me, that alone was more than enough to send me bragging to her boss.

At lunchtime by my reckoning, I spotted a joint called *Le Hamburger* and practically tripped over Sofia in my haste to get over there.

"Carlton, where are you going?"

"I'm starving," I hollered on the run. "I'm going to that place."

"*Le Hamburger?* But Carlton, this place is plain. You should have the lunch at the hotel."

"No, I should have *the* lunch right here. *This* is something I understand."

Sofia wasn't pleased with my choice, but she gave up the fight and got us in and seated. *Le Hamburger* was a shoebox of a place, staffed by dark-skinned people who might have been from Eastern Europe or thereabouts. Their French was as unintelligible as anyone else's, although the heavenly aroma of grilling meat was a universal language in itself.

"I want a cheeseburger and fries," I told Sofia in a rush. "And ketchup, lots of ketchup. None of that mayonnaise you all use."

She gave me a bewildered nod, then went up to the counter to order. I could hear her speaking almost apologetically with the line cook: "*Un hamburger avec fromage, et des frites avec...ketchup—*" She paused and looked over. "Carlton, what will you have to drink?"

"Gimmie a beer," I said, my mouth already watering. "Anything."

"*Et un Kronenbourg, s'il vous plaît,*" she added.

She returned and settled in across from me, checked her phone and then put it away.

"Expecting a call?" I asked her.

"*Non*, it is only a habit."

The grill sizzled as my patty was slapped down. I leaned back and inhaled in ecstasy.

"What did you order?" I asked her after that moment of bliss.

"Oh, nothing for me. It is too early for the lunch."

"Nonsense."

"No, Carlton. Not to worry, it is fine for me."

"Well I'm not eating alone," I grumbled. "Go up there and order something. It's on me."

"*Merci*, but I think this is not proper to pay for me."

"It's not in the program, huh?"

"The clients do not have to make these expenses. It is not in the contract."

"Don't care. Go order something. Don't eat it if you don't want to, but order *something*."

She considered me skeptically, and there was that anxious look again, as if she were being forced to satisfy either me or her employer. She got up with a perplexed sigh, then went on up to order something for herself. When she came back she seemed uncomfortable.

"Ease up, Sofia," I said. "Where I come from, picking up the tab for lunch is a kind of tradition. And you're learning about Americans, yes?"

"Yes, maybe this is so." She relaxed a little. "Where are you from in *Les États-Unis*, um, the United States?"

"I'm from Tennessee. Nashville."

"Ah, Tennessee! Davy Crocket, yes?"

"Yes, Davy Crocket," I chuckled, "a long time ago. How about you? Where do you live?"

"In Saint-Denis," which sounded like *Saw-Denee*. I'd never heard of it.

"Is it far from here?"

"No, on the Metro it is not too long."

"Hmm, I see..."

I trailed off then as our hamburgers came. Suspicions about Sofia were coalescing in my mind. These suspicions were even further reinforced when she went after her hamburger as if she had just come off the trail. She'd devoured it and was licking her fingers before I was even half done with mine. And I'm the one who was supposed to have been hungry. She was clearly embarrassed in the aftermath, her pale cheeks reddening, her eyes dark and worried, and not a crumb left on her plate.

"So see?" I said with a lighthearted smile, hoping to ease her discomfort. "Now you're learning about Americans."

She smiled, thank goodness, and I hurried through my own burger. I was beginning to pity her, especially now that I thought I had a pretty good idea about what was going on. I warned myself not to get involved, while at the same time I scolded myself that it wasn't right to do nothing at all. I finished my beer, and we resumed our trek to the Arc de Triomphe. Sofia slipped back into her tour-guide persona, but I wasn't listening now, I was debating what to do.

* * *

We returned to the hotel as the sun was lazing toward the left bank of the Seine, after a wearying day that took us past practically every landmark in my tourist brochure. We had eventually used the Metro to get around, this to speed up our progress and also to give my aching feet a rest. Sofia's feet must have ached as well, but she soldiered on without complaint, probably too afraid of scoring poorly with her employer otherwise. The Metro itself was an adventure for me, having never ridden a subway before. The warren of tubes beneath the streets was like another Paris of its own. I looked for postcards along our route, but never found any. Gracie would be disappointed. Sofia said she hadn't seen postcards in years.

Sofia walked me to my door, where I inserted my card key and paused with the door cracked open. Sofia looked as beat as a truck-stop waitress at the end of her shift, and yet when I met her eyes she put on a game smile that tried to hide her condition but didn't succeed. *Don't get involved*, I told myself in one thought; and then in the next thought, *I should help her because I can.*

"So," she said, "I hope your tour was good?"

"Yes, Sofia. It was excellent."

She let out a long sigh of relief, as if she'd had that bottled up all day.

"I am glad," she went on. "Tonight your supper will be downstairs at 2100, um, at nine o' clock, and in the morning we must go to the *gare*, the station, at eight o' clock for the journey to the *cimetière*. So, I will see you in the morning, yes?"

"Okay, Sofia. Thanks."

"*De rien*, Carlton. *Bonsoir.*"

She turned and made for the elevator, swaying wearily as she went. I reached out a hand, checked myself, but then bit my lip and plunged in.

"Sofia, one more thing." She halted and looked back, so tired and beaten down that my doubts were erased at a glance. "Please come inside for a minute."

"Is there a difficulty with your room, Carlton?"

"Uh, no. I just need to speak with you."

She trudged past me into the room, and I stood with the door ajar so she wouldn't get the wrong impression.

"Listen, Sofia—I need to go downstairs and talk to the desk clerk, and while I'm gone I want you to go in and use the shower. Take all the time you need."

She took on a cornered look of fear.

"No, I cannot do that," she protested. "It is not proper."

This was when I had to remember what it was like to be a father, to be able to put my foot down and be stern.

"I don't care if it's proper or not. I want you to do it, and I don't want to argue about it."

"But *Monsieur* Jeffries—"

"I think I know what's going on, Sofia. This isn't something I can just stand by and ignore."

"*Oh, pas de.*"

She seemed to wilt, covering her face and lowering herself onto the corner of the bed. Tears dripped from her palms.

"It's going to be okay, Sofia," I consoled her, uncertain of my own emotions. "Just do what I ask. Please."

I left her then, pulling the door behind me, and I could hear her crying as I went down the hall.

I returned more than an hour later and rapped lightly at the door.

"Sofia?"

The door eased open and Sofia greeted me, freshly showered and trembling. She was wearing one of the complimentary terry-cloth robes, her hair wrapped up in a towel. Her bare feet were as small as the rest of her. She looked younger now, like a teenager. I felt a pang of memory.

"Feel better?" I asked her.

"Yes," she answered guardedly. I knew what this must look like to her, so I went right away for the card key in my pocket.

"Here," I said, offering her the key. "This is the key to your room. It's just down the hall. They should be by with some clothes in a little while."

"But *Monsieur* Jeffries—"

"It's Carlton, or did you forget?"

"No," her cheeks trembled, "I did not forget...Carlton. But I do not understand."

"I saw you sleeping in the lobby last night."

"Oh," she mouthed and turned away.

"It's okay, Sofia. It's all very proper. They don't know the room is for you, so please go use it. And I want to go out of the hotel for dinner tonight, so I would like you to be back at eight—not nine, but eight—and show me where to go. Will you do that for me?"

"Yes, Carlton," she answered numbly.

She gathered her clothes, and I held the door as she padded to her room; and then I fell onto the bed, as exhausted as if I had just hiked thirty miles.

* * *

I know what the concierge had thought when I asked him to rustle up some women's clothes. He figured that I had hooked up with a prostitute and was trying to dress her up for a night on the town. And I know that you must be thinking the same thing, but believe me when I say that seducing Sofia was the furthest thing on my mind. I was *sixty-two years old*, for God's sake, and Sofia wasn't much older than Rachel had been when...well, some people are fine with relationships like that, but I'm not one of them.

That concierge had also taken my simple instructions about as far as he possibly could, no doubt lining his pockets along the way. The clothes Sofia showed up in were on the high end of high-class, transforming her from a struggling working girl into a high-caliber *Parisienne*. She was dressed in a spring fashion despite the chill in the air: a belted yellow polka-dotted dress with wide lapels and a high collar, white heels on her feet, matching gloves, and a swooping white hat that had a brim wider than a sombrero. If the wind caught it, it would be gone. It was a fabulous ensemble but she would freeze outside, so I draped one of my blazers over her shoulders. The pensive look she gave me said she was thinking along the same lines as the concierge, so I dashed that notion right off the bat.

"Look, Sofia—don't make too much of this. I'm not after anything, I just think you're going through some hard times. And I don't like the way your employer treats you. When this is over I think I'll go down there and give them hell."

You would have thought an elevator had slipped its cables the way she reacted.

"No, Carlton! You would not do that!"

"Of course not," I laughed. "I'm joking. I wouldn't want to get you in trouble."

She laughed with me after a moment to work it out, and that put being more than my guide for the evening out of her mind. But I won't deny that if I had been younger...she really could be pretty with a bright smile, a sparkle in her eye and her hair up off her neck.

"Shall we?" I asked then.

"Yes. Where would you like to go?"

"I don't care. Someplace quiet. And someplace where I can get a drink."

We slipped out the back way so that she wouldn't be spotted in the lobby. She knew the desk clerk, she said, and he knew her employer. I'd assumed as much. We wound up in an alley that smelled worse than a kennel full of peeing puppies, but got away unnoticed. Sofia steered us through the misty evening, clutching my blazer around her shoulders to ward off the chill. After several blocks we turned down a narrow side street to a basement-level restaurant called—and this made my jaw drop—*Le Tennessee.*

"You've gotta be kidding me!" I exclaimed.

"When you say you are from Tennessee, I thought you would like this place."

"Sure," I said, dumbfounded, "but...*Le Tennessee?* In Paris?"

"It is clever marketing, yes?"

"I'd say."

We went down the steps and inside, past a small Jack Daniels sign that added even further to the incongruity of the whole thing. The place had tavern-style decor, with low lighting, dark woods, a menu of steaks and burgers, and a mirrored shelf behind the bar lined with bottles of Jack Daniels, George Dickel, and the others. The irony was that I had never seen a place like this in Tennessee, but I wasn't complaining.

There were no other patrons, so we sat ourselves in a dusky far corner. The rose hue of a streetlight through a window at the low ceiling burnished Sofia's cheeks.

"There's nobody here," I said, glancing around for signs of life. "Is the place open?"

"Yes, not to worry. It is too soon for the other people, but a waiter should come."

"Why do you folks eat so late? Back home I'd be getting ready for bed about now."

"It is different customs for us. I think in Tennessee I would find it strange."

"Yeah, well, anyway—oh, there's somebody."

A waiter came out, or perhaps a bartender. He wore a loose white shirt with a black armband, like something out of *Gunsmoke.* They were really playing it up. I chuckled, and he noticed us with a start.

"*Bonsoir,*" he said, hustling over with a pair of menus.

Sofia took over from there, talking a mile a minute, making inquisitive gestures at the menu, brows rising and falling. It seemed like a lot of talk just to get something to eat. I wanted a burger and fries, which Sofia thought was nuts—or as she said, *étrange*—considering what we'd had for lunch. She ordered a steak, I couldn't make out what kind. I added a straight Jack over ice before our waiter departed, and he got my meaning just fine.

I sat back and relaxed then. Sofia gazed around at the bric-a-brac on the walls, the kinds of things you used to see when there were Cracker Barrel restaurants: old cigarette signs, small farm implements, black and white photos. They all looked authentic. The waiter dropped off my whiskey without a word, then took off. Sofia eyed me as I lifted the tumbler to my lips.

"You like whiskey?" she asked.

"Yes I do. How about you?"

"*Non.* It burns too much in the throat."

I laughed and took a sip, sighed at the familiar warmth.

"Well," I said then, "if you can't feel it going down then what's the point?"

"I do not understand this."

"Of course not." Her brows dipped in puzzlement. "*Not to worry*," I added with a smile.

She smiled too, and then we had silence to contend with. I gazed out the window at the street above. It was really deserted out there, which seemed, well, *étrange*.

"Sofia?" I asked while looking out. "What's going on over here?"

"It is as I told you."

"I think it must be more than that."

"Yes," she said. I turned to meet her eyes. She kept them hidden beneath the brim of her hat. "It is all these things together. When Putin went to the Baltic countries the Euro lost its value, and the *Califat* in *La Syrie* made too many immigrants. Do you not know this from your country?"

I looked away guiltily and said, "I guess I haven't been keeping up."

"It is as I say. And the winter was bad for the farmers and the people. I am afraid—"

Our waiter brought the food, so we hushed that talk, as if we were conspirators discussing state secrets. My burger was open-faced, dripping with mushrooms and caramelized onions. Sofia's steak lapped over the edge of her plate, which seemed to go contrary to the food shortages she'd told me about but then I hadn't checked the prices, which were probably shocking. Her steak was so large that even I would have had trouble getting it down, but she tore into it like a hollow-eyed East German just over the wall.

We ate in silence. I refreshed my whiskey when I was done, and Sofia finished her steak shortly thereafter. Our waiter cleared our table then. There were still no other patrons in the place. I began to get a sad sense of decline, that Paris—and perhaps Europe as a whole—was staggering toward hard times that would last a while. Of course you know that it was worse even than that, but this was only the beginning. To us these were just events in passing, no different than the scores of crises that were always popping up. But in retrospect—even though I avoided the news as much as possible—I still heard enough of it that I experienced my own unease at the gathering chaos: the Russians, the South China Sea, the refugees swarming Western countries, the unending insurgency in the Middle East, our shameful government back home—and especially the weather.

I shook off those thoughts. In the here and now, I wanted to know more about Sofia. The way she kept her eyes on her hands, she must have known that the time had come for an explanation.

"So, Sofia," I said after a jolt of whiskey. "Tell me about yourself."

"I do not know what you mean."

"Yes you do. Tell me about your phone."

She had it with her, although it was turned off. Nevertheless her hand was always near it, hovering, ready to spring. She sighed.

"I am supposed to check with them often," she said, still avoiding my eyes.

"Why?"

"To tell them where I have taken you so they can get the...*gratuity* from the business."

"Uh, huh, that's what I thought. That hamburger joint today was off-route, wasn't it?"

"Yes."

"And what about the hotel?"

"The hotel has paid this gratuity already, so I am told to have you eat the food there so they can charge you the money. If I do this they will let me have some food, and they will let me sleep there, as you saw me."

"Damn, Sofia—"

"*Monsieur* Jeffries, um, *Carlton*—they are not cheating you, they are only having you to pay the money at their places." Her eyes were glistening now.

"And what about this place?"

"This is not one of their places."

"Won't this get you in trouble?"

"I do not know." She fixed me with reddening eyes and a face of fear. "Carlton, there are no jobs. There is no money. I have to do this."

"Okay, okay. Settle down. We'll figure a way to keep your employer happy. But Sofia...how long have you had to do this?"

She wiped her nose with her napkin. "You are my first time. I had a job in the bank, doing interpretation for the British clients. But the bank was closed so I had no more job, and the immigrants in Saint-Denis made the riot and my apartment was burned. There was no place to sleep. No food."

"Don't you have family to help you?"

"*Non.* My father is in Lyon. It is worse there. He is very sick."

Now that it was all out, I really wished I hadn't tugged at that thread, but I had. And now I was in it—involved. I shook my head.

"Okay, Sofia, look—here's what we'll do: I'll go to the hotel restaurant and have a snack or something. That should get you off the hook with them. And then tomorrow...do they have this arrangement with the cemetery as well?"

"No, it is only here."

"Good. Then at least you can be out of it for a couple of days." I put down my card and signaled for the bill. "We can worry about the rest later."

* * *

I slept poorly, but was showered and had everything packed when Sofia met me at the door at 0800. She was back in her previous clothes, laundered and fresh now, and her perfume was just the hint that it should have been. She was unexpectedly cheerful.

"*Bonjour,* Carlton! Are you ready for the train?"

She explained the day's procedure: a stop in the hotel restaurant for coffee and croissant—she gave me a wry wink at that—the Metro to Gare de l'Est, and then a four-hour train ride to Verdun, where a hotel was booked for us and a taxi would take us to the cemetery. I had all of this in my itinerary, of course, but it was confusing, which is why I had asked for a guide in the first place. I was anxious to get moving, if only to escape the subtle corruption I now saw in every pair of eyes I met.

The train ride was bleak. We were shooting into the Lorraine region, an important agricultural area, and yet the fields were brown and fallow. Fresh-cut logs littered the sidings like discarded bodies, these from the trees that had fallen across the tracks during the winter. The sky was a uniform gray. I often saw knots of people waiting at the crossings, cold, disheveled, like refugees during the war. It was unsettling.

Sofia kept up her commentary, describing scenes from summers past when fields of wheat and barley waved in the breeze, and black-and-white *Vosgienne* cattle huddled with their backsides to the sun. Not anymore. It was cold outside, chilly in our car. Sofia scooted up next to me and took my hand in a proprietary way that felt off. I pulled my hand back and found a magazine to occupy it, slipped on my reading glasses, smiled awkwardly then flipped pages.

Verdun was a pretty town on a river, with crenelated gate towers and the Old-World architecture that I was beginning to take for granted. The sun was breaking through in places, brief moments of warmth. We checked in at the *Hotel de Ville* and dropped our bags. My room was on the second floor, hers on the third. Our taxi was waiting when we got back outside.

It took the better part of an hour to reach the cemetery. Although it was only about twenty-five miles away, our route was slow, wandering lazily through quaint villages and between bucolic hills that were more in line with how I had pictured France. Things did not seem as dire here. Perhaps it was the sun finally breaking through, or perhaps the American cemetery had created a local bubble of sustained economy. Sofia's commentary along the way seemed to defy the idyllic setting. This area had been a crossroads of warring armies for centuries, she said. Plows turned up bones all the time.

The Meuse-Argonne Cemetery was a startling oasis of green set within the winter-ravaged fields and hillsides. The perimeter was densely wooded with evergreens, the lawns maintained with a precision that only the military could achieve. The place was vast, the largest American cemetery abroad. It took my breath, it really did.

There were more than fourteen thousand men buried here, Sofia informed me as we passed between the elaborate gatehouses at the entrance; fourteen thousand men who died during the final months of World War One. A thousand more were listed on plaques, although their bodies had never been found.

We cut to the left toward the visitor center, through a forest as remarkable for its healthy green canopy as its sober calm. Dad should have come, I thought. He shouldn't have put it off. In my mind I played a scene, Dad and me here, witnessing this together. His eyes would have filled, I know they would have. Instead my eyes filled for him.

We met a Mr. Phillips in the visitor center, an American somewhat older than me but with a rigid military bearing and an immaculately-pressed black suit. I had expected him to be in uniform, but no, he said, only on special occasions; and of course tomorrow—Memorial Day. There was no time for small talk, unfortunately. His stiff, professional demeanor revealed no hint of urgency, but his eyes swept a lobby crowded with waiting visitors, and this told all. We went out right away, down a grassy path through the woods, around a circular pool and fountain, and then into a checker-board of burial plots divided by hedgerows. My forehead became damp because of our pace, and this despite the cool breeze. We weaved between crosses that stood in ordered lines like the almond orchards I remembered from the San Joaquin Valley. I understood the need for an appointment now—I would never have found it on my own.

"Here he is," said Mr. Phillips. He stood back as I dropped to a knee. Sofia put a steadying hand on my shoulder. "I'll leave you now," he went on. "You have an hour and a half before the cemetery closes, so take your time. And please stop by the visitor center before you go. You can sign the register then, and we can answer any questions you might have."

I thanked him with a mumble, lost in feelings I hadn't expected.

"This is your grandfather?" Sofia asked somberly.

"Yes."

I put a hand on the cross and kept it there, as if Dad might feel it through my memory. I read the words out loud:

> *Sergt. Tom Carlton*
> *16th Inf. 1 Div.*
> *Tennessee Oct 7, 1918*

And then I was thrown back in time, in a rush that actually made me dizzy. Dad was there, younger than I was now, handsome, taciturn, smoking a Carlton.

"I didn't forget, Dad," I muttered through trembling lips. Tears pattered off my cheeks. "I didn't forget."

My knees began to ache, so Sofia helped me up, supporting me close to her side.

"Every generation," I said, lifting my face to the mottled sun to dry my tears. "My grandfather, my dad, my brother—my son." Sofia squeezed my arm tighter when she heard that.

"You have a son in the *Armée?*"

"Had. Iraq."

"I am so sorry, Carlton. He must have been very brave."

"I'm the only one who didn't go," I said numbly. "Dad didn't want that. Now I think I understand."

"May I take a photo?" she asked.

"Sure."

She held up her phone and took the photo. I didn't own a cell phone, and I hadn't brought a camera. My memory was all I needed. With nothing else to say or do, we returned to the visitor center, where the crowd had thinned considerably. Mr. Phillips was nowhere to be seen, so I signed the register and we left.

* * *

Back at the hotel, I paused at the entrance to the bar and turned to Sofia.

"Go on up," I told her. "I'm going to stop in for a drink."

"Then I should stay with you," she said, which is what I had expected.

"That's not necessary. I think I can make them understand me." I could have added, *I prefer to be alone,* but that would have led to a debate I didn't have the energy to engage in right then.

"Not to worry, Carlton." She took my arm as if I might get away. "It is why I am here."

The bar was small, a cafe really, with a few round tables, a pastry case and espresso machine, and a single shelf of spirits behind the counter. Two couples of retirement age were sitting around a table by the window, making low conversation over their flutes of wine. The rolls of flab beneath the men's polo shirts, as well as the ladies' brassy bouffant hair, identified them as Americans. We turned our backs to them and went to the counter.

"I'd like a—"

Sofia cut in before I could say another word, rattling off in French to a youngish guy who had good looks and a discerning gaze.

"Yes, it is my pleasure," he said in English with a sharp glance at Sofia, as if she had interrupted him as well.

He handed me my whiskey, passed Sofia a bottle of mineral water. "Thank you," I said to him, and then we heard a call from behind us.

"Hey, an American. What a relief. Bring it over here, pal. We could use a friendly voice."

I turned with a groan. All four of them were looking at me with expectant grins, scooting around to make room at their table. The place was too small to offer escape or privacy, so I relented and went to join them. Sofia edged in right next to me, shuffling her chair until we were all in and settled.

"I'm Vince," one of the men said.

"And I'm Rob," said the other.

"We're twins. Can you tell?" said Vince.

"Fraternal twins," said Rob.

I looked the men over. One had a full head of auburn hair streaked with silver, the other a few strands combed across. I wouldn't have identified them as brothers let alone twins.

"And these are our wives, Fran and Blanche," Rob added. Both ladies smiled lightly and waved.

"I'm Fran."

"I'm Blanche."

"Nice to meet you."

"So what's your name, pal?" I think that was Vince.

"Carlton."

"Nice to meet you, Carlton." It was Rob that time.

"And I am Sofia," Sofia interjected, scooting a bit closer to me. The ladies' brows went up as if they detected some gossip in the making.

"You French?" one of the men asked Sofia.

"*Oui.*"

"Well..." Vince it was. His eyes grazed Sofia speculatively, and then he fixed them on me. "So where you from, Carlton?"

"Tennessee."

"I knew it!" he snapped his fingers, "what with that accent. We're from Colorado Springs. Ever been there?"

"No, I haven't."

"You should come out then. It's a great place."

"Except for the fires," Rob added.

"Yeah, they're bad this year," one of the ladies said, I think Blanche.

"Really bad," said Fran.

"We thought we'd come over, get away from the smoke for a while, you know?" said Vince.

"We've been talking about this forever," said Rob. "Our great-grandfather is buried here."

"Wow," I muttered without enthusiasm, downing my whiskey all at once. The ladies looked bored all of a sudden. They had probably jiggled in excitement at the prospect of visiting France, only to find themselves part of a brotherly pilgrimage to a country that couldn't seem to get rid of winter.

"Carlton's grandfather is there also," Sofia chimed in, bristling when no one seemed to pay her any mind. If she edged any closer to me she would be in my lap.

"That so."

"Yeah," I said, rattling the ice in my empty glass. "My father told me about this when I was a boy."

"Hey, us too. Why'd it take us all so long to come see for ourselves?"

"Don't know," I shrugged. "I never thought I would. It was a last-minute thing."

"Carlton, do you want one more?" Sofia asked then, pointing to my glass.

"Yes, please. That would be great."

She took my glass and hopped up to the counter. All four pairs of eyes were back on me. Vince leaned in close.

"That's a cute little *fräulein* you've got there," he winked. The ladies scowled, and I winced inwardly. No wonder the world hated Americans. Too many of us were so damned ignorant.

"Yeah, she's really latched onto you," Rob added to that.

"Real possessive," Fran added in turn.

I gritted my teeth and took a breath.

"No, that's not it. She's my guide—from the travel agency."

"Now that's smart," Blanche said, slapping the table for emphasis. "We should have gotten ourselves one, Vince."

"What for?"

"So we could *do* something," she pouted. "I can't understand a word of this gibberish."

"You all could probably hire a guide in Paris," I said.

"Naw," said Rob. "We're not going back there till we fly out."

"We've only got a few more days," said Vince. "We rented a car, and were just going to drive around and see all the battle sites around here—"

"But we keep getting lost," Rob finished for him.

"Every day's the same," Fran moaned. "We go out and get lost and don't see anything."

"And it's so cold," Blanche said, hugging her arms to prove the point.

"What global warming?" Vince commented smugly.

I shook my head at that. Considering the fires they'd left behind in Colorado, there was no point getting into it. Then I had a thought.

"You could use Sofia," I said.

"Your guide?" asked Vince. "What about you?"

"I'm only here for one more day. I can find my way around."

"Hmm." Vince rubbed his chin in thought. "Is she expensive?"

"I think you would find her rates very reasonable."

"We'll think about it."

Sofia rejoined us then, so the conversation steered away from that in a hurry.

"I want to go up and lay down," Blanche said. "I'm worn out."

"Okay, hun," said Vince. They all stood. "Well, Carlton, nice to meet you. We'll talk about what you said. Oh—where are you eating dinner tonight?"

"I haven't thought about it."

"There's a place up the street. Why don't you meet us here, say seven-thirty, and we'll all go?"

The last thing I wanted to do was spend an evening with these people, but I had an idea swirling in my mind that just might work.

"Sure," I said. "See you then."

I was still reeling from that dizzying repartee a few minutes later. The whiskey helped. It was just us in the bar now, plenty of room, but Sofia stayed right up against me. I scooted away from her, and held out a restraining hand when she tried to scoot with me.

"Sofia? What's going on with you?"

"I do not know what it is you mean?"

"Yeah you do. You've been on me like a jealous schoolgirl all day."

"I am not a *zhelous* school girl." She crossed her arms and fumed.

"Then what is it?"

"It is nothing."

"Bull."

"Bull? What is bull? I do not understand this."

"It means you're not telling me the truth." Her eyes filled as unexpectedly as a flash flood. "Aw, hell. What's the matter now?"

"It is nothing," she sobbed.

The bartender looked over and shook his head, as if he were well versed in the vagaries of French women and pitied my predicament. I sighed and rubbed at a headache that was long overdue.

"Sofia, stop that right now and tell me what's wrong."

"It is only—" She dabbed at her eyes and sniffed before going on. "—it is only that no man has ever been good to me before."

And with that her eyes welled again. Damn, this was even worse than I thought. Being sympathetic wasn't the way to go. She would latch onto that and run with it, so I dialed up the tension instead.

"So what? So you think you can trap me in a corner? I'm not fallin' for that hurt little-girl ploy, so cut it out."

"*Ooh*," she squealed, covering her face to hide whatever was going on there, embarrassment I hoped. Finally she whispered through her fingers, "You are a good man."

My head throbbed.

"I'm not a good man."

"You must be."

This was going nowhere. I could have used another whiskey.

"Look, Sofia—forget about that. I have a job for you."

She lowered her hands and looked up at me timidly, her lips forming a hopeful smile.

"Yes, Carlton. Anything for you."

"Those people need a guide. I want you to go out with them tomorrow."

"But no!" she exclaimed, her hopes dashed. "I am only *your* guide. It is in the contract."

"I don't care. I want you to do it."

"But it would not be proper." She went off in French then, and my head pounded worse.

"Sofia, I—" I raised a hand, frustrated enough to slam it on the table, but then Rachel appeared in my mind, shrewdly weaving between my arguments, and I had to smile. I let out a long breath and said gently, "Look, Sofia—think about it. You need money, right? Well here's a way to get some extra. Your employer doesn't need to know."

"But I have tomorrow to show you Lorraine."

"To tell you the truth, honey, I'd rather sleep late. I've seen what I came for."

Sofia reached out a hand and I let her. "You are tired," she said.

"Yes, very tired." The headache was closing in behind my eyes. I squeezed and rolled them against the pain.

"*Très bien.* If it is what you want."

"Good," I breathed in relief. "Now go up and get ready for dinner. We'll meet here."

"*Oui,* Carlton."

She rose limply and headed for the stairs, and I called after her: "And Sofia? Make a good impression. Okay?"

* * *

I never left the bar. The bartender was attentive. He refreshed my whiskey when needed, but otherwise left me alone. At last, thank God. I sipped as the sun set, running through memories that played like films, sometimes smiling, sometimes laughing, and sometimes wiping at my eyes. The foursome came down first and jogged me out of that state.

"Hey there, Carlton," Vince boomed from the foot of the stairs. "All set?"

They gathered around me, showered, perfumed and casually dressed.

"I'm just waiting on Sofia," I said.

Rob glanced impatiently at his watch. "Okay."

I had no conversation to make, so sat there pushing my glass around with a finger while they talked among themselves. And then Sofia came down the stairs. She was decked out in her Paris clothes, except for the hat, which she'd had the sense to leave behind. Her white sweater was arranged over her shoulders in a way that did not detract from the elegance of her ensemble at all. Her hair was up, her neck long and lovely.

"*Ahlo,*" she said, smiling as prettily as Audrey Hepburn to Humphrey Bogart. The ladies were impressed, no doubt wondering where they could find that dress. The men were more so. Vince and Rob stumbled over one another to reach her first, wound up taking an arm on either side of her. And the ladies didn't seem to mind.

"*Bonsoir,* Carlton," Sofia paused between them to say. "Are we ready to go?"

I stood, a hand on the table for support.

"Look y'all," I said, trying to conceal my wobble. "I'm not feeling well. Sorry. You all go on without me."

Sofia's brows dipped but she didn't say anything.

"Sorry about that, pal," Vince said. "Maybe it was something you ate."

"Maybe."

"Okay then. Well, uh, maybe we'll see you tomorrow."

They went out as a group, Sofia looking at me over her shoulder. I rubbed my eyes and sighed, and then I went up to bed.

* * *

The next morning was remarkable, still cool but there was sun, real sun. I slept luxuriously late, crawling out of bed only when the bright morning insisted. I ordered breakfast on my own and savored it. There was a note for me at the desk: Sofia had gone off with the group; they would be back by dinner. I walked out of the hotel feeling free, hailed a taxi and had it take me to the Meuse-Argonne Cemetery.

The place was even more spectacular on that bright day, every color enriched, every shadow in striking contrast. I walked the grounds. Hundreds of local people were placing little American flags next to each cross, bending over as if they were working the fields. The flags fluttered dizzyingly in the breeze, like a plain of nesting gulls. A ceremony was underway, solemn and dignified; crisp uniforms, trumpets and waving flags. I'd seen ceremonies, plenty of them. Instead I went to my grandfather's cross and sat in the grass.

The day went long, eventually becoming warm. April would be seventeen in a couple of weeks. I thought about her, how much she would have liked to see this; how I wouldn't be here if not for her. I thought about Dad, and about Tom Carlton. What kind of man had he been? He must have been like Dad, only in an earlier time. Was I like Dad? Then that would mean that I was like Tom Carlton, too. I reached for his cross and tried to pull him through the years. We had no photos of him. There might have been some once, but if so they were lost to time. When I thought of him I pictured Dad in a Doughboy uniform, a black and white image, dignified and optimistic.

Evening came on with a chill. I hauled myself up, took a taxi back to the hotel and went to the bar. The same bartender was there. He slid a glass of whiskey across as I came in.

"Thanks," I said.

"*De rien.*"

The sun was low enough to cast the bar in a salmon glow. I watched it set, dipping slowly beyond a far hill. I felt warm.

When Vince and family came in with Sofia they were chattering with excitement, the ladies going on as if this had been their first fine day in France. I smiled in satisfaction and lowered my eyes to my whiskey.

"Carlton! There you are," Vince announced. "Feeling better?"

"Much better," I answered distantly.

"What a great day," he went on. "What a great idea, Carlton. This little gal knows her stuff!"

"I thought you would like her," I said to my glass.

Sofia stood before me, a placid look on her face.

"Are you feeling well, Carlton?" she asked.

"Yes. How did it go?"

"I think very well."

"Better than that, pal," Vince cut in. "Look, we wonder if she can take us out again tomorrow."

I nodded before he finished, anticipating that he would ask that.

"Good," he said then. "Well, okay everybody. Upstairs and get ready for dinner."

"She was really sweet," Fran leaned in as they were turning to leave. "Thank you so much."

Once they were gone I looked up to see Sofia still standing there, gazing at me curiously.

"Carlton, are you certain you are fine?" she asked, taking a seat across from me.

"Yes, Sofia. I'm fine." I reached behind my lapel and pulled out an envelope. "This is your tip, Sofia. We Americans do that, so don't argue with me about it." She frowned and stared at the envelope. "Take it," I said. "You'll find that it's generous." Her fingers crept reluctantly for the envelope, and I stood. "It's not my business," I said then, "but the hell with your employer. If I were you I would use that to set up shop here for the summer. There'll be more people like these along, and in the winter I would go south, someplace warm." I patted her hand and smiled, and her eyes were wet. "Goodnight, Sofia."

In the deepest part of night, when the darkness feels eternal and even the insects are quiet, there came a soft rapping at my door. I hadn't been asleep, had instead been floating in a waking dream. I slipped through the darkness, opened the door and found Sofia there in shadow.

"May I come inside?" she asked as softly as a caress.

"Yes," I said, still shrouded in a dream of forests and mountains and thunder, a silhouette limned in heavenly light.

Her scent was clean and fresh, no perfume, just skin and hair and perhaps salty tears. She came to me and rested her face against my chest, warm and trembling, and for a moment I held someone else.

I sighed in memory and closed the door.

TWENTY-SIX

Poor, sweet Sofia. She made love like a rambunctious teenager, but she was so earnest in her searching expression and desire to please that I went along as if she were the most experienced lover in the world. It felt strange at first. Notwithstanding the difference in our ages, I hadn't been with a woman since Judith; and in truth had never intended to be with a woman again. Still, I'm glad it happened. It reminded me what it felt like to be young.

I thought about Sofia often, especially after that next devastating winter descended on Europe. If she took my advice, she went south where it was warm. On cold evenings in the den, the fireplace hissing and with a whiskey in my hand, I envisioned her in Spain or Italy, smiling brightly in the sun and with some color on her cheeks. I did make an effort to check up on her that winter, did a web search on her name but got a million returns with no way to sort them out. The travel agency in Paris was no help. I never found her, and over time, just like the others, she slipped into memory.

Both April and Tom Junior graduated from high school the following spring, and both were enrolled in college for the fall semester. Thomas called to tell me that April had been accepted at Boston University, and that she didn't appear to be interested in the Appalachian Trail. His sigh of relief was genuine and deep, while mine was laced with a regret that took effort to conceal. Despite our talk that time, I had quietly hoped that April would take off for the trail, would walk in her mother's steps and perhaps establish what might have become a family tradition. April wanted to be a school teacher, though. There was something.

Tom Junior enrolled at UT Knoxville, majoring in economics. Gracie was enormously proud of him, of course. I guess I was proud, too. Tom Junior and I had never been close, but he was Tommy's son, a Jeffries. The future would carry on through him. I sent letters of congratulation to both of them, along with checks in amounts sufficient for the occasion. April hand-wrote me a nice thank you note. Tom Junior thanked me in an email.

It was another hot and dry summer. Despite what was happening out west, a city like Nashville would never run short of water. Just the same, having to drag hundreds of feet of garden hose across the hill to water the flower gardens and privet hedge was a pain compounded by a water bill that demonstrated in real dollars how much it was costing to keep that hedge green. In the heat of August, I hired a crew to install a rainwater-collection tank up the hill at the property line, not too far from where the old water tank had been located. Actually, I had them put the tank over the line a little bit in order to clear the dog cemetery. Few if any people visited the park up there anymore, so the verges had become densely overgrown. No one would know or even care that I had encroached onto the park's grounds, and besides, it wasn't long before the brush closed in and the tank was barely visible anyway. Our first good rains in September filled it, and with irrigation lines buried in the soil I was able to keep the privet watered from then on with little effort.

Time eases along. There was always something to keep up with, be it the puppies or the greenhouse or whatnot. I filled my days. Gracie retired in 2024, and afterward began to spend more time at the house, sleeping over often enough that she kept some cosmetics and extra clothes in the guestroom. I didn't mind. With no family left in Nashville, she was alone but for me. And then she had come to know my nature well, could tell at a glance whether to join me or leave me alone. We fell into routines, breakfast in the mornings when she slept over, sunsets on the deck if the weather permitted. She came and went as she pleased, no need to announce her arrival or departure. We could pass the entire day without seeing one another, spend our evenings in silence or in conversation.

It was a comfortable arrangement until one morning in the summer of 2026. We were at the breakfast table, quietly sipping our coffees. Gracie was reading the news on her tablet while I thumbed through a *National Geographic* magazine.

"Get this," she blurted, breaking the silence. I gazed at her over the tops of my bifocals. Her eyes were fixed on her tablet, a finger hovering, ready to scroll.

"What?"

"Some British doctors have injected a woman with nanites."

"Nanites?"

She looked up and smiled. "Molecular machines, Carlton. You need to keep up."

I sighed and pushed my magazine aside. "How can I? There's no newspaper anymore."

"Watch the news on TV then."

I scowled. "It's all politics and people shouting at each other. No thanks."

She rolled her eyes and grinned sarcastically, waving her tablet. "Then get one of these."

"I miss my newspaper," I grumbled. "I don't like reading the news on computers."

"Why not?"

"Because you can't hold them open. You can't fold the pages over, and you can't see where you've been and where you're going. It's just not the same. And all those ads and flashing banners hurt my eyes."

"You're too old-fashioned, Carlton. Anyway, these nanites are supposed to fix wrinkles and things." She frowned and probed at her cheeks. "Maybe I should do it."

That thought struck me with horror for some reason.

"God, why?"

"You'd know if you weren't so...I mean *look at you*. You could still pass for fifty. It's not fair."

"I don't *feel* like I could pass for fifty."

Becoming old didn't bother me so much as the little annoyances that came with it: the constant ringing in my ears, the stiff joints, having to wear bifocals, and worst of all, needing to pee all the time. Otherwise I was in pretty good shape I guess. As far as how I looked, I couldn't have cared less.

"I bet you feel better than I do," Gracie fired back.

"C'mon, Gracie, you look great and you know it. Sometimes people can't tell if Angelina's your daughter or your sister."

That tugged a thin smile out of her lips. Those were the words she needed to hear, and as far as I was concerned they were true. Gracie did look great for sixty-eight years old. Her face was still petite, but with a dignified, matronly bearing. Sure she colored her hair these days, but so what? She did have a little droop in her cheeks and some wrinkles above her lips, but not such that most would notice.

"Don't ever let Angelina hear you say that," she chided me with a laugh. She returned her attention to her tablet; then: "Uh, oh."

"What is it now?"

"The new administration wants to send troops back to Iraq."

That turned us onto a sore topic.

"I figured that would happen if they got back in," I spat. "You'd think that business with the Chinese would have slowed them down a little."

"Yeah," Gracie sighed sadly. An aircraft carrier had been driven out of the South China Sea by a swarm of Chinese gunships. The blow went deeper than the few lives that were lost. "I'm glad Tommy isn't interested in the military," she went on. "I was afraid...you know, because of his father."

"At least we have that to be grateful for."

"Speaking of Tommy, he's taking his next semester in Mexico City."

"Really? Why?"

"For some international credibility. It looks good on a CV."

"Huh."

"And..." She set her tablet down and crossed her arms on the table, her expression vague. I eyed her with sudden apprehension."

"And?"

"And, well...Angelina's husband is going to be posted there, too."

"In Mexico City?"

"Yeah, chief of operations for the bank."

"When?"

"Right away."

"That must be hard on Angelina."

"It is. The suddenness, you know? They've been talking about it for a long time, and then it just happens. No warning."

"What's she going to do?"

"It'll take her a few months to arrange things, but then she and the kids are moving down there, too."

"Oh, no, Gracie—I'm so sorry."

"It'll be okay."

She was looking at her hands now, pondering something. That stretched out as I looked on, and then she turned to me with eyes that said it would not be okay.

"Gracie, what is it?" I asked, worried for some reason.

"I have cousins down there, you know," she said, averting her eyes. "All the Quinterras are there."

"Yeah—"

"Angelina wants me to come live with them."

I groaned. Now I understood.

"And what do you want to do?"

"I don't know, Carlton. They're my family. No one's left here...except you."

That hung over us as she laced and unlaced her fingers. I meant to say something, opened my mouth to speak but no words formed.

"I would stay with you, Carlton," she whispered to her hands. "If you wanted me to I would."

"Gracie, I—"

When she looked up her eyes were wet.

"Carlton, can't you...isn't there *anything*?"

"Gracie, I—I mean, you know..."

"It's been *twenty years*, Carlton."

"It's not that." I felt as if my guts were being pulled out. "I just can't—"

"Can't you at least *pretend*?"

Anger flared in her eyes—anger or disgust, one. I squirmed and looked up at the ceiling.

"Gracie, it's not...that's not the way it is with us."

She sniffed and wiped her eyes, put on a fake smile.

"I know, Carlton. I know."

Gracie left for Mexico City in September, a week before my sixty-eighth birthday. I saw her off at the airport. We hugged like the old friends that we were, perhaps holding on a bit longer. She pushed back and searched my eyes, raised a hand gently to my face.

"Oh, Carlton," she said sadly. "Who's going to look after you?"

"You know me, Gracie. I'll be fine."

"I know," she whispered with a mournful nod.

She gave me a last glance as she went to board her plane, a glance that held decades of longing; a glance that said goodbye forever. I stood there for the longest time, dismal in my thoughts, and then I went home, not lonely but alone nonetheless.

* * *

The months flickered past like a train at a night crossing, another mild winter into an early spring. The woods up the hill were changing. The view I had seen out the kitchen window every morning for a good part of my life was off somehow, something about the colors. My hickory tree toppled in a February storm.

I did miss Gracie. I had to admit that.

I started keeping Bentley in the house. He was the oldest of my dogs, a good fella who liked to rest his head on my lap when I sat on the deck in the evenings. We watched the sun go down together. Bentley came from Beauregard, who was up in the cemetery now.

I flew to Boston in May to see April receive her diploma. We sat together as a group in the Walter Brown Arena, Thomas, Pam and their four kids: a teenaged boy who resembled the Tollbooth Tom I'd met all those years ago, and three cute girls of elementary-school age, none of whom had red hair. I sat on the end with Thomas, his little girls bouncing in and out of his lap. His devotion to them was obvious from the joy in his eyes, but the look of adoration he cast at April as she walked across the stage revealed his first love.

I wiped my eyes and slipped into memory. I saw Rachel, of course; Rachel with red hair and, if anything, a freer disposition. April walked loosely across the stage, swinging her arms, hair blazing from under her cap and with a grin that rivaled the bright lights above. She accepted her diploma with proper decorum, but then turned and swung it with both hands as if she were batting a fly ball out of the arena. Everyone erupted in laughter, perhaps Thomas most of all.

April introduced me to her boyfriend when we met up later. They stood closely together, still dressed in their red graduation gowns. No one had told me anything about this, but I could tell from the proprietary way Patrick had his arm around April that he was more than just a boy friend.

"Grampa, this is Patrick," she beamed.

"Hello, Patrick," I said, shaking his hand.

"Mr. Jeffries. It's so good to finally meet you."

Patrick had a square jaw and the ruddy complexion that went with a lot of these Boston people. He smiled easily and his eyes were blue. I liked him right off. Thomas on the other hand...

"Congratulations Patrick," Thomas said stiffly.

"Thank you, Mr. Tiller," Patrick said just as stiffly.

I asked Thomas about Patrick once we were alone.

"I take it you don't like Patrick."

"No, he's okay. I've met his parents. They're good people."

"Then what is it?"

"April never told you?"

"Told me what?"

"That they've been living together for almost two years."

"No, she never told me that. This bothers you, I guess. She *is* an adult, Thomas."

He read my look of amusement and shook his head.

"You don't understand, Carlton. It's not that, it's just...they don't want to get married."

"So? Maybe they're not ready."

"That's not it. None of the kids want to get married these days."

"Hmm. Why is that?"

"Who knows? It's wicked strange."

"Well, they're big kids. They get to do what they want."

"If you say so."

A little over a year later, two days shy of her twenty-fourth birthday, April gave birth to twin boys, my first great-grandchildren. Their names were Richard and James—*Jeffries*.

* * *

I returned home from Boston to another hot summer. Dust hung in the languid air from day to day. The mornings and evenings were bearable outdoors, but the baking afternoons reminded me of Fresno. I set up a water sprinkler out back for the dogs, watched them through the kitchen window as they played. They were like eager children dancing in the spray. It made me smile.

Alfonso and his crew showed up toward the end of June to grind the hickory stump. They'd cut and cleared the tree for me back in February right after it fell, but Alfonso didn't own a stump grinder so that part of the task had been pushed off until later. We had also intended to replant the section of privet hedge that had been taken out by the hickory, however we both agreed that it was now too hot to put new plants in the ground. We would save that for fall when it cooled off a little.

I put on a wide-brimmed hat before going out to watch. There wasn't any shade in the front yard anymore. Alfonso stood off to the side with a man I didn't know, supervising as his guys wheeled the stump grinder into place. They had their shirts off, brown backs already slick with sweat. It was going to be a big job, made worse by the heat.

"Hello, Mr. Jeffries," Alfonso greeted me as I approached.

"Afternoon, Alfonso." I wiped my brow with my fingers and flicked the sweat into the parched grass. "Maybe you should have done this first thing in the morning."

"It'll be okay, boss. These men are from Mexico. They're used to it."

"Just the same, I think I'll run a water hose down here, something they can cool off with."

"They'll appreciate that."

Someone cranked the stump grinder and it roared to life. Wood chips began to fly. The three of us went down to Alfonso's truck, away from the noise. Alfonso's dog, Jalisco, had his head out the window, dripping tongue hanging like a pink fish. Alfonso petted his dog fondly. Jalisco had come from Bentley and a Louisiana female, and had since sired his own pups.

"Mr. Jeffries," Alfonso said, gesturing to the man at his side, "this is my cousin, Hector."

"Nice to meet you, Hector."

"*Y tu también*, Mr. Jeffries," he said with a deferent nod.

"Hector is from Matamoros," Alfonso explained. "My father's brother is Hector's father."

"Oh," I said to Hector. "So that means Hermano was your grandfather, too."

"*Sí*, he was my grandfather."

"Well, I liked him a lot."

"He like you too, Mr. Jeffries. He talk about you sometimes."

"Did he?"

"*Sí*."

Hector was older than Alfonso by a few years, with the presence of a man of business rather than a laborer. He spoke English well enough, but heavily accented. Alfonso had been raised in Nashville, while his cousin had obviously been raised in Old Mexico.

"I told Hector that you used to be in the liquor business," Alfonso said then.

"Yes I was—out in California."

"Hector is here to open a business."

"Is that right?"

"*Sí señor*," Hector spoke up. "A place to sell liquor and beer."

"Well, it's a good business. I wish you luck."

"Actually, Mr. Jeffries," Alfonso stepped forward, "I think you know the place he wants to buy."

"I do?"

"Yeah. ABC Spirits on Harding Place?"

"I do know that place. I go there from time to time. Didn't know it was for sale, though. It's a good location. You'll do well."

"*Sí*, it is a good opportunity," said Hector.

"There's only one problem," Alfonso added.

I studied them both curiously. Something was up.

"And what's that?" I asked with a note of suspicion.

"Hector is—" Alfonso said evasively, "—well, Mr. Jeffries, I think you know."

"Uh, huh." I turned to Hector but kept my eyes on Alfonso. "No green card, right?"

"*Sí*, Mr. Jeffries—"

"So the Tennessee Alcohol Control Board won't give you a license."

"That is correct, *señor*."

"Jesus Alfonso—"

"Mr. Jeffries," Alfonso spoke quickly, "it's a good business with little risk—"

"Unless someone finds out about Hector."

"They wouldn't if—"

"If the business was in my name, right?"

"Yes, sir."

I sighed, but then I thought about it. The stock market was erratic as hell, Europe was a mess, and my principal was lying as dormant as a seventeen-year cicada.

"Hmm," I scratched my chin then fixed my eyes on Hector and Hector alone. "How about a silent partner, Hector?"

And that's how I came to be part owner of a liquor store where one could get good Tennessee whiskey.

* * *

There was one more event to mark that summer, an event that still intrudes into my dreams even now.

It was a little after ten on a Wednesday night. I had already been in bed for a while, and was just dozing off when the phone rang. That yanked me out of my torpor. My phone seldom rang, and when it did it was either Sadie, Thomas or April who, what with the time difference, never called later than early evening. When a phone wakes you up at night it usually means something bad has happened, so I answered it with foreboding.

"Hello?"

"Mr. Carlton Jeffries?"

It was a woman's voice, with a nasal, institutional quality that only reinforced my anxiety.

"Yes, this is he."

"I'm Laquiesha Mays, calling from Nashville-Meharry General Hospital. We have an indigent patient who has listed you as contact in the event of death."

"What?" I sat up and rubbed the sleep out of my eyes. "Who?"

"Do you know a Mr. Kenneth Batista?"

"*Kenny?*"

"Then you do know him, sir?"

"Well, uh...not for a long time. Did you say he's *dead?*"

"No, sir. I said you are his contact in the event of death."

I shook my head at that and rubbed at my eyes some more.

"Miss, uh—"

"Mays."

"Yes—Miss Mays. Then why are you calling me?"

"Mr. Batista asked us to reach out to you. He would like to see you if possible."

"*Huh?*" I searched my memory. When had I seen Kenny last? Decades? "Uh, Miss Mays...I don't know. I haven't seen him in more than thirty years."

"I understand, Mr. Jeffries. This is common in these cases."

"*In these cases?* Common how?"

"I'm not at liberty to discuss a patient's history, but if you would come to the hospital I'm sure Mr. Batista would discuss it with you himself."

"Uh—when?"

"Now would be best."

"*Now?*"

"And Mr. Jeffries? You should probably hurry."

* * *

I stood outside Kenny's door while a male nurse in yellow scrubs tapped his foot and grew impatient.

"Mr. Jeffries...?"

"Yeah, I know. I'm sorry, but I'm just not sure about this."

"You came to the hospital, Mr. Jeffries, so you must have been sure at some point."

His tone was biting, not soothing. If I weren't so muddled I would have snapped back at him.

"I tell you what," he went on with a quick glance at a wall clock. It was past midnight. "Why don't you have a seat and think about it. If you change your mind, just tell them over at the desk."

He dismissed me and turned on his heels.

"No, wait—I'll go in."

He sighed at the inconvenience. "Very well, Mr. Jeffries."

I was led into a poorly lit room that smelled like feces, with an underlying odor not unlike what turkey vultures peck at in the middle of the road. There were two beds, both occupied by cadaverous bodies with white sheets tucked around them, only their heads showing. I couldn't make out their features in the weak light.

The nurse tapped at a tablet. "He's the one on the right, sir." He went to the monitor and examined the display. "This says he's awake. Try not to get him excited, and please remember that there's another patient in the room."

He spun around in a hurry and left. In the silence that followed I could hear a pair of rasping breaths that sounded of disease and imminent death. I swallowed an urge to run, and with that meager fortification approached Kenny hesitantly.

I wouldn't have recognized him, not even if he were sitting across from me in a well-lit room. His face looked like a deflated walnut topped by patchy tufts of white hair. I stood there feeling nauseous while he struggled to breathe. The smell coming off of him was sickening. I didn't know this man. I had no business being here. I warred with that as the monitors beeped their somber tone. I edged closer until I could just make out his eyes, flinched when I saw that they were open.

"Carlton," he spoke weakly. His voice was like mush. He had no teeth. "I didn't think you would come."

"Kenny?"

"Yeah, man." He smacked his gums and made what might have been a smile. Drool ran out the corner of his mouth.

"Kenny, what's wrong with you?"

He gurgled as if he were drowning, coughed in a phlegmy spasm and said, "Everything, man." I came a little closer. His eyes were on me, dark as swamp water, unblinking "Man," he said in what passed for an astounded tone. "You look the same."

He coughed again and I backed up a little.

"Kenny, I—"

"It's okay, man. I got nothing you can catch. I wanted to see you before...you know."

"Why?"

"To settle things."

"Oh, damn, Kenny. That was so long ago."

"Naw, man. Like yesterday."

"So what? You want me to feel guilty?"

He shook his head, which seemed to take more strength than he possessed. He rasped a few breaths before going on.

"You tried, man. I know you tried."

That was not what I was expecting to hear. Memories rushed in like a flood. I felt a cold place in my stomach.

"Maybe not enough, Kenny," I admitted weakly.

"More than anybody else. This is on me, Carlton. Not you."

Guilt was tearing at my insides. He was wrong. I hadn't helped him, I had walked away. There was nothing he could say to absolve me of that.

"I heard about little Tommy," he went on, "and your wife and daughter. I'm so sorry. I wish I could have known them." That pulled a tear out of the corner of my eye.

"Judith wanted to meet you," I said shakily. "But—"

"I know. You were right, though. The way I was...it wouldn't have been good. Gracie's gone, too. Yeah?"

"She went to Mexico."

"There's nobody left, then. Just us."

Until then I had never thought about it that way. I swept through my memory, everyone gone away or gone for good. Even Evelyn had left Nashville. I had no idea where she was, whether she was alive or gone for good as well. Everything seemed so long ago, so far away. I saw Kenny as a gangly boy, our fort on the hill, our picture in the paper, Tommy laughing and bouncing on Kenny's knee. I wiped my eyes.

"Yeah, Kenny. It's just us."

"All alone. I never thought..."

"It's okay, Kenny."

"...all alone."

A tear tracked a course through the fissures in his cheek. He struggled to pull a hand free from the sheet. What came out looked like brittle sticks under desiccated skin. After several tries, he managed to steer a knuckle and dab at his eye.

"I'm tired, Carlton. So tired. I'm ready to go—"

I thought he meant to sleep. I started to turn.

"Okay, Kenny."

"No—" His hand reached for me. I eyed it with a loathing that felt despicable when I realized that he could see the expression on my face. If that pained him, I couldn't tell.

"I just wish," he said, and more tears ran. "I just wish...I'm nothing, Carlton. *Nothing.*"

The soul-wrenching emptiness in that crushed my heart, provoked memories that I had kept carefully tucked away. He had squandered sixty-nine years, and would die with that as his legacy unless...

"No, Kenny, that's not true." I blurted this even as I debated whether or not he deserved to know. His hand tottered in the air like an unsteady drunk, grasping for something, anything. I gulped against my disgust and took it, felt how weak it was; how sickly fragile. I leaned over him, wrinkled my nose at the smell. "You have a daughter, Kenny," I whispered. "And grandchildren."

His face screwed up into something that was even uglier to witness. The hollows of his eyes filled, wells of tears.

"Gracie?" he cried.

"Yeah."

"Oh my God. Oh my God."

The monitors began to beep urgently. Kenny let go my hand, his arm dropping lifelessly to his side. I shouldn't have told him. It was a mistake; another mistake. The nurse rushed in and shouldered me aside.

"Okay Mr. Jeffries," he barked. "You'd better leave now."

I backed away as the nurse worked on Kenny, made it to the door when I heard faintly, "*Carlton—thanks.*"

Kenny didn't die that night. He continued for three more days, conscious and alert according to the hospital people, and then he went to sleep and didn't wake up. I paid to have him buried next to his mother and father at Woodlawn. I was the only mourner at the service.

* * *

The stock market crashed on Monday, October 29, 2029. Any fool could have seen it coming. It had been drummed into school kids of my era that the stock market crash of October 29, 1929 had led to the Great Depression. This might be only so much esoteric ancient history to you, but for us of that generation the stock market crash of 1929, although occupying some nebulous place in the distant past, is what led to everything: from Franklin Roosevelt to World War Two; then the atom bomb, the Cold War, landing on the moon, and in the process creating what we called the Greatest Generation. My father belonged to that generation. Looking back now, as only I can, his generation *was* great; greater than mine for sure, and greater than any of the others that have come along in my lifetime.

It was because of this imprinted curiosity that I relented and looked at the news, as if I might glean some connection with that distant time my father knew. Best I could gather, it was the pundits who drove the world to this, harping with lustful zeal about the similarities between then and now: a broken Europe and squalid Russia, power consolidated in a totalitarian state—in this case China—and in the middle a right-leaning, circumspect America.

On the street, though, things were going along more or less normally. There was no single event or series of events that led to the crash, only self-aggrandizing and ridiculously irresponsible buffoons on the television and in Congress. People doing what people do—which is to jerk their knees at the least bit of information—they herded together at the banks to yank out their money. They dumped their stocks at a loss and did all the other predictable things, and this while the pundits wrung their hands and bemoaned the loss of American greatness. What greatness? More than a quarter of the way into the twenty-first century, America was still being run on abortion and guns, as if there weren't more important things to be focused on. I could just picture the Chinese wringing their hands, too—in disbelief and delight.

On my hill the weather was actually pleasant, and I swore off the news once more. It was telling that in the midst of all of that, people still bought their booze. Hector and I had five locations now. I couldn't have cared less about the stock market.

* * *

Sadie came in May 2032 to give the commencement address at Lipscomb University. She had become the *Grande Dame* of feminist letters, a revered presence in literary circles even though she hadn't turned out a new book since before Mama died. She gave speeches, edited anthologies, and every once in a while returned to Dartmouth to hold lectures in packed halls. She and Ryan had retired in the teens, and were living on his family's land in Vermont near Sherburne Pass. It had been a long time since we had seen one another.

I picked her up at the airport, and when she saw the Pontiac she smiled in touching remembrance.

"I can't believe you still have it," she said.

"I can't believe how good you look," I said in return.

Sadie was eighty years old that May, soon to be eighty-one, but to look at her you couldn't have guessed. Her skin was smooth, her hair bobbed as always. She wore black pants and a white pullover that formed around a figure that was remarkably svelte considering her age. Her collar was tall in the latest urban fashion, lending her a stately, dignified appearance. She moved nimbly, her hands flexible and slender. I was amazed.

"You look pretty well yourself," she said with a chuckle. "Come on, let's get out of this heat."

The drive home was depressing because of the state of things. Panhandlers were camped out in the medians. Families lived in cardboard boxes with flaps cut to let in the stifling air. On some of them, children had colored doors and window frames, trees and flowers. Sadie looked out at this with a sorrowful gaze, elbow on the door, her chin resting on her fingers, the air conditioner ruffling her hair.

"Isn't it like this in Vermont, too?" I asked her.

"Not as bad," she said to the window and the scene beyond. "Some in Rutland and Bennington. Montpelier, too. The smaller villages are pretty much normal. Families are farming again."

"I wonder if people still hike the trail."

"Maybe...or maybe not. Hanover won't let them hike through town anymore, can't tell the vagrants from the hikers. They have to go around. It's probably like that all up and down the trail. Anyway, there are people living in the shelters now. They tried to revive that CCC thing, at least put those people to work keeping the trail up. The president vetoed it. He said people needed real jobs."

"Sounds pretty typical."

We left the squalor and that conversation behind when the gate opened and we turned up the hill.

"It's like Hong Kong," she mused.

"What do you mean?"

"Before World War Two. China was in chaos, but the British had their enclave, everything normal. This is like your enclave."

"This is my home," I retorted testily.

"I know." She looked at me and smiled in contrition. "I didn't mean anything, just wandering thoughts." She looked around. "I'm still sorry about your tree. I think I miss it as much as anything."

"It's been a long time."

"It has. Is your hedge dying?"

"I hope not. The tank's getting low so I've been rationing. Alfonso has this idea to plant cactus and things that don't need as much water."

"That sounds weird."

"Well I'm still thinking about it. By the way, which room do you want?"

"How about my old room?"

"I thought so," I grinned. "I've got it all ready for you."

She grinned back, with a visage that was so youthful it was startling. I puzzled that over, tried to form the last picture I had of her for comparison. I shook that off and we went inside.

While Sadie settled in, I slipped out back to see to the dogs. Princess Grace practically jumped me when I opened the door to the kennel. She was four years old and had already made two litters, but despite that she still seemed to have a lot of puppy in her.

"What's her name?" Sadie asked from behind me, causing me to jump.

"Oh! You surprised me. I thought you would be lying down for a while. Aren't you tired from the flight?"

"No, I'm fine. So what's her name?"

"This little hellion is Princess Grace."

"Princess Grace?" Sadie looked either dubious or amused.

"Oh, she's a princess alright. Holds her nose in the air when she's stubborn, and pitches a fit if I don't pay attention to her.

Sadie surveyed the eight dogs and puppies vying for my attention, "And all these dogs go back to Langley?"

"Yep, well some of them—to Langley and Mirabel. This girl does." I frisked Princess Grace's neck, and she responded with an eager, slobbering pant. "I traded with the breeders in Louisiana for some unrelated dogs, you know, to keep them from getting inbred."

"Dad would be amazed."

"Mama too, I think."

"Yes, I'm sure she would."

Sadie looked up at the tinder-dry hill. "Everything is so brown"

"Yeah. There hasn't been much rain since March."

"It's strange. The weather's normal in Vermont, maybe even a little cooler than usual."

"That *is* strange. I don't know...it's been unpredictable. It can be like this and then come a deluge that fills the water tank in minutes. The summers have been mostly dry, though. We still get a lot of rain in the fall."

"Do you ever go up the hill anymore?"

"Sometimes. I take the dogs up to run."

"Can we go up there?"

"Now?"

"I'd like to."

"Yeah, okay. If you want. They've more or less let the park go, but the grass isn't too high yet. It's steep though. Sure you can make it?"

"I'm sure. Let's go."

I would have taken the dogs with us but Sadie seemed to be in a mood for reflection. We took the path around back of the kennel and made our way up, pausing at the dog cemetery where Sadie sat to rest.

"Do you remember Bentley?" I asked her.

"Of course I remember Bentley."

"He's over there next to Beauregard. And then Dolly and Daisy, and well..."

"And Langley."

"Yeah."

"There are so many. It feels like the cemetery in Smith County."

"It feels like it's almost as big as the cemetery in Smith County. Keeping it mowed is a lot of work, even when it's dry like this."

She pointed toward an open area just ahead of us. "I can almost envision Elizabeth right there, and Mom and Daddy...and Leavitt. Can you still picture him, Carlton? Leavitt I mean?"

"Yeah," I answered with a sigh.

"I can't see his face anymore. I have to look at a picture, as if he were one of our distant relatives and not our brother."

"It *has* been more than sixty years, Sadie."

"*Sixty years*...it's like another life, as if it weren't me at the mailbox but someone else. Do you ever feel that way?"

"No." I shook my head. "If I think about it I go right back there, like it was me now."

"That must be a lot to cope with. Maybe if you weren't so alone."

"It doesn't bother me."

"Still..." She bit off that thought. "Do you ever see Tommy?"

"Tom Junior? No, he's in Mexico City. He got married down there."

"I know. Luke told me about it when I was in Seattle."

"You didn't tell me you saw Luke." She caught the edge in my voice.

"Oh, Carlton. Why can't you let it go?"

Luke had moved to Washington State soon after Mama's funeral so that he and his boyfriend could get married. That kind of business wasn't allowed in Tennessee at the time. I wouldn't go, of course, which drove the wedge even deeper. But times had changed. That whole thing didn't really bother me these days, but there was more to it than just that.

"Sadie, things were never right between us. I could tell that from the day he was born."

"But he's your *son*, Carlton."

"Yeah, that was proved. But he never acted like my son; and his...*husband*, I guess—I met him that one time. I didn't like him and he didn't like me."

"Nick's sweet. They have a good life."

"I'm happy for them."

"They have two *kids*, Carlton. Your grandchildren."

"I've never seen them. And anyway, I don't know that I have any real relation to them."

She scowled at that.

"You should call him."

"He knows where I live."

"I don't understand you, Carlton. You have so much, and I..." She clammed up then, just sat there in brooding silence.

"C'mon, Sadie. It's nothing to get upset about."

"No, that's not it."

"What, then?"

She exhaled a long breath and wiped at her eyes before answering.

"Ryan has Alzheimer's."

"Oh, Sadie." I slipped an arm around her shoulders and she leaned into me. "How bad is it?"

"Bad enough. We're trying to get him into an experimental program."

"What kind of program?"

"Nanites. They're supposed to be able to remove the plaques."

"*Nanites?*" I pulled my arm away. "Are those things safe?"

She looked me over sharply.

"Are you a doctor now, Carlton?"

"C'mon, Sadie, I didn't mean that. It's just...they scare me."

"You've been watching too many movies."

"I wouldn't want them in me."

"You might feel different if you had Alzheimer's."

"I hope I don't have to make that choice."

"Someone might have to make it for you."

This had become heated for some reason. I studied her in confusion, trying to grasp why she was so touchy about the subject. It was only then that I realized she wasn't wearing her glasses.

"Are you wearing contacts now?" I asked her.

"No."

She didn't elaborate, which left me hanging for an explanation.

"Did you get Lasik or something?"

"No, Carlton."

"Then what—"

"Is it your business?" she unexpectedly snapped. I flinched back.

"Hey, I'm sorry."

"No, Carlton, I'm sorry." She looked away for a moment, seemed to be weighing something, then turned back to me. "Look, Carlton, *I've* had nanite treatments."

"*Oh, Sadie...*"

"It was about a year ago, at a cosmetic clinic in Britain. And I'm fine. I haven't felt this well since...I can't even remember."

My expression told all.

"There's nothing wrong with it," she went on defensively. "You'd see that if you weren't so old-fashioned—and if you weren't so lucky. You've never even been sick. You don't *know* how lucky you are. The doctors would say you have long telomeres. I don't know why I don't have them, too. I'm *eighty*, Carlton. I'm not ready to be this old."

"But Sadie—"

"Forget it." She stood in a huff. "We'd better get back down now."

If you had asked me, I couldn't have told you what it was about nanites that disturbed me so much. Of course the ones that Sadie used were first-generation, little specks of free-floating matter imprinted with proteins, nothing like what came later. The next day she gave her speech to rapturous applause, an eighty-year-old woman with the drive and enthusiasm of someone much younger. People fawned over her, praised her courage. Afterward I drove her to the airport, searching the silence for what it was we had lost up on the hill. I drew back reflexively when she leaned in to kiss me goodbye. Just the barest brush of her lips reached my cheek. I felt bad about that for a while, and then it didn't matter anymore.

* * *

Depending on where you live you might not know the truth about the Needles Incident, but considering how that singularly reckless episode pretty much created the mess we're living in now, I think I should spare a little of this paper to tell it to you straight.

It happened on the Fourth of July following Sadie's visit. Just after sunrise, a murky state-sovereignty agitator named Jimmy Lee Paul blew up a water-pumping station on the California side of the Colorado River, or what passed for a river at that point. He fled at high speed in a relic SUV, eastbound on Interstate 40, with as many as a dozen California Highway Patrol cruisers and a few drones chasing after him. He shot off the interstate at Needles, California, zigzagged through town—sideswiping an electric two-seater and killing a lady—then blasted across the Highway 95 bridge into Arizona.

The California Highway Patrol stayed right with him, crossed the Arizona line in hot pursuit, but were stopped by ranks of Arizona lawmen who stood across the highway like cowboys at high noon, their weapons drawn and aimed at the Californians. It was a standoff like nothing seen since the Wild West. The Californians were driven back. When the Feds came in, they were driven back as well.

In quick response, the hardest of the hardline states, whipped up by the swaggering governor of Arizona, banded together into what they called the *Tenth Amendment Alliance*. They disbanded their National Guards and reformed them as state militias, seized control of their national parks and federal buildings, diverted traffic at their state lines, then dared the federal government to try and do something about it. But after years of austerity, budget cuts and laissez-faire leadership, the federal government couldn't do much more than posture and make threats. It fell to the more moderate states to try to rein all of this in, but they had no choice but to react in kind. There were skirmishes along state lines throughout the country, the bloodiest between California and Arizona. Some braggarts from Texas invaded New Mexico at Hobbs, raised an 1830s Republic of Texas flag over that dusty town, then as if reenacting the Battle of the Alamo, were gunned down to the last man. It was a long, burning summer of armed stand-offs, bombings, shootings, righteous chest thumping and all the rest. Disgraceful. I tried to avoid the news, but events this shameful seemed to spill their sorry particulars from the very air.

When Congress reconvened in August, a senator from Texas proposed the USA Freedom and Cooperation Act. The Act would, he argued disingenuously, reestablish order, promote commerce, and ultimately preserve the Union. It figures the Texans would be the ones to come up with this Orwellian piece of work. God, I dislike them so much. What the Act actually did was devolve power to the states, granting those of a certain political bent the victory over the federal government that they had been fighting for continuously since Franklin Roosevelt was president. Among other things, it established border checkpoints between rival states, independent immigration policy, and the authority to print local currency. The members of the Tenth Amendment Alliance, mainly composed of the mid and southern states—including Tennessee—giddily used their new authority to call for a constitutional convention, and actually issued passports to their residents.

What followed could have been foreseen, and perhaps was. Various states banded together by political ideology, like nations within the nation. Disenfranchised and disempowered, millions of people migrated to the states more akin to their way of thinking, flooding across state lines like Dust-Bowl refugees. Texas and Arizona sealed their borders with Mexico and harried their immigrant populations. The Mexicans didn't need much encouragement to get out of those places, a sentiment that would eventually reach Hector, although that was still a little way off at the time. The Chinese took advantage of our disunity to dredge one of their islands from a seamount some two hundred miles off of Hawaii. Even the Canadians got into it, nosing around the north slope of Alaska while their southern neighbors were in a froth and not paying attention.

Everything eventually settled out into an uneasy status quo. The ideology that drove all of this is obsolete now—you would find it laughably quaint—but the bureaucracies and the legacies it created became entrenched. They're still with us, which is why you need papers to travel, why there are still sporadic food shortages, why you instinctively loathe people from certain parts of the country, and why we lost Hawaii and Alaska.

I was untouched on my hill, as if all of this were going on across the ocean somewhere. I should have paid more attention. When Sadie died suddenly of a stroke on her eighty-third birthday, I couldn't go because I didn't hold a Tennessee passport. Ryan was alive but incapable. Some of Sadie's former students saw to it all. They had her buried in the Pine Knoll Cemetery in Hanover, a mile south of Dartmouth College and near the new, de facto route of the Appalachian Trail. I was told there were hundreds of mourners.

I hope I can find her grave when I get down there, pay my respects. I can still see her clearly at our last parting, how hurt she was when I pulled away from her goodbye kiss. It was the nanites that did it, both my reaction then and her stroke later. Who knows how long she would have lived otherwise.

T WENTY-SEVEN

I've been in and out of a fever, radiating heat while shivering at the same time. I have hugged Sam close when the shivering was the worst, only to push him away later when the sweat began to roll out of me. The aspirins aren't helping. I don't know what to make of it. And there's a smell in here now, a smell that reminds me of Kenny's hospital room. I think something must have crawled under the shelter, something old and ready to die. I'm afraid that by tomorrow the odor will be unbearable. This is my sixth day here, six days that would have seen me out of the wilderness by now if not for the weather.

But the sun did break through briefly as it set this evening. I was curled inside my dank sleeping bag, shivering and hugging myself when I felt dapples of light on my face, like the gentle touch of a mother's fingertips. I opened my sticky eyes on a dim sunset that was no less blazing in its intensity. It could have been a feverish dream, but no, Sam saw it too. He was prancing in the way of excited dogs, wagging his tongue and tumbling over me. I saw soft rays lancing through the trees, scattering off the rushing stream in a glittering spectacle; and in those moments the birds found their voices at last, celebrating the sun with a spontaneous chorus.

But only briefly. By the time I had summoned the energy to heave myself up on my elbows, the sun was gone.

Now it's late. The birds are silent once more and the stream is as dark as oil. And yet there is light. The clouds are flowing like a tide, with stars wandering in and out like ships in a fog. For a short time there was even a sliver of moon! Suddenly I feel renewed, like a sunrise over Mt. Washington. Even my fever has broken. The sore on my backside is worrisome, but I'll make do. It's time to continue. There's not much paper left. Sam ruined some of it when he was prancing around, but I couldn't bring myself to scold him, not when I would have pranced with him if I had been able. What remains will have to be enough. There's still much to tell, but then not really. Paragraphs as years, time speeding along. I need to finish this, to get moving again. The sun will rise in the morning, I *know* it will, and then I'll go.

* * *

The years eased along, punctuated by things you know as well as some you don't. An asteroid came close in 2036. The Chinese launched the rockets that deflected it. They also landed on Mars, although not one of their crew survived the journey. What a bleak place. No one wanted to go back. Why bother? That seemed to crush more hopes that the crash of '29.

April's boys turned ten in 2038. I saw them on the computer, identical little guys with an innocent enthusiasm that defied the state of things. I couldn't tell which one was which, and I think they were teasing me, swearing one was the other and so on. April leaned into view to sort that out for me, smiling with a motherly aspect but still freckled and youthfully pretty. I would have sent them birthday cards, but the Postal Service had been shut down. The private companies that had taken over had yet to pass my mailbox.

Tennessee did not participate in the 2040 census. Between that and the loss of the mail, I never saw another property tax notice. Government computer systems were so antiquated by then that heavy-handed state revenuers were sent out to canvas the neighborhoods and collect the taxes in person, but there was such little left of my neighborhood by then that I think I was overlooked and forgotten. It was because of the ants.

Of the three disasters that savaged Nashville, this is one you've probably never heard of even though it did its fair share of damage. I first spotted the ants on a summer morning in 2039. Princess Grace and I were on the deck, taking in the morning before it got too hot. I was sipping coffee while surveying the new landscaping that Alfonso had put in, the cactus, the agave and rock gardens. The privet hedge looked like a line of intertwined skeletons, a few feeble leaves struggling to persevere. The hedge was so sparse that I could see through it to the McMansions across the street. They had been vacant since about the second year after the crash, and had gone derelict.

The neighboring house to the west of me was also vacant. The old folks had died, their kids unable to press a successful claim since they lived on the wrong side of a state line. There were a few people hanging on up and down the street. I didn't know any of them. My neighbor to the east, Guy Meadows, was a widower like me. We seldom spoke. For years his house had been hidden by a line of trees, later by my privet hedge, but now I could see his house clearly, as if it had been plunked down whole in the night. From the bedroom window that I had once pulled Evelyn through, I could make out his backyard and windows, see into his private places. It wasn't that I was peeping, only that I had never needed to keep those curtains closed in the past. Sometimes he would see me looking out, would put on an indignant face and yank his blinds.

On that morning I was just looking around, not trying to pry, only filling the time. I noticed a mound of soil against Guy's brick wall, thought it peculiar but shrugged it off until I spotted another mound in my dying hedge. My first thought was that groundhogs had moved in, and I groaned. Groundhogs can be pesky varmints. They will root in your garden and tunnel under your foundation. Given enough time they can drop the corner of a house. I went down with Princess Grace to investigate, took a stick and poked at the mound—and when I did a million tiny ants swarmed out in a living mat, surging up the stick toward my hand.

Princess Grace yelped and began to roll in the grass. I threw down the stick, not quite sure what I was seeing. Within a week of that there were mounds all over the yard and against the house as well. I went into the cabinet under the kitchen sink for something or other and discovered a mound rising up from the water pipes. The damned ants were in my house!

There were at least two kinds of ants involved. What had set them off was never clear. I looked them up on the computer. The fire ants—*Solenopsis invicta*—had come from South America via Mississippi. The crazy ants—*Nylanderia fulva*—were from the same place and were apparently so aggressive that they actually preyed on the fire ants. There had been fire ants in Nashville at least since the turn of the century, migrating north with the retreating winters. I had read about them in the paper but I had never seen them. And I had never even *heard* of crazy ants. Nevertheless, both had somehow become immune to the most common insecticides and were exploding across Nashville unchecked. And the little bastards had a sting as bad as a hornet. Some people were allergic to the sting and could die. With no idea what to do, I called Alfonso.

Alfonso came right out and walked my property with a gleaming metal can and a spray wand, delivering liquid death to every mound he came across. He vacuumed the mound out of my kitchen cabinet then caulked the pipes. When he was done I gave him a cold coke and we sat at the kitchen table.

"I hope this works," he said, not sounding confident at all.

"That stuff smells potent," I said, wrinkling my nose, "like what they used to spray on the tobacco fields."

"Yeah, and that may be where the problem started. The ants seem to have become immune to it."

"What if it doesn't work?"

"I don't know, Mr. Jeffries. People are trying everything: orange oil, boric acid—I know a couple of guys that got ahold of some Diazinon and *it* didn't work."

"Sounds bad."

"Yeah." He finished off his coke in a long gulp then stood. "I've gotta get going. People are calling from all over the place."

"Okay, Alfonso. Thanks."

Alfonso's spray didn't work. The ants got into the kennel, seemed to build a mound up the wall overnight. I vacuumed that up, but they were back the next day. Desperate people were even pouring gasoline on the mounds and setting them on fire, but this seemed to only spread the ants faster. A few mornings later an ambulance pulled up to Guy's house and carried him away. I don't know what happened to him, stung by ants, perhaps. He never returned.

The ants killed one of my puppies. Poor Jackie. I had planned to keep her. I carried her up to the dog cemetery, sidestepping ant mounds as I went. I hacked at the ground with arms that hadn't been strong enough for such work in a while but were powered by anger. When Jackie was properly buried I leaned on my shovel, wiped my brow, and remembered something from long ago, something ironic now that I thought about it.

I went into the garage, searching it as well as my vaguest memories. There was just the Pontiac in there now, along with the water heater and the back-up batteries for the solar system. I paused to form the image in my mind. They had to be here somewhere. Where else would they have gone? My eyes settled on the low door to Dad's storm shelter.

I hadn't opened that door in years, had no reason to. It was full of junk: old lawn chairs and bicycles, coffee cans and cardboard boxes. Until then it would have taken more effort than it was worth to empty it, but suddenly I was yanking things out in a frenzy, tossing them behind me as I burrowed deeper. Dust rose in a suffocating fog but I pressed on, convinced of my certainty, and then I found them, stacked in a corner—the two olive-green cans of DDT that Dad had used to kill termites.

DDT was a powerful insecticide that could linger in the environment for decades. It had been banned in the 1970s because it weakened the shells of birds' eggs and had almost wiped out bald eagles, falcons, and other species of raptors. Rachel Carson had warned about this in her book, *Silent Spring*. I remembered Mr. Fennick stiffly teaching us about this in the fifth grade, and Judith had adopted the book as her bible. Judith had never used insecticides on her garden, nor did I use them now, but then DDT had also wiped out malaria in the United States. Maybe—just maybe—it would work on these ants. I offered a silent apology to Judith, Mr. Fennick, and Rachel Carson as I took up those cans of DDT and set to work.

I took perverse pleasure in watching those ants die, as if they had come after me personally. I cleared them off my property and the surrounding properties. The stuff worked fast, but not fast enough to spare my neighbors. The ants had infested walls and attics, and people had emptied so many cans of bug spray that their houses had become toxic. Everyone on my street had fled the ants, and before long their properties were overgrown and gone wild. Elsewhere in the city, the ants had nested in transformers and electrical panels, shorting circuits and starting fires that swept through parched woods and neighborhoods like what we used to see in California. Alfonso told me that the ants had even undermined a bridge embankment, causing the bridge to collapse.

I gave Alfonso what was left of the DDT. He used it on his customers' properties, charging a hefty fee that he offered to share with me. I declined. He had done enough for me, I felt I owed him. When word got out, the state found some old DDT barrels on a military base somewhere and used them to eradicate the ants in

Nashville. They even spared a little of the DDT for Memphis. Nashville slowly recovered, although the houses on my street were never reoccupied. I felt like a pioneer then, alone in the wilderness. And I didn't mind.

* * *

The position of State Revenuer was a coveted job that attracted the finest men; men of character and duty and fairness. Unfortunately these were not the men who got the job, but rather the opposite. The revenuers who combed through the state, from the remotest hollow to the densest city block, were thugs and marauders who vied fiercely for their positions because of what they could skim for themselves. I bought a rifle against their eventual visit, but that never came to pass. Instead they found Hector.

The ants were still being eradicated when Hector came to see me. It was the first week of December in 2040. The air was cool and humid and we'd seen some rain, so Hector and I settled in the den to talk. I offered him a whiskey but he declined. I poured one for myself and sat.

"Mr. Jeffries," he said, avoiding my eyes. I had repeatedly asked him to call me Carlton—we were business partners after all, and had been for thirteen years—but something in his upbringing refused to allow him. He rubbed his hands and laced his fingers before going on. "There is trouble with these tax *hombres*."

"Oh?" I said, sitting up at that.

"*Sí*. They have been to all of our stores and take our money."

"Oh." I sat back then and waved it off. "It's a cost of doing business, Hector. Just pay them off and get them out." Our stores were ridiculously profitable. It chafed to have to pay those hefty state taxes, but then there were all the other taxes and fees that we *didn't* have to pay these days in light of everything that had happened. To me it was pretty much a wash.

"*No señor*. They will take only US dollars."

"Hmm." That was more worrisome. Most people still paid in dollars, but we were bound by law to accept Tennessee scrip, which was worth about as much as Confederate notes. Converting these to dollars was expensive, like having a fifty-percent-off sale every day, and we had quit using banks after the crash. We were fortunate that there was such a deep network of Mexicans in Nashville to help us filter this money, but I had discovered that trundling all that cash around was complicated just the same. "Well," I said after a sip of whiskey, "that could be a problem."

"There is more."

"Huh?"

"*Señor*, they have discovered my status. They are bad to the latinos always, but now they charge extra from me. Soon they will ruin us. *Los gringos pendejos!*" He looked to spit but checked himself when he remembered that he was indoors.

"Uh, oh." I leaned forward. "What can we do?"

"*Señor*—Mr. Jeffries, I think we should close the stores and I should take my family to Mexico. It is not safe here."

"But—" That took my breath before I could think of a reply which, after a few moments of watching the frost condense on my glass, still didn't come. "But Hector—"

"It is the only way, Mr. Jeffries. Today we have stock and much cash, but tomorrow," he shrugged his shoulders, "*posiblemente no.*"

I downed my whiskey and gritted my teeth. Hector was right. These revenuers were real trash. Sooner or later they would take everything we had, and they did treat the Mexicans like dirt. They were due for the same surprise the Texans had discovered, that without workers and the money they generated there was little left. But I liked Hector—I liked his family. They felt like my own. I was missing him already.

"When do you want to do it?" I asked, resigned to the situation.

"Immediately, Mr. Jeffries. There is no time to lose. They will be back in January, so it must all be gone before that time."

I mulled that while standing to pour another whiskey.

"So sell off the inventory, divide the cash? Is that what you have in mind?"

"*Sí señor.*"

"Damn, Hector." I fell onto the Barcalounger. "I'm gonna miss you."

"*Y tu también, pero* we have done well, no?"

"Yes, Hector, we have done well. Listen, uh...load up all the whiskey and bring it here."

"*All of it, señor?*"

"Just the Tennessee whiskey, the JD and the rest. I don't want to have to buy it from the competition, I'd rather just buy my own. I'll pay for your portion"

"As you wish, Mr. Jeffries."

Hector got to work right away, and I looked for a place to put all of that whiskey. The storm shelter was the best option. It was cool in there, out of the way, and I had mostly cleared it out during my search for the DDT. There wasn't much left in there now, so I went in to finish the job.

As much as children seek out any hiding place they can find, I wondered why I had never played in there as a boy. Perhaps it was because of the damp, musty smell, or perhaps simply because it was indoors. It had always been Dad's place. I don't think Mama ever once went in herself. And so this time, without the urgency of a search in progress, I felt as if I were intruding into a secret place that Dad had reserved for himself.

The light came from a single old-style fluorescent fixture, and the cement walls still looked as if they had been freshly poured. I hauled out what remained, and in a corner found Dad's old tackle box. Dad had loved to fish, I think even more than he had loved golf. I remembered that he had wanted me to take up fishing. Too bad I had never found the time. I smiled wistfully at the memory and went to grab the box. When I did I almost jerked my arm out of its socket. The box was as heavy as a cement block!

I rubbed my shoulder and stood back, eyeing the box with confounded curiosity. I took it firmly by the handle and managed to lift it, but dropped it with a clunk when I felt a muscle going in my back. A cloud of dust wafted up, forcing me to step out for air.

This was damned strange.

I went back in and lowered to my knees, waving the dust out of my face. The hasp was rusty and didn't want to open so I went after it with a hammer. That made a lot of noise and stirred up more dust, but by then solving this mystery had become an urgent obsession. I wailed at the thing until the hasp broke, but then found that the hinges were frozen. It took a crowbar to finally get the box open, and what I discovered inside were dozens of plastic tubes that were as long as my fingers and about as big around as a pair of thumbs. I hefted one of the tubes in my hand. It was solid and heavy, like a bar of steel. There was a red plastic cap in one end, which I pried off with my pocket knife. I upended the tube...and gold coins spilled out, one after another in a steady cascade.

I stared in dumb disbelief for some time, even after the coins had settled firmly in the dust. I knew *what* they were, I just didn't know *why* they were. Why did Dad have a tackle box full of gold coins down here? I picked up one of the coins and examined it. It was a ten-dollar piece dated 1984, imprinted with *Los Angeles XXIII Olympiad*. I shook my head to clear it. I remembered those Olympics, they were the ones the Russians had boycotted. And I remembered...a long-ago conversation between Dad and Eugene, a conversation about gold. Dad thought the prices were too erratic, he preferred real estate. I chuckled. It looked as if Dad had hedged his bets after all.

There was a yellowing note with my name on it, which I regarded with the same dizzy confusion as all the rest of it. It was hand-written from Dad, as if he were reaching to me across the decades. It read:

Carlton, these are off the books. Divide them evenly between the three of you and save them for the future. Some day they might be worth something. Love, Dad.

And then it hit me, the reason Dad had asked me in his will to go fishing. He'd assumed I would go looking for his tackle box and would find his stash of gold. He'd also assumed that I would do as he asked. I shook my head guiltily.

"Sorry, Dad," I sighed, but then I lit up at the possibilities. When Hector was done we would literally have boxes of cash, both US dollars and Tennessee scrip. But cash wasn't like gold, it wasn't a guarantee of security, not the way things were now. Dad had probably lost money on this hoard, but today these coins were worth... *hundreds of thousands of dollars*. And no one knew they were here, not the state, not the revenuers—*no one*. Except me. I laughed giddily, put the coins and the note back and closed the box.

* * *

I didn't see much of Alfonso anymore. There was no yard work to keep up with now, and I could handle the dogs myself. He came by from time to time with a new puppy. He had his own breeding program going on, and we swapped dogs the way I used to with the Louisiana breeders. Alfonso made good money selling his coonhounds in rural areas, where subsistence hunting was the only way some people could survive. He would have been in bad shape otherwise, since his landscaping business had pretty much collapsed. Not that he could have found workers any-way—they had mostly been driven back to Mexico.

"It's the stupidest thing, man," he groused during one visit. "Hector invited us to come stay with him in Matamoros, but get this: the Mexicans won't let me in because I'm *American*. Can you believe it? They call us *pochos*." He spat that as if something nasty were on his tongue. "Now they've closed the border. No more wet-backs, they say—and especially no *gringos*."

I had to laugh, but then I had to apologize to Alfonso. I wasn't laughing at his predicament, I said, only at the ironic reversal of things.

* * *

When April came to visit for my ninetieth birthday, it was the first time we had seen one another in person since the twins were four. Now they were twenty and out on their own. Jaime, Alfonso's son, picked her up at the bus station and brought her to the house. When I met them out front I hugged April hard enough to break something if I weren't careful.

"Gosh, Grampa, I can't breathe."

"I'm sorry, sweetie, it's just that I haven't seen you in so long."

"C'mon, we talk all the time."

"It's not the same on the computer."

"I know," she said with a sigh, her warm breath on my ear. She pushed back then and we held one another at arm's length. "You look great, Grampa."

"You do, too, sweetie." And she did, mostly. She was sticky in the heat, and there were dark circles under her eyes, probably from the long trip. She seemed thin. "Was the trip hard?"

"It wasn't great." She pursed her lips and frowned. "Could have been worse, I guess."

"No trouble at the border?"

"Not really. They held me up to check my papers, and grilled me about why I was going to Tennessee. I told them it was to see family. I gave them Jaime's name like you said." She looked at Jaime and smiled. "Thank you, Jaime."

"Yeah, thanks, Jaime," I said as well. The revenuers already knew about his fami-ly's business, but they didn't know about me and I meant to keep it that way.

"*De nada* Mr. Jeffries; Miss April. I'd better get going now. Everything should be okay. I don't think they'll bother to follow up, but if they do I'll make up a story."

Things had settled down over the past few years, but the state homeland agencies still flexed their muscles, as if to create the very need for their existence.

"That's good, Jaime. I appreciate it. Tell your father hello for me."

"I will, sir."

Jaime was about the same age as April's boys, dark complected like his father and with an entrenched southern accent. He drove an old white Ford pick-up that he and his father had converted to electric. We watched him as he silently backed down the driveway.

"Grampa, I don't even recognize the place," April said, shielding her eyes as she scanned back and forth. The hedge was gone, the street buried under leaves and duff. The gate hung rusting off its hinges, while prickly pear cactus waved their spikey paddles in the breeze.

"It's been a long time, sweetie. At least the house is the same. Let's get you inside where it's cool."

I had April lie down on the couch in the living room while I put her things away. Afterward I brought out a pitcher of cold sweet tea and sat across from her. She had her flimsy out and was working at it with a frown.

"I can't get a signal in here, Grampa."

"That's because I don't have one of those wireless things."

"You don't? Then how do you get connected?"

"Over the telephone."

"*The telephone?* You mean it still *works?*"

"It works fine, always has."

"How is that possible?"

"I don't know. I think they forgot to turn it off when they converted everything over, and now nobody even remembers it's there." I shrugged. "I mean, the cables are still in the ground. They have to be going somewhere."

"But then that means...*you're still using that antique computer?*"

"Yeah."

"Grampa, that thing's older than I am. No wonder the picture is so bad when I call you." She rolled up her flimsy and waved it at me. "You should get one of these."

"That's just another gadget," I grumbled. "No thanks. My computer does everything I need it to do."

"But it's too old to stream vids and things. What do you do for entertainment?"

"I read my father's books, or I look at the television."

"*Television?*"

"I've got an antenna, April. There are still a couple stations, more like kids' hobbies, I think, but I look at them every now and then."

"You're *so* old fashioned," she smiled. "I don't know how you get along."

"I got along fine before there were computers. Still do. Now drink your tea."

She hung there a moment while she puzzled over that concept, then picked up her tea and took a sip.

"This is great, Grampa. Thanks."

Princess Grace hobbled in to see what was going on in her domain. April stared in disbelief.

"Is this—"

"Yep, Princess Grace."

"My God, she was practically a puppy."

"She's an old lady now, almost twenty. She's older than me in dog years."

"Come over here, Princess Grace."

Princess Grace was too feeble to hop on the couch, so April got down on her knees to pet the dog. Princess Grace thumped her tail in response, but didn't have the strength for much more than that.

"She's such a sweet dog, Grampa."

"They all were, sweetie." My eyes misted. Watching dogs grow old is practice for the people in your life, but that doesn't temper the sorrow, only moves it to a manageable place. "How are the boys?" I asked to get away from those thoughts. April looked up and smiled.

"Doing well. They're both in love." She batted her eyes. "Ricky wants to move in with his girlfriend, so of course Jimmy wants to move in with his. Patrick thinks it's okay, but I told them they were too young."

I chuckled. "That's what I told your mother, and that's what my mother told me. It doesn't seem to make a difference. Grandmother Villetta, on the other hand, would tell them to make their own choices and get in the mud with it if they had to."

There was a picture of Grandmother Villetta on the mantle. April wandered over and gazed at it with her arms crossed, as if she were studying a portrait in a gallery.

"She was born in 1890," April mused. "Just think of the things she'd seen in her life."

"Just think of the things you've seen in *your* life," I said.

She rounded on me. "It's not the same."

"She wouldn't say that."

"What would she say then?"

"Probably that times always look more interesting to people who weren't in them."

April considered that for a moment.

"What was she like?"

"Hmm...She was a proper lady, hard and soft at the same time, and she could tell stories. If anything happened, good or bad, she had a story for it—and she had a way of turning what you thought back on you."

April smiled and sidled on over, sat on the arm of my chair and rested a hand on my shoulder.

"I wish I could have heard her stories," she said.

"I've told you a lot of them."

"Yeah," she looked off in thought, "but never *your* stories. Not even the Appalachian Trail. Dad still talks about that all the time."

"Well," I looked down, "my stories just aren't as good as Grandmother's were."

"I don't believe that." She got up and went to the couch. "Grampa, why don't you write them down?"

"Oh, I don't think so, sweetie."

"Why not? A narrative from you would be an important historical record. I could use it in my classroom, and I'm sure the boys would appreciate it. People don't know how it was. You could tell them. You could tell *me*."

"I haven't done anything worth telling people."

"That's not true, Grampa."

"It is true. Look—you should have asked your Aunt Sadie before she died. *She* was the famous writer."

April frowned. "I did ask her, a long time ago. She wouldn't do it."

"Did she say why?"

"Only that she wasn't interested in dredging up the past. I don't know what she meant by that. So? Will you do it?"

The expression on her freckled, trusting face said she was certain that I would acquiesce, and so I knew I was going to have to watch that expression turn to disappointment. I couldn't give her what she wanted. Even though I felt well, my days had to be drawing to a close, and when they did all of this would finally be over, all of the pain and regret erased by time, nothing left for others to pick over. That was the only thought that gave me peace.

"No," I said sharply, wincing as I did but I had to cut this off or else she would keep at it. "I'm sorry, but no."

She wasn't just disappointed, if anything she was shattered. I wasn't prepared for that. Her cheeks flushed and her hopeful smile fell. Something in her eyes seemed to be crying out for consolation, but all I could do was look down at my hands and hope this would end it.

When April left me that last time, the light seemed to have gone out of her.

"Come again soon, sweetie," I said, holding her and not wanting to let go. "Bring the boys."

"If I can."

There was a finality in her tone that caught uneasily in my stomach. She pecked my cheek in a somber farewell, and Jaime drove her to the station.

When April died of her breast cancer the following spring, it was Thomas who called me.

"*April's gone, Carlton,*" he cried. "*Rachel's baby is gone.*"

Thomas was in his sixties by then, gray and drawn with grief, although his voice could still be the one that had greeted me in Fresno, so many years ago now that it didn't seem possible. I wobbled and held onto the computer screen, as if Thomas could reach through to support me. I couldn't breathe.

"Thomas, I...I..."

He wiped his nose and leaned closer to the camera.

"Even though we knew it was coming, I wanted to think they'd made a mistake, you know?"

My lungs were burning. I forced myself to exhale, as if I had been punched in the stomach, and only then managed enough breath to cry out, "*Why didn't you tell me?*"

It hurt just to get those words out. There was a crushing weight on my head. Thomas seemed confused.

"*She didn't tell you?* That was why she wanted to see you so badly last year."

I could feel my face go white, and everything inside me run onto the floor. I mumbled something.

"*Oh my God, oh my God...*Carlton—"

I just covered my face and cried.

Thomas emailed me photos of the service. I looked at them with hollow eyes, then went to my room and crawled into bed.

* * *

Jaime looked after the dogs. He made runs to the store for me, and took care of burying Princess Grace. I stayed in bed with the curtains drawn, days passing into winter, willing myself to die. Jaime was patient. Alfonso, too. It seemed unreal to me that I was still alive. I had dreams, forests and mountains and the crack of thunder, a silhouette limned in heavenly light. Sometimes Grandmother Villetta came to my dreams. She would sit me on her knee and rock silently, brushing the hair from my eyes or the tears from my cheeks.

"*Why*, Grandmother?" I beseeched her.

"There's no answer for that, boy. We abide what we can. Some things take time. I'm here, so just rest. Rest till you're ready."

Outside, spring came on with a touch of green that we hadn't seen for a while. The air was mild. A pair of mockingbirds nested beyond my window. I watched them. I watched as their chicks suddenly raised clamoring beaks above the edge of the nest. I watched the chicks grow, awkward and downy and with stubby tail feathers. I watched them hop onto the edge of their nest and flap their adolescent wings. I watched them leap and flutter, and then they were gone.

I raised myself from bed and plodded out onto the deck.

It was morning, warm but not hot. The air was particularly clean. I breathed deeply and sat. I felt too fatigued for more than that, but it was a good morning, good to be outdoors. Later I rummaged through the kitchen, wrote out a list of necessities, folded the list around a generous amount of cash and gave it to Jaime when he came.

"Please go buy these things for me, Jaime," I said. "Keep whatever's leftover for yourself. Just leave the stuff at the mailbox. I'll go down to pick it up. Thanks for everything, but I need to be alone for a while."

His look of concern was as deep as if we shared common blood, but he didn't argue or even make to argue.

Summer came on, as hot as ever. I was surprised how well I could make it up and down the hill, carrying a list down to leave in the mailbox, carrying my groceries up in canvas totes. In the evenings I had my whiskey on the deck. A few years sped by. I buried another dog.

And then another spring, hot and sweltering, the kind of weather that made being outdoors pure misery. I was on the deck, about to go inside when the morning light went dim, as if the moon were passing across the sun. Frigid gusts suddenly blew in from the northwest. Isabel, one of Princess Grace's granddaughters, wrapped herself around my legs and tucked her tail.

"Now, now, Isabel. It's nothing."

I scratched her behind the ears, then craned my neck trying to see over the roof at what was coming. Rain would be welcome, although even a solid downpour wouldn't make much of a difference in our arid conditions. It was more the novelty of it, a cool wind, rain to wash the air, the speckles of green that would pop up in the yard almost immediately afterward. But I couldn't see anything from that side of the house.

"C'mon, Isabel. Let's go up the hill and have a look."

I slapped my thigh for her to follow, then went out the back and started up the hill. A line of clouds cut a diagonal across the sky, like a coal-black shade drawn on the morning. The sky was blue to the south, as bright and clear as a day at the beach, while to the north it was eerily dark, advancing like oil in a pan; and with that the cold gusts whipping through the treetops, rustling their limbs with invisible force. I wouldn't be able to see much more until we made it into the meadow.

The wind ceased abruptly before we got there, as if a giant fan had been un-plugged. Everything went still then. Sounds were sharp, the squeak of my shoes, Is-abel's panting breath. No birds. My ears popped as we entered the meadow. I worked my jaw to clear them, and looked up at an ominous black sky that was tinged with green. The ceiling was low, charcoal clouds moving across like a bore tide. I felt a stirring in my belly. Isabel cowered at my feet. I recognized that sky. It was possible that I was the only one left who did.

The trees across the way blocked my view. I could see the sky, but not what it was bringing. I went to the old ash tree and considered whether or not I could possibly climb it. I could see the limb high above where I had climbed as a boy, but reaching it now seemed as impossible as scaling sheer cliff. There were some lower branches I could reach, a crook to put my foot. I took hold of a limb and pulled myself up, grunting at the effort. I reached for another limb and pulled again. Isabel whimpered below me, nosing around the tree as if trying to find her own way up. One more limb, that was about all the breath I had, but I managed to straddle it and lift my head for a better view—

—and what I saw was God smiting Nashville with his omnipotent fingers.

The scale of it overwhelmed me and I almost fell. Funnel clouds dangled from the sky like beastly udders, not one, not two, but more than I could take in. Fingers of death ripped wantonly at the land, some joining together to tear a wider swath before parting again on their own courses, skipping from hilltop to hilltop, others plowing between the hills as if to carve those valleys deeper. A sudden spattering of rain stuck me like icy needles, blown away by a gust before they could even dampen my shirt. A roar steadily grew, like a train coming closer.

I have never known such fear, such primal, gut-tingling terror. I scrambled down without care, lost my grip on a lower limb and fell. I struck the ground. The air was driven out of me and I felt an ankle twist, but the need to flee coursed through me so deeply that I rolled through the grass, rolled over and over until I reached the tree line and could pull myself up.

"Hurry, Isabel! Hurry!"

I went down the hill mostly sliding on my backside, with Isabel taking the lead now. I passed the kennel and let out a sob. There was no time to save the dogs, not even enough time to look up at the sky. I could feel the pressure at my back, a remorseless predator right on me, my ears popping, hail slanting in like cold bullets. I kicked into the garage, dove into the storm shelter amidst my whiskey and gold, clutched Isabel to my chest as if she were the last living thing on earth, and covered my ears when the roar became so loud it was unbearable.

It was over in minutes, less than minutes. I was rocking with Isabel in my lap, my eyes tightly closed, and then I noticed...it was quiet. No sound. I ventured to open my eyes. New light shone through the garage-door windows, casting across the Pontiac to lay golden pools on the cement floor. There was a tang of ozone in the air, but otherwise everything felt as calm as a perfect morning. I stood, limped outside and gazed up at a partition of gray that was speeding off even as I watched. Everything looked fine. The garden shed, the greenhouse...both untouched. I hobbled around the greenhouse to check on the kennel, breathed the deepest sigh of relief when I saw that it was perfectly intact. Up the hill, the woods, the water tank—all fine.

It seemed incredible. I went back around to look down the hill. The derelict McMansions were gone, the hill torn and splintered and seeming to bleed from furrows of red clay. Off in the distance—a surreal scene of devastation.

I went inside, took some aspirins and wrapped my ankle. I needed a whiskey after that. I sat on the deck and sipped my whiskey, Isabel back to her old self at my side. It wasn't even noon yet. The scene before me was apocalyptic, but if I were inside with the curtains drawn I could easily have pretended that nothing at all was out of the ordinary.

The storm had come across in a wall that was miles long, fueled by a dip in the jet stream that had brought a front of cold arctic air into collision with the hot, climate-altered air of the south. It was the most powerful storm ever recorded up to that time. Tornadoes had followed courses as if with a purpose. At least one stabbed into downtown, running along 21ˢᵗ Avenue, across the Four-Forty Parkway and then down Hillsboro Pike, ripping the heart out of Green Hills. Others jumped from hilltop to hilltop, obliterating everything on the northwest sides, sparing those structures providentially located in just the right places on the southeast sides. Two twisters had merged into a mile-wide vortex that homed in with preternatural accuracy on J. Percy Priest Dam. It was the breaching of that dam that flooded downtown Nashville, and to this day, with a starved federal government unable to assist, that dam has never been rebuilt.

Up on the hill, that old Civil War cannon had been yanked from its carriage and driven into the ground like a post. The ash tree had lost some mighty limbs, ripped away as if by a careless butcher, but the tree still stood. My house was completely intact, no damage except for one shattered solar panel. But Green Hills as I knew it, as my father had helped build it, was gone.

* * *

Tens of thousands had died. Green Hills, with its over-built corridor along Hillsboro Pike, and with its McMansions crowded onto single lots, suffered casualties on the scale of a third-world tsunami, which is why Green Hills is remembered along with the Titanic and Pompeii for epic catastrophe. At the same time, though, many tens of thousands had survived elsewhere in the city. I saw some of them through binoculars out on the deck, people picking their way through streets clogged with rubble, mangled bodies, and other things blown in from far away; small, indistinguishable figures from my height, carrying loved ones in their arms, huddling in ragged and filthy groups. The destruction was even apparent at night, total darkness but for the flickering stars above and the equally numerous campfires below. I often heard sporadic gunfire, distant popping like fireworks.

Water mains were broken, water towers toppled, the pumping stations wrecked or gone completely. Splicing the line from my water tank into my house's plumbing was simple. I was never short of water or electricity, and with my greenhouse I was never short of food.

Miraculously, my telephone and internet still worked. Wireless towers lay folded and crumpled against their hilltop mounts, but those forgotten underground cables still carried current. I tried to call Alfonso and Jaime, but only heard a shrill whine on the other end.

It was a week or more later when Jaime climbed my hill. Isabel announced Jaime's presence out front with a couple of barks. I spotted Jaime through the living room windows and hurried down to meet him before he reached the door.

"Mr. Jeffries, thank God you're okay," he said in a breathless voice, sweat beading his forehead. He had a bandage above his right eye.

"Jaime! I tried to call—"

"The phones are down, sir."

"Mine isn't."

"It's not?"

"How is your father? Is everyone all right?"

"We're all fine. We got to the basement in time."

"You look hot. Come in, come in."

We went upstairs to the kitchen, where I sat him down at the table and brought a pitcher of sweet tea from the refrigerator. Jaime eyed this with incredulity combined with a look of longing that bordered on jealousy. He licked his dry lips as I poured him a glass, which he gulped down as if he had just come across a desert. I poured him another.

"How do you do it, Mr. Jeffries? This is amazing." He held the cool glass to his forehead and closed his eyes.

"I just got lucky, Jamie. Tell me what's happening out there."

"It's bad, sir. Our neighborhood is pretty much okay, but there's no electricity or water. There are gangs running around, gotta watch out for them." He lifted his shirt to reveal a sinister-looking automatic pistol. "Papa sent me up to check on you. There are trees down all over the place. I had to hike in from I-65. Everything's gone, all the houses, everything. I don't think the gangs will come here. They won't think there's anything left."

"I'm just glad you all made it."

"You should come out with me, sir. You can't stay here by yourself."

"Yes I can, Jaime. I'm not going anywhere."

Jaime finished off his second glass then stood.

"I'd better get back then, sir."

"Okay, Jaime." I walked with him to the stairs but then pulled up before going down. "Wait a minute. How are you all going to get by?"

"I don't know, sir." He put on a worried expression. "We'll figure something out."

"Look, I need some things, sugar and coffee and such. Can you try to get them for me?"

"I can try, sir, but—"

"Just wait here, Jaime. I'll be right back."

I rushed to the kitchen, wrote out a quick list and wrapped it around one of my gold coins. Cash wouldn't go far now, not in the medieval conditions I could see from the deck. Alfonso and his family would need something more basic and time-less to help sustain them. I returned to Jaime with the list.

"Take this," I said, closing his hand on the list and the coin. "See what you can find, and keep what you think is fair for yourself. Just leave it at my mailbox as al-ways."

Jaime unfolded the list and saw the coin. His eyes went wide.

"Mr. Jeffries—"

"Can you do this for me, Jaime?"

"Yes, sir." He seemed uncertain. "If that's what you want."

"Okay, then." I smiled and patted his back. "Please be careful."

* * *

There were areas of town that were completely intact. I couldn't see them from my side of the hill, but they were there. I heard gunfire during the nights, and shout-ing that carried all the way up to me. Isabel was my alarm system, and I kept my rifle close, but no one ever came, only Jaime to drop off whatever goods he had been able to find for me. He would wave at the house, then reach into the mailbox for another list, another gold coin, seem to consider it all blankly then turn around and leave.

I relished the solitude, days in my greenhouse cultivating tomatoes and beans, squash and okra. I froze or canned this bounty, always more than I needed. I shot groundhogs for the dogs. There were always plenty of groundhogs.

A semblance of city government formed up within the first month or so, using Andrew Jackson's Hermitage as the new municipal building. Somehow that old mansion had come through unscathed. There was less gunfire at night. Order was being reestablished block by block. Winter came on, not nearly as cold as winters I had known but cold enough to throw the city into a panic. The hydroelectric power stations were gone, the grid in a shambles. Many people could burn wood for heat, but most surviving homes weren't equipped for that. There was no gas in the lines. That was a utility that had been shut off at my house years ago. I couldn't use my gas fireplace, but I had electric heat. I was warm and comfortable, but the people out there...

The city got one of the old coal power plants working, ran wires to a few substations and spliced in others. I saw it on the television, a jubilant crowd cheering as switches were thrown. There was one television station operating, powered by solar cells. For people who had mostly forgotten about television, people who took their information from the air through their flimsies, it must have been like stepping back into the nineteenth century and trying to figure out how old tools worked. No one knew how to build or even repair a television, but fortunately there were enough of the old sets still lying around to deflect that problem. An old-fashioned television was suddenly worth as much as one of my gold coins.

But what coal had been scavenged didn't last long. As we moved into January there were emotional debates and much hand wringing. Someone with a grim imagination had run the numbers and concluded that embalmed cadavers would burn long enough, and hot enough, to fuel the station, at least for a while—and Nashville was a city full of mausoleums. The religious folks were aghast, and most people simply couldn't reconcile themselves to the idea, but when the power finally sputtered out on a bitterly cold day their minds changed in a hurry. The interim mayor said she would call up the fires of hell if that's what it took to heat the city.

Squads of volunteers were organized to raid the mausoleums, bringing the bodies out in gruesome chain gangs. Hastily-cobbled rules stated that the bodies were to be handled respectfully, and that some body part, usually a snipped off finger, was to be left behind in deference to the memory of the deceased; but what I saw on the television was a frenzied rout by mobs driven mad by this grisly work. Bodies were tossed from hand to hand, some dropped to the ground, obscenely contorted.

They got their station running again. On hazy days I stayed indoors, afraid that I might unknowingly breathe in Mr. Gorman. Just the thought made me sick to my stomach.

* * *

The bodies kept Nashville warm that winter, and then a deal was struck for coal from Kentucky. Nashville began to recover, in a patchwork of neighborhoods interspersed between devastated areas that the mayor vowed to reclaim someday. They could take their time with Green Hills as far as I was concerned. What confounded me was the priority given to the digital network. The resources and manpower required to raise new towers and reestablish the nodes were enormous. People might do without hospitals and proper sanitation, they might live in shacks without running water, but by God they couldn't do without their flimsies and other gadgets.

I celebrated my one hundredth birthday with a whiskey over ice in the company of Isabel and Nellie, a female from Isabel's final litter. It was a warm day, overcast, but I took my whiskey outside on the deck and surveyed my hill. Scrub had covered the wounds below, and brushy trees were sprouting, trees that Alfonso identified as mesquite. He didn't plant them, he said. How they got there was anyone's guess.

I thought long and hard that day. I thought how it might be for other centenarians, with great-grandchildren clamoring for attention, family by the dozens gathered in praise, competing with one another as surely as the kids. Did I wish I had that for myself? Maybe if...but then no. I wouldn't let those thoughts in. I had everything I needed, peace and quiet, something to do, and companions that didn't ask for more than I could give.

My one hundred and third birthday gave me pause. I had lived longer than Grandmother Villetta. It didn't seem right, cruel fate, and yet I watched where I put my feet just the same.

Nellie bore her final litter the following year. There was one cute little female in that litter, the runt, really. When her siblings scrambled to nurse, this puppy would get pushed aside, weak and whimpering. It was the natural order of things, but I felt for that pup. When I went into the kennel she would come to me, head bobbing, eyes barely open, then lay her head on my shoe and fall asleep as if she sensed safety in my presence. Later I kept her in the house, even let her sleep on my bed. She stayed near me always, and with a proper diet grew to a good size. She was a smart girl. I named her Penny.

I had too many dogs. I had just about wiped out the groundhog population, and although there were deer all over the place, butchering them for the dogs was more work than I had the strength to keep up with. I waited by the mailbox one morning for Jaime, which would take him by surprise but I needed to speak with him. I noticed while standing there that the brush and the cactus and the rest had grown so tall that the house was almost completely camouflaged. I couldn't see down the hill anymore. That brush had grown thick as well. My street was like a path through the woods, like those portions of the Appalachian Trail in Virginia that follow old roads from the 1930s, roads that had once led to chestnut farms and such and were discernable only because of their regular lines and the occasional stone embankment.

The trees that had fallen in the storm were going back to nature quickly, rotting and covered with moss. It was a wilderness, and yet in the distance I could hear heavy equipment creaking and grinding, working to reclaim the streets. Someday they would reach my hill, but I was sure that I wouldn't be around then.

I was sitting against the mailbox post, dozing with Penny by my side when she barked, two quick barks to announce that someone was coming. I looked up to see a boy of eight or nine years old wearing shorts and an old white T-shirt, and for a confused moment I thought I was dreaming of Kenny, the way he was when we were kids. The boy paused warily at Penny's bark, so I hauled myself up with effort and beckoned him to come on.

"Who are you?" I asked. Penny wasn't bristling, but she was attentive. The boy eyed Penny and looked as if he were about to run.

"I'm Raphael. *Mi papa* told me to come."

"Jaime is your father?"

"*Sí*. You are his friend?"

"I am. Why didn't your father come?"

"*Porque mi abuelo* died three days ago and Papa has to do everything now."

"*Your grandfather?* Alfonso has died?"

"*Sí.*"

"I'm sorry, Raphael. Your grandfather was a good man. I knew him for a long time."

Despite that exchange, Raphael still seemed nervous.

"I am supposed to take a list," he said.

"Yeah, here it is." I handed him my list and a gold coin. "Be careful with that." Raphael held the coin to his eye and studied it closely, seeming fascinated. "And tell your father that I want him to take some of my dogs."

"*Sí señor.*"

He pocketed the coin and sprinted off, as carefree as if all of this were normal.

I gave up all the dogs except for Isabel, Nellie, Penny, and a male named Emilio. That made my work easier. I suddenly had more free hours than chores, so I looked for other activities. I carved hiking staffs from downed limbs, tried to make sugar from beets. I pruned and rooted rose canes, hoping to get the roses started around the house again. When Raphael told me that paper was scarce, I tried to make my own. I chipped up some of the fallen limbs from the ash tree, boiled the chips and spread the resulting pulp on a window screen to dry. That didn't turn out well, as I have said, but then I wouldn't be writing this otherwise.

2064 was a milestone of sorts. I remembered reading somewhere, a long time ago, that the Census Bureau figured the last baby boomer, those born between 1946 and 1964, would die right about now. Not hardly. While I sat on my hill, the few other survivors of my generation were spending their children's and grandchildren's inheritances on the latest bio-tech, on anything that would extend their lives. A continuous flood of devices came out of China, not the least of which were the programmable nanites. Well...

I buried Isabel. Penny bore a litter a few seasons later. I chose one female from that litter and sent the rest back with Raphael. That little puppy reminded me of Princess Grace, awkward and clumsy and yet seeming to hold herself above her siblings. If she was crowded out while trying to nurse, she would yip and snap, not at her siblings but at me, as if I were derelict in my duty. And then I would reach in to make room for her, and she would burrow in as if she were at the center of everything. She was like the belle of the ball, so that's what I named her.

* * *

I lost track of the days, the years. My age felt like a running irony. I sat on the deck, sipped my whiskey and waited for the stroke that never came. I was certain to be the last baby boomer now, after what the hackers did to those old folks with the nanites, making them pirouette in public, jump up and down until those 3-D replacement hearts pounded, turning their victims into fools before walking them into traffic. It was disgusting how the mobs cheered as this went on, as if those geriatric marionettes were French nobility bound for the guillotine; as if the mobs never considered that a hacker could do the same to them.

I saw on the computer that Luke had died. It wasn't tragic and it wasn't unexpected. He had lived a long and full life, longer than most. I had followed him on the computer over the years, watched his children grow; watched their children grow. There must have been something of me in him after all, since he refused to be treated with nanites or the other things. Or maybe it was because of what had happened to Sadie. Nevertheless I had always thought, in some deep place, that he would come to me one day, that we would put aside everything and become the father and son that we had never been. Best I could tell, though, he didn't even know that I was still alive. This made me despondent until the whiskey did its work and I realized that they must all be gone by now, that there was no one left for me to atone to. When I carried Nellie up to the cemetery I noticed that I walked more erect, that her weight didn't wear me down, that the air smelled particularly sweet. I slept through the nights without dreams, awoke feeling refreshed. It was liberating.

Dexter came. He had only been able to reach me because of all the road work they were doing on Harding Place. Parts of Green Hills were being repopulated now, although they didn't call it Green Hills anymore, too much stigma was attached to that name. Now they called it *Battle Hills*, a great place to buy real estate, a place with a future. I could hear them working in the distance, inexorably bearing my way. I would have thought I would be gone before they could get here, but of late I wasn't as sure.

I needed to keep busy, to distract myself from all of that. I asked Raphael, now a young man, to bring up a mate for Belle, and soon thereafter Belle bore a litter of frolicking pups that made me smile. It was good to have puppies around again. I played with them. When they were old enough I sent them all with Raphael except for one, my favorite of the pack, a male that I had named Samuel.

* * *

The final disaster occurred on a sultry night in August. I was asleep when it happened, didn't even know for days. It was the quiet that eventually caught my notice, the absence of far-off sounds, of construction equipment and distant traffic. Damned strange. I tried the computer but it wouldn't come on. Neither would the television. While I could normally do without the news, I was suddenly desperate for an explanation for all of this. I went into the attic to find Dad's old short-wave radio, which is also when I found the trove of paper that most of this is written on. Over the radio I learned that an electromagnetic pulse device had been set off near Nashville; that the city had gone black; that airplanes had fallen out of the sky like dead birds; that thousands of people with nanites or other electronic augmentation had dropped dead where they stood. Horrible.

I remembered reading about EMP weapons, how they fried just about everything electronic without directly harming people or buildings; but the likelihood of one going off in Nashville had always seemed about as improbable as a volcano popping up on the Cumberland Plateau.

I still wonder—why *Nashville* of all places? Personally I think it was an accident. The device must have been bound for somewhere else, in a strike against America that would exceed the all but forgotten attacks on 9-11. It could have inadvertently gone off in transit, perhaps on the way to Washington DC or New York City, where the death toll would have been as bad as if from an atom bomb. But even that doesn't really make sense. Who would've still had it in for us? We had dethroned ourselves years ago, after all. Nevertheless someone *did* do it, some terrorist from the Middle East, some disunionist here at home, or some state actor out there who hated us not because of our former power but because of the vacuum we had left. Oh, I don't know—maybe it *was* meant for Nashville, set off by some nut still in a lather about all those bodies that were desecrated in the 50s.

Raphael never made it up my hill again. I waited for him as the days wore on, as my supplies dwindled. I quit looking for him after a time. The city was dead. I felt like a castaway then, not secluded by my choice but because I *had* no choice. I did have food and water and a long supply of whiskey, everything I needed to live, although I soon missed coffee and milk and luxuries like that.

* * *

A dozen years can pass as nothing. It was just Sam and me now. I had worked my way through all of Dad's books, and was on the deck reading *Robinson Crusoe* for the third or fourth time when I spotted dust rising from the brush down the hill and off a way. Sam gave a low growl and stood to attention. After so long alone, I regarded what I was seeing as if it were an hallucination, a waking dream, but then I heard whistling, a chipper tune, and I sat bolt upright.

The cloud of dust wafted on the tepid breeze. Brush parted, and with that the crunch of footsteps. Sam went rigid. I took up my rifle and we went down to investigate.

The clots of prickly pear cactus offered perfect concealment, and the homemade moccasins I wore made no sound. I rounded a cactus, peering between the spines, Sam at my side ready to do whatever needed to be done. A figure came into view, a strapping young man with long dark hair and a thin beard under a floppy hat, a pack on his back, a hiking staff in his hand. He meandered along, whistling, following what still resembled a path through the woods. I cocked my rifle and he froze, his lips still pursed to whistle but with nothing coming through them, not even breath.

We held that pose for some moments, and then he dropped his staff and slowly raised his hands.

"I am only a *voyageur*, um, a traveler," he said to the air, in a voice that was heavily accented. "I have no things to steal."

"You a foreigner?" I hollered.

"Yes. *Je suis de la France*, um, I am from France."

"*France?* What are you doing *here?*"

"I am traveling to see the world, and I have come to this place."

"What's your name, boy?"

"I am Jean-Carl."

"Jean-Carl, huh?" He seemed harmless. I couldn't spot any weapons on him. He looked like nothing more than a weary hiker, the way I had looked once. "Come on over here and let me have a look at you."

He left his staff where it lay and edged around the cactus with his hands still in the air. He gulped when he saw my rifle aimed at his chest, and gulped again when he noticed how tensely-wound Sam was.

"I make no problems, *monsieur*," he said shakily. Maybe so, but he had the rugged look of someone who had been on the trail for a long time, wiry but tough, tough enough to overpower me in a second. I eyed him about as menacingly as someone my age could muster, but when his stomach rumbled loud enough for even my aged ears to hear, a ravenous sound I remembered all too well, I dropped my suspicions and lowered my rifle. He exhaled a sigh of relief and guardedly lowered his hands.

"You're a long way from anywhere, Jean-Carl," I said.

"Yes, this is true." He examined me curiously. "And you are very old."

That came out as an innocent statement, nothing meant to cause offense.

"I am *very* old," I emphasized with a half smile.

It seemed as if there was nothing more to say. We studied one another for a few long moments, and then he shrugged.

"If it is okay," he said, "I will go now."

"Hmpf. Sure, go ahead on."

I gestured with my lowered barrel and he went around to retrieve his staff, returning a moment later as if to say goodbye.

"I will go now," he said without conviction. His rumbling stomach could have rivaled Indian drums. He cast expectant looks my way, looks that stoked a memory, and then I had it. It was the old Appalachian Trail dodge, a way to be offered charity from strangers without having to ask. A hiker just had to look pitiful, in need, speaking little except with the eyes. Somehow this got through to people, caused them to offer up more than they would give a starving child: food, shelter, sometimes money. Hikers called it *yogiing*, as in to *yogi* someone for a meal. It almost always worked. It had worked for me on both hikes.

"You must be hungry," I said. He perked up.

"Yes, I am very hungry."

You see? It was working now. But more than that, I suddenly found myself in need of company, if only for a short time. And then there was his lyrical French accent, which I had found charming once, and was drawn to now for some reason.

"My house is up the hill," I said. "Come on up."

* * *

I led him onto the deck and sat him in the shade of the umbrella. Sam had accepted Jean-Carl now, and was lazing in the shade as well.

"I'll find you something to eat," I said. "Be right back."

I filled a tall glass with ice water, rustled up a hank of venison and carried these out to him. He stared as if astonished.

"You have ice? Oh—" He gushed some appreciative words in French, then gulped down the water, seeming to marvel at the ice. "This is *fantasteek, Monsieur...*?"

"It's Jeffries."

"*Je Freece?*" He threw me another of those curious looks.

"That's right."

"*Mon dieu.*"

"What is it?"

He looked away. "It is nothing."

I had brought out a whiskey over ice for myself. I sat back and sipped while he ripped a bite of venison and chewed heartily.

"So, *Monsieur* Jeffries," he said after he got that down, "you have seen France?"

"Yes, a long time ago. I was in Paris."

"*Oui*, Paris. It is not so good there now."

"Where do you live in France?"

"Near Carcassonne. It is in the south. You know this place?" I shook my head. "It is a warm place. The north is very cold. This is because of the ices in Greenland being no more. It has changed the ocean."

"I remember it being cold when I was there."

"Yes, this has happened for a long time."

"How old are you, Jean-Carl?"

"I am twenty-one years. And you are how old?"

"Older than you can imagine. So what brings you here?"

"Well, you know, I want to see the world, and this place where the terrible thing happened."

"You came all the way over here to see what's left of Nashville?"

"*Oui*, and other things."

His gaze lingered on me long enough to make me uncomfortable. I sat my whiskey down and leaned forward.

"What other things?"

"It is...I must show you." He reached into his pack and brought out a photo, considered it inwardly for a moment before he showed it to me. "Do you know this photo?"

A chill passed through me quickly enough to make me dizzy. I could only sputter. "That's...that's..."

"*Oui. Meuse-Argonne Cimetière Américain.* This is you, no?" He held the photo up for comparison and smiled.

"*What...how...Where did you get that?*"

Sam jerked his head up at my tone, ready to pounce if I but snapped my fingers. This caused Jean-Carl to back up a bit. He went on quickly.

"*Mon grand-père*, um, my grandfather...he gave it to me."

"*Your grandfather?*"

"*Oui*. He is the son of some person you know. She is Sofia Fontanier."

"Sofia—"

"*Oui. Mon arrière-grand-mère*, um, my great-grandmother."

"*Sofia is your great-grandmother?*"

"*Oui*. I am Jean-Carl Fontanier-Jeffries

"*Jeffries?*"

I collapsed onto the deck. Jean-Carl rushed to my side, a look of guilt on his face that admitted he'd blundered badly. He got an arm under and lifted me, held me as if I were a child.

"*Monsieur* Jeffries," he hollered. "*Désolé*. I did not know this would make you fall."

I cried into my hands.

"*Sofia had a child?*"

"*Oui. Mon grand-père*. He is Jacques-Carl."

"Then you're my...*my great-grandson?*"

"*Oui, Monsieur* Jeffries."

"*Oh my God!*"

Despite the shock, I was still able to work through the implications. I had a child I had never known, an entire family that had gone on without my knowledge. And Sofia—I could still see her clearly, her earnest eyes and innocent naiveté. And she had been so alone.

Jean-Carl got me into my chair, where I downed the last of my whiskey. I waved him into the house for another. He returned with the entire bottle, which was prescient of him. I slurped down a jolt as quickly as I could pour it, and then another. Once the warm numbness spread through me I felt able to continue.

"How did you find me?" I asked weakly.

"*Mon arrière-grand-mère*, um, Sofia—she saw the man on the net say your name. She was very excited. It seemed not possible to her. I was only a boy when this happened. She told *mon père*, um, my father—she told him to come here, but the terrible thing happened to your city and he could not do it. So now I am no longer a boy and it is for me to try it."

"But...you couldn't know I would still be alive."

"This is true, but maybe I would find some persons of your family and they would know there are persons of your family in France also. *Arrière-grand-mère* wanted this. It is what she said when I was a boy."

"Sofia..." I looked up with blurry eyes. "How is she?"

"She is no longer living."

That drew a sob out of me.

"And your grandfather? My...son?"

"He is good. He no longer must work, so now he is happy."

"And his name is Jacques-Carl?"

"*Oui.*"

It was more than I could bear. Even Sam could tell something was off. He had wrapped himself around my legs and was shivering.

"I need to lay down for a while, Jean-Carl."

He hustled over to support me, walked me to my room and helped me into bed. I lay there but I didn't sleep. The sun set and rose again, and still I was awake.

* * *

Jean-Carl stayed for one week. I gave him a tour of the house, walked him up the hill. In the evenings we sat on the deck. I told him stories, which he absorbed as if he were starved for them. I told him everything. When the day came for him to leave I felt what seemed like the greatest loss yet.

We were out front, the heat coming up with the sun.

"Be careful," I told him.

"Yes, *Grand-père.*" That's what he called me. The other was a mouthful.

"Tell your grandfather that I wish...I wish..."

My face broke then and he took me in his arms.

"I know what to say, *Grand-père*. It is okay."

He hugged me then, something I hadn't felt in so long; something I hadn't known I needed. I pushed back and searched his face. He had a hawkish nose and high cheeks, and brown eyes that were rimmed red with emotion. There really was no resemblance, no feature that I could label as belonging to me, and yet I felt close to him, as close as if he were Rachel or April.

"This place," I said, waving my hand at the house. "This is our place. Someday it should be yours." I handed him my field bag, Tommy's bag, heavy from the gold coins I had put inside it. Also some papers, a set of keys. "Take this and promise to come back."

His eyes glistened.

"This I promise."

* * *

I quit drinking after Jean-Carl left. I can't say why. The whiskey just didn't taste right anymore.

I resumed my routines, passing my days by rote. The house felt empty. A week of Jean-Carl's youthful optimism had seemed to permeate every room, to light every corner that had lain in curtained shadow for so long. In his absence the curtains had been drawn closed once more, shadows rising up the walls.

I wandered into the garage one morning with no thought in mind, only to pass the time. The Pontiac rested on jacks there, its wheels removed and stacked on a pallet to protect them from dry rot. It had been years—no decades—since the Pontiac had last powered up the hill. It was coated in dust, and yet light still glinted off the chrome in places, flickering like a faint heartbeat.

The door screeched when I opened it, hinges as stiff as my old joints. The musty smell of Naugahyde came out on a waft of preserved air, like the first exhalation of a long-sealed tomb. I lowered myself inside and pulled the door. The layers of dust on the windows closed out everything beyond, leaving me cocooned with my thoughts. I rested my hands on the wheel and closed my eyes. I saw all of them then, moments in time that played in my mind like a scratchy 8mm film: Dad smoking a cigarette; Kenny tapping out a tune on the dash; Gracie in a white dress, insecure but proud just the same; Evelyn in a ponytail, when she was young and fresh; Tommy and Luke, as babies and toddlers all at once; Rachel, preening like a queen; Judith...

The keys dangled in the ignition. I turned them, yearning for a spark even as I knew full well that the life had long since drained from this dinosaur.

I sighed and got out, took a towel and absently began to wipe away the dust. Sam was there, thumping his tail uncertainly at this curious new activity. I wasn't thinking of anything, just wiping dust. I lifted the hood by old habit, smelled the varnish of stale gasoline. I took off the air filter and pumped the carburetor linkage. I connected the battery, which was as dead and cold as a block of stone in a cave.

I hovered there, wondering what I was doing, and then determination coursed through me in a jolt. I felt twenty years slide off my shoulders, perhaps more. I dusted my hands and swore to myself—I could do it, I could make the Pontiac run. I could hear it roar once more!

I attached a charger to the battery, brought out my tools and took the carburetor apart to clean it. I filed and readjusted the ignition points, went underneath and drained foul-smelling gasoline into buckets. I worked for days, often late into the night, cleaning and lubricating, dragging off to bed with grease on my hands and brow. I polished the paint until it gleamed, the chrome until it sparkled. I skimmed the moisture off the surface of the gasoline in the buckets, poured what remained through old T-shirts to filter out the sediment. And last the wheels, which were a challenge because of their weight. But I got them on, my back twinging at the strain. I aired them up with a hand pump. When I removed the jacks the Pontiac settled on creaky springs, looking as if it were ready to pounce. I primed the carburetor and got inside. The dome light came on, which gave me hope. I reached for the key and took a breath.

The engine was slow to crank, like a millwheel being turned by an aging horse, but it did crank, coughing at the bad gas, popping through the carburetor, catching for a moment before giving up. I sat back to let the battery cool and then tried again, and when the engine caught and roared I hooted and slapped the wheel and tears filled my eyes. Sam was terrified by the sudden thunderous exhaust, a sound he had never heard. He raced to a corner with his tail tucked. Acrid fumes filled the garage. Holding my breath, I shuffled over to open the garage doors. The smoke that billowed out was black and pungent, but the Pontiac purred where it idled, as if resurrected and ready to prowl.

Once all of this was done, and I had gotten the last of the grease from beneath my fingernails, I fell back into my usual routines, tending the greenhouse, preserving food, and cleaning; always cleaning. Spring moved toward summer, which was only a shift from one kind of heat to another. I often went into the garage and started the Pontiac just to hear it run, with Sam next to me where his ancestor had once sat. It was soothing, that throaty, melodious sound. It made the hill seem small, the house a prison, the world a place I could venture into once again.

The decision to go was another unconscious action. I awoke one morning and just began to fill a backpack, crossing the house back and forth in search of this piece or that. I hummed as I worked, a peppy tune that set Sam jumping with excitement. Something was up, something new. He could sense it.

I had a dream that last night, of forests and mountains and the crack of thunder, a silhouette limned in heavenly light. I awoke with tears and a pounding heart, or maybe that was also a dream.

I left a note on my desk, and then I put Sam in the Pontiac and we backed out of the garage. I locked the house, as if we were only going on an errand, and then we crunched through the scrub to the base of the hill.

Negotiating our way onto a passable street was slow and difficult. We edged around fallen trees. Sometimes I had to stop and lever rotted logs out of the way. I found that Nashville wasn't completely abandoned. People had staked claims in places, living like pioneers in cabins that they had knocked together in the scrubby hollows where McMansions had once been crowded wall to wall. Other people occupied former apartment complexes and office buildings, going about their business as if this were yesterday. They swept and painted and mowed, tended garden plots and gawked as we rolled by. Many of the streets were clear. Children and adults went by on bicycles, always gawking. I saw solar panels and windmills, the beginnings of a new infrastructure. Time would tell.

What I had hoped—and what proved to be the case—was that the border checkpoints were only on the interstates and main transit lines, where the chargers are located for electric vehicles. There was no need for the states to spend resources to garrison the back roads. No one would dare venture too far afield for fear of running their batteries dry. But I was driving a gasoline-powered car, a vehicle so archaic that none of these people had ever even seen one. At the same time, a lot of the old farm equipment still ran on gasoline or diesel, so by working my way through farm country I was able to find fuel for the Pontiac while also avoiding the checkpoints.

Local folk came out to stare, lining fences and roadsides as if a parade were going past. Some of the older ones would give me the thumbs-up. A few had tears in their eyes. They waved American flags at me, the old flags with fifty stars.

I crossed from Tennessee into Virginia and followed the spine of the Appalachians north, along rutted roads that I knew were within a breath of the old Appalachian Trail. It was slow going. At night I would find a secluded place to park the car, then sleep in the back seat. I kept Sam inside with me so that he wouldn't get himself into trouble. The forest became denser and greener as I went on, a sight that filled me like cold sweet tea on a hot day. The aridness back home had come on so gradually that I had forgotten the lushness of a green forest, the calming cool of a dense canopy.

The effects of the EMP were not as far-ranging as I had feared. I skirted rural towns that looked as healthy and enterprising as they had ever been. I was passed by drones, by electric cars and scooters, and people often didn't even stop to stare, as if there were nothing unique at all about a lumbering old car. I didn't linger in these towns for fear of being spotted by local law enforcement. Without papers, I would certainly be carted off to jail. It turned out that most of the policing had been handed off to drones and auto-recognition cameras, which hadn't been programmed to recognize something as old as the Pontiac. I did see one sheriff. This was in some little town in Pennsylvania that I couldn't find a way around. He locked eyes on me and I tensed, preparing for the worst, but then he just smiled with a kind of nostalgic sigh and waved me on.

The weather turned in New England, becoming wet and cold. The villages were farther between, the woods dark. I considered trying to find Sadie's grave, but then thought better of it. I would stand out too much in a town the size of Hanover.

I encountered fewer people in the state of Maine. Perhaps the longer winters had made life untenable. The towns were mostly empty, clapboard buckling, paint peeling in long flakes. In the gray mist they were eerily reminiscent of that coal town in Sadie's first book. The Kennebec River was lifeless, running with silt. Ice still glazed the north sides of trees. The highway resembled nothing more than a parting of the wilderness, trees overhanging, moose scattering ahead of me with their comical gallop. Millinocket was deserted, falling down. That's where I ran out of gas. I left the Pontiac in front of a once-grand house, hefted my backpack, and Sam and I set out on foot. You know the rest.

* * *

I'm on my last piece of paper and I'm running out of space, so let these be my final thoughts from Rainbow Stream. I hope thru-hikers return one day, that they will leave their gadgets behind and experience the trail with their own senses. And I hope they'll add something of themselves to this, draw pictures or write poems, the way it used to be.

Right now the sky is full of stars. They look so close that I could just reach up and swirl them with my fingers. The stream is burbling in a calming flow, as I remember it from before. It will be morning soon. This fever has me shivering, and the sore on my backside hurts terribly, but I'll feel better when the sun comes up. The sun—just to feel its warmth again is all I need. And then I'll go.

I've given myself another trail name, a name that brings me home to the place that gave me the life I've had. What would I have been without it? Less, I think; less than I am now because I wouldn't have had them, even if only for a short time. Here, I can just squeeze it in. Call me—

The Appalachian, ME=>GA '76, ME=>GA '08, ME=>GA '87

$\mathscr{E}PILOGUE$

June 27, 2087 - Evening

I'm writing this on the back of one of those pages I took out of that journal. I hated to do it, but I don't have anything else. The handwriting on the other side is in a patient, flowing script; every i dotted, every t crossed, every loop perfectly formed. I had never thought to see that handwriting again. This had been Judith's journal, actually more of a day planner. On the first few pages are some shopping lists and Thanksgiving recipes, a flight number and arrival time for Thomas. I must have swept the journal up when I cleaned out the Fresno house, and then Sadie found it later. She handed it to me that day, and I stuck it in my backpack. I wish I had taken the time to look at it then.

The sun did rise. I waited for it, sitting up despite the pain, rocking with my sleeping bag around my shoulders. My eyes were heavy but I wouldn't let them close, not when the sky was beginning to glow in heavenly lavender and pink; not when the stars were winking their last and the trees were rising from the mist to reveal their living green. Everything was soft, like a winter's dream of spring. The first rays canted through the treetops, scattering on jeweled drops of dew. And then the sun crowned and the forest erupted in a blaze of light. Oh my God how beautiful; how beautiful.

Rays reached the front of the shelter at last, like tentative fingers getting the feel of the place. Against the pain and the fever, I shuffled over to lie in them. I felt their warm caress and I moaned, as if they were Judith's own hands comforting me. I lay there shivering, bundled in my sleeping bag, but none of that mattered now that there was sun. I closed my eyes to dancing shadows and a blessed feeling of contentment.

Judith wrote this in her journal, dated November 18, 2006:

Carlton will be fine.

Just that by itself, underlined twice, as if this were something she was trying to convince herself of. The rest of the page is taken up with lists, dress sizes and the like, the name of a bridal shop in San Jose. I understood it then, the plans they were making, not in secret but only waiting for me to catch up.

I awoke with a start and gazed around in confusion. The sun was high, its warmth enveloping. Sam was out of the shelter, tugging at his leash. I groaned at the pain in my backside, deep and stabbing now, like an ice pick grinding against my bones. I was soaked with sweat, enough to have dampened the floor where my face had lain. Every movement was a painful thrust into my hip. I couldn't sit up. I managed to fish a mirror out of my backpack and get a look at the sore on my backside. What I saw caused a chill to fill the hollows of my bones.

I fell back exhausted, the sweat coming out of me like salty rain. Dizziness over-whelmed me and I must have passed out.

This time the sun is beyond the roof of the shelter, casting shadows the other way. The stream sounds distant. I'm shivering and burning at the same time, trying to focus but everything is a blur. I must have been dreaming, or perhaps it was delir-ium. Was I humming or was that in my mind? I must have been humming because Sam is watching me with excited eyes, expecting to go.

Evening light, pale amber. I've been out again. I had a dream, so real, of forests and mountains and the crack of thunder, a silhouette limned in heavenly light. There was a voice, sweet and familiar. It spoke to me:

Are you ready?

The voice was comforting, made me feel like another person from another time, in the full sun under a cloudless sky and without pain. I answered:

I'm resting, just for a little while, not too long.

Go ahead and rest, Carlton. Just rest till you're ready.

How will I know?

Oh, baby, you'll know. Sing with me now. Sing with me.

Sam is curled by my side. I'm not shivering anymore. I'm out of my sleeping bag, must have done that in my sleep. I feel warm, a kind of fuzzy tremor on my skin. The ache in my backside seems far away. She's singing her song, I can hear it in the trees, in the breeze, in the flow of the stream and in the setting sun.

Ba-by, ba-by....

I want to cry, but at the same time I want to cry out.

I would sing it with you, baby, but I'm so tired—so tired.

Just rest, Carlton, and you'll be fine.

Will I?

Colors have blended into a vivid blur, greens and blues and streaks of amber. Night is coming.

I think I'll let Sam off his leash—

$\mathcal{A}$CKNOWLEDGEMENTS

While *The Appalachian* is a work of fiction, I strove for the greatest accuracy I could achieve in the backgrounds and settings of the various eras this story encompasses. Residents of Nashville, Tennessee and Fresno, California might recognize some of the particulars of their cities in my story, hopefully with fond recollection. Also, many of the tertiary characters are real people. I will leave it to the reader to puzzle out which. The houses in Nashville, Smith County and Fresno exist more or less as described (or at least as of the last time I visited them some years ago). There is a Shy's Hill, and there is a park on top dedicated to the Battle of Nashville. As a teenager, I combed those woods myself in search of Civil War artifacts, and came down with the chigger bites to prove it. The old ash tree, however, is fiction. All of the schools I have included by name are real, with students attending them today. Sadly, Hillsboro High School in Green Hills may meet its demise in the next few years as developers make the land worth more than its history.

As for the Appalachian Trail, I have hiked it twice, southbound both times. Thru-hikers might appreciate that the idea for this novel came to me in 2008 while I was sheltering overnight in the Fire Warden's Cabin in New Hampshire, mile 418.5 going south, mile 1757.7 going north. The other shelters I have described are real; the trail conditions are real; the weight loss is real; the uplifting sense of spiritual clarity is real; and the end-of-trail depression is likewise real. This is not a guide for hiking the trail, although the information I have included to move the plot along is accurate as of this writing.

Let me say that while I deliver a brutal fate to the city of Nashville, it is and continues to be a fantastic city; likewise Fresno, California, where I spent several memorable years.

There are many I must thank for their assistance. My sister Charlyne, who was raised in Nashville, helped me with the specifics of teenage life in Green Hills during the 1960s and 1970s. If 1970s graduates of Hillsboro High School find themselves reminiscing about Carlton's high school days, it is due to my sister's efforts. Jill Thaxton, my editor, never shied away from telling it to me straight. Judith thanks her for that, too. Dusty Guthier, an old friend, brought me up to date on events in Fresno, which has really changed since I lived there. The American Battle Monuments Commission patiently described the Meuse-Argonne American Cemetery to me, as well as their procedures. Doug Dolan of the Maine Appalachian Trail Club, and Daniel Chazin of New York-New Jersey Trail Conference, diligently searched the available literature as well as the personal recollections of their predecessors, enabling me to accurately describe the Appalachian Trail of the 1970s. The Appalachian Trail Conservancy, the Fresno Unified School District, and Nashville Public Schools all took the time to fill me in on the myriad little details that will make Carlton's world familiar to many readers. And finally Villetta Roberts (pronounced *Vill-ett*), for letting me use her beautiful name.

Without all of this help I simply could not have achieved the level of authenticity that I felt was essential to this book. Nevertheless, if something's off it's on me, not them.

Oh, and Wiebke helped. *Takk skal du ha.*

Kirk Ward Robinson
Smith County, Tennessee
June 2015

ABOUT THE AUTHOR

Kirk Ward Robinson was born and raised in south Texas, and has since lived in every continental American time zone. He is an inveterate hiker and cyclist who prefers to travel and explore the world that way. His wide-ranging career has included roles as a chief operating officer, bookstore manager, stagehand, bicycle mechanic, and executive director of an educational non-profit organization in cooperation with the National Park Service. Robinson has been twice named to Kirkus Reviews' *Best Books*: in 2012 for *Life in Continuum*, and in 2015 for *The Appalachian*. He earned five stars from Foreword Clarion Reviews for his novel *The Latter Half of Inglorious Years*.

These days he maintains a small ancestral farm in the hills of Tennessee.

www.kirkwardrobinson.com